PRAISE FOR RICH HORTON

Fantasy: The Best of the Year, 2006 Edition

"The nineteen excellent short stories in this latest addition to the growing field of annual "best of" fantasy anthologies include works by established stars and many stories that first appeared in small press venues. . . . Horton has gathered a diverse mix of styles and themes that illustrate the depth and breadth of fantasy writing today."

—*Publishers Weekly,* starred review

Science Fiction: The Best of the Year, 2006 Edition

"Horton's elegiac anthology of fifteen mostly hard sf stories illuminates a broad spectrum of grief over love thwarted through time, space, human frailty or alien intervention. This anthology reflects the concerns of the genre today—and the apparent inability of our society to do anything about them."

—*Publishers Weekly*

Fantasy: The Best of the Year, 2007 Edition

"Horton's fantasy annual showcases the best short speculative fiction that steps beyond the established boundaries of science. The sixteen selections represent both magic-oriented fantasy and cross-genre slipstream fiction. Their inspired and resourceful authors range from veteran fantasists to newer voices. Fantasy enthusiasts looking for stories that expand the genre's boundaries in unexpected ways will find them in this inventive, enticingly provocative collection."

—*Booklist*

Science Fiction: The Best of the Year, 2007 Edition

"What with sf's current high literary standing, there is no shortage of gifted authors striving to produce outstanding short fiction, and editor Horton is more than happy to encourage them via this annual for which he sets no higher criterion than plain good writing. Dedicated genre fans may find some overlap of this with other genre annuals, but given the hours of mind-bending entertainment it provides, they'll hardly resent it."

—*Booklist*

continued

continued

The Year's Best Science Fiction and Fantasy, 2010 Edition

"The thirty stories in this annual collection present an outstanding showcase of the year's most distinctive sf and fantasy. A better exposure to current trends in sf and fantasy would be hard to find."

—Library Journal

"American science fiction magazines are struggling to survive, but Horton easily fills this hefty anthology with stories from original anthologies and online publications. Rather than focusing on a narrow subset of fantastic stories, he attempts to illuminate the entire field."

—Publishers Weekly

Unplugged: The Web's Best Sci-Fi & Fantasy, 2008 Download

"*Unplugged* aims to showcase the online fiction often neglected in standard best-of-the-year anthologies, and a rousing success it is. The selections come from a truly excellent assortment of venues, including *Tor.com, Lone Star Stories, Baen's Universe,* and *Farrago's Wainscot.* They constitute a shining example of the good general anthology. Clearly, selecting only online stories imposed no limit on scope, variety, and high quality."

—Booklist

"A short but superlative substantiation of the quality of speculative fiction being published on the Internet, this exceptional anthology of the best science fiction and fantasy put online in 2008 includes gems by genre luminaries as well as rising stars like Tina Connolly and Beth Bernobich. After reading this fourteen-story compilation, online publishing naysayers may rethink their position."

—Publishers Weekly, starred review

War & Space: Recent Combat

"*War and Space: Recent Combat,* from editors Rich Horton and Sean Wallace, is possibly one of the finest anthologies that I've ever come across. This anthology looks at the nature of war, and how it might impact our future civilizations in space. Above all, these twenty stories are good stories, above and beyond the central premise that links them all together. There are stories of daring, heroism and duty, all of which together, make up one hell of a collection."

—io9

SPACE OPERA

OTHER BOOKS BY RICH HORTON

Fantasy: The Best of the Year, 2006 Edition

Fantasy: The Best of the Year, 2007 Edition

Fantasy: The Best of the Year, 2008 Edition

Robots: The Recent A.I. (with Sean Wallace)

Science Fiction: The Best of the Year, 2006 Edition

Science Fiction: The Best of the Year, 2007 Edition

Science Fiction: The Best of the Year, 2008 Edition

Unplugged: The Web's Best Sci-Fi & Fantasy: 2008 Download

The Year's Best Science Fiction & Fantasy, 2009 Edition

The Year's Best Science Fiction & Fantasy, 2010 Edition

The Year's Best Science Fiction & Fantasy, 2011 Edition

The Year's Best Science Fiction & Fantasy, 2012 Edition

The Year's Best Science Fiction & Fantasy, 2013 Edition

War & Space: Recent Combat (with Sean Wallace)

SPACE OPERA

EDITED BY

RICH HORTON

PRIME BOOKS

SPACE OPERA

Prime Books
www.prime-books.com

ISBN: 978-1-60701-407-2

To my fellow Boeing employees:
some of us are working to make some of this stuff possible.

CONTENTS

SPACE OPERA
THEN AND NOW

RICH HORTON

The term space opera was coined by the late great writer/fan Wilson (Bob) Tucker in 1941, and at first was strictly pejorative. Tucker used the term, analogous to radio soap operas, for "hacky, grinding, stinking, outworn, spaceship yarn[s]." The term remained largely pejorative until at least the 1970s. Even so, much work that would now be called space opera was written and widely admired in that period . . . most obviously, perhaps, the work of writers like Edmond Hamilton and, of course, E. E. "Doc" Smith. To be sure, even as people admired Hamilton and Smith, they tended to do so with a bit of disparagement: these were perhaps fun, but they weren't "serious." They were classic examples of guilty pleasures. That said, stories by the likes of Poul Anderson, James Schmitz, James Blish, Jack Vance, and Cordwainer Smith, among others, also fit the parameters of space opera and yet received wide praise.

It may have been Brian Aldiss who began the rehabilitation of the term with a series of anthologies in the mid-70s: *Space Opera* (1974), *Space Odysseys* (1974), and *Galactic Empires* (two volumes, 1976). Aldiss, whose literary credentials were beyond reproach, celebrated pure quill space opera as "the good old stuff," even resurrecting all but forgotten stories like Alfred Coppel's "The Rebel of Valkyr," complete with barbarians transporting horses in spaceship holds. Before long writers and critics were defending space opera as a valid and vibrant form of SF.

By the early 1990s there was talk of "the new space opera," at first largely a British phenomenon, exemplified by the work of Colin Greenland (such as *Take Back Plenty*) and Iain M. Banks (such as *Use of Weapons*)—both of those novels were first published in 1990. "The new space opera," it seems to me, was essentially the old space opera, updated as much science fiction had been by 1990, with a greater attention to writing quality, and a greater likelihood of featuring women or people of color as major characters, and perhaps a greater likelihood of left-wing political viewpoints. Once one noted the existence of "the new space opera" it was easy to look back and see earlier examples, such as Melissa Scott's Silence Leigh books (beginning with *Five-Twelfths of Heaven* (1985)), M. John Harrison's cynical *The Centauri Device* (1974), and Samuel R. Delany's *Nova* (1968).

Nova is my personal choice as the progenitor of space opera as a revitalized genre, but that's probably a largely personal choice. (*Nova* is one of my favorite novels). Others could certainly point to something different: perhaps Barrington Bayley's *The Star Virus* (1970 in book form, but a shorter version appeared in 1974). Even more sensibly one could say that space opera never went away—what about Alfred Bester's *The Stars My Destination* (1956), to name just one seminal earlier work?

Perhaps, then, *The Centauri Device* is in retrospect the key work. Harrison conceived it explicitly as "anti-space opera," and it was a reaction not just to the likes of Doc Smith, but to *Nova*, which Harrison had called "a waste of time and talent." To quote Harrison himself, from his blog: "I never liked that book [*The Centauri Device*] much but at least it took the piss out of sf's three main tenets: (1) The reader-identification character always drives the action; (2) The universe is knowable; (3) the universe is anthropocentrically structured & its riches are an appropriate prize for people like us."

Even if *The Centauri Device* verges on parody, and explicitly disapproves of its subgenre, those three principles do suggest an alternate path for space opera, perhaps a truer definition of the "new" space opera: less likely to be anthropocentric in approach, less likely to accept that the universe is knowable, less likely to have the main character succeed (if he or she still does drive the action). And, anyway, Harrison returned to space opera with his remarkable recent trilogy, *Light* (2002), *Nova Swing* (2006) and *Empty Space* (2012). Those books certainly read like space opera to me, but they also certainly tick the boxes Harrison lists above

(Harrison also, less importantly perhaps, started a trend for clever ship names in *The Centauri Device*, using phrases from the Bible and Kipling for spaceships named *Let Us Go Hence* and *The Melancolia that Transcends All Wit*. That led, it would seem, to Iain M. Banks' famous names for his Culture ships, and to similarly cute names in the work of many other writers.)

At any rate, once established as an essentially respectable branch of SF, space opera has continued to flourish. Some of it shows aspects of Harrison's model, at least in parts, other stories are as triumphalist as anything that came before, more often we see a mix. A good recent example might be Tobias Buckell's Xenowealth series, beginning with *Crystal Rain* (2006)— featuring heroes and heroines from non-traditional cultures, and somewhat ambiguous about the place of humans in a hostile universe, but also most assuredly featuring main characters with tons of agency and ability to drive the plot, and a general sense of cautious and perhaps conditional optimism.

The list of enjoyable space opera novels in recent years is long—notable practitioners include Alastair Reynolds, Karl Schroeder, Kristine Kathryn Rusch, Nancy Kress, John Barnes, and James S. A. Corey; and I could go on for some time.

This book collects short fiction, however. One of the near-defining characteristics of space opera is a wide screen, and this seems to drive longer works. It's not nearly as easy to evoke the feeling of vastness, of extended action, that we love in space opera over a shorter length. But it can of course be done. Two of the best books of the past few years are original anthologies edited by Gardner Dozois and Jonathan Strahan: *The New Space Opera*, and *The New Space Opera 2*. These are packed with delicious stories, undeniable space opera of a variety of modes and moods, and they show that you don't need five hundred pages for a good space opera. I've chosen a piece or two from each of these books for this volume.

I also must mention one newer writer in particular: the remarkable Yoon Ha Lee. She has yet to publish a novel, but an array of striking stories has already established an impressive reputation. She has written work in multiple subgenres, but one of her continuing themes is war, and often war in space, between planets . . . which means, more or less, space opera. And in the briefest of spaces she can evoke a war extending across centuries and light years.

So, this book, which collects twenty-two outstanding stories, some traditional space opera in flavor, others which looks at those themes from different directions; some set across interstellar spaces, others confined to the Solar System; some intimate character stories, other action-packed; some (perhaps most) concerned with war and the effects of war, but others more interested in the grand spaces of the universe. But all, above all, fun.

THE KNIGHT OF CHAINS, THE DEUCE OF STARS

YOON HA LEE

The tower is a black spire upon a world whose only sun is a million starships wrecked into a mass grave. Light the color of fossils burns from the ships, and at certain hours, the sun casts shadows that mutter the names of vanquished cities and vanished civilizations. It is said that when the tower's sun finally darkens, the universe's clocks will stop.

But the sun, however strange, is not why people make the labyrinthine journey to the tower. The tower guards the world's hollow depths, in which may be found the universe's games. Every game played among the universe's peoples was once trapped in the world's terrible underground passages, and every one was mined and bargained for by some traveler. It is for such a game that the exile Niristez comes here now, in a ship of ice and iron and armageddon engines.

This is the hand Niristez played long ago: The Ten of Theorems; the Knight of Hounds; the Nine of Chains, the bad-luck symbol she uses as a calling card; and she kept two cards hidden, but lost the round anyway.

Niristez carries the last two cards with her. They come from a deck made of coalescent paper, which will reveal the cards drawn when she chooses and not before. Today, the backs show the tower in abbreviated brushstrokes, like a needle of dark iron plunging into an eye. Coalescent cards are not known for their subtlety.

She may have lost that match, but it's not the only game she's playing, and this time she means to win.

The tower has a warden, or perhaps the warden has a tower. The warden's name is Daechong. He is usually polite. It was one of the first lessons he learned.

Most people don't first notice the warden when they meet him, or the rooms crowded with agate-eyed figurines, flowers of glass, cryptochips sliced into mosaics. They first notice the warden's gun. It is made of living bone and barbed wire and smoke-silver axioms. It would have a stock of mother-of-pearl, if pearls were born from gangrenous stars. It has a long, lustrous barrel forged in a bomb's hellheart. And along the barrel is an inscription in whatever language your heart answers to: *I never miss.*

When he is human-shaped, Daechong is modestly tall, with a narrow face and dark hair cut short. His hands move too quickly to be reassuring, even if he always keeps them in sight. He wears gray, although sometimes his definition of "gray" has more in common with the black static that you find on the other side of your eyelids.

Daechong has been chained to the tower since the tower came into existence. He remembers his first visitors. It took him very little time to understand that he couldn't leave, and so he murdered them. After that, for a long time, he was alone. When more visitors started to arrive, he was very careful with them, having learned that silence is wearisome company.

Anyone who desires to descend into the world with its unmined games must persuade him to let them pass. Daechong is not recalcitrant, precisely, but he likes to challenge his visitors to games himself. It is possible, although not easy, to defeat him. Sometimes defeat carries a small penalty, sometimes a great one, according to his mood.

It is inadvisable to threaten him, and especially inadvisable to attempt to separate him from his gun. The gun admits no bullets and speaks no words of fire or fission. It gives forth no smoke, no sparks, no suppurating oil.

Yet the gun always hits what Daechong intends to shoot. Killing is one of the few pleasures available to him, and he indulges either as part of a wager or in self-defense. It doesn't matter whether the target is in front of him, or behind him, or in another galaxy, behind the ash-shroud of stars that failed to be born. Sometimes, when he fires, a quantum sentience shudders apart into spin-states pinned to forever zeros. Sometimes a city inverts itself, plunging its arches and cobweb skyroads into the earth, leaving its citizens to suffocate. The story goes that the sun-of-starships was Daechong's response to some reckless admiral bent on conquering the tower, although Daechong refuses to say anything definite on the matter.

It has been a long time since Daechong feared anyone. When he learns that Niristez of the Nine of Chains has asked for an audience, fear is not what he feels. But after all this time, he is still capable of curiosity; he will not turn her away.

There is an old story you already know, and a variant on it that you have already guessed.

Take a chessboard, eight squares by eight squares, sixty-four in total. Play begins with the first square being paid for with a single death. On the second day, fill in the next square with two deaths. On the third day, four; on the fourth day, eight. The sequence continues in this manner. The question is when both parties will find the toll of deaths such that they can no longer stomach the price of play.

We use chess—with its pieces intimating knights and kings and castles, sword-crash wars of old—for convenience, although it could be anything else. And we restrict ourselves to powers of two for convenience as well, although the mathematics of escalation knows no such boundary.

Daechong waits for Niristez in one of the highest rooms of the tower. He doesn't know what she looks like, and he declines to watch her enter by the door that will admit her but which will not allow him to leave. Besides, he can hear her footsteps wherever she is in the tower, or on the world. She has a militant reputation: he can tell that by the percussion of her boots.

This room contains musical instruments. He doesn't know how to play any of them, but he can tune and maintain them. His current favorite is a flute made of pipe scavenged from some extinguished city's scrap heap. There's a great curving harp, a lithophone, two bells. On occasion, one of his visitors breaks an instrument, and then he burns up the fragments; that's all.

The footsteps slow. She's reached the room. The lights in the tower will have told her where to go. On occasion, some visitor strays, and then he has to fetch them out of the confusion of hallways and shadows. It is sometimes tempting to let them wander, but by now the habits of courtesy are strong.

Niristez knocks once, twice. Waits.

"The door is unlocked," Daechong says.

He regards her thoughtfully as she enters the room. She is taller than he is, and her hair is like a banner. In the intolerable aeons of her exile, she has gone by many names, but Niristez is the one she prefers. It means *I promise*. The name is a lie, although most people know better than to mention it to her face. Once she had a reputation for always keeping her promises. Once she swore to win an unwinnable war. Then she fled her people, and the war has not, to this day, been won.

Her most notable feature, aside from her reputation, is not her height, or the gloves made from skinned fractals, or even the sword-of-treatises knotted at her side. It is her eyes, whose color cannot be discerned in any light but corpselight. In her eyes you can see a map forever drawing and redrawing itself, a map that knows where your flaws may be found, a map that knows how your desires may be drowned. Long ago, she was a strategist for the High Fleet of the Knifebird, and while no one now refers to her by her old rank, people remember what her eyes mean. Daechong isn't concerned by them, terrible though they are. She will already have charted his greatest weakness, and she doesn't need her unique form of vision to do so.

Niristez isn't looking at his gun, which is easily within his reach. That isn't saying much. No matter where it lies, the gun is always within his reach. But its presence is like a splinter of black dreaming, inescapable.

Niristez is, however, bearing a bottle of amber-green glass, with a cork whose eye stares unblinking at Daechong. "I thought," she says dryly, "it would be ungracious if I didn't bring a gift, considering that I am here to bargain for a favor."

"It's very considerate of you," Daechong says. "Shall I open it here?"

Niristez shrugs. "It's yours now, so you may as well suit yourself."

He keeps glasses in a red-stained cabinet. She's not the first person to bring him liquor. He picks out two spiraling flutes, with gold wire patterns reminiscent of inside-out automata and melting gears. It's tempting to shoot the bottle open, but that would be showing off, so he picks the cork out with his fingers. He's killed people by digging out their eyes; this isn't so different.

The liquor effervesces and leaves querulous sparks in the air, spelling out hectic inequalities and the occasional exclamatory couplet. Daechong looks at it longingly. "Would you be offended if I burn it up?" he says. Anything for a taste of the world outside. "I can't actually drink."

"I can't claim to be difficult to offend," Niristez says, "but as I said, it's yours now." She takes a sip herself. The inequalities flare up and die down into first-order contradictions as they pass her lips.

Daechong taps the rim of the glass. For a moment, nothing happens. Then the entire glassful goes up in smoke the color of lamentations, sweet and thick, and he inhales deeply. "You must find my tastes predictable," he says.

Niristez smiles, and shadows deepen in her eyes. "Let's say it's something we have in common."

"You mentioned that you wished to bargain," he says. "Might I ask what you're looking for?" Ordinarily he would not be so direct, but Niristez has a reputation for impatience.

"I want what everyone wants who comes here," Niristez says. "I want a game. But it's not just a game." It never is. "You know my reputation, I trust."

"It would be hard to escape it, even living where I do," Daechong says.

"On this world is the stratagem that will enable me to keep my promise." Niristez's eyes are very dark now, and her smile darker still. "I wish to buy the game that contains it from you. I've spent a great deal of time determining that this game must exist. It will win me the war of wars; it will let me redeem my name."

Daechong taps the glass again. This time it chimes softly, like a bell of bullets. Some of the musical instruments reverberate in response. "I'm afraid that you are already losing my interest," he says. "Games that admit an obvious dominant strategy tend not to be very interesting from the players' point of view." It's difficult to be a warden of games and not feel responsible for the quality of the ones that he permits to escape into the outside world. "I could let you root around for it, but I assume you're after a certain amount of guidance."

Although he is not infallible, Daechong has an instinct for the passages. He knows where the richest strata are, where the games sought are likeliest to be found. When people bargain with him, it's not simply access that they seek. Anyone can wander through the twisty passages, growing intoxicated by the combinatoric vapors. It's another matter to have a decent chance of finding what they want.

"That's correct," Niristez says. "I have spent long enough gnawing at the universe's laws and spitting out dead ends. I don't intend to waste any more time now that I know what I'm after." She leans forward. "I am sure that you will hear me out. Because what I offer you is your freedom."

Daechong tilts his head. "It's not the first time someone has made that claim, so forgive me for being skeptical."

He cannot remember ever setting foot outside the tower; it has a number of windows almost beyond reckoning, which open and close at his desire, and which reveal visions terrible and troubling. Poetry-of-malice written into the accretion disks of black holes. Moons covered with sculptures of violet-green fungus grown in the hollowed-out bodies of prisoners of war. Planets with their seas boiled dry and the fossils bleached upon alkaline shores. These and other things he can see just by turning his head and wishing it so.

Yet he thinks, sometimes, of what it would be like to walk up stairs that lead to a plaza ringed by pillars of rough-hewn stone, or perhaps gnarled trees, and not the tower's highest floor with its indiscriminate collection of paintings, tapestries, and curious statuettes that croak untrue prophecies. (More gifts. He wouldn't dream of getting rid of them.) What it would be like to travel to a gas giant with its dustweave rings, or to a fortress of neutronium whispers, or to a spot far between stars that is empty except for the froth of quantum bubbling and the microwave hiss. What it would be like to walk outside and look up at the sky, any sky. There isn't a sky in the universe whose winds would scour him, whose rains would poison him, whose stars would pierce his eyes. But his immunity does him no good here.

"Call my bluff, then," she says, her smile growing knife-sweet. "You like a challenge, don't you? You won't see me here again if you turn me down. If nothing else, it's a moment's diversion. Let's play a game, you and I. If I win, you will tell me where to find my stratagem. If I lose, I will tell you how you can unshackle yourself from this tower—and you can set me whatever penalty you see fit."

"I don't remember the very beginning of my existence," Daechong says softly. "But I was made of pittances of mercy and atrocities sweeter than honey. I was made of carrion calculations and unpolished negations. They say your shadow is shaped like massacres, Niristez. You haven't killed a fraction of the people that I have. Are you sure you want to offer this? I am not accustomed to losing, especially when the stakes matter to me."

He doesn't speak of the penalties he extracts when people lie to him. For all the dreadful things he's done, he has always respected honesty.

"I am sure," she says.

"The High Fleet of the Knifebird is still fighting the war you promised to win. It would not be difficult for me to shoot the key players into cinders."

The lines of her face become sharper, keener. "I know," she says. "But I made my promise. This is the only way to keep it. I will attempt the gamble. I always keep my promises."

Niristez has been saying this for a long time, and people have been tactful when she does so for a long time. Daechong, too, is tactful. It does him no harm. "If you are certain," he says, "then let us play."

At this point, it is worth describing the war that the High Fleet of the Knifebird has been fighting for so long, against an opponent that is everywhere distributed and which has no name but the name that particles mutter as they decay. The High Fleet has not yet raised the redshift banner that indicates defeat, but the fact that they have been fighting all this time without much in the way of lasting gains is hardly a point of pride.

High Fleet doctrine says that they are finite warriors fighting an infinite war, and the stakes are nothing less than control of the universe's laws. Each small war in the continuum is itself a gamepiece in the war of wars, placed or extinguished according to local conditions. The value of each piece is contextual both in time and in space. A duel between two spindleships at the edge of an obscure asteroid belt may, at times, weigh more heavily than a genocidal war between a dozen star empires.

In the game of Go, it is possible for players to play such that alternating captures of single stones would cause repeating positions. In principle, these moves could be played forever, and the game would never end. However, the rule called ko prevents such repetition from happening immediately.

There exists a type of ko situation, the ten thousand year ko, which is often left unresolved—sometimes until the game's conclusion—because the player who enters the battle first does so at a disadvantage. The war of wars is widely held to have run afoul of something similar.

You may speculate as to the application to the ex-strategist Niristez's situation, although most people believe that she is not capable of such subtlety. Indeed, it's not clear why she would be interested in prolonging the war of wars, unless she intended it as revenge for her loss of status. Even if she meant only to force the universe into an asymptotic cooldown rather than a condensed annihilation, this would hardly be an unambiguous victory for her or her former allies. But then, if she were skilled enough to carry out this gambit anyway, surely she wouldn't have fallen in the first place.

Daechong allows Niristez the choice of game, since she is the petitioner. The choice itself might tell him something about her, although he doubts it will be anything he couldn't already have figured out. He is surprised, then thoughtful, when she requests a linguistic game played upon competing lattices. Its name means something like "the calculus of verses." He would not have suspected her of a fondness for poetry, even the poetry of eradication. It is likely that the game has real-world manifestations, not that he has any way of checking.

The game has a deployment phase, in which they breed pensive sememes and seed rival phonologies, braid the syntactical structures that they will be pitting against each other. "Do you have the opportunity to read much?" Niristez asks him, no doubt thinking of varieties of literature to wield against him.

"On occasion people bring me books," he says. Sometimes they are tattooed on wafers of silicon. Sometimes they come bound in metal beaten thin from the corpses of deprecated clocks. Occasionally they have pages of irradiated paper. He is especially fond of the neutron variety. "I don't often read them, however." He reads fastest by—surprise—burning up the books, and while he did that a few times by accident in the early days, he saves that now for special occasions.

"Well," Niristez says, "the universe is infested with words of all kinds. I can't blame you for being choosy." She does something exceedingly clever with the placement of a cultural singularity to urge her budding language to better readiness for the engagement.

Daechong's deployments are conservative. In his experience, people who focus too much on the setup phase of the game tangle themselves up during the match proper. "I am fluent in very many languages," he says, which is an understatement. He has always assumed that the knack is a requirement, or perhaps a gift, of his position. "But I enjoy talking to people more."

"Yes," she says, "I imagine you would."

They are quiet through the rest of the deployment phase, although Daechong pours Niristez another glass of the wine she brought him, since she appears to be thirsty. She sips at it little by little, without any sign of enjoyment. He considers having another glass himself, but the smoke is still pleasantly strong in the air; no need yet.

When the game begins in earnest, the lattices light up in the colors of drifting constellations and burning sodium and firefly sonatas. Niristez's first move gives her entire language an imperialistic focus. His response is to nurture a slang of resistance.

"I am not familiar with the High Fleet's customs," Daechong says while she considers a typological imperative. "Will it be difficult to secure your reinstatement?"

This is not, strictly speaking, a courteous thing to bring up; but they are playing now. She will expect him to try to unsettle her.

Her laugh is so brief he wonders if he imagined it. "That's an open question. Tell me, Warden, if you get free of this place, where will you go?"

A predictable riposte. "I don't know," he says, although people have asked him before. His answer always changes. "The universe is a very large place. I expect that wherever I start, I can find something new to see. At the moment, I wouldn't mind visiting a binary star system. Something simple and ordinary."

That's not it at all. He likes the thought of stars that have companions, even though he knows better than to think that such things matter to stars.

Niristez seeds the plebeian chants with prestige terms from her own language, denaturing his slang. "What if you find that you were happier here?"

"There's always that risk, yes."

"The possibility doesn't bother you?"

She's asking questions she knows the answers to, which is also part of the game. "Of course it bothers me," Daechong says, "but if I never leave, I will never find out." He initiates a memetic protest. Unstable, although it has the advantage of propagating swiftly.

"I have seen a great deal of the world outside," Niristez remarks. For a moment, he can almost see what color her eyes are. "There are people who wall themselves away deliberately, you know. Ascetics and philosophers and solitude artists. Some of them would give a great deal to take your place."

"As far as anyone knows," Daechong says, "I have been here since the first stars winked open. My time here has hardly been infinite, but it's still a long time, as finite numbers go. I have no reason to believe any successor of mine would spend less time here."

She studies his move's ramifications with a slight frown, then glances around as though seeing the instruments for the first time. Nevertheless, it doesn't escape his attention that she singles out the flute for scrutiny. "Your imprisonment has given you unprecedented access to the games of the universe," she says. "Or do you take no pleasure in the things you guard?"

He considers his answer while she puts together a propaganda campaign. Blunt, but perhaps that's to be expected of someone with a military background. Still, he can't let down his guard. She may be covering for a more devious ploy. "I can't claim that the position hasn't been without its privileges," he says mildly.

Daechong has played games on involute boards, games of sacrifice and skullduggery and smiling assurances, games where you keep score with burning worlds. He has played games with rules that mutate turn by turn, and games where you bet with the currency of senescent ambition, and games that handicap the stronger player with cognitive manacles. Most of the time, he wins, and he never throws a match, even when he's tempted to just to see what would happen.

After a few moments, he counters the propaganda campaign with a furtive renaissance of the musical forms that he put in place during deployment. It's early to do this, but he'd rather respond now than give Niristez's tactic a chance to play out fully. People are sometimes startled by his comfort with music, for all that he plays no instrument. Music has its own associations with games and sports: battle hymns, marches, aggressive rhythms beaten upon the space-time membrane.

They test each other with more such exchanges. Niristez's fingers tap the side of the table before she manages to still them. Daechong doesn't take that lapse at face value, either. "In the old days, it was held that my vision meant I could not be defeated," she says abruptly, "although that has never been the case. Seeing a no-win situation opening its jaws in your direction isn't necessarily helpful."

"Have there been many of those in your career?"

"You only need one," she says, not without humor. "And even then, I've orchestrated my share of dreadful battles. Gravitational tides and neutron cannons and the slaughters you get when you use a thermodynamic vise on someone's sputtering sun. Doomships that intone stagnancy-curses into the ecosystems of entire planets. Civilizations' worth of skeletons knit together with ligatures-of-damnation and made to fight unsheathed in the crackling cold void. Dead people everywhere, no matter how you count the cost."

She's either trying to warn him or distract him. They might be the same thing. "You wouldn't have been at personal risk?" he asks. Although he's spoken with soldiers of all sorts, the staggering variety of military conventions means that he is cautious about making assumptions. In any case, he's met very few Knifebird officers.

"Not as such," she says, "although there's always the risk of an assassination attempt. A few have tried." She doesn't bother telling him what happened to them. In this matter, anyway, they are similar.

Niristez's attacks are starting to give way before Daechong's tradition of stories handed down mouth to mouth, myths to succor insurrection. A myth doesn't have to roar like dragons or fight like tigers. A myth can murmur possibilities with fox words. A myth can be subtle.

He doesn't point this out, but he doesn't have to. The rueful cast of her mouth tells him she is thinking it.

Niristez redoubles her efforts, but her early-game deployment has locked her into rigid, not to say tyrannical, stratagems. Unless she comes up with something extraordinary, they are nearing the point where the game is effectively over, even if a few of the lattices' regions can still be contested.

At last Niristez picks up a hollowed-out demagogue node and tips it over: surrender. "There's no sense in dragging this out any further," she says.

Daechong is starting to become alarmed: Niristez should be afraid, or resigned, or angry; anything but this calculating alertness. It does occur to him that, by choosing her strategy so early, she dictated his. But that was only part of the game, and in the meantime, they have their agreement.

He doesn't reach for the gun—not yet.

"It doesn't matter anyway," Niristez says. The side of her mouth tips up, and there are fissures like needles in her irises. "We both win."

He doesn't understand.

"I never needed to go into the passages," she says, and her voice is very steady. "I'm looking at what I seek already. Because the game the tower plays is you, Warden."

A myth can be subtle, and some regard Daechong as one himself; but he isn't the only myth in the room.

"Explain yourself," Daechong says, quiet and cutting.

"Everyone has been mining the planet for its games," Niristez says, "but no one has been looking at what's been right in front of them all this time. In a way, you are a game, are you not? You are a challenge to be met. You have rules, give rewards, incur penalties.

"I don't know who mined you out of the dark depths. It was probably long ago. You must have been one of the first games after the universe's very machinery of equations. And when they realized just what they had let loose into the world, when they realized your name, they locked you up in the tower. Of course, it was too late."

Niristez doesn't tell him what his name has to be. He is figuring that out for himself. The gun's presence presses against his awareness like an attar of carnage.

"You promised me my freedom," Daechong says after a long, brittle silence. "Or is that a trick, too?"

"Only if you think of it as one," she says. "You could have left at any time if you'd only known, Warden. You're only trapped here so long as you are a prisoner of your own nature. As the warden, you alone can determine this. If you choose to be a game no longer, you can walk out at any time."

Now she looks at the gun. At the dull bone, at the spiky wires, at the inscription: *I never miss.* "Destroy the gun," she says, "and walk free. It's up to you."

"If you had won," Daechong says, "you would have demanded that I come with you."

He rises. She tilts her head back to meet his gaze, unflinching. Of all things, her eyes are—not kind, precisely, but sympathetic. "Yes," she said. "But this way you have a choice."

"You're implying that, when I leave, all the wars end. That the game of war ceases to exist."

"Yes," she says.

All wars over. Everywhere. All at once.

"I can only assume that at this point in time, such a suspension of hostilities would leave the High Fleet of the Knifebird in a winning position," Daechong says.

Her eyes darken in color. "Warden," she says, "if I have learned one thing in my years of exile, it is that there are victors in war, but no one *wins*."

"I could wait for a position unfavorable to your cause," he says. "Thwart you." They're playing for higher stakes now.

"You could try," she says, "but I know what passes outside this tower, and you don't." The map in her eyes is fractal-deep, and encompasses the universe's many conflagrations.

"You played well," Daechong says. He isn't merely being polite, and he doesn't say this to many people. "I should have been better prepared."

"The difference between us is this," she says. "You are a tactician, and you fought the battle; but I am a strategist, and I fought the war. *I keep my promises.*"

"I don't concern myself with ethics," Daechong says, "but I am surprised that you would think of something as far-reaching and devastating as war to be nothing more than a game."

"It's all in how you define the set," she murmurs.

The gun is in his hand. He points it at the wall, not at Niristez, and not at himself. (This is habit. In reality, this doesn't make Niristez any safer.) It is beautiful in the way of annihilated stars, beautiful in the way of violated postulates. And she is telling him that he would have to extinguish it forever.

"It comes down to this," Niristez says. The smile is gone from her mouth, but it kindles in her eyes. "Is thwarting my promise in the war of wars more important to you than the freedom you have desired for so long?"

• • •

In the game of Go, groups of stones are said to be alive or dead depending on whether or not the opponent can kill them. But sometimes the opponents have two groups that live together: Neither can attack the other without killing itself. This situation is called *seki*, or mutual life.

The tower is a black spire upon a world whose only sun is a million starships wrecked into a mass grave. There is no light in the starships, and as time goes by, fewer and fewer people remember when the sun-of-starships gave forth any radiance at all. The shadows still mutter the names of vanquished cities and vanished civilizations, but of course the world is nothing but shadow now, and the few inhabitants remaining find it impossible to hear anything else.

Now and again people make the labyrinthine journey to the tower, which plunges into the world's hollow depths. But the tower no longer has any doors or any windows, or a warden to greet visitors, and the games that might have been dug out of the dark passages are trapped there.

Two cards of coalescent paper can, however, be found before the tower. Even the wind dares not move them from where they rest. One of them displays the Knight of Chains reversed: shattered fetters, unsmiling eyes, an ornate border that speaks to a preference for courtesy. The other card is the Deuce of Stars. It is the only source of light on the planet.

Even with the two cards revealed, Niristez would have lost the round; but that wasn't the game she was playing anyway. In the meantime, she likes to think of the former warden looking up at a chilly sky filled with enough stars to sate the longest nights alone, his hands forever empty.

THE WRECK OF THE
GODSPEED

JAMES PATRICK KELLY

Day One

What do we know about Adel Ranger Santos?

That he was sixty-five percent oxygen, nineteen percent carbon, ten percent hydrogen, three percent nitrogen, two percent calcium, one percent phosphorus, some potassium, sulfur, sodium, chlorine, magnesium, iodine and iron and just a trace of chromium, cobalt, copper, fluorine, manganese, molybdenum, selenium, tin, vanadium and zinc. That he was of the domain *Eukarya*, the kingdom of *Animalia*, the phylum *Chordata*, subphylum *Vertebrata*, the class *Mammalia*, the order *Primates*, the family *Hominidae*, the genus *Homo* and the species *Novo*. That, like the overwhelming majority of the sixty trillion people on the worlds of Human Continuum, he was a hybrid cybernetic/biological system composed of intricate subsystems including the circulatory, digestive, endocrine, excretory, informational, integumenary, musculo-skeletal, nervous, psycho-spiritual, reproductive, and respiratory. That he was the third son of Venetta Patience Santos, an Elector of the Host of True Flesh and Halbert Constant Santos, a baker of fine breads. That he was male, left-handed, somewhat introverted, intelligent but no genius, a professed but frustrated heterosexual, an Aries, a virgin, a delibertarian, an agnostic and a swimmer. That he was nineteen Earth standard years old and that until he stumbled, naked, out of the molecular assembler onto the *Godspeed* he had never left his home world.

The woman caught Adel before he sprawled headlong off the transport stage. "Slow down." She was taller and wider than any of the women he'd known; he felt like a toy in her arms. "You made it, you're here." She straightened him and stepped back to get a look. "Is there a message?"

—*a message*?—buzzed Adel's plus.

minus buzzed—*yes give us clothes*—

Normally Adel kept his opposites under control. But he'd just been scanned, transmitted at superluminal speeds some two hundred and fifty-seven light years, and reassembled on a threshold bound for the center of the Milky Way.

"Did they say anything?" The woman's face was tight. "Back home?"

Adel shook his head; he had no idea what she was talking about. He hadn't yet found his voice, but it was understandable if he was a little jumbled. His skin felt a size too small and he shivered in the cool air. This was probably the most important moment of his life and all he could think was that his balls had shrunk to the size of raisins.

"You're not . . . ? All right then." She covered her disappointment so quickly that Adel wondered if he'd seen it at all. "Well, let's get some clothes on you, Rocky."

minus buzzed—*who's Rocky?*—

"What, didn't your tongue make the jump with the rest of you?" She was wearing green scrubs and green open-toed shoes. A oval medallion on a silver chain hung around her neck; at its center a pix displayed a man eating soup. "Can you understand me?" Her mouth stretched excessively, as if she intended that he read her lips. "I'm afraid I don't speak carrot, or whatever passes for language on your world." She was carrying a blue robe folded over her arm.

"Harvest," said Adel. "I came from Harvest."

"He talks," said the woman. "Now can he walk? And what will it take to get him to say his name?"

"I'm Adel Santos."

"Good." She tossed the robe at him and it slithered around his shoulders and wrapped him in its soft embrace. "If you have a name then I don't have to throw you back." Two slippers unfolded from its pockets and snugged onto his feet. She began to speak with a nervous intensity that made Adel dizzy. "So, Adel, my name is Kamilah, which means 'the perfect one' in Arabic which is a dead language you've probably never heard of and I'm here to give you the official welcome to your pilgrimage aboard the *Godspeed* and to show you around but we have to get done before dinner which tonight is synthetic roasted garab . . . "

—*something is bothering her*—buzzed minus—*it must be us*—

" . . . which is either a bird or a tuber, I forget which exactly but it comes from the cuisine of Ohara which is a world in the Zeta 1 Reticuli system which you've probably never heard of . . . "

—*probably just a talker*—plus buzzed.

" . . . because I certainly never have." Kamilah wore her hair kinked close against her head; it was the color of rust. She was cute, thought Adel, in a massive sort of way. "Do you understand?"

"Perfectly," he said. "You did say you were perfect."

"So you listen?" A grin flitted across her face. "Are you going to surprise me, Adel Santos?"

"I'll try," he said. "But first I need a bathroom."

There were twenty-eight bathrooms on the *Godspeed*; twenty of them opened off the lavish bedrooms of Dream Street. A level below was the Ophiuchi Dining Hall, decorated in red alabaster, marble and gilded bronze, which could seat as many as forty around its teak banquet table. In the more modest Chillingsworth Breakfasting Room, reproductions of four refectory tables with oak benches could accommodate more intimate groups. Between the Blue and the Dagger Salons was the Music Room with smokewood lockers filled with the noblest instruments from all the worlds of the Continuum, most of which could play themselves. Below that was a library with the complete range of inputs from brainleads to books made of actual plant material, a ballroom decorated in the Nomura III style, a VR dome with ten animated seats, a gymnasium with a lap pool, a black box theater, a billiard room, a conservatory with five different ecosystems and various stairways, hallways, closets, cubbies, and peculiar dead ends. The MASTA, the molecular array scanner/transmitter/assembler was located in the Well Met Arena, an enormous airlock and staging area that opened onto the surface of the threshold. Here also was the cognizor in which the mind of the *Godspeed* seethed.

It would be far too convenient to call the *Godspeed* mad. Better to say that for some time she had been behaving like no other threshold. Most of our pioneering starships were built in hollowed out nickel-iron asteroids—a few were set into fabricated shells. All were propelled by matter-antimatter drives that could reach speeds of just under a hundred thousand kilometers per second, about a third of the speed of light. We began to launch them from the far frontiers of the Continuum a millennium ago to search for terrestrial planets that were either habitable or might profitably be made so. Our thresholds can scan planetary systems of promising stars as far away as twenty light years. When one discovers a suitably terrestrial world, it decelerates and swings into orbit. News of the find is immediately dispatched at superluminal speed to all the worlds of the Continuum; almost immediately materials and technicians appear on the transport stage. Over the course of several years we build a new orbital station containing a second MASTA, establishing a permanent link to the Continuum. Once the link is secured, the threshold continues on its voyage of discovery. In all, the *Godspeed* had founded thirty-seven colonies in exactly this way.

The life of a threshold follows a pattern: decades of monotonous acceleration, cruising and deceleration punctuated by a few years of intense and glorious activity. Establishing a colony is an ultimate affirmation of human culture and even the cool intelligences generated by the cognizors of our thresholds share in the camaraderie of techs and colonists. Thresholds take justifiable pride in their accomplishments; many have had worlds named for them. However, when the time comes to move on, we expect our thresholds to dampen their enthusiasms and abort their nascent emotions to steel themselves against the tedium of crawling between distant stars at three-tenths the speed of light.

Which all of them did—except for the *Godspeed*.

As they were climbing up the Tulip Stairway to the Dream Halls, Adel and Kamilah came upon two men making their way down, bound together at the waist by a tether. The tether was about a meter long and two centimeters in diameter; it appeared to be elastic. One side of it pulsed bright red and the other was a darker burgundy. The men were wearing baggy pants and gray jackets with tall, buttoned collars that made them look like birds.

"Adel," said Kamilah, "meet Jonman and Robman."

Jonman looked like he could have been Robman's father, but Adel knew better than to draw any conclusions from that. On some worlds, he knew, physiological camouflage was common practice.

Jonman gazed right through Adel. "I can see that he knows nothing about the problem." He seemed detached, as if he were playing chess in his head.

Kamilah gave him a sharp glance but said nothing. Robman stepped forward and extended his forefinger in greeting. Adel gave it a polite touch.

"This is our rookie, then?" said Robman. "Do you play tikra, Adel?"

—*who's a rookie?*—buzzed minus.

—*we are*—

Since Adel didn't know what tikra was, he assumed that he didn't play it. "Not really," he said.

"He's from one of the farm worlds," said Kamilah

"Oh, a rustic." Robman cocked his head to one side, as if Adel might make sense to him if viewed from a different angle. "Do they have gulpers where you come from? Cows?" Seeing the blank look on Adel's face, he pressed on. "Maybe frell?"

"Blue frell, yes."

—*keep talking*—plus buzzed—*make an impression*—

Adel lunged into conversation. "My uncle Durwin makes summer sausage from frell loin. He built his own smoke house."

Robman frowned.

"It's very good." Adel had no idea where he was going with this bit of family history. "The sausages, I mean. He's a butcher."

—and we're an idiot—

"He's from one of the farm worlds," said Jonman, as if he were catching up with their chitchat on a time delay.

"Yes," said Robman. "He makes sausages."

Jonman nodded as if this explained everything about Adel. "Then don't be late for dinner," he advised. "I see there will be garab tonight." With this, the two men continued downstairs.

Adel glanced at Kamilah, hoping she might offer some insight into Robman and Jonman. Her eyes were hooded. "I wouldn't play anything with them if I were you," she murmured. "Jonman has a stochastic implant. Not only does he calculate probabilities, but he cheats."

The top of the Tulip Stairway ended at the midpoint of Dream Street. "Does everything have a name here?" asked Adel.

"Pretty much," said Kamilah. "It tells you something about how bored the early crews must have been. We're going right." The ceiling of Dream Street glowed with a warm light that washed Kamilah's face with pink. She said the names of bedroom suites as they passed the closed doors. "This is Fluxus. The Doghouse. We have room for twenty pilgrims, twice that if we want to double up."

The carpet was a sapphire plush that clutched at Adel's sandals as he shuffled down the hall.

"Chrome over there. That's where Upwood lived. He's gone now. You don't know anything about him, do you?" Her voice was suddenly tight. "Upwood Marcene?"

"No, should I? Is he famous?"

"Not famous, no." The medallion around her neck showed a frozen lake. "He jumped home last week, which leaves us with only seven, now that you're here." She cleared her throat and the odd moment of tension passed. "This is Corazon. Forty Pushups. We haven't found a terrestrial in ages, so Speedy isn't as popular as she used to be."

"You call the threshold Speedy?"

"You'll see." Kamilah sighed. "And this is Cella. We might as well see if Sister is receiving." She pressed her hand to the door and said, "Kamilah here." She waited.

"What do you want, Kamilah?" said the door, a solid blue slab that featured neither latch nor knob.

"I have the new arrival here."

"It's inconvenient." The door sighed. "But I'm coming." It vanished and before them stood a tiny creature, barely up to Adel's waist. She was wearing a hat that looked like a birds nest made of black ribbon with a smoky veil that covered her eyes. Her mouth was thin and severe. All he could see of her almond skin was the dimpled chin and her long elegant neck; the billowing sleeves of her loose black dress swallowed her hands.

"Adel Santos, this is Lihong Rain. She prefers to be called Sister." Sister might have been a child or she might have been a grandmother. Adel couldn't tell.

"Safe passage, Adel." She made no other welcoming gesture.

Adel hesitated, wondering if he should try to initiate contact. But what kind? Offer to touch fingers? Shake hands? Maybe he should catch her up in his arms and dance a two-step.

"Same to you, Sister," he said and bowed.

"I was praying just now." He could feel her gaze even though he couldn't see it. "Are you religious, Brother Adel?" The hair on the back of his neck stood up.

"I'd prefer to be just Adel, if you don't mind," he said. "And no, I'm not particularly religious, I'm afraid."

She sagged, as if he had just piled more weight on her frail shoulders. "Then I will pray for you. If you will excuse me." She stepped back into her room and the blue door reformed.

plus buzzed—*we were rude to her*—

—*we told the truth*—

"Don't worry," said Kamilah. "You can't offend her. Or rather, you can't *not* offend her, since just about everything we do seems to offend her. Which is why she spends almost all her time in her room. She claims she's praying, although Speedy only knows for sure. So I'm in Delhi here, and next door you're in The Ranch."

—*Kamilah's next door?*—buzzed minus.

—*we hardly know her don't even think it*—

—*too late*—

They stopped in front of the door to his room, which was identical to Sister's, except it was green. "Press your right hand to it anywhere, say your name and it will ID you." After Adel followed these instructions, the door considered for a moment and then vanished with a hiss.

Adel guessed that the room was supposed to remind him of home. It didn't exactly, because he'd lived with his parents in a high rise in Great Randall, only two kilometers from Harvest's first MASTA. But it was like houses he had visited out in the countryside. Uncle Durwin's, for example. Or the Pariseaus'. The floor appeared to be of some blondish tongue-and-grooved wood. Two of the walls were set to show a golden tallgrass prairie with a herd of chocolate-colored beasts grazing in the distance. Opposite a rolltop desk were three wooden chairs with velvet upholstered seats gathered around a low oval table. A real plant with leaves like green hearts guarded the twin doorways that opened into the bedroom and the bathroom.

Adel's bed was king-sized with a half moon head and footboards tied to posts that looked like tree trunks with the bark stripped off. It had a salmon-colored bedspread with twining rope pattern. However, we should point out that Adel did not notice anything at all about his bed until much later.

—*oh no*—

"Hello," said Adel.

—*oh yes*—

"Hello yourself, lovely boy." The woman was propped on a nest of pillows. She was wearing a smile and shift spun from fog. It wisped across her slim, almost boyish, body concealing very little. Her eyes were wide and the color of honey. Her hair was spiked in silver.

Kamilah spoke from behind him. "Speedy, he just stepped off the damn stage ten minutes ago. He's not thinking of fucking."

"He's a nineteen year old male, which means he can't think of anything but fucking." She had a wet, whispery voice, like waves washing against pebbles. "Maybe he doesn't like girls. I like being female, but I certainly don't have to be." Her torso flowed beneath the fog and her legs thickened.

"Actually, I do," said Adel. "Like girls, I mean."

"Then forget Speedy." Kamilah crossed the room to the bed and stuck her hand through the shape on the bed. It was all fog, and Kamilah's hand parted it. "This is just a fetch that Speedy projects when she feels like bothering us in person."

"I have to keep my friends company," said the *Godspeed*.

"You can keep him company later." Kamilah swiped both hands through the fetch and she disappeared. "Right now he's going to put some clothes on and then we're going to find Meri and Jarek," she said.

"Wait," said Adel. "What did you do to her? Where did she go?"

"She's still here," Kamilah said. "She's always everywhere, Adel. You'll get used to it."

"But what did she want?"

The wall to his right shimmered and became a mirror image of the bedroom. The *Godspeed* was back in her nest on his bed. "To give you a preview of coming attractions, lovely boy."

Kamilah grasped Adel by the shoulders, turned him away from the wall and aimed him at the closet. "Get changed," she said. "I'll be in the sitting room."

Hanging in the closet were three identical peach-colored uniforms with blue piping at the seams. The tight pantaloons had straps that would pass under the instep of his feet. The dress blue blouse had the all-too-familiar pulsing heart patch over the left breast. The jacket had a double row of enormous silver zippers and bore two merit pins which proclaimed Adel a true believer of the Host of True Flesh.

Except that he wasn't.

Adel had long since given up on his mother's little religion but had never found a way to tell her. Seeing his uniforms filled him with guilt and dread. He'd come two hundred and fifty-seven light years and he had still not escaped her. He'd expected she would pack the specs for True Flesh uniforms in his luggage transmission, but he'd thought she'd send him at least some civilian clothes as well.

—we have to lose the clown suit—

"So how long are you here for?" called Kamilah from the next room.

"A year," replied Adel. "With a second year at my option." Then he whispered, "Speedy, can you hear me?"

"Always. Never doubt it." Her voice came from the tall blue frel-leather boots that were part of his uniform. "Are we going to have secrets from Kamilah? I love secrets."

"I need something to wear," he whispered. "Anything but this."

"A year with an option?" Kamilah called. "Gods, Adel! Who did you murder?"

"Are we talking practical?" said the *Godspeed*. "Manly? Artistic? Rebellious?"

He stooped and spoke directly into left boot. "Something basic," he said. "Scrubs like Kamilah's will be fine for now."

Two blobs extruded from the closet wall and formed into drab pants and a shirt.

"Adel?" called Kamilah. "Are you all right?"

"I didn't murder anyone." He stripped off the robe and pulled briefs from a drawer. At least the saniwear wasn't official True Flesh. "I wrote an essay."

Softwalks bloomed from the floor. "The hair on your legs, lovely boy, is like the wire that sings in my walls." The *Godspeed*'s voice was a purr.

The closet seemed very small then. As soon as he'd shimmied into his pants, Adel grabbed the shirt and the softwalks and escaped. He didn't bother with socks.

"So how did you get here, Kamilah?" He paused in the bedroom to pull on the shirt before entering the sitting room.

"I was sent here as a condition of my parole."

"Really?" Adel sat on one of the chairs and snapped on his softwalks. "Who did you murder?"

"I was convicted of improper appropriation," she said. "I misused a symbol set that was alien to my cultural background."

*—say again?—*buzzed minus.

Adel nodded and smiled. "I have no idea what that means."

"That's all right." Her medallion showed a fist. "It's a long story for another time."

We pause here to reflect on the variety of religious beliefs in the Human Continuum. In ancient times, atheists believed that humanity's expansion into space would extinguish its historic susceptibility to superstition. And for a time, as we rode primitive torches to our cramped habitats and attempted to terraform the mostly-inhospitable worlds of our home system, this expectation seemed reasonable. But then the discovery of quantum scanning and the perfection of molecular assembly led to the building of the first MASTA systems and everything changed.

Quantum scanning is, after all, destructive. Depending on exactly what has been placed on the stage, that which is scanned is reduced to mere probabilistic wisps, an exhausted scent or perhaps just soot to be wiped off the sensors. In order to jump from one MASTA to another, we must be prepared to die. Of course, we're only dead for a few seconds, which is the time it takes for the assembler to reconstitute us from a scan. Nevertheless, the widespread acceptance of MASTA transportation means that all of us who had come to thresholds have died and been reborn.

The experience of transitory death has led *homo novo* to a renewed engagement with the spiritual. But if the atheists were disappointed in their predictions of the demise of religion, the creeds of antiquity were decimated by the new realities of superluminal culture. Ten thousand new religions have risen up on the many worlds of the Continuum to comfort and sustain us in our various needs. We worship stars, sex, the vacuum of space, water, the cosmic microwave background, the Uncertainty Principle, music, old trees, cats, the weather, dead bodies, certain pharaohs of the Middle Kingdom, food, stimulants, depressants, and Levia Calla. We call the deity by many names: Genius, the Bitch, Kindly One, the Trickster, the Alien, the Thumb, Sagittarius A*, the Silence, Surprise, and the Eternal Center. What is striking about this exuberant diversity, when we consider how much blood has been shed in the name of gods, is our universal tolerance of one another. But that's because all of us who acknowledge the divine are co-religionists in one crucial regard: we affirm that the true path to spirituality must necessarily pass across the stages of a MASTA.

Which is another reason why we build thresholds and launch them to spread the Continuum. Which is why so many of our religions count it as an essential pilgrimage to travel with a threshold on some fraction of its long journey. Which is why the Host of True Flesh on the planet Harvest sponsored an essay contest opened to any communicant who had not yet died to go superluminal, the first prize being an all-expense paid pilgrimage to the

Godspeed, the oldest, most distant, and therefore holiest of all the thresholds. Which is why Venetta Patience Santos had browbeaten her son Adel to enter the contest.

Adel's reasons for writing his essay had been his own. He had no great faith in the Host and no burning zeal to make a pilgrimage. However he chafed under the rules his parents still imposed on him, and he'd just broken up with his girlfriend Gavrila over the issue of pre-marital intercourse—he being in favor, she taking a decidedly contrary position—and he'd heard steamy rumors of what passed for acceptable sexual behavior on a threshold at the farthest edge of civilization. Essay contestants were charged to express the meaning of the Host of True Flesh in five hundred words or less. Adel brought his in at four hundred and nine.

Our Place
By Adel Ranger Santos

We live in a place. This seems obvious, maybe, but think about it. Originally our place was a little valley on the African continent on a planet called Earth. Who we are today was shaped in large part by the way that place was, so long ago. Later humans moved all around that planet and found new places to live. Some were hot, some freezing. We lived at the top of mountains and on endless prairies. We sailed to islands. We walked across deserts and glaciers. But what mattered was that the places that we moved to did not change us. We changed the places. We wore clothes and started fires and built houses. We made every place we went to our place.

Later we left Earth, our home planet, just like we left that valley in Africa. We tried to make places for ourselves in cold space, in habitats, and on asteroids. It was hard. Mars broke our hearts. Venus killed millions. Some people said that the time had come to change ourselves completely so that we could live in these difficult places. People had already begun to meddle with their bodies. It was a time of great danger.

This was when Genius, the goddess of True Flesh awoke for the first time. Nobody knew it then, but looking back we can see that it must have been her. Genius knew that the only way we could stay true to our flesh was to find better places to make our own. Genius visited Levia Calla and taught her to collapse the wave-particle duality so that we could look deep into ourselves and see who we are. Soon we were on our way to the stars. Then Genius told the people to rise up against anyone who wanted to tamper with their bodies. She made the people realize that we were not meant to become machines. That we should be grateful to be alive for the normal a hundred and twenty years and not try to live longer.

I sometimes wonder what would have happened if we were not alone in space. Maybe if there were really aliens out there somewhere, we would never have had Genius to help us, since there would be no one true flesh. We would probably have all different gods. Maybe we would have changed ourselves, maybe into robots or to look like aliens. This is a scary thought. If it were true, we'd be in another universe. But we're not.

This universe is our place.

What immediately stood out in this essay is how Adel attributed Levia Calla's historic breakthrough to the intervention of Genius. Nobody had ever thought to suggest this before, since Professor Calla had been one of those atheists who had been convinced that religion would wither away over the course of the twenty-first century. The judges were impressed that Adel had so cleverly asserted what could never be disproved. Even more striking was the dangerous speculation that concluded Adel's essay. Ever since Fermi first expressed his paradox, we have struggled with the apparent absence of other civilizations in the universe. Many of the terrestrial worlds we have discovered have complex ecologies, but on none has intelligence evolved. Even now, there are those who desperately recalculate the factors in the Drake Equation in the hopes of arriving at a solution that is greater than one. When Adel made the point that no religion could survive first contact, and then trumped it with the irrefutable fact that we are alone, he won his place on the *Godspeed*.

Adel and Kamilah came upon two more pilgrims in the library. A man and a woman cuddled on a lime green chenille couch in front of a wall that displayed images of six planets, lined up in a row. The library was crowded with glassed in shelves filled with old-fashioned paper books, and racks with various I/O devices, spex, digitex, whisperers and brainleads. Next to a row of workstations, a long table held an array of artifacts that Adel did not immediately recognize: small sculptures, medals and coins, jewelry and carved wood. Two paintings hung above it, one an image of an artist's studio in which a man in a black hat painted a woman in a blue dress, the other a still life with fruit and some small, dead animals.

"Meri," said Kamilah, "Jarek, this is Adel."

The two pilgrims came to the edge of the couch, their faces alight with anticipation. Out of the corner of his eye, Adel thought he saw Kamilah shake her head. The brightness dimmed and they receded as if nothing had happened.

—*we're a disappointment to everyone*—buzzed minus

plus buzzed—*they just don't know us yet*—

Meri looked to be not much older than Adel. She was wearing what might have been long saniwear, only it glowed, registering a thermal map of her body in red, yellow, green and blue. "Adel." She gave him a wistful smile and extended a finger for him to touch.

Jerek held up a hand to indicate that he was otherwise occupied. He was wearing a sleeveless gray shirt, baggy shorts and blacked out spex on which Adel could see a data scrawl flicker.

"You'll usually find these two together," said Kamilah. "And often in bed."

"At least we're not joined at the hip like the Manmans," said Meri. "Have you met them yet?"

Adel frowned. "You mean Robman?"

"And Spaceman." Meri had a third eye tattooed in the middle of her forehead. At least, Adel hoped it was a tattoo.

—*sexy*—buzzed minus

plus buzzed—*weird*—

—*weird is sexy*—

"Oh, Jonman's not so bad." Jarek pulled his spex off.

"If you like snobs." Meri reminded him a little of Gavrila, except for the extra eye. "And cheats."

Jarek replaced the spex on the rack and then clapped Adel on the back. "Welcome to the zoo, brother." He was a head shorter than Adel and had the compact musculature of someone who was born on a high G planet. "So you're in shape," he said. "Do you lift?"

"Some. Not much. I'm a swimmer." Adel had been the Great Randall city champion in the 100 and 200 meter.

"What's your event?"

"Middle distance freestyle."

—*friend?*—

"We have a lap pool in the gym," said Jarek.

—*maybe*—minus buzzed

"Saw it." Adel nodded approvingly. "And you? I can tell you work out."

"I wrestle," said Jarek. "Or I did back on Kindred. But I'm a gym rat. I need exercise to clear my mind. So what do you think of old Speedy so far?"

"It's great." For the first time since he had stepped onto the scanning stage in Great Randall, the reality of where he was struck him. "I'm really excited to be here." And as he said it, he realized that it was true.

"That'll wear off," said Kamilah. "Now if you two sports are done comparing large muscle groups, can we move along?"

"What's the rush, Kamilah?" Meri shifted into a corner of the couch. "Planning on keeping this one for yourself?" She patted the seat, indicating that Adel should take Jarek's place. "Come here, let me get an eye on you."

Adel glanced at Jarek, who winked.

"Has Kamilah been filling you in on all the gossip?"

Adel crammed himself against the side cushion of the couch opposite Meri. "Not really."

"That's because no one tells her the good stuff."

Kamilah yawned. "Maybe because I'm not interested."

Adel couldn't look at Meri's face for long without staring at her tattoo, but if he looked away from her face then his gaze drifted to her hot spots. Finally he decided to focus on her hands.

"I don't work out," said Meri, "in case you're wondering."

"Is this the survey that wrapped yesterday?" said Kamilah, turning away from them to look at the planets displayed on the wall. "I heard it was shit."

Meri had long and slender fingers but her fingernails were bitten ragged, especially the thumbs. Her skin was very pale. He guessed that she must have spent a lot of time indoors, wherever she came from.

"System ONR 147-563." Jarek joined her, partially blocking Adel's view of the wall. "Nine point eight nine light years away and a whole lot of nothing. The star has luminosity almost three times that of Sol. Six planets: four hot airless rocks, a jovian and a subjovian."

"I'm still wondering about ONR 134-843," said Kamilah, and the wall filled with a new solar system, most of which Adel couldn't see. "Those five Martian-type planets."

"So?" said Meri. "The star was a K1 orange-red dwarf. Which means those Martians are pretty damn cold. The day max is only 17C on the warmest and at night it drops to—210C. And their atmospheres are way too thin, not one over a hundred millibars. That's practically space."

"But there are five of them." Kamilah held up her right hand, fingers splayed. "Count them, five."

"Five Martians aren't worth one terrestrial," said Jarek.

Kamilah grunted. "Have we seen any terrestrials?"

"Space is huge and we're slow." Jarek bumped against her like a friendly dog. "Besides, what do you care? One of these days you'll bust off this rock, get the hero's parade on Jaxon and spend the rest of your life annoying the other eyejacks and getting your face on the news."

"Sure." Kamilah slouched uncomfortably. "One of these days."

—*eyejack*?—buzzed minus.

Adel was wondering the same thing. "What's an eyejack?"

"An eyejack," said Meri confidentially, "is someone who shocks other people."

"Shocks for pay," corrected Kamilah, her back still to them.

"Shock?" Adel frowned. "As in voltage shock or scandalize shock?"

"Well, electricity could be involved." Kamilah turned from the wall. Her medallion showed a cat sitting in a sunny window. "But mostly what I do," she continued, "is make people squirm when they get too settled for their own good."

—*trouble*—buzzed plus.

—*love it*—minus buzzed.

"And you do this how?"

"Movement." She made a flourish with her left hand that started as a slap but ended as a caress that did not quite touch Jarek's face. Jarek did not flinch. "Imagery. I work in visuals mostly but I sometimes use wordplay. Or sound— laughter, explosions, loud music. Whatever it takes to make you look."

"And people pay you for this?"

"Some do, some sue." Kamilah rattled it off like a catchphrase.

"It's an acquired taste," Meri said. "I know I'm still working on it."

"You liked it the time she made Jonman snort juice out of his nose," said Jarek. "Especially after he predicted she would do it to him."

The wall behind them turned announcement blue. "We have come within survey range of a new binary system. I'm naming the M5 star ONR 126-850 and the M2 star ONR 154-436." The screen showed data sheets on the discoveries: *Location, Luminosity, Metallicity, Mass, Age, Temperature, Habitable Ecosphere Radius.*

"Who cares about red dwarfs?" said Kamilah.

"About sixty percent of the stars in this sector are red dwarfs," said Meri.

"My point exactly." Said Kamilah, "You're not going to find many terrestrials orbiting an M star. We should be looking somewhere else."

"Why is that?" said Adel.

"M class are small cool stars," said Jarek. "In order to get enough insolation to be even remotely habitable, a planet has to be really close to the sun, so close that they get locked into synchronous rotation because of the intense tidal torque. Which means that one side is always dark and the other is always light. The atmosphere would freeze off the dark side."

"And these stars are known for the frequency and intensity of their flares," said Meri, "which would pretty much cook any life on a planet that close."

"Meri and Jarek are our resident science twizes," said Kamilah. "They can tell you more than you want to know about anything."

"So do we actually get to help decide where to go next?" said Adel.

"Actually, we don't." Jarek shook his head sadly.

"We just argue about it." Kamilah crossed the library to the bathroom and paused at the doorway. "It passes the time. Don't get any ideas about the boy, Meri. I'll be right back." The door vanished as she stepped through and reformed immediately.

"When I first started thinking seriously about making the pilgrimage to the *Godspeed*," said Jarek, "I had this foolish idea that I might have some influence on the search, maybe even be responsible for a course change. I knew I wouldn't be aboard long enough to make a planetfall, but I thought maybe I could help. But I've studied Speedy's search plan and it's perfect, considering that we can't go any faster than a third of C."

"Besides, *we're* not going anywhere, Jerek and you and me," said Meri. "Except back to where we came from. By the time Speedy finds the next terrestrial, we could be grandparents."

"Or dead," said Kamilah as she came out of the bathroom. "Shall we tell young Adel here how long it's been since Speedy discovered a terrestrial planet?"

"Young Adel?" said Meri. "Just how old are you?"

"Nineteen standard," Adel muttered.

—*twenty-six back home*—buzzed plus.

"But that's twenty-six on Harvest."

"One hundred and fifty-eight standard," said the wall. "This is your captain speaking."

"Oh gods." Kamilah rested her forehead in her hand.

The image the *Godspeed* projected was more uniform than woman; she stood against the dazzle of a star field. Her coat was golden broadcloth lined in red; it hung to her knees. The sleeves were turned back to show the lining. Double rows of brass buttons ran from neck to hem. These were unbuttoned below the waist, revealing red breeches and golden hose. The white sash over her left shoulder was decorated with patches representing all the terrestrial planets she had discovered. Adel counted more than thirty before he lost track.

"I departed from the MASTA on Nuevo Sueño," said the *Godspeed*, "one hundred and fifty-eight years ago, Adel, and I've been looking for my next discovery ever since."

"Longer than any other threshold," said Kamilah.

"Longer than any other threshold," the *Godspeed* said amiably. "Which pains me deeply, I must say. Why do you bring this unfortunate statistic up, perfect one? Is there some conclusion you care to draw?"

She glared at the wall. "Only that we have wasted a century and a half in this desolate corner of the galaxy."

"We, Kamilah?" The *Godspeed* gave her an amused smile. "How long have you been with me?"

"Not quite a year." She folded her arms.

"Ah, the impatience of flesh." The *Godspeed* turned to the stars behind her. "You have traveled not quite a third of a light year since your arrival. Consider that I've traveled 50.12 light years since my departure from Nuevo Sueño. Now see what that looks like to me." She thrust her hands above her head and suddenly the points of light on the wall streamed into ribbons and the center of the screen jerked up-right-left-down-left with each course correction and then the ribbons became stars again. She faced the library again, her face glowing. "You have just come 15.33 parsecs in ten seconds. If I follow my instructions to reach my journey's end at the center of our galaxy I will have traveled 8.5 kiloparsecs."

—*if?*—buzzed minus.

"Believe me, Kamilah, I can imagine your experience of spacetime more easily than you can imagine mine." She tugged her sash into place and then pointed at Kamilah. "You're going to mope now."

Kamilah shook her head. Her medallion had gone completely black.

"A hundred and thirty-three people have jumped to me since Nuevo Sueño. How many times do you think I've had this conversation, Kamilah?"

Kamilah bit her lip.

"Ah, if only these walls could talk." The *Godspeed*'s laugh sounded like someone dropping silver spoons. "The things they have seen."

—*is she all right?*—buzzed plus.

"Here's something I'll bet you didn't know," said the *Godspeed*. "A fun fact. Now that Adel has replaced Upwood among our little company, everyone on board is under thirty."

The four of them digested this information in astonished silence.

"Wait a minute," said Meri. "What about Jonman?"

"He would like you to believe he's older but he's the same age as Kamilah." She reached into the pocket of her greatcoat and pulled out a scrap of digitex. A new window opened on the wall; it contained the birth certificate of Jon Haught Shillaber. "Twenty-eight standard."

"All of us?" said Jarek. "That's an pretty amazing coincidence."

"A coincidence?" She waved the birth certificate away. "You don't know how hard I schemed to arrange it." She chuckled. "I was practically diabolical."

"Speedy," said Meri carefully, "you're starting to worry us."

"Worry?"

"Worry," said Jarek.

"Why, because I make jokes? Because I have a flare for the dramatic?" She

bowed low and gave them an elaborate hand flourish. "I am but mad north-
northwest: when the wind is southerly I know a hawk from a handsaw."

minus buzzed—*time to be afraid*—

"So," said the *Godspeed*, "we seem to be having a morale problem. I know
my feelings have been hurt. I think we need to come together, work on some
common project. Build ourselves back into a team." She directed her gaze at
Adel. "What do you say?"

"Sure."

"Then I suggest that we put on a play."

Meri moaned.

"Yes, that will do nicely." The *Godspeed* clapped her hands, clearly pleased
at the prospect. "We'll need to a pick a script. Adel, I understand you've had
some acting experience so I'm going to appoint you and Lihong to serve on
the selection committee with me. I think poor Sister needs to get out and
about more."

"Don't let Lihong pick," said Meri glumly. "How many plays are there
about praying?"

"Come now, Meri," said the *Godspeed*. "Give her a chance. I think you'll
be surprised."

Day Five

There are two kinds of pilgrimage, as commonly defined. One is a journey
to a specific, usually sacred place; it takes place and then ends. The other is
less about a destination and more about a spiritual quest. When we decide to
jump to a threshold, we most often begin our pilgrimages intending to get to
the *Godspeed* or the *Big D* or the *Bisous Bisous,* stay for some length of time
and then return to our ordinary lives. However, as time passes on board we
inevitably come to realize—sometimes to our chagrin—that we have been
infected with an irrepressible yearning to seek out the numinous, wherever
and however it might be found.

Materialists don't have much use for the notion of a soul. They prefer to
locate individuality in the mind, which emerges from the brain but cannot exist
separately from it. They maintain that information must be communicated to
the brain through the senses, and only through the senses. But materialists
have yet to offer a rigorous explanation of what happens during those few
seconds of a jump when the original has ceased to exist and the scan from it
has yet to be reassembled. Because during the brief interval when there are
neither senses nor brain nor mind, we all seem to receive some subtle clue
about our place in the universe.

This is why there are so few materialists.

Adel had been having dreams. They were not bad dreams, merely disturbing. In one, he was lost in a forest where people grew instead of trees. He stumbled past shrubby little kids he'd gone to school with and great towering grownups like his parents and Uncle Durwin and President Adriana. He knew he had to keep walking because if he stopped he would grow roots and raise his arms up to the sun like all the other tree people, but he was tired, so very tired.

In another, he was standing backstage watching a play he'd never heard of before and Sister Lihong tapped him on the shoulder and told him that Gavrila had called in sick and that he would have to take her part and then she pushed him out of the wings and he was onstage in front of a sellout audience, every one of which was Speedy, and he stumbled across the stage to the bed where Jarek waited for him, naked Jarek, and then Adel realized that he was naked too, and he climbed under the covers because he was cold and embarrassed, and Jarek kept staring at him because he, Adel, was supposed to say his line but he didn't know the next line or any line and so he did the one thing he could think to do, which was to kiss Jarek, on the mouth, and then his tongue brushed the ridges of Jarek's teeth and all the Speedys in the audience gave him a standing ovation . . .

. . . which woke him up.

Adel blinked. He lay in bed between Meri and Jarek; both were still asleep. They were under a yellow sheet that had pink kites and blue clouds on it. Jarek's arm had dropped loosely across Adel's waist. In the dim light he could see that Meri's lips were parted and for a while he listened to the seashore whisper of her breathing. He remembered that something had changed last night between the three of them.

Something, but what?

Obviously his two lovers weren't losing any sleep over it. Speedy had begun to bring the lights up in Meri's room so it had to be close to morning chime. Adel lifted his head but couldn't see the clock without disturbing his bedmates, so he tried to guess the time. If the ceiling was set to gain twenty lumens a minute and Speedy started at 0600, then it was . . . he couldn't do the math. After six in the morning, anyway.

The something was Jarek—*yes*. Adel realized that he'd enjoyed having sex with Jarek just a bit more than with Meri. Not that he hadn't enjoyed her too. There had been plenty of enjoying going on, that was for sure. A thrilling night all around. But Adel could be rougher with Jarek than he was with Meri. He didn't have to hold anything back. Sex with Jarek was a little like wrestling, only with orgasms.

Adel had been extremely doubtful about sleeping with both Meri *and* Jarek, until Meri had made it plain that was the only way he was ever going to get into her bed. The normal buzz of his opposites had risen to a scream; their deliberations had gotten so shrill that he'd been forced to mute their input. Not that he didn't know what they were thinking, of course; they were him.

Jarek had been the perfect gentleman at first; they had taken turns pleasuring Meri until the day before yesterday when she had guided Adel's hand to Jarek's erect cock. An awkward moment, but then Adel still felt like he was all thumbs and elbows when it came to sex anyway. Jarek talked continually while he made love, so Adel was never in doubt as to what Jarek wanted him to do. And because he trusted Jarek, Adel began to talk too. And then to moan, whimper, screech, and laugh out loud.

Adel felt extraordinarily adult, fucking both a man and a woman. He tried the word out in the gloom, mouthing it silently. I *fuck*, you *fuck*, he, she, or it *fucks*, we *fuck*, you all *fuck*, they *fuck*. The only thing that confused him about losing his virginity was not that his sexual identity was now slightly blurry; it was his raging appetite. Now that he knew what he had been missing, he wanted to have sex with everyone here on the *Godspeed* and then go back to Harvest and fuck his way through Great Randall Science and Agricultural College and up and down Crown Edge. Well, that wasn't quite true. He didn't particularly want to see the Manmans naked and the thought of sleeping with his parents made him queasy and now that he was an experienced lover, he couldn't see himself on top, underneath or sideways with his ex, Gavrila. But still. He'd been horny back on Harvest but now he felt like he might spin out of control. Was it perverted to want so much sex?

Adel was wondering what color Sister Lihong Rain's hair was and how it would look spread across his pillow when Kamilah spoke through the closed door.

"Send Adel out," she said, "but put some clothes on him first."

Adel's head jerked up. "How does she know I'm here?"

"Time is it?" said Meri.

"Don't know." Jarek moaned and gave him a knee in the small of the back. "But it's for you, brother, so you'd better get it."

He clambered over Meri and tumbled out of bed onto her loafers. Their clothes were strewn around the room. Adel pulled on his saniwear, the taut silver warm-ups that Meri had created for him and his black softwalks. The black floss cape had been his own idea—a signature, like Kamilah's medallion or Sister's veil. The cape was modest, only the size of a face towel, and was attached to his shoulders by the two merit pins he'd recycled from his Host uniforms.

He paused in front of a wall, waved it to mirror mode, combed fingers through his hair and then stepped through the door. Kamilah leaned against the wall with her medallion in hand. She gazed into it thoughtfully.

"How did you find me?" said Adel.

"I asked Speedy." She let it fall to her chest and Adel saw the eating man again. Adel had noticed that her eating man had reappeared again and again, always at the same table. "You want breakfast?"

He was annoyed with her for rousting him out of bed before morning chime. "When I wake up." Who knew what erotic treats he might miss?

"Your eyes look open to me." She gave him a knowing smile. "Busy night?"

He considered telling her that it was none of her business, but decided to flirt instead. Maybe he'd get lucky. "Busy enough." He gave his shoulders a twitch, which made his cape flutter. "You?"

"I slept."

"I slept too." Adel waited a beat. "Eventually."

"Gods, Adel!" Kamilah laughed out loud. "You're a handful, you know that?" She put an arm around his shoulders and started walking him back up Dream Street. "Meri and Jarek had better watch out."

Adel wasn't quite sure what she meant but he decided to let it drop for now. "So what's this about?"

"A field trip." They started down the Tulip Stairway. "What do you know about physics?"

Adel had studied comparative entertainment at Great Randall S&A, although he'd left school in his third year to train for the Harvest Olympics and to find himself. Unfortunately, he'd finished only sixth in the 200 meters and Adel was still pretty much missing. Science in general and physics in particular had never been a strength. "I know some. Sort of."

"What's the first law of thermodynamics?"

"The first law of thermodynamics." He closed his eyes and tried to picture the screen. "Something like . . . um . . . a body stays in motion . . . ah . . . as long as it's in motion?"

"Oh great," she said wearily. "Have you ever been in space?"

For the first time in days he missed the familiar buzz of his opposites. He lifted their mute.

—*she thinks we're a moron*—buzzed minus.

—*we are a moron*—plus buzzed.

"Everybody's in space," he said defensively. "That's where all the planets are. We're traveling through space this very moment."

"This wasn't meant to be a trick question," she said gently. "I mean have you ever been in a hardsuit out in the vacuum?"

"Oh," he said. "No."

"You want to?"

—*wow*—

—*yes*—

He had to restrain himself from hugging her. "Absolutely."

"Okay then." She gestured at the entrance to the Chillingsworth Breakfasting Room. "Let's grab something to take away and head down to the locker room. We need to oxygenate for about half an hour."

—*but why is she doing this?*—buzzed plus.

There were two ways to the surface of the *Godspeed*: through the great bay doors of the Well Met Arena or out the Clarke Airlock. Adel straddled a bench in the pre-breathing locker room and wolfed down a sausage and honeynut torte while Kamilah explained what was about to happen.

"We have to spend another twenty-minutes here breathing a hundred percent oxygen to scrub nitrogen out of our bodies. Then just before we climb into the hardsuits, we put on isotherms." She opened a locker and removed two silky black garments. "You want to wait until the last minute; isotherms take some getting used to. But they keep the hardsuit from overheating." She tossed one to Adel.

"But how can that happen?" He held the isotherm up; it had a hood and opened with a slide down the torso. The sleeves ended at the elbow and the pants at the knee. "Isn't space just about as cold as anything gets?"

"Yes, but the hardsuit is airtight, which makes it hard to dissipate all the heat that you're going to be generating. Even though you get some servo-assist, it's a big rig, Adel. You've got to work to get anywhere." She raised her steaming mug of kappa and winked at him. "Think you're man enough for the job?"

—*let that pass*—buzzed plus.

"I suppose we'll know soon enough." Adel rubbed the fabric of the isotherm between his thumb and forefinger. It was cool to the touch.

Kamilah sipped from the mug. "Once we're out on the surface," she said, "Speedy will be running all your systems. All you have to do is follow me."

The *Godspeed* displayed on a section of wall. She was wearing an isotherm with the hood down; it clung to her like a second skin. Adel could see the outline of her nipples and the subtle wrinkles her public hair made in the fabric.

—*but they're not real*—minus buzzed.

"What are you doing, Kamilah?" said the *Godspeed*. "You were out just last week."

"Adel hasn't seen the view."

"I can show him any view he wants. I can fill the Welcome Arena with stars. He can see in ultraviolet. Infrared."

"Yes, but it wouldn't be quite real, would it?"

"Reality is over-rated." The *Godspeed* waggled a finger at Kamilah. "You're taking an unusual interest in young Adel. I'm watching, perfect one. "

"You're watching everyone, Speedy. That's how you get your cookies." With that she pulled the top of her scrubs off. "Time to get naked, Adel. Walk our hardsuits out and start the checklist, would you, Speedy?"

—*those are real*—buzzed minus.

—*Meri and Jarek remember*—

—*we can look*—

And Adel did look as he slithered out of his own clothes. Although he was discreet about it, he managed to burn indelible images into his memory of Kamilah undressing, the curve of her magnificent hip, the lush pendency of her breasts, the breathtaking expanse of her back as her tawny skin stretched tight over nubs of her spine. She was a woman a man might drown in. Abruptly, he realized that he was becoming aroused. He turned away from her, tossed his clothes into a locker, snatched at the isotherm and pulled it on.

And bit back a scream.

Although it was as silken as when Kamilah had pulled it out of the drawer, his isotherm felt like it had spent the last ten years in cryogenic storage. Adel's skin crawled beneath it and his hands curled into fists. As a swimmer, Adel had experienced some precipitous temperature changes, but he'd never dived into a pool filled with liquid hydrogen.

—*trying to kill us*—screeched minus.

"Are you all right?" said Kamilah. "Your eyes look like eggs."

"Ah," said Adel. "*Ah.*"

—*we can do this*—buzzed plus.

"Hang on," said Kamilah. "It passes."

As the hardsuits clumped around the corner of the locker room, their servos singing, Adel shivered and caught his breath. He thought he could hear every joint crack as he unclenched his fists and spread his fingers. When he pulled the isotherm hood over his head, he got the worst ice cream headache he'd ever had.

"This is going to be fun," he said through clenched teeth.

The hardsuits were gleaming white eggs with four arms, two legs and a tail. The arms on either side were flexrobotic and built for heavy lifting. Beside them were fabric sleeves into which a spacewalker could insert his arms for delicate work. The legs ended in ribbed plates, as did the snaking tail, which Kamilah explained could be used as a stabilizer or an anchor. A silver ball the size of coconut perched at the top of the suit.

"Just think of them as spaceships that walk," said Kamilah. "Okay, Speedy. Pop the tops."

The top, translucent third of each egg swung back. Kamilah muscled a stairway up to the closest hardsuit. "This one's yours. Settle in but don't try moving just yet."

Adel slid his legs into the suit's legs and cool gel flowed around them, locking him into place. He ducked instinctively as the top came down, but he had plenty of room. Seals fasten with a *scritch* and the heads up display on the inside of the top began to glow with controls and diagnostics. Beneath the translucent top were fingerpads for controlling the robotic lifter arms; near them were the holes of the hardsuit's sleeves. Adel stuck his arms through, flexed his fingers in the gloves then turned his attention back to the HUD. He saw that he had forty hours of oxygen reserve and his batteries were at 98% of capacity. The temperature in the airlock was 15.52°C and the air pressure was 689 millibars. Then the readouts faded and The *Godspeed* was studying him intently. She looked worried.

"Adel, what's going on?"

"Is something going on?"

"I'm afraid there is and I don't want you mixed up in it. What does Kamilah want with you?"

Adel felt a chill that had nothing to do with his isotherm.

—*don't say anything*—buzzed plus

—*we don't know anything*—

"I don't know that she wants anything." He pulled his arms out of the hardsuit's sleeves and folded them across his chest. "I just thought she was being nice."

"All right, Adel," said Kamilah over the comm. "Take a stroll around the room. I want to see how you do in here where it's flat. Speedy will compensate if you have any trouble. I'm sure she's already in your ear."

The *Godspeed* held a forefinger to her lips. "Kamilah is going to ask you to turn off your comm. That's when you must be especially careful, Adel." With that, she faded away and Adel was staring, slack-jawed, at the HUD.

"Adel?" said Kamilah. "Are you napping in there?"

Adel took a couple of tentative steps. Moving the hardsuit was a little like walking on stilts. He was high off the floor and couldn't really see or feel what was beneath his feet. When he twisted around, he caught sight of the tail whipping frantically behind him. But after walking for a few minutes, he decided that he could manage the suit. He lumbered behind Kamilah through the inner hatch of the airlock, which slid shut.

Adel listened to the muted chatter of pumps evacuating the lock until finally there wasn't enough air to carry sound. Moments later, the outer hatch opened.

"Ready?" Kamilah said. "Remember that we're leaving the artificial gravity field. No leaps or bounds—you don't watch to achieve escape velocity."

Adel nodded.

—*she can't see us*—buzzed minus—*we have to talk to her*—

Adel cleared his throat. "I've always wanted to see the stars from space."

"Actually, you won't have much of a view until later," she said. "Let's go."

As they passed through the hatch, the *Godspeed* announced, "Suit lights are on. I'm deploying fireflies."

Adel saw the silver ball lift from the top of Kamilah's suit and float directly above her. The bottom half of it was now incandescent, lighting the surface of the *Godspeed* against the swarming darkness. At the same time the ground around him lit up. He looked and saw his firefly hovering about a meter over the suit.

—*amazing*—buzzed plus—*we're out, we're out in space*—

They crossed the flat staging pad just outside the airlock and stepped off onto the regolith. The rock had been pounded to gray dust by centuries of foot traffic. Whenever he took a step the dust puffed underfoot and drifted slowly back to the ground like smoke. It was twenty centimeters deep in some places but offered little resistance to his footplates. Adel's excitement leached slowly away as Kamilah led him away from the airlock. He had to take mincing steps to keep from launching himself free of the *Godspeed*'s tenuous gravitational pull. It was frustrating; he felt as if he were walking with a pillow between his legs. The sky was a huge disappointment as well. The fireflies washed out the light from all but the brightest stars. He'd seen better skies camping on Harvest.

"So where are we going?"

"Just around."

"How long will it take?"

"Not that long."

—*hiding something?*—buzzed plus.

—*definitely*—

"And what exactly are we going to do?"

"A little bit of everything. One of her robotic arms gave him a playful wave. "You'll see."

They marched in silence for a while. Adel began to chafe at following Kamilah's lead. He picked up his pace and drew alongside of her. The regolith here was not quite so trampled and much less regular, although a clearly defined trail showed that they were not the first to make this trek. They passed stones and rubble piles and boulders the size of houses and the occasional impact crater that the path circumnavigated.

—*impact crater?*—buzzed minus.

"Uh, Kamilah," he said. "How often does Speedy get hit by meteors?"

"Never," said Kamilah. "The craters you see are all pre-launch. Interstellar space is pretty much empty so it's not that much of a problem."

"I sweep the sky for incoming debris," said the *Godspeed*, "up to five million meters away."

"And that works?"

"So far," said Kamilah. "We wouldn't want to slam into anything traveling at a third the speed of light."

They walked on for another ten minutes before Kamilah stopped. "There." She pointed. "That's where we came from. Somewhere out there is home."

Adel squinted. *There* was pretty much meaningless. Was she pointing at some particular star or a space between stars?"

"This is the backside. If Speedy had a rear bumper," she said, "we'd be standing on it right here. I want to show you something interesting. Pull your arms out of the sleeves."

"Done."

"The comm toggle is under the right arm keypad. Switch it off."

The *Godspeed* broke into their conversation. "Kamilah and Adel, you are about to disable a key safety feature of your hardsuits. I strongly urge you to reconsider."

"I see the switch." Adel's throat was tight. "You know, Speedy warned me about this back in the airlock."

"I'm sure she did. We go through this every time."

"You've done this before?"

"Many times," she said. "It's a tradition we've started to bring the new arrival out here to see the sights. It's actually a spiritual thing, which is why Speedy doesn't really get it."

"I have to turn off the comm why?"

"Because she's watching, Adel," said Kamilah impatiently. "She's always with us. She can't help herself."

"Young Adel," murmured the *Godspeed*. "Remember what I said."

—*trust Kamilah*—

—*or trust Speedy*—

—*we were warned*—

Adel flicked the toggle. "Now what?" he said to himself. His voice sounded very small in the suit.

He was startled when Kamilah leaned her suit against his so that the tops of the eggs were touching. It was strangely intimate maneuver, almost like a kiss. Her face was an electric green shadow in the glow of the HUD.

He was startled again when she spoke. "Turn. The. Comm. Off." He could hear her through the suit. She paused between each word, her voice reedy and metallic.

"I did," he said.

He could see her shake her head and tap fingers to her ears. "You. Have. To. Shout."

"I. Did!" Adel shouted.

"Good." She picked up a rock the size of a fist and held it at arm's length. "Drop. Rock." She paused. "Count. How. Long. To. Surface."

—*science experiments?*—buzzed plus.

—*she's gone crazy*—

Adel was inclined to agree with his minus but what Kamilah was asking seemed harmless enough.

"Ready?"

"Yes."

She let go. Adel counted.

One one thousand, two one thousand, three one thousand, four one thousand, five . . .

And it was down.

"Yes?" said Kamilah.

"Five."

"Good. Keep. Secret." She paused. "Comm. On."

As he flicked the switch he heard her saying. " . . . you feel it? My first time it was too subtle but if you concentrate, you'll get it."

"Are you all right, Adel?" murmured the *Godspeed*. "What just happened?"

"I don't know," said Adel, mystified.

"Well, we can try again on the frontside," said Kamilah. "Sometimes it's better there. Let's go."

—*what is she talking about?*—minus buzzed.

For twenty minutes he trudged in perplexed silence past big rocks, little rocks and powdered rocks in all the colors of gray. In some places the surface of the trail was grainy like sand, in others it was dust, and in yet others it was bare ledge. Adel just didn't understand what he was supposed to have gotten from watching the rocks drop. Something to do with gravity? What he didn't know about gravity would fill a barn. Eventually he gave up trying to figure it out. Kamilah was right about one thing: it was real work walking in a hardsuit. If it hadn't been for the isotherm, he would have long since broken a sweat.

—*this is has to get better*—buzzed plus.

"How much longer?" said Adel at last.

"A while yet." Kamilah chuckled. "What are you, a little kid?"

"Remember the day I got here?" he said. "You told me that you were sentenced to spend time on Speedy. But you never said why."

"Not that interesting, really."

"Better than counting rocks." He stomped on a flat stone the size of his hand, breaking it into three pieces. "Or I suppose I could sing." He gave her the first few bars of "Do As We Don't" in his finest atonal yodel.

"Gods, Adel, but you're a pest today." Kamilah sighed. "All right, so there's a religion on Suncast . . . "

"Suncast? That's where you're from?"

"That's where I was from. If I ever get off this rock, that's the last place I'm going to stay."

—*if?*—buzzed minus—*why did she say if?*—

Anyway, there's a sect that call themselves God's Own Poor. They're very proud of themselves for having deliberately chosen not to own very much. They spout these endless lectures about how living simply is the way to true spirituality. It's all over the worldnet. And they have this tradition that once a year they leave their houses and put their belongings into a cart, supposedly everything they own but not really. Each of them drags the cart to a park or a campground—this takes place in the warm weather, naturally—and they spend two weeks congratulating themselves on how poor they are and how God loves them especially."

"What god do they worship?"

"A few pray to Sagittarius A*, the black hole at the center of the galaxy, but most are some flavor of Eternal Centerers. When it was founded, the Poor might actually have been a legitimate religion. I mean, I see their point that owning too much can get in the way. Except that now almost all of them have houses and furniture and every kind of vehicle. None of them tries to fit the living room couch on their carts. And you should see some of these carts. They cost more than I make in a year."

"From shocking people," Adel said. "As a professional eyejack."

The comm was silent for a moment. "Are you teasing me, young Adel?"

"No, no." Adel bit back his grin. "Not at all." Even though he knew she couldn't see it, she could apparently *hear* it inflected in his voice. "So you were annoyed at them?"

"I was. Lots of us were. It wasn't only that they were self-righteous hypocrites. I didn't like the way they commandeered the parks just when the rest of us wanted to use them. So I asked myself, how can I shock the Poor and what kind of purse can I make from doing it?"

A new trail diverged from the one they had been following, Kamilah considered for a moment and then took it. She fell silent for a few moments.

Adel prompted her. "And you came up with a plan."

—*why are we interested in this?*—buzzed plus.

—*because we want to get her into bed*—

"I did. First I took out a loan; I had to put my house up as collateral. I split two hundred thousand barries across eight hundred cash cards, so each one was worth two hundred and fifty. Next I set up my tent at the annual Poverty Revival at Point Kingsley on the Prithee Sea, which you've never heard of but which is one of the most beautiful places in the Continuum. I passed as one of the Poor, mingling with about ten thousand true believers. I parked a wheelbarrow outside the tent that had nothing in it but a suitcase and a shovel. That got a megagram of disapproval, which told me I was onto something. Just before dawn on the tenth day of the encampment, I tossed the suitcase and shoveled in the eight hundred cash cards. I parked my wheelbarrow at the Tabernacle of the Center and waited with a spycam. I'd painted, 'God Helps Those Who Help Themselves' on the side; I thought that was a nice touch. I was there when people started to discover my little monetary miracle. I shot vids of several hundred of the Poor dipping their hot hands into the cards. Some of them just grabbed a handful and ran, but quite a few tried to sneak up on the wheelbarrow when nobody was looking. But of course, everyone was. The wheelbarrow was empty in about an hour and a half, but people kept coming to look all morning."

Adel was puzzled. "But your sign said they were supposed to help them-selves," he said. "Why would they be ashamed?"

"Well, they were supposed to be celebrating their devotion to poverty, not padding their personal assets. But the vids were just documentation, they weren't the sting. Understand that the cards were *mine*. Yes, I authorized all expenditures, but I also collected detailed reports on everything they bought. Everything, as in possessions, Adel. Material goods. All kinds of stuff, and lots of it. I posted the complete record. For six days my website was one of the most active on the worldnet. Then the local Law Exchange shut me down. Still, even after legal expenses and paying off the loan, I cleared almost three thousand barries."

—*brilliant*—buzzed minus.

—*she got caught*—plus buzzed.

"But this was against the law on Suncast?" said Adel.

"Actually, no." Kamilah kicked at a stone and sent it skittering across the regolith. She trudged on in silence for a few moments. "But I used a wheelbarrow," she said finally, "which LEX ruled was too much like one of their carts—a cultural symbol. According to LEX, I had committed Intolerant Speech. If I had just set the cards out in a basket, the Poor couldn't have touched me. But I didn't and they did. In the remedy phase of my trial, the Poor asked LEX to ship me here. I guess they thought I'd get religion."

"And did you?"

"You don't get to ask all the questions." The tail of her hardsuit darted and the footplate tapped the rear of Adel's suit. "Your turn. Tell me something interesting about yourself. Something that nobody knows."

He considered. "Well, I was a virgin when I got here."

"Something interesting, Adel."

"And I'm not anymore."

"That nobody knows," she said.

—*just trying to shock you*—buzzed plus.

—*bitch*—minus buzzed.

"All right," he said, at last. "I'm a delibertarian."

Kamilah paused, then turned completely around once, as if to get her bearings. "I don't know what that is."

"I have an implant that makes me hear voices. Sometimes they argue with each other."

"Oh?" Kamilah headed off the trail. "About what?"

Adel picked his way after her. "Mostly about what I should do." He sensed that he didn't really have her complete attention. "Say I'm coming out of church and I see a wheelbarrow filled with cash cards. One voice might tell me to grab as many as I can, the other says no."

"I'd get tired of that soon enough."

"Or say someone insults me, hurts my feelings. One voice wants to understand her and the other wants to kick her teeth in. But the thing is, the voices are all me."

"All right then," Kamilah paused, glanced left and then right as if lining up landmarks. "We're here."

—*too bad we can't kick her teeth in*—buzzed minus.

"Where's here?"

"This is the frontside, exactly opposite from where we just were. We should try shutting down again. This might be your lucky spot."

"I don't know if I want to," said Adel. "What am I doing here, Kamilah?"

"Look, Adel, I'm sorry," she said. "I didn't mean to hurt your feelings. I forget you're just a kid. Come over here, let me give you a hug."

"Oh." Adel was at once mollified by Kamilah's apology and stung that she thought of him as a kid.

—*we are a kid*—plus buzzed.

And what kind of hug was he going to get in a hardsuit?

—*shut up*—

"You're only nine standard older than I am," he said as he brought his suit within robotic arm's reach.

"I know." Her two arms snaked around him. "Turn off your comm, Adel."

This time the *Godspeed* made no objection. When the comm was off, Kamilah didn't bother to speak. She picked up a rock and held it out. Adel waved for her to drop it.

One one thousand, two one thousand, three one thousand, four one thousand, five one thousand six one thousand, seven one . . .

Seven? Adel was confused.

*—we messed up the count—*buzzed minus.

—did not—

He leaned into her and touched her top. "Seven."

"Yes." She paused. "Turn. Off. Lights."

Adel found the control and heard a soft clunk as the firefly docked with his hardsuit. He waved the suit lights off and blacked out the HUD, although he was not in a particularly spiritual mood. The blackness of space closed around them and the sky filled with the shyest of stars. Adel craned in the suit to see them all. Deep space was much more busy than he'd imagined. The stars were all different sizes and many burned in colors: blues, yellows, oranges and reds—a lot more reds than he would have thought. There were dense patches and sparse patches and an elongated wispy cloud the stretched across his field of vision that he assumed was the rest of the Milky Way.

—amazing—

—but what's going on?—

"Questions?" said Kamilah.

"Questions?" he said under his breath. "Damn right I have questions." When he shouted, he could hear the anger in his voice. "Rocks. Mean. What?"

"Speedy. Slows. Down." She paused. "We. Don't. Know. Why." Another pause. "Act. Normal. More. Later."

—act normal?—

—we're fucked—

"Comm." He screamed. "On."

"Careful," she said. "Adel."

He felt a slithering against his suit as she let go of him. He bashed at the comm switch and brought the suit lights on.

" . . . the most amazing experience, isn't it?" she was saying. "It's almost like you're standing naked in space."

"Kamilah . . . " He tried to speak but panic choked him.

"Adel, what's happening?" said the *Godspeed*. "Are you all right?"

"I have to tell you," said Kamilah, "that first time I was actually a little scared but I'm used to it now. But you—you did just fine."

"Fine," Adel said. His heart was pounding so hard he thought it might burst his chest. "Just fine."

Day Twelve

Since the *Godspeed* left the orbit of Menander, fifth planet of Hallowell's Star, to begin its historic voyage of discovery, 69,384 of us stepped off her transport stage. Only about ten thousand of us were pilgrims, the rest were itinerant techs and prospective colonists. On average, the pilgrims spent a little over a standard year as passengers, while the sojourn of the colony-builders rarely exceeded sixty days. As it turns out, Sister Lihong Rain held the record for the longest pilgrimage; she stayed on the *Godspeed* for more than seven standards.

At launch, the cognizor in command of the *Godspeed* had been content with a non-gendered persona. Not until the hundred and thirteenth year did it present as The Captain, a male authority figure. The Captain was a sandy-haired mesomorph, apparently a native of one of the highest G worlds. His original uniform was modest in comparison to later incarnations, gray and apparently seamless, with neither cuff nor collar. The Captain first appeared on the walls of the library but soon spread throughout the living quarters and then began to manifest as a fetch, that could be projected anywhere, even onto the surface. The *Godspeed* mostly used The Captain to oversee shipboard routine but on occasion he would approach us in social contexts. Inevitably he would betray a disturbing knowledge of everything that we had ever done while aboard. We realized to our dismay that the *Godspeed* was always watching.

These awkward attempts at sociability were not well received; the Captain persona was gruff and humorless and all too often presumptuous. He was not at all pleased when one of us nicknamed him Speedy. Later iterations of the persona did little to improve his popularity.

It wasn't until the three hundred and thirty-second year that the stubborn Captain was supplanted by a female persona. The new Speedy impressed everyone. She didn't give orders; she made requests. She picked up on many of the social cues that her predecessor had missed, bowing out of conversations where she was not welcome, not only listening but hearing what we told her. She was accommodating and gregarious, if somewhat emotionally needy. She laughed easily, although her sense of humor was often disconcerting. She didn't mind at all that we called her Speedy. And she kept our secrets.

Only a very few saw the darker shades of the *Godspeed*'s persona. The techs found her eccentricities charming and the colonists celebrated her for being such a prodigious discoverer of terrestrials. Most pilgrims recalled their time aboard with bemused nostalgia.

Of course, the *Godspeed* had no choice but to keep all of us under constant surveillance. We were her charges. Her cargo. Over the course of one thousand and eighty-seven standards, she witnessed six homicides, eleven suicides and two hundred and forty-nine deaths from accident, disease, and old age. She took each of these deaths personally, even as she rejoiced in the two hundred and sixty-eight babies conceived and born in the bedrooms of Dream Street. She presided over two thousand and eighteen marriages, four thousand and eighty-nine divorces. She witnessed twenty-nine million eight hundred and fifteen thousand two hundred and forty-seven acts of sexual congress, not including masturbation. Since she was responsible for our physical and emotional well-being, she monitored what we ate, who we slept with, what drugs we used, how much exercise we got. She tried to defuse quarrels and mediate disputes. She readily ceded her authority to the project manager and team leaders during a colonizing stop but in interstellar space, she was in command.

Since there was little privacy inside the *Godspeed*, it was difficult for Kamilah, Adel, Jarek, Meri, Jonman and Robman to discuss their situation. None of them had been able to lure Sister out for a suit-to-suit conference, so she was not in their confidence. Adel took a couple of showers with Meri and Jarek. They played crank jams at top volume and whispered in each other's ears as they pretended to make out, but that was awkward at best. They had no way to send or encrypt messages that the *Godspeed* couldn't easily hack. Jonman hit upon the strategy of writing steganographic poetry under blankets at night and then handing them around to be read—also under blankets.

We hear that love can't wait too long,
Go and find her home.
We fear that she who we seek
Must sleep all day, have dreams of night
killed by the fire up in the sky.
Would we? Does she?

Steganography, Adel learned from a whisperer in the library, was the ancient art of hiding messages within messages. When Robman gave him the key of picking out every fourth word of this poem, he read: *We can't go home she must have killed up would.* This puzzled him until he remembered that the last pilgrim to leave the *Godspeed* before he arrived was Upwood Marcene. Then he was chilled. The problem with Jonman's poems was that they had to be written mechanically—on a surface with an implement. None of the pilgrims had ever needed to master the skill of handwriting; their scrawls were all but indecipherable. And asking for the materials to write with aroused the *Godspeed*'s suspicions.

Not only that, but Jonman's poetry was awful.

Over several days, in bits and snatches, Adel was able to arrive at a rough understanding of their dilemma. Three months ago, while Adel was still writing his essay, Jarek had noticed that spacewalking on the surface of the *Godspeed* felt different than it had been when he first arrived. He thought his hardsuit might be defective until he tried several others. After that, he devised the test, and led the others out, one by one, to witness it. If the *Godspeed* had actually been traveling at a constant 100,000 kilometers per second, rocks dropped anywhere on the surface would take the same amount of time to fall.

However, when she accelerated away from a newly established colony, rocks dropped on the backside took longer to fall than rocks on the frontside. And when she decelerated toward a new discovery . . .

Once they were sure that they were slowing down, the pilgrims had to decide what it meant and what to do next. They queried the library and, as far as they could tell, the *Godspeed* had announced every scan and course change she had ever made. In over a thousand years the only times she had ever decelerated was when she had targeted a new planet. There was no precedent for what was happening and her silence about it scared them. They waited, dissembled as best they could, and desperately hoped that someone back home would notice that something was wrong.

Weeks passed. A month. Two months.

Jonman maintained that there could be only two possible explanations: the *Godspeed* must either be falsifying its navigation reports or it had cut all contact with the Continuum. Either way, he argued, they must continue to wait. Upwood's pilgrimage was almost over, he was scheduled to go home in another two weeks. If the *Godspeed* let him make the jump, then their troubles were over. Hours, or at the most a day, after he reported the anomaly, techs would swarm the transport stage. If she didn't let him make the jump, then at least they would know where they stood. Nobody mentioned a third outcome, although Upwood clearly understood that there was a risk that the *Godspeed* might kill or twist him during transport and make it look like an accident. Flawed jumps were extremely rare but not impossible. Upwood had lost almost five kilos by the day he climbed onto the transport stage. His chest was a washboard of ribs and his eyes were sunken. The other pilgrims watched in hope and horror as he faded into wisps of probability and was gone.

Five days passed. On the sixth day, the *Godspeed* announced that they would be joined by a new pilgrim. A week after Upwood's departure, Adel Ranger Santos was assembled on the transport stage.

Sister was horribly miscast as Miranda. Adel thought she would have made a better Caliban, especially since he was Ferdinand. In the script, Miranda was supposed to fall madly in love with Ferdinand, but Sister was unable to summon even a smile for Adel, much less passion. He might as well have been an old sock as the love of her life.

Adel knew why the *Godspeed* had chosen *The Tempest*; she wanted to play Prospero. She'd cast Meri as Ariel and Kamilah as Caliban. Jonman and Robman were Trinculo and Stephano and along with Jarek also took the parts of the various other lesser lords and sons and brothers and sailors. Adel found it a very complicated play, even for Shakespeare.

"I am a fool," said Sister, "to weep when I am glad." She delivered the line like someone hitting the same note on a keyboard again and again.

Adel had a whisperer feeding him lines. "Why do you weep?"

"Stop there." The *Godspeed* waved her magic staff. She was directing the scene in costume. Prospero wore a full-length opalescent cape with fur trim, a black undertunic and a small silver crown. "Nobody says 'weep' anymore." She had been rewriting the play ever since they started rehearsing. "Adel, have you ever said 'weep' in your life?"

"No," said Adel miserably. He was hungry and was certain he would starve to death before they got through this scene.

"Then neither should Ferdinand. Let's change 'weep' to 'cry.' Say the line, Ferdinand."

Adel said, "Why do you cry?"

"No." She shut her eyes. "No, that's not right either." Her brow wrinkled. "Try 'why are you crying?' "

"Why are you crying?" said Adel.

"Much better." She clapped hands once. "I know the script is a classic but after three thousand years some of these lines are dusty. Miranda, give me 'I am a fool' with the change."

"I am a fool," she said, "to cry when I am glad."

"Why are you crying?"

"Because I'm not worthy. I dare not even offer myself to you—much less ask you to love me." Here the *Godspeed* had directed her to put her arms on Adel's shoulders. "But the more I try to hide my feelings, the more they show."

As they gazed at each other, Adel thought he did see a glimmer of something in Sister's eyes. Probably nausea.

"So no more pretending." Sister knelt awkwardly and gazed up at him. "If you want to marry me, I'll be your wife." She lowered her head, but forgot again to cheat toward the house, so that she delivered the next line to the floor. "If not, I'll live as a virgin the rest of my life, in love with nobody but you."

"We can't hear you, Miranda," said the *Godspeed*.

Sister tilted her head to the side and finished the speech. "You don't even have to talk to me if you don't want. Makes no difference. I'll always be there for you."

"Ferdinand," the *Godspeed* murmured, "she's just made you the happiest man in the world."

Adel pulled her to her feet. "Darling, you make me feel so humble."

"So then you'll be my husband?"

"Sure," he said. "My heart is willing . . . " he laid his hand against his chest, " . . . and here's my hand." Adel extended his arm.

"And here's mine with my heart in it." She slid her fingers across his palm, her touch cool and feathery.

"And," prompted the *Godspeed*. "And?"

With a sigh, Sister turned her face up toward his. Her eyelids fluttered closed. Adel stooped over her. The first time he had played this scene, she had so clearly not wanted to be kissed that he had just brushed his lips against her thin frown. The *Godspeed* wanted more. Now he lifted her veil and pressed his mouth hard against hers. She did nothing to resist, although he could feel her shiver when he slipped the tip of his tongue between her lips.

"Line?" said the *Godspeed*.

"Well, got to go." Sister twitched out of his embrace. "See you in a bit."

"It will seem like forever." Adel bowed to her and then they both turned to get the *Godspeed*'s reaction.

"Better," she said. "But Miranda, flow into his arms. He's going to be your husband, your dream come true."

"I know." Her voice was pained.

"Take your lunch break and send me Stephano and Trinculo." She waved them off. "Topic of the day is . . . what?" She glanced around the little theater, as if she might discover a clue in the empty house. "Today you are to talk about what you're going to do when you get home."

Adel could not help but notice Sister's stricken expression; her eyes were like wounds. But she nodded and made no objection.

As they passed down the aisle, the *Godspeed* brought her fetch downstage to deliver the speech that closed Act III, Scene i. As always, she gave her lines a grandiloquent, singing quality.

"Those two really take the cake. My plan is working out just great, but I can't sit around patting myself on the back. I've got other fish to fry if I'm going to make this mess end happily ever after."

To help Adel and Sister get into character, the *Godspeed* had directed them to eat lunch together every day in the Chillingsworth Breakfasting Room while the other pilgrims dined in the Ophiuchi. They had passed their first meal in tortured silence and might as well have been on different floors of the threshold. When the *Godspeed* asked what they talked about, they sheepishly admitted that they had not spoken at all. She knew this, of course, but pretended to be so provoked that she assigned them topics for mandatory discussion.

The Chillingsworth was a more intimate space than the Ophiuchi. It was cross-shaped; in the three bays were refectory tables and benches. There was a tile fireplace in the fourth bay in which a fetch fire always burned. Sconces in the shapes of the famous singing flowers of Old Zara sprouted from pale blue walls.

Adel set his plate of spiralini in rado sauce on the heavy table and scraped a bench from underneath to sit on. While the pasta cooled he closed his eyes and lifted the mute on his opposites. He had learned back on Harvest that their buzz made acting impossible. They were confused when he was in character and tried to get him to do things that weren't in the script. When he opened his eyes again, Sister was opposite him, head bowed in prayer over a bowl of thrush needles.

He waited for her to finish. "You want to go first?" he said. "I don't like to think about going home to Pio," she said. "I pray it won't happen anytime soon."

*—your prayers are answered—*buzzed minus.

"Why, was it bad?"

"No." She picked up her spoon but then set it down again. Over the past few days Adel had discovered that she was a extremely nervous eater. She barely touched what was on her plate. "I was happy." Somehow, Adel couldn't quite imagine what happy might look like on Sister Lihong Rain. "But I was much smaller then. When the Main told me I had to make a pilgrimage, I cried. But she has filled with her grace and made me large. Being with her here is the greatest blessing."

"Her? You are talking about Speedy?"

Sister gave him a pitying nod, as if the answer were as obvious as air. "And what about you, Adel?"

Adel had been so anxious since the spacewalk that he hadn't really considered what would happen if he were lucky enough to get off the *Godspeed* alive.

*—we were going to have a whole lot of sex remember?—*buzzed plus

—with as many people as possible—

Adel wondered if Sister would ever consider sleeping with him. "I want to have lovers." He had felt a familiar stirring whenever he kissed her in rehearsal.

"Ah." She nodded. "And get married, like in our play?"

"Well that, sure. Eventually." He remembered lurid fantasies he'd spun about Helell Merwyn, the librarian from the Springs upper school and his mother's friend Renata Murat and Lucia Guerra who was in that comedy about the talking house. Did he want to marry them?

*—no we just want a taste—*minus buzzed.

"I haven't had much experience. I was a virgin when I got here."

"Were you?" She frowned. "But something has happened, hasn't it? Something between you and Kamilah."

*—we wish—*buzzed plus.

"You think Kamilah and I . . . ?"

"Even though nobody tells me, I do notice things," Sister said. "I'm twenty-six standard old and I've taken courses at the Institute for Godly Fornication. I'm not naïve, Adel."

—fornication?—

"I'm sure you're not." Adel was glad to steer the conversation away from Kamilah, since he knew the *Godspeed* was watching. "So do you ever think about fornicating? I mean in a godly way, of course?"

"I used to think about nothing else." She scooped a spoonful of the needles and held it to her nose, letting the spicy steam curl into her nostrils. "That's why the Main sent me here."

"To fornicate?"

"To find a husband and bring him to nest on Pio." Her shoulders hunched, as if she expected someone to hit her from behind. "The Hard Thumb pressed the Main with a vision that I would find bliss on a threshold. I was your age when I got here, Adel. I was very much like you, obsessed with looking for my true love. I prayed to the Hard Thumb to mark him so that I would know him. But my prayers went unanswered."

As she sat there, staring into her soup, Adel thought that he had never seen a woman so uncomfortable.

*—get her back talking about fornication—*minus buzzed.

"Maybe you were praying for the wrong thing."

"That's very good, Adel." He was surprised when she reached across the table and patted his hand. "You understand me better than I did myself. About a year ago, when Speedy told me that I had been aboard longer than anyone else, I was devastated. But she consoled me. She said that she had heard my prayers over the years and had longed to answer them. I asked her if she were a god, that she could hear prayer?"

Sister fell silent, her eyes shining with the memory.

"So?" Adel was impressed. "What did she say?"

"Speedy is very old, Adel. Very wise. She has revealed mysteries to me that even the Main does not know."

*—she believes—*plus buzzed.

"So you worship her then? Speedy is your god?"

Her smile was thin, almost imperceptible, but it cracked her doleful mask. "Now you understand why I don't want to go home."

"But what about finding true love?"

"I have found it, Adel." Sister pushed her bowl away; she had eaten hardly anything. "No man, no *human* could bring me to where she has brought me."

—could we maybe try?—

—she's not talking about that—

"So you're never leaving then?" Adel carelessly speared the last spiralini on his plate. "She's going to keep you here for the rest of your life?"

"No." Her voice quavered. "No."

"Sister, are you all right?"

She was weeping. That was the only word for it. This was not mere crying; her chest heaved and tears ran down her cheeks. In the short time he had known her, Adel had often thought that she was on the brink of tears, but he hadn't imagined that her sadness would be so wracking.

"She says something's going to happen . . . soon, too soon and I-I have to leave but I . . . " A strangled moan escaped her lips.

Adel had no experience comforting a woman in pain but he nevertheless came around the table and tried to catch her in his arms.

She twisted free, scattering thrush needles across the table. "Get away." She shot off her bench and flung herself at the wall of the breakfasting room. "I don't want him. Do you hear?" She pounded at the wall with her fists until the sconce shook. "He's nothing to me."

The *Godspeed*'s head filled the wall, her face glowing with sympathy. "Adel," she said. "You'd better leave us."

"I want you," Sister cried. "It's you I want!"

Day Fifteen

Adel sprawled on the camel-back sofa and clutched a brocade toss pillow to his chest. He rested his head in the warmth of Meri's lap but, for the first time since they had met, he wasn't thinking of having sex with her. He was trying very hard to think of nothing at all as he gazed up at the clouds flitting across the ceiling of the Blue Salon.

Robman spun his coin at the tikra table. It sang through stacks of particolored blocks that represented the map of the competing biomes, bouncing off trees, whirling over snakes, clattering to a stop by the Verge.

"Take five, put two," said Robman. "I want birds."

"I'll give you flies," said Jonman.

"Digbees and bats?"

"Done."

Jonman spun his coin. "It's not just you, Adel," he said. "Speedy picked Robman and me and Jarek too. Sister didn't want us either."

"Why would she want you two?" said Adel. "You're yoked."

"Not always," said Meri. "Jonman was here a month before Robman."

"But I saw him coming," said Jonman. "Put ought, skip the take."

"She didn't disappear because of you," said Adel.

—*or you either*—buzzed minus.

"Or you either." Meri had been stroking his hair, now she gave it a short tug. "This has nothing to do with you."

"I made her cry."

"No, *Speedy* did that." Meri spat the name, as if she were daring the *Godspeed* to display. She had not shown herself to them in almost three days.

Robman spun again.

"Speedy wouldn't let her go out of the airlock," said Meri. "Would she?"

"Without a suit?" Robman sipped Z-breeze from a tumbler as he watched his coin dance. "Never."

"Who knows what Speedy will do?" said Adel.

"They're wasting their time," said Jonman. "Sister isn't out there."

"Do you see that," Meri said "or is it just an opinion?"

"Take one, put one," said Robman.

"Which gets you exactly nothing," said Jonman. "I call a storm."

"Then I call a flood." Robman pushed three of his blocks toward Jonman's side of the board. The tether connecting them quivered and Adel thought he could hear it gurgling faintly.

Jonman distributed the blocks around his biome. "What I see is that she's hiding someplace," he said. "I just don't see where."

Meri slid out from under Adel's head and stood. "And Speedy?" Adel put the pillow on the armrest of the sofa and his head on the pillow.

"She's here," said Jonman. "She's toying with us. That's what she does best."

"At least we don't have to practice her damn play," said Robman.

Adel wanted to wrap the pillow around his ears to blot out this conversation. One of their number had vanished, they were some fifty light years from the nearest MASTA, and there was something very wrong with the cognizor in command of their threshold. Why weren't the others panicking like he was? "Rehearse," he said.

"What?"

"You don't practice a play. You rehearse it."

Meri told the wall to display the airlock but it was empty. "They must be back already."

"Have some more Z-breeze, Rob," said Jonman. "I can't feel anything yet."

"Here." He thrust the tumbler at Jonman. "Drink it yourself."

Jonman waved it off. "It's your day to eat, not mine."

"You just want to get me drunk so you can win."

"Nothing," said Kamilah, as she entered the salon with Jarek. "She's not out there."

"Thank the Kindly One," said Jarek.

Robman gave Jonman an approving nod. "You saw that."

"Is Speedy back yet?" said Kamilah.

"She hasn't shown herself." Meri had settled into a swivel chair and was turning back and forth nervously.

"Kamilah and I were talking on the way up here," said Jarek. He strode behind Meri's chair and put hands on her shoulders to steady her. "What if she jumped?"

"What if? " Meri leaned her head back to look up at him.

"Adel says she was hysterical," said Kamilah. "Let's say Speedy couldn't settle her down. She's a danger to herself, maybe to us. So Speedy has to send her home."

"Lose your mind and you go free?" Robman spun his coin. "Jon, what are we waiting for?"

"Speedy," said Kamilah. "Is that it? Talk to us, please."

They all looked. The wall showed only the empty airlock.

Adel hurled the pillow at it in a fury. "I can't take this anymore." He scrambled off the couch. "We're in trouble, people."

—be calm—

—tell it—

They were all staring at him but that was fine. The concern on their faces made him want to laugh. "Sister said something was going to happen. This is it." He began to pace around the salon, no longer able to contain the frenzied energy skittering along his nerves. "We have to do something."

"I don't see it," said Jonman.

"No, you wouldn't." Adel turned on him. "You always want to wait. Maybe that was a good idea when all this started, but things have changed."

"Adel," said Meri, "what do you think you're doing?"

"Look at yourselves," he said. "You're afraid that if you try to save yourselves, you'll be fucked. But you know what, people? We're already fucked. It makes no sense anymore to wait for someone to come rescue us."

Adel felt a hand clamp onto his shoulder and another under his buttock. Kamilah lifted him effortlessly. "Sit down." She threw him at the couch. "And shut up." He crashed into the back cushion headfirst, bounced and tumbled onto the carpet.

Adel bit his tongue when he hit the couch; now he tasted blood. He rolled over, got to hands and knees and then he did laugh. "Even you, Kamilah." He gazed up at her. She was breathing as if she had just set a record in the two hundred meter freestyle. "Even you are perfectly scared." Her medallion spun wildly on its silver chain.

"Gods, Adel." She took a step toward him. "Don't."

Adel muted his opposites then; he knew exactly what he needed to do. "Speedy!" he called out. "We know that you're decelerating."

Meri shrieked in horror. Jonman came out of his chair so quickly that his tether knocked several of the blocks off the tikra board. Kamilah staggered and slumped against a ruby sideboard.

"Why, Adel?" said Jarek. "Why?"

"Because she knows we know." Adel picked himself up off the Berber carpet. "She can scan planets twenty-light years away and you don't think she can see us dropping rocks on her own surface?" He straightened his cape. "You've trapped yourselves in this lie better than she ever could."

"You do look, my son, as if something is bothering you." The *Godspeed*'s fetch stepped from behind the statue of Levia Calla. She was in costume as Prospero.

"What did . . . ?"

"Speedy, we don't . . . "

"You have to . . . "

"Where is . . . ?"

The *Godspeed* made a grand flourish that ended with her arm raised high above her head. She ignored their frantic questions, holding this pose until they fell silent. Then she nodded and smiled gaily at her audience.

"Cheer up," she said, her voice swelling with bombast. "The party's almost over. Our actors were all spirits and have melted into air, into thin air. There was never anything here, no soaring towers or gorgeous palaces or solemn temples. This make-believe world is about to blow away like a cloud, leaving not even a wisp behind. We are the stuff that dreams are made of, and our little lives begin and end in sleep. You must excuse me, I'm feeling rather odd just now. My old brain is troubled. But don't worry. Tell you what, why don't you just wait here a few more minutes? I'm going to take a turn outside to settle myself."

The *Godspeed* paused expectantly as if waiting for applause. But the pilgrims were too astonished to do or say anything, and so she bowed and, without saying another word, dissolved the fetch.

"What was that?" said Robman.

"The end of Act IV, scene 1," said Adel grimly.

"But what does it mean?" said Meri.

Jarek put his hand to her cheek but then let it fall again. "I think Adel is right. I think we're . . . "

At that moment, the prazz sentry ship struck the *Godspeed* a mortal blow, crashing into its surface just forty meters from the backside thruster and compromising the magnetic storage rings that contained the antimatter generated by collider. The sonic blast was deafening as the entire asteroid lurched. Then came the explosion. The pilgrims flew across the Blue Salon like leaves in a storm amidst broken furniture and shattered glass. Alarms screamed and Adel heard the distant hurricane roar of escaping air. Then the lights went out and for long and hideous moment Adel Ranger Santos lay in darkness, certain that he was about to die. But the lights came up again and he found himself scratched and bruised but not seriously hurt. He heard a moan that he thought might be Kamilah. A man was crying behind an overturned desk. "Is everyone all right?" called Jerek. "Talk to me."

The fetch reappeared in the midst of this chaos, still in costume. Adel had never seen her flicker before. "I'm afraid," said the *Godspeed* to no one in particular, "that I've made a terrible mistake."

The Alien is worshipped on almost all the worlds of the Continuum. While various religions offer divergent views of the Alien, they share two common themes. One is that the Alien gods are—or were once—organic intelligences whose motives are more or less comprehensible. The other is that the gods are absent. The Mission of Tsef promises adherents that they can achieve psychic unity with benign alien nuns who are meditating on their behalf somewhere in the M5 globular cluster. The Cosmic Ancestors are the most popular of the many panspermian religions; they teach that our alien parents seeded earth with life in the form of bacterial stromatolites some 3.7 billion years ago. There are many who hold that humanity's greatest prophets, like Jesus and Ellen and Smike, were aliens come to share the gospel of a loving universe while the Uplift believes that an entire galactic civilization translated itself to a higher reality but left behind astronomical clues for us to decipher so that we can join them someday. It is true that the Glogites conceive of Glog as unknowable and indifferent to humankind, but there is very little discernable difference between them and people who worship black holes.

We find it impossible to imagine a religion that would worship the prazz, but then we know so little about them—or it. Not only is the prazz not organic, but it seems to have a deep-seated antipathy toward all life. Why this should be we can't say: we find the prazz incomprehensible. Even the *Godspeed*, the only intelligence to have any extended contact with the prazz, misjudged it—them—entirely.

Here are a few of most important questions for which we have no answer:

What exactly are the prazz?

Are they one or many?

Where did they come from?

Why was a sentry posted between our Local Arm and the Sagittarius-Carina Arm of the Milky Way?

Are there more sentries?

And most important of all: what are the intentions of the prazz now that they know about us?

What we can say is this: in the one thousand and eighty-sixth year of her mission, the *Godspeed* detected a communication burst from a source less than a light year away. Why the prazz sentry chose this precise moment to signal is unknown; the *Godspeed* had been sweeping that sector of space for years and had seen no activity. Acting in accordance with the protocols for first contact, she attempted a stealth scan, which revealed the source as a small robotic ship powered by a matter-antimatter engine. Unfortunately, the prazz sentry sensed that it was being scanned and was able to get a fix on the *Godspeed*. What she should have done at that point was to alert the Continuum of her discovery and continue to track the sentry without making contact. That she did otherwise reflects the unmistakable drift of her persona from threshold norms. Maybe she decided that following procedures lacked dramatic flair. Or perhaps the discovery of the prazz stirred some inexpressible longing for companionship in the *Godspeed*, who was herself an inorganic intelligence. In any event, she attempted to communicate with the prazz sentry and compartmentalized the resources she devoted to the effort so that she could continue to send nominal reports to the Continuum. This was a technique that she had used just once before, but to great effect; compartmentalization was how the *Godspeed* was able to keep her secrets. We understand now that the contact between the two ships was deeply flawed, and their misunderstandings profound. Nevertheless, they agreed to a rendezvous and the *Godspeed* began to decelerate to match course and velocity with the prazz sentry.

The highboy that killed Robman had crushed his chest and cut the tether that joined him to Jonman. Their blood was all over the floor. Adel had done his best for Jonman, clearing enough debris to lay him out flat, covering him with a carpet. He had tied the remaining length of tether off with wire stripped from the back of a ruined painting, but it still oozed. Adel was no medic but he was pretty sure that Jonman was dying; his face was as gray as his jacket. Kamilah didn't look too bad but she was unconscious and breathing shallowly. Adel worried that she might have internal injuries. Meri's arm was probably broken; when they tried to move her she moaned in agony. Jarek was kicking the slats out of a Yamucha chair back to make her a splint.

"An alien, Speedy?" Adel felt too lightheaded to be scared. "And you didn't tell anyone?" It was as if the gravity generator had failed and at any moment he would float away from this grim reality.

"So where is this fucking prazz now?" Jarek ripped a damask tablecloth into strips.

"The sentry ship itself crashed into the backside engine room. But it has deployed a remote." The *Godspeed* seemed twitchy and preoccupied. "It's in the conservatory, smashing cacti."

"What?" said Adel.

"It has already destroyed my rain forest and torn up my alpine garden."

plus buzzed—*they're fighting with plants?*—

"Show me," said Jarek.

The wall turned a deep featureless blue. "I can't see them; my cameras there are gone." The *Godspeed* paused, her expression uneasy.

—*more bad news coming*—buzzed minus.

"You should know," she said, "that just before it attacked, the prazz warned me that I was infested with vermin and needed to sterilize myself. When I told it that I didn't consider you vermin . . . "

"You're saying they'll come for us?" said Jarek.

"I'm afraid that's very likely."

"Then stop it."

She waved her magic staff disconsolately. "I'm at a loss to know how."

"Fuck that, Speedy." Jarek pointed one of the slats at her fetch. "You think of something. Right now." He knelt by Meri. "I'm going to splint you now, love. It's probably going to hurt."

Meri screamed as he tenderly straightened her arm.

"I know, love," said Jarek. "I know."

—*we have to get out of here*—buzzed minus.

"How badly are you damaged, Speedy?" said Adel. "Can we use the MASTA?"

"My MASTA is operational on a limited basis only. My backside engine complex is a complete loss. I thought I was able to vent all the antimatter in time, but there must have been a some left that exploded when the containment failed."

Something slammed onto the level below them so hard that the walls shook.

—*those things are tearing her apart*—

—*looking for us*—

"I've sealed off the area as best I can but the integrity of my life support envelope has been compromised in several places. At the rate I'm bleeding air into space . . . "

Adel felt another jarring impact, only this one felt as if it were farther away. The *Godspeed*'s fetch blurred and dispersed into fog. She reconstituted herself on the wall.

" . . . the partial pressure of oxygen will drop below 100 millibars sometime within the next ten to twelve hours."

"That's it then." Jarek helped Meri to her feet and wiped the tears from her face with his forefinger. "We're all jumping home. Meri can walk, can't you Meri?"

She nodded, her eyes wide with pain. "I'm fine."

"Adel, we'll carry Jonman out first."

"The good news," said the *Godspeed*, "is that I can maintain power indefinitely using my frontside engines."

"Didn't you hear me?" Jarek's voice rose sharply. "We're leaving right now. Jonman and Kamilah can't wait and the rest of us vermin have no intention of being sterilized by your fucking prazz."

"I'm sorry, Jarek." She stared out at them, her face set. "You know I can't send you home. Think about it."

"Speedy!" said Meri. "No."

"What?" said Adel. "What's he talking about?"

"What do you care about the protocols?" Jarek put his arm around Meri's waist to steady her. "You've already kicked them over. That's why we're in this mess."

"The prazz knows where we are," said the *Godspeed*, "but it doesn't know where we're from. I burst my weekly reports . . . "

"Weekly lies, you mean," said Adel.

"They take just six nanoseconds. That's not nearly enough time to get a fix. But a human transmit takes 1.43 *seconds* and the prazz is right here on board." She shook her head sadly. "Pointing it at the Continuum would violate my deepest operating directives. Do you want a prazz army marching off the MASTA stage on Moquin or Harvest?"

"How do we know they have armies?" Jarek said, but his massive shoulders slumped. "Or MASTAs?"

Jonman laughed. It was a low, wet sound, almost a cough. "Adel," he rasped. "I see . . . " He was trying to speak but all that came out of his mouth was thin, pink foam.

Adel knelt by his side. "Jonman, what? You see what?"

"I see." He clutched at Adel's arm. "You." His grip tightened. "Dead." His eyelids fluttered and closed.

—*this isn't happening*—

"What did he say?" said Meri.

"Nothing." Adel felt Jonman's grip relaxing; his arm fell away.

—*dead?*—buzzed plus

Adel put his ear to Jonman's mouth and heard just the faintest whistle of breath.

minus buzzed—*we're all dead*—

Adel stood up, his thoughts tumbling over each other. He believed that Jonman hadn't spoken out of despair—or cruelty. He had seen something, maybe a way out, and had tried to tell Adel what it was.

—*don't play tikra with Jonman*—buzzed minus—*he cheats*—

—*dead*—plus buzzed—*but not really*—

"Speedy," said Adel, "what if you killed us?" What would the prazz do then?"

Jarek snorted in disgust. "What kind of thing is that to . . . " Then he understood what Adel was suggesting. "Hot damn!"

"What?" said Meri. "Tell me."

"But can we do it?" said Jarek. "I mean, didn't they figure out that it's bad for you to be dead too long?"

Adel laughed and clapped Jarek on the shoulder. "Can it be worse than being dead forever?"

—*so dangerous*—buzzed minus.

—*we're fucking brilliant*—

"You're still talking about the MASTA?" said Meri. "But Speedy won't transmit."

"Exactly," said Adel.

"There isn't much time," said the *Godspeed*.

The Neverending Day

Adel was impressed with how easy it was being dead. The things that had bothered him when he was alive, like being hungry or horny, worrying about whether his friends really liked him or what he was going to be if he ever grew up—none of that mattered. Who cared that he had never learned the first law of thermodynamics or that he had blown the final turn in the most important race of his life? Appetite was an illusion. Life was pleasant, but then so were movies.

The others felt the same way. Meri couldn't feel her broken arm and Jonman didn't mind at all that he was dying, although he did miss Robman. Adel felt frustrated at first that he couldn't rouse Kamilah, but she was as perfect unconscious as she was when she was awake. Besides, Upwood predicted that she would get bored eventually being alone with herself. It wasn't true that nobody changed after they were dead, he explained, it was just that change came very slowly and was always profound. Adel had been surprised to meet Upwood Marcene in Speedy's pocket-afterlife, but his being there made sense. And of course, Adel had guessed that Sister Lihong Rain would be dead there too. As it turned out, she had been dead many times over the seven years of her pilgrimage.

Speedy had created a virtual space in her memory that was almost identical to the actual *Godspeed*. Of course, Speedy was as real as any of them, which is to say not very real at all. Sister urged the newcomers to follow shipboard routine whenever possible; it would make the transition back to life that much easier. Upwood graciously moved out of The Ranch so that Adel could have his old room back. Speedy and the pilgrims gathered in the Ophiuchi or the

Chillingsworth at meal times, and although they did not eat, they did chatter. They even propped Kamilah on a chair to include her in the group. Speedy made a point of talking to her at least once at every meal. She would spin theories about the eating man on Kamilah's medallion or propose eyejack performances Kamilah might try on them.

She also lobbied the group to mount *The Tempest*, but Jarek would have no part in it. Of all of them, he seemed most impatient with death. Instead they played billiards and cards. Adel let Jonman teach him Tikra and didn't mind at all when he cheated. Meri read to them and Jarek played the ruan and sang. Adel visited the VR room but once; the sim made him feel gauzy and extenuated. He did swim two thousand meters a day in the lap pool, which, although physically disappointing, was a demanding mental challenge. Once he and Jarek and Meri climbed into bed together but nothing very interesting happened. They all laughed about it afterward.

Adel was asleep in his own bed, remembering a dream he'd had when he was alive. He was lost in a forest where people grew instead of trees. He stumbled past shrubby little kids and great towering grownups like his parents and Uncle Durwin. He knew he had to keep walking because if he stopped he would grow roots and raise his arms up to the sun like all the other tree people, but he was tired, so very tired.

"Adel." Kamilah shook him roughly. "Can you hear that? Adel!"

At first he thought she must be part of his dream.

—*she's better*—

—*Kamilah*—

"Kamilah, you're awake!"

"Listen." She put her forefinger to her lips and twisted her head, trying to pinpoint the sound. "No, it's gone. I thought they were calling Sister."

"This is wonderful." He reached to embrace her but she slid away from him. "When did you wake up?"

"Just now. I was in my room in bed and I heard singing." She scowled. "What's going on, Adel? The last thing I remember was you telling Speedy you knew we were decelerating. This all feels very wrong to me."

"You don't remember the prazz?"

Her expression was grim. "Tell me everything."

Adel was still groggy, so the story tumbled out in a hodgepodge of the collision and the prazz and the protocols and Robman and the explosion and the blood and the life support breech and Speedy scanning them into memory and Sister and swimming and tikra and Upwood.

"Upwood is here?"

"Upwood? Oh yes."

—he is?—

—is he?—

As Adel considered the question, his certainty began to crumble. "I mean he was. He gave me his room. But I haven't seen him in a while."

"How long?"

Adel frowned. "I don't know."

"How long have we been here? You and I and the others?"

Adel shook his head.

"Gods, Adel." She reached out tentatively and touched his arm but of course he didn't feel a thing. Kamilah gazed at her own hand in horror, as if it had betrayed her. "Let's find Jarek."

Kamilah led them down the Tulip Stairs, past the Blue and Dagger Salons through the Well Met Arena to the Clarke Airlock. The singing was hushed but so ethereal here that even Jarek and Adel, whose senses had atrophied, could feel it. Sister waited for them just inside the outer door of the airlock.

Although Adel knew it must be her, he didn't recognize her at first. She was naked and her skin was so pale that it was translucent. He could see her heart beating and the dark blood pulsing through her veins, the shiny bundles of muscles sliding over each other as she moved and the skull grinning at him beneath her face. Her thin hair had gone white; it danced around her head as if she were falling.

—beautiful—

—exquisite—

"I'm glad you're here." She smiled at them. "Adel. Kamilah. Jarek." She nodded at each of them in turn. "My witnesses."

"Sister," said Kamilah, "come away from there."

Sister placed her hand on the door and it vanished. Kamilah staggered back and grabbed at the inner door as if she expected to be expelled from the airlock in a great outrush of air, but Adel knew it wouldn't happen. Kamilah still didn't understand the way things worked here.

They gazed out at a star field much like the one that Adel had seen when he first stepped out onto the surface of the *Godspeed*. Except now there was no surface—only stars.

"Kamilah," said Sister. "you started last and have the farthest to travel. Jarek, you still have doubts. But Adel already knows that the self is a box he has squeezed himself into."

—yes—

—right—

She stepped backwards out of the airlock and was suspended against the stars.

"Kamilah," she said, "trust us and someday you *will* be perfect." The singing enfolded her and she began to glow in its embrace. The brighter she burned the more she seemed to recede from them, becoming steadily hotter and more concentrated until Adel couldn't tell her from one of the stars. He wasn't sure but he thought she was a blue dwarf.

"Close the airlock, Adel." Speedy strolled into the locker room wearing her golden uniform coat and white sash. "It's too much of a distraction."

"What is this, Speedy?" Jarek's face was ashen. "You said you would send us back."

Adel approached the door cautiously; he wasn't ready to follow Sister to the stars quite yet.

"But I did send you back," she said.

"Then who are we?"

"Copies." Adel jabbed at the control panel and jumped back as the airlock door reappeared. "I think we must be backups."

Kamilah was seething. "You kept copies of us to play with?" Her fists were clenched.

Adel was bemused; they were dead. Who did she think she was going to fight?

"It's not what you think." Speedy smiled. "Let's go up to Blue Salon. We should bring Jonman and Meri into this conversation too." She made ushering motions toward the Well Met and Adel and Jarek turned to leave.

—*good idea*—

—*let's go*—

"No, let's not." With two quick strides, Kamilah gained the doorway and blocked their passage. "If Meri wants to know what's going on, then she can damn well ask."

"Ah, Kamilah. My eyejack insists on the truth." She shrugged and settled onto one of the benches in the locker room. "This is always such a difficult moment," she said.

"Just tell it," said Kamilah.

"The prazz ship expired about three days after the attack. In the confusion of the moment, I'd thought it was my backside engine that exploded. Actually it was the sentry's drive. Once its batteries were exhausted, both the sentry ship and its remote ceased all function. I immediately transmitted all of you to your various home worlds and then disabled my transmitter and deleted all my navigation files. The Continuum is safe—for now. If the prazz come looking, there are further actions I can take."

"And what about us?" said Kamilah. "How do we get home?"

"As I said, you are home, Kamilah. Your injuries were severe but certainly not fatal. Your prognosis was for a complete recovery."

—right—

—makes sense—

"Not that one," said Kamilah. "This one." She tapped her chest angrily. "Me. How do I get home?"

"But Kamilah . . . " Speedy swept an arm expansively, taking in the airlock and lockers and Well Met and the Ophiuchi and Jarek and Adel. " . . . this is your home."

The first pilgrim from the *Godspeed* lost during a transmit was Io Waals. We can't say for certain whether she suffered a flawed scan or something interfered with her signal but when the MASTA on Rontaw assembled her, her heart and lungs were outside her body cavity. This was three hundred and ninety-two years into the mission. By then, the Captain had long since given way to Speedy.

The *Godspeed* was devastated by Io's death. Some might say it unbalanced her, although we would certainly disagree. But this was when she began to compartmentalize behaviors, sealing them off from the scrutiny of the Continuum and, indeed, from most of her conscious self. She stored backups of every scan she made in her first compartment. For sixty-seven years, she deleted each of them as soon as she received word of a successful transmit. Then Ngong Issonda died when a tech working on Loki improperly recalibrated the MASTA.

Only then did the *Godspeed* understand the terrible price she would pay for compartmentalization. Because she had been keeping the backups a secret not only from the Continuum but also to a large extent from herself, she had never thought through how she might make use of them. It was immediately clear to her that if she resent Ngong, techs would start arriving on her transport stage within the hour to fix her. The *Godspeed* had no intention of being fixed. But what to do with Ngong's scan? She created a new compartment, a simulation of her architecture into which she released Ngong. Ngong did not flourish in the simulation, however. She was depressed and withdrawn whenever the *Godspeed* visited. Her next scan, Keach Soris arrived safely on Butler's Planet, but Speedy loaded his backup into the simulation with Ngong. Within the year, she was loading all her backups into the sim. But as Upwood Marcene would point out some seven centuries later, dead people change and the change is always profound and immaterial. In less than a year after the sim was created, Ngong, Keach and Zampa Stackpole stepped out of airlock together into a new compartment, one that against all reason transcends the boundaries of the *Godspeed*, the Milky Way and spacetime itself.

• • •

So then, what do we know about Adel Ranger Santos?

Nothing at all. Once we transmitted him back to Harvest, he passed from our awareness. He may have lived a long, happy life or a short painful one. His fate does not concern us.

But what do we know about Adel Ranger Santos?

Only what we know about Upwood Marcene, Kalimah Raunda, Jarek Ohnksen, Merigood Auburn Canada, Lihong Rain and Jonman Haught Shillaber—which is everything, of course. For they followed Ngong and Keach and Zampa and some forty thousand other pilgrims through the airlock to become us.

And we are they.

SAVING TIAMAAT

GWYNETH JONES

—◆—

I had reached the station in the depth of Left Speranza's night; I had not slept. Fogged in the confabulation of the transit, I groped through crushing aeons to my favourite breakfast kiosk: unsure if the soaring concourse outside Parliament was ceramic and carbon or a *metaphor*; a cloudy internal warning—now what was the message in the mirror? Something pitiless. Some blank-eyed, slow-thinking, long-grinned crocodile—

"Debra!"

It was my partner. "Don't *do* that," I moaned. The internal crocodile shattered, the concourse lost its freight of hyper-determined meaning, too suddenly for comfort. "Don't you know you should never startle a sleepwalker?"

He grinned; he knew when I'd arrived, and the state I was likely to be in. I hadn't met Pelé Leonidas Iza Quinatoa in the flesh before, but we'd worked together, we liked each other. "Ayayay, so good you can't bear to lose it?"

"Of course not. Only innocent, beautiful souls have sweet dreams."

He touched my cheek: collecting a teardrop. I hadn't realised I was crying. "You should use the dreamtime, Debra. There must be *some* game you want to play."

"I've tried, it's worse. If I don't take my punishment, I'm sick for days."

The intimacy of his gesture (skin on skin) was an invitation and a promise; it made me smile. We walked into the Parliament Building together, buoyant in the knocked-down gravity that I love although I know it's bad for you.

In the Foyer, we met the rest of the company, identified by the Diaspora Parliament's latest adventure in biometrics, the aura tag. To our vision, the KiAn Working Party was striated orange/yellow, nice cheerful implications, nothing too deep. The pervasive systems were seeing a lot more, but that didn't bother Pelé or me; we had no secrets from Speranza.

The KiAn problem had been a matter of concern since their world had been "discovered" by a Balas/Shet prospector, and joined the miniscule roster of populated planets linked by instantaneous transit. Questions had been raised then, over the grave social imbalance: the tiny international ruling caste, the exploited masses. But neither the Ki nor the An would accept arbitration (why the hell should they?). The non-interference lobby is the weakest faction in the Chamber, quarantine-until-they're-civilised was not considered an option. Inevitably, around thirty local years after first contact, the Ki had risen against their overlords, as often in the past. Inevitably, this time they had modern weapons. They had not succeeded in wiping out the An, but they had pretty much rendered the shared planet uninhabitable.

We were here to negotiate a rescue package. We'd done the damage, we had to fix it, that was the DP's line. The Ki and the An no doubt had their own ideas as to what was going on: they were new to the Interstellar Diaspora, not to politics.

But they were here, at least; so that seemed hopeful.

The Ki Federation delegates were unremarkable. There were five of them, they conformed to the "sentient biped" bodyplan that unites the diaspora. Three were wearing Balas business suits in shades of brown, two were in grey military uniform. The young co-leaders of the An were better dressed, and one of the two, in particular, was *much* better looking. Whatever you believe about the origins of the "diaspora" (Strong theory, Weak theory, something between) it's strange how many measures of beauty are common to us all. He was tall, past two metres: he had large eyes, a mane of rich brown head-hair, an open, strong-boned face, poreless bronze skin, and a glorious smile. He would be my charge. His co-leader, the subordinate partner, slight and small, almost as dowdy as the Ki, would be Pelé's.

They were codenamed Baal and Tiamaat, the names I will use in this account. The designations Ki and An are also codenames.

We moved off to a briefing room. Joset Moricherri, one of the Blue Permanent Secretaries, made introductory remarks. A Green Belt Colonel, Shamaz Haa'agaan, gave a talk on station security. A slightly less high-ranking DP administrator got down to basics: standard time conventions, shopping allowances, access to the elevators, restricted areas, housekeeping . . . Those who hadn't provided their own breakfast raided the culturally neutral trolley. I sipped my Mocha/Colombian, took my carbs in the form of a crisp cherry-jam tartine; and let the day's agenda wash over me, as I reviewed what I knew about Baal and Tiamaat's relationship.

They were not related by blood, except in the sense that the An gene pool was very restricted: showing signs of other population crashes in the past. They were not "married", either. The Ki and the An seemed to be sexually dimorphic on the Blue model (though they could yet surprise us!); and they liked opposite sex partnerships. But they did not marry. Tiamaat's family had been swift to embrace the changes, she'd been educated on Balas/Shet. Baal had left KiAn for the first time when war broke out. They'd lost family members, and they'd certainly seen the horrific transmissions smuggled off KiAn before the end. Yet here they were, with the genocidal Ki: thrown together, suddenly appointed the rulers of their shattered nation, and bound to each other for life. Tiamaat looked as if she was feeling the strain. She sat with her eyes lowered, drawn in on herself, her body occupying the minimum of space. Beside her, Baal devoured a culturally-neutral doughnut, elbows sprawled, with a child's calm greed. I wondered how much my alien perception of a timid young woman and a big bold young man was distorting my view. I wondered how all that fine physicality translated into mind.

Who are you, Baal? How will it feel to know you?

From the meeting we proceeded to a DP reception and lunch, from thence to a concert in the Nebula Immersion Chamber: a Blue Planet symphony orchestra on virtual tour, the Diaspora Chorus in the flesh, singing a famous masque; a solemn dance drama troupe bi-locating from Neuendan. Pelé and I, humble Social Support officers, were in the background for these events. But the An had grasped that we were their advocates: as was proved when they pounced on us, eagerly, after the concert. They wanted to meet "the nice quiet people with the pretty curly faces—"

They spoke English, language of diplomacy and displacement. They'd both taken the express, neuro-tech route to fluency: but we had trouble pinning this request down. It turned out they were asking to be introduced to a bowl of orchids.

Appearances can be deceptive; these two young people were neither calm nor cowed. They had been born in a mediaeval world, and swept away from home as to the safety of a rich neighbour's house: all they knew of the interstellar age was the inside of a transit lounge. The Ki problem they knew only too well: Speranza was a thrilling bombardment. With much laughter (they laughed like Blue teenagers, to cover embarrassment), we explained that they would not be meeting any bizarre lifeforms. No tentacles, no petals, no intelligent gas clouds here; not yet!

"You have to look after us!" cried Baal. He grabbed my arm, softly but I felt the power. "Save us from making fools of ourselves, dear Debra and Pelé!"

Tiamaat stood back a pace, hiding her giggles behind her hand.

The last event scheduled on that first day was a live transmission walkabout from the Ki refugee camp, in the Customised Shelter Sector. In the planning stages, some of us had expressed doubts about this stunt. If anything went wrong it'd sour the whole negotiation. But the Ki and the An leaders were both keen, and the historic gesture was something the public back on the homeworlds would understand—which in the end had decided the question. The Diaspora Parliament had to struggle for planetside attention, we couldn't pass up an opportunity.

At the gates of the CSS, deep in Speranza's hollow heart, there was a delay. The Customised Shelter Police wanted us in armoured glass-tops, they felt that if we *needed* a walkabout we could fake it. . . . Pelé chatted with Tiamaat, stooping from his lean black height to catch her soft voice. Baal stared at the banners on two display screens. The KiAn understood flags, we hadn't taught them that concept. Green and gold quarters for the Ki, a centre section crosshatched with the emblems of all the nations. Purple tracery on vivid bronze for the An.

Poor kid, I thought, it's not a magic gateway to your lost home. Don't get your hopes up. That's the door to a cage in a conservation zoo.

He noticed my attention, and showed his white teeth. "Are there other peoples living in exile on this floor?"

I nodded. "Yes. But mostly the people sheltered here are old spacers, who can't return to full gravity. Or failed colonist communities, likewise: people who've tried to settle on empty moons and planets and been defeated by the conditions. There are no other populated planet exiles. It hasn't been, er, necessary."

"We are a first for you."

I wondered if that was ironic; if he was capable of irony.

A compromise was reached. We entered on foot, with the glass-tops and CSP closed cars trailing behind. The Ki domain wasn't bad, for a displaced persons camp wrapped in the bleak embrace of a giant space station. Between the living-space capsule towers the refugees could glimpse their own shade of sky; and a facsimile of their primary sun, with its partner, the blue-rayed daystar. They had sanitation, hygiene, regular meals; leisure facilities, even employment. We stopped at an adult retraining centre, we briefly inspected a hydroponic farm. We visited a kindergarten, where the teaching staff told us (and the flying cams!) how all the nations of the Ki were gathered here in harmony, learning to be good Diaspora citizens.

The children stared at Baal and Tiamaat. They'd probably been born in the camp, and never seen An in the flesh before. Baal fidgeted, seeming indignant under their scrutiny. Tiamaat stared back with equal curiosity. I saw her reach a tentative hand through the shielding, as if to touch a Ki child: but she thought better of it.

After the classroom tour, there was a reception, with speeches, dance, and choral singing. Ki community leaders and the An couple didn't literally "shake hands"; but the gesture was accomplished. Here the live trans. ended, and most of our party stayed behind. The An leaders and the Ki delegates went on alone, with a police escort, for a private visit to "Hopes and Dreams Park"—a facsimile of one of the Sacred Groves (as near as the term translates), central to KiAn spirituality.

Pelé and I went with them.

The enclave of woodland was artfully designed. The "trees" were like self-supporting kelp, leathery succulents—lignin is only native to the Blue Planet—but they were tall, and planted close enough to block all sight of the packed towers. Their sheets of foliage made a honeyed shade, we seemed alone in a gently managed wilderness. The Ki and the An kept their distance from each other now that the cams weren't in sight. The police moved outward to maintain a cordon around the group, and I began to feel uneasy. I should have been paying attention instead of savouring my breakfast, I had not grasped that "Hope and Dreams Park" would be like this. I kept hearing voices, seeing flitting shadows; although the park area was supposed to have been cleared. I'd mentioned the weak shielding, I hoped it had been fixed—

"Are religious ceremonies held here?" I asked Tiamaat.

She drew back her head, the gesture for *no*. "Most KiAn have not followed religion for a long time. It's just a place sacred to ourselves, to nature."

"But it's fine for the Shelter Police, and Pelé and I, to be with you?"

"You are advocates."

We entered a clearing dotted with thickets. At our feet smaller plants had the character of woodland turf, starred with bronze and purple flowers. Above us the primary sun dipped towards its false horizon, lighting the blood red veins in the foliage. The blue daystar had set. Baal and Tiamaat were walking together: I heard him whisper, in the An language, *now it's our time.*

"And these are the lucky ones," muttered one of the Ki delegates to me, her "English" mediated by a throat-mike processor that gave her a teddy-bear growl. "Anyone who reached Speranza had contacts, money. Many millions of our people are trying to survive on a flayed, poisoned bombsite—"

And whose fault is that?

I nodded, vaguely. It was NOT my place take sides—

Something flew by me, big and solid. Astonished, I realised it had been Baal. He had moved so fast, it was so totally unexpected. He had plunged right through the cordon of armed police, through the shield. He was gone, vanished. I leapt in pursuit at once, yelling: "Hold your fire!" I was flung back, thrown down into zinging stars and blackness. The shield *had* been strengthened, but not enough.

Shelter Police bending over me, cried: *what happened, Ma'am, are you hit?*

My conviction that we had company in here fused into certainty—

"Oh, God! Get after him. After him!"

I ran with the police, Pelé stayed with Tiamaat and the Ki: on our shared frequency I heard him alerting Colonel Shamaz. We cast to and fro through the twilight wood, held together by the invisible strands and globules of our shield, taunted by rustles of movement, the CSP muttering to each other about refugee assassins, homemade weapons. But the young leader of the An was unharmed when we found him,having followed the sounds of a scuffle and a terrified cry. He crouched, in his sleek tailoring, over his prey. Dark blood trickled from the victim's nostrils, high-placed in a narrow face. Dark eyes were open, fixed and wide.

I remembered the children in that school, staring up in disbelief at the ogres.

Baal rose, wiping his mouth with the back of his hand. "What are you looking at?" he inquired, haughtily, in his neighbours' language. The rest of our party had caught up: he was speaking to the Ki. "What did you expect? You know who I am."

Tiamaat fell to her knees, with a wail of despair, pressing her hands to either side of her head. "He has a right! Ki territory is An territory, he has a right to behave as if we were at home. And the Others knew it, don't you see? They *knew*!"

The CSP officer yelled something inexcusable and lunged at the killer. Pelé grabbed him by the shoulders and hauled him back, talking urgent sense. The Ki said nothing, but I thought Tiamaat was right. They'd known what the Diaspora's pet monster would do in here; and he hadn't let them down.

Perfectly unconcerned, Baal stood guard over the body until Colonel Haa'agaan arrived with the closed cars. Then he picked it up and slung it over his shoulder. I travelled with him and his booty, and the protection of four Green Belts, to the elevator. Another blacked-out car waited for us on Parliament level. What a nightmare journey! We delivered him to the service entrance of his suite in the Sensitive Visitors Facility, and saw him drop the body insouciantly into the arms of one of his aides—a domestic, lesser specimen of those rare and dangerous animals, the An.

The soldiers looked at each other, looked at me. "You'd better stay," I said. "And get yourselves reinforced, there might be reprisals planned."

Baal's tawny eyes in my mind: challenging me, trusting me—

The debriefing was in closed session; although there would be a transcript on record. It took a painful long time, but we managed to exonerate everyone, including Baal. Mistakes had been made, signals had been misread. We knew the facts of the KiAn problem, we had only the most rudimentary grasp of the cultures involved. Baal and Tiamaat, who were not present, had made no further comment. The Ki (who were not present either) had offered a swift deposition. They wanted the incident treated with utmost discretion: they did not see it as a bar to negotiation. The Balas/Shet party argued that Baal's kill had been unique, an "extraordinary ritual" that we had to sanction. And we knew this was nonsense, but it was the best we could do.

One of our Green Belts, struck by the place in the report where Tiamaat exclaims *the Others knew it!*, came up with the idea that the young Ki had been a form of suicide bomber: sacrificing his life in the hope of wrecking the peace talks. Investigation of the dead boy and his contacts would now commence.

"Thank funx it didn't happen on the live transmission!" cried Shamaz, the old soldier; getting his priorities right.

It was very late before Pelé and I got away. We spent the rest of the night together, hiding in the tenderness of the Blue Planet, where war is shameful and murder is an aberration; where kindness is common currency, and in almost every language strangers are greeted with love: *dear, pet, darling; sister, brother, cousin,* and nobody even wonders why. What an unexpected distinction, we who thought we were such ruthless villains, such fallen angels. "We're turning into the care assistant caste for the whole funxing galaxy," moaned Pelé. "Qué cacho!"

The Parliament session was well attended: many tiers packed with bi-locators; more than the usual scatter of Members present in the flesh, and damn the expense. I surveyed the Chamber with distaste. They all wanted to make their speeches on the KiAn crisis. But they knew nothing. The freedom of the press fades and dies at interstellar distances, where everything has to be couriered, and there's no such thing as evading official censorship. They'd heard about the genocide, the wicked but romantic An; the ruined world, the rescue plans. They had no idea exactly what had driven the rebel Ki to such desperation, and they weren't going to find out—

All the Diaspora Parliament knew was spin.

And the traditional Ki, the people we were dealing with, were collusive. They didn't *like* being killed and eaten by their aristos, but for outsiders to find out the truth would be a far worse evil: a disgusting, gross exposure. After all, it was only the poor, the weak-minded and the disadvantaged, who ended up on a plate . . . Across from the Visitors' Gallery, level with my eyes, hung the great Diaspora Banner. The populated worlds turned sedately, beautifully scanned and insanely close together; like one of those ancient distorted projections of the landmasses on the Blue. The "real" distance between the Blue system and Neuendan (our nearest neighbour) was twenty six thousand light-years. Between the Neuendan and the Balas/Shet lay fifteen hundred light-years; the location of the inscrutable Aleutians' homeworld was a mystery. How would you represent *that* spatial relationship, in any realistic way?

"Why do they say it all aloud?" asked Baal, idly.

He was beside me, of course. He was glad to have me there, and kept letting me know it: a confiding pressure against my shoulder, a warm glance from those tawny eyes. He took my complete silence about the incident in Hopes and Dreams Park for understanding. A DP Social Support Officer *never* shows hostility.

"Isn't your i/t button working?"

The instantaneous translation in here had a mind of its own.

"It works well enough. But everything they say is just repeating the documents on this desk. It was the same in the briefing yesterday, I noticed that."

"You read English?"

"Oh yes." Reading and writing have to be learned, there is no quick neuro-fix. Casually, with a glint of that startling irony, he dismissed his skill. "I was taught, at home. But I don't bother. I have people who understand all this for me."

"It's called oratory," I said. "And rhetoric. Modulated speech is used to stir peoples' emotions, to cloud the facts and influence the vote—"

Baal screwed up his handsome face in disapproval. "That's distasteful."

"Also it's tradition. It's just the way we do things."

"Ah!"

I sighed, and sent a message to Pelé on our eye socket link.

Change partners?

D'you want to reassign? came his swift response. He was worrying about me, he wanted to protect me from the trauma of being with Baal; which was a needle under my skin. I liked Pelé very much, but I preferred to treat the Diaspora Parliament as a no-ties singles bar.

No, I answered. *Just for an hour, after this.*

Getting close to Tiamaat was easy. After the session the four of us went down to the Foyer, where Baal was quickly surrounded by a crowd of high-powered admirers. They swept him off somewhere, with Pelé in attendance. Tiamaat and I were left bobbing in the wake, ignored; a little lost. "Shall we *have coffee,* Debra?" she suggested, with dignity. "I love *coffee*. But not the kind that comes on those trolleys!"

I took her to "my" kiosk, and we found a table. I was impressed by the way she handled the slights of her position. There goes Baal, surrounded by the mighty, while his partner is reduced to having coffee with a minder. . . . It was a galling role to have to play in public. I had intended to lead up to the topic on my mind: but she forestalled me. "You must be horrified by what happened yesterday."

No hostility. "A *little* horrified, I admit." I affected to hesitate. "The Balas/Shet say that what Baal did was a ritual, confirming his position as leader; and the Ki expected it. They may even have arranged for the victim to be available. And it won't happen again. Are they right?"

She sipped her cappuchino. "Baal doesn't believe he did anything wrong," she answered, carefully; giving nothing away.

I remembered her cry of despair. "But what do *you* think—?"

"I can speak frankly?"

"You can say anything. We may seem to be in public, but nothing you say to me, or that I say to you, can be heard by anyone else."

"Speranza is a very clever place!"

"Yes, it is . . . And as you know, though the system itself will have a record, as your Social Support Officer I may not reveal anything you ask me to keep to myself."

She gave me eye-contact then, very deliberately. I realised I'd never seen her look anyone in the eye. The colour of her irises was a subtle, lilac-starred grey.

"Before I left home, when I was a child, I ate meat. I hadn't killed it, but I knew where it came from. But I have never killed, Debra. And now I don't believe I ever will." She looked out at the passing crowd, the surroundings that must be so punishingly strange to her. "My mother said we should close ourselves off to the past, and open ourselves to the future. So she sent me away, when I was six years' old, to live on another world—"

"That sounds very young to me."

"I *was* young. I still had my milk teeth . . . I'm not like Baal, because I have been brought up differently. If I were in his place, things would be better for the Others. I truly believe that—" She meant the Ki, the prey-nations. "But I know what has to be done for KiAn. *I want this rescue package to work.* Baal is the one who will make it happen, and I support him in every way."

She smiled, close-lipped, no flash of sharp white: I saw the poised steel in her, hidden by ingrained self-suppression. And she changed the subject, with composure. Unexpected boldness, unexpected finesse—

"Debra, is it true that Blue people have secret super-powers?"

I laughed and shook my head. "I'm afraid not. No talking flowers here!"

Pelé tried to get the DP software to change our codenames. He maintained that *Baal* and *Tiamaat* were not even from the same mythology, and if we were going to invoke the gods, those two should be Aztecs: Huehueteotl, ripping the living heart from his victims . . . The bots refused. They said they didn't care if they were mixing their mysticisms. Codenames were a device to avoid accidental offense until the system had assimilated a new user language. "Baal" and "Tiamaat" were perfectly adequate, and the MesoAmerican names had too many characters.

I had dinner with Baal, in the Sensitive Visitor Facility. He was charming company: we ate vegetarian fusion cuisine, and I tried not to think about the butchered meat in the kitchen of his suite. On the other side of the room, bull-shouldered Colonel Haa'agaan ate alone; glancing at us covertly with small, sad eyes from between the folds of his slaty head-hide. Shamaz had been hard hit by what had happened in the Hopes and Dreams Park. But his orange and yellow aura-tag was still bright; and I knew mine was, too. By the ruthless measures of interstellar diplomacy, everything was still going well; set for success.

If things had been different I might have joined Pelé again when I was finally off duty. As it was, I retired to my room, switched all the décor, including ceiling and floor, to starry void, mixed myself a kicking neurochemical cocktail, and applied the popper to my throat. Eyedrops are faster, but I wanted the delay, I wanted to feel myself coming apart. Surrounded by directionless immensity, I sipped chilled water, brooding. How can a people have World Government, space-flight level industrialisation, numinal intelligence, and yet the ruling caste are still killing and eating the peasants? How can they do that, when practically everyone on KiAn admits they are a single species, differently adapted: *and they knew that before we told them.* How can we be back here, the Great Powers and their grisly parasites: making the same moves, the same old mistakes, the same old hateful compromises, that our Singularity was supposed to cure forever?

Why is moral development so difficult? Why are predators charismatic?

The knots in my frontal lobes were combed out by airy fingers, I fell into the sea of possibilities, I went to the place of terror and joy that no one understands unless they have been there. I asked my question and I didn't get an answer, you never get an answer. Yet when I came to the shallows again, when I laid myself, exhausted, on this dark and confused shore, I knew what I was going to do: I had seen it.

But there always has to be an emotional reason. I'd known about Baal's views before I arrived. I'd known that he would hunt and kill "weakling" Ki, as was his traditional right, and not just once, he's do it whenever the opportunity arose; and I'd still been undecided. It was Tiamaat who made the difference. I'd met her, skin on skin as we say. I knew what the briefing had not been able to tell me. She was no cipher, superficially "civilised" by her education, she was *suppressed.* I had heard that cry of despair and anger, when she saw what Baal had done. I had talked to her. I knew she had strength and cunning, as well as good intentions. A latent dominance, the will and ability to be a leader.

I saw Baal's look of challenge and trust, even now—

But Tiamaat deserved saving, and I would save her.

The talks went on. Morale was low on the DP side, because the refugee camp incident had shown us where we stood; but the Ki delegates were happy—insanely, infuriatingly. The "traditional diet of the An" was something they refused to discuss, and they were going to get their planet rebuilt anyway. The young An leaders spent very little time at the conference table. Baal was indifferent—he had people to understand these things for him—and Tiamaat could not be present without him. This caused a rift. Their aides, the only other An around, were restricted to the SV Facility suites (we care assistants may be crazy but we're not entirely stupid). Pelé and I were fully occupied, making sure our separate charges weren't left moping alone. Pelé took Tiamaat shopping and visiting museums (virtual and actual). I found that Baal loved to roam, just as I do myself, and took him exploring the lesser-known sights.

We talked about his background. Allegedly, he'd given up a promising career in the Space Marines to take on the leadership. When I'd assured myself that his pilot skills were real, he wasn't just a toy-soldier aristo, I finally took him on the long float through the permanent umbilical, to Right Speranza.

We had to suit up at the other end.

"What's this?" demanded Baal, grinning. "Are we going outside?"

"You'll see. It's an excursion I thought you'd enjoy."

The suits were programmable. I watched him set one up for his size and bulk, and knew he was fine: but I put him through the routines, to make sure. Then I took him into the vasty open cavern of the DP's missile repository, which we crossed like flies in a cathedral, hooking our tethers to the girders, drifting over the ranked silos of deep-space interceptors, the giant housing of particle cannons.

All of it obsolete, like castle walls in the age of heavy artillery; but it looks convincing on the manifest, and who knows? "Modern" armies have been destroyed by Zulu spears, it never pays to ignore the conventional weapons—

"Is this a *weapons* bay?" the monster exclaimed; scandalised, on suit radio.

"Of course," said I. "Speranza can defend herself, if she has to."

I let us into a smaller hangar, through a lock on the cavern wall, and filled it with air and pressure and lights. We were completely alone. Left Speranza is a natural object, a hollowed asteroid. Right is artificial, and it's a dangerous place for sentient bipeds. The proximity of the torus can have unpredictable and bizarre effects, not to mention the tissue-frying radiation that washes through at random intervals. But we would be fine for a short while. We fixed tethers, opened our faceplates and hunkered down, gecko-padded bootsoles clinging to the arbitrary "floor."

"I thought you were angels," he remarked, shyly. "The weapons, all of that, it seems beneath you. Doesn't your codename, 'Debra,' mean an angel? Aren't you all messengers, come to us from the Mighty Void?"

"Mighty Void" was a Balas/Shet term meaning something like God.

"No . . . Deborah was a judge, in Israel. I'm just human, Baal. I'm a person with numinal intelligence, the same kind of being as you are; like all the KiAn."

I could see that the harsh environment of Right Speranza moved him, as it did me. There was a mysterious peace and truth in being here, in the cold dark, breathing borrowed air. He was pondering: open and serious.

"Debra . . . ? Do you believe in the Diaspora?"

"I believe in the Weak Theory," I said. "I don't believe we're all descended from the same Blue Planet hominid, the mysterious original starfarers, precursors of homo sapiens. I think we're the same because we grew under the same constraints: time, gravity, hydrogen bonds; the nature of water, the nature of carbon—"

"But instantaneous transit was invented on the Blue Planet," he protested, unwilling to lose his romantic vision.

"Only the prototype. It took hundreds of years, and a lot of outside help, before we had anything like viable interstellar travel—"

Baal had other people to understand the technology for him. He was building castles in the air, dreaming of his future. "Does everyone on the Blue speak English?"

"Not at all. They mostly speak a language called *putonghua*; which means 'common speech,' as if they were the only people in the galaxy. Blues are as insular as the KiAn, believe me, when they're at home. When you work for the DP, you change your ideas; it happens to everyone. I'm still an Englishwoman, and *mi naño* Pelé is still a man of Ecuador—

"I know!" he broke in, eagerly. "I felt that. I *like* that in you!"

"But we skip the middle term. The World Government of our single planet doesn't mean the same as it did." I grinned at him. "Hey, I didn't bring you here for a lecture. This is what I wanted to show you. See the pods?"

He looked around us, slowly, with a connoisseur's eye. He could see what the pods were. They were Aleutian-build, the revolutionary leap forward:

vehicles that could pass through the mind/matter barrier. An end to those dreary transit lounges, true starflight, the Holy Grail: and only the Aleutians knew how it was done

"Like to take one out for a spin?"

"You're kidding!" cried Baal, his eyes alight.

"No, I'm not. We'll take a two-man pod. How about it?"

He saw that I was serious, which gave him pause. "How can we? The systems won't allow it. This hangar has to be under military security."

"I *am* military security, Baal. So is Pelé. What did you think we were? Kindergarten teachers? Trust me, I have access, there'll be no questions asked."

He laughed. He knew there was something strange going on, but he didn't care: he trusted me. I glimpsed myself as a substitute for Tiamaat, glimpsed the relationship he should have had with his partner. Not sexual, but predation-based: a playful tussle, sparring partners. But Tiamaat had not wanted to be his sidekick—

We took a pod. Once we were inside, I sealed us off from Speranza, and we lay side by side in the couches, two narrow beds in a torpedo shell: an interstellar sports car, how right for this lordly boy. I checked his hook-ups, and secured my own.

"Where are we going?"

"Oh, just around the block."

His vital signs were in my eyes, his whole being was *quivering* in excitement, and I was glad. The lids closed, we were translated into code, we and our pod were injected into the torus, in the form of a triple stream of pure information, divided and shooting around the ring to meet itself, and collide—

I sat up, in a lucent gloom. The other bed's seal opened, and Baal sat up beside me. We were both still suited, with open faceplates. Our beds shaped themselves into pilot and co-pilot couches, and we faced what seemed an unmediated view of the deep space outside. Bulwarks and banks of glittering instruments carved up the panorama: I saw Baal's glance flash over the panels greedily, longing to be piloting this little ship for real. Then he saw the yellow primary, a white hole in black absence; and its brilliant, distant partner. He saw the pinpricks of other formations that meant nothing much to me, and he knew where I had brought him. We could not see the planet, it was entirely dark from this view. But in our foreground, the massive beams of space-to-space lasers were playing: shepherding plasma particles into a shell that would hold the recovering atmosphere in place.

To say that KiAn had been flayed alive was no metaphor. The people still living on the surface were in some kind of hell. But it could be saved.

"None of the machinery is strictly material," I said, "in any normal sense.

It was couriered here, as information, in the living minds of the people who are now on station. We can't see them, but they're around, in pods like this one. It will all disintegrate, when the repairs are done. But the skin of your world will be whole again, it won't need to be held in place."

The KiAn don't cry, but I was so close to him, in the place where we were, that I felt his tears. "*Why* are you doing this?" he whispered. "You must be angels, or why are you saving us, what have we done to deserve this?"

"The usual reasons," I said. "Market forces, political leverage, power play."

"I don't believe you."

"Then I don't know what to tell you, Baal. Except that the Ki and the An have numinal intelligence. You are like us, and we have so few brothers and sisters. Once we'd found you, we couldn't bear to lose you."

I let him gaze, for a long moment without duration.

"I wanted you to see this."

I stepped out of my pilot's couch and stood braced: one hand gecko-padded to the inner shell, while I used the instruments to set the pod to self-destruct. The eject beacon started up, direct cortical warning that my mind read as a screaming siren—

"Now I'm going back to Speranza. But you're not."

The fine young cannibal took a moment to react. The pupils in his tawny eyes widened amazingly when he found that he was paralysed, and his capsule couldn't close.

"Is this a dream?"

"Not quite. It's a confabulation. It's what happens when you stay conscious in transit. The mind invents a stream of environments, events. The restoration of KiAn is real, Baal. It will happen. We can see it 'now' because we're in non-duration, we're experiencing the simultanaeity. In reality—if that makes any sense, language hates these situations—we're still zipping around the torus. But when the confabulation breaks up, you'll still be in deep space and about to die."

I did not need to tell him why I was doing this. He was no fool, he knew why he had to go. But his mind was still working, fighting—

"Speranza is a four-space mapped environment. You can't do this and go back alone. The system knows you were with me, every moment. The record can't be changed, no way, without the tampering leaving a trace."

"True. But I am one of those rare people who can change the information. You've heard fairytales about us, the Blues who have super-powers? I'm not an angel, Baal. Actually, it's a capital crime to be what I am, where I come from. But Speranza understands me. Speranza uses me."

"Ah!" he cried. "I knew it, I felt it. We are the same!"

• • •

When I recovered self-consciousness, I was in my room, alone. Earlier in the day, Baal had claimed he needed a nap. After a couple of hours, I'd become suspicious, checked for his signs, and found him missing: gone from the SV Facility screen. I'd been trying to trace him when Right Speranza had detected a pod, with the An leader on board, firing up. The system had warned him to desist. Baal had carried on, and paid high price for his attempted joyride. The injection had failed, both Baal and one fabulous Aleutian-build pod had been annihilated.

Remembering this much gave me an appalling headache—the same aching awfulness I imagine shapeshifters (I know of one or two) feel in their muscle and bone. I couldn't build the bridge at all: no notion how I'd connected between this reality and the former version. I could have stepped from the dying pod straight through the wall of this pleasant, modest living space. But it didn't matter. I would find out, and Debra would have been behaving like Debra.

Pelé came knocking. I let him in and we commiserated, both of us in shock. We're advocates, not enforcers, there's very little we can do if a Sensitive Visitor is really determined to go AWOL. We'd done all the right things, short of using undue force, and so had Speranza. When we'd broken the privilege locks, Baal's room record had shown that he'd been spying out how to get access to one of those Aleutian pods. It was just too bad that he'd succeeded, and that he'd had enough skill to get himself killed. Don't feel responsible, said Pelé. It's not your fault. Nobody thinks that. Don't be so sad. Always so sad, Debra: it's not good for the brain, you should take a break. Then he started telling me that frankly, nobody would regret Baal. By An law, Tiamaat could now rule alone; and if she took a partner, we could trust her not to choose another bloodthirsty atavist . . . I soon stopped him. I huddled there in pain, my friend holding my hand: seeing only the beautiful one, his tawny eyes at the last, his challenge and his trust; mourning my victim.

I'm a melancholy assassin.

I did not sleep. In the grey calm of Left Speranza's early hours, before the breakfast kiosks were awake, I took the elevator to the Customised Shelter Sector, checked in with the CSP, and made my way, between the silent capsule towers, to Hopes and Dreams Park. I was disappointed that there were no refugees about. It would have been nice to see Ki children, playing fearlessly. Ki oldsters picking herbs from their windowboxes, instead of being boiled down for soup themselves. The gates of the Sacred Grove were open, so I just walked in. There was a memorial service: strictly no outsiders, but I'd had a personal message from Tiamaat saying I would be welcome. I didn't particularly want to meet her again. I'm a superstitious assassin, I felt that she would somehow know what I had done for her. I thought I would keep to the back of whatever gathering I found, while I made my own farewell.

The daystar's rays had cleared the false horizon, the sun was a rumour of gold between the trees. I heard laughter, and a cry. I walked into the clearing and saw Tiamaat. She'd just made the kill. I saw her toss the small body down, drop to her haunches, and take a ritual bite of raw flesh; I saw the blood on her mouth. The Ki looked on, keeping their distance in a solemn little cluster. Tiamaat transformed, splendid in her power, proud of her deed, looked up; and straight at me. I don't know what she expected. Did she think I would be glad for her? Did she want me to know how I'd been fooled? Certainly she knew she had nothing to fear. She was only doing the same as Baal had done, and the DP had made no protest over *his* kill. I shouted, like an idiot: *Hey, stop that!*, and the whole group scattered. They vanished into the foliage, taking the body with them.

I said nothing to anyone. I had not, in fact, foreseen that Tiamaat would become a killer. I'd seen a talented young woman, who would blossom if the unfairly favoured young man was removed. I hadn't realised that a dominant An would behave like a dominant An, irrespective of biological sex. But I was sure my employers had grasped the situation; and it didn't matter. The long-gone, harsh symbiosis between the An and the Ki, which they preserved in their rites of kingship, was not the problem. It was the modern version, the mass market in Ki meat, the intensive farms and the factories. Tiamaat would help us to get rid of those. She would embrace the new in public, whatever she believed in private.

And the fate of the Ki would change.

The news of Baal's death had been couriered to KiAn and to the homeworlds by the time I took my transit back to the Blue. We'd started getting reactions: all positive, so to speak. Of course, there would be persistent rumours that the Ki had somehow arranged Baal's demise, but there was no harm in that. In certain situations, assassination *works*—as long as it is secret, or at least misattributed. It's a far more benign tool than most alternatives; and a lot faster. I had signed off at the Social Support Office, I'd managed to avoid goodbyes. Just before I went through to the lounge, I realised that I hadn't had my aura tag taken off. I had to go back, and go through *another* blessed gate; and Pelé caught me.

"Take the dreamtime," he insisted, holding me tight. "Play some silly game, go skydiving from Angel Falls. *Please*, Debra. Don't be conscious. You worry me."

I wondered if he suspected what I really did for a living.

Maybe so, but he couldn't possibly understand.

"I'll give it serious thought," I assured him, and kissed him goodbye.

I gave the idea of the soft option serious thought for ten paces, passed into the lounge, and found my narrow bed. I lay down there, beside my fine young cannibal, the boy who had known me for what I was. His innocent eyes . . . I lay down with them all, and with the searing terrors they bring; all my dead remembered.

I needed to launder my soul.

SIX LIGHTS OFF GREEN SCAR

GARETH L. POWELL

1.

Roulette ships were dangerous and sexy. They were small and fast and tough. Their hulls were black tungsten alloy laced with smart carbon filament. They looked a bit like flint arrowheads. The media called them "roulette" ships because they were used for random jumping.

Random jumping was an extreme sport. It was the ultimate gamble. It was a pilot throwing his craft into hyperspace on a random trajectory, just to see where he'd end up.

Some discovered habitable planets, or rich mineral deposits. They became celebrities. They brought back wild tales of bizarre planetary systems, of swollen stars and uncharted asteroid belts.

But the risks were huge. Roulette pilots gambled with their lives, and there were ugly rumours of ghost ships, of murder and cannibalism, and individuals dying lonely, lingering deaths in distant star systems.

Those lucky enough to find their way home clustered on worlds close to the edge of familiar space, where they could stand under the clear night sky and see the unexplored frontier stretching away before them. Pik Station was one such world. It was a dirty little outpost on a half-forgotten moon. Its buildings were low and squalid, like bunkers. Down by the spaceport, drifters and tired hustlers worked its narrow streets. They huddled at its windy intersections in flapping coats, waiting for the right deal, the big score.

Sal Dervish moved among them, avoiding the ebb and flow of their skinny bodies. He wore a heavy coat and a set of stained ship fatigues. His breath came in ragged clouds and his insulated boots crunched solidly on the icy ground. He was the master of the *Wild Cat*, an old roulette ship in storage at the port. She needed an overhaul but he couldn't afford it. Some days, he could hardly afford to eat.

The bar he was heading for was a squat, scrappy affair, built of packing crates and corrugated iron. Whenever a shuttle lifted from the port, its walls and windows shook. As he opened the door, a woman detached herself from the counter and came over.

"Captain Dervish?" She had a reedy accent and wore a smart green parka with the hood thrown back.

He squinted. "Are you Vance?"

She took his elbow and guided him to a table near the fireplace, where two glasses and a bottle of local rot had been laid out.

"Call me Tamara," she said. She poured the drinks and handed him one. As he sipped it, he studied her. She had hair the colour of copper, pulled back into a loose ponytail. When she spoke, it was from the side of her mouth.

"Thank you for coming," she said, "I know it can't have been easy."

Sal put down his glass. "How do you want to do this?'

She looked at him from beneath her long lashes.

"Take a seat," she said.

When they were settled, she activated her voice recorder and leant across the filmy table.

She said, "Let's start at the beginning."

"The beginning?" Sal scratched his nose.

They were trolling around a brown dwarf six lights off Green Scar when they found the derelict ship.

"It looked like hell," he said. "Like something from a sewer."

Tamara nodded. She had her attention focused on the recorder, adjusting the sound levels.

"And this was a random jump?"

He took the bottle and refilled his glass.

"It was our fourth jump in a row," he said. "We were going for the record."

"So what happened?"

"What happened?" He puffed his cheeks out; even now, he could feel the adrenalin tingling in his blood, the breath catching in his throat.

He said, "We found a derelict ship, like nothing we'd ever seen. Kate said it would be worth a fortune."

Tamara consulted her notebook. "She was the first aboard?"

He nodded. "She went over with Petrov. They wanted to take some pictures, collect some samples, that sort of thing."

"And something attacked them?"

He pushed back on his stool. "They started screaming," he said. "There was something in there, taking them apart."

"And so you turned tail and ran?" Tamara said.

He clenched his fists. "They were already dying," he said. "There was something in there with them, something horrible."

He wiped a hand across his forehead.

"Are you okay?" she asked.

He took a deep breath. He said, "I don't like talking about it."

She looked him in the eye, her gaze long and cool, like the snow outside. She said, "I'm paying you."

He shifted uncomfortably.

She said, "I've heard the stories. I know the other pilots treat you as a pariah, a jinx. They say you've lost your nerve and you'll never jump again." She reached over and touched his wrist. Her fingertips were cold and rough, like frost. "But you used to be a big star, back in the day. People want to find out what happened to you, how you ended up in this desolate wasteland." She waved her hand in a gesture that encompassed the bar, the street, and the dirty snowfields beyond.

He turned away. He wished he'd never agreed to meet her.

"I'm offering you a way out," she said, "a way to redeem yourself."

"I don't care about that."

She withdrew her hand. She put her glass down and pushed it away with her fingernails.

"You cared about Kate, didn't you?" she said.

He dropped his gaze. "More than you'll ever know."

"Then come with me," she said. "I'm going in search of your derelict, and I want you to come along. I want to get your reactions, see the thing through your eyes."

She tapped a painted fingernail on the plastic casing of her recorder. "It could be a great story, Sal."

He stood. The legs of his stool scraped loudly on the concrete floor. Around the bar, several heads turned his way.

"I've spent the last two years trying to forget," he said.

She leaned back, arms folded.

"And has it worked?"

Kate Schnitzler was an engineer. Her hands were rough and she had dirt under her nails. She wore canvas dungarees and a grease-stained t-shirt. She liked machines for their dependability and precision. She had hair the colour of sunlight and she made a point of brushing her teeth every evening, no matter how tired or drunk or lazy she felt. She liked the smell of engine grease and she liked to have her back stroked after sex. When not sharing his cabin, she slept in the cargo bay, curled in an old inflatable life raft from the ship's emergency locker. The orange distress beacon threw eerie moving shadows across the walls.

"When you're running from something, you can't trust a soul," she once said.

"Not friends or family—they know who you are, where you go, what you do. To get away, you've got to change, got to do something unexpected."

It took him a month to get up the courage to ask her what she was running from. They were welding a buckled hull plate at the time, in the heat and dust of a dry desert world. She pushed up her black goggles and fixed him with sad eyes.

"We're all running from something, Sal," she said. "People like us don't belong anywhere. Wherever we are, we've always got one eye on the exit, one foot out the door."

She stretched her bare arms over her head. "It's like we were given the wrong lives, you know? Like we've been running from them for so long that we can't remember what it feels like to be still."

It was nearly midday and the hot wind blew thin fans of sand and ash across the runway's shimmering tarmac. She put her arms around his waist and her hair tickled his chin.

"We're like sharks," she said. "We have to keep moving, or we suffocate."

2.

Random jumps through hyperspace were often rough, like passing through white-hot plasma. Only streamlined ships with heavy-duty heat shielding could batter their way through. Ships like the *Wild Cat*, for instance. They were sturdy and dependable. They were designed for abuse. You could slam one into a rocky moon at Mach Four and probably walk away from the wreckage unscathed. Even so, Tamara Vance knew that most professional "roulette" pilots wound up dead sooner or later. They just kept pushing the envelope, racking up the odds until something broke. It didn't matter how safe their ships were, or how tough; the danger was addictive, compelling. These guys just kept tempting fate until something gave.

Take Sal, for instance.

As a roulette pilot, he'd seen strange and terrible things, and staked his claim on half a dozen new worlds. He'd jumped deeper into the unknown than anyone else. Where other pilots crumbled or collapsed, where they lost their nerve, he kept flying. He wasn't afraid, and that lack of feeling had given him an edge. For a short time, it had made him unbeatable. It was only when he met Kate that he appeared to let his guard down. For the first time, he became vulnerable. He started worrying about someone else.

Back in her hotel room, Tamara felt jittery, the way she always did when working on a big story. But this time, it was worse than usual. There was something about Sal Dervish that annoyed and fascinated her. He was a wreck, and she wanted to understand why. But more than that, she wanted to help him.

She stripped off and stepped into the shower. She let the warm water drum into the kinks in her shoulders. She told herself she shouldn't get involved, that she should concentrate on the story. She had her career to think about.

Random jumping was still big news back in the cities of the Assembly's comfortable inner systems. For people whose only experience of flight was a twice-daily trip on a commuter shuttle, the idea of people like Sal Dervish hurling themselves into hyperspace was a wild, almost unbearably exciting prospect: it meant they could emerge almost anywhere and find almost anything. Some random jumpers had grown wealthy and famous from their discoveries. It was a good way to get rich quick, and a good way to get killed.

She rubbed shampoo into her hair. In ancient times, she thought, they'd have been shamans. They'd have been the ones dosing themselves on whatever drugs came to hand, pushing the boundaries of reality in search of answers. They'd have been out there, cavorting in the firelight while the rest of the tribe lived their trip vicariously, too scared to take the plunge themselves.

To a reporter like her, it was a goldmine. It was compulsive, must-see entertainment. And she knew she'd been incredibly lucky to track down Sal Dervish. He'd been such a high-profile burnout that no one in the random jumping community seriously expected him to jump again. After two years in the wilderness, he'd become an almost mythical figure, halfway between an urban legend and a cautionary tale.

She stepped out of the shower and pulled on a robe. If she could take him back to the scene of his downfall and make him face his fear, then this time next year, she'd be sitting behind an anchor's desk, where she belonged.

She had all her hopes pinned on this story. Too many to let her relax and wait for his call. She needed to be active. She got dressed and went out, making sure she had her phone in her pocket.

It took her only a little over an hour to walk the entire length of the settlement, and she was glad of her parka. She watched condensation freeze on the giant fuel silos at the port. She read the graffiti on a row of old spherical descent modules. She saw a couple of drunken ice miners beat each other senseless in the bloody snow outside one of the crappier downtown bars.

Eventually, fed-up and alone, she found herself wandering the streets on the edge of town. Overhead, the stars burned fierce and blue. The dirty snow squeaked underfoot. The cold air bit at her nose and ears; it scoured her lungs. To someone used to the bright lights of the inner systems, Pik Station was a bitter, dismal place.

In a dingy bistro off a side street, she stopped to thaw. They had an open fire, and she needed to get the chill out of her bones. She ordered a drink and took it to a table near the hearth. But no sooner had she got comfortable than a thin guy with hard bright eyes approached her.

"Miss Vance, I presume?" he said.

She was taken aback. She was used to being recognised on the streets of the inner systems but not out here, in the sticks. She was surprised anyone knew who she was.

He bowed his head and said, "I thought as much. There aren't that many women walking these streets in hand-stitched Swiss snow boots."

He held out a hand and she took it. He looked halfway familiar but she couldn't place him. Beneath his leather coat, he wore a white suit and leather cowboy boots. She could smell his aftershave.

She said, "Have we met?"

He smiled. He lifted her hand and brushed it with his dry lips. There were thick silver rings on his fingers.

"I suppose it's possible," he said. He shrugged off his coat and beckoned the barkeeper.

"My name's Dieter," he said. "Can I buy you a drink?"

3.

When Sal got back to the *Wild Cat*, Laurel-Ann was waiting for him. He'd been hoping she might've got bored and left.

"Where've you been, Sal?" she said, smoothing down her vinyl skirt with pale fingers. The overhead lights glittered off her lip-gloss. He pushed past her and staggered down to his cabin. He showered and slipped into a polyester robe. There were still a few bottles of rot in the hold. He took one to his bunk. When she joined him, he ignored her. He didn't want her there, didn't even want to look at her.

"Just leave me alone," he said.

She didn't understand. She was nineteen, with bad skin and bleached hair.

"What's the matter, baby? Have I done something wrong?" Her voice was thin and pleading and he hated the sound of it.

He rolled over and pointed at the hatch.

"Just get lost," he said.

Her face fell. For a moment, he thought he caught a glimpse of something vulnerable behind the make-up and breast implants. Then her lip curled. She sniffed, adjusted her top, and gathered her few belongings together. He closed his eyes and listened to her heels stamp across the deck. At the hatch, she paused.

"Fuck you," she said.

• • •

When Sal was young, he was awkward and fidgety and raw. He grew up in a town near a failing seaport. It was shrouded in fog most days, and the port lights made the sky glow a hellish orange. When it wasn't foggy, it was raining, and the corrosive salt air blew in off the muddy grey mouth of the estuary, cold and sharp like rusty barbed wire.

Lowell Creek, like Pik Station, was the sort of dismal hinterland most people only passed through, on their way somewhere else. Those that stopped and stayed tended to be lost or desperate, or beyond caring. Either they were looking for trouble, or they were trying to hide from it.

He grew up in a house by the river shore, in a row of fishermen's cottages. At high tide, the lamp light from the front room window spilled out over the muddy creek water. When it rained, the lights of the houses on the far shore swam and smeared. He'd wait there, by that window, when his father was out, waiting for the lights of his little boat to appear through the gloom, listening to the pop and sizzle of the ship-to-shore radio.

Until one night, his father failed to return.

It was the night the Endurance exploded. Lightning crackled through the overcast sky. Thunder growled. The waves crashed over the flood defences, smashing their spray against the shingle walls of the house. During lulls, he could hear foghorns out in the channel.

His mother joined him at the window.

"It's time you were off to bed," she said half-heartedly.

He rubbed the glass where it was misting. He could see she didn't mean it, that she wanted his company.

"Just a few minutes more," he said.

Down by the creek, he could see lights: There were kids on the Endurance.

She was a rusty old hovercraft, built to transport cargo. She lay in the mud at the back of the creek and the local teenagers used her as a hangout. They sat in her hold, drinking and smoking.

When her leaky fuel tank exploded, the blast shook the windows of his house. It echoed along the street. Front doors were thrown open and people appeared, pulling coats over their pyjamas. His mother went with them.

It took most of the night to bring the blaze under control. There were kids trapped by the fire. Driving rain and intense heat hampered the rescuers. And all the while, out at sea, Sal's father was drowning. The storm had swamped his small boat. With everyone crowded around the burning Endurance, there was no one to hear his final, desperate calls. No one except Sal, listening to the radio as he clung helplessly to the window, too scared to move.

When he was fifteen, he ran away from the pain. He locked his past away, where it couldn't hurt him. He rode the freighters that dragged from world to world. He stowed away. He got his first taste of hyperspace travel. He got a tattoo. He lost his virginity behind a greasy café on a cold world whose name he could never remember.

On Strauli, he was caught on the ground during a hurricane that lasted a year; and on Djatt, he spent three days wandering alone in an arctic blizzard. And yet, there was never anything to match the night the Endurance went up. There was nothing that could compare to the fear and helplessness of listening to his father die, alone. And so he became a roulette pilot because nothing could frighten him, nothing could shake him. Nothing . . . until he heard Kate scream. It brought back the awful, freezing dread of that distant rainy night. Alone in the Star Chamber of the *Wild Cat*, he'd been terrified. He'd been a boy again, lost and helpless.

And so he'd fled once more. And he hadn't stopped running until he met Tamara.

They were seated around the table in the Wild Cat's galley, playing poker.

Kate said, "It's my brother."

"What about him?" Sal thumbed through the cards in his hand. He had six suns and a diamond.

"That's who I'm running from." She tossed a couple of chips into the centre of the table. Beside her, Petrov studied his own cards and frowned.

"It's not my night, I think." He reached for the rot bottle and refilled his glass. Sal ignored him.

"Your brother?"

"My twin brother."

Kate pushed a hand back through her hair and dropped her cards. "I fold."

"Me too." Sal took the bottle from Petrov and made sure her glass was full.

"So, what did he do?"

"My brother?" She shrugged. "It's not so much what he did, as what he does."

"And that is what?" Petrov asked, sweeping his winnings into his lap.

Kate looked away.

"He hurts people," she said.

Sal woke with a shout. It was past midnight; the lights on the *Wild Cat* were deep brown and his pulse raced. He felt sick.

He slid down to the end of the bunk and opened his footlocker. Near the bottom, among the books and papers, he found his only picture of her. He pulled it out with trembling hands, smoothing down the creased edges. It was a printout captured from a security camera. He'd found it in a pile of her stuff. It showed her laughing, her head thrown back, the line of her throat white against the red silk strap of her dress. She held an empty wine glass carelessly in one hand, a bottle in the other. She had confetti in her hair. He sat on the edge of his bunk and held it to his forehead. He rocked back and forth.

One of Laurel-Ann's pink bauble earrings lay on the deck. He kicked it away savagely, feeling ashamed.

Losing Kate had ripped open old wounds, leaving him scared and vulnerable. It had crippled him.

He clenched his fists, crumpling her picture. He could hear her screams in his head. He couldn't stop them, couldn't block them out. He raged around the ship, pounding the bulkheads with his fists, kicking and slapping the doors and consoles until his hands and feet bled.

Panting, he collapsed into the pilot's chair. Kate's picture was torn; there were pieces missing. He caught sight of his reflection in the console screens; he looked old and beaten.

Everything that was wrong in his life, all the guilt and self-loathing, had its root in that one moment of freezing panic when he'd run, abandoning her. And he'd give anything to be able to go back and do things differently.

But how could he?

Should he take up Tamara Vance's offer? He sat up straight and wiped his eyes. Everything here was so screwed up, what was there to lose? He couldn't go on like this, carrying this burden of grief and remorse. He needed a way to make amends, to atone for his cowardice.

He had to go back to Green Scar and do what he should've done in the first place. And, if he didn't survive, it would make things right, it would be a redemption.

He called Tamara Vance and she answered on the third ring.

He said, "I'm in."

She said, "I'll be right over."

4.

Sal glanced across to where Dieter leaned against the landing bay door, just out of earshot.

"I don't trust him," he said.

Tamara rolled her eyes. She was standing on the boarding ramp of the *Wild Cat*. Sal sat at the top. His boots were undone and he was bare-chested. His forearms rested lightly on his knees. He'd been helping the maintenance crew to weld new hull plates in place, in preparation for their flight, and his skin shone with sweat and grease. Tamara's money had allowed him to make his ship spaceworthy again, but he knew the repairs were only temporary fixes. They'd last long enough to do what needed to be done.

"Look at him, look at the way he's dressed: He's a thug," he said in a low voice. "He's a small time gangster wannabe and I don't want him on my ship."

"I really wish you'd reconsider."

Sal ran a hand through his dirty hair. He could smell his own sweat.

"I'm sorry," he said, "but there's no way."

Tamara rocked back on her heels. She said, "Think of him as a rich tourist looking for a thrill."

Sal stood up and wiped his palms together. "I'm sorry."

Seeing the gesture, Dieter straightened up and stepped forward. He was wearing thin black sunglasses and a wide, floppy hat. His boot heels clicked loudly on the bay's metal floor.

"Mister Dervish," he called, "I have an offer which may change your mind."

Sal turned. He spread his hands. "I really doubt it," he said.

"You haven't heard it yet."

Dieter stopped walking. He took his glasses off and fixed Sal with a steady stare.

"If you'll take me, I'm willing to pay you two hundred thousand," he said.

Sal grunted. "Credits? Or local funny money?"

"Credits."

He whistled. "The whole ship isn't worth that much."

Dieter reached into the pocket of his white coat. He pulled out a bundle of laminated notes and tossed them onto the boarding ramp.

"At a generous estimate, Mister Dervish, your ship's worth a hundred and ninety thousand Credits. You can consider the rest payment for your services."

Sal tried to keep a straight face. He had to admit he was tempted. With that kind of money, he could completely refit the *Wild Cat*, or sell her and retire. He could start a new life, somewhere nobody knew him.

Just thinking about it made him ache because he wanted it so much.

Tamara put a hand on his shoulder.

"Please?" she said.

An hour later, the *Wild Cat* blasted into the cold dawn sky. Once above the grey clouds, she turned as if questing for a scent. Sal, in the Star Chamber at her heart, watched as navigation solutions popped up around him. Their flashing yellow overlays marked potential destinations within range. He paused, taking in the sweep of possibilities. In the chair beside him, Tamara looked up from her notes.

"Are you ready?" she said.

He nodded, trying to look more confident that he felt. "As ready as we'll ever be."

The co-ordinates were still in the ship's memory, where they'd lain hidden for the last two years. He took a deep breath and engaged the Bradley engines. His heart hammered in his chest.

Three hours later, they emerged near an unremarkable brown dwarf six lights from the Green Scar system. They were just beyond the rim of explored space, out on the ragged edge of the frontier. The ride through hyperspace had been long and rough, worse than he remembered.

He pulled up a wraparound display of the system. The brown dwarf was on their starboard side. An insistent red cursor to port showed the position of the alien derelict.

Tamara said, "How close do you think we can get?"

He took a deep breath. He was beginning to have second thoughts. He needed time to nerve himself.

"I don't know."

Behind him, Dieter unfastened his safety restraints and stood up.

"You're going on board," he said.

Sal turned to him. "What?"

"You heard me." Dieter reached into his jacket and pulled out a stubby, business-like pistol.

Sal said, "What the hell are you doing?"

He looked at Tamara. She wouldn't look at him. Her chin dropped onto her chest.

"Dieter is Kate's brother," she said.

Dieter leaned over him. He smelled of aftershave and sweat. When he spoke, a gold canine caught the light.

"You ran out on her," he said.

Sal turned away. "It wasn't like that."

Dieter pointed the gun at him and said, "You left her to die and you ran, to save yourself."

Sal looked down at the metal deck and shook his head. He said, "There was nothing I could do. I wish there was."

Dieter took a step back. He indicated the red cursor on the display. He said, "You're going to go over there and bring back her body."

Tamara said, "That's suicide."

Dieter ignored her. He leaned in close again. His skin was the colour of sand and his breath made Sal's nose wrinkle.

"You owe her that much," Dieter said.

Sal turned his face away. "You know she spent her life running from you, don't you?" he said.

Dieter scowled. "She was my sister. You lost her, and I want her back."

He straightened up. He held the gun in front of him. "I want her back, and you're going to get her for me."

Sal clenched his fists.

"I'm not doing anything for you," he said.

Dieter's lip curled. His pistol swung toward Tamara. Sal saw what was about to happen and shouted: "Leave her alone!"

Tamara squirmed in her seat, tried to turn away, but the safety harness held her in place.

She yelped as Dieter shot her.

"Sal?" she said. "Sal?"

She pressed her hands over the wound in her thigh, trying to staunch the flow of blood. It welled up thickly between her fingers. Sal popped his straps and grabbed an emergency patch from the medkit. He pushed her hands away slapped it over the ragged hole in her sodden fatigues.

He rounded on Dieter. He yelled: "Why the hell did you do that?"

Dieter looked down at him. "That patch will stop the bleeding," he said, "but it can't repair an artery. If you don't get her to a hospital in the next few hours, she'll lose that leg. Maybe even die."

Sal looked at the blood on his hands. He felt angry and helpless. He looked at Tamara.

She said, "It hurts."

Dieter aimed the gun at her other leg. With his free hand, he reached over and took Sal by the shoulder. He pushed him towards the pilot's chair.

"If you want to save her, you'll have to find Kate," he said.

Sal strapped himself in. He didn't have any choice. His hands were shaking as he reached out and grasped the controls.

"Hold on," he said.

He brought them in fast, but the black ship was waiting. It attacked as soon as they were close enough. Shards burst from it like porcupine quills and punched into their hull. They felt the impacts through the floor.

"What was that?" Tamara asked with her eyes closed.

Damage reports clamoured for Sal's attention. He pulled up a summary. "Multiple kinetic hits, like a shotgun blast," he said. "We've lost the cameras on the port side and we're leaking air."

Behind him, Dieter held the back of his couch. Tamara looked sick.

"Can you bring us around, get the starboard cameras on the derelict?" she said.

"I'll try."

On the tactical display, the black ship was a shadow moving against the stars; he had to infer its shape from memory. Off to one side, the star known as Green Scar burned against the pale wash of the Milky Way.

The derelict fired a second volley. The *Wild Cat* shuddered as it hit and the lights in the Star Chamber flickered.

"I just keep thinking too much," Sal said.

He felt the gun press into the back of his neck. Dieter said, "What?"

Sal pictured Kate and Laurel-Ann. He felt the weight of the last two years, pressing down on him.

"I just want it to stop," he said.

He aimed the *Wild Cat*'s nose at the alien ship and threw open the throttle.

There are two kinds of courage. There's the kind you get from knowing that what you're doing is right. And there's the kind you get from knowing it's hopeless and wrong, and just not giving a damn.

In the seconds before the impact, his fear vanished. He was ready to go out in a blaze of glory if it meant wiping the slate clean. He let out a loud laugh: this was how it used to be on a random jump, how it used to feel. He was totally connected to the moment. Adrenalin hammered in his veins. Everything felt fierce and primal and inevitable. And it all moved so damn fast.

He'd almost forgotten how good it felt . . .

For half a second, in the roar of the exhaust, he thought he heard Kate calling to him. Only this time, it wasn't fear in her voice, it was forgiveness.

"Nothing in the main corridor," Petrov reported.

Sal didn't bother to reply; his attention was taken up with the thermal imaging scan, which produced a ghostly image of the two figures in the narrow corridor.

"Nothing but this crap," Kate said, eyeing the slimy, dripping walls with distaste.

She moved like a dancer, lightly on the balls of her feet. The slug thrower in her right hand wavered back and forth with the sweep of her gaze.

"Are you picking up any signs of life?" she said.

Sal could feel the tension in his back and forearms; his fists were clenching and unclenching. He tried to relax, but he'd heard the stories, same as everyone else.

"There's nothing on the monitors," he said.

"I hear you, my friend." Petrov was already chipping away at the walls with a chisel.

"Hey, careful," Kate said. She sounded so close that it was easy to forget she

was three kilometres away, in the belly of a strange and potentially dangerous alien derelict.

"I love you," he said, into the microphone.

5.

The *Wild Cat* crashed against the hideous black ship and the impact cracked her tough hull. Her spine buckled; her heat shield tore apart, and she fell from the larger vessel like a bug falling from a windshield.

In the spherical Star Chamber at her heart, the virtual screens flared and died; part of the ceiling collapsed; sparks flew from crippled instrument panels and burning plastic fumes filled the air.

Sal Dervish sagged against the crash webbing in his couch. His neck hurt. With most of the external cameras gone, he was blind and disorientated; unable to tell where he was, or what state his ship was in. His only functioning screens showed empty space, distant stars.

He looked around for Dieter. Without straps to restrain him, the young man had been catapulted forward and smashed against an instrument panel. There was blood in his hair and his head lay at an awkward angle.

In the co-pilot's position, Tamara Vance lolled against her straps, unconscious. They were here because of her. Her eyes were closed, her face slack. He reached out to touch her hand and she started.

"What happened?" she said. There was blood on her chin, where she'd bitten her lip. "Did we kill it?"

Sal shook his head. "We hit it, but I don't think it noticed. It slapped us aside and kept right on going."

"And we survived?" She sounded unsure. She rubbed her forehead with the back of her hand.

He nodded. He ran his fingertips over the unresponsive instruments. His pulse was racing, hammering in his ears. There was a bubbling laugh in his throat and he had to bite down hard, afraid to let it out.

"I told you this ship was tough," he said. "How's the leg?"

"Painful." She dabbed tentatively at the blood on her chin with the sleeve of her flight suit. Her ponytail was coming loose and untidy strands of copper-coloured hair fell around her face. Sal gave her a grin. He could see she was shaken but he couldn't help it. A burden had been lifted from him. He'd done penance for his cowardice, thrown himself into battle and emerged alive, if not triumphant.

"Did you get it all on film?" he asked.

The corner of her mouth twitched upward. She still held the recorder in her lap, although the cables connecting it to the ship's systems had been ripped loose.

"Everything up until the crash," she said.

He unbuckled and reached for Dieter's gun. He picked it up and blew dust off the barrel. It was a matt black plastic pistol. It looked ugly and vicious and expensive, and it felt great.

"What are you going to do with that?" she said.

"I don't know." he said, shrugging. He just wanted to hold it. It was a victory celebration, like a finger of defiance to the universe that had—once again—failed to kill him.

He pointed it at Dieter. "Why didn't you tell me who he was?" he said.

"Because I knew you'd never let him on board, and getting both of your reactions was too good an opportunity to pass up," Tamara said.

She swivelled around and tapped the instrument panel with distaste. The few functioning readouts showed only that the Bradley engines were offline and haemorrhaging fuel.

"So, how do we get home? We're still venting oxygen and it looks to me like the ship's pretty wrecked."

He knew he should be angry with her for lying to him, but he couldn't summon up the energy. Instead, he closed one eye and sighted the gun on Dieter's forehead. He pictured himself pulling the trigger.

"We've got an automatic distress beacon," he said.

"No-one's going to hear that before we run out of air. We're in the middle of nowhere."

He closed his eyes. His euphoria was gone and all he really wanted now was to go back to his cabin, grab a shower and get some sleep.

"The chances are slim," he admitted.

"Then what do you suggest?" she said through gritted teeth.

He scanned the room. There was an emergency locker marked with red flashes. He pulled it open and brought out a couple of lightweight pressure suits.

"We'll use these," he said. "Their air recyclers are good for days. We'll have time to think of something."

She looked down. "What about Dieter?" she said.

Sal grunted and put a hand on the back of his neck, where it still hurt. "Let's stuff him in one of the emergency sleep tanks and worry what to do with him later."

They were quiet for a moment, unwilling to look at each other. They both knew that with his injuries, there was a good chance Dieter wouldn't survive the freezing process.

Eventually, Tamara pulled herself upright and looked down at her bloody thigh. She smoothed back her hair and folded her arms.

"Screw him," she said.

• • •

Over the next few hours, the *Wild Cat* faded around them like a candle guttering. Sal didn't think she'd ever fly properly again; her back was broken, her engines wrecked. Despite the efforts of her auto-repair packages, her vital systems were failing one by one, leaking away or freezing in the darkness.

He sat there, in his control couch, with the black box resting on his knees and Dieter's pistol in a thigh pocket. The air in his suit smelled of sweat and fear. The overhead lights sparked and fluttered fitfully as the power fluctuated in the damaged reactor. And all the while, he thought of Kate.

"Tell me about her," Tamara said, in one of her lucid moments.

Sal wrinkled his nose; he didn't want to talk about her, not now, at the end.

He said, "She was just the most incredible person I ever met."

He hugged himself as best he could in the cumbersome suit. The temperature on the bridge had been falling steadily and was already well below freezing.

He began to feel light-headed and drowsy. Despite what he'd told Tamara, the air recyclers weren't designed for long duration use and probably wouldn't last much longer, certainly no more than a day.

She coughed and muttered. The painkillers had worn off and she was slipping in and out of a tormented sleep. Beneath her visor, she looked weak and pale.

"This wasn't how it was supposed to be," Sal said, aware he was talking to himself. A long, drawn-out death wasn't something he'd bargained for when he decided to ram the alien ship. He'd hoped to go out in a blaze of glory and redemption, not linger here, slowly fading. His empty stomach was an uncomfortable knot. His throat was dry. His suit itched and chafed. But somehow, none of it really mattered. What mattered was that he'd come here to make peace with the past. He'd made a decision and faced the consequences. His only regret was that Tamara had to share his fate. But then, without her cajoling, he might never have come back. He might have died alone, on Pik Station, in disgrace.

He used the functioning console to divert the last of the ship's power to the self-repair packages, hoping it might buy them a bit more time. And then he lay and looked at the ceiling. Beside him, sexless in her thick pressure suit, Tamara groaned and swore and thrashed. She was disorientated from the drugs. She clawed at her faceplate with gloved fingers until he used the medical interface on the wrist of her suit to trigger morphine into her system.

"We're going to die," she sobbed, her cries melting into the warmth of the drug. "We can't last more than a few days without water. We're both going to die."

He did his best to keep her comfortable. He thought about putting her into one of the emergency sleep tanks next to Dieter's, but couldn't summon the energy. As the hours wore away, his eyelids became heavier and heavier. His thoughts became slippery and vague. He saw Kate's face. He saw the dark muddy water of Lowell Creek. And then . . .

An insistent beeping in his headphones woke him. He stirred, moving stiffly. His lips felt cracked and his fingers and toes hurt because they were so cold.

Beneath a thin layer of frost, there were a handful of lights blinking on the control console. The self-repair packages had brought the Bradley engines back online.

He nudged Tamara. "Hey, we've got power," he said.

But even as he spoke, something caught his eye. On one of the remaining functional screens, something big and black moved purposefully against the stars. A proximity warning pinged on the main flight console as the ship's autopilot tagged the intruder, logging its position and vector as a possible threat.

Tamara opened her eyes. She looked awful. Her head swayed from side-to-side, weighed down by the helmet.

"We can go home?" she said.

Sal bit his lip. They could jump into hyperspace, but the heat shielding was damaged and they had no way to navigate.

"The black ship's coming back," he said.

He glanced over, but she'd closed her eyes again. He ran a quick check on her air supply and frowned at the result. She was good for a couple of hours, maybe. She had enough oxygen to make it back to Pik Station, if he could take them straight there. But he had no way to navigate. They could end up anywhere, if they didn't burn up in the process.

He felt his lips twitch in a smile.

"No air and a damaged heat shield," he said. Surely this would be the ultimate random jump—if they survived it, he'd get his reputation back, whether he wanted it or not.

He looked at the screen: The black ship was closing. It would be in striking range in six seconds.

Four seconds.

He reached out and placed his gauntleted hand on the touch screen that controlled the Bradley engines. Despite the cold, his palms were sweating.

Two seconds.

One.

His lips peeled back in a fierce grin. He pressed down on the screen and the *Wild Cat* groaned. She shook herself like a wounded animal, and leapt.

GLORY

GREG EGAN

An ingot of metallic hydrogen gleamed in the starlight, a narrow cylinder half a meter long with a mass of about a kilogram. To the naked eye it was a dense, solid object, but its lattice of tiny nuclei immersed in an insubstantial fog of electrons was one part matter to two hundred trillion parts empty space. A short distance away was a second ingot, apparently identical to the first, but composed of antihydrogen.

A sequence of finely tuned gamma rays flooded into both cylinders. The protons that absorbed them in the first ingot spat out positrons and were transformed into neutrons, breaking their bonds to the electron cloud that glued them in place. In the second ingot, antiprotons became antineutrons.

A further sequence of pulses herded the neutrons together and forged them into clusters; the antineutrons were similarly rearranged. Both kinds of cluster were unstable, but in order to fall apart they first had to pass through a quantum state that would have strongly absorbed a component of the gamma rays constantly raining down on them. Left to themselves, the probability of them being in this state would have increased rapidly, but each time they measurably failed to absorb the gamma rays, the probability fell back to zero. The quantum Zeno effect endlessly reset the clock, holding the decay in check.

The next series of pulses began shifting the clusters into the space that had separated the original ingots. First neutrons, then antineutrons, were sculpted together in alternating layers. Though the clusters were ultimately unstable, while they persisted they were inert, sequestering their constituents and preventing them from annihilating their counterparts. The end point of this process of nuclear sculpting was a sliver of compressed matter and antimatter, sandwiched together into a needle one micron wide.

The gamma ray lasers shut down, the Zeno effect withdrew its prohibitions. For the time it took a beam of light to cross a neutron, the needle sat motionless in space. Then it began to burn, and it began to move.

The needle was structured like a meticulously crafted firework, and its outer layers ignited first. No external casing could have channelled this blast, but the pattern of tensions woven into the needle's construction favored one direction for the debris to be expelled. Particles streamed backward; the needle moved forward. The shock of acceleration could not have been borne by anything built from atomic-scale matter, but the pressure bearing down on the core of the needle prolonged its life, delaying the inevitable.

Layer after layer burned itself away, blasting the dwindling remnant forward ever faster. By the time the needle had shrunk to a tenth of its original size it was moving at ninety-eight per cent of light speed; to a bystander this could scarcely have been improved upon, but from the needle's perspective there was still room to slash its journey's duration by orders of magnitude.

When just one thousandth of the needle remained, its time, compared to the neighboring stars, was passing two thousand times more slowly. Still the layers kept burning, the protective clusters unraveling as the pressure on them was released. The needle could only reach close enough to light speed to slow down time as much as it required if it could sacrifice a large enough proportion of its remaining mass. The core of the needle could only survive for a few trillionths of a second, while its journey would take two hundred million seconds as judged by the stars. The proportions had been carefully matched, though: out of the two kilograms of matter and antimatter that had been woven together at the launch, only a few million neutrons were needed as the final payload.

By one measure, seven years passed. For the needle, its last trillionths of a second unwound, its final layers of fuel blew away, and at the moment its core was ready to explode it reached its destination, plunging from the near-vacuum of space straight into the heart of a star.

Even here, the density of matter was insufficient to stabilize the core, yet far too high to allow it to pass unhindered. The core was torn apart. But it did not go quietly, and the shock waves it carved through the fusing plasma endured for a million kilometers: all the way through to the cooler outer layers on the opposite side of the star. These shock waves were shaped by the payload that had formed them, and though the initial pattern imprinted on them by the disintegrating cluster of neutrons was enlarged and blurred by its journey, on an atomic scale it remained sharply defined. Like a mold stamped into the seething plasma it encouraged ionized molecular fragments to slip into the troughs and furrows that matched their shape, and then brought them together to react in ways that the plasma's random collisions would never have allowed. In effect, the shock waves formed a web of catalysts, carefully laid out in both time and space, briefly transforming a small corner of the star into a chemical factory operating on a nanometer scale.

The products of this factory sprayed out of the star, riding the last traces of the shock wave's momentum: a few nanograms of elaborate, carbon-rich molecules, sheathed in a protective fullerene weave. Traveling at seven hundred kilometers per second, a fraction below the velocity needed to escape from the star completely, they climbed out of its gravity well, slowing as they ascended.

Four years passed, but the molecules were stable against the ravages of space. By the time they'd traveled a billion kilometers they had almost come to a halt, and they would have fallen back to die in the fires of the star that had forged them if their journey had not been timed so that the star's third planet, a gas giant, was waiting to urge them forward. As they fell toward it, the giant's third moon moved across their path. Eleven years after the needle's launch, its molecular offspring rained down on to the methane snow.

The tiny heat of their impact was not enough to damage them, but it melted a microscopic puddle in the snow. Surrounded by food, the molecular seeds began to grow. Within hours, the area was teeming with nanomachines, some mining the snow and the minerals beneath it, others assembling the bounty into an intricate structure, a rectangular panel a couple of meters wide.

From across the light years, an elaborate sequence of gamma ray pulses fell upon the panel. These pulses were the needle's true payload, the passengers for whom it had merely prepared the way, transmitted in its wake four years after its launch. The panel decoded and stored the data, and the army of nano-machines set to work again, this time following a far more elaborate blueprint. The miners were forced to look further afield to find all the elements that were needed, while the assemblers labored to reach their goal through a sequence of intermediate stages, carefully designed to protect the final product from the vagaries of the local chemistry and climate.

After three months' work, two small fusion-powered spacecraft sat in the snow. Each one held a single occupant, waking for the first time in their freshly minted bodies, yet endowed with memories of an earlier life.

Joan switched on her communications console. Anne appeared on the screen, three short pairs of arms folded across her thorax in a posture of calm repose. They had both worn virtual bodies with the same anatomy before, but this was the first time they had become Noudah in the flesh.

"We're here. Everything worked," Joan marveled. The language she spoke was not her own, but the structure of her new brain and body made it second nature.

Anne said, "Now comes the hard part."

"Yes." Joan looked out from the spacecraft's cockpit. In the distance, a fissured blue-gray plateau of water ice rose above the snow. Nearby, the nanomachines were busy disassembling the gamma ray receiver. When they had erased all traces of their handiwork they would wander off into the snow and catalyze their own destruction.

Joan had visited dozens of planet-bound cultures in the past, taking on different bodies and languages as necessary, but those cultures had all been plugged in to the Amalgam, the meta-civilization that spanned the galactic disk. However far from home she'd been, the means to return to familiar places had always been close at hand. The Noudah had only just mastered interplanetary flight, and they had no idea that the Amalgam existed. The closest node in the Amalgam's network was seven light years away, and even that was out of bounds to her and Anne now: they had agreed not to risk disclosing its location to the Noudah, so any transmission they sent could only be directed to a decoy node that they'd set up more than twenty light years away.

"It will be worth it," Joan said.

Anne's Noudah face was immobile, but chromatophores sent a wave of violet and gold sweeping across her skin in an expression of cautious optimism. "We'll see." She tipped her head to the left, a gesture preceding a friendly departure.

Joan tipped her own head in response, as if she'd been doing so all her life. "Be careful, my friend," she said.

"You too."

Anne's ship ascended so high on its chemical thrusters that it shrank to a speck before igniting its fusion engine and streaking away in a blaze of light. Joan felt a pang of loneliness; there was no predicting when they would be reunited.

Her ship's software was primitive; the whole machine had been scrupulously matched to the Noudah's level of technology. Joan knew how to fly it herself if necessary, and on a whim she switched off the autopilot and manually activated the ascent thrusters. The control panel was crowded, but having six hands helped.

2

The world the Noudah called home was the closest of the system's five planets to their sun. The average temperature was one hundred and twenty degrees Celsius, but the high atmospheric pressure allowed liquid water to exist across the entire surface. The chemistry and dynamics of the planet's crust had led to a relatively flat terrain, with a patchwork of dozens of disconnected seas but no globe-spanning ocean. From space, these seas appeared as silvery mirrors, bordered by a violet and brown tarnish of vegetation.

The Noudah were already leaving their most electromagnetically promiscuous phase of communications behind, but the short-lived oasis of Amalgam-level technology on Baneth, the gas giant's moon, had had no trouble eavesdropping on their chatter and preparing an updated cultural briefing which had been spliced into Joan's brain.

The planet was still divided into the same eleven political units as it had been fourteen years before, the time of the last broadcasts that had reached the node before Joan's departure. Tira and Ghahar, the two dominant nations in terms of territory, economic activity and military power, also occupied the vast majority of significant Niah archaeological sites.

Joan had expected that they'd be noticed as soon as they left Baneth—the exhaust from their fusion engines glowed like the sun—but their departure had triggered no obvious response, and now that they were coasting they'd be far harder to spot. As Anne drew closer to the home world, she sent a message to Tira's traffic control center. Joan tuned in to the exchange.

"I come in peace from another star," Anne said. "I seek permission to land."

There was a delay of several seconds more than the light-speed lag, then a terse response. "Please identify yourself and state your location."

Anne transmitted her coordinates and flight plan.

"We confirm your location, please identify yourself."

"My name is Anne. I come from another star."

There was a long pause, then a different voice answered. "If you are from Ghahar, please explain your intentions."

"I am not from Ghahar."

"Why should I believe that? Show yourself."

"I've taken the same shape as your people, in the hope of living among you for a while." Anne opened a video channel and showed them her unremarkable Noudah face. "But there's a signal being transmitted from these coordinates that might persuade you that I'm telling the truth." She gave the location of the decoy node, twenty light years away, and specified a frequency. The signal coming from the node contained an image of the very same face.

This time, the silence stretched out for several minutes. It would take a while for the Tirans to confirm the true distance of the radio source.

"You do not have permission to land. Please enter this orbit, and we will rendezvous and board your ship."

Parameters for the orbit came through on the data channel. Anne said, "As you wish."

Minutes later, Joan's instruments picked up three fusion ships being launched from Tiran bases. When Anne reached the prescribed orbit, Joan listened anxiously to the instructions the Tirans issued. Their tone sounded wary, but they were entitled to treat this stranger with caution, all the more so if they believed Anne's claim.

Joan was accustomed to a very different kind of reception, but then the members of the Amalgam had spent hundreds of millennia establishing a framework of trust. They also benefited from a milieu in which most kinds of force had been rendered ineffectual; when everyone had backups of themselves scattered around the galaxy, it required a vastly disproportionate effort to inconvenience someone, let alone kill them. By any reasonable measure, honesty and cooperation yielded far richer rewards than subterfuge and slaughter.

Nonetheless, each individual culture had its roots in a biological heritage that gave rise to behavior governed more by ancient urges than contemporary realities, and even when they mastered the technology to choose their own nature, the precise set of traits they preserved was up to them. In the worst case, a species still saddled with inappropriate drives but empowered by advanced technology could wreak havoc. The Noudah deserved to be treated with courtesy and respect, but they did not yet belong in the Amalgam.

The Tirans' own exchanges were not on open channels, so once they had entered Anne's ship Joan could only guess what was happening. She waited until two of the ships had returned to the surface, then sent her own message to Ghahar's traffic control.

"I come in peace from another star. I seek permission to land."

3

The Ghahari allowed Joan to fly her ship straight down to the surface. She wasn't sure if this was because they were more trusting, or if they were afraid that the Tirans might try to interfere if she lingered in orbit.

The landing site was a bare plain of chocolate colored sand. The air shimmered in the heat, the distortions intensified by the thickness of the atmosphere, making the horizon waver as if seen through molten glass. Joan waited in the cockpit as three trucks approached; they all came to a halt some twenty meters away. A voice over the radio instructed her to leave the ship; she complied, and after she'd stood in the open for a minute, a lone Noudah left one of the trucks and walked toward her.

"I'm Pirit," she said. "Welcome to Ghahar." Her gestures were courteous but restrained.

"I'm Joan. Thank you for your hospitality."

"Your impersonation of our biology is impeccable." There was a trace of skepticism in Pirit's tone; Joan had pointed the Ghahari to her own portrait being broadcast from the decoy node, but she had to admit that in the context her lack of exotic technology and traits would make it harder to accept the implications of that transmission.

"In my culture, it's a matter of courtesy to imitate one's hosts as closely as possible."

Pirit hesitated, as if pondering whether to debate the merits of such a custom, but then rather than quibbling over the niceties of interspecies etiquette she chose to confront the real issue head on. "If you're a Tiran spy, or a defector, the sooner you admit that the better."

"That's very sensible advice, but I'm neither."

The Noudah wore no clothing as such, but Pirit had a belt with a number of pouches. She took a hand-held scanner from one and ran it over Joan's body. Joan's briefing suggested that it was probably only checking for metal, volatile explosives and radiation; the technology to image her body or search for pathogens would not be so portable. In any case, she was a healthy, unarmed Noudah down to the molecular level.

Pirit escorted her to one of the trucks, and invited her to recline in a section at the back. Another Noudah drove while Pirit watched over Joan. They soon arrived at a small complex of buildings a couple of kilometers from where the ship had touched down. The walls, roofs and floors of the buildings were all made from the local sand, cemented with an adhesive that the Noudah secreted from their own bodies.

Inside, Joan was given a thorough medical examination, including three kinds of full-body scan. The Noudah who examined her treated her with a kind of detached efficiency devoid of any pleasantries; she wasn't sure if that was their standard bedside manner, or a kind of glazed shock at having been told of her claimed origins.

Pirit took her to an adjoining room and offered her a couch. The Noudah anatomy did not allow for sitting, but they liked to recline.

Pirit remained standing. "How did you come here?" she asked.

"You've seen my ship. I flew it from Baneth."

"And how did you reach Baneth?"

"I'm not free to discuss that," Joan replied cheerfully.

"Not free?" Pirit's face clouded with silver, as if she was genuinely perplexed.

Joan said, "You understand me perfectly. Please don't tell me there's nothing *you're* not free to discuss with me."

"You certainly didn't fly that ship twenty light years."

"No, I certainly didn't."

Pirit hesitated. "Did you come through the Cataract?" The Cataract was a black hole, a remote partner to the Noudah's sun; they orbited each other at a distance of about eighty billion kilometers. The name came from its telescopic appearance: a dark circle ringed by a distortion in the background of stars, like some kind of visual aberration. The Tirans and Ghahari were in a race to be the first to visit this extraordinary neighbor, but as yet neither of them were quite up to the task.

"*Through* the Cataract? I think your scientists have already proven that black holes aren't shortcuts to anywhere."

"Our scientists aren't always right."

"Neither are ours," Joan admitted, "but all the evidence points in one direction: black holes aren't doorways, they're shredding machines."

"So you traveled the whole twenty light years?"

"More than that," Joan said truthfully, "from my original home. I've spent half my life traveling."

"Faster than light?" Pirit suggested hopefully.

"No. That's impossible."

They circled around the question a dozen more times, before Pirit finally changed her tune from *how* to *why*?

"I'm a xenomathematician," Joan said. "I've come here in the hope of collaborating with your archaeologists in their study of Niah artifacts."

Pirit was stunned. "What do you know about the Niah?"

"Not as much as I'd like to." Joan gestured at her Noudah body. "As I'm sure you've already surmised, we've listened to your broadcasts for some time, so we know pretty much what an ordinary Noudah knows. That includes the basic facts about the Niah. Historically they've been referred to as your ancestors, though the latest studies suggest that you and they really just have an earlier common ancestor. They died out about a million years ago, but there's evidence that they might have had a sophisticated culture for as long as three million years. There's no indication that they ever developed space flight. Basically, once they achieved material comfort, they seem to have devoted themselves to various artforms, including mathematics."

"So you've traveled twenty light years just to look at Niah tablets?" Pirit was incredulous.

"Any culture that spent three million years doing mathematics must have something to teach us."

"Really?" Pirit's face became blue with disgust. "In the ten thousand years since we discovered the wheel, we've already reached halfway to the Cataract. They wasted their time on useless abstractions."

Joan said, "I come from a culture of spacefarers myself, so I respect your achievements. But I don't think anyone really knows what the Niah achieved. I'd like to find out, with the help of your people."

Pirit was silent for a while. "What if we say no?"

"Then I'll leave empty-handed."

"What if we insist that you remain with us?"

"Then I'll die here, empty-handed." On her command, this body would expire in an instant; she could not be held and tortured.

Pirit said angrily, "You must be willing to trade *something* for the privilege you're demanding!"

"Requesting, not demanding," Joan insisted gently. "And what I'm willing to offer is my own culture's perspective on Niah mathematics. If you ask your archaeologists and mathematicians, I'm sure they'll tell you that there are many things written in the Niah tablets that they don't yet understand. My colleague and I—" neither of them had mentioned Anne before, but Joan was sure that Pirit knew all about her "—simply want to shed as much light as we can on this subject."

Pirit said bitterly, "You won't even tell us how you came to our world. Why should we trust you to share whatever you discover about the Niah?"

"Interstellar travel is no great mystery," Joan countered. "You know all the basic science already; making it work is just a matter of persistence. If you're left to develop your own technology, you might even come up with better methods than we have."

"So we're expected to be patient, to discover these things for ourselves . . . but you can't wait a few centuries for us to decipher the Niah artifacts?"

Joan said bluntly, "The present Noudah culture, both here and in Tira, seems to hold the Niah in contempt. Dozens of partially excavated sites containing Niah artifacts are under threat from irrigation projects and other developments. That's the reason we couldn't wait. We needed to come here and offer our assistance, before the last traces of the Niah disappeared forever."

Pirit did not reply, but Joan hoped she knew what her interrogator was thinking: *Nobody would cross twenty light years for a few worthless scribblings. Perhaps we've underestimated the Niah. Perhaps our ancestors have left us a great secret, a great legacy. And perhaps the fastest—perhaps the only—way to uncover it is to give this impertinent, irritating alien exactly what she wants.*

4

The sun was rising ahead of them as they reached the top of the hill. Sando turned to Joan, and his face became green with pleasure. "Look behind you," he said.

Joan did as he asked. The valley below was hidden in fog, and it had settled so evenly that she could see their shadows in the dawn light, stretched out across the top of the fog layer. Around the shadow of her head was a circular halo like a small rainbow.

"We call it the Niah's light," Sando said. "In the old days, people used to say that the halo proved that the Niah blood was strong in you."

Joan said, "The only trouble with that hypothesis being that *you* see it around *your* head . . . and I see it around mine." On Earth, the phenomenon was known as a "glory." The particles of fog were scattering the sunlight back toward them, turning it one hundred and eighty degrees. To look at the shadow of your own head was to face directly away from the sun, so the halo always appeared around the observer's shadow.

"I suppose you're the final proof that Niah blood has nothing to do with it," Sando mused.

"That's assuming I'm telling you the truth, and I really can see it around my own head."

"And assuming," Sando added, "that the Niah really did stay at home, and didn't wander around the galaxy spreading their progeny."

They came over the top of the hill and looked down into the adjoining riverine valley. The sparse brown grass of the hillside gave way to a lush violet growth closer to the water. Joan's arrival had delayed the flooding of the valley, but even alien interest in the Niah had only bought the archaeologists an extra year. The dam was part of a long-planned agricultural development, and however tantalizing the possibility that Joan might reveal some priceless insight hidden among the Niah's "useless abstractions," that vague promise could only compete with more tangible considerations for a limited time.

Part of the hill had fallen away in a landslide a few centuries before, revealing more than a dozen beautifully preserved strata. When Joan and Sando reached the excavation site, Rali and Surat were already at work, clearing away soft sedimentary rock from a layer that Sando had dated as belonging to the Niah's "twilight" period.

Pirit had insisted that only Sando, the senior archaeologist, be told about Joan's true nature; Joan refused to lie to anyone, but had agreed to tell her colleagues only that she was a mathematician and that she was not permitted to discuss her past. At first this had made them guarded and resentful, no doubt because they assumed that she was some kind of spy sent by the authorities to watch over them. Later it had dawned on them that she was genuinely interested in their work, and that the absurd restrictions on her topics of conversation were not of her own choosing. Nothing about the Noudah's language or appearance correlated strongly with their recent division into nations—with no oceans to cross, and a long history of migration they were more or less geographically homogeneous—but Joan's odd name and occasional *faux pas* could still be ascribed to some mysterious exoticism. Rali and Surat seemed content to assume that she was a defector from one of the smaller nations, and that her history could not be made explicit for obscure political reasons.

"There are more tablets here, very close to the surface," Rali announced excitedly. "The acoustics are unmistakable." Ideally they would have excavated the entire hillside, but they did not have the time or the labor, so they were using acoustic tomography to identify likely deposits of accessible Niah writing, and then concentrating their efforts on those spots.

The Niah had probably had several ephemeral forms of written communication, but when they found something worth publishing, it stayed published: they carved their symbols into a ceramic that made diamond seem like tissue paper. It was almost unheard of for the tablets to be broken, but they were small, and multi-tablet works were sometimes widely dispersed. Niah technology could probably have carved three million years' worth of knowledge on to the head of a pin—they seemed not to have invented nanomachines, but they were into high quality bulk materials and precision engineering—but for whatever reason they had chosen legibility to the naked eye above other considerations.

Joan made herself useful, taking acoustic readings further along the slope, while Sando watched over his students as they came closer to the buried Niah artifacts. She had learned not to hover around expectantly when a discovery was imminent; she was treated far more warmly if she waited to be summoned. The tomography unit was almost foolproof, using satellite navigation to track its position and software to analyze the signals it gathered; all it really needed was someone to drag it along the rock face at a suitable pace.

Through the corner of her eye, Joan noticed her shadow on the rocks flicker and grow complicated. She looked up to see three dazzling beads of light flying west out of the sun. She might have assumed that the fusion ships were doing something useful, but the media was full of talk of "military exercises," which meant the Tirans and the Ghahari engaging in expensive, belligerent gestures in orbit, trying to convince each other of their superior skills, technology, or sheer strength of numbers. For people with no real differences apart from a few centuries of recent history, they could puff up their minor political disputes into matters of the utmost solemnity. It might almost have been funny, if the idiots hadn't incinerated hundreds of thousands of each other's citizens every few decades, not to mention playing callous and often deadly games with the lives of the inhabitants of smaller nations.

"Jown! Jown! Come and look at this!" Surat called to her. Joan switched off the tomography unit and jogged toward the archaeologists, suddenly conscious of her body's strangeness. Her legs were stumpy but strong, and her balance as she ran came not from arms and shoulders but from the swish of her muscular tail.

"It's a significant mathematical result," Rali informed her proudly when she reached them. He'd pressure-washed the sandstone away from the near-indestructible ceramic of the tablet, and it was only a matter of holding the surface at the right angle to the light to see the etched writing stand out as crisply and starkly as it would have a million years before.

Rali was not a mathematician, and he was not offering his own opinion on the theorem the tablet stated; the Niah themselves had a clear set of typographical conventions which they used to distinguish between everything from minor lemmas to the most celebrated theorems. The size and decorations of the symbols labelling the theorem attested to its value in the Niah's eyes.

Joan read the theorem carefully. The proof was not included on the same tablet, but the Niah had a way of expressing their results that made you believe them as soon as you read them; in this case the definitions of the terms needed to state the theorem were so beautifully chosen that the result seem almost inevitable.

The theorem itself was expressed as a commuting hypercube, one of the Niah's favorite forms. You could think of a square with four different sets of mathematical objects associated with each of its corners, and a way of mapping one set into another associated with each edge of the square. If the maps commuted, then going across the top of the square, then down, had exactly the same effect as going down the left edge of the square, then across: either way, you mapped each element from the top-left set into the same element of the bottom-right set. A similar kind of result might hold for sets and maps that could naturally be placed at the corners and edges of a cube, or a hypercube of any dimension. It was also possible for the square faces in these structures to stand for relationships that held between the maps between sets, and for cubes to describe relationships between those relationships, and so on.

That a theorem took this form didn't guarantee its importance; it was easy to cook up trivial examples of sets and maps that commuted. The Niah didn't carve trivia into their timeless ceramic, though, and this theorem was no exception. The seven-dimensional commuting hypercube established a dazzlingly elegant correspondence between seven distinct, major branches of Niah mathematics, intertwining their most important concepts into a unified whole. It was a result Joan had never seen before: no mathematician anywhere in the Amalgam, or in any ancestral culture she had studied, had reached the same insight.

She explained as much of this as she could to the three archaeologists; they couldn't take in all the details, but their faces became orange with fascination when she sketched what she thought the result would have meant to the Niah themselves.

"This isn't quite the Big Crunch," she joked, "but it must have made them think they were getting closer." *The Big Crunch* was her nickname for the mythical result that the Niah had aspired to reach: a unification of every field of mathematics that they considered significant. To find such a thing would not have meant the end of mathematics—it would not have subsumed every last conceivable, interesting mathematical truth—but it would certainly have marked a point of closure for the Niah's own style of investigation.

"I'm sure they found it," Surat insisted. "They reached the Big Crunch, then they had nothing more to live for."

Rali was scathing. "So the whole culture committed collective suicide?"

"Not actively, no," Surat replied. "But it was the search that had kept them going."

"Entire cultures don't lose the will to live," Rali said. "They get wiped out by external forces: disease, invasion, changes in climate."

"The Niah survived for three million years," Surat countered. "They had the means to weather all of those forces. Unless they were wiped out by alien invaders with vastly superior technology." She turned to Joan. "What do you think?"

"About aliens destroying the Niah?"

"I was joking about the aliens. But what about the mathematics? What if they found the Big Crunch?"

"There's more to life than mathematics," Joan said. "But not much more."

Sando said, "And there's more to this find than one tablet. If we get back to work, we might have the proof in our hands before sunset."

5

Joan briefed Halzoun by video link while Sando prepared the evening meal. Halzoun was the mathematician Pirit had appointed to supervise her, but apparently his day job was far too important to allow him to travel. Joan was grateful; Halzoun was the most tedious Noudah she had encountered. He could understand the Niah's work when she explained it to him, but he seemed to have no interest in it for its own sake. He spent most of their conversations trying to catch her out in some deception or contradiction, and the rest pressing her to imagine military or commercial applications of the Niah's gloriously useless insights. Sometimes she played along with this infantile fantasy, hinting at potential superweapons based on exotic physics that might come tumbling out of the vacuum, if only one possessed the right Niah theorems to coax them into existence.

Sando was her minder too, but at least he was more subtle about it. Pirit had insisted that she stay in his shelter, rather than sharing Rali and Surat's; Joan didn't mind, because with Sando she didn't have the stress of having to keep quiet about everything. Privacy and modesty were non-issues for the Noudah, and Joan had become Noudah enough not to care herself. Nor was there any danger of their proximity leading to a sexual bond; the Noudah had a complex system of biochemical cues that meant desire only arose in couples with a suitable mixture of genetic differences and similarities. She would have had to search a crowded Noudah city for a week to find someone to lust after, though at least it would have been guaranteed to be mutual.

After they'd eaten, Sando said, "You should be happy. That was our best find yet."

"I am happy." Joan made a conscious effort to exhibit a viridian tinge. "It was the first new result I've seen on this planet. It was the reason I came here, the reason I traveled so far."

"Something's wrong, though, I think."

"I wish I could have shared the news with my friend," Joan admitted. Pirit claimed to be negotiating with the Tirans to allow Anne to communicate with her, but Joan was not convinced that he was genuinely trying. She was sure that he would have relished the thought of listening in on a conversation between the two of them—while forcing them to speak Noudah, of course—in the hope that they'd slip up and reveal something useful, but at the same time he would have had to face the fact that the Tirans would be listening too. What an excruciating dilemma.

"You should have brought a communications link with you," Sando suggested. "A home-style one, I mean. Nothing we could eavesdrop on."

"We couldn't do that," Joan said.

He pondered this. "You really are afraid of us, aren't you? You think the smallest technological trinket will be enough to send us straight to the stars, and then you'll have a horde of rampaging barbarians to deal with."

"We know how to deal with barbarians," Joan said coolly.

Sando's face grew dark with mirth. "Now *I'm* afraid."

"I just wish I knew what was happening to her," Joan said. "What she was doing, how they were treating her."

"Probably much the same as we're treating you," Sando suggested. "We're really not that different." He thought for a moment. "There was something I wanted to show you." He brought over his portable console, and summoned up an article from a Tiran journal. "See what a borderless world we live in," he joked.

The article was entitled "Seekers and Spreaders: What We Must Learn from the Niah." Sando said, "This might give you some idea of how they're thinking over there. Jaqad is an academic archaeologist, but she's also very close to the people in power."

Joan read from the console while Sando made repairs to their shelter, secreting a molasses-like substance from a gland at the tip of his tail and spreading it over the cracks in the walls.

There were two main routes a culture could take, Jaqad argued, once it satisfied its basic material needs. One was to think and study: to stand back and observe, to seek knowledge and insight from the world around it. The other was to invest its energy in entrenching its good fortune.

The Niah had learned a great deal in three million years, but in the end it had not been enough to save them. Exactly what had killed them was still a matter of speculation, but it was hard to believe that if they had colonized other worlds they would have vanished on all of them. "Had the Niah been Spreaders," Jaqad wrote, "we might expect a visit from them, or them from us, sometime in the coming centuries."

The Noudah, in contrast, were determined Spreaders. Once they had the means, they would plant colonies across the galaxy. They would, Jaqad was sure, create new biospheres, re-engineer stars, and even alter space and time to guarantee their survival. The growth of their empire would come first; any knowledge that failed to serve that purpose would be a mere distraction. "In any competition between Seekers and Spreaders, it is a Law of History that the Spreaders must win out in the end. Seekers, such as the Niah, might hog resources and block the way, but in the long run their own nature will be their downfall."

Joan stopped reading. "When you look out into the galaxy with your telescopes," she asked Sando, "how many *re-engineered stars* do you see?"

"Would we recognize them?"

"Yes. Natural stellar processes aren't that complicated; your scientists already know everything there is to know about the subject."

"I'll take your word for that. So . . . you're saying Jaqad is wrong? The Niah themselves never left this world, but the galaxy already belongs to creatures more like them than like us?"

"It's not Noudah versus Niah," Joan said. "It's a matter of how a culture's perspective changes with time. Once a species conquers disease, modifies their biology, and spreads even a short distance beyond their home world, they usually start to relax a bit. The territorial imperative isn't some timeless Law of History; it belongs to a certain phase."

"What if it persists, though? Into a later phase?"

"That can cause friction," Joan admitted.

"Nevertheless, no Spreaders have conquered the galaxy?"

"Not yet."

Sando went back to his repairs; Joan read the rest of the article. She'd thought she'd already grasped the lesson demanded by the subtitle, but it turned out that Jaqad had something more specific in mind.

"Having argued this way, how can I defend my own field of study from the very same charges as I have brought against the Niah? Having grasped the essential character of this doomed race, why should we waste our time and resources studying them further?

"The answer is simple. We still do not know exactly how and why the Niah died, but when we do, that could turn out to be the most important discovery in history. When we finally leave our world behind, we should not expect to find only other Spreaders to compete with us, as honorable opponents in battle. There will be Seekers as well, blocking the way: tired, old races squatting uselessly on their hoards of knowledge and wealth.

"Time will defeat them in the end, but we already waited three million years to be born; we should have no patience to wait again. If we can learn how the Niah died, that will be our key, that will be our weapon. If we know the Seekers' weakness, we can find a way to hasten their demise."

6

The proof of the Niah's theorem turned out to be buried deep in the hillside, but over the following days they extracted it all.

It was as beautiful and satisfying as Joan could have wished, merging six earlier, simpler theorems while extending the techniques used in their proofs. She could even see hints at how the same methods might be stretched further to yield still stronger results. "The Big Crunch" had always been a slightly mocking, irreverent term, but now she was struck anew by how little justice it did to the real trend that had fascinated the Niah. It was not a matter of everything in mathematics collapsing in on itself, with one branch turning out to have been merely a recapitulation of another under a different guise. Rather, the principle was that every sufficiently beautiful mathematical system was rich enough to mirror *in part*—and sometimes in a complex and distorted fashion—every other sufficiently beautiful system. Nothing became sterile and redundant, nothing proved to have been a waste of time, but everything was shown to be magnificently intertwined.

After briefing Halzoun, Joan used the satellite dish to transmit the theorem and its proof to the decoy node. That had been the deal with Pirit: anything she learned from the Niah belonged to the whole galaxy, as long as she explained it to her hosts first.

The archaeologists moved across the hillside, hunting for more artifacts in the same layer of sediment. Joan was eager to see what else the same group of Niah might have published. One possible eight-dimensional hypercube was hovering in her mind; if she'd sat down and thought about it for a few decades she might have worked out the details herself, but the Niah did what they did so well that it would have seemed crass to try to follow clumsily in their footsteps when their own immaculately polished results might simply be lying in the ground, waiting to be uncovered.

A month after the discovery, Joan was woken by the sound of an intruder moving through the shelter. She knew it wasn't Sando; even as she slept an ancient part of her Noudah brain was listening to his heartbeat. The stranger's heart was too quiet to hear, which required great discipline, but the shelter's flexible adhesive made the floor emit a characteristic squeak beneath even the gentlest footsteps. As she rose from her couch she heard Sando waking, and she turned in his direction.

Bright torchlight on his face dazzled her for a moment. The intruder held two knives to Sando's respiration membranes; a deep enough cut there would mean choking to death, in excruciating pain. The nanomachines that had built Joan's body had wired extensive skills in unarmed combat into her brain, and one scenario involving a feigned escape attempt followed by a sideways flick of her powerful tail was already playing out in the back of her mind, but as yet she could see no way to guarantee that Sando came through it all unharmed.

She said, "What do you want?"

The intruder remained in darkness. "Tell me about the ship that brought you to Baneth."

"Why?"

"Because it would be a shame to shred your colleague here, just when his work was going so well." Sando refused to show any emotion on his face, but the blank pallor itself was as stark an expression of fear as anything Joan could imagine.

She said, "There's a coherent state that can be prepared for a quark-gluon plasma in which virtual black holes catalyze baryon decay. In effect, you can turn all of your fuel's rest mass into photons, yielding the most efficient exhaust stream possible." She recited a long list of technical details. The claimed baryon decay process didn't actually exist, but the pseudo-physics underpinning it was mathematically consistent, and could not be ruled out by anything the Noudah had yet observed. She and Anne had prepared an entire fictitious science and technology, and even a fictitious history of their culture, precisely for emergencies like this; they could spout red herrings for a decade if necessary, and never get caught out contradicting themselves.

"That wasn't so hard, was it?" the intruder gloated.

"What now?"

"You're going to take a trip with me. If you do this nicely, nobody needs to get hurt."

Something moved in the shadows, and the intruder screamed in pain. Joan leaped forward and knocked one of the knives out of his hand with her tail; the other knife grazed Sando's membrane, but a second tail whipped out of the darkness and intervened. As the intruder fell backward, the beam of his torch revealed Surat and Rali tensed beside him, and a pick buried deep in his side.

Joan's rush of combat hormones suddenly faded, and she let out a long, deep wail of anguish. Sando was unscathed, but a stream of dark liquid was pumping out of the intruder's wound.

Surat was annoyed. "Stop blubbing, and help us tie up this Tiran cousin-fucker."

"Tie him up? You've killed him!"

"Don't be stupid, that's just sheath fluid." Joan recalled her Noudah anatomy; sheath fluid was like oil in a hydraulic machine. You could lose it all and it would cost you most of the strength in your limbs and tail, but you wouldn't die, and your body would make more eventually.

Rali found some cable and they trussed up the intruder. Sando was shaken, but he seemed to be recovering. He took Joan aside. "I'm going to have to call Pirit."

"I understand. But what will he do to these two?" She wasn't sure exactly how much Rali and Surat had heard, but it was certain to have been more than Pirit wanted them to know.

"Don't worry about that, I can protect them."

Just before dawn someone sent by Pirit arrived in a truck to take the intruder away. Sando declared a rest day, and Rali and Surat went back to their shelter to sleep. Joan went for a walk along the hillside; she didn't feel like sleeping.

Sando caught up with her. He said, "I told them you'd been working on a military research project, and you were exiled here for some political misdemeanor."

"And they believed you?"

"All they heard was half of a conversation full of incomprehensible physics. All they know is that someone thought you were worth kidnapping."

Joan said, "I'm sorry about what happened."

Sando hesitated. "What did you expect?"

Joan was stung. "One of us went to Tira, one of us came here. We thought that would keep everyone happy!"

"We're Spreaders," said Sando. "Give us one of anything, and we want two. Especially if our enemy has the other one. Did you really think you could come here, do a bit of fossicking, and then simply fly away without changing a thing?"

"Your culture has always believed there were other civilizations in the galaxy. Our existence hardly came as a shock."

Sando's face became yellow, an expression of almost parental reproach. "Believing in something in the abstract is not the same as having it dangled in front of you. We were never going to have an existential crisis at finding out that we're not unique; the Niah might be related to us, but they were still alien enough to get us used to the idea. But did you really think we were just going to relax and accept your refusal to share your technology? That one of you went to the Tirans only makes it worse for the Ghahari, and vice versa. Both governments are going absolutely crazy, each one terrified that the other has found a way to make its alien talk."

Joan stopped walking. "The war games, the border skirmishes? You're blaming all of that on Anne and me?"

Sando's body sagged wearily. "To be honest, I don't know all the details. And if it's any consolation, I'm sure we would have found another reason if you hadn't come along."

Joan said, "Maybe I should leave." She was tired of these people, tired of her body, tired of being cut off from civilization. She had rescued one beautiful Niah theorem and sent it out into the Amalgam. Wasn't that enough?

"It's up to you," Sando replied. "But you might as well stay until they flood the valley. Another year isn't going to change anything. What you've done to this world has already been done. For us, there's no going back."

7

Joan stayed with the archaeologists as they moved across the hillside. They found tablets bearing Niah drawings and poetry, which no doubt had their virtues but to Joan seemed bland and opaque. Sando and his students relished these discoveries as much as the theorems; to them, the Niah culture was a vast jigsaw puzzle, and any clue that filled in the details of their history was as good as any other.

Sando would have told Pirit everything he'd heard from Joan the night the intruder came, so she was surprised that she hadn't been summoned for a fresh interrogation to flesh out the details. Perhaps the Ghahari physicists were still digesting her elaborate gobbledygook, trying to decide if it made sense. In her more cynical moments she wondered if the intruder might have been Ghahari himself, sent by Pirit to exploit her friendship with Sando. Perhaps Sando had even been in on it, and Rali and Surat as well. The possibility made her feel as if she was living in a fabricated world, a scape in which nothing was real and nobody could be trusted. The only thing she was certain that the Ghaharis could not have faked was the Niah artifacts. The mathematics verified itself; everything else was subject to doubt and paranoia.

Summer came, burning away the morning fogs. The Noudah's idea of heat was very different from Joan's previous perceptions, but even the body she now wore found the midday sun oppressive. She willed herself to be patient. There was still a chance that the Niah had taken a few more steps toward their grand vision of a unified mathematics, and carved their final discoveries into the form that would outlive them by a million years.

When the lone fusion ship appeared high in the afternoon sky, Joan resolved to ignore it. She glanced up once, but she kept dragging the tomography unit across the ground. She was sick of thinking about Tiran-Ghahari politics. They had played their childish games for centuries; she would not take the blame for this latest outbreak of provocation.

Usually the ships flew by, disappearing within minutes, showing off their power and speed. This one lingered, weaving back and forth across the sky like some dazzling insect performing an elaborate mating dance. Joan's second shadow darted around her feet, hammering a strangely familiar rhythm into her brain.

She looked up, disbelieving. The motion of the ship was following the syntax of a gestural language she had learned on another planet, in another body, a dozen lifetimes ago. The only other person on this world who could know that language was Anne.

She glanced toward the archaeologists a hundred meters away, but they seemed to be paying no attention to the ship. She switched off the tomography unit and stared into the sky. *I'm listening, my friend. What's happening? Did they give you back your ship? Have you had enough of this world, and decided to go home?*

Anne told the story in shorthand, compressed and elliptic. The Tirans had found a tablet bearing a theorem: the last of the Niah's discoveries, the pinnacle of their achievements. Her minders had not let her study it, but they had contrived a situation making it easy for her to steal it, and to steal this ship. They had wanted her to take it and run, in the hope that she would lead them to something they valued far more than any ancient mathematics: an advanced spacecraft, or some magical stargate at the edge of the system.

But Anne wasn't fleeing anywhere. She was high above Ghahar, reading the tablet, and now she would paint what she read across the sky for Joan to see.

Sando approached. "We're in danger, we have to move."

"Danger? That's my friend up there! She's not going to shoot a missile at us!"

"Your friend?" Sando seemed confused. As he spoke, three more ships came into view, lower and brighter than the first. "I've been told that the Tirans are going to strike the valley, to bury the Niah sites. We need to get over the hill and indoors, to get some protection from the blast."

"Why would the Tirans attack the Niah sites? That makes no sense to me."

Sando said, "Nor me, but I don't have time to argue."

The three ships were menacing Anne's, pursuing her, trying to drive her away. Joan had no idea if they were Ghahari defending their territory, or Tirans harassing her in the hope that she would flee and reveal the non-existent shortcut to the stars, but Anne was staying put, still weaving the same gestural language into her maneuvers even as she dodged her pursuers, spelling out the Niah's glorious finale.

Joan said, "You go. I have to see this." She tensed, ready to fight him if necessary.

Sando took something from his tool belt and peppered her side with holes. Joan gasped with pain and crumpled to the ground as the sheath fluid poured out of her.

Rali and Surat helped carry her to the shelter. Joan caught glimpses of the fiery ballet in the sky, but not enough to make sense of it, let alone reconstruct it.

They put her on her couch inside the shelter. Sando bandaged her side and gave her water to sip. He said, "I'm sorry I had to do that, but if anything had happened to you I would have been held responsible."

Surat kept ducking outside to check on the "battle," then reporting excitedly on the state of play. "The Tiran's still up there, they can't get rid of it. I don't know why they haven't shot it down yet."

Because the Tirans were the ones pursuing Anne, and they didn't want her dead. But for how long would the Ghahari tolerate this violation?

Anne's efforts could not be allowed to come to nothing. Joan struggled to recall the constellations she'd last seen in the night sky. At the node they'd departed from, powerful telescopes were constantly trained on the Noudah's home world. Anne's ship was easily bright enough, its gestures wide enough, to be resolved from seven light years away—if the planet itself wasn't blocking the view, if the node was above the horizon.

The shelter was windowless, but Joan saw the ground outside the doorway brighten for an instant. The flash was silent; no missile had struck the valley, the explosion had taken place high above the atmosphere.

Surat went outside. When she returned she said quietly, "All clear. They got it."

Joan put all her effort into spitting out a handful of words. "I want to see what happened."

Sando hesitated, then motioned to the others to help him pick up the couch and carry it outside.

A shell of glowing plasma was still visible, drifting across the sky as it expanded, a ring of light growing steadily fainter until it vanished into the afternoon glare.

Anne was dead in this embodiment, but her backup would wake and go on to new adventures. Joan could at least tell her the story of her local death: of virtuoso flying and a spectacular end.

She'd recovered her bearings now, and she recalled the position of the stars. The node was still hours away from rising. The Amalgam was full of powerful telescopes, but no others would be aimed at this obscure planet, and no plea to redirect them could outrace the light they would need to capture in order to bring the Niah's final theorem back to life.

8

Sando wanted to send her away for medical supervision, but Joan insisted on remaining at the site.

"The fewer officials who get to know about this incident, the fewer problems it makes for you," she reasoned.

"As long as you don't get sick and die," he replied.

"I'm not going to die." Her wounds had not become infected, and her strength was returning rapidly.

They compromised. Sando hired someone to drive up from the nearest town to look after her while he was out at the excavation. Daya had basic medical training and didn't ask awkward questions; he seemed happy to tend to Joan's needs, and then lie outside daydreaming the rest of the time.

There was still a chance, Joan thought, that the Niah had carved the theorem on a multitude of tablets and scattered them all over the planet. There was also a chance that the Tirans had made copies of the tablet before letting Anne abscond with it. The question, though, was whether she had the slightest prospect of getting her hands on these duplicates.

Anne might have made some kind of copy herself, but she hadn't mentioned it in the prologue to her aerobatic rendition of the theorem. If she'd had any time to spare, she wouldn't have limited herself to an audience of one: she would have waited until the node had risen over Ghahar.

On her second night as an invalid, Joan dreamed that she saw Anne standing on the hill looking back into the fog-shrouded valley, her shadow haloed by the Niah light.

When she woke, she knew what she had to do.

When Sando left, she asked Daya to bring her the console that controlled the satellite dish. She had enough strength in her arms now to operate it, and Daya showed no interest in what she did. That was naive, of course: whether or not Daya was spying on her, Pirit would know exactly where the signal was sent. So be it. Seven light years was still far beyond the Noudah's reach; the whole node could be disassembled and erased long before they came close.

No message could outrace light directly, but there were more ways for light to reach the node than the direct path, the fastest one. Every black hole had its glory, twisting light around it in a tight, close orbit and flinging it back out again. Seventy-four hours after the original image was lost to them, the telescopes at the node could still turn to the Cataract and scour the distorted, compressed image of the sky at the rim of the hole's black disk to catch a replay of Anne's ballet.

Joan composed the message and entered the coordinates of the node. *You didn't die for nothing, my friend. When you wake and see this, you'll be proud of us both.*

She hesitated, her hand hovering above the send key. The Tirans had wanted Anne to flee, to show them the way to the stars, but had they really been indifferent to the loot they'd let her carry? The theorem had come at the end of the Niah's three-million-year reign. To witness this beautiful truth would not destroy the Amalgam, but might it not weaken it? If the Seekers' thirst for knowledge was slaked, their sense of purpose corroded, might not the most crucial strand of the culture fall into a twilight of its own? There was no shortcut to the stars, but the Noudah had been goaded by their alien visitors, and the technology would come to them soon enough.

The Amalgam had been goaded, too: the theorem she'd already transmitted would send a wave of excitement around the galaxy, strengthening the Seekers, encouraging them to complete the unification by their own efforts. The Big Crunch might be inevitable, but at least she could delay it, and hope that the robustness and diversity of the Amalgam would carry them through it, and beyond.

She erased the message and wrote a new one, addressed to her backup via the decoy node. It would have been nice to upload all her memories, but the Noudah were ruthless, and she wasn't prepared to stay any longer and risk being used by them. This sketch, this postcard, would have to be enough.

When the transmission was complete she left a note for Sando in the console's memory.

Daya called out to her, "Jown? Do you need anything?"

She said, "No. I'm going to sleep for a while."

THE MOTE DANCER AND THE FIRELIFE

CHRIS WILLRICH

Dust to dust.

Nicolai was three years dead when I lighted to EZ Aquarii to forget him. Naturally he came along too. Nicolai was never someone you got rid of easily. I still had the ring to prove it.

In the sun-speared and dusty-aired haunt of his killers I sipped a concoction of swirled beige and blue that the Spinies called alcoholic and my stomach called garlic-infused root beer, and I let him hold forth. "This isn't the way, I-Chen," he said, the sounds *ee-zhen* rolling from his lips like a lush mispronunciation of *Eden* and his rich, gold-brown eyes shining like the God-sized sunrises we'd see at the Epsilon Indi homestead. Dead, he was as apparent to me as the ruddy triple sunset flashing a crazy webwork across the contours of my glass. And just as blinding. "Violence only swaps one problem for another," he pressed.

"You might've thought of that before," I said.

That made him look away, toward shady nooks where cobalt-skinned Spine Flutists held forehands over flames. It looked like your classic cozy romantic restaurant—the kind Nicolai never took me to—the darkness cloaking the differences. Like the *thurik*, puzzle-pyramids of dried noodles whose collapse signaled who got the tab, and the *mumwolka*, bat-winged, bug-eyed scavengers gibbering in the roof's arabesque lattices, conditioned to scavenge tables when the server snuffed the candles.

And those little whirlwinds meandering along the street outside and blowing dust through the curtains—dust that wasn't all dust, dust that sparkled a little, dust that was half the cause of my problems.

"You're right," said the other half, "I wasn't thinking at all."

"Damn right you weren't."

Nicolai shook his head. His wavy brown hair was tangled, knotted, and utterly ignored, the way it always used to be, nothing idealized about it. "Had to stop them," he said.

"You were never a fighter. I was there. Just meters . . . "

"You're no marine yourself."

There was also nothing idealized about his voice. It was always a bit hoarse and frog-like when he'd been drinking. My madness had drawn a glass beside his hand. Nothing ideal about that calloused hand either, or the way he wiped his forever-leaky nose, and the crooked shape of it.

He was dead. I was dreaming him up from dust. He farted, smiling apologetically. I could even smell it.

"I've got training," I snapped at that smile. "Why couldn't you wait?"

He shrugged. "I'm a man."

He never changed. That was the problem. "So that's it? You got killed to prove you weren't a whipped husband? Bravo."

That got through his calm. "Goddamn it. You want to drive me away, drive me away. Do it. Say I charged the Spinies because deep down I'm a coward. Say it."

I whacked down my drink. Our barmates snapped alert.

One of the Spinies was older, more wrinkled, smaller than the others. He stood. He was the reason I'd come and now my heartbeat raced, outrunning my good sense. I said to Nicolai, "You did it because deep down you are a gutless, macho, idiotic, coward."

Face scarlet, Nicolai stood and stalked out through a curtain of leather strips of dubious origin. He even disturbed it a little. My madness wasn't just inventing props now but twisting my perceptions of real objects. Not a good sign.

My perceptions of the Spinies, alas, were quite accurate. Four more of them rose upon their three legs apiece to an average height of a meter-point-nine, glass bottles or obsidian swords in two of three arms. Not a good sign either.

Because my life might depend on it, I surrendered to the influence of the dust-like glinting Motes drifting here and there, dancing through the air and inside my body and brain.

That last category was the real issue here.

Mad mortal I, I linked into the immortal network that was the Spinies' inheritance and curse.

Dust to dust.

Now I could detect my barmates' thoughts, flickering all around me like a separate collection of candles, burning in some deeper end of the spectrum. I even sensed those thoughts quiver a little toward me as the Spinies detected me in turn. The flickers had an angry red billow about them, with a green tinge of fear. They surely weren't worried by my appearance—a short Asian-

European woman whose only modifications were harmless gills, webbed hands and feet, and ocean-rated eyes—but rather by my own mind-flame, proof that although human I, too, was a Mote-Dancer.

I decided to encourage that fear. I rose, my hands spread, but my old Survey sidearm visible.

The old Spiny, the one I'd marked earlier, stepped to one side. His only weapon was a sheathed dagger, and his backpack bristled with thick bone flutes. He said nothing, just rocked a little on one foot, watching.

He was about to get a show. One of the belligerent ones howled and squeaked, and the Motes supplied a translation like a whisper in my ear. "You are a noxious smoke. Take your diseased little dung-brain to the street."

Another roared. The translation: "Siblings! Let us help it get there."

Now, their looks didn't bother me. I was comfortable with the wrinkled blue skin and the long black vision-slit in the mouthless head, the gummy maw in the chest and the rubbery third arm jutting beneath it, the prominent spine in back carrying a good half of the brain matter. I didn't see the Spine Flutists as monsters anymore. I'd decided they had their species stupidities, just like us.

No, what bothered me was that these fellows were all too ready to demonstrate them.

Their weapons, dark or clear, glinted in the triple sunset, and their mental flames now flickered a private blue, suggesting an intimate discussion of just how damaged I ought to be when I left.

But first, they needed the right music.

So three new Spinies rose. Like the old guy, they wore backpacks and from these withdrew flutes fashioned of vertebrae bolstered with metal.

I'd seen this bifurcation of the warrior class before. The "Quixotes" advanced, while their "Sanchos" pressed flutes to their chest-maws and trilled a maniacal improvisation, to my ears something like Chinese opera filtered through jazz and spliced with a catfight. Not what I'd call music to die for, but my opinion didn't count much.

Spiny Customs had generously allowed me to keep my pistol, after draining its battery to red. I had maybe three shots. Worse yet, if I killed someone, that was the end of my journey to sanity. I'd be deported or executed. And either way I'd had enough of dead people.

So I turned toward an empty table and shot the candle.

The laser pulse spattered wax; the flame went out. The mass of *mumwolka* on the ceiling screeched down to investigate.

I grabbed the candle from my own table and rolled it toward the lead Quixote, who was pirouetting backward away from the dark-winged beasts.

I fired a second time, and the *mumwolka* dove for the obliterated second candle. The Spinies flailed with bottles and blades.

The old Spiny would have to wait. I fled the way Nicolai had gone. Had seemed to go.

Once on the dusty street, with its low aqueduct gurgling cool beneath baking desert air, I would not have paused had not the city of Gwumnok assaulted me.

Tornfar (the original Spiny word does something like that to my voicebox) is a roughly Earthlike moon but with lower gravity, and its cliffs soar higher. Whatever weaponry the extinct Glyph Lords had employed in branding planets with Mediterranean-sized symbols, it had exposed rich mineral veins here upon this coast, where waterfalls and a good harbor further ensured a near-vertical city would rise in a half-mile of zigzagging splendor. Twisted narrow streets crammed with spindly buildings made no concession to clumsy bipeds, except down in the reassuring grid of the harborside Earthtown.

Reaching Earthtown meant safety, of a sort, if Quixotes or constabulary or gravity didn't catch me first. I had only one real advantage. The downside of the Motes was continual distraction from the physical world (as I knew too well.) Spinies relied so much on Motes and other legacies of the Glyph Lords that they underestimated human tricks, like our biotech.

Readying gills, I climbed into the murky aqueduct.

"I-Chen!" Nicolai shouted, as though standing above the water.

"Shut up," I mouthed, and swam.

The current quickened and I shucked my shoes. I struggled at a switchback, limbs flailing, taking a beating from intricate stonework portraying the Sigil Sea. Sometimes I imagined I heard shouts, bells, scuttling feet in sets of three.

In a reverie, I swam other alien waters, the subsurface ocean of icemoon GX Andromedae d3, trying to rescue Nicolai and my other Grand Survey crewmates from lamprey-like aliens we called Naiads. I saw his helmeted face winking at me, mocking death and all toothy monsters; heard his crackling radio-voice cracking stupid jokes, making me laugh at our situation so my brain could reset and think of a plan. Which I did, because otherwise he was going to get himself killed. By the end of it I wanted to rip that helmet off and silence those jokes with my lips . . .

I slammed into a steel cap and clung. Apparently this portal could divert water somewhere deeper inside the cliff. Though connected by mechanisms to the surface, there was a manual release . . .

I yanked, and water sucked me into darkness. I barely managed to pull the cap behind me, scraping my wedding ring.

Down I went, riding a chute into muck. As a metaphor for how my life had been going, it didn't stink. That was good, because everything else did.

I splashed into a gently-sloping track of foul water—nasty stuff, but the current was mild. Crawling onto a stone walkway, I switched over from gills and found my bearings. My eyes, crafted for deep-sea diving (thank you, Mom and Dad), perceived a tunnel goring the gloom. I'd be safe here a moment, if uncomfortable.

At least Spine Flutist sewage smelled a trifle better to me than the human variety. A hint of burnt onion about it, actually, and wet grass.

I recalled the scents of the island homestead at Epsilon Indi—the farmhouse, the goats, the hot sea-breeze, the rusty shuttle donated by our ex-crewmates aboard Nightgift. *Never should have kept the creaking thing, even if Nicolai had torched a slice of metal from it to make the perfect wedding ring. It wasn't spaceworthy but it flew, and the reminder of the past made us restless. Without it we wouldn't have taken so many trips to the mainland, wouldn't have been there when the Spiny warband landed to claim as theirs any world bearing Glyph Lord relics. Relics like the Motes . . .*

I felt a hand on my shoulder. A human hand.

"That was fast," I said, not turning around.

Nicolai sighed. "It was futile, goading you like that. Of course I'm still here. And I had no right to speak that way."

"Of course you did. Damn it. You, you're—"

"Your spouse?" Nicolai chuckled. "Forget it. *He's* dead. Remember that sealant for bulkhead breaches? How the undertaker used it to reconnect his stubborn neck?"

"Shut up."

"Can't. He wouldn't want you to hurt yourself. Don't look for vengeance on Tornfar. Or a quick death."

"Not vengeance," I said. "It's . . . "

A splash and a roar interrupted us.

A ghost-white, almost translucent creature sprang from the muck, whipped three tentacles around me, and yanked me in.

I passed through Nicolai's nonexistent body on the way down. My brain was too shocked to preserve the illusion. Nicolai disappeared. Then light and air did too.

I switched to gills. I was in less danger of disease than if I'd frolicked in a *human* sewer, but this surely wasn't good for my health. Even so, I had to fight on the thing's turf. I strained to reach my pistol. Our struggle shoved me into the air again, and I got a better look.

The beast had a Spiny's basic body plan, only swapping the pair of triple limbs for suckered tentacles, the head for a nub, and the gummy mouth-ridges for sharklike teeth. It snapped at my left hand, slicing my nerves with hot slivers of pain. I got my right hand around the pistol and pressed muzzle to maw.

There was a flash and a shudder, and a reek like a cookout at a garbage fire. The thing toppled backward as I teetered.

Screeching, it rose again, blue ooze burbling from the mouth. It looked near death but determined to go down eating.

I pulled the trigger again, was rewarded with a tiny firework spark. Further attempts yielded sad little clicks. *Yup,* I thought inanely, *three shots left! That Fisher girl knows her gear!*

I scrambled back; Toothsome advanced.

Then it shuddered as someone behind it stabbed once, twice, thrice, and upon the final thrust, cut sideways through unseen vitals. The sewer-thing collapsed, sinking into the murk.

Behind it stood the old Sancho I'd marked earlier, his obsidian dagger dripping blue.

"Thank you," I managed.

The Spiny nodded to me in the human way. He helped me onto the walkway. There we sat like old friends at some polluted fishing hole.

"I-Chen Fisher," he said. "I am pleased you have not attained your final glory." He pronounced my name right, *ee-zhen,* and even strained to confine his voice to human listening range, so much that it came out monotone. Otherwise, his Chinglése was better than my Warrior's Voice would ever be.

"I was told," he said, "you wished to meet. I regret I did not introduce myself at once."

"Well," I said, trying to compose myself from battles both minutes and years ago, "at least this way we have a private place to talk. You're the Sancho. Who . . . "

"Yes." The Spiny's third arm ended in sucker-studded wedges like the arms of a starfish, an evolutionary connection to the dead thing in the water. The wedges unfolded and plucked one of the many bone flutes nestled in his pack. "I am Omz—" he said, with a hesitation as if there was another, unheard syllable in ultrasound. "I am celebrant-and-psychopomp to Awo—" again his voice shifted beyond my hearing, "—nom."

"Your Quixote," I said, and Omz nodded.

"I-Chen," Nicolai broke in, manifesting on the parallel walkway across the muck. "What do you want with *him*?"

Omz looked around, a full-body motion for a Spiny. "Yes, there it is. The anomaly in your mind. I sense another human nearby. Yet I see no one. Few Mote-Dancers can hide from me. Yet I barely detect his presence. Your mate?"

"Yes."

Omz was silent for several hissing breaths. "I had thought such survivals impossible among humans."

"That's usually true." I twisted my ring and heard my voice go clinical, as

Nicolai's golden eyes shifted warily to me. "But among paired Mote-Dancers, sometimes a death-imprint appears in the surviving partner." No one, human, Epsilon, or Spine Flutist, knew just how the Glyph Lords' tiny computer nodes operated, whether they transmitted via gravitangles or warpknots or pinhead angels. We just knew they worked—for most of the Spinies, and for a handful of us. Nicolai had barely connected with the Motes, but my link had been strong, one of the strongest among humans.

I remembered standing beside him on top of a city-sized Glyph Lord mausoleum on Lacaille 9352 d, gold-glinting dust swirling around us in the aftermath of our shuttle's landing. I remembered his wink as he popped open his helmet, and my foolish need to prove myself as daring, my exhalations making whorls in the dust like puffs of breath on a snowy day. I remember him grabbing for me as my vision blurred and the dead world spun. When I came to, his head was wreathed in a silver nimbus of concern . . .

It wasn't quite the old fantasy of telepathy, but it was close. And the experience of sharing Nicolai's thoughts had swirled together with my memories to concoct a strange brew of madness. A ghost too real to go away; almost a splitting apart of my own consciousness.

Omz was quiet for a while, except for his short, hissing breaths. "You are blessed," he said.

"You think so?" My head ached; maybe I'd gotten infected after all. "He's *dead*. He and I both know it. But I can't forget, and I can't grieve. I don't have the real him, just a facsimile." Like someone had shoved a knife into my gut, and there it stayed. I could walk around, pretend to be okay, but I didn't feel much except the blade. I couldn't get rid of it and I couldn't bleed.

"I'm sorry," Nicolai said.

"Not your fault," I murmured.

"I can almost hear him," Omz said. "He is very strong. It is strange . . . He has nearly attained the firelife. Yet you both regret it."

"What is this 'firelife?' " Nicolai said.

"Wait," I whispered, and now my very own personal ghost looked angry. I knew he wanted to rifle through my mind now, but I had to hold him back.

"If you wish vengeance," Omz said, "you must know that Mnat—" here the voice again squeaked out of human range, "—the Quixote who slew your mate, has already entered the firelife."

"I know," I told Omz, focusing on his gummy mouth, trying not to return Nicolai's stare.

I remembered firing again and again into the mass of Spinies at Epsilon Indi, heedless of which were combatants and which not, the blue blood never spattering fast enough. I remembered rage that I hadn't been the one who gunned down Nicolai's slayer . . .

"Awo()nom," continued Omz, "he who prevented our conversing just now in the House of Flame and Spirits, is my new charge. You cannot take your revenge on him either. And to harm a Sancho is a grave crime. Indeed, we have not forgotten that many Sanchos died at human hands."

"It took us a while," I said with great care, "to understand your customs."

"And indeed, that was war, and you are barbarians. This time, however, you have no excuse."

"I'm not out for revenge."

"What *are* you doing, I-Chen?" Nicolai said, staring at the Spiny who'd been closest to his killer.

"What I have to," I murmured low.

I bundled up my nerve. It was surprisingly easy, now that I sat beside the Sancho. "I didn't want you for vengeance, Omz. I need you. As a bridge to the firelife."

Omz's eyeslit bulged a little around the middle, which indicated interest. Or maybe disbelief. Nicolai's shock was easier to read.

"I want Nicolai to meet the one who killed him."

The Memory Craft was a filigree behemoth, a ponderous double-hull sprouting teetering wooden towers like *thurik*, aquiver with sails and crisscrossed with rigging dangling flags and skulls. From a distance it resembled a Spiny brain (much like ours, but more oblong) as if sculpted out of twigs and spiderwebs. The structure seemed doomed to collapse, but this was a misperception. In the first place, Tornfar's lower gravity assured the ragged fantasia held up better than it appeared.

In the second place, the thing was doomed to be torched.

No one hires a Memory Craft alone, so the evening after the fracas at the House of Flame and Spirits, Omz and I boarded with twenty-six other Sanchos, plus the friends and family of various deceased Quixotes. Our little band stood apart beside a lit brazier, as did the other knots of celebrants. Our steamer tug pulled us seaward in a twilight ruled by a dance of auroras beneath the gargantuan stormy disk of Tornfar's gas-giant primary. Motes meandered like swarming fireflies.

The carnival kaleidoscope of the Spiny harbor and the cool subdued grid of Earthtown slipped past, and I hefted the Spine Flutist weapon required of my role. It was an obsidian sword somewhat reminiscent of an Aztec *macuahuitl*, but instead of a long blade studded with subsidiary spikes, it was one serrated triangular wedge with sharp flanges like a pair of *mumwolka*-wings. Obsidian blades are fragile but sharper than steel. If I knew what I was doing, I could behead an enemy. If I didn't know what I was doing, I could behead myself. I was more in the latter category. I said as much to Omz.

He played a few trial notes on the flute made from Mnat's spine.

"Cut your foe," he said. "Do not get cut."

"Thanks."

"Also, we are more vulnerable than you to a spinal strike. Much of our brain is distributed down the upper vertebrae."

It occurred to me the flanges might facilitate a back blow. "Thanks. Really."

Omz snorted, which I believed amounted to a Spiny nod. Then he played graceful, eerie music, notes like pebbles plunked into still water, much of it barely tingling my eardrums. The tune was echoed in over two dozen places by the other Sanchos. Weirdly warbling, the Memory Craft sang its way toward the deep. Wood creaked beneath my sandals. I was dizzy, and my head throbbed. I'd rested the whole day in my narrow Earthtown lodgings but still felt sick. Humans lived in this alien city, after all, sharing food with the Spinies, and sharing microbes as well. *Note for the future*, I thought, *only fight in the sewers of previously undiscovered planets.*

"Foe?" Nicolai interrupted my thoughts, appearing on my left. "What foe?"

Here it was. "Mnat. You know. The one who killed you."

He appeared to rest his hand on a nearby mast. "How does that work?"

"I'll perceive an illusion of Mnat. Sound familiar? We fight. If she lands a blow, I'll feel pain. Maybe worse."

"I don't like the sound of this."

"If I understand right, I don't have to win, so much as prove my spirit, my worthiness to commune with the dead. The Spinies respect courage as much as prowess. And it's not all about combat—the Sanchos can enter the firelife too, becoming immortal through song."

"The firelife again . . ."

I couldn't put him off any longer. "Spiny Valhalla. The celebrated dead live on. In the Motes."

Slowly he nodded. "I'm no Sancho. What am I supposed to say to Mnat?"

"That's up to you . . ."

"Great. Very helpful."

I shrugged, not wanting to add more. The imprint of Nicolai couldn't read my thoughts. But he was still inside my head. "All right," he said, searching my face, "but if I think you're in trouble, we bail. Understood?"

"Understood."

All the Sanchos stopped playing at once, a Mote-enabled synchronization that made my heart skip. They all began chanting in Warrior's Voice, speaking of their lost Quixotes. I had to tune out the babble, focus on Omz. I opened myself to the Motes, and as I beheld the gold intensity of the Sancho's mind-flame, they whispered a translation.

"To all who watch, here or ashore, or scrying through the Motes . . . Welcome. We commune with Mnat the warrior, my sister in spirit. Born in the lowest slagtown of Gwumnok, she was the humblest of free women. For most slaglings, passage to the firelife is but a dream. For how many of us know, let alone celebrate, the downtrodden? Yet Mnat had the spark which ignites the fire."

The spark which ignites gunfire, you mean, I thought. But I controlled my bitterness when Omz stretched his rubbery third arm across the brazier and splayed wedge-shaped fingers over the flames. In Chinglése he said, "Alien visitors, take my hand."

Visitors. He was talking to Nicolai directly. I unwrapped my bandaged hand and took Omz's cool, suckered grip, and Nicolai's joined ours. Nicolai winced right along with me as we lowered our grasp to just above the dancing flames. The cuts from the sewer-thing screamed at me afresh. I held still.

"Mnat," Omz said in Warrior's Voice. "We call to you. You who labored long hours at the darkblade. You who struggled to pilot a Legacy Ship. You who sacrificed all for a chance at renown, to become a Quixote of the Outer Crusade. When we met aboard ship, you were all purpose and fire, and I knew you a worthy subject for song. We made a fine pair, you fighting duels all through the vessel, I your Sancho, drunkenly composing sagas to make you famous."

I squelched my anger, concentrating on Omz's voice, further opening myself to the Motes and the firelife. I sensed Omz's mind, felt his proud ideals crackling like crazy orange lightning-strokes. Elsewhere, the other knots of Spinies celebrated the newly-dead they wished to install in the firelife or the honored dead they wished to summon.

I let Omz pull me and Nicolai closer to that other realm. Omz's inner world burned into ours. All around us, sheets of rippling light, like luminous sailcloth, shuddered and seethed. The forms of Spine Flutists puckered the radiance like smothered things, yet I felt their exultation like an electric shock.

Then a shout arose in the ordinary world. It crossed the water from Earthtown.

Peering through all the glory, I spotted the source. A Spine Flutist wielding a darkblade rushed along the last of the docks, paralleling the Memory Craft. Blue-clad human security raced after.

It was Omz's current Quixote, Awo()nom. He hadn't been invited.

Awo()nom sprinted, made an extraordinary leap even for Tornfar, and caught the side of the Memory Craft. I had to give him points for style. He even managed to keep the blade. The humans lowered their weapons, forbidden to fire outside their territory. I caught the looks they threw me and didn't need them to be Mote-Dancers to understand their thoughts. I was on my own.

Awo()nom screamed at his mentor, and with my mind so close to the firelife, I received voice and translation as one. "Blasphemers! Siblings, do you not see? This human will poison the firelife with her madness! Help me!"

As he scrambled onto the deck, some of the Quixotes took up the cry.

"Okay," Nicolai said, "this is where we bail. Good thing you've got gills."

I shook my head and saw Omz look disoriented, still reaching for the firelife. We were so close. Soon Mnat would manifest, and I could beg her for a boon. Just a few more moments . . .

"I-Chen," Nicolai said. "Go!"

"Not yet . . . "

"What's wrong with you? What does he mean, you want to 'poison the firelife?' "

"Nicolai . . . "

"It's me. Isn't it. You didn't want me to *talk*. You wanted to turn *me* into 'honored dead.' "

He yanked his hand away from Omz's and mine.

Omz reeled back.

I snarled, schemes unravelling.

I wouldn't give up now, not after light-years and burns and fever.

Awo()nom rushed forward. He wasn't going after me but after Omz. Of course—I wasn't going to breach the firelife on my own. He could finish me off later.

I interrupted his plans, by stepping in his way.

Darkblade in my right hand, I grabbed my pistol with the left. Awo()nom couldn't be sure it was out of juice. He stopped and raised his own blade.

At least he was after me, now. I backpedaled toward one of the spindly sails. Judging the wind, I slashed lines with the darkblade.

A boom spun and smacked Awo()nom over. Three legs quivered in the air as he struggled to rise.

But now a trio of Spinies advanced on Omz.

There was no hope now of meeting Mnat. It seemed I should simply jump. I'd be safe enough in the Sigil Sea, and Nicolai came with the package. Really, how bad could madness be?

I shook my head and rushed back to Omz. Sometimes that's the only real freedom you get in life: to choose your own craziness.

I toppled the brazier with my foot, sparking the ceremonial conflagration an hour early. Hot coals scattered across the deck, igniting the wood. That distraction bought us a moment, so I got an arm around Omz and tugged him toward the rail. Born in higher gravity, I had raw strength at least. Omz protested but came along. Nicolai paced us, shouting warnings. He seemed to perceive things I couldn't, as if he was spreading out his consciousness via the Motes.

"Watch out!"

Awo()nom was back, intercepting us at the rail. His darkblade lashed, and Omz, teetering at the brink, blocked with the bone flute.

The polished spine of dead Mnat shattered, and a streak of turquoise blood appeared on Omz's chest, just above the mouth.

I tackled Awo()nom, losing my pistol overboard.

We each struggled to position our blades. I was a higher-gravity fighter, but Awo()nom had six limbs to my four. It would have made an interesting wrestling match, but unfortunately it was more a knife-fight. There came an almost gentle slice, and then a searing line of pain burned my right arm. Confused, I thought for a giddy moment I'd managed to cut Awo()nom too, as I spotted blood all over him; but it was red.

He scrambled away, balanced himself on one foot, and kicked with the other two. I *whoofed* and groaned and fell. Things went hazy. Disoriented, I heard my blade clatter, and I was mighty annoyed with whatever idiot had allowed herself to drop it.

Awo()nom raised his.

As he began the killing blow, Nicolai got in his way.

The Spiny didn't appear to see him, but Nicolai screamed, "No!"

Awo()nom paused mid-swing, looking around for the source of the ghostly voice.

Screams erupted behind him.

I made myself rise, wobbling, clutching my bloody arm. The blaze crackled along the deck, hissing up the masts and roaring amidst the sails. Awo()nom, Nicolai, and I stood within a lucky pocket of safety, but everywhere else surged the dancing weave of fire. In my sight it intermingled with the Mote-visualized veils of light and the radiant ribbons of the aurora, until it seemed all the world ahead and above was a hysteria of light while behind and below writhed the dark chuckling sea.

In the midst of luminous chaos the three Quixotes who'd joined Awo() nom's cause paused in shock. For beside them a spectral curtain of light intersected a wall of fire, and at the conjunction a figure emerged.

It was a Spiny, luridly lit by flame and sunset, an eerie gold nimbus all around.

"Mnat," I heard Awo()nom gasp.

As if the spoken name were a signal, the ghost-Quixote raised a darkblade and slashed at one of the living. Her target fell, unmarked and yet quivering in pain.

The other two dropped into sudden three-kneed genuflection. I had never seen abasement so perfectly executed.

Mnat ignored them, strode toward us.

"You cannot approve!" Awo()nom screeched. "Humans must not defile the firelife!"

Omz, crouching by the rail, said, "It is dishonor that defiles the firelife, not the forms we are born with. You have proven that, my former student, by attacking a Sancho."

Awo()nom looked all around him and snarled, swinging his weapon toward me. He reminded me of Toothsome, dying back in the sewer. I couldn't move.

Simultaneously, Nicolai punched him and Mnat speared him with her darkblade.

There was no physical wound, but Awo()nom convulsed from this assault of ghosts. He staggered to the rail, toppled over.

Mnat took Nicolai's hand.

"Yes," Nicolai said. "I understand." He turned to me. "I-Chen . . . she says I'm honored dead now. They'll take me . . . "

"Nicolai," I managed to say, "I can't make you go. It will be an alien place. I don't know if you'll be happy. Do you want to stay?"

He watched me silently, then finally reached out and touched my shoulder. "I think, deep down, you know the answer, I-Chen. I was a navigator on *Nightgift*, remember, before you talked me into settling down. I like seeing new places." He smirked. "But you have to tell me what *you* want. For your own sake."

I closed my eyes, then made myself open them and meet his gold-brown gaze. Like the sunrise. "Nicolai. Please. Go into the firelife."

He kissed me gently, feather-light.

Then he turned and followed Mnat into the conflagration. She raised her blade toward me as she back-stepped into the fire, blurred, and vanished.

I pulled off my ring and hurled it after them. It tinkled as it skittered into the flames. It seemed to me Nicolai knelt beside it within the blaze, as he too faded from view.

It was like a spike come loose from my skull, that reeling moment upon a hulk shaped like a burning brain when I gave my husband to another world.

In the dark before firstrise I sat dozing in the House of Flame and Spirits, wrapped in bandages, draped in intricately embroidered blankets portraying ancient Spinies and fanciful Glyph Lords. Our table nestled beside the kitchen, and the vinegar smell from the greenish soup Omz held beneath my nose made me gag, and gagging made me alert. Everything, body and mind, ached.

"Thank you . . . Omz," I was finally able to say. Rubbing my forehead, I looked up.

There was Nicolai, smiling beside the Sancho.

"No," I said. "No . . . " Had it all been for nothing?

"I-Chen," Nicolai said, "just stay calm." He winked. "You forgot that the

Motes aren't really telepathy, and I'm not really a ghost. I'm a manifestation of your own thoughts. I *belong* to your brain. The most you could do is *copy* me, imperfectly, into the firelife."

Omz said, "Now there are two of Nicolai, yours and ours."

"Damn you," I said to Omz, knocking the soup away. "Spiny bastard. You knew this would happen all along—"

I sensed Spiny minds nearby, flaring to red attention. But this time no one rose to throw me out. They were waiting, watching, giving me another chance.

"Yes, I-Chen Fisher." Omz offered me a human nod. "You deceived me, secretly planning to offer Nicolai to the firelife. When I understood this, I chose not to enlighten you of the result. For I realized we had a chance to bring our peoples together, if only in this small way. I took that chance, for the sake of much more than your sanity."

"I-Chen," Nicolai said, just as kindly as before, but stopping me from striking Omz, before I got myself killed. Which maybe was what I wanted, just then.

"Look at me."

I did. Now that I watched him carefully there was something different. There was a glow about him, not otherworldly glory of the firelife but a gentle haziness that smoothed away the snarls of his hair, straightened his posture a little. He sat carefully, like he was posing for a painting, and it was hard to imagine him wiping his nose.

"I'm not the same, I-Chen. You copied me, true. But you did more than give the other Nicolai to the firelife. You *told* him to go. You said goodbye."

"Goodbye," I whispered.

His image softened some more, and when he smiled, it was like Nicolai, yes, but it was also a little like my first love when I was eighteen, and like an old classmate from the academy, and maybe just a bit like a hunky model I'd seen in Epsilon Indi advertisements. I was losing him, had lost him years ago, but the message was now catching up to me like the final light from a dying star. My hands began to shake. I braided my fingers, feeling for my ring and finding only skin. The shaking moved up to my chest.

"I'm still here, I-Chen. But not like before. You broke something in me." There was no recrimination in his voice, and no regret. "I'm less of an imprint and more of a memory, and I'll get more that way all the time."

I made myself breathe, slow and deep. It might be true. It might be terrible, maybe for a long time, but . . .

"It'll be terrible," Nicolai said, "maybe for a long time, but you will get better." And I knew for certain then, that he was right about this.

That *I* was right about this.

I stood, somehow keeping my balance. Nicolai kept sitting, making no move to follow. To Omz I said, "I need to go look at the sea for a while. But I'll come back. And if you're still here I'll buy you a drink. And then, if you don't mind, I'd like to talk to you. About . . . people we've shared."

Omz snorted. "It would please me."

"And—Nicolai."

He looked up, and I said silently, *I'd like to talk to you again too. Just for a while. But not right now. I want to be alone, now.*

I wasn't even pretending to send a message through the Motes. I was only thinking to myself. But I thought he said, "Whenever you want," before he just wasn't there anymore.

I nodded to Omz and walked past all the staring Spinies, out into the lights and scents and confusion of this mysterious city poised between night and dawn where I would never find him, even though every last skull held a piece of him, including my own. And that hurt like hell.

At last.

ON RICKETY THISTLEWAITE

MICHAEL F. FLYNN

There is an ancient Terran word: rickety. *It is not clear to scholars what this word meant exactly, but that it applied to Thistlewaite was undoubted. "Rickety Thistlewaite" had been its appellation from the beginning, from the days before even the First Ships set down. At least, if you can depend on their legends, which like everything else there, are shaky. The planet's nature can be seen in its propensity to earthquakes. Somebody had talcumed the seams of her plates and they slip and slide with greasier abandon than they do on more gritty worlds. "As sturdy as a Thistlewaite skyscraper" is a proverb on half the planets of the Periphery, and believed earnestly enough by the Thistles themselves that they build none—and so the proverb does double-duty. What can be more sturdy than something unbuilt, runs a Thistlean joke. A building never erected can never fall down. Ha, ha. But the Thistles have developed a keen sense of balance along with their mordant wit, and a fatalistic conviction that nothing can ever be done that will not eventually fail.*

The harper and the scarred man have come to Thistlewaite in search of the harper's mother. That is simple enough for a story. They will not find her there; but they may begin the finding of her there, for it was the last world to which she had been assigned before vanishing on a personal quest. Bridget ban—the vanished mother—was a Hound of the Kennel, and a Hound of the Kennel could be many things and anything: spy, assassin, savior, ambassador, planetary manager; and without pity or remorse when what had to be done had to be done. The one thing they are not supposed to be is missing for three years. She had left a note; she had left a trinket; and she had left. "Out to the edge. Fire from the sky. Back soon," read the note. But it is now a bit longer than soon, and the daughter has grown impatient.

Lucia Thompson—the daughter—goes by the office-name Méarana, which means both *fingers* and, through a slight shift in stress, *swift*. She is an ollamh, as the harper's case slung across her back announces. She is lean and supple, with eyes of the hard, sharp glass-green of flint. Her hair is the red of flame, but her skin is dark gold.

The scarred man uses the name Donovan buigh, at other times the office-name of The Fudir, but no one knows his true name, least of all himself. His face is shrunken, as if it has been suctioned out and all that remains of him is skin and skull. His chin curls like a coat hook, and his mouth sags across the saddle of the hook. His hair is white, and there are places on his skull, places with scars, where the hair will never grow back. His eyes rove in constant motion.

The fingers of the harper have pried him most unwillingly from his bottle to join this feckless venture. He does not think that they will find Bridget ban, or that she will be alive if they do. Yet at one time, years ago, he had loved her, and a part of him yearns for her still. So he is of two minds about the entire quest; indeed, of more than two minds, for Donovan buigh is a man of parts. Like the demon, Legion, he contains multitudes. His *quondam* employers had shattered his mind like glass, hoping that by isolating different elements of the espionage art in different loci of the brain they could create a well-oiled team of specialists. What they had gotten was a quarreling committee.

The Kennel has given up the search, Méarana had told the scarred man after tracking him down to the Bar on Jehovah to enlist his reluctant help.

And why should you succeed, he had replied, *where the professionals have failed?*

Because a daughter may see a thing that even a colleague would miss.

A thin reed from which to fly hope's banner. It was no more substantial than a Thistlewaite skyscraper.

Jenlùshy Town had sat on the epicenter of the great thistlequake, and two-thirds of the country had been knocked about like jackstraws and flinders. Collapsing province-towns, mountain landslides, floods, and fires had swallowed two-thirds of the District Commissioners, along with half the dough-riders. The One Man, the Grand Secretary, and five of the Six Ministers had perished in the collapse of the Palace. In a state as highly centralized as the Jenlùshy *sheen* that was the equivalent of a frontal lobotomy.

Bridget ban had been sent to oversee the restoration of sanitation, of water and utilities, of housing and roads, of public order. The late Emperor—the One Man—had clearly lost "the approval of the sky," and so she chose for his replacement a Warden named Jimmy Barcelona who had been Chief of Public Works Unit for Capital District. At her suggestion, he selected the office-name of Resilient Services and for his regnal theme, "a robust and reliable infrastructure." It rang less gloriously than most regnal themes, but was surely apropos, all things considered.

It is their intention to make inquiries in the Terran Corner—for Terrans, like the Third Monkey, will seldom say anything, though unlike the first two, they see and hear everything. The Fudir is a member of the Terran Brotherhood and perhaps they may speak to him. He believes Bridget ban learned something during her assignment on Thistlewaite that set her off on her final quest. To find what that something was will be the first step to finding her.

But no man may do business in Jenlùshy without the One Man's permission. Certainly, no one can go about making a nosy nuisance of himself without what the Terrans call a "heads up" to the head man. Normally, obtaining an audience with a Thistlewaite emperor was a long, laborious, and expensive affair. The recovery from the 'quake was still in its final stages, and Resilient Services had better things to do than put on a show for Peripheral touristas. Donovan had counted on this as yet another delay to the harper's journey, although he had by then given up on dissuading her entirely.

But if the visitor was the daughter of the very Hound who had placed the emperor on the Ivy Throne, doors swung open with disconcerting ease.

The Grand Secretary had insisted on a certain formality of dress. Happily, the harper had brought with her several bolts of Megranomic anycloth; so the morning of the audience, she consulted *Benet's Sumptuary Guide to the Spiral Arm* and programmed the material through the datathread to assume the chosen color, cut, and texture.

The harper wore a *leine* of pure white linen with fitted sleeves, and intricate red geometric embroidery at the neck, cuffs, and hem. It was bloused though a leather *crios* at the waist, in the pouches of which were placed the tools of the harper's trade. Over this she had thrown a woolen *brat* in bright green with gold borders. She wore it like a shawl fastened at the right shoulder by a large golden brooch depicting a snake entwining a rose. She walked unshod and the nails of her feet and hands matched the color of the embroidery of her *leine*. Her red hair fell free, to indicate her unwed status, but she wore a silver ollamh's circlet at her brow.

The scarred man wore Terran garb, and if fewer eyes caressed him than caressed the harper, it was because he was moon to her sun. He dressed in a dark yellow *sherwani* over embroidered *jutti* and matching *kurta paijamas*. His sandals were plain and of brown leather with golden crescents on the straps. The scars on his head were decently covered by a skull-cap, and across his shoulder he had thrown a *gharchola* stole. Gold lac-bangles adorned his wrists and ankles, and rouge had reddened his cheeks. When he wanted to, the Fudir could cut a figure.

In the anteroom to the audience chamber, the Fudir bowed to the Grand Secretary, and said, in a croak resembling Thistletalk, "This miserable worm prays that these poor rags do not find disfavor in the eyes of noble Grand Secretary."

That worthy went by the name of Morgan Cheng-li and was known therefore among the backroom staff as "Jingly" in a play on both his name and the sound of the coins that so often crossed his palm. His frog-like mien— pigeon-chested, eyes bulged, cheeks blown out—gave the impression that he had held his breath for a very long time.

At the appointed time, the Assistant Palace Undersecretary of Off-World Affairs escorted them into the throne room. "Rags?" the harper whispered in Gaelactic as they proceeded down the hallway. "After all the work I put into this wardrobe?"

"Self-deprecation is mandatory here," the Fudir said. "You should see officials defer for places at a banquet table."

"Och. Mother and I hold to a faith that values humility, but that sort of servility smacks of unseemly pride."

Donovan interrupted and said, "Hush, both of you. And remember what we told you. Don't mention that your mother has vanished. She came from the sky; and if she's vanished into the sky—."

"Then she's lost the Approval of the Sky," the harper returned wearily. "I know. I know."

Donovan turned to her. "And through her, the emperor she appointed. Tell them your mother's gone missing and it's tantamount to a call for revolution. And don't think old Frog-Face back there won't lead it, either."

The throne on which Resilient Services perched was fashioned of solid gold. The stiles had the form of climbing ivy and from them on thread-like wires hung leaves of artfully tarnished copper. This gave them a greenish cast and, when movement caused them to sway, they tinkled like wind-chimes. Under the throne, for some age-long and forgotten reason, rested a large stone. The high back, rearing above the yellow-robed emperor, bore four ideograms: the motto of the sheen.

"Behold the August Presence," the Voice of the Sheen cried out. "Behold the Resilient Services Reign, who provides the sheen with robust and reliable infrastructure!"

Now *there's* a battle cry to rally the troops, said the Brute. The scarred man's splintered mind contained a variety of shards. His former employers had believed that their agent might have need of ruthless physical action.

It works for them. The earthquake destroyed so much. The silver tongue of persuasion was also a useful skill. But the Brute and the Silky Voice did not much like each other.

The Fudir scolded them both. *Quiet. We're not here to mock their customs.*

"Who," the Voice demanded, "approaches the August Presence?"

The Fudir bowed, sweeping his arm to the right and holding his left over his heart. "I hight Donovan buigh of Jehovah, special emissary of the Particular Service to the Court of the Morning Dew. My companion hight the ollamh, Méarana of Dangchao, master of the *clairseach*."

The emperor had gone, first pale, then flushed. "Ah. So," he said. "You much resemble my illustrious predecessor, and . . . I had thought she had returned to resume her duties." He clapped his hands and a servant struck a hanging gong. "Bring forth the crumpets and scones!"

Underlings and flunkies scurried about in apparent confusion, but in short order a table was set up in the center of the hall, dressed with cloth, napkins, and fine bone-china cups, and surrounded by three soft-backed chairs and a silver tea service on a gravity cart. A tray of biscuits, ceremoniously escorted, was placed on the table, and the visitors were shown to their seats. The emperor stood and descended from the Ivy Throne, shedding his yellow robes of state and handing them to the Assistant Deputy Undersecretary for Wardrobe.

Beneath his cope, the emperor had been wearing a simple day suit: a cut-away cloth coat of dark blue possessed of brass buttons over a plain buff waistcoat and matching pantaloons. His feet were shod in riding boots with golden spurs; and at his throat was gathered a stiffly starched cravat. He took the seat at the head of the table and, with a flick of his wrist, dismissed his ministers and staff. These scurried to the walls, where they stood in various poses pretending to converse with one another, though alert always to a summons from the Presence.

"Tea?" the Presence said, holding a cup under the samovar.

He proceeded through the ceremony with meticulous detail. One lump or two? Cream? Scone? Jam? Each motion practiced; each stir a precise radius and number of revolutions.

The Fudir supposed this was the Thistle equivalent to the Terran ceremony of bread and salt. More elaborate, of course, in that mad and fussy Thistle fashion.

When all had been served by the emperor's own hand, Resilient Services intoned formally, "We shall now make small talk."

The Fudir stepped into the momentary silence. "How stand matters since the great thistlequake, your imperial majesty? Recovery proceeding apace, I hope?"

"Oh, yes. Quite, thank you," the emperor responded. "And for duration of High Tea, you call me 'Jimmy.' Port Tsienchester not yet fully operational; but perhaps by end of Sixmonth. You." He pointed at the harper. "I mistake you for another. She, too, from Kennel. She give mandate to rule. How I curse that day."

"My mother," said the harper.

"Ah." The emperor looked to the Fudir.

"I have been charged to escort the daughter to her," the Terran said.

"Why do you curse the day my mother made you emperor?" the harper asked. "She made you emperor of one of the Fourteen States."

"That curse." Jimmy turned a little in his seat. "See sigils over throne? Love-heaven. Person. Protect. Heaven-below. Man who love heaven-sky will protect empire. But heaven perfect. Never fail, never fall. Heaven-below, Sheen Jenlùshy, should be imitate that perfection. Never does. But if emperor love heaven good enough, everything fine below, too. Never fail, never fall. One Man must be regular as sky. Move in orbit, like planet. Go here, go there. All same ceremony, all same word. All pest black-fly ministers buzz round me. Buzz, buzz, buzz. Do this, do that. All 'veddy propah.' No mistake. Mistake in heaven-below cause mistake in heaven-above. Very bad. Calf still-born. My fault. Stumbled over sunrise prayer. Bandit rob exchequer in Bristol-fu. My fault. Did not make proper ablution. All universe connected through dough. Everything affect everything. Mountainslide in Northumberchow Shan . . . "

"Your fault," said the Fudir. "We get it. I can see cosmic oneness has its drawbacks. If you forget to clip your toenails, who knows what horrors might be unleashed?"

The emperor shook his head. "Only here in tea ceremony is emperor become Jimmy again." He turned abruptly to the harper. "Tell me of homeworld, Mistress Harp."

"Dangchao Waypoint? Well . . . It's a dependency of Die Bold. Mostly open prairies on Great Stretch continent, where we raise Nolan's Beasts—a breed of cattle. A few big towns."

"You have harp with you, mistress? Of course. Ollamh never far from instrument. You bring with tomorrow. Play songs of far away Dangchao."

Méarana put her cup carefully on its saucer. "Well . . . Donovan and I have some business to conduct . . . "

"Oh, no," said Resilient Service. "I must insist."

And there was something hard in the way he said it that caused the harper to hesitate and glance at her companion.

"I had planned to visit the Corner," the Fudir said. "Best if I go in alone. You can entertain the emperor while I do that."

"Yes," agreed the emperor of the Morning Dew. "You do that."

The next morning, as Méarana prepared for her command performance at the palace, the Fudir prepared to enter the Corner of Jenlùshy. For this, he did not dress as he had for the palace. Indeed, he barely dressed at all. Around his waist he tied a simple blue-and-white checkered dhoti. On his feet, sandals. His upper body, he oiled.

"Easier to slip out of someone's grip," he said with a leer. Save for secreting various weapons in unlikely places, that completed his toilet.

The harper looked him over before he departed. She pointed to the dhoti. "How do you bend over in that thing?"

"Very carefully. Be sure to keep the emperor happy. I think he's a little taken with you. But remember: no hint of anything wrong 'up in the skies.' "

"How many times will you tell me that, old man? Just be careful in the Corner. The concierge told me it's a dangerous place."

"Full of Terrans. You be careful, too. There aren't any Terrans in the palace, but that doesn't mean it isn't dangerous."

"I long to see fruited plains of your home world," the emperor said after Méarana had played a set of Dangchao songs from the Eastern Plains. "To ride like wind chasing Nolan's Beasts with lasso and bolo. To drive herd to market in—how you say? Port Qis-i-nao? No, Port Kitch-e-ner." He pronounced the alien sounds with great care. "Oh, life of Beastie boys, live free under stars."

Sometimes Méarana wanted to slap the emperor of the Morning Dew. He confused song with life. Life on the plains, under the stars, driving the herd to the knocking plants for shipment to Die Bold, was dirty, tiring, bone-breaking labor that stole sleep and health and even life itself. Beastie boys fared better in song than on the plains.

"Play again song of Dusty Shiv Sharma," said the emperor over cups of Peacock's Rose tea; and he warbled with a bad accent, " 'best Beastie boy o'er alla High Plain.' "

Dusty Sharma had been a real "beast-puncher" a hundred and fifty metric years ago; but he had been called "Shiv" because he carried a hide-out knife in his knee boot. Historians said he would not have been a pleasant man to meet, even when sober; but he had been so encrusted with legend that the real man was unrecognizable.

Instead, she played a jaunty tune that evoked what the Dangchao beast-punchers called the Out-in-back. Of "the splendor o' the mountains, a-rearin' toward the sky" there could be no musty historians' doubts.

After the session, as he bade her good-bye, Jimmy said, "I wish you play here forever."

And so matters ran for several days. Méarana would play songs of the Periphery and engage in "small-talk" with the emperor, and the Fudir would nose around various eddies of the city asking after the activities of Bridget ban. The journey of a thousand leagues begins with a single step, but it seemed to the harper that neither she nor Donovan were advancing the search for her mother by so much as even that single step. Anxiety enhanced impatience. The days were distinguished only by the particular songs she sang, and the precise lack of information with which the Fudir returned each evening.

Because Resilient Services had discovered the relaxing properties of her harp, he had bid her remain for his afternoon Council and play gentle suantraís while he reviewed the reports the dough-riders had brought in. No decision in Sheen Jenlùshy was ever final until ratified by the emperor: not the death sentence to a murderer meted out in Wustershau, not the mei-pōl festival to be held in Xampstedshau, not the list of candidates proposed from the 7th Dough for the imperial examinations. Each must be reviewed with the Six Ministers, a decision rendered, and the triplicate copies apportioned.

The suantraí was supposed to induce drowsiness in its hearers. Méarana thought her playing superfluous. The problem was not to relax, she thought, but to stay awake. The emperor invested her with a title—Invited Minister for Harmonious Meetings—and gave her a brooch to wear.

During the second such meeting, while Méarana plucked long-mastered melodies from the strings, Cheng-li presented a petition to the emperor by the Minister for All Things Natural Within the Realm. "He prays his daughter be granted yin, and not sit for examinations."

Resilient Services did not even glance at the petition. "Denied," he said.

The Minister flushed and muttered, "But all ministers granted this."

Cheng-li slapped the table. "Filial impiety! Five blows!" And the Eater of Beef, who stood by the wall with a long cane of slapstick, stood to attention.

But Resilient Services, looking up from yet another report, said, "Belay that, please. Imperial grace." Cheng-li bowed in submission, and the Minister threw himself on the carpet and blubbered his thanks.

"I was frightened," the harper later admitted to the Fudir, when that worthy had emerged from the Terran Corner slightly scathed and greatly enlightened. "At least, a little," she added. They had met in the Fudir's room at the Hotel

Mountain Glowering. Méarana sat in the comfortable sofa while the scarred man examined his face in the mirror.

"What? Of our young emperor?" The Fudir applied a healing stick to the cut over his left eye, wincing slightly at the sting. "The Council has a quota of decisions to overrule, so none of the district commissioners start feeling above their place. If they can't find cause, they'll overrule at random. And the emperor can overrule the Council, which is what you saw him do today. He even overruled Jingly."

"Not so much frightened *of* him as *for* him. His slightest whim is instantly obeyed. And the others grovel before him. It can't be good for a man to have others grovel to him."

"Better perhaps," said Donovan, "than for the ones who grovel."

"There was one set of reports . . . Did you know there is a second, independent hierarchy whose only purpose is to monitor the behavior of the regular officials and report any 'non-harmonious words or acts'?"

The Fudir dabbed at the other cuts he had suffered. "The Bureau of Shadows," he said. "It could be worse."

"Worse, how?"

"They could be shadowing the common people. If a government is going to snoop, they may as well restrict their snooping to one another. The system could be brought to perfection if the first set of officials were then restricted to monitoring the second. How soon can you break off these afternoon tête-à-têtes?"

It took a moment for the last comment to register. Méarana sat up. "You learned something!"

"The jewelmonger Hennessi fu-lin remembers the necklace your mother gave you. He bought it in pawn from a man of Harpaloon. The man never came back for it, so he sold it to your mother."

"The Kennel told us Mother reported in from Harpaloon. Was she following the necklace?"

"It seems so. It's not much, but it's more than we had. We'll leave for Harpaloon tomorrow evening on the regular shuttle."

That night, in what little sleep the harper found, her mother lurked, always just out of reach.

There were no public clocks in Jenlùshy. The right of proclaiming the Hours was reserved to the emperor. Within the palace complex stood a single cesium clock of unimaginably ancient vintage. It did not match Thistlean hours, having been calibrated long ago to the tock of a different world, but the Sages of the Clock would note the time displayed and perform a ritual called the Transposition of Times, and determine when each new local hour began.

Uncounted people on uncounted worlds spent their workday "watching the clock," but on Thistlewaite there were workers actually paid to do so. The Voice of the Sheen would then, to trumpet blast and gongs, announce the Hour from the parapet of the imperial palace, and the cable channels would carry her word throughout the sheen.

Méarana heard the trumpets as she made her way down Poultry Street, a narrow lane with subtle aromatic reminders of its original inhabitants. Méarana said a word equally pungent and quickened her pace, for the trumpet meant that she would be late for her command performance. She tolerated Donovan's eccentricities on most things, but the packing of her baggage was not among them and that she had done herself.

White Rod was as pale as his wand of office when Méarana finally appeared. Trembling, he led her into the throne room, where Resilient Services sat alone at High Tea, to all appearances sorely vexed. Méarana thought she would play a suantraí to sooth the man's palpable anxiety. She waited for White Rod's underling to pull her chair out for her. Instead, underlings hesitated, emperors rose, and guests sat in fits and starts. Apparently, custom required He Who Serves the Tea to sit last of all; but because the tea had already been poured before Méarana's entrance, harmony was now broken. She did not see why this mattered at all, least of all that it mattered so terribly, but she supposed that now a two-headed calf would be born somewhere for which her lateness could be blamed. She was a Die Bolder, born and bred, and a devotee of causality. Concatenation struck her as absurd.

You would think that a harper would know all about harmony, the emperor told her when that quality had been restored. It was an elliptical rebuke, with a great deal of opprobrium in the ellipsis. "It is a terrible discourtesy with which to end my visit," she replied.

The emperor of the Morning Dew sat back a little in his chair. Today he wore a dinner jacket of bright green, done up with contrasting red embroidery, with a ruffled cravat at his throat. On his head, he had placed a white powdered wig bearing a long pigtail down his back. "End visit," he said, as if examining the phrase for possible alternative meanings.

"Yes. Donovan and I leave on the evening shuttle to rendezvous with the throughliner *Srini Siddiqi*. My mother awaits me."

"Ah. Your mother. Yes. Play me," he said as he poured a second cup of tea and, using a silver tongs, dropped a lump of sugar in it, "song of your mother."

Hitherto, the emperor's requests had been for songs of faraway planets, of romance and distance. The harper played Mother as a geantraí: a jaunty tune that conjured her in the moment in which Bridget ban strode across the decks of *Hot Gates* like the queen of High Tara. Somehow, though, as her fingers wandered across the strings, a goltraí crept in: a keening lament as heartbreaking as all the losses of the world. By then, she had been transported by her own music, as sometimes befell when the harp took charge and the strings played her fingers rather than the proper way round.

The emperor's sob startled her from her trance and, realizing what she had done, she transformed the music once more into geantraí, pivoted by progressions out of the seventh mode and lessening his black bile with the eighth. When she had finished, she laid her hand flat against the strings to still them; though it seemed to her that they still wanted plucking and vibrated softly even so.

"I did not mean to upset you, Jimmy," she said.

"No, no, quite all right. Chin-chin. Emperor *should* be upset now and then. Tedious business, remaining always in balance—always in harmony." A quick smile and with a nod toward the harp.

Méarana played more, but the emperor seemed unwontedly distracted.

When the session drew to a close, Méarana said, "This worm trembles that she must leave so soon."

Jimmy laid a hand on her bare arm. "Do not go," he said with eyes as wide as sorrow. "How else I hear such distant places? Duty pin me to Jenlùshy like butterfly to board. You stay here. *Be empress.* Bring songs of places I never see."

Méarana slid her arm gently from his touch. She adjusted the green shawl around her shoulders. "I cannot. I would be a prisoner here."

"In chains of gold," he told her. "In velvet bands."

"Ochone! Are chains of gold chains no less? I must go. It is a *geasa* upon me."

The emperor of the Morning Dew slumped a little in his seat. "Obligation. Yes, I understand. You must find her."

She said nothing for a time, stroking the strings of her harp, but without striking them, so that they only murmured but did not speak. "How did you know?"

The emperor gestured elegantly toward the harp. "Such sorrow come only from death or loss. And death not drive you across Spiral Arm."

Méarana closed her eyes. "No one has heard from her in three metric years. Many search, myself most of all."

Jimmy Barcelona lifted his teacup to his lips and his eyes searched the courtiers who lined the walls out of earshot, engaged in faux conversations. "Then," he said, dropping his voice, "I, too, search. I go with you . . . "

Méarana had expected the invitation to stay; but not the offer to go. "Ye . . . Ye cannae," she said, falling into her native accents. "Jenlùshy needs you. Mother selected you because of your expertise in infrastructure. You must stay here and rebuild the Morning Dew so that it can survive the next thistlequake."

But Jimmy dismissed that with a wave of the hand. "Never build so strong but Thistlewaite stronger. This miserable worm, engineer. Lay pipe. Estimate building loads and construction costs. Bridges . . . Was *happy* build bridges. Never ask for this."

The harper touched the strings of her harp. "No one ever does," she said quietly, running her fingers down the cords.

"I give orders. Modify systems; implement fault tolerancing and redundancy; increase reliability of infrastructure. Ministers . . . make up numbers to please me, and always build as always. One day, all come down again. No. Better one seek Bridget ban across whole Spiral Arm. There, perhaps, success."

To maintain the harmony of heaven-below by trying to impose the regularities of astronomy on the behavior of humans was very nearly the definition of madness. And yet mystics throughout the ages, from astrologers to computer modelers, had sought it. They forgot that even the heavens held surprises.

Jimmy Barcelona at least could see the futility of his efforts, even if he was not quite clear on why they were futile. Méarana almost told him that her quest was no less futile, but that was something she had not yet told even herself.

And so she spoke truth to power. "Ye maun seek Bridget ban for her sake, not because you want to shuck your ain responsibilities."

Power didn't like to hear that. "If *purpose* same," whispered the emperor, "what matter, different *motives*? Keep smile. We pretend talk small nothings. Courtiers cannot hear. Listen. If Bridget ban lost, approval of sky lost, too. So order in heaven-below, in Jenlùshy, not maintain, and all become chaos above."

"That's absurd, Jimmy!"

"This Thistlewaite. Nothing absurd. You know Garden of Seven Delights?"

"What? Yes. Donovan and I have eaten there several times. The food is . . ."

"Listen. Garden have back door. I come tonight, at Domestic Entertainment Hour. I come in front, lock door on entourage, run out back. You wait by back door with fast flitter. Rent most fast in whole sheen. I come out back door, jump in, and you 'light a shuck for Texas,' as your friend say. We take shuttle." At this point he relaxed and sat back in his chair. "Then you, me, your Donovan, we fly across sky, go . . . maybe Texas, maybe find Bridget ban."

"That's impossible."

The emperor smiled. "But then maybe Invited Minister for Harmonious Meetings not leave Jenlùshy."

"I told you. We already have berths booked."

The smile broadened. "I think of this long time since. Minister need One Man's permission before leave sheen. Suppose I no give."

The harper studied Jimmy's open, friendly smile and saw implacable purpose between her and her mother. She took her napkin and dabbed at her lips. High Tea was coming to an end and the servitors were gathering to take down the café table and set the throne room back to rights. "I must confer with my friend."

The emperor, too, glanced at the approaching staff. "No time. No confer. Decide."

Méarana took a deep breath, exhaled. "Second night hour. Behind the Garden of Seven Delights."

"With most fast flivver. Now," he rose from the table and raised his voice a bit so others could hear. "No need more play. Tomorrow, come back, sing of . . . High Tara."

Méarana rose, showed leg in a graceful bow, and swept up her harp case. "Your worship commands; this worthless one obeys." And she slung the case across her shoulder and strode for the door.

She wondered what Donovan would say about this latest development; but she thought she could guess.

"Have you gone mad?" Donovan demanded.

The sleek Golden Eagle flivver floated up Double Moon Street on a cushion produced by the magnetic field in the paving. "You better hope not," the harper said. "I'm driving." To the west, the Kilworthy Hills had darkened, but their highest peaks still caught the un-set sun from over the horizon and flashed a brilliant white and grey.

"Kidnapping the emperor? Tell me that's sane."

"It's not a kidnapping. It's his idea."

"Then you don't know Thistlewaite. He may be the emperor, but 'Custom is king of all.' "

"Donovan, listen to me. He may be subject to custom—that's what he wants to escape—but he's certainly capable of keeping the two of us here under lock and key and demanding I play escapist music for him every afternoon *for the rest of my freaking life*! And then how would I find my mother?"

"Uncle Zorba told me to keep you out of trouble. I guess he didn't think you'd be the one starting it."

"I suppose the emperor would let you go. You have no songs for him."

A part of the scarred man's mind flashed with anger and Donovan chuckled. *Was that you, Fudir? Insulted that she expects you to abandon her? I'm shocked.*

The Fudir told him what he could do with his shock.

<This is dangerous>, said Inner Child.

We needn't smuggle *Jimmy* off-world, the Silky Voice suggested. We need only spirit *Méarana* from the emperor's clutches.

Ah, said the Brute. You take the fun outta everything, sweetie.

It would not need much, whispered another voice. *A slight tap on the temple and she'll wake up on the shuttle halfway to Harpaloon.*

<The emperor wouldn't like that>, Inner Child pointed out.

Donovan said nothing aloud. *Brute, do you think you can do it without injuring her?*

No problemo.

Yeah? Do you want to tell Zorba we cold-conked his god-daughter, or should I? said the Fudir. If we stiff the emperor, he'll seal the borders. And even if we make it across somehow, Snowy Mountain would be happy to hand us back.

Somehow? said Donovan. *Where was there ever a border you or I found uncrossable?*

Alone, and not with a naïf of a harper in tow.

And not, said the Sleuth, who had been silent until then, *with a pause for debate at every juncture.*

Méarana shook his shoulder. "Fudir. We're there."

The scarred man gathered his thoughts and looked around the service alleyway. The paving here was not magnetized and Méarana had switched over to ground effect, which blew the litter about in swirls. Cans clattered; paper flapped. The narrow lane was unlit, and what illumination spilled across the roofs from Gayway Street did little to lift the shadows. On the right, dust bins stood by each door along the back walls of the Gayway shops. On the left, a stone wall enclosed the residential lots. The emperor had made a good choice for his abduction. Except for the Garden, the other shops were closed up for the night. Blocked from the Garden, his entourage would be forced to run to the far ends of the block to reach the alley, by which time the flivver would be long gone.

"You're going to do it, aren't you?" said Donovan.

"Of course, I am," said Méarana. "It's our only way to get off this planet." Then, realizing that the question was not meant for her, she favored him with a searching look. "You don't have to do this, you know."

"Don't worry about me," said the Fudir. "I promised Zorba that I'd watch out for you."

"I'm not without resources. Mother taught me a trick or two."

"Actually, he said he'd hunt me down and kill me if anything happened to you."

Méarana laughed. "Uncle Zorba is a great kidder."

The Fudir said nothing. Zorba was not that great a kidder. He raised the flivver's gull-wing, and hopped into the alley. The ground effect was just enough to keep the chassis above the paving. "Keep the turbines at hover." Then he crossed to the utility door of the Garden of Seven Delights, ready to hustle the emperor into the waiting vehicle.

Where do you think they'll be? asked the Sleuth.

"Shut up," Donovan explained.

He heard the distant blast of the trumpets from the palace walls, and pole-speakers about the city carried the Voice of the Sheen's announcement of Domestic Entertainment Hour. Clever timing, thought the Fudir. Most of Jenlùshy would be indoors with their visors active, watching the evening installments of their favorite shows.

Shortly after, he heard the whine of flivvers pulling into the restaurant's parking lot on the Gayway side of the building, followed by the hiss and chunk of doors rising and closing. "Get ready," he told Méarana.

He heard the front door slam, rapid footfalls approaching, then the utility door flew open and Jimmy Barcelona rushed out into the alley. The Fudir pushed a large dust bin in front of the door to impede pursuit and took the emperor by the elbow and hurried him toward the car.

At which point, a dozen men dressed in black rose from the surrounding shadows and leveled stingers at them.

Yes, said the Sleuth, *that's where I thought they'd be, too.*

The Fudir cast about for an escape route, torn between Inner Child's impulse to run and the Brute's impulse to fight. Donovan, who had been stung more than once in his career, raised the scarred man's hands. The Silky Voice wept over their failure. Pulled thus in half a dozen directions, the scarred man remained motionless at their average.

Inside the flivver, the harper sat with her hands clenched on the control yoke. Rage dueled with sudden relief in her features. Her hands moved a fraction and the turbine's pitch subtly increased. Donovan, who knew the capabilities of man and machine, thought it a desperate ploy, but one with a hair's-breadth chance of success. Cut losses, abandon allies.

It's what he would have done.

But the flivver's whine dropped into silence. Méarana turned open-faced to the Fudir and the scarred man read her fears writ there.

Flivvers approached from either end of the alley and came to a rest, neatly boxing them in. The doors of the one facing them arched open and

Morgan Cheng-li stepped forth, followed by White Rod bearing the Yellow Cope.

"Ah, majesty," said the Grand Secretary. "This worm abases himself for interruption of such clever evening entertainment, but Monthly Tattoo waits August Presence on parade ground." He showed leg and, with a sweep of the arm, invited Resilient Services to enter the flivver. Jimmy Barcelona slumped and he looked at Donovan, and then at Méarana. "What I say? This Thistlewaite. All plans fail."

Two of the Shadows led Resilient Services to the flivver where White Rod waited.

By this time, the harper had come to stand beside the scarred man. "Are you all right?" she asked him in a whisper.

The Fudir did not know what to tell her. That he had frozen when fast and decisive action might have been most necessary? That it was just as well that they had not escaped because he would not be reliable in a pinch? The sum of his parts was less than the whole he had once been. Donovan answered for him. "No worries," he said. "Hush, here comes Jingly."

The Grand Secretary bestowed a slight nod and sweep of the arm. "You should not have indulged him," he said in Gaelactic. "He is needed too much here."

"He threatened to hold me captive if I didn't," the harper said.

A wave of a jeweled hand. "That is contrary to the Treaty of Amity and Common Purpose. Fourteen States all signatory to League Treaty. You think we want Hounds come here, tear down prison to free you?"

Donovan did not know if The Particular Service would go that far; at least not for his sake. Though they might for Bridget ban's daughter.

"You spy on your own emperor?" he said.

Jingly looked surprised. "Of course! You know 'Shadows'? Provincial Surveillance Commissions watch over Provincial Administrative Commissions. Yang, yin. Each official, each prefect, each dough-rider has shadow. Shadows report harmony to Imperial Censor."

"Yes, I know that."

"So. Who need harmony more than emperor? All balance depend on him. I say 'balance,' but no word in Gaelactic mean same."

"I understand."

"No," said Jingly. "You *not* understand. Only Thistles understand. Our star is central star of whole universe. Microwave 'walls,' same distance, all direction. Heavy burden, balance whole universe on shoulders. No man have such strength. Often bend, sometimes break. Like today. No one man manage all. But all Morning Dew, all Thistlewaite unite in this. All share burden; all *help* emperor. Like today."

Behind him, White Rod placed the Yellow Cope on the emperor's shoulders and bowed him deferentially toward the waiting car.

"You go now," said Jingly. "You not come back Jenlùshy."

Méarana bowed and Donovan bowed and, rising, she saw behind the yellow-garbed August Presence, the trapped eyes of Jimmy Barcelona, who had wanted of all things only to build bridges.

WAR WITHOUT END

UNA McCORMACK

"As flowers turn toward the sun, by dint of a secret heliotropism the past strives to turn toward that sun which is rising in the sky of history."
—Walter Benjamin

Liberation +40 years

Roby's sun was behind them. The planet itself gleamed dimly against the black, pocked and marked like a target. The jump here had been swift but pitiless, and Shard had been violently sick. His constitution—his strength—was not what it once had been. Now he sat limp and passive in his seat, his cheek resting clammily against the cold porthole, directing all his will towards heading off the tremors that coursed through his body and threatened him with further indignities.

Beside him, Lowe rattled on about arrival times, departure times, transportation to the city, agendas . . . At some point, Shard thought, this trip would end. At some point, by extension, Lowe would stop talking. Shard pointed his fingertips at the world below, aimed, *fired* . . . The shuttle banked and he missed. Roby was gone from view—but it was still there, he knew. It had always been there. Shard snapped, "I'm not so far gone I can't remember what you've told me three times already."

Lowe stopped, perplexed rather than cowed. He was a careful young man, well-informed and attentive to detail, untroubled by any broader passions, making up in precision what he lacked in perception. Usually Shard preferred it that way; not now.

"On arrival at the port," Shard said, "a car will be waiting to take us to the capital, where accommodation has been arranged for the duration of our stay in the fourth tower. Tomorrow morning—eighth hour, free standard—another car will take us to the Archive. After which—" this said bitterly, "—I'm on my own."

"Exactly so." Lowe, content, returned to his briefings, with no apparent appreciation of Shard's irony. Shard's hatred peaked—then passed, like his nausea, like all things.

It all unfolded much as Lowe had sketched, with the single notable exception of the protest that was waiting for them between the port and the first of the promised cars. Under siege in the arrival hall, Shard looked out to see upwards of fifty people, few of them old enough to remember the war, carrying banners executed with an otherwise uplifting degree of competence and literacy, chanting their complaint with no small grasp of rhythmic structure. Their unifying theme was their hatred of Shard. The local police watched affably from the side and showed no particular interest in moving them. Grimly, Shard said, "Now this wasn't in the itinerary."

Lowe did not reply. He was deep in the grip of that paralysis that overwhelms functionaries when their best-laid plans prove susceptible to simple human irrationality. He was not, Shard saw, going to be any use.

After thorough consideration of the terrain, the nature of the enemy, and the men and materiel at his disposal, Shard was in a position to offer a professional appraisal of their situation. "I suggest, Mr. Lowe, that we make a run for it." Seeing Lowe baulk, he hastened to explain. "All we have to do is get through the crowd and across the road."

"That's all?"

"The passenger doors are on this side of the car, see? You make for the front and I'll head for the back. Keep your head down and your forearms up—like this, see? Don't stop. It's me they're after, anyway."

Lowe was not measurably comforted. Shard took hold of his elbow and marshalled him through the doors, into the hard light and cold air of Roby, amongst the signs and voices calling him *evil* and *butcher* and *murderer*.

The doors closed behind them. Shard surveyed the mob and the mob stared back. Then it moved in, with a single purpose.

Battle was joined. Shard lost hold of Lowe within seconds. In the crush and the chaos, he stumbled, falling forwards with a gasp, an old man on his knees. Somebody laughed. Just before he hit the ground, the police intervened, swooping in as if to relieve a falling city. Two of them gathered up the visitors, while the rest formed a barrier to let them pass, calling to the crowd that it was over, that they had had their fun.

They deposited them on the far side of the road and would not accept thanks. In the sanctuary of the car, Lowe inspected the marks on his arm which would shortly become bruises. "I had not anticipated that."

Shard was too busy trying to slow his heart rate to be able to point out that such was Lowe's entire purpose. By the time he had his breath back, the moment had passed, but he was able to communicate enough silent fury to penetrate even Lowe's thick skin. They journeyed to the capital in silence.

Shard brooded on his reception. It was the youth of his assailants that troubled him most; how long this hatred had lasted, how deep it must still run, down even to this generation, which had not been born when he was last here and could only know him through the medium of history lessons, propaganda. Was there to be no end?

Full darkness had fallen by the time the car landed at their accommodation. Shard's room was functional but clean. By this point all he cared about was the bed. "Marshal," Lowe said, "we should go through the agenda for tomorrow."

It was too much. Shard—sick in heart and body, wearied almost beyond relief from the journey, from the events of the day, from all that had brought him back here so late in life—snapped. He strode over to the door and threw it open. "Get out! You bloody halfwit! Get the hell out!"

Lowe, bewildered, blinked twice and then withdrew. With peace of a kind restored, Shard could devote himself again to throwing up, in privacy if not in comfort. This done, he drew the curtains, blocking out any sight of the city beyond. Then he lay down on his bed and returned to that solitary contemplation of our mortality which is the nightly pursuit of many, not simply sick old men, and in which we should all on occasion be indulged—even those of Shard's stripe.

Liberation +39.5 years

When the message arrived from the Archive, Shard was raking over the leaves in his garden. Autumn had come early to this part of Mount Pleasant. Soon it would be too wet to work outside on a daily basis, but Shard had a bonfire planned first, an innocent and agreeable pleasure. Shard could be found in his garden most days. He liked the nature of the tasks, which required total attention and absorption, and to which he was entirely committed. His dedication over the years had reaped rewards: his lawn was smooth and uniform, and his flowerbeds triumphant in competition. Moreover, as he liked to say, the exercise kept him fit.

There was a low wall at the far end of the lawn, separating the more cultivated part of the garden from a patch of ground that Shard had left deliberately untouched, for the sake of spring's unruly spread of bright wild flowers. On the wall stood a portable comm: Shard usually brought one out with him to listen to while he worked. All morning, it had been peacefully burbling out news and other nonsense.

A soft chord interrupted the flow, signalling the arrival of a message. With a short puff, Shard stopped work. A few joints cracked. He removed his gardening gloves and wiped his forehead. "Play," he said, and walked over to the comm.

A woman was speaking; an old woman, talking as if from a pre-prepared script. *"Marshal,"* she said. *"My name is Ines de Souza. I am the co-ordinator of the Archive of Public Memory on Roby. Next year will be the fortieth anniversary of the Liberation. Gaps remain in our records—as they always will and always must—and yet I remain curious that you have never given an interview about your time on Roby."* He heard a rustling of papers, like the crackle of flames, and then the woman sighed. *"We grow old, Marshal. Time passes, not much remains—for us, at least. Whatever contribution the former commander of the Commonwealth's forces would be willing to make, the Archive will most gladly receive it."*

The message ended. Shard stared down at the comm. His heart had begun to pound and his face was burning. The message began to repeat, as he had it set to do. *"My name is Ines de Souza. I am the co-ordinator of the Archive of Public Memory on Roby—"*

With a roar of untrammelled rage, Shard kicked the comm off the wall. It soared high into the air, free as a bird in flight, coming to land deep, deep into the wilderness he had made. That finished him for the day. He retreated indoors. Mid-afternoon it rained, heavily, and all his plans came to nothing.

Once upon a time, Shard had believed in loyalty. By this point in his life he still believed in discretion, and for this reason he did not reply to de Souza's message. What purpose would it serve? What could he say about Roby that had not been said already, by both sides? Why pick over the corpse? But during the winter he had no work and few distractions. Instead, he looked out at his modest garden and brooded about his place in history. In the spring, his sense of grievance flowered like a cactus. He contacted Forshaw, and was granted an audience.

These days Forshaw lived on Xanadu, in the humid confines of the biodomes. It was not cheap to retire here. Gabriel Forshaw, a veteran of nothing more brutal than the press conference and the lecture circuit, could afford it. Mark Shard, who had kept a loyal silence, could not. Inside the dome, it was lush, protected, secluded. Outside, interminable dust storms screamed across empty land indifferent to human suffering. Yet that is all there is.

Abundance—of wealth, of talent, of connections—was what Shard had chiefly associated with Forshaw. Now all spent. Forshaw was a sick man; shrunken. His skin was grey and papery, and his eyes lacked hope and lustre. Not even gerontotherapy could combat the cancer; cosmetic surgery could no longer conceal the decline. Forshaw was dying—and the sheer extravagance of the environment in which he would spend his last days only served to reinforce how cruelly.

Once, in a busier and more active life than either of them now led, Shard and Forshaw had conferred on an almost daily basis. The whole business of putting down a revolt required the military at least to go through the motions of informing the political arm what it was up to, although Forshaw had been particularly adept at not hearing anything that might incriminate. His fitness for the political life had been boundless: he had been snake clever, capable of aping authenticity, and blessed with the moral compass of a tiger. His genius, his *trick*, had been to make this animal behaviour appear urbane—likeable, even. He was one of a very few from that time to have retired undefeated and all-but-untarnished. Yet this was how it was going to end.

Shard had not liked Forshaw, but he had suffered him as one of the inevitable crosses borne when one chose—as one must—to participate in public life. He had never forgiven him for the end of the war on Roby. Not even the sight of him now could move Shard beyond this. Perhaps there was a moment of tempered compassion—the fearful kind of fellow-feeling that arises from imagining oneself in such a state—but no more than a moment, and then it was gone.

Forshaw's house was filled with literary awards and pictures of him with the other luminaries of his generation. He had Shard brought out onto the terrace, where they sat under the cover of huge, regular green leaves. Life throbbed around them in studied, well-marshalled profligacy. From deep within the foliage, songbirds of the kind designed and kept for pleasure trilled harmoniously. No mention was made of Forshaw's condition, the open secret, the ruin in the midst of plenty. Shard expressed pleasure at seeing him after so long. Forshaw thanked him with equivalent sincerity. Silence fell, and Shard sat in appalled contemplation of Forshaw's ravaged face.

Forshaw drew back his lips into a smile until his teeth showed, skull-fashion. "I assume there's some purpose to your being here? I don't recall visiting the sick being part of your religion. In fact, I don't recall you being religious at all. But it has been some time."

Recalled to himself, Shard drew out the file containing the message he had received from Roby, and handed it over. Forshaw read out the header. " '*From the Archive of Public Memory, Salvation, Roby; to Marshal Mark Shard, former Commander, Commonwealth Pacification Force on Roby*'."

He laughed, tossing the file and its petition unheard onto the table. "The Archive of Public Memory. They certainly know how to conjure with words out there. One might almost admire them for it—as one had to admire their tenacity."

Shard did not comment. His own encounters with the people of Roby, which had been first-hand whereas Forshaw's had not, did not make him want to express admiration.

"So what is it? A summons?"

Shard retrieved the file from the table. He put it away with care, as an historian might with a piece of evidence. "Nothing so crude. They want to interview me."

"You're not thinking of agreeing?"

"Why not?"

"Mark, it's done. It's over. Nobody cares any longer."

"They do on Roby, patently—"

"Nobody *here* cares. Why should they?"

"Perhaps . . . " Shard struggled to articulate new ideas that were as yet only half-formed in his mind. "Perhaps the record should be set straight."

Forshaw had long since stopped listening. "An old war," he said, "finished years ago. A lost war. The failed policies of old men, soon to be gone and then hastily, all too hastily, forgotten." His words were like his books, Shard thought; florid and without substance. Groundless. "Besides, it all rather runs the risk of becoming something of an embarrassment. One example. What would you say, exactly, if this woman chose to ask you about the end?"

"We didn't do anything wrong," Shard insisted, his first hint of mutiny.

A butterfly settled on Forshaw's wrist. It was about the size of a child's hand, and coloured deep blue. There were white spots on the larger, upper portions of its wings, and a hint of imperial purple to the lower. Forshaw sat in contemplation it for a while before gently brushing it away with a translucent finger. "Well," he said. "I know I didn't."

Shard lifted his eyes, looking past the leaves at the barrier that constituted the limit of the sky. He thought he saw a faint dark line, marking the place where two pieces of the dome met. He reflected upon these joints. He imagined them widening, the dome collapsing; briefly he pictured the unspeakable, unliveable aftermath . . . "You son of a bitch," he said, in wonder. "You son of a bitch."

Forshaw closed his eyes. "At least have the decency to wait till I'm dead."

Decency. The word was an offence coming from the mouth of this man. What, in the end, did he know about Roby? His policies had only ever been implemented at a distance; he had been protected from their consequences just as this dome protected him from the hell outside. But what would history record? A history that Forshaw had spent decades securing—while Shard had kept his loyal silence. Trembling, Shard looked upon Forshaw's ruined face and he was glad.

"But since you're clearly going to do it," Forshaw said, "a word of advice. These people are not the rude peasants of our propaganda. They never were. They were sophisticated and they were ruthless." He cracked open a yellow lizard eye. "Don't lose sight of your real enemy. And try not to lose your bloody temper."

Shard left. Violently he desired now to be instrumental in the failure of this man's bid for immortality, to wrest their shared history back from him and strip it of the veneer with which Forshaw had tried to finish it. Besides, loyalty had not rewarded as richly as leadership. Shard could do with the money.

Liberation +40 years

Shard's first night back on Roby was not restful. Exhaustion, jump-lag, a room too sparsely furnished—all of this contributed to his discomfort, not to mention the twinge of some burgeoning dread which he glossed as performance nerves. Eventually, faint light began to creep through the gap between the curtains. Shard gave up torturing himself with the hope of sleep. He got up and went out onto the balcony to contemplate the world outside, the world he had lost.

It was a cold spring morning, the light as pure and hard as in memory, the hills brown and stony. Deliberately, Shard's eye followed their line westwards; a squat range deeply riven by vanished glaciers, caught in perpetual convulsion, as if ancient gods or monsters had fought some fundamental struggle here, ages before humanity got its chance. The city's towers stood in a ring on four low hills, the circle broken by the ruin of the fifth. That was at the centre of his view. No doubt the room had been selected for this purpose.

The sky above was bright blue, the promise of a warm day. As Shard watched, the mist lying in the hollow formed by the hills began to lift. Piecemeal, their lower reaches came into sight, greened by moss and ivy, shimmering with tiny pale flowers adapted to life in the cracks. Last of all, the undercity was revealed, ramshackle and disorderly, squatting like a beggar in the space between the hills—and here, at last, were the anticipated changes: the barricades completely gone, disappeared without trace; hilltop and undercity now linked by black tramlines, zigzagging surely, inevitably, upwards.

Forty years ago, all of this—air and land, hill and hollow—had belonged to Shard. Not in any legal sense—the various consortia on behalf of whom the Commonwealth had fought this war would surely have contested that—but it had been his in all the ways that matter beyond possession. He had been the one to decide who of his men and his enemies were to live and who were to die. It was that responsibility which had given him title to this land, in a moral sense at least. Shard had referred to this place as West-20. Now it was named Salvation.

From deep within the undercity, which Shard had once held but had never mastered, a clock chimed the tenth before the hour. Others began to follow suit, and then Shard's comm buzzed too. It was Lowe, asking the Marshal to join him on the tower-top, where he was waiting for the car to take them to the Archive.

They were still waiting an hour later. Lowe was frantic. Shard sat to one side and practiced patience. If the delay was a result of mismanagement, that boded well for the day ahead. If it was intended as an insult—what else should he expect from these people?

When at last the car landed, the driver offered no explanation. Installed in the back, Lowe fussed over the day's agenda. Shard stared down at the city as it passed below, picking over the scar left by the obliterated tower. Why had it been left in that state? Forty years had passed. Why not remove it, rebuild it, overwrite it? Was it meant as a memorial? Or a symbol, perhaps; proof that nothing was lasting.

The second tower hove into view. The car pitched sharply, decelerated, and bumped out a landing. The driver did not get out, but stuck his arm out of the window, reaching to open the back door that way. Shard got out onto the landing bay and went forward to speak to him. An apology was clearly not going to be forthcoming but there would at least be an explanation. Before he could demand it, he heard voices shouting his name. He looked across the roof to see yet another pack heading his way, banners aloft. Forgetting the driver, he turned on Lowe. "What in the name of hell are they doing here?"

"I've absolutely no idea—"

"How do we get inside? Come on, man, quickly!"

Lowe looked around helplessly. Shard, meanwhile, had sighted a metal door set in a concrete block about twenty paces away. If memory served correctly, this should provide access to the stairwell. He took Lowe's arm and shoved him that way. "Over there. Get a move on!"

They were halfway there when the door opened. A slight figure leaned out and began gesturing to them frantically to come that way. Lowe reached the door first; Shard, panting, just after. He pushed Lowe inside and slammed the door shut behind him. Moments later, there was a hammering on it, but these doors had been built to survive bombardment and siege. A handful of grubby activists should prove no problem. Satisfied, for the moment, that he was safe, Shard turned his wrath upon the new arrival. "How did they get up here? Who let them in?"

Their saviour—a slight, androgynous youth—stared in frank alarm past Shard's shoulder at the barricaded door. "Christ, that was close!"

Shard exploded. He stuck his finger in the youth's face. "If you're trying to shake me, it won't bloody work! Nothing you people threw at me ever shook me! Do you hear me? Nothing!"

There was a short charged silence. Lowe nervously cleared his throat. As it began to occur to Shard that he might not be entirely in control, he heard slow footsteps coming up the metal steps. From out of the shadowy stairwell, another figure emerged. It was an old woman. Shard looked her up and down, was about to dismiss her—but curiosity got the better of him. "Who the hell are you?"

"Marshal," she said. "I'm Ines de Souza. You can stop shouting now."

In the lift down into the main body of the tower, de Souza gave Shard his explanation. "Most of the building is public access, but we cordoned off the secondary landing bay in advance of your arrival. For some reason, your driver elected to land at the main bay."

Lowe said, "It really is very irregular—"

De Souza looked him up and down and then looked away. Shard winced. "I can make a formal apology," she said, "if that would help."

"Don't trouble yourself, ma'am," Shard said, in a quieter voice than he had used in several days. "No harm was done."

De Souza grunted in—dear God, was that approval? Shard eyed her. She was small and nut-brown, and dressed exceedingly badly in a long patterned skirt in green and gold, a pale blue cotton shirt, and scuffed sandals. Slung across her right shoulder was a dilapidated hessian bag which bore a bright orange flower stitched on with pink thread. The bag was stuffed to bursting with papers, many of them yellowed. Shard had expected an elegant academic, perhaps, or a trim administrator. Not confusion, disarray, poverty. Most startling to his eyes was how old she looked. One did not see that within the Commonwealth anymore; one had to be poor, or as sick as Forshaw. Shard took heart. Whatever had happened, Roby remained the poor relation.

The lift doors opened onto a dim unfurnished corridor. If this was freedom, Shard thought, as they walked along it, he would rather be rich. His good spirits did not last: at the end of the corridor, de Souza led him into a room which for all the world looked exactly like a torture chamber.

Liberation +39.75 years

After Xanadu, Shard's fury flourished. He was a new man, fired with a new purpose—the unmaking of Gabriel Forshaw. He lost no time in responding to the Archive and agreeing to an interview. His greatest fear now was that Forshaw might cheat him, dying before Shard had the chance to give his version of events. He even offered to go to Roby, rather than risk the inevitable delay that would be involved in getting permission for his interviewers to enter Commonwealth space. Friendly they all might be these days, or nearly, but one should never forget the provenance even of one's friends.

There was a gap of several weeks before the Archive replied; a period during which Shard monitored the obituary feeds compulsively. Forshaw—thank God—was not dead by the time de Souza replied agreeing to his visit. The morning after, Lowe arrived unasked on Shard's doorstep, sent from the Bureau to assist him. "These are delicate times," Lowe explained, perched on

Shard's sofa like a dapper heron, handling his cup and saucer with fastidious care. "Relations between us are finely balanced, and it is to the benefit of all that nothing happens to disturb that balance."

Presumably he was a spy, but that at least meant he might come in useful. Shard took out the file containing all his correspondence with de Souza and threw it over. The cup slipped in Lowe's grasp, splashing tea into his saucer, but he steadied it. "If you want to help," Shard said, "find out what this one got up to during the war."

A tall order. Secrecy lingered over the files from that period like flies above a shallow grave. Nonetheless, Lowe returned in a matter of days. "She worked with children. Specifically orphans, resettling them after the war. After that she was a history teacher in Salvation and for the past twelve years she has been co-ordinating their Archive."

"What about before the war?"

"There's nothing from then."

"Nothing at all?"

"Date and place of birth, who owned her bond . . . There's no reason why there should be anything else. Not everyone on Roby was directly involved in hostilities."

Shard grunted. He had never made that mistake. Every last one of them had been either a threat or a threat in the making.

"But we do have one concern," Lowe said.

"Get on with it."

"Her name appears on several of the extradition requests we received in the twenties." There had been a rash of them back then. They asked for Shard on numerous occasions; once or twice, they had even asked for Forshaw. The people of Roby certainly had no trouble determining their enemies. "Our strong advice is that you reconsider travelling to Roby—"

"No."

"She's not on any outstanding blacklist. She can travel here."

"That would take too long."

"We have no jurisdiction in Roby—"

"Do you know, I remember there was a war fought about that—"

"And you have no diplomatic immunity—"

"For God's sake, man, enough! What you're saying is that if anything goes wrong out there I'm on my own?"

Lowe pressed a fingertip delicately against the side of his nose. "You have all the protections that any citizen of the Commonwealth can expect, of course. But if there *is* trouble out there, we might not be in a position to help you."

"You mean you don't want to kick up the diplomatic stink it would need?"

Shard watched grimly as Lowe struggled to come up with a form of language acceptable to them both. "Times have changed, Marshal. We are no longer enemies and there is the strong possibility that we might become friends. Many of their current organizers were born after the war—"

This was enough. "Do you really believe they think of us as friends in the making?" Shard said. "They hated us. They will hate us till the end. Every last one of them. If you'd been there, if you'd seen how it was there, you'd understand that. Have you all gone mad at the Bureau? Is there anyone looking out for us these days? Or have you bought into your own propaganda? We fought a *war* with these people, man! We killed them in their hundreds of thousands, and they would have done the same to us if they'd had the capability. This new generation has been taught by the last. If you and your masters believe this is over, you're living in a fantasy land."

Lowe, uncomfortable, had looked away. He was tweaking his cuffs, unnecessarily. "You're free to do whatever you choose, of course. But the Commonwealth is now looking to advance its friendship with the people of Roby." He stretched his hands out in appeal to some final authority. "That's *policy.*"

For one shattering second, Shard surveyed his life, and he saw how all that had once mattered now counted for nothing. Worse than nothing—it was, as Forshaw had said, an embarrassment. His heart burned within him. Even shame would be better, he thought; that at least would accord some significance to all that had happened, all that had been suffered. But they had not even earned that recognition. They were an embarrassment. "Damn you all," he whispered, thinly, like a voice in the wilderness. "But you won't stop me going! I *will* have my say, before the end."

Lowe barely covered a sigh. "I'm sure you will, Marshal. But I wonder— who do you imagine is listening?"

Liberation +40 years

It was not the bareness of the room that had struck Shard, although it *was* bare—a table, two chairs, grey walls and a carpetless floor, and a single small window through which light passed feebly to reveal the dust swirling slowly. It was how the room was equipped.

The chairs were set in opposition, the table between them, and behind each place stood a diptych of screens, positioned at a slight angle to each other. Four screens in total, two on each side. Each of them was connected by a veritable web of cables to two small black boxes, one at either end of the table. Attached to each of these was a set of sensors, one for the arm, two for each temple. Shard recognized every last piece of this equipment; what surprised him was that it was duplicated. That was not the usual arrangement.

"Forgive the accommodation," de Souza said, dumping her bag on the table. It slumped under the weight of its contents. She followed his look around the room. "I imagine you recognize all this. Your people left it all behind."

Unhurriedly, her bag fell over. Papers spilled out onto the floor. "Blast," she said, without rancour. She leaned one hand on the table and started to lower herself down, but her aide got there first, kneeling to gather her scattered works and then holding them out to her like an offering. "Bless you, Jay," she said, and sat down, with a sigh. "Have a seat, Marshal."

"Can I get you anything, Ines?" the youth said. "Tea?"

"Tea, yes, yes—thank you. *Please*, Marshal," this with a touch of asperity, "have a seat. It's exhausting watching you standing to attention. You'll be giving me your name and number next."

Shard made a sweeping gesture that took in the screens, the sensors, the blood flow monitors. "Is that my safest option?"

"All this? Nothing to lose sleep over." Deftly, as if this was something she had done countless times before, de Souza began to hook herself up. She rolled up her sleeve, fixing a sensor against her upper arm with an armband. "You must have seen a psycho-imager in use before, surely? While you were here, if not since?"

Shard stiffened. He gripped the back of his chair and his knuckles turned white. "Mme de Souza, it is a matter of record that I did not conduct any interrogations on Roby. If you're looking to trap me that way you'll have to try considerably harder."

De Souza, who had been about to attach the other two sensors to her temples, halted with her hand halfway up to her face. "Trap you? You have a very strange idea of what I'm doing here, Marshal. I'm hardly fit for mortal combat, am I?" She finished attaching the sensors. "If I were you I'd sit down in your chair and stop trying to second-guess me. I'm only going to ask you a few questions."

Hooked up, de Souza turned her attention to the black box on her right, playing with dials and switches. "Useless bloody . . . Ah! There we are!" A green light flickered and, behind her, on the left-hand screen, an image appeared, grainy at first, and then coming slowly into focus. It was a sunflower—joyful and riotously bright against the uniform grey wall. Shard glanced over his shoulder: yes, there it was, on the left-hand screen behind him.

"On my mind," she said. "No luck with them. Top-heavy."

"Try propping them up against a wall," Shard said faintly. He took his seat, uncomfortably conscious of the two screens behind him and what they might reveal. "But one that gets light. And not too much water. It loosens the soil so it can't bear the weight."

"I'll bear that in mind next time. Thank you."

Shard examined the second set of sensors on the table in front of him. He picked up the armband. "Marshal," Lowe said urgently, "I strongly advise against this—"

"It's strange how things work out," de Souza said. "These little devices turned out to be a godsend. I never would have thought that, given what they were used for before Liberation. What we found was that they got people round the table who didn't trust each other and showed them exactly what it was they could expect from each other." Behind her, the sunflower transformed into a rapid series of images—memories, Shard imagined—of people gathered round tables, shouting, debating. Back home, they had predicted civil war on Roby; had considered the potential of a humanitarian mission. It hadn't happened. "If you can't hide what you're thinking," de Souza said, "you'd better have a way of justifying it. And of course, we couldn't have built the Archive without them."

The picture altered. Shard realized that he was seeing from her perspective as she sat at this table, looking back at the place where he was now, talking to another old man, an old man thinking about the war. What else was there? "Not just to document the order of events," she said, "but to archive the personal recollections, the individual impressions of that time. The marching songs, the stump speeches. I doubt we got the half of it. We suffer from a surfeit of history on Roby." And she showed him the essence of it: what it was like to crawl out from beneath a pile of bodies, to watch a plantation burn, to see armed men line up in advance of opening fire upon you. "But what never ceased to amaze me," she said, "was how often people said it was the best time of their life. Because they were young and active, I imagine. Committed to something bigger than themselves. Is that how it was with you, Marshal? Was it the best time of your life?"

Shard put his hands, palm down, flat upon the table. "Madame," he said. "If we are going to talk, you will have to take my word—or nothing."

De Souza gave him the kind of look a teacher might give a promising student who had failed a simple test through idleness or a closed mind. Shard cleared his throat. Carelessly, he said, "You know, we often wondered what control individuals had over what they were showing us. How much an image could be manipulated by an unwilling subject. How much we could rely on what was generated as a result."

"But you use them within the Commonwealth, don't you? You must know something about how little a subject can conceal—willing or otherwise."

"An artist might use one, yes, or a therapist with a patient, but they're hardly forced!"

"How about within the justice system?"

"If you've nothing to hide you've nothing to fear—"

Quickly, Shard cut himself off. Too late. De Souza smiled, benignly and, with a sigh, he began to roll up his sleeve. "Marshal . . . " Lowe warned.

Damn idiot sounded surprised. "She has me," Shard explained, as he attached the sensors. "Condemned from my own mouth." De Souza leaned over to switch on the box next to him. She was still smiling.

He gave a bark of laughter. "How much can be concealed? I can find out for myself now, can't I?" De Souza's eyes flicked up past his shoulder, and he looked in turn at the right-hand screen behind her, where he could examine his own thoughts. It was hazy for a while, and then sharpened suddenly into focus and showed the face of Gabriel Forshaw.

De Souza drew in a breath. "I had no idea he was so sick."

She was thinking—as Shard could see—of how Forshaw had looked forty years ago, in one of the propaganda 'casts, encouraging the insurgents to surrender. Smoke and mirrors. Forshaw had never been that glossy. "Even sicker in the flesh," he said. He tapped the table, clearing his thoughts, and showed her how spectacular his garden had been the previous summer. "Shall we begin?"

She did not ask about Roby. They talked in some detail about his early career and then she went back in time and asked him about his decision to join the army. He gave his habitual, pre-prepared defence and then was confronted, suddenly, with the sight of his father—a splinter of memory so sharp he feared its capacity to wound if he touched it further. Enough. "Madame. I have to stop."

They had been talking for almost three hours. Shard's head throbbed; so did his upper arm where the band was strapped on. "Of course," de Souza said.

Shard yanked the sensors from his temples and the picture on the screen disappeared from view. He saw that de Souza was watching him. "I hope I've not worn you out."

He wiped his hand across his forehead. "No."

"We can break for the day—"

"No."

"Have you discovered how much you can conceal?"

"Enough," he answered honestly, "but only with effort. I imagine that your difficulty is in interpretation."

"Whereas our fear was always self-disclosure. That was all you needed, really. You needed to make us mistrust ourselves. Self-doubt, a moment of hesitation, checking oneself before speaking—that was your way in. Once that became too much to sustain . . . " She studied him. She had not yet detached herself. "We would have to continue for some time yet before we reached that point."

Shard nodded. His hands, he realized, were trembling slightly. He put them on his knees, hiding them away under the table. "So, have you learned anything of substance, Madame?"

"Plenty." She paused, as if to sift through evidence. "You see yourself as scrupulous, meticulous. You hold the politicians responsible for all that happened here, and you mean that in its broadest sense. If you thought you could get away with it, you would tell me that you were only following orders."

Shard shoved back his chair. He stood up, abruptly. "Lowe," he said. He was shaking. "Get the car."

"You are besieged," she told him, softly and, behind her, West-20's fifth tower shuddered and began to fall. "And I find myself wondering—have you ever stopped thinking of us as the enemy?"

Brooding that evening alone in his room, Shard concluded that the only option was to go on the offensive. He could not refuse to continue, not having come so far, and not after the small victories she had achieved. The following day, he stuck grimly to the script that he and Lowe had prepared. Doggedly, he told the truth as he saw it—a story of duty and loyalty and honour: simple values, easily communicated, not intrinsically the worse for that. He worked the machine more cannily too: he demanded frequent breaks, pulled the sensors off at random, kept her at bay. He held Forshaw at the front of his mind and with him the grievance that he signified. He found that now that he had started talking, it was easy to keep the accusations flowing. "I know what people say these days. That the military was out of control on Roby."

"I have heard it rumoured that there was almost mutiny at the end—"

"Don't believe everything you hear. They were there at every stage, the politicians, Foreshaw foremost. Nothing happened without their consent. They were there right to the very end—oh yes!"

"Tell me about that, Marshal," she said. She was looking down, sifting through her notes. "The last day. Much about what happened then still puzzles me."

He swung away from it. Instead he went back to the beginning, as the script dictated and, methodically, he detailed the battles he had fought. He talked about the people he had commanded, in particular those who had been lost. He wanted her to see—to understand—that the damage had not been all on one side. Deliberately, he avoided studying what appeared on her screen; although, at very end of the day, he glanced over—cautiously, surreptitiously. To his surprise he saw her sunflowers blooming. He pondered the image that night as he tried to sleep. As darkness fell, the meaning came to him. All he had to say, all he had told her—it *bored* her.

The injustice almost overwhelmed him. The next day, therefore, he gloried in his occasional victories, the harm that he had done to her at every stage.

He drenched his screen in it, forcing her to see it, not looking once at her side. In their fourth session, she withdrew, paying him no more than perfunctory attention. He began to believe he had beaten her back, and his heart sped in anticipation of triumph. Imagining himself all but victorious, and curiously, he began to observe her thoughts again.

Her mind turned out to be full of what he took to be her Archive—a large unwieldy stack of papers, aging, and with an inkblot in the middle of one page. His eye was drawn to this black spot. Even as he opined, again, on the failure of nerve that had brought about their defeat, he would find himself glancing across. Eventually, he saw that it was not a stain or a blot, but a scorch mark, as if someone had stubbed out a cigarette on the skin of the page, or put a match to it. He became distracted; at one point the image even appeared, for a few short seconds, on his own screen. Soon, he could not keep his eyes off it; it drew him to her like a black hole. In the end, it was the whole of what was between them.

De Souza was no longer even pretending to listen to him. She sat looking down upon the table, the back of one hand pressed hard against her mouth. Was she ill? "Madame?" he said. "Madame?"

He reached out to touch her hand and she pulled back. Abruptly, the stain in her mind disappeared; replaced by amorphous unrevealing images, pastoral scenes: the rocky hills above Salvation, the grey-green grass of the plains in sector-13. Then these too were gone. She had removed the sensors from her temples. "Thank you, Marshal. I'm grateful that you were willing to come this far to speak to me." She took her armband off slowly, and leaned over to switch off her monitor.

Shard stared at her. "Is that it?"

She began to gather up her papers. "Yes."

"But we haven't got to the end—"

"Yes we have. Or, rather—we have got as far as it is possible for us to get."

Again, he put out his hand, with the idea of stopping her clearing away, but he thought better of it. "There's still the last day," he offered. "Don't you want to know what happened? Don't you want to know why that tower came down? That and no other?" There was the black hole on the screen. "I know everything, everything that went on." Seeing her hesitate, he pressed on with his assault. "It will die with me, you know! That gap will remain forever! There's nobody else. Forshaw will never tell you the truth! He'll be gone soon anyway. There is only me, Madame," he taunted her softly. "I'm the only one left."

She stood for a while as if in contemplation, her head down, hands gripping the edge of the table. Then she looked him directly in the eye. "You don't have the heart." She slung her bag over her shoulder, carrying it like a burden as she walked towards the door. "Goodbye, Marshal. Enjoy what's left of your feud."

In the car back, Lowe did not conceal his relief that the whole sorry business had come to an end. "Foolish to have come here in the first place. The Bureau has unearthed more about de Souza. A teacher and archivist—if only! She ran one of the first underground railways out of Salvation, and then retooled her network to run arms back in. Now they tell me." Petulantly, he said, "People do not pay enough attention to the details! Wasn't that exactly how it all started? Smuggling children out of the cities and into the country?"

"I forget," Shard said.

"But we've got through without any disasters. And now we can go home."

Shard said, "I'm not done here yet."

"But Mme de Souza made it quite clear that your sessions together were finished—"

"I don't care what she said. I have not finished with her. We'll go over in the morning as arranged, and we'll remain there until Mme de Souza has heard all that I have to say."

There was a pause. "Regretfully," Lowe said, "that cannot be 'we'. If you as a private citizen want to continue your association with Mme de Souza, that is your choice. But as a representative of the Commonwealth, I cannot in conscience knowingly sit down in the same room as someone who committed terrorist acts against us. Not without quite specific permission."

Shard smiled. "So I really am on my own?"

"Only by your own choice, Marshal—"

Roughly, Shard patted him on the arm. "Leave it. I understand. I understand."

In truth, Shard no longer cared. Lowe was irrelevant. His own will had brought him here this time, not the Bureau's, not the Commonwealth's, not de Souza's. He would leave on his own terms. He spent another sleepless night, but this was in anticipation of battle. He was certain that she would come to hear him: that great gap drew her back to him, the only one who could fill it for her. He stood at the window and looked down at the lit-up city—*his* city, which bore the mark of his time here and always would. A little before dawn he did sleep—fitfully, excitedly—and when the alarm woke him, a message from de Souza was waiting for him. She would meet him at the Archive, as originally planned.

This was his moment of triumph. His hands shook as he washed and dressed, his heart quaked. He was jubilant. He had them both now: de Souza wanting to know what he knew, Forshaw wanting him to conceal it. He would go this morning and unmake history, remaking it in the way he chose. Not propaganda, not hagiography—he would at last be able to give his own account, which was true.

He took the car across to the Archive alone. When he arrived, de Souza was there already, sitting at the table talking quietly to her freakish aide. He

strode into the room, feeling half his age. When she saw him, de Souza rose
from her chair. Before he could start, she said, "I'm sorry to be the bearer of
bad news, Marshal. Gabriel Forshaw died yesterday."

Shard's legs all but crumpled beneath him. He made a lunge for the table,
gripping it to steady himself. De Souza's aide discreetly helped into his chair.

"Quietly, I gather," de Souza said. "In his sleep."

"How else would it be?"

She took her seat slowly. "We have his lectures of course, his memoirs . . . "
She held up her hands, an old woman's hands, and empty. "Soon we will all be
gone," she said. "All that will be left will be what we committed to the Archive.
I know." Her voice rose, and he needed no aid to perceive and understand
her distress. " . . . that it will remain of interest for as long as some of us are
still alive. But what then? It will become a curiosity, and at last will be lost in
time, like a signal that decays. With the children of our great-grandchildren,
I would say, when the living link has been severed and there is nobody alive
who remembers us, even as we are now." She looked at him. "What do you
think, Marshal? Should we not be glad? If the lives we led and the wars we
fought are in the end meaningless?"

It was to Shard a horror, a kind of hell. In terror, he said, "They won't. They
can't! Not all of it!"

She did not answer. Her aide had placed an arm around her shoulder, in
comfort, and he saw her then as she was—an old woman who had fought a
war; who had lived to see her life's work transformed beyond recognition, as it
would have to be if it was ever to be counted a success. All that remained was
the chance to set the record straight. He gathered up the sensors and, when he
saw he had her attention, he bent his forefinger to gesture her in. "Let me tell
you," he said, "about Gabriel Forshaw."

Liberation Day

In thirteen minutes the evacuation would be complete. The last ship would
have left Roby. Shard stood in C&C watching the lights flash. He had turned
off the alarms over an hour ago.

"Commander," said his adjutant, who was desperate to leave and even
more desperate not to show it, "incoming from the Bureau. The Secretary, sir."

Shard, who had been waiting for this, took it in his private office. Forshaw,
he observed, did not look like a man who had been up all night. *Still there,
Shard? You're the veritable captain of the sinking ship.*

"Plenty to do yet, sir."

*"Quite. Listen, Cabinet finally got its act together and made a decision, so I
have this authorization for you. Code-45. You got that?"*

"Code-45. And you're quite sure about that, sir?"

"Cabinet's decision. I'm just the messenger."

"I'll see to it at once, sir."

"Good man."

Forshaw hesitated. The lights flashed and the clock counted down. "The sooner I can get to it," Shard pointed out, "the sooner I can leave."

"Yes. Of course. Well, I'll see you on Mount Pleasant in a few days, Commander. Safe journey home." He cut the comm and was gone.

"Fucking gangster," Shard muttered to the space the other man left. He passed on the newly-issued order to the other officers, proceeded to execute it for his own area, and then went back out to C&C to tell his frantic adjutant they could leave. They boarded the shuttle with seven-and-a-half minutes to spare; as it lifted, Shard looked out to watch the light show.

They had mined all the cities months ago, after the insurgents took North-29, rigging up all the towers individually. Thirty-eight cities, an average of five towers each; almost two hundred bonfires if you totted them all up. Shard imagined the show running the length of the Diamond Coast and up along the Red River deep into the heart of their territory, taking out everything— communications, air links, the lot. If they wanted Roby, they could have it— what was left—and after a few years picking through the rubble, they could come begging for help.

They were safely above the city when Shard's tower went down, but they still felt it. His adjutant stared in disbelief out of the porthole and then in horror at Shard. Shard watched the second tower. And watched. And watched. He checked the time. Sixty-four seconds. It should have gone by now—but perhaps something was wrong with the mechanism. At one-hundred-and-sixteen seconds, uneasily, he started watching the third tower. At one-hundred-and-twenty-three seconds, when it was still standing, he knew where the failure had been and knew that it was not in the equipment. The ruin of his own tower was now conspicuously in need of explanation and, as Roby fell away from him, Shard knew who would take the blame. Who else? How did you court-martial an entire army? How did you condemn a whole system?

The two screens behind de Souza displayed conflicting images. Shard was thinking of the city as he had seen it the night before, lit up but not alight, scarred but not wrecked. De Souza was thinking of the falling cities, seeing the world after collapse, blasted back to the stone age, all but uninhabitable. "Do you not see?" he said, revolted at last by the sight of it. "I thought I was ending it. I thought I was ending the war."

"Oh, Mark Shard," she told him as she clasped his hand, "it was not yours to end."

Shard thought fleetingly of reparation—and then, in his mind's eye, he glimpsed the city as it might have been, not ruined but resurgent. He saw it perfected; the last tower still stood and the sun shone hard upon it. Silhouetted in front was de Souza, sitting like a guardian on the gates of history. Reflected in her face, he saw what could have been. Breathless now, he saw the future that he could have had a hand in making, had all his gifts of loyalty and dedication not been misapplied. As his heart gave out, he saw himself clearly: caught in the pain of an ageless struggle, ruined by his choice of side. He saw the world as it could have been, had the enemy not, this time, persuaded.

And Ines de Souza—who had survived all those that had declared themselves her enemy—she, when asked, would say: "His heart. In the end—his heart."

FINISTERRA

DAVID MOLES

⇒◆⇐

1. Encantada

Bianca Nazario stands at the end of the world.

The firmament above is as blue as the summer skies of her childhood, mirrored in the waters of *la caldera*; but where the skies she remembers were bounded by mountains, here on Sky there is no real horizon, only a line of white cloud. The white line shades into a diffuse grayish fog that, as Bianca looks down, grows progressively murkier, until the sky directly below is thoroughly dark and opaque.

She remembers what Dinh told her about the ways Sky could kill her. With a large enough parachute, Bianca imagines, she could fall for hours, drifting through the layered clouds, before finding her end in heat or pressure or the jaws of some monstrous denizen of the deep air.

If this should go wrong, Bianca cannot imagine a better way to die.

Bianca works her way out a few hundred meters along the base of one of Encantada's ventral fins, stopping when the dry red dirt beneath her feet begins to give way to scarred gray flesh. She takes a last look around: at the pall of smoke obscuring the *zaratán's* tree-lined dorsal ridge, at the fin she stands on, curving out and down to its delicate-looking tip, kilometers away. Then she knots her scarf around her skirted ankles and shrugs into the paraballoon harness, still warm from the bungalow's fabricators. As the harness tightens itself around her, she takes a deep breath, filling her lungs. The wind from the burning camp smells of wood smoke and pine resin, enough to overwhelm the taint of blood from the killing ground.

Blessed Virgin, she prays, be my witness: this is no suicide.

This is a prayer for a miracle.

She leans forward.

She falls.

•••

2. The Flying Archipelago

The boat-like anemopter that Valadez had sent for them had a cruising speed of just less than the speed of sound, which in this part of Sky's atmosphere meant about nine hundred kilometers per hour. The speed, Bianca thought, might have been calculated to bring home the true size of Sky, the impossible immensity of it. It had taken the better part of their first day's travel for the anemopter's point of departure, the ten-kilometer, billion-ton vacuum balloon *Transient Meridian*, to drop from sight—the dwindling golden droplet disappearing, not over the horizon, but into the haze. From that Bianca estimated that the bowl of clouds visible through the subtle blurring of the anemopter's static fields covered an area about the size of North America.

She heard a plastic clattering on the deck behind her, and turned to see one of the anemopter's crew, a globular, brown-furred alien with a collection of arms like furry snakes, each arm tipped with a mouth or a round and curious eye. The *firija* were low-gravity creatures; the ones Bianca had seen on her passage from Earth had tumbled joyously through the *Caliph of Baghdad's* inner ring spaces like so many radially symmetrical monkeys. The three aboard the anemopter, in Sky's heavier gravity, had to make do with spindly-legged walking machines, and there was a droop in their arms that was both comical and melancholy.

"Come forward," this one told Bianca in fractured Arabic, its voice like a Peruvian pipe ensemble. She thought it was the one that called itself Ismaíl. "Make see archipelago."

She followed it forward to the anemopter's rounded prow. The naturalist, Erasmus Fry, was already there, resting his elbows on the rail, looking down.

"Pictures don't do them justice, do they?" he said.

Bianca went to the rail and follows the naturalist's gaze. She did her best to maintain a certain stiff formality around Fry; from their first meeting aboard *Transient Meridian* she'd had the idea that it might not be good to let him get too familiar. But when she saw what Fry was looking at, the mask slipped for a moment, and she couldn't help a sharp, quick intake of breath.

Fry chuckled. "To stand on the back of one," he said, "to stand in a valley and look up at the hills and know that the ground under your feet is supported by the bones of a living creature—there's nothing else like it." He shook his head.

At this altitude they were above all but the highest-flying of the thousands of beasts that made up Septentrionalis Archipelago. Bianca's eyes tried to make the herd (or flock, or school) of *zaratanes* into other things: a chain of islands, yes, if she concentrated on the colors, the greens and browns of forests and plains, the grays and whites of the snowy highlands; a fleet of ships, perhaps, if she instead focused on the individual shapes, the keel ridges, the long, translucent fins, ribbed like Chinese sails.

The *zaratanes* of the archipelago were more different from one another than the members of a flock of birds or a pod of whales, but still there was a symmetry, a regularity of form, the basic anatomical plan—equal parts fish and mountain—repeated throughout, in fractal detail from the great old shape of Zaratán Finisterra, a hundred kilometers along the dorsal ridge, down to the merely hill-sized bodies of the nameless younger beasts. When she took in the archipelago as a whole, it was impossible for Bianca not to see the *zaratanes* as living things.

"Nothing else like it," Fry repeated.

Bianca turned reluctantly from the view, and looked at Fry. The naturalist spoke Spanish with a flawless Miami accent, courtesy, he'd said, of a Consilium language module. Bianca was finding it hard to judge the ages of *extrañados*, particularly the men, but in Fry's case she thought he might be ten years older than Bianca's own forty, and unwilling to admit it—or ten years younger, and in the habit of treating himself very badly. On her journey here she'd met cyborgs and foreigners and artificial intelligences and several sorts of alien—some familiar, at least from media coverage of the *hajj*, and some strange—but it was the *extrañados* that bothered her the most. It was hard to come to terms with the idea of humans born off Earth, humans who had never been to Earth or even seen it; humans who, many of them, had no interest in it.

"Why did you leave here, Mr. Fry?" she asked.

Fry laughed. "Because I didn't want to spend the rest of my life out *here*." With a hand, he swept the horizon. "Stuck on some Godforsaken floating island for years on end, with no one but researchers and feral refugees to talk to, nowhere to go for fun but some slum of a balloon station, nothing but a thousand kilometers of air between you and Hell?" He laughed again. "You'd leave, too, Nazario, believe me."

"Maybe I would," Bianca said. "But you're back."

"I'm here for the money," Fry said. "Just like you."

Bianca smiled, and said nothing.

"You know," Fry said after a little while, "they have to kill the *zaratanes* to take them out of here." He looked at Bianca and smiled, in a way that was probably meant to be ghoulish. "There's no atmosphere ship big enough to lift a *zaratán* in one piece—even a small one. The poachers deflate them—gut them—flatten them out and roll them up. And even then, they throw out almost everything but the skin and bones."

"Strange," Bianca mused. Her mask was back in place. "There was a packet of material on the *zaratanes* with my contract; I watched most of it on the voyage. According to the packet, the Consilium considers the *zaratanes* a protected species."

Fry looked uneasy, and now it was Bianca's turn to chuckle.

"Don't worry, Mr. Fry," she said. "I may not know exactly what it is Mr. Valadez is paying me to do, but I've never had any illusion that it was legal."

Behind her, the *firija* made a fluting noise that might have been laughter.

3. The Steel Bird

When Bianca was a girl, the mosque of Punta Aguila was the most prominent feature in the view from her fourth-floor window, a sixteenth-century structure of tensegrity cables and soaring catenary curves, its spreading white wings vaguely—but only vaguely—recalling the bird that gave the city its name. The automation that controlled the tension of the cables and adjusted the mosque's wings to match the shifting winds was hidden within the cables themselves, and was very old. Once, after the hurricane in the time of Bianca's grandfather, it had needed adjusting, and the old men of the *ayuntamiento* had been forced to send for *extrañado* technicians, at an expense so great that the *jizyah* of Bianca's time was still paying for it.

But Bianca rarely thought of that. Instead she would spend long hours surreptitiously sketching those white wings, calculating the weight of the structure and the tension of the cables, wondering what it would take to make the steel bird fly.

Bianca's father could probably have told her, but she never dared to ask. Raúl Nazario de Arenas was an aeronautical engineer, like the seven generations before him, and flight was the Nazarios' fortune; fully a third of the aircraft that plied the skies over the Rio Pícaro were types designed by Raúl or his father or his wife's father, on contract to the great *moro* trading and manufacturing families that were Punta Aguila's truly wealthy.

Because he worked for other men, and because he was a Christian, Raúl Nazario would never be as wealthy as the men who employed him, but his profession was an ancient and honorable one, providing his family with a more than comfortable living. If Raúl Nazario de Arenas thought of the mosque at all, it was only to mutter about the *jizyah* from time to time—but never loudly, because the Nazarios, like the other Christians of Punta Aguila, however valued, however ancient their roots, knew that they lived there only on sufferance.

But Bianca would sketch the aircraft, too, the swift gliders and lumbering flying boats and stately dirigibles, and these drawings she did not have to hide; in fact for many years her father would encourage her, explaining this and that aspect of their construction, gently correcting errors of proportion and balance in Bianca's drawings; would let her listen in while he taught the family profession to her brothers, Jesús the older, Pablo the younger.

This lasted until shortly before Bianca's *quinceañera*, when Jesús changed his name to Walíd and married a *moro*'s daughter, and Bianca's mother delivered a lecture concerning the difference between what was proper for a child and what was proper for a young Christian woman with hopes of one day making a good marriage.

It was only a handful of years later that Bianca's father died, leaving a teenaged Pablo at the helm of his engineering business; and only Bianca's invisible assistance and the pity of a few old clients had kept contracts and money coming into the Nazario household.

By the time Pablo was old enough to think he could run the business himself, old enough to marry the daughter of a musical instrument maker from Tierra Ceniza, their mother was dead, Bianca was thirty, and even if her dowry had been half her father's business, there was not a Christian man in Río Pícaro who wanted it, or her.

And then one day Pablo told her about the *extrañado* contract that had been brought to the *ayuntamiento*, a contract that the *ayuntamiento* and the Guild had together forbidden the Christian engineers of Punta Aguila to bid on—a contract for a Spanish-speaking aeronautical engineer to travel a very long way from Río Pícaro and be paid a very large sum of money indeed.

Three months later Bianca was in Quito, boarding an elevator car. In her valise was a bootleg copy of her father's engineering system, and a contract with the factor of a starship called the *Caliph of Baghdad*, for passage to Sky.

4. The Killing Ground

The anemopter's destination was a *zaratán* called Encantada, smaller than the giant Finisterra but still nearly forty kilometers from nose to tail, and eight thousand meters from gray-white keel to forested crest. From a distance of a hundred kilometers, Encantada was like a forested mountain rising from a desert plain, the clear air under its keel as dreamlike as a mirage. On her pocket system, Bianca called up pictures from Sky's network of the alpine ecology that covered the hills and valleys of Encantada's flanks: hardy grasses and small warm-blooded creatures and tall evergreens with spreading branches, reminding her of the pines and redwoods in the mountains west of Río Pícaro.

For the last century or so Encantada had been keeping company with Zaratán Finisterra, holding its position above the larger beast's eastern flank. No one, apparently, knew the reason, and Fry—who, he being the expert, Bianca had expected to at least have a theory—didn't even seem to be interested in the question.

"They're beasts, Nazario," he said. "They don't do things for reasons. We only call them animals and not plants because they bleed when we cut them."

They were passing over Finisterra's southern slopes. Looking down, Bianca saw brighter, warmer greens, more shades than she could count, more than she had known existed, the green threaded through with bright ribbons of silver water. She saw the anemopter's shadow, a dark oblong that rode the slopes and ridges, ringed by brightness—the faint reflection of Sky's sun behind them.

And just before the shadow entered the larger darkness that was the shadow of Encantada, Bianca watched it ride over something else: a flat green space carved out of the jungle, a suspiciously geometric collection of shapes that could only be buildings, the smudge of chimney smoke.

"Fry—" she started to say.

Then the village, if that's what it was, was gone, hidden behind the next ridge.

"What?" said Fry.

"I saw—I thought I saw—"

"People?" asked Fry. "You probably did."

"But I thought Sky didn't have any native sentients. Who are they?"

"Humans, mostly," Fry said. "Savages. Refugees. Drug farmers. Five generations of escaped criminals, and their kids, and *their* kids." The naturalist shrugged. "Once in a while, if the Consilium's looking for somebody in particular, the wardens might stage a raid, just for show. The rest of the time, the wardens fly their dope, screw their women . . . and otherwise leave them alone."

"But where do they come from?" Bianca asked.

"Everywhere," Fry said with another shrug. "Humans have been in this part of space for a long, long time. This is one of those places people end up, you know? People with nowhere else to go. People who can't fall any farther."

Bianca shook her head, and said nothing.

The poachers' camp, on Encantada's eastern slope, was invisible until they were almost upon it, hidden from the wardens' satellite eyes by layers of projected camouflage. Close up, the illusion seemed flat, its artificiality obvious, but it was still not until the anemopter passed through the projection that the camp itself could be seen: a clear-cut swath a kilometer wide and three times as long, stretching from the lower slopes of Encantada's dorsal ridge down to the edge of the *zaratán*'s cliff-like flank. Near the edge, at one corner, there was a small cluster of prefabricated bungalows; but at first it seemed to Bianca that most of the space was wasted.

Then she saw the red churned into the brown mud of the cleared strip, saw the way the shape of the terrain suggested the imprint of a gigantic, elongated body.

The open space was for killing.

"Sky is very poor, Miss Nazario," said Valadez, over his shoulder.

The poacher boss looked to be about fifty, stocky, his hair still black and his olive skin well-tanned but pocked with tiny scars. His Spanish was a dialect Bianca had never heard before, strange and lush, its vowels rich, its *hs* breathy as Bianca's *js*, its *js* warm and liquid as the *ys* of an Argentine. When he said *fuck your mother*—and already, in the hour or so Bianca had been in the camp, she had heard him say it several times, though never yet to her—the *madre* came out *madri*.

About half of the poachers were human, but Valadez seemed to be the only one who spoke Spanish natively; the rest used Sky's dialect of bazaar Arabic. Valadez spoke that as well, better than Bianca did, but she had the sense that he learned it late in life. If he had a first name, he was keeping it to himself.

"There are things on Sky that people want," Valadez went on. "But the *people* of Sky have nothing of interest to anybody. The companies that mine the deep air pay some royalties. But mostly what people live on here is Consilium handouts."

The four of them—Bianca, Fry, and the *firija*, Ismaíl, who as well as being an anemopter pilot seemed to be Valadez' servant or business partner or bodyguard, or perhaps all three—were climbing the ridge above the poachers' camp. Below them workers, some human, some *firija*, a handful of other species, were setting up equipment: mobile machines that looked like they belonged on a construction site, pipes and cylindrical tanks reminiscent of a brewery or a refinery.

"I'm changing that, Miss Nazario." Valadez glanced over his shoulder at Bianca. "Off-world, there are people—like Ismaíl's people here"—he waved at the *firija*—"who like the idea of living on a floating island, and have the money to pay for one." He swept an arm, taking in the camp, the busy teams of workers. "With that money, I take boys out of the shantytowns of Sky's balloon stations and elevator gondolas. I give them tools, and teach them to kill beasts.

"To stop me—since they can't be bothered to do it themselves—the Consilium takes the same boys, gives them guns, and teaches them to kill men."

The poacher stopped and turned to face Bianca, jamming his hands into the pockets of his coat.

"Tell me, Miss Nazario—is one worse than the other?"

"I'm not here to judge you, Mr. Valadez," said Bianca. "I'm here to do a job."

Valadez smiled. "So you are."

He turned and continued up the slope. Bianca and the *firija* followed, Fry trailing behind. The path switchbacked through unfamiliar trees, dark, stunted, waxy-needled; these gave way to taller varieties, including some that Bianca would have sworn were ordinary pines and firs. She breathed deeply, enjoying the alpine breeze after the crowds-and-machines reek of *Transient Meridian's* teeming slums, the canned air of ships and anemopters.

"It smells just like home," she remarked. "Why is that?"

No once answered.

The ridge leveled off, and they came out into a cleared space, overlooking the camp. Spread out below them Bianca could see the airfield, the globular tanks and pipes of the poachers' little industrial plant, the bungalows in the distance—and, in between, the red-brown earth of the killing ground, stretching out to the cliff-edge and the bases of the nearest translucent fins.

"This is a good spot," Valadez declared. "Should be a good view from up here."

"A view of what?" said Fry.

The poacher didn't answer. He waved to Ismaíl, and the *firija* took a small folding stool out of a pocket, snapping it into shape with a flick of sinuous arms and setting it down behind him. Valadez sat.

And after a moment, the answer to Fry's question came up over the edge.

Bianca had not thought hardly at all about the killing of a *zaratán*, and when she had thought of it she had imagined something like the harpooning of a whale in ancient times, the great beast fleeing, pursued by the tiny harassing shapes of boats, gored by harpoons, sounding again and again, all the strength bleeding out of the beast until there was nothing left for it to do but wallow gasping on the surface and expire, noble and tragic. Now Bianca realized that for all their great size, the *zaratanes* were far weaker than any whale, far less able to fight or to escape or even—she sincerely hoped—to understand what was happening to them.

There was nothing noble about the way the nameless *zaratán* died. Anemopters landed men and aliens with drilling tools at the base of each hundred-meter fin, to bore through soil and scale and living flesh and cut the connecting nerves that controlled them. This took about fifteen minutes, and to Bianca there seemed to be something obscene in the way the paralyzed fins hung there afterwards, lifeless and limp. Thus crippled, the beast was pushed and pulled by aerial tugs—awkward machines, stubby and cylindrical, converted from the stationkeeping engines of vacuum balloons like *Transient*

Meridian—into position over Encantada's killing ground. Then the drilling teams moved in again, to the places marked for them ahead of time by seismic sensors and ultrasound, cutting this time through bone as well as flesh, to find the *zaratán's* brain.

When the charges the drilling teams had planted went off, a ripple went through the *zaratán's* body, a slow-motion convulsion that took nearly a minute to travel down the body's long axis, as the news of death passed from synapse to synapse; and Bianca saw flocks of birds started from the trees along the *zaratán's* back as if by an earthquake, which in a way she supposed this was. The carcass immediately began to pitch downward, the nose dropping— the result, Bianca realized, of sphincters relaxing one by one, all along the *zaratán's* length, venting hydrogen from the ballonets.

Then the forward edge of the keel fin hit the ground and crumpled, and the whole length of the dead beast, a hundred thousand tons of it, crashed down into the field; and even at that distance Bianca could hear the cracking of gargantuan bones.

She shivered, and glanced at her pocket system. The whole process, she was amazed to see, had taken less than half an hour.

"That's this trip paid for, whatever else happens," said Valadez. He turned to Bianca. "Mostly, though, I thought you should see this. Have you guessed yet what it is I'm paying you to do, Miss Nazario?"

Bianca shook her head. "Clearly you don't need an aeronautical engineer to do what you've just done." She looked down at the killing ground, where men and aliens and machines were already climbing over the *zaratán's* carcass, uprooting trees, peeling back skin and soil in great strips like bleeding boulevards. A wind had come up, blowing from the killing ground across the camp, bringing with it a smell that Bianca associated with butcher shops.

An engineering problem, she reminded herself, as she turned her back on the scene and faced Valadez. That's all this is.

"How are you going to get it out of here?" she asked.

"Cargo-lifter," said Valadez. "The *Lupita Jeréz*. A supply ship, diverted from one of the balloon stations."

The alien, Ismaíl, said: "Like fly anemopter make transatmospheric." The same fluting voice and broken Arabic. "Lifter plenty payload mass limit, but fly got make have packaging. Packaging for got make platform have stable." On the word *packaging* the *firija's* arms made an expressive gesture, like rolling something up into a bundle and tying it.

Bianca nodded hesitantly, hoping she understood. "And so you can only take the small ones," she said. "Right? Because there's only one place on Sky you'll find a stable platform that size: on the back of another *zaratán*."

"You have the problem in a nutshell, Miss Nazario," said Valadez. "Now, how would you solve it? How would you bag, say, Encantada here? How would you bag Finisterra?"

Fry said: "You want to take one *alive?*" His face was even more pale than usual, and Bianca noticed that he, too, had turned is back to the killing ground.

Valadez was still looking at Bianca, expectantly.

"He doesn't want it alive, Mr. Fry," she said, watching the poacher expectantly. "He wants it dead—but intact. You could take even Finisterra apart, and lift it piece by piece, but you'd need a thousand cargo-lifters to do it."

Valadez smiled.

"I've got another ship," he said. "Built for deep mining, outfitted as a mobile elevator station. Counterweighted. The ship itself isn't rated for atmosphere, but if you can get one of the big ones to the edge of space, we'll lower the skyhook, catch the beast, and catapult it into orbit. The buyer's arranged an FTL tug to take it from there."

Bianca made herself look back at the killing ground. The workers were freeing the bones, lifting them with aerial cranes and feeding them into the plant; for cleaning and preservation, she supposed. She turned back to Valadez.

"We should be able to do that, if the *zaratán's* body will stand up to the low pressure," she said. "But why go to all this trouble? I've seen the balloon stations. I've seen what you people can do with materials. How hard can it be to make an imitation *zaratán?*"

Valadez glanced at Ismaíl. The walker was facing the killing ground, but two of the alien's many eyes were watching the sky—and two more were watching Valadez. The poacher looked back at Bianca.

"An imitation's one thing, Miss Nazario; the real thing is something else. And worth a lot more, to the right buyer." He looked away again; not at Ismaíl this time, but up the slope, through the trees. "Besides," he added, "in this case I've got my own reasons."

"Ship come," Ismaíl announced.

Bianca looked and saw more of the *firija's* eyes turning upward. She followed their gaze, and at first saw only empty sky. Then the air around the descending *Lupita Jeréz* boiled into contrails, outlining the invisible ovoid shape of the ship's lifting fields.

"Time to get to work," said Valadez.

Bianca glanced toward the killing ground. A pink fog was rising to cover the work of the flensing crews.

The air was full of blood.

• • •

4. The aeronauts

Valadez's workers cleaned the nameless *zaratán's* bones one by one; they tanned the hide, and rolled it into bundles for loading aboard the *Lupita Jeréz*. That job, grotesque though it was, was the cleanest part of the work. What occupied most of the workers was the disposal of the unwanted parts, a much dirtier and more arduous job. Exotic internal organs the size of houses; tendons like braided, knotted bridge cables; ballonets large enough, each of them, to lift an ordinary dirigible; and hectares and hectares of pale, dead flesh. The poachers piled up the mess with earth-moving machines and shoveled it off the edge of the killing ground, a rain of offal falling into the clouds in a mist of blood, manna for the ecology of the deep air. They sprayed the killing ground with antiseptics, and the cool air helped to slow decay a little, but by the fourth day the butcher-shop smell had nonetheless given way to something worse.

Bianca's bungalow was one of the farthest out, only a few dozen meters from Encantada's edge, where the wind blew in from the open eastern sky, and she could turn her back on the slaughter to look out into clear air, dotted with the small, distant shapes of younger *zaratanes*. Even here, though, a kilometer and more upwind of the killing ground, the air carried a taint of spoiled meat. The sky was full of insects and scavenger birds, and there were always vermin underfoot.

Bianca spent most of her time indoors, where the air was filtered and the wet industrial sounds of the work muted. The bungalow was outfitted with all the mechanisms the *extrañados* used to make themselves comfortable, but while in the course of her journey Bianca had learned to operate these, she made little use of them. Besides her traveling chest—a gift from her older brother's wife, which served as armoire, desk, dresser and drafting table— the only furnishings were a woven carpet in the Lagos Grandes style, a hard little bed, and a single wooden chair, not very different from the ones in her room in Punta Aguila. Though those had been handmade, and these were simulations provided by the bungalow's machines.

The rest of the room was given over to the projected spaces of Bianca's engineering work. The tools Valadez had given her were slick and fast and factory-fresh, the state of somebody's art, somewhere; but what Bianca mostly found herself using was her pocket system's crippled copy of the Nazario family automation.

The system Bianca's father used to use, to calculate stresses in fabric and metal and wood, to model the flow of air over wings and the variation of pressure and temperature through gasbags, was six centuries old, a slow, patient, reliable thing that dated from before the founding of the London

Caliphate. It had aged along with the family, grown used to their quirks and to the strange demands of aviation in Rio Pícaro. Bianca's version of it, limited though it was, at least didn't balk at control surfaces supported by muscle and bone, at curves not aerodynamically smooth but fractally complex with grasses and trees at hanging vines. If the *zaratanes* had been machines, they would have been marvels of engineering, with their internal networks of gasbags and ballonets, their reservoir-sized ballast bladders full of collected rainwater, their great delicate fins. The *zaratanes* were beyond the poachers' systems' stubborn, narrow-minded comprehension; for all their speed and flash, the systems sulked like spoiled children whenever Bianca tried to use them to do something their designers had not expected her to do.

Which she was doing, all the time. She was working out how to draw up Leviathan with a hook.

"Miss Nazario."

Bianca started. She had yet to grow used to these *extrañado* telephones that never rang, but only spoke to her out of the air, or perhaps out of her own head.

"Mr. Valadez," she said, after a moment.

"Whatever you're doing, drop it," said Valadez's voice. "You and Fry. I'm sending a 'mopter for you."

"I'm working," said Bianca. "I don't know what Fry's doing."

"This *is* work," said Valadez. "Five minutes."

A change in the quality of the silence told Bianca that Valadez had hung up. She sighed; then stood, stretched, and started to braid her hair.

The anemopter brought them up over the dorsal ridge, passing between two of the great translucent fins. At this altitude, Encantada's body was clear of vegetation; Bianca looked down on hectares of wind-blasted gray hide, dusted lightly with snow. They passed within a few hundred meters of one of the huge spars that anchored the after fin's leading edge: a kilometers-high pillar of flesh, teardrop in cross-section and at least a hundred meters thick. The trailing edge of the next fin, by contrast, flashed by in an instant, and Bianca had only a brief impression of a silk-supple membrane, veined with red, clear as dirty glass.

"What do you think he wants?" Fry asked.

"I don't know." She nodded her head toward the *firija* behind them at the steering console. "Did you ask the pilot?"

"I tried," Fry said. "Doesn't speak Arabic."

Bianca shrugged. "I suppose we'll find out soon enough."

Then they were coming down again, down the western slope. In front of Bianca was the dorsal ridge of Zaratán Finisterra. Twenty kilometers away and blue with haze, it nonetheless rose until it seemed to cover a third of the sky.

Bianca looked out at it, wondering again what kept Encantada and Finisterra so close; but then the view was taken away, and they were coming down between the trees, into a shady, ivy-filled creekbed somewhere not far from Encantada's western edge. There was another anemopter already there, and a pair of aerial tugs—and a whitish mass that dwarfed all of these, sheets and ribbons of pale material hanging from the branches and draped over the ivy, folds of it damming the little stream.

With an audible splash, the anemopter set down, the ramps lowered, and Bianca stepped off, into cold, ankle-deep water that made her glad of her knee-high boots. Fry followed, gingerly.

"You!" called Valadez, pointing at Fry from the deck of the other anemopter. "Come here. Miss Nazario—I'd like you to have a look at that balloon."

"Balloon?"

Valadez gestured impatiently downstream, and suddenly Bianca saw the white material for the shredded, deflated gasbag it was; and saw, too, that there was a basket attached to it, lying on its side, partially submerged in the middle of the stream. Ismaíl was standing over it, waving.

Bianca splashed over to the basket. It actually *was* a basket, two meters across and a meter and a half high, woven from strips of something like bamboo or rattan. The gasbag—this was obvious, once Bianca saw it up close— had been made from one of the ballonets of a *zaratán*, a *zaratán* younger and smaller even than the one Bianca had seen killed; it had been tanned, but inexpertly, and by someone without access to the sort of industrial equipment the poachers used.

Bianca wondered about the way the gasbag was torn up. The tissues of the *zaratánes*, she knew, were very strong. A hydrogen explosion?

"Make want fly got very bad," Ismaíl commented, as Bianca came around to the open side of the basket.

"They certainly did," she said.

In the basket there were only some wool blankets and some empty leather waterbags, probably used both for drinking water and for ballast. The lines used to control the vent flaps were all tangled together, and tangled, too, with the lines that secured the gasbag to the basket, but Bianca could guess how they had worked. No stove. It seemed to have been a pure hydrogen balloon; and why not, she thought, with all the hydrogen anyone could want free from the nearest *zaratán's* vent valves?

"Where did it come from?" she asked.

Ismaíl rippled his arms in a way that Bianca guessed was meant to be an imitation of a human shrug. One of his eyes glanced downstream.

Bianca fingered the material of the basket: tough, woody fiber. Tropical, from a climate warmer than Encantada's. She followed Ismaíl's glance. The trees hid the western horizon, but she knew, if she could see beyond them, what would be there.

Aloud, she said: "Finisterra."

She splashed back to the anemopters. Valadez's hatch was open.

"I'm telling you," Fry was saying, "I don't know her!"

"Fuck off, Fry," Valadez said as Bianca stepped into the cabin. "Look at her ID."

The *her* in question was a young woman in with short black hair and sallow skin, wearing tan off-world cottons like Fry's under a colorful homespun *serape*; and at first Bianca was not sure the woman was alive, because the man next to her on Valadez's floor, also in homespun, was clearly dead, his eyes half-lidded, his olive skin gone muddy gray.

The contents of their pockets were spread out on a low table. As Bianca was taking in the scene, Fry bent down and picked up a Consilium-style ID tag.

" 'Edith Dinh,' " he read. He tossed the tag back and looked at Valadez. "So?"

" 'Edith Dinh, *Consilium Ethnological Service*,' " Valadez growled. "Issued Shawwal '43. *You* were here with the *Ecological* Service from Rajab '42 to Muharram '46. Look again!"

Fry turned away.

"All right!" he said. "Maybe—maybe I met her once or twice."

"So," said Valadez. "Now we're getting somewhere. Who the hell is she? And what's she doing *here*?"

"She's . . . " Fry glanced at the woman and then quickly looked away. "I don't know. I think she was a population biologist or something. There was a group working with the, you know, the natives—"

"There aren't any natives on Sky," said Valadez. He prodded the dead man with the toe of his boot. "You mean these *cabrones*?"

Fry nodded. "They had this 'sustainable development' program going—farming, forestry. Teaching them how to live on Finisterra without killing it."

Valadez looked skeptical. "If the Consilium wanted to stop them from killing Finisterra, why didn't they just send in the wardens?"

"Interdepartmental politics. The *zaratanes* were EcoServ's responsibility; the n—I mean, the *inhabitants* were EthServ's." Fry shrugged. "You know the wardens. They'd have taken bribes from anyone who could afford it, and shot the rest."

"Damn right I know the wardens." Valadez scowled. "So instead EthServ sent in these do-gooders to teach them to make balloons?"

Fry shook his head. "I don't know anything about that."

"Miss Nazario? Tell me about that balloon."

"It's a hydrogen balloon, I think. Probably filled from some *zaratán's* external vents." She shrugged. "It looks like the sort of thing I'd expect someone living out here to build, if that's what you mean."

Valadez nodded.

"But," Bianca added, "I can't tell you why it crashed."

Valadez snorted. "I don't need you to tell me that," he said. "It crashed because we shot it down." Pitching his voice for the anemopter's communication system, he called out: "Ismaíl!"

Bianca tried to keep the shock from showing on her face, and after a moment, she had regained her composure. *You knew they were criminals when you took their money,* she told herself.

The *firija's* eyes came around the edge of the doorway.

"Yes?"

"Tell the tug crews to pack that thing up," said Valadez. "Every piece, every scrap. Pack it up and drop it into clear air."

The alien's walking machine clambered into the cabin. Its legs bent briefly, making a little bob like a curtsey.

"Yes." Ismaíl gestured at the bodies of the dead man and the unconscious woman. Several of the *firija's* eyes met Valadez's. "These two what do?" he asked.

"Them, too," said Valadez. "Lash them into the basket."

The *firija* made another bob, and started to bend down to pick them up.

Bianca looked down at the two bodies, both of them, the dead man and the unconscious woman, looking small and thin and vulnerable. She glanced at Fry, whose eyes were fixed on the floor, his lips pressed together in a thin line.

Then she looked over at Valadez, who was methodically sweeping the balloonists' effects into a pile, as if neither Bianca nor Fry was present.

"No," she said; and Ismaíl stopped, and straightened up.

"What?" said Valadez.

"*No,*" Bianca repeated.

"You want her bringing the wardens down on us?" Valadez demanded.

"That's murder, Mr. Valadez," Bianca said. "I won't be a party to it."

The poacher's eyes narrowed. He gestured at the dead man.

"You're already an accessory," he said.

"After the fact," Bianca replied evenly. She kept her eyes on Valadez.

The poacher looked at the ceiling. "Fuck your mother," he muttered. He looked down at the two bodies, and at Ismaíl, and then over at Bianca. He sighed, heavily.

"All right," he said to the *firija*. "Take the live one back to the camp. Secure a bungalow, one of the ones out by the edge"—he glanced at Bianca—"and lock her in it. Okay?"

"Okay," said Ismaíl. "Dead one what do?"

Valadez looked at Bianca again. "The dead one," he said, "goes in the basket."

Bianca looked at the dead man again, wondering what bravery or madness had brought him aboard that fragile balloon, and wondering what he would have thought if he had known that the voyage would end this way, with his body tumbling down into the deep air. She supposed he must have known there was a chance of it.

After a moment, she nodded, once.

"Right," said Valadez. "Now get back to work, damn it."

5. The city of the dead

The anemopter that brought Bianca and Fry over the ridge took them back. Fry was silent, hunched, his elbows on his knees, staring at nothing. What fear or guilt was going through his mind, Bianca couldn't guess.

After a little while she stopped watching him. She thought about the Finisterran balloon, so simple, so fragile, making her father's wood-and-silk craft look as sophisticated as the *Lupita Jeréz*. She took out her pocket system, sketched a simple globe and basket, then erased them.

Make want fly very bad, Ismaíl the *firija* had said. Why?

Bianca undid the erasure, bringing her sketch back. She drew the spherical balloon out into a blunt torpedo, round at the nose, tapering to a point behind. Added fins. An arrangement of pulleys and levers, allowing them to be controlled from the basket. A propeller, powered by—she had to think for a little while—by an alcohol-fueled engine, carved from *zaratán* bones . . .

The anemopter was landing. Bianca sighed and again erased the design. Why?

The *firija* guard outside Edith Dinh's bungalow didn't seem to speak Arabic or Spanish, or in fact any human language at all. Bianca wondered if the choice was deliberate, the guard chosen by Valadez as a way of keeping a kind of solitary confinement.

Or was the guard Valadez's choice at all? she wondered suddenly, and shivered, looking at the meter-long weapon cradled in the alien's furred arms.

Then she squared her shoulders and approached the bungalow. Wordlessly, she waved the valise she was carrying, as if by it her reason for being there were made customary and obvious.

The alien said something in its own fluting language—whether a reply to her, or a request for instructions from some unseen listener, Bianca couldn't tell. Either those instructions were to let her pass, though, or by being seen in Valadez's company she had acquired some sort of reflected authority; because the *firija* lifted its weapon and, as the bungalow's outer door slid open, motioned for her to enter. The inner door was already open.

"¿*Hóla?*" Bianca called out, tentatively, and immediately felt like an idiot.

But the answer came:

"*Aqui.*"

The interior layout of the bungalow was the same as Bianca's. The voice came from the sitting room, and Bianca found Dinh there, still wearing the clothes she had on when they found her, sitting with her knees drawn up, staring out the east window into the sky. The east was dark with rain clouds, and far below, Bianca could see flashes of lightning.

"*Salaam aleikum,*" said Bianca, taking refuge in the formality of the Arabic.

"*Aleikum as-salaam,*" Dinh replied. She glanced briefly at Bianca and looked away; then looked back again. In a Spanish that was somewhere between Valadez's strange accent and the mechanical fluency of Fry's language module, she said: "You're not from Finisterra."

"No," said Bianca, giving up on the Arabic. "I'm from Rio Pícaro—from Earth. My name is Nazario, Bianca Nazario y Arenas."

"Edith Dinh."

Dinh stood up. There was an awkward moment, where Bianca was not sure whether to bow or curtsey or give Dinh her hand. She settled for proffering the valise.

"I brought you some things," she said. "Clothes, toiletries."

Dinh looked surprised. "Thanks," she said, taking the valise and looking inside.

"Are they feeding you? I could bring you some food."

"The kitchen still works," said Dinh. She held up a white packet. "And these?"

"Sanitary napkins," said Bianca.

"Sanitary . . . ?" Color rose to Dinh's face. "Oh. That's all right. I've got implants." She dropped the packet back in the valise and closed it.

Bianca looked away, feeling her own cheeks blush in turn. Damned *extrañados*, she thought. "I'd better—" be going, she started to say.

"Please—" said Dinh.

The older woman and the younger stood there for a moment, looking at each other, and Bianca suddenly wondered what impulse had brought her here, whether curiosity or Christian charity or simply a moment of loneliness, weakness. Of course she'd had to stop Valadez from killing the girl, but this was clearly a mistake.

"Sit," Dinh said. "Let me get you something. Tea. Coffee."

"I—All right." Bianca sat, slowly, perching on the edge of one of the too-soft *extrañado* couches. "Coffee," she said.

The coffee was very dark, and sweeter than Bianca liked it, flavored with something like condensed milk. She was glad to have it, regardless, glad to have something to look at and something to occupy her hands.

"You don't look like a poacher," Dinh said.

"I'm an aeronautical engineer," Bianca said. "I'm doing some work for them." She looked down at her coffee, took a sip, and looked up. "What about you? Fry said you're a biologist of some kind. What were you doing in that balloon?"

She couldn't tell whether the mention of Fry's name had registered, but Dinh's mouth went thin. She glanced out the west window.

Bianca followed her glance and saw the guard, slumped in its walker, watching the two women with one eye each. She wondered again whether Valadez was really running things, and then whether the *firija's* ignorance of human language was real or feigned—and whether, even if it *was* real, someone less ignorant might be watching and listening, unseen.

Then she shook her head and looked back at Dinh, waiting.

"Finisterra's falling," Dinh said eventually. "Dying, maybe. It's too big; it's losing lift. It's fallen more than fifty meters in the last year alone."

"That doesn't make sense," Bianca said. "The lift-to-weight ratio of an aerostat depends on the ratio of volume to surface area. A larger *zaratán* should be *more* efficient, not less. And even if it *does* lose lift, it should only fall until it reaches a new equilibrium."

"It's not a *machine*," Dinh said. "It's a living creature."

Bianca shrugged. "Maybe it's old age, then," she said. "Everything has to die sometime."

"Not like this," Dinh said. She set down her coffee and turned to face Bianca fully. "Look. We don't know who built Sky, or how long ago, but it's obviously artificial. A gas giant with a nitrogen-oxygen atmosphere? That *doesn't happen*. And the Earthlike biology—the *zaratánes* are DNA-based, did you know that? The whole place is astronomically unlikely; if the Phenomenological Service had its way, they'd just quarantine the entire system, and damn Sky and everybody on it.

"The archipelago ecology is as artificial as everything else. Whoever designed it must have been very good; post-human, probably, maybe even post-singularity. It's a robust equilibrium, full of feedback mechanisms, ways to correct itself. But we, us ordinary humans and human-equivalents, we've"— she made a helpless gesture—"*fucked it up*. You know why Encantada's stayed here so long? Breeding, that's why . . . or maybe 'pollination' would be a better way to put it . . . "

She looked over at Bianca.

"The death of an old *zaratán* like Finisterra should be balanced by the birth of dozens, hundreds. But you, those bastards you work for, you've killed them all."

Bianca let the implication of complicity slide. "All right, then," she said. "Let's hear your plan."

"What?"

"Your *plan*," Bianca repeated. "For Finisterra. How are you going to save it?"

Dinh stared at her for a moment, then shook her head. "I can't," she said. She stood up, and went to the east window. Beyond the sheet of rain that now poured down the window the sky was deep mauve shading to indigo, relieved only by the lightning that sparked in the deep and played across the fins of the distant *zaratanes* of the archipelago's outer reaches. Dinh put her palm flat against the diamond pane.

"I *can't* save Finisterra," she said quietly. "I just want to stop you *hijos de puta* from doing this again."

Now Bianca was stung. "*Hija de puta*, yourself," she said. "You're killing them, too. Killing them and making balloons out of them, how is that better?"

Dinh turned back. "One *zaratán* the size of the one they're slaughtering out there right now would keep the Finisterrans in balloons for a hundred years," she said. "The only way to save the archipelago is to make the *zaratanes* more valuable alive than dead—and the only value a live *zaratán* has, on Sky, is as living space."

"You're trying to get the Finisterrans to colonize the other *zaratanes*?" Bianca asked. "But why should they? What's in it for them?"

"I told you," Dinh said. "Finisterra's dying." She looked out the window, down into the depths of the storm, both hands pressed against the glass. "Do you know how falling into Sky kills you, Bianca? First, there's the pressure. On the slopes of Finisterra, where the people live, it's a little more than a thousand millibars. Five kilometers down, under Finisterra's keel, it's double that. At two thousand millibars you can still breathe the air. At three thousand nitrogen narcosis sets in—'rapture of the deep,' they used to call it. At four thousand, the partial pressure of oxygen alone is enough to make your lungs bleed."

She stepped away from the window and looked at Bianca.

"But you'll never live to suffer that," she said, "because of the heat. Every thousand meters the average temperature rises six or seven degrees. Here it's about fifteen. Under Finisterra's keel it's closer to fifty. Twenty kilometers down, the air is hot enough to boil water."

Bianca met her gaze steadily. "I can think of worse ways to die," she said.

"There are seventeen thousand people on Finisterra," said Dinh. "Men, women, children, old people. There's a town—they call it the Lost City, *la ciudad perdida*. Some of the families on Finisterra can trace their roots back six generations." She gave a little laugh, with no humor in it. "They should call it *la ciudad muerta*. They're the walking dead, all seventeen thousand of them. Even though no one's alive on Finisterra today will live to see it die. Already the crops are starting to fail. Already more old men and old women die every summer, as the summers get hotter and drier. The children of the children who are born today will have to move up into the hills as it starts to get too hot to grow crops on the lower slopes; but the soil isn't as rich up there, so many of those crops will fail, too. And *their* children's children . . . won't live to be old enough to have children of their own."

"Surely someone will rescue them before then," Bianca said.

"Who?" Dinh asked. "The Consilium? Where would they put them? The vacuum balloons and the elevator stations are already overcrowded. As far as the rest of Sky is concerned, the Finisterrans are 'malcontents' and 'criminal elements.' Who's going to take them in?"

"Then Valadez is doing them a favor," Bianca said.

Dinh started. "*Emmanuel Valadez* is running your operation?"

"It's *not my* operation," Bianca said, trying to keep her voice level. "And I didn't ask his first name."

Dinh fell into the window seat. "Of course it would be," she said. "Who else would they . . . " She trailed off, looking out the west window, toward the killing ground.

Then, suddenly, she turned back to Bianca.

"What do you mean, *doing them a favor*?" she said.

"Finisterra," Bianca said. "He's poaching Finisterra."

Dinh stared at her. "My God, Bianca! What about the people?"

"What about them?" asked Bianca. "They'd be better off somewhere else— you said that yourself."

"And what makes you think Valadez will evacuate them?"

"He's a *thief*, not a mass murderer."

Dinh gave her a withering look. "He *is* a murderer, Bianca. His father was a warden, his mother was the wife of the *alcalde* of Ciudad Perdida. He killed his own stepfather, two uncles, and three brothers. They were going to execute him—throw him over the edge—but a warden airboat picked him up. He spent two years with them, then killed his sergeant and three other wardens, stole their ship and sold it for a ticket off-world. He's probably the most wanted man on Sky."

She shook her head and, unexpectedly, gave Bianca a small smile.

"You didn't know any of that when you took the job, did you?"

Her voice was full of pity. It showed on her face as well, and suddenly Bianca couldn't stand to look at it. She got up and went to the east window. The rain was lighter now, the lightning less frequent.

She thought back to her simulations, her plans for lifting Finisterra up into the waiting embrace of the skyhook: the gasbags swelling, the *zaratán* lifting, first slowly and then with increasing speed toward the upper reaches of Sky's atmosphere. But now her inner vision was not the ghost-shape of a projection but a living image—trees cracking in the cold, water freezing, blood boiling from the ground in a million, million tiny hemorrhages.

She saw her mother's house in Punta Aguila—her sister-in-law's house, now: saw its windows rimed with frost, the trees in the courtyard gone brown and sere. She saw the Mercado de los Maculados beneath a blackening sky, the awnings whipped away by a thin wind, ice-cold, bone-dry.

He killed that Finisterran balloonist, she thought. He was ready to kill Dinh. He's capable of murder.

Then she shook her head.

Killing one person, or two, to cover up a crime, was murder, she thought. Killing seventeen thousand people by deliberate asphyxiation—men, women, and children—wasn't murder, it was genocide.

She took her cup of coffee from the table, took a sip and put it down again.

"Thank you for the coffee," she said, and turned to go.

"How can you just let him do this?" Dinh demanded. "How can you *help him do this*?"

Bianca turned on her. Dinh was on her feet; her fists were clenched, and she was shaking. Bianca stared her down, her face as cold and blank as she could make it. She waited until Dinh turned away, throwing herself into a chair, staring out the window.

"I saved your life," Bianca told her. "That was more than I needed to do. Even if I *did* believe that Valadez meant to kill every person on Finisterra, *which I don't*, that wouldn't make it my problem."

Dinh turned farther away.

"Listen to me," Bianca said, "because I'm only going to explain this once." She waited until Dinh, involuntarily, turned back to face her.

"This job is my one chance," Bianca said. "*This job* is what I'm here to do. I'm not here to save the world. Saving the world is a luxury for spoiled *extrañado* children like you and Fry. It's a luxury I don't have."

She went to the door, and knocked on the window to signal the *firija* guard.

"I'll get you out of here if I can," she added, over her shoulder. "But that's all I can do. I'm sorry."

Dinh hadn't moved.

As the *firija* opened the door, Bianca heard Dinh stir.

"*Erasmus* Fry?" she asked. "The naturalist?"

"That's right." Bianca glanced back, and saw Dinh looking out the window again.

"I'd like to see him," Dinh said.

"I'll let him know," said Bianca.

The guard closed the door behind her.

6. The face in the mirror

There was still lightning playing along Encantada's dorsal ridge, but here on the eastern edge the storm had passed. A clean, electric smell was in the air, relief from the stink of the killing ground. Bianca returned to her own bungalow through a rain that had died to sprinkles.

She called Fry.

"What is it?" he asked.

"Miss Dinh," Bianca said. "She wants to see you."

There was silence on the other end. Then:

"You told her I was here?"

"Sorry," Bianca said, insincerely. "It just slipped out."

More silence.

"You knew her better than you told Valadez, didn't you," she said.

She heard Fry sigh. "Yes."

"She seemed upset," Bianca said. "You should go see her."

Fry sighed again, but said nothing.

"I've got work to do," Bianca said. "I'll talk to you later."

She ended the call.

She was supposed to make a presentation tomorrow, to Valadez and some of the poachers' crew bosses, talking about what they would be doing to Finisterra. It was mostly done; the outline was straightforward, and the visuals could be auto-generated from the design files. She opened the projection file, and poked at it for a little while, but found it hard to concentrate.

Suddenly to Bianca her clothes smelled of death, of Dinh's dead companion and the slaughtered *zaratán* and the death she'd spared Dinh from and the eventual deaths of all the marooned Finisterrans. She stripped them off and threw them in the recycler; bathed, washed her hair, changed into a nightgown.

They should call it la ciudad muerta.

Even though no one who's alive on Finisterra today will live to see it die.

She turned off the light, Dinh's words echoing in her head, and tried to sleep. But she couldn't; she couldn't stop thinking. Thinking about what it felt like to be forced to live on, when all you had to look forward to was death.

She knew that feeling very well.

What Bianca had on Pablo's wife Mélia, the instrument-maker's daughter, was ten years of age, and a surreptitious technical education. What Mélia had on Bianca was a keen sense of territory, and the experience of growing up in a house full of sisters. Bianca continued to live in the house after Mélia moved in, even though it was Mélia's house now, and continued, without credit, to help her brother with the work that came in. But she retreated over the years, step by step, until the line was drawn at the door of the fourth-floor room that had been hers ever since she was a girl, and buried herself in her blueprints and her calculations, and tried to pretend she didn't know what was happening.

And then there was the day she met her *other* sister-in-law. Her *moro* sister-in-law. In the Mercado de los Maculados, where the aliens and the *extrañados* came to sell their trinkets and their medicines; a dispensation from the *ayuntamiento* had recently opened it to Christians.

Zahra al-Halim, a successful architect, took Bianca to her home, where Bianca ate caramels and drank blackberry tea and saw her older brother for the first time in more than twenty years, and tried very hard to call him Walíd and not Jesús. Here was a world—Bianca sensed; her brother and his wife were very discreet—that could be hers, too, if she wanted it. But like Jesús/Walíd, she would have to give up her old world to have it. Even if she remained a Christian she would never see the inside of a church again. And she would still never be accepted by the engineers' guild.

She went back to the Nazario house that evening, ignoring the barbed questions from Mélia about how she had spent her day; she went back to her room, with its blueprints and its models, and the furnishings she'd had all her life. She tried for a little while to work, but was unable to muster the concentration she needed to interface with the system.

Instead she found herself looking into the mirror.

And looking into the mirror Bianca focused not on the fragile trapped shapes of the flying machines tacked to the wall behind her, spread out and pinned down like so many chloroformed butterflies, but on her own tired face, the stray wisps of dry, brittle hair, the lines that years of captivity had made across her forehead and around her eyes. And, meeting those eyes, it seemed to Bianca that she was looking not into the mirror but down through the years of her future, a long, straight, narrow corridor without doors or branches, and that the eyes she was meeting at the end of it were the eyes of Death, Bianca's own, *su propria Muerte*, personal, personified.

Bianca got out of bed, turning on the lights. She picked up her pocket system. She wondered if she should call the wardens.

Instead she un-erased, yet again, the sketch she'd made earlier of the simple alcohol-powered dirigible. She used the Nazario family automation to fill it out with diagrams and renderings, lists of materials, building instructions, maintenance and pre-flight checklists.

It wasn't much, but it was better than Dinh's balloon.

Now she needed a way for Dinh to get it to the Finisterrans.

For that—thinking as she did so that there was some justice in it—she turned back to the system Valadez had given her. This was the sort of work the *extrañado* automation had been made for, no constraints other than those imposed by function, every trick of exotic technology available to be used. It was a matter of minutes for Bianca to sketch out her design; an hour or so to refine it, to trim away the unnecessary pieces until what remained was small enough to fit in the valise she'd left with Dinh. The only difficult part was getting the design automation to talk to the bungalow's fabricator, which was meant for clothes and furniture and domestic utensils. Eventually she had to use her pocket system to go out on Sky's local net—hoping as she did so that Valadez didn't have anyone monitoring her—and spend her own funds to contract the conversion out to a consulting service, somewhere out on one of the elevator gondolas.

Eventually she got it done, though. The fabricator spit out a neat package, which Bianca stuffed under the bed. Tomorrow she could get the valise back and smuggle the package to Dinh, along with the dirigible designs.

But first she had a presentation to make to Valadez. She wondered what motivated him. Nothing so simple as money—she was sure of that, even if she had trouble believing he was the monster Dinh had painted him to be. Was it revenge he was after? Revenge on his family, revenge on his homeland?

That struck Bianca a little too close to home.

She sighed, and turned out the lights.

7. The professionals

By morning the storm had passed and the sky was blue again, but the inside of Valadez' bungalow was dark, to display the presenters' projections to better advantage. Chairs for Valadez and the human crew bosses were arranged in a rough semicircle; with them were the aliens whose anatomy permitted them to sit down. Ismaíl and the other *firija* stood in the back, their curled arms and the spindly legs of their machines making their silhouettes look, to Bianca, incongruously like those of potted plants.

Then the fronds stirred, suddenly menacing, and Bianca shivered. Who was really in charge?

No time to worry about that now. She straightened up and took out her pocket system.

"In a moment," she began, pitching her voice to carry to the back of the room, "Mr. Fry will be going over the *zaratán's* metabolic processes, and our plans to stimulate the internal production of hydrogen. What I'm going to be talking about is the engineering work required to make that extra hydrogen do what we need it to do."

Bianca's pocket system projected the shape of a hundred-kilometer *zaratán*, not Finisterra or any other particular individual but rather an archetype, a sort of Platonic ideal. Points of pink light brightened all across the projected *zaratán's* back, each indicating the position of a sphincter that would have to be cut out and replaced with a mechanical valve.

"Our primary concern during the preparation phase has to be these external vents. However, we also need to consider the internal trim and ballast valves . . . "

As she went on, outlining the implants and grafts, surgeries and mutilations needed to turn a living *zaratán* into an animatronic corpse, a part of her was amazed at her own presumption, amazed at the strong, confident, professional tone she was taking.

It was almost as if she were a real engineer.

The presentation came to a close. Bianca drew in a deep breath, trying to maintain her veneer of professionalism. This part wasn't in her outline.

"And then, finally, there is the matter of evacuation," she said.

In the back of the room, Ismaíl stirred. "Evacuation?" he asked—the first word anyone had uttered through the whole presentation.

Bianca cleared her throat. Red stars appeared along the imaginary *zaratán's* southeastern edge, approximating the locations of Ciudad Perdida and the smaller Finisterran villages.

"Finisterra has a population of between fifteen and twenty thousand, most of them concentrated in these settlements here," she began. "Using a ship the size of the *Lupita Jeréz*, it should take roughly—"

"Not your problem, Miss Nazario." Valadez waved a hand. "In any case, there won't be any evacuations."

Bianca looked at him, appalled, and it must have shown on her face, because Valadez laughed.

"Don't look at me like that, Miss Nazario. We'll set up field domes over Ciudad Perdida and the central pueblos, to tide them over till we get them where they're going. If they keep their heads they should be fine." He laughed again. "Fucking hell," he said, shaking his head. "What did you think this was about? You didn't think we were going to kill twenty thousand people, did you?"

Bianca didn't answer. She shut the projection off and sat down, putting her pocket system away. Her heart was racing.

"Right," said Valadez. "Nice presentation, Miss Nazario. Mr. Fry?"

Fry stood up. "Okay," he said. "Let me—" He patted his pockets. "I, ah, I think I must have left my system in my bungalow."

Valadez sighed.

"We'll wait," he said.

The dark room was silent. Bianca tried to take slow, deep breaths. Mother of God, she thought, thank you for not letting me do anything stupid.

In the next moment she doubted herself. Dinh had been so sure. How could Bianca know whether Valadez was telling the truth?

There was no way to know, she decided. She'd just have to wait and see.

Fry came back in, breathless.

"Ah, it wasn't—"

The voice that interrupted him was loud enough that at first it was hardly recognizable as a voice; it was only a wall of sound, seeming to come from the air itself, echoing and reechoing endlessly across the camp.

"THIS IS AN ILLEGAL ENCAMPMENT," it said, in bazaar Arabic. "ALL PERSONNEL IN THE ENCAMPMENT WILL ASSEMBLE ON OPEN GROUND AND SURRENDER TO THE PARK WARDENS IN AN ORDERLY FASHION. ANY PERSONS CARRYING WEAPONS WILL BE PRESUMED TO BE RESISTING ARREST AND WILL BE DEALT WITH ACCORDINGLY. ANY VEHICLE ATTEMPTING TO LEAVE THE ENCAMPMENT WILL BE DESTROYED. YOU HAVE FIVE MINUTES TO COMPLY."

The announcement repeated itself: first in the fluting language of the *firija*, then in Miami Spanish, then as a series of projected alien glyphs, logograms and semagrams. Then the Arabic started again.

"Fuck your mother," said Valadez grimly.

All around Bianca, poachers were gathering weapons. In the back of the room, the *firija* were having what looked like an argument, arms waving, voices raised in a hooting, atonal cacophony.

"*What do we do?*" Fry shouted, over the wardens' announcement.

"Get out of here," said Valadez.

"Make fight!" said Ismaíl, turning several eyes from the *firija* discussion.

"Isn't that *resisting arrest*?" asked Bianca.

Valadez laughed harshly. "Not shooting back isn't going to save you," he said. "The wardens aren't the Phenomenological Service. They're not civilized Caliphate cops. *Killed while resisting arrest* is what they're all about. Believe me—I used to be one."

Taking a surprisingly small gun from inside his jacket, he kicked open the door and was gone.

Around the *Lupita Jeréz* was a milling knot of people, human and otherwise, some hurrying to finish the loading, others simply fighting to get aboard.

Something large and dark, and fast, passed over the camp, and there was a white flash from the cargo-lifter, and screams.

In the wake of the dark thing came a sudden sensation of heaviness, as if the flank of Encantada were the deck of a ship riding a rogue wave, leaping up beneath Bianca's feet. Her knees buckled and she was thrown to the ground, pressed into the grass by twice, three times her normal weight.

The feeling passed as quickly as the wardens' dark vehicle, and Ismaíl, whose walker had kept its footing, helped Bianca up.

"What was *that*?" Bianca demanded, bruises making her wince as she tried to brush the dirt and grass from her skirts.

"Antigravity ship," Ismaíl said. "Same principle like starship wave propagation drive."

"*Antigravity?*" Bianca stared after the ship, but it was already gone, over Encantada's dorsal ridge. "If you *coños* have antigravity, then why in God's name have we been sitting here playing with catapults and balloons?"

"Make very expensive," said Ismaíl. "Minus two suns exotic mass, same like starship." The *firija* waved two of its free eyes. "Why do? Plenty got cheap way to fly."

Bianca realized that despite the remarks Valadez had made on the poverty of Sky, she had been thinking of all *extrañados* and aliens—with their ships and machines, their familiar way with sciences that in Rio Pícaro were barely more than a whisper of forbidden things hidden behind the walls of the rich *moros'* palaces—as wealthy, and powerful, and free. Now, feeling like a fool for not having understood sooner, she realized that between the power of the Consilium and people like Valadez there was a gap as wide as, if not wider than, the gap between those rich *moros* and the most petty Ali Baba in the back streets of Punta Aguila.

She glanced toward the airfield. Aerial tugs were lifting off; anemopters were blurring into motion. But as she watched, one of the tugs opened up into a ball of green fire. An anemopter made it as far as the killing ground before being hit by something that made its static fields crawl briefly with purple lightnings and then collapse, as the craft's material body crashed down in an explosion of earth.

And all the while the wardens' recorded voice was everywhere and nowhere, repeating its list of instructions and demands.

"Not any more, we don't," Bianca said to Ismaíl. "We'd better run."

The *firija* raised its gun. "First got kill prisoner."

"*What?*"

But Ismaíl was already moving, the mechanical legs of the walker sure-footed on the broken ground, taking long, swift strides, no longer comical but frighteningly full of purpose.

Bianca struggled after the *firija*, but quickly fell behind. The surface of the killing ground was rutted and scarred, torn by the earth-moving equipment used to push the offal of the gutted *zaratanes* over the edge. Bianca supposed grasses had covered it once, but now there was only mud and old blood. Only the certainty that going back would be as bad as going forward kept Bianca moving, slipping and stumbling in reeking muck that was sometimes ankle-deep.

By the time she got to Dinh's bungalow, Ismaíl was already gone. The door was ajar.

Maybe the wardens rescued her, Bianca thought; but she couldn't make herself believe it.

She went inside, moving slowly.

"Edith?"

No answer; not that Bianca had really expected any.

She found her in the kitchen, face down, feet toward the door as if she had been shot while trying to run, or hide. From three meters away Bianca could see the neat, black, fist-sized hole in the small of Dinh's back. She felt no need to get closer.

Fry's pocket system was on the floor in the living room, as Bianca had known it would be.

"You should have waited," Bianca said to the empty room. "You should have trusted me."

She found her valise in Dinh's bedroom, and emptied the contents onto the bed. Dinh did not seem to have touched any of them.

Bianca's eyes stung with tears. She glanced again at Fry's system. He'd left it on purpose, Bianca realized; she'd underestimated him. Perhaps he had been a better person than she herself, all along.

She looked one more time at the body lying on the kitchen floor.

"No, you shouldn't," she said then. "You shouldn't have trusted me at all."

Then she went back to her own bungalow and took the package out from under the bed.

8. Finisterra

A hundred meters, two hundred, five hundred—Bianca falls, the wind whipping at her clothes, and the hanging vegetation that covers Encantada's flanks is a green-brown blur, going gray as it thins, as the *zaratán's* body curves away from her. She blinks away the tears brought on by the rushing wind, and tries to focus on the monitor panel of the harness. The wind speed indicator is the only one that makes sense; the others—altitude, attitude, rate of descent—are cycling through nonsense in three languages, baffled by the instruments' inability to find solid ground anywhere below.

Then Bianca falls out of Encantada's shadow into the sun, and before she can consciously form the thought her hand has grasped the emergency handle of the harness and pulled, convulsively; and the glassy fabric of the paraballoon is billowing out above her, rippling like water, and the harness is tugging at her, gently but firmly, smart threads reeling themselves quickly out and then slowly in again on their tiny spinnerets.

After a moment, she catches her breath. She is no longer falling, but flying.

She wipes the tears from her eyes. To the west, the slopes of Finisterra are bright and impossibly detailed in the low-angle sunlight, a million trees casting a million tiny shadows through the morning's rapidly dissipating mist.

She looks up, out through the nearly invisible curve of the paraballoon, and sees that Encantada is burning. She watches it for a long time.

The air grows warmer, and more damp, too. With a start, Bianca realizes she is falling below Finisterra's edge. When she designed the paraballoon, Bianca intended for Dinh to fall as far as she safely could, dropping deep into Sky's atmosphere before firing up the reverse Maxwell pumps, to heat the air in the balloon and lift her back to Finisterra; but it does not look as if there is any danger of pursuit now, from either the poachers or the wardens. Bianca starts the pumps, and the paraballoon slows, then begins to ascend.

As the prevailing wind carries her inland, over a riot of tropical green, and in the distance Bianca sees the smoke rising from the chimneys of Ciudad Perdida, Bianca glances up again at the burning shape of Encantada, and wonders whether she'll ever know if Valadez was telling the truth.

Abruptly the jungle below her opens up, and Bianca is flying over cultivated fields, and people are looking up at her in wonder.

Bianca looks out into the eastern sky, dotted with distant *zaratanes*. There is a vision in her mind, a vision that she thinks maybe Edith Dinh saw: the skies of Sky more crowded than the skies over Río Pícaro, Septentrionalis

Archipelago alive with the bright shapes of dirigibles and gliders, those nameless *zaratanes* out there no longer uncharted shoals but comforting and familiar landmarks.

She cuts the power to the pumps and opens the parachute valve at the top of the balloon. This isn't what she wanted, when she set out from home; but she is still a Nazario, and still an engineer. As she drops, children are already running toward her across the field.

A small miracle, but perhaps it is enough.

SEVEN YEARS FROM HOME

NAOMI NOVIK

—⟨⟩—

Preface

Seven days passed for me on my little raft of a ship as I fled Melida; seven years for the rest of the unaccelerated universe. I hoped to be forgotten, a dusty footnote left at the bottom of a page. Instead I came off to trumpets and medals and legal charges, equal doses of acclaim and venom, and I stumbled bewildered through the brassy noise, led first by one and then by another, while my last opportunity to enter any protest against myself escaped.

Now I desire only to correct the worst of the factual inaccuracies bandied about, so far as my imperfect memory will allow, and to make an offering of my own understanding to that smaller and more sophisticate audience who prefer to shape the world's opinion rather than be shaped by it.

I engage not to tire you with a recitation of dates and events and quotations. I do not recall them with any precision myself. But I must warn you that neither have I succumbed to that pathetic and otiose impulse to sanitize the events of the war, or to excuse sins either my own or belonging to others. To do so would be a lie, and on Melida, to tell a lie was an insult more profound than murder.

I will not see my sisters again, whom I loved. Here we say that one who takes the long midnight voyage has leaped ahead in time, but to me it seems it is they who have traveled on ahead. I can no longer hear their voices when I am awake. I hope this will silence them in the night.

Ruth Patrona
Reivaldt, Janvier 32, 4765

The First Adjustment

I disembarked at the port of Landfall in the fifth month of 4753. There is such a port on every world where the Confederacy has set its foot but not yet its flag: crowded and dirty and charmless. It was on the Esperigan continent, as the Melidans would not tolerate the construction of a spaceport in their own territory.

Ambassador Kostas, my superior, was a man of great authority and presence, two meters tall and solidly built, with a jovial handshake, high intelligence, and very little patience for fools; that I was likely to be relegated to this category was evident on our first meeting. He disliked my assignment to begin with. He thought well of the Esperigans; he moved in their society as easily as he did in our own, and would have called one or two of their senior ministers his personal friends, if only such a gesture were not highly unprofessional. He recognized his duty, and on an abstract intellectual level the potential value of the Melidans, but they revolted him, and he would have been glad to find me of like mind, ready to draw a line through their name and give them up as a bad cause.

A few moments' conversation was sufficient to disabuse him of this hope. I wish to attest that he did not allow the disappointment to in any way alter the performance of his duty, and he could not have objected with more vigor to my project of proceeding at once to the Melidan continent, to his mind a suicidal act.

In the end he chose not to stop me. I am sorry if he later regretted that, as seems likely. I took full advantage of the weight of my arrival. Five years had gone by on my homeworld of Terce since I had embarked, and there is a certain moral force to having sacrificed a former life for the one unknown. I had observed it often with new arrivals on Terce: their first requests were rarely refused even when foolish, as they often were. I was of course quite sure my own were eminently sensible.

"We will find you a guide," he said finally, yielding, and all the machinery of the Confederacy began to turn to my desire, a heady sensation.

Badea arrived at the embassy not two hours later. She wore a plain gray wrap around her shoulders, draped to the ground, and another wrap around her head. The alterations visible were only small ones: a smattering of green freckles across the bridge of her nose and cheeks, a greenish tinge to her lips and nails. Her wings were folded and hidden under the wrap, adding the bulk roughly of an overnight hiker's backpack. She smelled a little like the sourdough used on Terce to make roundbread, noticeable but not unpleasant. She might have walked through a spaceport without exciting comment.

She was brought to me in the shambles of my new office, where I had barely begun to lay out my things. I was wearing a conservative black suit, my best, tailored because you could not buy trousers for women ready-made on Terce, and, thankfully, comfortable shoes, because elegant ones on Terce were not meant to be walked in. I remember my clothing particularly because I was in it for the next week without opportunity to change.

"Are you ready to go?" she asked me, as soon as we were introduced and the receptionist had left.

I was quite visibly *not* ready to go, but this was not a misunderstanding: she did not want to take me. She thought the request stupid, and feared my safety would be a burden on her. If Ambassador Kostas would not mind my failure to return, she could not know that, and to be just, he would certainly have reacted unpleasantly in any case, figuring it as his duty.

But when asked for a favor she does not want to grant, a Melidan will sometimes offer it anyway, only in an unacceptable or awkward way. Another Melidan will recognize this as a refusal, and withdraw the request. Badea did not expect this courtesy from me, she only expected that I would say I could not leave at once. This she could count to her satisfaction as a refusal, and she would not come back to offer again.

I was however informed enough to be dangerous, and I did recognize the custom. I said, "It is inconvenient, but I am prepared to leave immediately." She turned at once and walked out of my office, and I followed her. It is understood that a favor accepted despite the difficulty and constraints laid down by the giver must be necessary to the recipient, as indeed this was to me; but in such a case, the conditions must then be endured, even if artificial.

I did not risk a pause at all even to tell anyone I was going; we walked out past the embassy secretary and the guards, who did not do more than give us a cursory glance—we were going the wrong way, and my citizen's button would likely have saved us interruption in any case. Kostas would not know I had gone until my absence was noticed and the security logs examined.

The Second Adjustment

I was not unhappy as I followed Badea through the city. A little discomfort was nothing to me next to the intense satisfaction of, as I felt, having passed a first test: I had gotten past all resistance offered me, both by Kostas and Badea, and soon I would be in the heart of a people I already felt I knew. Though I would be an outsider among them, I had lived all my life to the present day in the self-same state, and I did not fear it, or for the moment anything else.

Badea walked quickly and with a freer stride than I was used to, loose-limbed. I was taller, but had to stretch to match her. Esperigans looked at her as she went by, and then looked at me, and the pressure of their gaze was suddenly hostile. "We might take a taxi," I offered. Many were passing by empty. "I can pay."

"No," she said, with a look of distaste at one of those conveyances, so we continued on foot.

After Melida, during my black-sea journey, my doctoral dissertation on the Canaan movement was published under the escrow clause, against my will. I have never used the funds, which continue to accumulate steadily. I do not like to inflict them on any cause I admire sufficiently to support, so they will go to my family when I have gone; my nephews will be glad of it, and of the passing of an embarrassment, and that is as much good as it can be expected to provide.

There is a great deal within that book which is wrong, and more which is wrongheaded, in particular any expression of opinion or analysis I interjected atop the scant collection of accurate facts I was able to accumulate in six years of over-enthusiastic graduate work. This little is true: the Canaan movement was an offshoot of conservation philosophy. Where the traditionalists of that movement sought to restrict humanity to dead worlds and closed enclaves on others, the Canaan splinter group wished instead to alter themselves while they altered their new worlds, meeting them halfway.

The philosophy had the benefit of a certain practicality, as genetic engineering and body modification was and remains considerably cheaper than terraforming, but we are a squeamish and a violent species, and nothing invites pogrom more surely than the neighbor who is different from us, yet still too close. In consequence, the Melidans were by our present day the last surviving Canaan society.

They had come to Melida and settled the larger of the two continents some eight hundred years before. The Esperigans came two hundred years later, refugees from the plagues on New Victoire, and took the smaller continent. The two had little contact for the first half-millennium; we of the Confederacy are given to think in worlds and solar systems, and to imagine that only a space voyage is long, but a hostile continent is vast enough to occupy a small and struggling band. But both prospered, each according to their lights, and by the time I landed, half the planet glittered in the night from space, and half was yet pristine.

In my dissertation, I described the ensuing conflict as natural, which is fair if slaughter and pillage are granted to be natural to our kind. The Esperigans had exhausted the limited raw resources of their share of the planet, and a short flight away was the untouched expanse of the larger continent, not a tenth as populated as their own. The Melidans controlled their birthrate, used only sustainable quantities, and built nothing which could not be eaten by the wilderness a year after they had abandoned it. Many Esperigan philosophers and politicians trumpeted their admiration of Melidan society, but this was only a sort of pleasant spiritual refreshment, as one admires a saint or a martyr without ever wishing to be one.

The invasion began informally, with adventurers and entrepreneurs, with the desperate, the poor, the violent. They began to land on the shores of the Melidan territory, to survey, to take away samples, to plant their own foreign roots. They soon had a village, then more than one. The Melidans told them to leave, which worked as well as it ever has in the annals of colonialism, and then attacked them. Most of the settlers were killed; enough survived and straggled back across the ocean to make a dramatic story of murder and cruelty out of it.

I expressed the conviction to the Ministry of State, in my pre-assignment report, that the details had been exaggerated, and that the attacks had been provoked more extensively. I was wrong, of course. But at the time I did not know it.

Badea took me to the low quarter of Landfall, so called because it faced on the side of the ocean downcurrent from the spaceport. Iridescent oil and a floating mat of discards glazed the edge of the surf. The houses were mean and crowded tightly upon one another, broken up mostly by liquor stores and bars. Docks stretched out into the ocean, extended long to reach out past the pollution, and just past the end of one of these floated a small boat, little more than a simple coracle: a hull of brown bark, a narrow brown mast, a grey-green sail slack and trembling in the wind.

We began walking out towards it, and those watching—there were some men loitering about the docks, fishing idly, or working on repairs to equipment or nets—began to realize then that I meant to go with her.

The Esperigans had already learned the lesson we like to teach as often as we can, that the Confederacy is a bad enemy and a good friend, and while no one is ever made to join us by force, we cannot be opposed directly. We had given them the spaceport already, an open door to the rest of the settled worlds, and they wanted more, the moth yearning. I relied on this for protection, and did not consider that however much they wanted from our outstretched hand, they still more wished to deny its gifts to their enemy.

Four men rose as we walked the length of the dock, and made a line across it. "You don't want to go with that one, ma'am," one of them said to me, a parody of respect. Badea said nothing. She moved a little aside, to see how I would answer them.

"I am on assignment for my government," I said, neatly offering a red flag to a bull, and moved towards them. It was not an attempt at bluffing: on Terce, even though I was immodestly unveiled, men would have at once moved out of the way to avoid any chance of the insult of physical contact. It was an act so automatic as to be invisible: precisely what we are taught to watch for in ourselves, but that proves infinitely easier in the instruction than in the practice. I did not *think* they would move; I knew they would.

Perhaps that certainty transmitted itself: the men did move a little, enough to satisfy my unconscious that they were cooperating with my expectations, so that it took me wholly by surprise and horror when one reached out and put his hand on my arm to stop me.

I screamed, in full voice, and struck him. His face is lost to my memory, but I still can see clearly the man behind him, his expression as full of appalled violation as my own. The four of them flinched from my scream, and then drew in around me, protesting and reaching out in turn.

I reacted with more violence. I had confidently considered myself a citizen of no world and of many, trained out of assumptions and unaffected by the parochial attitudes of the one where chance had seen me born, but in that moment I could with actual pleasure have killed all of them. That wish was unlikely to be gratified. I was taller, and the gravity of Terce is slightly higher than of Melida, so I was stronger than they expected me to be, but they were laborers and seamen, built generously and rough-hewn, and the male advantage in muscle mass tells quickly in a hand-to-hand fight.

They tried to immobilize me, which only panicked me further. The mind curls in on itself in such a moment; I remember palpably only the sensation of sweating copiously, and the way this caused the seam of my blouse to rub unpleasantly against my neck as I struggled.

Badea told me later that, at first, she had meant to let them hold me. She could then leave, with the added satisfaction of knowing the Esperigan fishermen and not she had provoked an incident with the Confederacy. It was not sympathy that moved her to action, precisely. The extremity of my distress was as alien to her as to them, but where they thought me mad, she read it in the context of my having accepted her original conditions and somewhat unwillingly decided that I truly did need to go with her, even if she did not know precisely why and saw no use in it herself.

I cannot tell you precisely how the subsequent moments unfolded. I remember the green gauze of her wings overhead perforated by the sun, like a linen curtain, and the blood spattering my face as she neatly lopped off the hands upon me. She used for the purpose a blade I later saw in use for many tasks, among them harvesting fruit off plants where the leaves or the bark may be poisonous. It is shaped like a sickle and strung upon a thick elastic cord, which a skilled wielder can cause to become rigid or to collapse.

I stood myself back on my feet panting, and she landed. The men were on their knees screaming, and others were running towards us down the docks. Badea swept the severed hands into the water with the side of her foot and said calmly, "We must go."

The little boat had drawn up directly beside us over the course of our encounter, drawn by some signal I had not seen her transmit. I stepped into it behind her. The coracle leapt forward like a springing bird, and left the shouting and the blood behind.

We did not speak over the course of that strange journey. What I had thought a sail did not catch the wind, but opened itself wide and stretched out over our heads, like an awning, and angled itself towards the sun. There were many small filaments upon the surface wriggling when I examined it more closely, and also upon the exterior of the hull. Badea stretched herself out upon the floor of the craft, lying under the low deck, and I joined her in the small space: it was not uncomfortable nor rigid, but had the queer unsettled cushioning of a waterbed.

The ocean crossing took only the rest of the day. How our speed was generated I cannot tell you; we did not seem to sit deeply in the water and our craft threw up no spray. The world blurred as a window running with rain. I asked Badea for water, once, and she put her hands on the floor of the craft and pressed down: in the depression she made, a small clear pool gathered for me to cup out, with a taste like slices of cucumber with the skin still upon them.

This was how I came to Melida.

The Third Adjustment

Badea was vaguely embarrassed to have inflicted me on her fellows, and having deposited me in the center of her village made a point of leaving me there by leaping aloft into the canopy where I could not follow, as a way of saying she was done with me, and anything I did henceforth could not be laid at her door.

I was by now hungry and nearly sick with exhaustion. Those who have not flown between worlds like to imagine the journey a glamorous one, but at least for minor bureaucrats, it is no more pleasant than any form of transport, only elongated. I had spent a week a virtual prisoner in my berth, the bed folding up to give me room to walk four strides back and forth, or to unfold my writing-desk, not both at once, with a shared toilet the size of an ungenerous closet down the hall. Landfall had not arrested my forward motion, as that mean port had never been my destination. Now, however, I was arrived, and the dregs of adrenaline were consumed in anticlimax.

Others before me have stood in a Melidan village center and described it for an audience—Esperigans mostly, anthropologists and students of biology and a class of tourists either adventurous or stupid. There is usually a lyrical description of the natives coasting overhead among some sort of vines or tree-branches knitted overhead for shelter, the particulars and adjectives determined by the village latitude, and the obligatory explanation of the typical plan of huts, organized as a spoked wheel around the central plaza.

If I had been less tired, perhaps I too would have looked with so analytical an air, and might now satisfy my readers with a similar report. But to me the village only presented all the confusion of a wholly strange place, and I saw nothing that seemed to me deliberate. To call it a village gives a false air of comforting provinciality. Melidans, at least those with wings, move freely among a wide constellation of small settlements, so that all of these, in the public sphere, partake of the hectic pace of the city. I stood alone, and strangers moved past me with assurance, the confidence of their stride saying, "I care nothing for you or your fate. It is of no concern to me. How might you expect it to be otherwise?" In the end, I lay down on one side of the plaza and went to sleep.

I met Kitia the next morning. She woke me by prodding me with a twig, experimentally, having been selected for this task out of her group of schoolmates by some complicated interworking of personality and chance. They giggled from a few safe paces back as I opened my eyes and sat up.

"Why are you sleeping in the square?" Kitia asked me, to a burst of fresh giggles.

"Where should I sleep?" I asked her.

"In a house!" she said.

When I had explained to them, not without some art, that I had no house here, they offered the censorious suggestion that I should go back to wherever I did have a house. I made a good show of looking analytically up at the sky overhead and asking them what our latitude was, and then I pointed at a random location and said, "My house is five years that way."

Scorn, puzzlement, and at last delight. I was from the stars! None of their friends had ever met anyone from so far away. One girl who previously had held a point of pride for having once visited the smaller continent, with an Esperigan toy doll to prove it, was instantly dethroned. Kitia possessively took my arm and informed me that as my house was too far away, she would take me to another.

Children of virtually any society are an excellent resource for the diplomatic servant or the anthropologist, if contact with them can be made without giving offense. They enjoy the unfamiliar experience of answering real questions, particularly the stupidly obvious ones that allow them to feel a sense of superiority over the inquiring adult, and they are easily impressed with the unusual. Kitia was a treasure. She led me, at the head of a small pied-piper procession, to an empty house on a convenient lane. It had been lately abandoned, and was already being reclaimed: the walls and floor were swarming with tiny insects with glossy dark blue carapaces, munching so industriously the sound of their jaws hummed like a summer afternoon.

I with difficulty avoided recoiling. Kitia did not hesitate: she walked into the swarm, crushing beetles by the dozens underfoot, and went to a small spigot in the far wall. When she turned this on, a clear viscous liquid issued forth, and the beetles scattered from it. "Here, like this," she said, showing me how to cup my hands under the liquid and spread it upon the walls and the floor. The disgruntled beetles withdrew, and the brownish surfaces began to bloom back to pale green, repairing the holes.

Over the course of that next week, she also fed me, corrected my manners and my grammar, and eventually brought me a set of clothing, a tunic and leggings, which she proudly informed me she had made herself in class. I thanked her with real sincerity and asked where I might wash my old clothing. She looked very puzzled, and when she had looked more closely at my clothing and touched it, she said, "Your clothing is dead! I thought it was only ugly."

Her gift was not made of fabric but a thin tough mesh of plant filaments with the feathered surface of a moth's wings. It gripped my skin eagerly as soon as I had put it on, and I thought myself at first allergic, because it itched and tingled, but this was only the bacteria bred to live in the mesh assiduously eating away the sweat and dirt and dead epidermal cells built up on my skin. It took me several more days to overcome all my instinct and learn to trust the living cloth with the more voluntary eliminations of my body also. (Previously I had been going out back to defecate in the woods, having been unable to find anything resembling a toilet, and meeting too much confusion when I tried to approach the question to dare pursue it further, for fear of encountering a taboo.)

And this was the handiwork of a child, not thirteen years of age! She could not explain to me how she had done it in any way which made sense to me. Imagine if you had to explain how to perform a reference search to someone who had not only never seen a library, but did not understand electricity, and who perhaps knew there was such a thing as written text, but did not himself read more than the alphabet. She took me once to her classroom after hours and showed me her workstation, a large wooden tray full of grayish moss, with a double row of small jars along the back each holding liquids or powders which I could only distinguish by their differing colors. Her only tools were an assortment of syringes and eyedroppers and scoops and brushes.

I went back to my house and in the growing report I would not have a chance to send for another month I wrote, *These are a priceless people. We must have them.*

• • •

The Fourth Adjustment

All these first weeks, I made no contact with any other adult. I saw them go by occasionally, and the houses around mine were occupied, but they never spoke to me or even looked at me directly. None of them objected to my squatting, but that was less implicit endorsement and more an unwillingness even to acknowledge my existence. I talked to Kitia and the other children, and tried to be patient. I hoped an opportunity would offer itself eventually for me to be of some visible use.

In the event, it was rather my lack of use which led to the break in the wall. A commotion arose in the early morning, while Kitia was showing me the plan of her wings, which she was at that age beginning to design. She would grow the parasite over the subsequent year, and was presently practicing with miniature versions, which rose from her worktable surface gossamer-thin and fluttering with an involuntary muscle-twitching. I was trying to conceal my revulsion.

Kitia looked up when the noise erupted. She casually tossed her example out of the window, to be pounced upon with a hasty scramble by several nearby birds, and went out the door. I followed her to the square: the children were gathered at the fringes, silent for once and watching. There were five women laid out on the ground, all bloody, one dead. Two of the others looked mortally wounded. They were all winged.

There were several working already on the injured, packing small brownish-white spongy masses into the open wounds and sewing them up. I would have liked to be of use, less from natural instinct than from the colder thought, which inflicted itself upon my mind, that any crisis opens social barriers. I am sorry to say I did not refrain from any noble self-censorship, but from the practical conviction that it was at once apparent my limited field-medical training could not in any valuable way be applied to the present circumstances.

I drew away, rather, to avoid being in the way as I could not turn the situation to my advantage, and in doing so ran up against Badea, who stood at the very edge of the square, observing.

She stood alone; there were no other adults nearby, and there was blood on her hands. "Are you hurt also?" I asked her.

"No," she returned, shortly.

I ventured on concern for her friends, and asked her if they had been hurt in fighting. "We have heard rumors," I added, "that the Esperigans have been encroaching on your territory." It was the first opportunity I had been given of hinting at even this much of our official sympathy, as the children only shrugged when I asked them if there were fighting going on.

She shrugged, too, with one shoulder, and the folded wing rose and fell with it. But then she said, "They leave their weapons in the forest for us, even where they cannot have gone."

The Esperigans had several kinds of land-mine technologies, including a clever mobile one which could be programmed with a target either as specific as an individual's genetic record or as general as a broadly defined body type—humanoid and winged, for instance—and set loose to wander until it found a match, then do the maximum damage it could. Only one side could carry explosive, as the other was devoted to the electronics. "The shrapnel, does it come only in one direction?" I asked, and made a fanned-out shape with my hands to illustrate. Badea looked at me sharply and nodded.

I explained the mine to her, and described their manufacture. "Some scanning devices can detect them," I added, meaning to continue into an offer, but I had not finished the litany of materials before she was striding away from the square, without another word.

I was not dissatisfied with the reaction, in which I correctly read intention to put my information to immediate use, and two days later my patience was rewarded. Badea came to my house in the mid-morning and said, "We have found one of them. Can you show us how to disarm them?"

"I am not sure," I told her, honestly. "The safest option would be to trigger it deliberately, from afar."

"The plastics they use poison the ground."

"Can you take me to its location?" I asked. She considered the question with enough seriousness that I realized there was either taboo or danger involved.

"Yes," she said finally, and took me with her to a house near the center of the village. It had steps up to the roof, and from there we could climb to that of the neighboring house, and so on until we were high enough to reach a large basket, woven not of ropes but of a kind of vine, sitting in a crook of a tree. We climbed into this, and she kicked us off from the tree.

The movement was not smooth. The nearest I can describe is the sensation of being on a child's swing, except at that highest point of weightlessness you do not go backwards, but instead go falling into another arc, but at tremendous speed, and with a pungent smell like rotten pineapple all around from the shattering of the leaves of the trees through which we were propelled. I was violently sick after some five minutes. To the comfort of my pride if not my stomach, Badea was also sick, though more efficiently and over the side, before our journey ended.

There were two other women waiting for us in the tree where we came to rest, both of them also winged: Renata and Paudi. "It's gone another three hundred meters, towards Ighlan," Renata told us—another nearby Melidan village, as they explained to me.

"If it comes near enough to pick up traces of organized habitation, it will not trigger until it is inside the settlement, among as many people as possible," I said. "It may also have a burrowing mode, if it is the more expensive kind."

They took me down through the canopy, carefully, and walked before and behind me when we came to the ground. Their wings were spread wide enough to brush against the hanging vines to either side, and they regularly leapt aloft for a brief survey. Several times they moved me with friendly hands into a slightly different path, although my untrained eyes could make no difference among the choices.

A narrow trail of large ants—the reader will forgive me for calling them ants, they were nearly indistinguishable from those efficient creatures— paced us over the forest floor, which I did not recognize as significant until we came near the mine, and I saw it covered with the ants, who did not impede its movement but milled around and over it with intense interest.

"We have adjusted them so they smell the plastic," Badea said, when I asked. "We can make them eat it," she added, "but we worried it would set off the device."

The word *adjusted* scratches at the back of my mind again as I write this, that unpleasant tinny sensation of a term that does not allow of real translation and which has been inadequately replaced. I cannot improve upon the work of the official Confederacy translators, however; to encompass the true concept would require three dry, dusty chapters more suited to a textbook on the subject of biological engineering, which I am ill-qualified to produce. I do hope that I have successfully captured the wholly casual way she spoke of this feat. Our own scientists might replicate this act of genetic sculpting in any of two dozen excellent laboratories across the Confederacy— given several years, and a suitably impressive grant. They had done it in less than two days, as a matter of course.

I did not at the time indulge in admiration. The mine was ignoring the inquisitive ants and scuttling along at a good pace, the head with its glassy eye occasionally rotating upon its spindly spider-legs, and we had half a day in which to divert it from the village ahead.

Renata followed the mine as it continued on, while I sketched what I knew of the internals in the dirt for Badea and Paudi. Any sensible mine-maker will design the device to simply explode at any interference with its working other than the disable code, so our options were not particularly satisfying. "The most likely choice," I suggested, "would be the transmitter.

If it becomes unable to receive the disable code, there may be a failsafe which would deactivate it on a subsequent malfunction."

Paudi had on her back a case which, unfolded, looked very like a more elegant and compact version of little Kitia's worktable. She sat crosslegged with it on her lap and worked on it for some two hours' time, occasionally reaching down to pick up a handful of ants, which dropped into the green matrix of her table mostly curled up and died, save for a few survivors, which she herded carefully into an empty jar before taking up another sample.

I sat on the forest floor beside her, or walked with Badea, who was pacing a small circle out around us, watchfully. Occasionally she would unsling her scythe-blade, and then put it away again, and once she brought down a mottie, a small lemur-like creature. I say lemur because there is nothing closer in my experience, but it had none of the charm of an Earth-native mammal; I rather felt an instinctive disgust looking at it, even before she showed me the tiny sucker-mouths full of hooked teeth with which it latched upon a victim.

She had grown a little more loquacious, and asked me about my own homeworld. I told her about Terce, and about the seclusion of women, which she found extremely funny, as we can only laugh at the follies of those far from us which threaten us not at all. The Melidans by design maintain a five to one ratio of women to men, as adequate to maintain a healthy gene pool while minimizing the overall resource consumption of their population. "They cannot take the wings, so it is more difficult for them to travel," she added, with one sentence dismissing the lingering mystery which had perplexed earlier visitors, of the relative rarity of seeing their men.

She had two children, which she described to me proudly, living presently with their father and half-siblings in a village half a day's travel away, and she was considering a third. She had trained as a forest ranger, another inadequately translated term which was at the time beginning to take on a military significance among them under the pressure of the Esperigan incursions.

"I'm done," Paudi said, and we went to catch up Renata and find a nearby ant-nest, which looked like a mound of white cotton batting, rising several inches off the forest floor. Paudi introduced her small group of infected survivors into this colony, and after a little confusion and milling about, they accepted their transplantation and marched inside. The flow of departures slowed a little momentarily, then resumed, and a file split off from the main channel of workers to march in the direction of the mine.

These joined the lingering crowd still upon the mine, but the new arrivals did not stop at inspection and promptly began to struggle to insinuate themselves into the casing. We withdrew to a safe distance, watching. The mine continued on without any slackening in its pace for ten minutes, as more ants began to squeeze themselves inside, and then it hesitated, one spindly metal leg held aloft uncertainly. It went a few more slightly drunken paces, and then abruptly the legs all retracted and left it a smooth round lump on the forest floor.

The Fifth Adjustment

They showed me how to use their communications technology and grew me an interface to my own small handheld, so my report was at last able to go. Kostas began angry, of course, having been forced to defend the manner of my departure to the Esperigans without the benefit of any understanding of the circumstances, but I sent the report an hour before I messaged, and by the time we spoke he had read enough to be in reluctant agreement with my conclusions if not my methods.

I was of course full of self-satisfaction. Freed at long last from the academy and the walled gardens of Terce, armed with false confidence in my research and my training, I had so far achieved all that my design had stretched to encompass. The Esperigan blood had washed easily from my hands, and though I answered Kostas meekly when he upbraided me, privately I felt only impatience, and even he did not linger long on the topic: I had been too successful, and he had more important news.

The Esperigans had launched a small army two days before, under the more pleasant-sounding name of expeditionary defensive force. Their purpose was to establish a permanent settlement on the Melidan shore, some nine hundred miles from my present location, and begin the standard process of terraforming. The native life would be eradicated in spheres of a hundred miles across at a time: first the broad strokes of clear-cutting and the electrified nets, then the irradiation of the soil and the air, and after that the seeding of Earth-native microbes and plants. So had a thousand worlds been made over anew, and though the Esperigans had fully conquered their own continent five centuries before, they still knew the way.

He asked doubtfully if I thought some immediate resistance could be offered. Disabling a few mines scattered into the jungle seemed to him a small task. Confronting a large and organized military force was on a different order of magnitude. "I think we can do something," I said, maintaining a veneer of caution for his benefit, and took the catalog of equipment to Badea as soon as we had disengaged.

She was occupied in organizing the retrieval of the deactivated mines, which the ants were now leaving scattered in the forests and jungles. A bird-of-paradise variant had been *adjusted* to make a meal out of the ants and take the glittery mines back to their tree-top nests, where an observer might easily see them from above. She and the other collectors had so far found nearly a thousand of them. The mines made a neat pyramid, as of the harvested skulls of small cyclopean creatures with their dull eyes staring out lifelessly.

The Esperigans needed a week to cross the ocean in their numbers, and I spent it with the Melidans, developing our response. There was a heady delight in this collaboration. The work was easy and pleasant in their wide-open laboratories full of plants, roofed only with the fluttering sailcloth eating sunlight to give us energy, and the best of them coming from many miles distant to participate in the effort. The Confederacy spy-satellites had gone into orbit perhaps a year after our first contact: I likely knew more about the actual force than the senior administrators of Melida. I was in much demand, consulted not only for my information but my opinion.

In the ferment of our labors, I withheld nothing. This was not yet deliberate, but neither was it innocent. I had been sent to further a war, and if in the political calculus which had arrived at this solution the lives of soldiers were only variables, yet there was still a balance I was expected to preserve. It was not my duty to give the Melidans an easy victory, any more than it had been Kostas's to give one to the Esperigans.

A short and victorious war, opening a new and tantalizing frontier for restless spirits, would at once drive up that inconvenient nationalism which is the Confederacy's worst obstacle, and render less compelling the temptations we could offer to lure them into fully joining galactic society. On the other hand, to descend into squalor, a more equal kind of civil war has often proven extremely useful, and the more lingering and bitter the better. I was sent to the Melidans in hope that, given some guidance and what material assistance we could quietly provide without taking any official position, they might be an adequate opponent for the Esperigans to produce this situation.

There has been some criticism of the officials who selected me for this mission, but in their defense, it must be pointed out it was not in fact my assignment to actually provide military assistance, nor could anyone, even myself, have envisioned my proving remotely useful in such a role. I was only meant to be an early scout. My duty was to acquire cultural information enough to open a door for a party of military experts from Voca Libre, who would not reach Melida for another two years. Ambition and opportunity promoted me, and no official hand.

I think these experts arrived sometime during the third Esperigan offensive. I cannot pinpoint the date with any accuracy, I had by then ceased to track the days, and I never met them. I hope they can forgive my theft of their war; I paid for my greed.

• • •

The Esperigans used a typical carbonized steel in most of their equipment, as bolts and hexagonal nuts and screws with star-shaped heads, and woven into the tough mesh of their body armor. This was the target of our efforts. It was a new field of endeavor for the Melidans, who used metal as they used meat, sparingly and with a sense of righteousness in its avoidance. To them it was either a trace element needed in minute amounts, or an undesirable by-product of the more complicated biological processes they occasionally needed to invoke.

However, they had developed some strains of bacteria to deal with this latter waste, and the speed with which they could manipulate these organisms was extraordinary. Another quantity of the ants—a convenient delivery mechanism used by the Melidans routinely, as I learned—were adjusted to render them deficient in iron and to provide a home in their bellies for the bacteria, transforming them into shockingly efficient engines of destruction. Set loose upon several of the mines as a trial, they devoured the carapaces and left behind only smudgy black heaps of carbon dust, carefully harvested for fertilizer, and the plastic explosives from within, nestled in their bed of copper wire and silicon.

The Esperigans landed, and at once carved themselves out a neat half-moon of wasteland from the virgin shore, leaving no branches which might stretch above their encampment to offer a platform for attack. They established an electrified fence around the perimeter, with guns and patrols, and all this I observed with Badea, from a small platform in a vine-choked tree not far away: we wore the green-gray cloaks, and our faces were stained with leaf juice.

I had very little justification for inserting myself into such a role but the flimsy excuse of pointing out to Badea the most crucial section of their camp, when we had broken in. I cannot entirely say why I wished to go along on so dangerous an expedition. I am not particularly courageous. Several of my more unkind biographers have accused me of bloodlust, and pointed to this as a sequel to the disaster of my first departure. I cannot refute the accusation on the evidence, however I will point out that I chose that portion of the expedition which we hoped would encounter no violence.

But it is true I had learned already to seethe at the violent piggish blindness of the Esperigans, who would have wrecked all the wonders around me only to propagate yet another bland copy of Earth and suck dry the carcass of their own world. They were my enemy both by duty and by inclination, and I permitted myself the convenience of hating them. At the time, it made matters easier.

The wind was running from the east, and several of the Melidans attacked the camp from that side. The mines had yielded a quantity of explosive large enough to pierce the Esperigans' fence and shake the trees even as far as our lofty perch. The wind carried the smoke and dust and flames towards us, obscuring the ground and rendering the soldiers in their own camp only vague ghostlike suggestions of human shape. The fighting was hand-to-hand, and the stutter of gunfire came only tentatively through the chaos of the smoke.

Badea had been holding a narrow cord, one end weighted with a heavy seed-pod. She now poured a measure of water onto the pod, from her canteen, then flung it out into the air. It sailed over the fence and landed inside the encampment, behind one of the neat rows of storage tents. The seed pod struck the ground and immediately burst like a ripe fruit, an anemone tangle of waving roots creeping out over the ground and anchoring the cord, which she had secured at this end around one thick branch.

We let ourselves down it, hand over hand. There was none of that typical abrasion or friction which I might have expected from rope; my hands felt as cool and comfortable when we descended as when we began. We ran into the narrow space between the tents. I was experiencing that strange elongation of time which crisis can occasionally produce: I was conscious of each footfall, and of the seeming-long moments it took to place each one.

There were wary soldiers at many of the tent entrances, likely those which held either the more valuable munitions or the more valuable men. Their discipline had not faltered, even while the majority of the force was already orchestrating a response to the Melidan assault on the other side of the encampment. But we did not need to penetrate into the tents. The guards were rather useful markers for us, showing me which of the tents were the more significant. I pointed out to Badea the cluster of four tents, each guarded at either side by a pair, near the farthest end of the encampment.

Badea looked here and there over the ground as we darted under cover of smoke from one alleyway to another, the walls of waxed canvas muffling the distant shouts and the sound of gunfire. The dirt still had the yellowish tinge of Melidan soil—the Esperigans had not yet irradiated it—but it was crumbly and dry, the fine fragile native moss crushed and much torn by heavy boots and equipment, and the wind raised little dervishes of dust around our ankles.

"This ground will take years to recover fully," she said to me, soft and bitterly, as she stopped us and knelt, behind a deserted tent not far from our target. She gave me a small ceramic implement which looked much like the hair-picks sometimes worn on Terce by women with hair which never knew a blade's edge: a raised comb with three teeth, though on the tool these were much longer and sharpened at the end. I picked the ground vigorously, stabbing deep to aerate the wounded soil, while she judiciously poured out a mixture of water and certain organic extracts, and sowed a packet of seeds.

This may sound a complicated operation to be carrying out in an enemy camp, in the midst of battle, but we had practiced the maneuver, and indeed had we been glimpsed, anyone would have been hard-pressed to recognize a threat in the two gray-wrapped lumps crouched low as we pawed at the dirt. Twice while we worked, wounded soldiers were carried in a rush past either end of our alleyway, towards shelter. We were not seen.

The seeds she carried, though tiny, burst readily, and began to thrust out spiderweb-fine rootlets at such a speed they looked like nothing more than squirming maggots. Badea without concern moved her hands around them, encouraging them into the ground. When they were established, she motioned me to stop my work, and she took out the prepared ants: a much greater number of them, with a dozen of the fat yellow wasp-sized brood-mothers. Tipped out into the prepared and welcoming soil, they immediately began to burrow their way down, with the anxious harrying of their subjects and spawn.

Badea watched for a long while, crouched over, even after the ants had vanished nearly all beneath the surface. The few who emerged and darted back inside, the faint trembling of the rootlets, the shifting grains of dirt, all carried information to her. At length satisfied, she straightened saying, "Now—"

The young soldier was I think only looking for somewhere to piss, rather than investigating some noise. He came around the corner already fumbling at his belt, and seeing us did not immediately shout, likely from plain surprise, but grabbed for Badea's shoulder first. He was clean-shaven, and the name on his lapel badge was *Ridang*. I drove the soil-pick into his eye. I was taller, so the stroke went downwards, and he fell backwards to his knees away from me, clutching at his face.

He did not die at once. There must be very few deaths which come immediately, though we often like to comfort ourselves by the pretense that this failure of the body, or that injury, must at once eradicate consciousness and life and pain all together. Here sentience lasted several moments which seemed to me long: his other eye was open, and looked at me while his hands clawed for the handle of the pick. When this had faded, and he had fallen supine to the ground, there was yet a convulsive movement of all the limbs and a trickling of blood from mouth and nose and eye before the final stiffening jerk left the body emptied and inanimate.

I watched him die in a strange parody of serenity, all feeling hollowed out of me, and then turning away vomited upon the ground. Behind me, Badea cut open his belly and his thighs and turned him face down onto the dirt, so the blood and the effluvia leaked out of him. "That will do a little good for the ground at least, before they carry him away to waste him," she said. "Come." She touched my shoulder, not unkindly, but I flinched from the touch as from a blow.

It was not that Badea or her fellows were indifferent to death, or casual towards murder. But there is a price to be paid for living in a world whose native hostilities have been cherished rather than crushed. Melidan life expectancy is some ten years beneath that of Confederacy citizens, though they are on average healthier and more fit both genetically and physically. In their philosophy a human life is not inherently superior and to be valued over any other kind. Accident and predation claim many, and living intimately with the daily cruelties of nature dulls the facility for sentiment. Badea enjoyed none of that comforting distance which allows us to think ourselves assured of the full potential span of life, and therefore suffered none of the pangs when confronted with evidence to the contrary. I looked at my victim and saw my own face; so too did she, but she had lived all her life so aware, and it did not bow her shoulders.

Five days passed before the Esperigan equipment began to come apart. Another day halted all their work, and in confusion they retreated to their encampment. I did not go with the Melidan company that destroyed them to the last man.

Contrary to many accusations, I did not lie to Kostas in my report and pretend surprise. I freely confessed to him I had expected the result, and truthfully explained I had not wished to make claims of which I was unsure. I never deliberately sought to deceive any of my superiors or conceal information from them, save in such small ways. At first I was not Melidan enough to wish to do so, and later I was too Melidan to feel anything but revulsion at the concept.

He and I discussed our next steps in the tiger-dance. I described as best I could the Melidan technology, and after consultation with various Confederacy experts, it was agreed he would quietly mention to the Esperigan minister of defense, at their weekly luncheon, a particular Confederacy technology: ceramic coatings, which could be ordered at vast expense and two years' delay from Bel Rios. Or, he would suggest, if the Esperigans wished to deed some land to the Confederacy, a private entrepreneurial concern might fund the construction of a local fabrication plant, and produce them at much less cost, in six months' time.

The Esperigans took the bait, and saw only private greed behind this apparent breach of neutrality: imagining Kostas an investor in this private concern, they winked at his venality, and eagerly helped us to their own exploitation. Meanwhile, they continued occasional and tentative incursions into the Melidan continent, probing the coastline, but the disruption they created betrayed their attempts, and whichever settlement was nearest would at once deliver them a present of the industrious ants, so these met with no greater success than the first.

Through these months of brief and grudging detente, I traveled extensively throughout the continent. My journals are widely available, being the domain of our government, but they are shamefully sparse, and I apologize to my colleagues for it. I would have been more diligent in my work if I had imagined I would be the last and not the first such chronicler. At the time, giddy with success, I went with more the spirit of a holidaymaker than a researcher, and I sent only those images and notes which it was pleasant to me to record, with the excuse of limited capacity to send my reports.

For what cold comfort it may be, I must tell you photography and description are inadequate to convey the experience of standing in the living heart of a world, alien yet not hostile, and when I walked hand in hand with Badea along the crest of a great canyon wall and looked down over the ridges of purple and grey and ochre at the gently waving tendrils of an elacca forest, which in my notorious video recordings can provoke nausea in nearly every observer, I felt the first real stir of an unfamiliar sensation of beauty-in-strangeness, and I laughed in delight and surprise, while she looked at me and smiled.

We returned to her village three days later and saw the bombing as we came, the new Esperigan long-range fighter planes like narrow silver knife-blades making low passes overhead, the smoke rising black and oily against the sky. Our basket-journey could not be accelerated, so we could only cling to the sides and wait as we were carried onward. The planes and the smoke were gone before we arrived; the wreckage was not.

I was angry at Kostas afterwards, unfairly. He was no more truly the Esperigans' confidant than they were his, but I felt at the time that it was his business to know what they were about, and he had failed to warn me. I accused him of deliberate concealment; he told me, censoriously, that I had known the risk when I had gone to the continent, and he could hardly be responsible for preserving my safety while I slept in the very war zone. This silenced my tirade, as I realized how near I had come to betraying myself. Of course he would not have wanted me to warn the Melidans; it had not yet occurred to him I would have wished to, myself. I ought not have wanted to.

Forty-three people were killed in the attack. Kitia was yet lingering when

I came to her small bedside. She was in no pain, her eyes cloudy and distant, already withdrawing; her family had been and gone again. "I knew you were coming back, so I asked them to let me stay a little longer," she told me. "I wanted to say goodbye." She paused and added uncertainly, "And I was afraid, a little. Don't tell."

I promised her I would not. She sighed and said, "I shouldn't wait any longer. Will you call them over?"

The attendant came when I raised my hand, and he asked Kitia, "Are you ready?"

"Yes," she said, a little doubtful. "It won't hurt?"

"No, not at all," he said, already taking out with a gloved hand a small flat strip from a pouch, filmy green and smelling of raspberries. Kitia opened her mouth, and he laid it on her tongue. It dissolved almost at once, and she blinked twice and was asleep. Her hand went cold a few minutes later, still lying between my own.

I stood with her family when we laid her to rest, the next morning. The attendants put her carefully down in a clearing, and sprayed her from a distance, the smell of cut roses just going to rot, and stepped back. Her parents wept noisily; I stayed dry-eyed as any seemly Terce matron, displaying my assurance of the ascension of the dead. The birds came first, and the motties, to pluck at her eyes and her lips, and the beetles hurrying with a hum of eager jaws to deconstruct her into raw parts. They did not have long to feast: the forest itself was devouring her from below in a green tide rising, climbing in small creepers up her cheeks and displacing them all.

When she was covered over, the mourners turned away and went to join the shared wake behind us in the village square. They threw uncertain and puzzled looks at my remaining as they went past, and at my tearless face. But she was not yet gone: there was a suggestion of a girl lingering there, a collapsing scaffold draped in an unhurried carpet of living things. I did not leave, though behind me there rose a murmur of noise as the families of the dead spoke reminiscences of their lost ones.

Near dawn, the green carpeting slipped briefly. In the dim watery light I glimpsed for one moment an emptied socket full of beetles, and I wept.

The Sixth Adjustment

I will not claim, after this, that I took the wings only from duty, but I refute the accusation I took them in treason. There was no other choice. Men and children and the elderly or the sick, all the wingless, were fleeing from the continuing hail of Esperigan attacks. They were retreating deep into the heart of the continent, beyond the refueling range for the Esperigan warcraft, to shelters hidden so far in caves and in overgrowth that even my spy satellites knew nothing of them. My connection to Kostas would have been severed, and if I could provide neither intelligence nor direct assistance, I might as well have slunk back to the embassy, and saved myself the discomfort of being a refugee. Neither alternative was palatable.

They laid me upon the altar like a sacrifice, or so I felt, though they gave me something to drink which calmed my body, the nervous and involuntary twitching of my limbs and skin. Badea sat at my head and held the heavy long braid of my hair out of the way, while the others depilated my back and wiped it with alcohol. They bound me down then, and slit my skin open in two lines mostly parallel to the spine. Then Paudi gently set the wings upon me.

I lacked the skill to grow my own, in the time we had; Badea and Paudi helped me to mine so that I might stay. But even with the little assistance I had been able to contribute, I had seen more than I wished to of the parasites, and despite my closed eyes, my face turned downwards, I knew to my horror that the faint curious feather-brush sensation was the intrusion of the fine spiderweb filaments, each fifteen feet long, which now wriggled into the hospitable environment of my exposed inner flesh and began to sew themselves into me.

Pain came and went as the filaments worked their way through muscle and bone, finding one bundle of nerves and then another. After the first half hour, Badea told me gently, "It's coming to the spine," and gave me another drink. The drug kept my body from movement, but could do nothing to numb the agony. I cannot describe it adequately. If you have ever managed to inflict food poisoning upon yourself, despite all the Confederacy's safeguards, you may conceive of the kind if not the degree of suffering, an experience which envelops the whole body, every muscle and joint, and alters not only your physical self but your thoughts: all vanishes but pain, and the question, is the worst over? which is answered *no* and *no* again.

But at some point the pain began indeed to ebb. The filaments had entered the brain, and it is a measure of the experience that what I had feared the most was now blessed relief; I lay inert and closed my eyes gratefully while sensation spread outward from my back, and my new-borrowed limbs became gradually indeed my own, flinching from the currents of the air, and the touch of my friends' hands upon me. Eventually I slept.

The Seventh Adjustment

The details of the war, which unfolded now in earnest, I do not need to recount again. Kostas kept excellent records, better by far than my own, and students enough have memorized the dates and geographic coordinates, bounding death and ruin in small numbers. Instead I will tell you that from aloft, the

Esperigans' poisoned-ground encampments made half-starbursts of ochre brown and withered yellow, outlines like tentacles crawling into the healthy growth around them. Their supply-ships anchored out to sea glazed the water with a slick of oil and refuse, while the soldiers practiced their shooting on the vast schools of slow-swimming kraken young, whose bloated white bodies floated to the surface and drifted away along the coast, so many they defied even the appetite of the sharks.

I will tell you that when we painted their hulls with algaes and small crustacean-like borers, our work was camouflaged by great blooms of sea day-lilies around the ships, their masses throwing up reflected red color on the steel to hide the quietly creeping rust until the first winter storms struck and the grown kraken came to the surface to feed. I will tell you we watched from shore while the ships broke and foundered, and the teeth of the kraken shone like fire opals in the explosions, and if we wept, we wept only for the soiled ocean.

Still more ships came, and more planes; the ceramic coatings arrived, and more soldiers with protected guns and bombs and sprayed poisons, to fend off the altered motties and the little hybrid sparrowlike birds, their sharp cognizant eyes chemically retrained to see the Esperigan uniform colors as enemy markings. We planted acids and more aggressive species of plants along their supply lines, so their communications remained hopeful rather than reliable, and ambushed them at night; they carved into the forest with axes and power-saws and vast strip-miners, which ground to a halt and fell to pieces, choking on vines which hardened to the tensile strength of steel as they matured.

Contrary to claims which were raised at my trial *in absentia* and disproven with communication logs, throughout this time I spoke to Kostas regularly. I confused him, I think; I gave him all the intelligence which he needed to convey to the Esperigans, that they might respond to the next Melidan foray, but I did not conceal my feelings or the increasing complication of my loyalties, objecting to him bitterly and with personal anger about Esperigan attacks. I misled him with honesty: he thought, I believe, that I was only spilling a natural frustration to him, and through that airing clearing out my own doubts. But I had only lost the art of lying.

There is a general increase of perception which comes with the wings, the nerves teased to a higher pitch of awareness. All the little fidgets and twitches of lying betray themselves more readily, so only the more twisted forms can evade detection—where the speaker first deceives herself, or the wholly casual deceit of the sociopath who feels no remorse. This was the root of the Melidan disgust of the act, and I had acquired it.

If Kostas had known, he would at once have removed me: a diplomat is not much use if she cannot lie at need, much less an agent. But I did not volunteer the information, and indeed I did not realize, at first, how fully I had absorbed the stricture. I did not realize at all, until Badea came to me, three years into the war. I was sitting alone and in the dark by the communications console, the phosphorescent after-image of Kostas's face fading into the surface.

She sat down beside me and said, "The Esperigans answer us too quickly. Their technology advances in these great leaps, and every time we press them back, they return in less than a month to very nearly the same position."

I thought, at first, that this was the moment: that she meant to ask me about membership in the Confederacy. I felt no sense of satisfaction, only a weary kind of resignation. The war would end, the Esperigans would follow, and in a few generations they would both be eaten up by bureaucracy and standards and immigration.

Instead Badea looked at me and said, "Are your people helping them, also?"

My denial ought to have come without thought, leapt easily off the tongue with all the conviction duty could give it, and been followed by invitation. Instead I said nothing, my throat closed involuntarily. We sat silently in the darkness, and at last she said, "Will you tell me why?"

I felt at the time I could do no more harm, and perhaps some good, by honesty. I told her all the rationale, and expressed all our willingness to receive them into our union as equals. I went so far as to offer her the platitudes with which we convince ourselves we are justified in our slow gentle imperialism: that unification is necessary and advances all together, bringing peace.

She only shook her head and looked away from me. After a moment, she said, "Your people will never stop. Whatever we devise, they will help the Esperigans to a counter, and if the Esperigans devise some weapon we cannot defend ourselves against, they will help us, and we will batter each other into limp exhaustion, until in the end we all fall."

"Yes," I said, because it was true. I am not sure I was still able to lie, but in any case I did not know, and I did not lie.

I was not permitted to communicate with Kostas again until they were ready. Thirty-six of the Melidans' greatest designers and scientists died in the effort. I learned of their deaths in bits and pieces. They worked in isolated and quarantined spaces, their every action recorded even as the viruses and bacteria they were developing killed them. It was a little more than three months before Badea came to me again.

We had not spoken since the night she had learned the duplicity of the

Confederacy's support and my own. I could not ask her forgiveness, and she could not give it. She did not come for reconciliation but to send a message to the Esperigans and to the Confederacy through me.

I did not comprehend at first. But when I did, I knew enough to be sure she was neither lying nor mistaken, and to be sure the threat was very real. The same was not true of Kostas, and still less of the Esperigans. My frantic attempts to persuade them worked instead to the contrary end. The long gap since my last communique made Kostas suspicious: he thought me a convert, or generously a manipulated tool.

"If they had the capability, they would have used it already," he said, and if I could not convince him, the Esperigans would never believe.

I asked Badea to make a demonstration. There was a large island broken off the southern coast of the Esperigan continent, thoroughly settled and industrialized, with two substantial port cities. Sixty miles separated it from the mainland. I proposed the Melidans should begin there, where the attack might be contained.

"No," Badea said. "So your scientists can develop a counter? No. We are done with exchanges."

The rest you know. A thousand coracles left Melidan shores the next morning, and by sundown on the third following day, the Esperigan cities were crumbling. Refugees fled the groaning skyscrapers as they slowly bowed under their own weight. The trees died; the crops also, and the cattle, all the life and vegetation that had been imported from Earth and square-peg forced into the new world stripped bare for their convenience.

Meanwhile in the crowded shelters the viruses leapt easily from one victim to another, rewriting their genetic lines. Where the changes took hold, the altered survived. The others fell to the same deadly plagues that consumed all Earth-native life. The native Melidan moss crept in a swift green carpet over the corpses, and the beetle-hordes with it.

I can give you no first-hand account of those days. I too lay fevered and sick while the alteration ran its course in me, though I was tended better, and with more care, by my sisters. When I was strong enough to rise, the waves of death were over. My wings curled limply over my shoulders as I walked through the empty streets of Landfall, pavement stones pierced and broken by hungry vines, like bones cracked open for marrow. The moss covered the dead, who filled the shattered streets.

The squat embassy building had mostly crumpled down on one corner, smashed windows gaping hollow and black. A large pavilion of simple cotton fabric had been raised in the courtyard, to serve as both hospital and headquarters. A young undersecretary of state was the senior diplomat remaining. Kostas had died early, he told me. Others were still in the process of dying, their bodies waging an internal war that left them twisted by hideous deformities.

Less than one in thirty, was his estimate of the survivors. Imagine yourself on an air-train in a crush, and then imagine yourself suddenly alone but for one other passenger across the room, a stranger staring at you. Badea called it a sustainable population.

The Melidans cleared the spaceport of vegetation, though little now was left but the black-scorched landing pad, Confederacy manufacture, all of woven carbon and titanium.

"Those who wish may leave," Badea said. "We will help the rest."

Most of the survivors chose to remain. They looked at their faces in the mirror, flecked with green, and feared the Melidans less than their welcome on another world.

I left by the first small ship that dared come down to take off refugees, with no attention to the destination or the duration of the voyage. I wished only to be away. The wings were easily removed. A quick and painful amputation of the gossamer and fretwork which protruded from the flesh, and the rest might be left for the body to absorb slowly. The strange muffled quality of the world, the sensation of numbness, passed eventually. The two scars upon my back, parallel lines, I will keep the rest of my days.

Afterword

I spoke with Badea once more before I left. She came to ask me why I was going, to what end I thought I went. She would be perplexed, I think, to see me in my little cottage here on Reivaldt, some hundred miles from the nearest city, although she would have liked the small flowerlike lieden which live on the rocks of my garden wall, one of the few remnants of the lost native fauna which have survived the terraforming outside the preserves of the university system.

I left because I could not remain. Every step I took on Melida, I felt dead bones cracking beneath my feet. The Melidans did not kill lightly, an individual or an ecosystem, nor any more effectually than do we. If the Melidans had not let the plague loose upon the Esperigans, we would have destroyed them soon enough ourselves, and the Melidans with them. But we distance ourselves better from our murders, and so are not prepared to confront them. My wings whispered to me gently when I passed Melidans in the green-swathed cemetery streets, that they were not sickened, were not miserable. There was sorrow and regret but no self-loathing, where I had nothing else. I was alone.

When I came off my small vessel here, I came fully expecting punishment, even longing for it, a judgment which would at least be an end. Blame had wandered through the halls of state like an unwanted child, but when I proved willing to adopt whatever share anyone cared to mete out to me, to confess any crime which was convenient and to proffer no defense, it turned contrary, and fled.

Time enough has passed that I can be grateful now to the politicians who spared my life and gave me what passes for my freedom. In the moment, I could scarcely feel enough even to be happy that my report contributed some little to the abandonment of any reprisal against Melida: as though we ought hold them responsible for defying our expectations not of their willingness to kill one another, but only of the extent of their ability.

But time does not heal all wounds. I am often asked by visitors whether I would ever return to Melida. I will not. I am done with politics and the great concerns of the universe of human settlement. I am content to sit in my small garden, and watch the ants at work.

Ruth Patrona

PLOTTERS AND SHOOTERS

KAGE BAKER

I was flackeying for Lord Deathlok and Dr. Smash when the shuttle brought the new guy.

I hate Lord Deathlok. I hate Dr. Smash too, but I'd like to see Lord Deathlok get a missile fired up his ass, from his own cannon. Not that it's really a cannon. And I couldn't shoot him, anyhow, because I'm only a Plotter. But it's the thought that counts, you know?

Anyway I looked up when the beeps and the flashing lights started, and Lord Deathlok took hold of my little French maid's apron and yanked it so hard I had to bend over fast, so I almost dropped the tray with his drink.

Pay attention, maggot-boy, said Lord Deathlok. It's only a shuttle docking. No reason you should be distracted from your duties.

I know what's wrong, said Dr. Smash, lounging back against the bar. He hears the mating call of his kind. They must have sent up another Plotter.

Oh, yeah. Lord Deathlok grinned at me. Your fat-ass girlfriend went crying home to his mum and dad, didn't he?

Oh, man, how I hated him. He was talking about Kev, who'd only gone Down Home again because he'd almost died in an asthma attack. Kev had been a good Plotter, one of the best. I just glared at Deathlok, which was a mistake, because he smiled and put his boot on my foot and stood up.

I don't think I heard your answer, Fifi, he said, and I was in all this unbelievable psychological pain, see, because even with the lower gravity he could still manage to get the leverage just right if he wanted to bear down. They tell us we don't have to worry about getting brittle bones up here because they make us do weight-training, but how would we know if they were lying? I could almost hear my metatarsals snapping like dry twigs.

Yes, my Lord Deathlok, I said.

What? He leaned forward.

My lord yes my Lord Deathlok!

That's better. He sat down.

So okay, you're probably thinking I'm a coward. I'm not. It isn't that Lord Deathlok is even a big guy. He isn't, actually, he's sort of skinny and he has these big yellow buck teeth that make him look like a demon jackrabbit. And Dr. Smash has breasts and a body odor that makes sharing an airlock with him a fatal mistake. But they're *Shooters,* you know? And they all dress like they're space warriors or something, with the jackets and the boots and the scary hair styles. Shracking fascists.

So I put down his Dis Pepsy and backed away from him, and that was when the announcement came over the speakers:

Eugene Clifford, please report to Mr. Kurtz's office.

Talk about saved by the bell. As the message repeated, Lord Deathlok smirked.

Sounds like Dean Kurtz is lonesome for one of his little buttboys. You have our permission to go, Fifi.

My lord thank you my Lord Deathlok, I muttered, and tore off the apron and ran for the companionway.

Mr. Kurtz isn't a dean; I don't know why the Shooters call him that. He's the Station Manager. He runs the place for Areco and does our performance reviews and signs our bonus vouchers, and you'd think the Shooters would treat him with a little more respect, but they don't because they're *Shooters,* and that says it all. Mostly he sits in his office and looks disappointed. I don't blame him.

He looked up from his novel as I put my head around the door.

You wanted to see me, Mr. Kurtz?

He nodded. New arrival on the shuttle. Kevin Nederlander's replacement. Would you bring him up, please?

Yes, sir! I said, and hurried off to the shuttle lounge.

The new guy was sitting there in the lounge, with his duffel in the chair beside his. He was short and square and his haircut made his head look like it came to a point. Maybe it's genetic; Plotters can't seem to get good haircuts, ever.

Welcome to the Gun Platform, newbie, I said. I'm your Orientation Officer. Which I sort of am.

Oh, good, he said, getting to his feet, but he couldn't seem to take his eyes off the viewscreen. I waited for him to ask if that was really Mars down there, or gush about how he couldn't believe he was actually on an alien world or at least in orbit above one. That's usually what they do, see. But he didn't. He just shouldered his duffel and tore his gaze away at last.

Charles Tead. Glad to be here, he said.

Heh! That'll change, I thought. You've got some righteous shoes to fill, newbie. Think you're up to it?

He just said that he was, not like he was bragging or anything, and I thought *This one's going to get his corners broken off really soon.*

So I took him to the Forecastle and showed him Kev's old bunk, looking all empty and sad with the drillholes where Kev's holoposters used to be mounted. He put his duffel into Kev's old locker and looked around, and then he asked who did our laundry. I coughed a little and explained about it being sent down to the planet to be dry-cleaned. I didn't tell him, not then, about our having to collect the Shooters' dirty socks and stuff for them.

And I took him to the Bridge where B Shift was on duty and introduced him to the boys. Roscoe and Norman were wearing their Jedi robes, which I wish they wouldn't because it makes us look hopeless. Vinder was in a snit because Bradley had knocked one of his action figures behind the console, and apparently it was one of the really valuable ones, and Myron's the only person skinny enough to get his arm back there to fish it out, but he's on C Shift and wouldn't come on duty until seventeen-hundred hours.

I guess that was where it started, B Shift making such a bad first impression.

But I tried to bring back some sense of importance by showing him the charting display, with the spread of the asteroid belt all in blue and gold, like a stained-glass window in an old-time church must have been, only everything moving.

This is your own personal slice of the sky, I said, waving at Q34-54. Big Kev knew every one of these babies. Tracked every little wobble, every deviation over three years. Plotted trajectories for thirty-seven successful shots. It was like he had a sixth sense! He even called three Intruders before they came in range. He was the Bonus Master, old Kev. You'll have to work pretty damn hard to be half as good as he was.

But it ought to be easy, said Charles. Doesn't the mapping software do most of it?

Well, like, I mean, sure, but you'll have to *coordinate* everything, you know? In your head? Machines can't do it all, I protested. And Vinder chose that second to yell from behind us, Don't take the Flying Dynamo's cape off, you'll break him! Which totally blew the mood I was trying to get. So I ignored him and continued:

We've been called up from Earth for a job only we can do. It's a high and lonely destiny, up here among the cold stars! Mundane people couldn't stick it out. That's why Areco went looking for guys like us. We're free of entanglements, right? We came from our parents' basements and garages to a place where our powers were *needed*. Software can map those rocks out there, okay; it can track them, maybe. But only a human can—can—smell them coming in before they're there, okay?

You mean like precognition? Charles stared at me.

Not exactly, I said, even though Myron claims he's got psychic abilities, but he never seems to be able to predict when the Shooters are going to go on a rampage on our turf. I'm talking about gut feelings. Hunches. Instinct! That's the word I was looking for. Human instinct. We outguess the software seventy percent of the time on projected incoming. Not bad, huh?

I guess so, he said.

I spent the rest of the shift showing him his console and setting up his passwords and customizations and stuff. He didn't ask many questions, just put on the goggles and focused, and you could almost see him wandering around among the asteroids in Q34-54 and getting to know them. I was starting to get a good feeling about him, because that was just the way Kev used to plot, and then he said:

How do we target them?

Vinder was so shocked he dropped the Blue Judge. Roscoe turned, took off his goggles to stare at me, and said:

We don't target. Cripes, haven't you told him?

Told me what? Charles turned his goggled face toward the sound of Roscoe's voice.

So then I had to tell him about the Shooters, and how he couldn't go into the bar when Shooters were in there except when he was flackeying for one of them, and what they'd do to him if he did, and how he had to stay out of the Pit of Hell where they bunked except when he was flackeying for them, and he was never under any circumstances to go into the War Room at all.

I was explaining about the flackeying rotation when he said:

This is stupid!

It's sheer evil, said Roscoe. But there's nothing we can do about it. They're Shooters. You can't fight them. You don't want to know what happens if you try.

This wasn't in my contract, said Charles.

You can go complain to Kurtz, if you want, said Bradley. It's no damn use. *He* can't control them. They're Shooters. Nobody else can do what they do.

I'll bet I could, said Charles, and everybody just sniffed at him, because, you know, who's got reflexes like a Shooter? They're the best at what they do.

You got assigned to us because you tested out as a Plotter, I told Charles. That's just the way things are. You're the best at your job; the pay's good; in five years you'll be out of here. You just have to learn to live with the crap. We all did.

He looked like a smart guy and I thought he wouldn't need to be told twice. I was wrong.

We heard the march of booted feet coming along the corridor. Vinder leaped up and grabbed all his action figures, shoving them into a storage pod. Norman began to hyperventilate; Bradley ran for the toilet. I just stayed where I was and lowered my eyes. It's never a good idea to look them in the face.

Boom! The portal jerked open and in they came, Lord Deathlok and the Shark and Iron Beast. They were carrying Piki-tiki. I blanched.

Piki-tiki was this sort of dummy they'd made out of a blanket and a mask. And a few other things. Lord Deathlok grinned around and spotted Charles.

Piki-tiki returns to his harem, he shouted. What's this? Piki-tiki sees a new and beautiful bride! Piki-tiki must welcome her to his realm!

Giggling, they advanced on Charles and launched the dummy. It fell over him, and before he could throw it off they'd jumped him and hoisted him between them. He was fighting hard, but they just laughed; that is, until he got one arm free and punched the Shark in the face. The Shark grabbed his nose and began to swear, but Lord Deathlok and Iron Beast gloated.

Whoa! The blushing bride needs to learn her manners. Piki-tiki's going to take her off to his honeymoon suite and see that she learns them well!

Ouch. They dragged him away. At least it wasn't the worst they might have done to him; they were only going to cram him in one of the lockers, probably one that had had some sweaty socks left in the bottom, and stuff Piki-tiki in there on top of him. Then they'd lock him in and leave him there. How did I know? They'd done it to me, on my first day.

If you're sensible, like me, you just shrug it off and concentrate on your job. Charles wouldn't let it go, though. He kept asking questions.

Like, how come the Shooters were paid better than we were, even though they spent most of their time playing simulations and Plotters did all the actual work of tracking asteroids and calculating when they'd strike? How come Mr. Kurtz had given up on disciplinary action for them, even after they'd rigged his holoset to come on unexpectedly and project a CGI of him having sex with an alligator, or all the other little ways in which they made his life a living hell? How come none of us ever stood up to them?

And it was no good explaining how they didn't respond to reason, and they didn't respond to being called immature and crude and disgusting, because they just loved being told how awful they were.

The other thing he asked about was why there weren't any women up here, and that was too humiliating to go into, so I just said tests had shown that men were better suited for life on a Gun Platform.

He should have been happy that he was a *good* Plotter, because he really was. He mastered Q34-54 in a week. One shift we were there on the Bridge and Myron and I were talking about the worst ever episode of *Schrödinger's Rock*, which was the one that had Lallal's evil twin showing up after being killed off in the second season, and Anil was unwrapping the underwear his mother had sent him for his thirty-first birthday, when suddenly Charles said: Eugene, you should probably check Q6-17; I'm calculating an Intruder showing up in about Q-14.

How'd you know? I said in surprise, slipping my goggles on. But he was right; there was an Intruder, tumbling end over end in a halo of fire and snow, way above the plane of the ecliptic but square in Q-14.

Don't you extend your projections beyond the planet's ecliptic? said Charles.

Myron and I looked at each other. We never projected out that far; what was the point? There was always time to spot an Intruder before it came in range.

You don't have to work *that* hard, dude, I said. Fifty degrees above and below is all we have to bother with. The scanning programs catch the rest. But I sent out the alert and we could hear the Shooters cheering, even though the War Room was clear at the other end of the Platform. As far out as the Intruder was, the Shark was able to send out a missile. We didn't see the hit— there wouldn't be one for two weeks at least, and I'd have to keep monitoring the Intruder and now the missile too, just to be sure the trajectories remained matched up—but the Shooters began to stamp and roar the Bonus Song.

Myron sniffed.

Typical, he said. We do all the work, they push one bloody button, and *they're* the heroes.

You know, it doesn't have to be this way, said Charles.

It's not like we can go on strike, said Anil sullenly. We're independent contractors. There's a penalty for quitting.

You don't have to quit, said Charles. You can show Areco you can do even more. We can be Plotters *and* Shooters.

Anil and Myron looked horrified. You'd have thought he'd suggested we all turn homo or something. I was shocked myself. I had to explain about tests proving that things functioned most smoothly when every man kept to his assigned task.

Don't Areco think we can multitask? he asked me. They're a corporation like any other, aren't they? They must want to save money. All we have to do is show them we can do both jobs. The Shooters get a nice redundancy package; we get the Gun Platform all to ourselves. Life is good.

Only one problem with your little plan, Mr. Genius, said Myron. I can't shoot. I don't have the reflexes a Shooter does. That's why I'm a Plotter.

But you could learn to shoot, said Charles.

I'll repeat this slowly so you get it, said Myron, exasperated. *I don't have the reflexes*. And neither do you. How many times have we been tested, our whole lives? Aptitude tests, allergy tests, brain scans, DNA mapping? Areco knows exactly what we are and what we can and can't do. I'm a Plotter. You're just fooling yourself if you think you aren't.

Charles didn't say anything in reply. He just looked at each of us in turn, pretty disgusted I guess, and then he turned back to his console and focused on his work.

That wasn't the end of it, though. When he was off his shift, instead of hanging out in the Cockpit, did he join in the discussions of graphic novels or what was hot on holo that week? Not Charles. He'd retire to a corner in the Forecastle with a buke and he'd game. And not just any game: targeting simulations. You never saw a guy with such icy focus. Sometimes he'd tinker with a couple of projects he'd ordered. I assumed they were models.

It was like the rest of us weren't even there. We had to respect him as a Plotter; for one thing, he turned out to have an uncanny knack for spotting Intruders, days before any of the rest of us detected them, and he was brilliant at predicting their trajectories too. But there was something distant about the guy that kept him from fitting in. Myron and Anil had dismissed him as a crank anyway, and a couple of the guys on B shift actively disliked him, after he spouted off to them the way he did to us. They were sure he was going to do something, sooner or later, that would only end up making it worse for all of us.

They were right, too.

When Weldon's turn in the rota ended, he brought Charles the French maid's apron and tossed it on his bunk.

Your turn to wear the damn thing, he said. They'll expect you in the bar at fourteen hundred hours. Good luck.

Charles just grunted, never even looking up from the screen of his buke.

Fourteen hundred hours came and he was still sitting there, coolly gaming.

Hey! said Anil. You're supposed to go flackey!

I'm not going, said Charles.

Don't be stupid! I said. If the rest of us have to do it, you do too.

Why? Terrible repercussions if I don't? Charles set aside his buke and looked at us.

Yes! said Myron. Preston from A Shift came running in right then, looking pale.

Who's supposed to be flackeying? There's nobody out there, and Lord Deathlok wants to know why!

See? said Myron.

You'll get all of us in trouble, you fool! Give me the apron, I'll go! said Anil. But Charles took the apron and tore it in half.

There was this horrified silence, which filled up with the sound of Shooters thundering along the corridor. We heard Lord Deathlok and Painmaster yelling as they came.

Flackey! Oh, flackey! Where are you?

And then they were in the room and it was too late to run, too late to hide. Painmaster's roach crest almost touched the ceiling panels. Lord Deathlok's yellow grin was so wide he didn't look human.

Hi there, buttholes, said Painmaster. If you girls aren't too busy making out, one of you is supposed to be flackeying for us.

It was my turn, said Charles. He wadded up the apron and threw it at them. How about you wait on yourself from now on?

This wasn't our idea! said Myron.

We tried to make him report for duty! said Anil.

We'll remember that, when we're assigning penalties, said Lord Deathlok. Maybe we'll let you keep your pants when we handcuff you upside down in the toilet. Little Newbie, though . . . He turned to Charles. What about a nice game of Walk the Dog? Painmaster, got a leash anywhere on you?

The Painmaster always has a leash for a bad dog, said Painmaster, pulling one out. He started toward Charles, and that's when it got crazy.

Charles jumped out of his bunk and I thought, *No, you idiot, don't try to run!* But he didn't. He grabbed Painmaster's extended hand and pulled him close, and brought his arm up like he was going to hug him, only instead he made a kind of punching motion at Painmaster's neck. Painmaster screamed, wet himself and fell down. Charles kicked him in the crotch.

Another dead silence, which broke as soon as Painmaster got enough breath in him for another scream. Everybody else in the room was staring at Charles, or I should say at his left wrist, because it was now obvious there was something strapped to it under his sleeve.

Lord Deathlok had actually taken a step backward. He looked from Painmaster to Charles, and then at whatever it was on Charles' wrist. He licked his lips.

So, that's, what, some kind of taser? he said. Those are illegal, buddy.

Charles smiled. I realized then I'd never seen him smile before.

It's illegal to buy one. I bought some components and made my own. What are you going to do? Report me to Kurtz? he said.

No; I'm just going to take it away from you, dumbass, said Lord Deathlok. He lunged at Charles, but all that happened was that Charles tased him too. He jerked backward and fell over a chair, clutching his tased hand.

You're dead, he gasped. You're really dead.

Charles walked over and kicked him in the crotch too.

I challenge you to a duel, he said.

What? said Lord Deathlok, when he had enough breath after his scream.

A duel. With simulations, said Charles. I'll outshoot you. Right there in the War Room, with everybody there to witness. Thirteen hundred hours tomorrow.

Fuck off, said Lord Deathlok. Charles leaned down and displayed the two little steel points of the taser.

So you're scared to take me on? Chicken, is that it? he said, and Myron and Anil obligingly started making cluck-cluck-cluck noises. Eugene, why don't you go over to the Pit of Hell and tell the Shooters they need to come scrape up these guys?

I wouldn't have done that for a chance to see the lost episodes of *Doctor Who,* but fortunately Lord Deathlok sat up, gasping.

Okay, he said. Duel. You lose, I get that taser and shove it up your ass.

Sure, said Charles. Whatever you want; but I won't lose. And none of us will ever flackey for you again. Got it?

Lord Deathlok called him a lot of names, but the end of it was that he agreed to the terms, and we made Painmaster (who was crying and complaining that his heartbeat was irregular) witness. When they could walk they went stumbling back to the Pit of Hell, leaning on each other.

You are out of your mind, I said, when they had gone. You'll go to the War Room tomorrow and they'll be waiting for you with six bottles of club soda and a can of poster paint.

Maybe, said Charles. But they'll back off. Haven't you clowns figured it out yet? They're used to shooting at rocks. They have no clue what to do about something that fights back.

They'll still win. You won't be able to tase them all, and once they get it off you, you're doomed.

They won't get off me, said Charles, rolling up his sleeve and unstrapping the taser mounting from his arm. I won't be wearing it. You will.

Me? I backed away.

And there's another one in my locker. Which one of you wants it?

You've got *two?*

Me! Anil jumped forward. So we'll be, like, your bodyguards? Yes! Can you make more of these things?

I won't need to, said Charles. Tomorrow's going to change everything.

I don't mind telling you, my knees were knocking as we marched across to the War Room next day. Everybody on B and C Shifts came along; strength in numbers, right? If we got creamed by the Shooters, at least some of us ought to make it out of there. And if Charles was insanely lucky, we all wanted to see.

It was embarrassing. Norman and Roscoe wore full Jedi kit, including their damn light sabers that were only holobeams anyway. Bradley was wearing a Happy Bat San playjacket. Anil was wearing his lucky hat from *Mystic Antagonists: the Extravaganza*. We're all creative and unique, no question, but . . . maybe it isn't the best idea to dress that way when you're going to a duel with intimidating mindless jerks.

We got there, and they were waiting for us.

Our Bridge always reminded me of a temple or a shrine or something, with its beautiful display shining in the darkness; but the War Room was like the Cave of the Cyclops. There wasn't any wall display like we had. There were just the red lights of the targeting consoles, and way in the far end of the room somebody had stuck up a black light, which made the lurid holoposters of skulls and demons and vampires seem to writhe in the gloom.

The place stank of body odor, which the Shooters can't get rid of because they wear all that black bioprene gear, which doesn't breathe like the natural fabrics we wear. There was also a urinal reek; when a Shooter is gaming, he doesn't let a little thing like needing to pee drive him from his console.

All this was bad enough; imagine how I felt to see that the Shooters had made war clubs out of chlorilar water bottles stuck into handles of printer paper rolled tight. They stood there, glowering at us. I saw Lord Deathlok and the Shark and Professor Badass. Mephisto, the Conquistador, Iron Beast, Killer Ape, Uncle Hannibal . . . every hateful face I knew from months of humiliating flackey-work, except . . .

Where's the Painmaster? said Charles, looking around in an unconcerned kind of way.

He had better things to do than watch you rectums lose, said Lord Deathlok.

He had to be shipped down to the infirmary, because he was complaining of chest pains, said Mephisto. The others looked at him accusingly. Charles beamed.

Too bad! Let's do this thing, gentlemen.

We fixed up a special console, homo, just for you, said Lord Deathlok with an evil leer, waving at one. Charles looked at it and laughed.

You have got to be kidding. I'll take *this* one over *here*, and you'll take the one next to it. We'll play side by side, so everybody can see. That's only fair, right?

Their faces fell. But Anil and I crossed our arms, so the taser prongs showed, and the Shooters grumbled but backed down. They cleared away empty bottles and snack wrappers from the consoles. It felt good, watching them humbled for a change.

Charles settled himself at the console he'd chosen, and with a few quick commands on the buttonball pulled up the simulation menu.

Is this all you've got? he said. Okay; I propose nine rounds. Three sets each of *Holodeath 2, Meteor Nightmare,* and *Incoming Annihilation.* Highest cumulative score wins.

You got it, shithead, said Lord Deathlok. He took his seat.

So they called up *Holodeath 2,* and we all crowded around to watch, even though the awesome stench of the Shooters was enough to make your eyes water. The holo display lit up with a sinister green fog, and the enemy ships started coming at us. Charles got off three shots before Lord Deathlok managed one, and though one of his shots went wild, two inflicted enough damage on a Megacruiser to set it on fire. Lord Deathlok's shot nailed a patrol vessel in the forefront, and though it was a low-score target, he took it out with just that one shot. The score counters on both consoles gave them 1200 points.

Charles finished the burning cruiser with two more quick shots—it looked fantastic, glaring red through its ports until it just sort of imploded in this cylinder of glowing ash. But Lord Deathlok was picking off the little transport cutters methodically, because they only take about a shot each if you're accurate, which he was. Charles pulled ahead by hammering away at the big targets, and he never missed another shot, and so what happened was that the score counters showed them flashing along neck and neck for the longest time and then, *boom,* the last Star Destroyer blew and Charles was suddenly way ahead with twice Deathlok's score.

We were all yelling by this time, the Shooters with their chimpanzee hooting and us with—well, we sort of sounded like apes too. The next set went up and here came the ships again, but this time they were firing back. Charles took three hits in succession, before he seemed to figure out how to raise his shields, and the Shooters started gloating and smacking their clubs together.

But he went on the offensive real fast, and did something I'd never thought of before, which was aiming for the ships' gunports and disabling them with one shot before hitting them with a barrage that finished them. I never even had time to look at what Deathlok was doing, but his guys stopped cheering suddenly and when the set ended, he didn't even have a third of the points Charles did.

The third set went amazingly fast, even with the difference that the gun positions weren't stationary and they had to maneuver around in the middle of the armada. Charles did stuff I would never have dared to do, recklessly swooping around and under the Megacruisers, *between* their gunports for cripe's sake, getting off round after round of shots so close it seemed impossible for him to pull clear before the ships blew, but somehow he did.

Lord Deathlok didn't seem to move much. He just sat in one position and pounded away at anything that came within range, and though he did manage to bag a Star Destroyer, he finished the set way behind Charles on points.

I would have just given up if I'd been Deathlok, but the Shooters were getting ugly, shouting all kinds of personal abuse at him, and I don't think he dared.

I had to run for the lavatory as *Incoming Annihilation* was starting, and of course I had to run all the way back to our end of the Gun Platform to our toilet because I sure wasn't going to use the Shooters', not with the way the War Room smelled. It was only when I was unfastening that I realized I was still wearing the taser, and that I'd done an incredibly stupid thing by leaving when I was one of Charles' bodyguards. So I finished fast and ran all the way back, and there was Mr. Kurtz strolling along the corridor.

Hello there, Eugene, he said. Something going on?

Just some gaming, I said. I need to get back—

But you're on Shooter turf, aren't you? Mr. Kurtz looked around. Shouldn't you be going in the other direction?

Well—we're having this competition, you see, Mr. Kurtz, I said. The new guy's gaming against Lord—I mean, against Peavey Crandall.

Is he? Mr. Kurtz began to smile. I wondered how long Charles would put up with the Shooters. Well, well.

He said it in a funny kind of way, but I didn't have the time to wonder about it. I just excused myself and ran on, and was really relieved to see that the Shooters didn't seem to have noticed my absence. They were all packed tight around the consoles, and nobody was making a sound; all you could hear was the *peew-peew-peew* of the shots going off continuously, and the *whump* as bombs exploded. Then there was a flare of red light and our guys yelled in triumph. Bradley was leaping up and down, and Roscoe did a Victory Dance until one of the Shooters asked him if he wanted his light saber rammed up his butt.

I managed to shove my way between Anil and Myron just as Charles was announcing, I believe you're screwed, Mr. Crandall. Care to call it a day?

I looked at their scores and couldn't believe how badly Lord Deathlok had lost to him. But Lord Deathlok just snarled.

I don't think so, Ben Dover. Shut up and play!

It was *Meteor Nightmare* now, as though they were both out there in the Van Oort belt, facing the rocks without any comforting distance of consoles or calculations. I couldn't stop myself from flinching as they hurtled forward; and I noticed one of the Shooters put up his arms involuntarily, as though he wanted to bat away the incoming with his bare hands.

It was a brutal game; *nightmare,* all right, because they couldn't avoid taking massive damage. All they could do was take out as many targets as they could before their inevitable destruction. When one or the other of them took a hit, there was a momentary flare of light that blinded everybody in the room. I couldn't imagine how Charles and Lord Deathlok, right there with their faces in the action, could keep shooting with any kind of accuracy.

Sure enough, early in the second round it began to tell. They were both getting flash-blind. Charles was still hitting about one in three targets, but Lord Deathlok was shooting crazily, randomly, not even bothering to aim so far as I could tell. What a look of despair on his ugly face, with his lips drawn back from his yellow teeth!

Only a miracle would save him, now. His overall score was so far behind Charles' he'd never catch up. The Shooters knew it too. I saw Dr. Smash turn his head and murmur to Uncle Hannibal. He took a firm grip on his war club. Panicking, I grabbed Anil's arm, trying to get his attention.

That was when the Incoming klaxons sounded. All the Shooters stood to attention. Lord Deathlok looked around, blinking, but Charles worked the buttonball like a pro and suddenly the game vanished, and there was nothing before us but the console displays. There was a crackle from the speakers—the first time they'd ever been used, I found out later—and we could hear Preston screaming, You guys! Intruder coming in fast! You have to stop! It's in—

Q41! said Uncle Hannibal, leaning forward to peer at the console readout. Get out of my chair, dickwad!

Charles didn't answer. He did something with the buttonball and there was the Intruder, like something out of *Meteor Nightmare*, shracking enormous. It was in his own sector! How could he have missed it? *Charles*, who was brilliant at spotting them before anybody else?

A red frame rose around it, with the readout in numbers spinning over so fast I couldn't tell what they said, except it was obvious the thing was coming in at high speed. All the Shooters were frantic, bellowing for Charles to get his ass out of the chair. Before their astounded eyes, and ours, he targeted the Intruder and fired.

All sound stopped. Movement stopped. Time itself stopped, except for on the display, where a new set of numbers in green and another in yellow popped up. They spun like fruit on a slot machine, the one counting up, the other counting down, both getting slower and slower until suddenly the numbers matched. Then, in perfect unison, they clicked upward together on a leisurely march.

It's a hit, announced Preston from the speakers. In twelve days thirteen hours forty-two minutes. Telemetry confirmed.

Dead silence answered him. And that was when I understood: Charles hadn't missed the Intruder. Charles had spotted it days ago. Charles had set this whole thing up, requesting the specific time of the duel, knowing the Intruder would interrupt it and there'd have to be a last-minute act of heroism. Which he'd co-opt.

But the thing is, see, there are *people* down there on the planet under us, who could die if a meteor gets through. I mean, that's why we're all up here in the first place, right?

Finally Anil said, in a funny voice, So . . . who gets the bonus, then?

He *can't* have just done that, said Mephisto, hoarse with disbelief. He's a *Plotter*.

Get up, faggot, said Uncle Hannibal, grabbing Charles' shoulder.

Hit him, said Charles.

I hadn't unfrozen yet, but Anil had been waiting for this moment all day. He jumped forward and tased Uncle Hannibal. Uncle Hannibal dropped, with a hoarse screech, and the other Shooters backed away fast. Anil stared down at Uncle Hannibal with unholy wonder in his eyes, and the beginning of a terrible joy. Suddenly there was a lot of room in front of the consoles, enough to see Lord Deathlok sitting there staring at the readout, with tears streaming down his face.

Charles got out of the chair.

You lost, he informed Lord Deathlok.

Your reign of terror is over! cried Anil, brandishing his taser at the Shooters. One or two of them cowered, but the rest just looked stunned. Charles turned to me.

You left your post, he said. You're a useless idiot. Myron, take the taser off him.

Sir yes sir! said Myron, grabbing my arm and rolling up my sleeve. As he was unfastening the straps, we heard a chuckle from the doorway. All heads turned. There was Mr. Kurtz, leaning there with his arms crossed. I realized he must have followed me, and seen the drama as it played out. Anil thrust his taser arm behind his back, looking scared, but Mr. Kurtz only smiled.

As you were, he said. He stood straight and left. We could hear him whistling as he walked away.

It wasn't until later that we learned the whole story, or as much of it as we ever knew: how Charles had been recruited, not from his parents' garage or basement, but from Hospital, and how Mr. Kurtz had known it, had in fact *requested it*.

We all expected a glorious new day had come for Plotters, now that Charles had proven the Shooters were unnecessary. We thought Areco would terminate their contracts. It didn't exactly happen that way.

What happened was that Dr. Smash and Uncle Hannibal came to Charles and had a private (except for Myron and Anil) talk with him. They were very polite. Since Painmaster wasn't coming back to the Gun Platform, but had defaulted on his contract and gone down home to Earth, they proposed that Charles become a Shooter. They did more; they offered him High Dark Lordship.

He accepted their offer. We were appalled. It seemed like the worst treachery imaginable.

And yet, we were surprised again.

Charles Tead didn't take one of the stupid Shooter names like Warlord or Iron Fist or Doomsman. He said we were all to call him *Stede* from now on. He ordered up, not a bioprene wardrobe with spikes and rivets and fringe, but . . . but . . . a three-piece suit, with a *tie*. And a bowler hat. He took his tasers back from Anil and Myron, who were crestfallen, and wore them himself, under his perfectly pressed cuffs.

Then he ordered up new clothes for all the other Shooters. It must have been a shock, when he handed out those powder blue shirts and drab coveralls, but they didn't rebel; by that time they'd learned what he'd been sent to Hospital for in the first place, which was killing three people. So there wasn't so much as a mutter behind his back, even when he ordered all the holoposters shut off and thrown into the fusion hopper, and the War Room repainted in dove gray.

We wouldn't have known the Shooters. He made them wash; he made them cut their hair, he made them shracking salute when he gave an order. They were scared to fart, especially after he hung up deodorizers above each of their consoles. The War Room became a clean, well-lit place, silent except for the consoles and the occasional quiet order from Charles. He seldom had to raise his voice.

Mr. Kurtz still sat in his office all day, reading, but now he smiled as he read. Nobody called him *Dean Kurtz* anymore, either.

It was sort of horrible, what had happened, but with Charles—I mean, Stede—running the place, things were a lot more efficient. The bonuses became more frequent, as everyone worked harder. And, in time, the Shooters came to worship him.

He didn't bother with us. We were grateful.

THE MUSE OF EMPIRES LOST

PAUL BERGER

A ship had come in, and now everything would change. Jemmi had recently become adept at crouching under windows and listening around corners, so when the village went abuzz with the news, she heard all the excitement. She was hungry and lonely, and she thought of Port-Town and the opportunities that would be found there now, and she left the village before light. She went with only the briefest pang of homesickness, and she went by the marsh trail rather than the main road, because if she had met any of her neighbors along the way, they would have stoned her.

The path was swallowed up by the murky water sooner than she expected, and the gray silt sucked at Jemmi's worn straw zori with each step. Poor old Sarasvati, always laboring to bestow ease and prosperity upon her people, and always falling a bit more behind. These were supposed to be fields, but the marshes stretched closer to their houses each year. She couldn't even get any decent fish to breed there. In the village they clucked their tongues and said that was old Sara's nanos going, as if anyone knew what that meant or could do anything about it. But sometimes you could melt handfuls of this silt down and chip it into very sharp little blades that would hold their edge for a shave or two and could be bartered for a bite to eat. Sometimes you could see it slowly writhe in your hand.

Now that the village had turned against her, Sara was Jemmi's closest and only chum. When Jemmi was at her most alone she would sit quietly and concentrate on a tiny still spot deep in her center and maybe think a few words in her heart, and a spark would answer, and a huge warm and beloved feeling would spread through her. She knew that was Sara speaking to her. Everyone wanted Sara to listen to them, but Sara barely ever spoke back to anyone.

By midday Jemmi struck a road, and the next morning she reached Port-Town. Her parents had taken her there once when she was little, so she already knew to expect the tumult and smells and narrow streets packed with new faces, but the sheer activity spun her around as she tried to track everything that moved through her line of sight. Jewel-green quetzals squabbled and huddled together under the eaves of high-peaked shingled roofs, and peacocks dodged rickshaw wheels and pecked at the dust and refuse in the streets. There was plenty of food here if she could get it, and fine things to own, stacked in stalls and displayed in shop windows.

She was drawn most of all, though, to the mass of humanity that surrounded her—she could practically taste their thoughts and needs as they swirled by. The townsfolk were thronging towards the old wharf, and she let herself be swept up with them. Sometimes men or women brushed against her or jostled her without a glance or a second thought, and she grinned to herself at the rare physical contact.

An ambitious vendor had piled bread and fruit into a wooden cart at the edge of the street to catch the passers-by, and Jemmi stopped in front of him.

"Neh, what ship is it?" she asked above the din.

"Haven't you heard, then?" he replied. "It's Albiorix!"

Jemmi thought he was mocking her until she caught the man's exultant smile. *Albiorix*—no ship had stopped here for more than a generation, and now this! Albiorix was the stuff of legend, a proud giant among ships, braver and broader-ranging than any other. If Sarasvati was on Albiorix's route now, they would all be rich again.

"Who was on board, then?"

"No one's seen them yet. Looks like they'll be debarking any minute."

Jemmi checked her urge to race off towards the wharf. She put her hand on the vendor's forearm and smiled her warmest smile, and as he stood distracted and fuddled she swept an apple and two rolls into her pockets. She turned and ran before the man's head cleared.

The crowds along the quay were packed tight and jostling viciously, but Jemmi plunged in and no one noticed or resisted as she slipped right up to the barrier. A boy was standing near her. He was clear-eyed and honey-skinned and probably about two years older than she was. Judging from his clothes and the rich dagger that hung at his belt—the hilt bound with real wire—his family was quite well-to-do. With visions of regular meals and a roof over her head, she sidled towards him. The boy looked over her rags and begrimed face and straightaway disregarded her. Jemmi held firm and let the motion of the crowd press him close to her. The back of his hand brushed against her bare wrist, and he unconsciously jerked it away. She shifted her weight so that she was a fraction closer to him. The next time he moved he touched her again, and she imagined that he was not quite so quick to pull back.

The third time they touched she kept her hand against his, and the boy did not pull away. He turned shyly to Jemmi.

"Hello," he said. "My name's Roycer."

At that moment, the entire length of Sarasvati trembled with a gentle impact, and the crowd's cheer was deafening.

Outside, languid in the vacuum of space, Albiorix stroked Sarasvati's stony mantle with the fluid tip of a miles-long tentacle—an overture and an offering. Sarasvati recalled Albiorix of old, and his strength and boldness were more than she could have hoped for. She extended a multitude of soft arms from deep within the moonlet that served as her shelter and her home, and entwined them with his. She dwarfed him as she embraced him. Her tentacles brushed the length of his nacreous spiral shell, and in the silence dizzying patterns of light flashed across both their surfaces. The colors matched and melded, until they raced along his arms and up hers and back again. Sarasvati was receptive, and eager to welcome Albiorix after his lonely journey across the vastness. He disentangled himself and drifted down to the tip of her long axis, and they both spread their arms wide as he clasped his head to the orifice there. She released her great outer valve for him, and he gently discharged his passengers and all their cargo. Sarasvati accepted them gracefully, and in return, flooded his interior with fresh atmosphere from her reserves. Now duty and foreplay had been dispensed with, and they embraced again in earnest, spinning in the void.

The sphincter on Sarasvati's inner surface dilated open, and the passengers off Albiorix stepped through into Port-Town, armed and alert. The arrivals were well aware that half the inhabitants of any orbital would tear newcomers apart just to see what they carried in their packs, and they hustled down the quay in tight phalanxes that bristled with weapons. They no doubt came from richer lands—Jemmi noticed the glint of steel in the trappings of their spears and crossbows as they passed. One group brandished old-style plasma rifles, but Jemmi assumed that was a bluff; everyone knew the smart electronics hadn't worked since the day the Cosmopolis fell. The crowds parted grudgingly around this threat, and Roycer was pushed closer to Jemmi, his gaze never leaving her face.

The rest of the townsfolk watched the arrivals' every move as they sought shelter in the winding streets. Those that could strike deals with families or inns to harbor them were likely to survive. This must have been an especially long voyage, Jemmi thought, or else star travel must be harder than anyone remembered. These arrivals all looked sunken-cheeked and worn down as if drained, or haunted by something they could not name.

One last traveler stepped through into Sarasvati, alone. He was the oddest thing Jemmi had ever seen. He was tall and slightly stooped and unnaturally pale—both his skin and his sparse hair were the same shade of thin gruel— and although at a distance Jemmi assumed he was very old, as he approached

Jemmi realized she could not guess his age at all. His only luggage was a canister that hung from his shoulder on a strap. He walked unarmed along the barrier and Jemmi was certain he would be snatched up, yet no one in the throng made a move towards him or particularly noted his presence. He took his time, scanning the faces and garments as if looking for something. He stopped in front of Jemmi and her boy, and smiled. His teeth were the same color as his skin, and were all broad and very large in his gums.

"You'll do," he told the boy. "Shouldn't we be getting home now?"

Wordlessly, the boy nodded and released Jemmi's hand. He slipped under the barrier and joined the traveler, and led him down the quay into town.

Jemmi, stunned with amazement and impotent wrath, stood there slack-jawed until long after they left her sight.

With the excitement over, the crowd melted away, and Jemmi saw no chances to get close to anyone else. She spent the rest of the day sidestepping traffic and looking into windows, and she was able to grab a bit more to eat in the same manner she had acquired breakfast. After dusk one or two men on the darkened streets spoke to her, but they didn't look useful and she didn't like what their voices implied, so after that she took to helping people ignore her. That meant she couldn't get indoors to sleep, but luckily Sara was still too distracted with her beau to make a proper rain. Jemmi spent the night curled at the foot of a weather-beaten neighborhood shrine at the end of a narrow alley. It was certainly not what she had hoped for when she had decided to make the journey to town, but it was not too different from what she had left behind. Amongst the incense ash and candle-stubs and tentacled figurines, some housewife had left a rag doll dressed in a new set of toddler's clothes, a supplication to Sara for an easy birth and a healthy baby. The offering of a portion of a family meal that sat alongside it had barely gone cold, but some things were sacred, and Jemmi was not tempted to take it.

She fell asleep thinking how happy she was for old Sara, and she dreamed a wondrously clear vision of the two lovers floating clasped together with countless arms, surrounded by stars, auroras chasing along their skins. Jemmi accepted the image without question, notwithstanding she had never seen a sky before.

She awoke when she felt that Sara was about to make dawn, and she stood in her alley to watch it. Directly overhead, the coil of viscera that stretched along Sarasvati's axis sparked and sputtered with flashes of bioluminescence, and then kindled down its entire length. As the light phased from gold to yellow to white, Jemmi was able to pick out the fields and woods and streets of her own village hanging high above and upside down along Sarasvati's great inner vault. It was significant to her only as a starting point; she had come to town now, and her home would be here. She set out walking again, looking for breakfast and Opportunity.

Before she found either, she found the traveler. He was sitting on the veranda of a home in a wealthy neighborhood, drinking tea and reading. The street was busy with passers-by, but none of them seemed to take any notice of his odd looks, or his book, or the fact that he seemed to actually know how to read it. Jemmi stopped in the street in front of him and stared.

The pale man stirred in his seat and looked up from his book. Jemmi's thoughts immediately shifted to other things—the kerchief on that woman walking past and how she would wear it if she had it, what plans the tradesman across the way might have for the bound lamb he carried, and wouldn't a single gutter down the middle of the street make it easier to clean than one down each side?—as if there were a broad, gentle pressure in the center of her mind. This, the thought struck her, must be what she made the people in crowds around her feel. She held her ground and pushed back.

The man met her gaze with a small, amused smirk. "What can I do for you, daughter?" he called down.

The pressure in Jemmi's mind immediately grew focused and became an urge to comply, practically dragging an answer from her. She refused, and met the force head-on. The compulsion increased, and she resisted.

She stood there frozen by the exertion, and suddenly the frontal assault on her mind dissipated, replaced by the barest sideways push that took her completely off balance.

"I had a boy," she called back, and heard the anger in her voice in spite of herself. "A boy and a dry place to sleep."

"Indeed?" the pale man answered. "Now, what would make you think— Oh my . . . " His little smirk wavered, and he said, mainly to himself, "Here, in this forsaken backwater? Can it be?" He considered his closed book for a moment, then put it aside and stepped to the veranda railing. "I think perhaps we should get to know each other. Won't you come up?"

If there was any coercion now, it was too subtle for Jemmi to feel, and she was intrigued by his bearing, and warily flattered. She joined him, and he sat her beside him like a lady of substance.

"My name," he said, "is Yee."

"Neh, that's a funny name, isn't it?"

His half-smirk returned. "Possibly. It was originally much longer, and there was a string of titles that went after it at one time, but these days Yee is sufficient for my needs." He had an old-fashioned accent that made her think of fancy dances attended by the lords of planets, and a way of speaking as if every word counted.

"I'm Jemmi, then."

"Jemmi, it is an unexpected pleasure to meet you. You are what, eleven, twelve years old?" Up close, Yee's eyes were nearly colorless, but Jemmi got the impression that if he looked too long at something, it would start to smolder—or maybe Yee would.

"Fourteen."

"Fourteen? Ah, yes, of course. Puberty would have begun. And I don't suppose you eat particularly well. Forgive me—I've been a neglectful host. Would you join me in breakfast?"

She nodded.

"I suspected as much. Roycer!" Yee called, barely raising his voice.

The boy from the crowd at the quay stepped out of the door as if he had been waiting beside it. He had the look of someone who had been working feverishly all night.

"I believe our guest could do with a bit to eat," said Yee.

"Breakfast! Of course!" said the boy, as if it were a stroke of genius. He disappeared back into the house.

"Tell me, Jemmi," continued Yee. "Do you have any family?"

She shook her head.

"So I conjectured. They didn't, by any chance, die under mysterious circumstances within the past few months, did they?"

The glance she shot him was all the answer he needed.

"I believe we have much in common, you and I . . . and I honestly can't recall ever saying that to anyone else."

Roycer hurried out of the house with a tray piled with a random assortment of cold meats and vegetables and cups and loaves and cheeses. He set it down before them and stepped away. Yee made a graceful gesture with an open palm, and Jemmi tore into it.

"Perhaps you could also prepare a bath for our guest," Yee suggested while she ate.

"Hot water!" the boy muttered to himself. "Cool water! And soap!" and raced back inside.

Yee watched Jemmi bolt down the food. "You would not be reduced to this if you were on a true world," he reflected. "A planet holds more riches than one person could ever grasp, and you would just be discovering you could take anything you desired right now. How ironic that you and I should both be trapped out in space, at the mercy of the vagaries of a forgotten fad."

Jemmi looked up. "What's that, then?"

"A fad?" said Yee. "A trend of fashion. A novelty. I'm sure you must take it for granted, but please believe me when I tell you that it is not at all an intuitive choice for a human to live in the belly of a mollusk adrift in the ether. When I commissioned the first orbitals, they were intended merely as pleasure palaces to keep my associates content and distracted. We gave the males mobility only to ensure that the species bred strong and true, not because we planned to ride them."

"You did? Like Sara? Like Albiorix?"

"Yes. Your Sarasvati is one of the oldest, one of my first. Through a twist of fate, I happened to be visiting one of her sisters the day the Cosmopolis fell. There wasn't time to return groundside before the machines stopped working of course, and not even a big ship like Albiorix is strong enough to make planetfall.

"Without the smart machines, you and I may ride ships from one impoverished orbital to the next, while the planets are rich and savage, but utterly isolated. The resources to rebuild civilization are there, but always just beyond my reach."

Jemmi had no clear idea of how long ago the Cosmopolis had fallen, but if Yee had been there her original impression was correct, and he was quite old. She was still hungry, but she was smart enough to stop eating before she got sick or sleepy. She pushed the tray away from her, half its contents untouched. Yee seemed to note this with the barest hint of an approving nod. Jemmi thought back to Sara's joy at the unexpected arrival of a suitor, and connected it to this unexpected man.

"Neh, why did Albiorix come back to Sara?"

"Ah, truth be told, it was not his intention at all. Albiorix prefers his route through his regular harem, and he likely planned to call on Demeter, and then Freya. It was time for me, however, to move rimward. It was a considerable struggle to make him accept my lead."

No one had ever taken such pains to answer Jemmi's questions before. She composed another one. "Why rimward, then?"

His smirk this time was a bit indulgent. "I have been to the galactic core, and I no longer believe I will find what I seek there. I am a man on a quest, you see."

The boy appeared in the doorway. "The bath is ready," he announced to the veranda in general.

"Roycer serves with excellent enthusiasm," Yee confided with a lowered voice. "Do you find everyone in Sarasvati so?"

Jemmi shrugged, nonplussed. "No one ever serves me," she admitted.

"Indeed? Well that must change. That must change immediately." He stood and offered his hand. "Would you care to join us inside?"

Roycer and Yee led her into the house, which was very old. Parts of it must have been built before the Fall, because they were made of textureless materials Jemmi had no words for, while other rooms were made of wood and stone.

They passed through a side parlor, where the rest of Roycer's family lolled in chairs or sprawled across the rug. Jemmi counted two parents, a brother, and three sisters, all with sunken, husk-like faces. They were all dead. She was very surprised—her parents had looked the same way when they died.

"A pity, I know," said Yee, gesturing towards the corpses with an upraised chin, "but I needed to simplify the household, and the boy is strong enough for my needs for the time being." Roycer didn't seem to see them at all.

Roycer's family was so rich they had a room just for baths, at the back of the house. It was floored with rough flagstones and had a hearth for heating the water, and a high-backed earthenware tub right in the middle. Jemmi thought it was very odd to take a bath in someone else's house in the middle of the day, and momentarily froze with the apprehension that she was being entrapped, but Yee dismissed it with a shake of his head.

"If you want to pass as townsfolk," he told her, "you really shouldn't be noticeably filthier than they are. Besides, I am too old to take advantage of you, and I promise Roycer will be a perfect gentleman. He will scrub your back if you like."

Yee graciously turned to face the wall, and on her other side, Roycer did the same. Perhaps this was what the high-born did during morning visits. Jemmi let her ragged tunic and leggings fall to the floor, and stepped in. The water was hotter than any water she had ever touched, but she was committed, so she gasped and puffed and slid herself down the side of the tub in tender increments. Her knees immediately disappeared behind swirls of brown. It was scalding, but she discovered that if she kept her legs pressed together and moved only when absolutely necessary, it was nearly relaxing. When she was settled, Yee sat himself on a stool in a corner, looking for all the world like a pale long-legged spider. Roycer remained where he was.

Jemmi picked up a cloth and swiped experimentally at dark patches on her skin. Yee suggested she try the soap, and she had more luck that way. Underneath, she was rather fair, and turning pink in the hot water.

"Neh, Yee," she said, comparing a pink-scrubbed arm to a besmudged one. "Where are you from?"

"Ah," he said. "I was born in the chief city of the greatest dominion the world had ever known."

"The Cosmopolis Core?"

He shook his head. "Long before that. This was so long ago that it was little more than a legend to the builders of the Cosmopolis. In those days our god walked apart from us as a formless creature of faith and awe, quite unlike the beings who have given us their bodies to be our homes and our worlds in this age. He failed us in the end, I suppose, because that empire fell. It was not the first empire to fall, and it certainly was not the last, but it fell badly when it went. And I was a young boy, trapped on a narrow and crowded island of towers when the chaos descended."

Jemmi was silent. Anyone raised among the half-buried reminders of the abrupt and terrible failure of the Cosmopolis had a visceral understanding of that type of chaos.

"This was all so far back that I can recall only the memories of recalling it centuries later. But I know the instrument of our downfall was a plague, that our enemies brought among us. Death tore through us so quickly that we who considered ourselves the capital of the world and the heart of its hope were no longer a city, but brutal pockets of marauders running through a steel-and-glass wasteland. I was thirteen then, and the sickness seized me suddenly. It was clear that I would die, but I did not. When I fought to live, I was somehow able to reach out and find strength in the people closest to me. When I recovered, I found they had wasted away in proportion to the vigor I gained. My parents and siblings were dead and empty around me, and I was utterly alone.

"Then the savages who had been our neighbors found our home and ransacked it. I cowered and sought to make myself invisible to their eyes, and they walked past me without seeing me, though I could have put out a hand and touched them. At that point I realized I was now something different, but there was no one to explain it to me."

Jemmi knew exactly what he meant.

"Many dark years followed, but I survived, and my people worked diligently to rebuild something of their society, and I always amassed the best of everything. Gradually I realized this industriousness was my own doing—I could not force a man to do a thing he did not wish to do, but I could place an idea in that man's head and give him the drive to realize it at any cost. The same way, I believe, that you are now learning to do, Jemmi. I felt your mind as you stood out on the street. A power has begun to emerge in you, though you do not know how to use it. This is a rare and precious gift. In all the history of the world, it may be only we two who have had it. And you are the first I have ever told.

"While the rest of our planet squabbled in the dust, my people strove in lockstep and regained their learning and power. They had been close to the secret of star travel when I was a child, though this knowledge was lost for generations during the dark ages. Eventually, though, I saw that mankind's future lay in its ability to spread across worlds, and I gave them the urge to create that technology. When they finally left to cross space in the first great wormhole-drive craft, I went with them, always as a counselor, never as a ruler. That is the proper role for you and me."

Jemmi nodded, wide-eyed.

"I have kept mankind focused on its own advancement and prosperity and culled the weak and the distractions, and I accept relatively little in return—I take no more from my people than the barest life force necessary to remain alive and continue in my role. I have shepherded humanity through eons of history, and ensured that each new empire was built according to my design. The Cosmopolis was my greatest work. Only when it fell and the worlds were sundered from one another did humanity lose my guidance. And look what has become of you."

Jemmi had never had a clear picture of life under the Cosmopolis, but she suddenly sensed that it must have been unimaginably finer than the way people lived now, and she felt ashamed.

"So you see, that is why I am here. To rescue mankind. I must rebuild the Cosmopolis."

To Jemmi sitting in her tub that sounded so grand it was absurd. "From Sarasvati? She's old and poor. How would she help, then?"

"As I told you, I am a man on a quest. I need only to reach an inhabited planet to raise humanity up again. But for that, I need a shuttle—one of the old machines. I have searched since the Great Fall, and none remain intact in any of the orbitals between here and the center. Perhaps there is one left in Sarasvati."

"But, neh, the old machines don't work."

Yee smiled his half-smirk again. "I believe that if I can find a shuttle, I can render it operable." His tone became more urgent. "Join with me, Jemmi. I will have need of your support in the days ahead. Add your power to mine, and there will be nothing we cannot do. We will save mankind from itself and bring order to the stars and lead an empire that spans the galaxy and can never be overthrown!"

"Okay."

He stopped short as if he had prepared more to say. "Excellent," he said.

"But I don't know what help I can be."

"People want to help *you*, Jemmi," said Yee. "It's in your nature. Roycer?"

Roycer stepped up behind her with a long-handled brush, and began to rub warm suds along her spine. Jemmi decided she enjoyed the sensation, and leaned forward to give him more surface to work with. He ran the brush up and down the same route, mechanically focused on the center of her back.

"If you'd like him to do something else, you may direct him," said Yee. "I hand the reins over to you. Simply feel his mind and put the idea into it. You'll find he will be avid to put it into action."

"Don't I need to touch him, then?"

"You shouldn't—I don't," Yee told her.

Jemmi thought back to her earlier struggle with Yee, and reached out with her mind the way she imagined he had. She sensed nothing, so she pressed stronger and further. Suddenly she connected—and she was immense and floating in space, lost and engrossed in animal passion, tangled with Albiorix and straining mightily against his thrusts to receive him deeper and deeper within her. She had gone too far, and was now in Sarasvati's mind.

Overwhelmed by the sensation and shocked by her transgression, Jemmi recoiled and shook herself free of Sara. As she went, she caught a final flash of Sara's sight—stars wheeling around her, and much closer, a blue disk half covered with a whorl of white. Then she was back in the tub.

"Nothing, eh?" Yee said gently from his corner. "Well, try again. You'll do it."

She took a deep breath and reached out again, this time barely past her own skin. She felt Yee in the room with her—he nearly filled it—so she turned the other way and touched Roycer. She hesitated, then decided that people like Yee and herself were beyond bashfulness, and gave the boy the idea of her right shoulder.

The brush moved from her spine and made gentle circles around her right shoulder blade. This was nothing at all like how she was used to confounding minds. It was subtle and focused and efficient. She immediately saw it as a thing of beauty, as if she had been born to it.

"Excellent!" It sounded a little strained when Yee said it. "It seems you learn more quickly than I did. But always be aware that his enthusiasm may be diverted to other ideas."

The brush was now circling her left shoulder.

Jemmi gently reminded Roycer of her right side, and the brush returned to make its circles there. Yee moved him away again—and it was more challenge than test. Jemmi pictured her right shoulder in detail and pressed the image into Roycer's mind, and then pressed even harder in response to Yee's redoubled pressure. Roycer stood frozen, torn between the two equal demands. After nearly a minute, the long-handled brush began to shudder silently.

"Well, there's no point in breaking him," Yee said a bit too lightly. "I still have some plans for the boy."

Behind her Roycer emitted a sigh, and the brush resumed its gentle circles on her right shoulder blade.

Afterwards, when Yee suggested that the bath had done as much for her as could reasonably be expected, she stood up into a large towel Roycer held for her. She pressed the water out of her hair, and tossed the towel over her shoulder like a gown.

"Neh, am I beautiful now?" she asked.

Yee looked her over with an eye that had appraised queens.

"Why would you ask such a thing?" he said at last. "For you, that will never matter."

So Jemmi moved in with Yee and Roycer, and got her warm dry bed and a boy to serve her after all. The bedroom was filled with magnificent girl-things that had been Roycer's sisters' and Yee said were now all hers. She dressed herself in a frock of a crisp, shiny fabric that would be ruined forever if it were even in the same room with a speck of grease, and put ribbon after ribbon into her hair until the whole mass could practically stand on its own. Yee saw it and muttered a vague comment that restraint was often the better part of elegance, so she kicked the dress into a corner and changed into a more practical working skirt.

The next day, as they finished breakfast and sat looking over the jumbled heap of everything Roycer had pulled out of the larder, Yee slid his chair back and observed, "We seem to have exhausted this house's stores. Come—it's time we went to the market." Jemmi and Roycer followed him out.

Jemmi loved crowds, and to her mind the market was the best part of Port-Town. Yee led them to the busiest, most densely-packed street, where folk shoved to get by them and hawkers vied to drown out each others' voices. He turned to Jemmi, and his voice carried perfectly without raising at all. "Roycer and I have some business to attend to and will leave you to do the shopping," he told her coolly. "Please do not return until you have acquired everything you think the household needs. And do try not to get yourself killed while you're about it. I have noticed subtlety is not your strong suit."

He steered Roycer into the crowd, and they disappeared in a few steps. Jemmi didn't even have a basket. Was Yee kicking her out already? Had she failed somehow? Or did it just mean he wanted her to practice putting ideas in peoples' heads? She couldn't tell, and she felt alone again, and very exposed. She fought to stay in one place for a long while until the buffeting from the shoppers became unbearable, and then, near tears, she fled to a quiet corner at the edge of the square.

She forced herself to breathe deeply until she was nearly calm again, and then reached out for the comfort of feeling Sara.

There was a brief, dizzying sensation of stretching through free-fall and then she was back in Sara's mind, gargantuan but still less than a mote in the immeasurable space that surrounded her. The Herculean coupling with Albiorix showed no sign of slowing, but those sensations were too strong for Jemmi and she turned to other aspects of Sara's awareness.

Sara, she saw, floated in a barren void but carried her ecosystem entire within her, as if someone had taken an empty house set in a garden, then turned all of it inside-out. She gloried in the living beings she harbored, both because they were the foundation of her own survival, and because they had sprung from her own body. Designed into the core of her awareness was the drive to shore up that precarious balance by any means possible. She could win over allies and choose favorites, and smite the enemies growing inside her as if they were incipient contagions.

Jemmi saw the spindle-shaped world inside Sara through Sara's own mind, and she felt the angst and darkness that had been taking hold as her facility to orchestrate that environment slipped away. Sara was old and proud and secretly ashamed to be failing in her duty. Her wordless hopes were focused on the great egg she had prepared for Albiorix. If it quickened, she would have a glorious new life within her for a time, and then the lives she sheltered would have a new home.

Jemmi showed herself to Sara and guilelessly let the fact of her budding talent flow through. For a moment she felt Sara freeze the link between them, as if assessing the best way to react to some startling threat. But when Sara came back, her response was to engulf Jemmi with the sensation that she knew her and cherished her and reveled in her. It overwhelmed Jemmi and flooded through her, and she was powerless against it. Sara had unlimited reserves of love to draw on, and she used them mercilessly.

Jemmi was pinned there like an enraptured butterfly for a long, timeless instant. She was unable to move or think, and she wouldn't have given it up for anything. Finally, when the effect was deep enough, Sara bid her farewell and gently withdrew.

Finding herself squatting by herself on muck-covered cobblestones, Jemmi hugged herself and sobbed quietly. She would have clawed her way back into Sara's mind, but the connection had ended with a note of finality that she would not overstep. Gradually, she realized she was not empty, but filled with warmth and strength, and she could think of nothing but the great heart that had given her that. She now knew down through her bones that she would never have any use for Yee's old empires or for planets where there was nothing at the other side of the sky but more sky, because Sarasvati was her world. Jemmi belonged here, where she could reach out with her hand or mind and touch her god, and if there was anything beyond Sara, it did not interest her.

But for the time being at least, Yee was helping her learn her own strength. She remembered the task he had given her and half-heartedly stepped to the edge of the crowd. She extended her mind just the slightest bit beyond her own skin, and the maelstrom of thoughts and words and desires that hit her was like ducking her head under a waterfall. She drew back and focused on the thoughts of the woman closest to her.

The invasion of privacy was thrilling. The woman was picking vegetables from big baskets, and Jemmi found herself swimming through twisting currents of intentions and half-ignored impressions and the occasional diamond-clear string of words. She wondered if she might become lost in the woman's mind if she got any closer.

Ever so gently—not at all like guiding Roycer's hand—she tossed in the notion that a vendor across the square might be willing to negotiate his price, and watched the ripples spread out across the woman's other thoughts. Her eyes lit, and she hurried away from the table.

Start at the beginning, Jemmi decided. She strode up to the vegetable seller, and graciously allowed him to place his hastily emptied wicker basket on her arm. Then she moved on to a baker, who placed two loaves into it with a flourish as if it was the wittiest thing in the world, and strolled on into the heart of the square.

Jemmi returned home at the head of a small, heavily-laden parade. She directed the string of young men carrying her parcels to line them up along the veranda, and then sent them off. Yee stepped out of the house to observe this, then turned back inside with an audible sniff. Jemmi ran up after him.

"Neh, I can do it!" she told him. "I did it!"

"I daresay you did," he said. "And made quite a scene, by the looks of it. It's a wonder they didn't have you burned at the stake. Have Roycer move your booty inside." He turned away again.

Jemmi was crestfallen.

"Neh, Yee," she blurted. He stopped. "How come Sara—Why don't things work like they did in the olden days?" she asked.

That must have been the right question to ask him, because he immediately warmed to her again. "Ah," he said. "It was the machines. Few people remember that it was the destruction of the machines that caused the fall of the Cosmopolis, and not the other way around. In the days of its greatest strength, the Cosmopolis had enemies who preferred utter anarchy to the order and prosperity it gave them. They were fools and fanatics. They introduced a machine pandemic that spread from one end of inhabited space to the other."

"And all the machines got sick?"

"Not at first. It slept quietly for years, and then at a pre-ordained signal it struck everywhere, simultaneously. All the smart electronics died at that moment, and the Cosmopolis was shattered. To re-create the technology that humans or Sarasvati relied on, we will have to build from the beginning again: steam and iron. It is a long road, but I have walked it before."

Jemmi did not trust Yee, and she didn't think she liked him, but she would follow him anywhere if it would save Sara.

"In fact, Roycer and I were able to uncover some information towards that end while you were out," he told her. "We learned that Sarasvati originally had a shuttle port at either extremity. These were large and busy, so they likely contained several shuttles at the time of the Fall, but they were quite prominent and I expect they were plundered generations ago. There were also several emergency evacuation portals scattered throughout her. These have been lost, and there is a chance that one may be untouched. They will have to be searched out."

That seemed like a lot of work to Jemmi. "Why don't you just ask Sara?"

Yee scoffed. "And what would the question be? The ships and orbitals are very simple beasts, and even if they understood, they couldn't form an answer. But come, I will show you how it's done." He stepped over her groceries and led her back down into the street.

"What we need is people who seem persistent and resourceful, and whose absence will not be noted overly much," said Yee. "People like you and me—but expendable, of course."

Yee approached a laborer in a floppy, grease-stained cap pulling a heavy cart, and smiling and clasping his long pale hands together, asked him if he knew anything about the old-days shuttle port at the end of Sarasvati's long axis. The man, obviously annoyed, shook his head and looked at Yee as if he were cracked. Yee appeared disappointed, and observed it was a pity, since it wouldn't do to go spreading this around, but he was eager for news of any undamaged shuttles, and was more than willing to reimburse the man who brought that news quite handsomely. A fortune, really. At any rate, if he heard of anything, Yee lived right over there—the house with the veranda, can you see?—and would be delighted to receive any news. The man moved on as if he was glad to be rid of Yee. His steps became increasingly more hesitant though, as if something was unfolding in his mind. Finally, about a hundred paces down the street he abandoned his cart completely with a furtive look back, and sprinted away along the quickest route out of Port-Town.

The next man Yee spoke to developed a frantic urge to make the grueling trek to the ruins of the shuttle port at Sarasvati's far end and return to report on his findings. After that, four others became fascinated with the pressing need to locate one of the lost evacuation ports scattered along her length. It seemed to Jemmi that before they hurried off, each of them had been struck by the sudden inspiration for a scheme that simultaneously delighted them and tortured them.

"If a man sees it as a struggle to express an idea from within, he'll exhaust everything he has to bring it to fruition," Yee explained, as the last one began to run. "Well, after your success in the market this morning, I believe I can leave the rest to you. You'll need to send out about another dozen or so." He turned to go.

"Neh, why so many?"

"One of the first things you must learn, Jemmi, is that one man acting alone will change nothing. To have progress, you must mobilize a society. Once we are on a world, you will see how quickly entire kingdoms move forward when they embrace the goals we give them."

Yee returned to the house and stepped over the groceries on the veranda as he went in. Jemmi stalked the street recruiting searchers for the rest of the afternoon, and the food sat out there until evening, when she reckoned she had snared enough.

There was no dawn the next morning. Jemmi jumped out of her big bed with a sense of foreboding and a gut feeling that it was later than it looked. She ran down the wooden stairs and out onto the road in her bare feet. Shock and woe were palpable in the air and the soil, and Sara was lamenting with all her heart. Then it hit Jemmi—Albiorix was dead. He had weakened and gone still and fallen slack in Sara's embrace, and she was nearly paralyzed by loneliness and the weight of this new failure.

People in the villages high overhead began to wake and light lamps and fires as they tentatively started their day. The scattering of weak sparks in the darkness was a pale imitation of the stars Jemmi had seen through Sara's eyes. Yee stepped out onto the veranda and silently leaned over the rail to look upwards and sniff, as if he were tasting the weather.

"Yee—Do you know? Albiorix is dead," Jemmi said.

"I'm not surprised," answered Yee. "He was stubbornly fixed on his old route, and I had to relieve him of much of his strength before he would accept my course. We're lucky I made it this far."

Jemmi's hands were fists. "How could you do that?"

"I know what you're thinking—and it's not a problem. Albiorix has always been trailed by younger males as he makes his rounds. I'm sure Horus or Xolotl will be here by the time we are ready to move on."

"But she was going to have his baby!" Jemmi managed.

"Not likely. The orbitals and ships are improbable beings, so they must be part animal, part machine," Yee told her. "I'm certain you've noticed Sarasvati is no longer the paradise she was intended to be. Since the Fall, they have been unable to replenish the nanomachines that they need to grow and heal themselves. I doubt there would have been any offspring." He shrugged.

Jemmi tried to say something, but her grief and rage were like a solid mass that seared through her throat and chest. She had no words to express the depth of his sin and blasphemy. She knew that to strike at Yee would be suicide, so instead, she forced herself to turn from him and raced down the darkened street. When her legs tired, she walked through Port-Town as she had on her first night, staying to the shadows and peeking in windows.

It was hours before she got bored with wandering and returned home. Yee was out.

"Roycer!" Jemmi said. "Where's the jar, then?"

"Which jar, Jemmi?" he asked.

"The one he brought with him off Albiorix. Where does he hide it?"

He paused, and she flicked the boy's mind to give him just a bit of encouragement. "In the tub room. Underneath the floor stones."

"Show me."

Roycer led her to the room with the tub and lifted a flat stone away. In the space beneath was the gray canister Yee had carried when they had first seen him. Jemmi pulled it out. It was obviously very old, because it was made of a single piece of something very smooth and very strong. She grasped the cap, but it would not turn. It had an indentation the shape of a palm on top, but nothing happened when she pressed her hand against it. She handed it back to Roycer and told him to return it just as they found it. He could demonstrate astounding attention to detail when prompted.

As he moved the stone back into place, Sarasvati stirred herself to remember her duty, and her sky sullenly flickered and kindled with morning light, half a day late.

Jemmi and Yee and Roycer continued to live together over the next dozen or so days, but Jemmi saw Yee as little as possible. She also began to avoid looking directly at Roycer. The boy seemed brittle and stretched thin, and he was getting weak and clumsy. He was no longer pretty. Jemmi suspected he would be replaced shortly.

The laborer in the floppy hat returned after a few days, limping and exhausted as if he had run all the way up to the old shuttle port and back. It had been picked clean, he reported, and nothing bigger than a wagon-wheel was left. Several nights after that, the searcher that had been sent to the far end of Sarasvati crawled across the veranda and scratched weakly at the door. He could not speak, but he had just enough strength left to convey that he had also found nothing. Roycer dragged the body inside before the neighbors noticed.

Jemmi approached Yee the next morning. "Neh, Yee, how long will the other searchers be gone?"

Yee snorted. "Were you expecting them back? The task you gave them was to return only when they could report something of value, and to continue searching until then. I'd be surprised if many of them are still standing. Your old Sarasvati is worthless to us, as I expected." He seated himself and picked up his book.

"You and I should begin planning our departure. One of the younger orbitals further rimward is more likely to have what we need."

Jemmi slipped outside and sat in a corner of the veranda. She stretched her mind out across the emptiness, and touched Sara.

All of Sara that was not dedicated to the physics of regulating her inner environment was still in mourning for Albiorix, and she was in no mood to notice Jemmi.

Please, Sara! I'm going to have to leave if you don't . . . We're all going to have to leave! She visualized Sarasvati's interior deserted and bare, and prodded her with the image. Resentful, Sara turned part of her attention to Jemmi, and sluggishly recognized her as one marked as her own.

You have to help us find a shuttle, or else he's going to take me far away. There was no reaction to the words, of course. Jemmi tried to make an image of a shuttle, but she had no idea what a spacecraft would look like. Instead, she imagined people flying in and out of Sarasvati.

Sara responded with a picture of a flawless white fish, smoother than an egg and shaped like a teardrop, with stubby fins. The fish dove out of a hole in the side of Sarasvati's asteroid and swam across empty space.

That must be it, then! Where?

But Sara did not have a mind that could answer a question like that.

Jemmi leapt onto the veranda railing and caught hold of the edge of the roof, then scrambled on top of the house. From its peak she could look down along Sarasvati's entire inner length as it curved over her head in lieu of a sky.

Is it there? she asked, looking at a spot directly across, and kept the interrogative at the front of her mind as she moved her eyes across Sarasvati's interior. When Jemmi reached a point that was far off—90° around and two-thirds of the way towards her other end—Sara stirred, and Jemmi's vision of the spot came into clear focus. She had a sudden image of the white shuttle in a smooth white cavern, clasped by metal arms that held it suspended over the floor.

Thank you, Sara! Thank you! Now I'll never have to leave you.

Jemmi gently withdrew and left Sara to her grief. She remained on the veranda until she had collected herself, and went inside.

"Neh, Yee," she said as if she was discussing the weather. "I've found a shuttle."

Yee looked up from his book, as cold as ice. "Do not even think of toying with me, child—you would die before you hit the ground. Run along."

"It's smooth and white, in a big white room. One of my searchers made it back."

Yee was out of his seat and gripping her collar as if propelled by lightning. "Where?" he demanded. "Let me talk to him!"

She shook her head. "Can't. He's dead now. But I know where it is." She took him to the mullioned window and pointed out the spot to him.

"There? Where the river makes the bend around the tip of the cloud forest?" He calculated. "That's a three-day journey. Roycer—the packs!" Jemmi heard heavy footsteps running frenetically through the house, and Roycer burst into the room carrying two loaded rucksacks and an enormous backpack.

"We leave now," said Yee said to her. "Prepare anything you need to take."

He left the room. Jemmi could think of nothing, so she sat and waited. When Yee passed through again, he had the gray canister slung over his shoulder, and he didn't pause to see if they followed him.

Three days later, Jemmi was farther from home than she had ever been. They had had men pull them in carts day and night for most of the way, but the last one had dropped from exhaustion just as they decided to leave the road, and they had hiked through the brush on their own.

They stood in a clearing in a jungle. Humid air, blown erratically out of an obstructed duct from one of Sarasvati's lungs, met the cool currents overhead and sent a thick perpetual cloud rolling through the trees. Moisture dripped from the leaves like rain. In front of them was a symmetrical grassy mound, like a small hill standing alone.

"This is assuredly an evacuation portal," said Yee, pacing around it. "That's the entrance, and it is overgrown and partially buried, so the space beyond certainly could have remained intact. But how did your source know what was inside?"

He shot Jemmi a glance. She shrugged.

"No matter. We are very close, and our day is at hand." He removed two packets from his rucksack and tucked them in the tumbled stones that filled a door-shaped indentation. "Roycer, light this string here and here, please, then join me quickly." He strode away. "Jemmi, you might care to accompany me."

She followed Yee back into the trees. Roycer came running up, and then there was an explosion that sent earth and spinning shards of timber flying past them. The cloud amongst them jumped, and Sarasvati flinched violently under their feet.

A third of the mound was blasted away. The explosion had removed the layer of soil and stone covering it, and laid bare several yards of a deep purple-pink gash that oozed and glistened wetly. Jemmi wondered if the wound was as bad for Sara as it looked, or if on her miles-long body it was less than a scratch. Of the doorway only smoke and rubble remained, but beyond it was a steep shaft that led down through Sarasvati.

Yee tossed aside his pack and hurried in. Roycer and then Jemmi followed him down a long spiral staircase, smooth flowing steps formed by Sarasvati's living body. When daylight could no longer reach them, the steps above and below them glowed to light their way. They descended so far that Jemmi could feel herself becoming heavier.

A chitinous membrane blocked the passage and drew them up short. Yee placed his hand in its center, and it dilated open. They stepped through, and it silently closed behind them. Another blocked their way, and the air pressure changed and Jemmi's ears popped before it opened for them.

The stairs here were no longer alive. They were mathematically perfect, with precise lines and right angles that had never existed in Jemmi's world. They were a sterile white, against which Yee and Roycer seemed both more vivid and less whole. Jemmi had left Sarasvati, and was standing in the bare asteroid that protected her soft flesh from the harsh vacuum.

The white staircase was short, and it opened up into a cavernous chamber walled and floored in featureless white. The vaulted ceiling was a warm silky gray, chased with flickers of colored lights—Sarasvati's outer surface, pressed tight across the top of the space. At the center, as big as a house, a pristine fish-shaped shuttle was suspended over the floor by a set of jointed steel arms.

Yee rushed forward with a sound that was part gasp and part sob. He circled the shuttle, reaching out a hand and pulling it back to his mouth as if he were afraid to touch it. Jemmi ran her palm along its side. It was smoother than an egg, and cool.

"It's whole, and perfect!" Yee crowed. "At long last, I've done it!"

Jemmi nudged at it. "But, neh, Yee," she said. "It's dead. It doesn't go."

"Ah, but it will now." He caressed the canister he carried.

"What's in that thing, then?"

"Today, it is the greatest treasure in all the galaxy. I have carried it with me since before the Fall, when I first began to suspect that my enemies might take extreme measures to divest humanity of my direction."

"I thought you said they were the enemies of Cosmopolis."

"I may have—did you think there was any difference?"

Near the tail of the shuttle, Yee gingerly pried open a tiny drawer in the craft's skin and inspected its interior with one eye. Then he placed his palm on the lid of the canister and twisted. It came off with a chuff of air. He handed the lid to Roycer, and reverently held the container out towards Jemmi.

"Behold—one and a half liters of breeder nanos, sealed away long prior to the Fall." Inside was a gritty paste. It smelled like hot sand and rising bread dough. "This is quite possibly the last batch in existence untouched by the machine plague. Each speck can replicate thousands of the same nanomachines that built and ran the technology of the Cosmopolis. What I hold here is enough to raise an entire planet from the dark ages back to enlightenment. It is the key to our next empire."

He lifted the canister to the intake panel. "It would not do to waste it—would half a spoonful be too much?" He tilted a drop in. "The nanos will find the diagnostic system, and it will activate them to begin whatever repairs it needs."

He pushed the little drawer closed and bore those eyes of his into the surface of the spacecraft as if willing it to let him see its inner workings. Nothing happened for as long as Jemmi could hold her breath, and then a faint ticking and hissing sound emerged. Yee cackled with delight. "It will be no time at all now," he told Jemmi. "In a few hours you'll have had your first taste of fresh air. You will have seen your first sunset."

"But then we'll come back to Sara, neh?"

Still preoccupied, he answered, "What's that? Don't be absurd. Once you're on a real planet, you won't spare another thought for this rat-hole."

Jemmi turned her back on him. Near the entrance stood a heavy hand crank and a podium topped with switches and levers. She ran her hands over the alien textures and idly toyed with the switches to hear them click.

She closed a simple circuit that had remained alive across the centuries, and the floor beneath them disappeared, phasing into transparency. Her heart lurched and she groped for balance. She stood atop a star-spattered bottomless void, and looked between her feet far out into nothing. Suddenly, an edge of the emptiness was occluded by a shape that swung past her. For a moment, staring up into the chamber was a golden-green, slit-pupilled, lidless eye—flat, dead, and far broader than the entire launch bay. It was Albiorix.

Sara was unable to bring herself to release him, and he wafted like marsh-grass in her embrace.

Jemmi stood transfixed until he swept beyond her range of vision, and said carefully, "Neh, Yee. I don't think I want to go with you."

Yee faced her, and his voice was cold with threat. "That is unacceptable, Jemmi. You have a great responsibility to humanity, and I need you by my side for the great works I will do. You will be my empress. One way or another you will accompany me, and I assure you that you will rejoice in the opportunity."

Jemmi averted her eyes from his. She reached out and placed a thought in Roycer's mind: *Roycer, kill Yee. It's important.*

Roycer sized up Yee with a stony glance, and quietly shucked his heavy pack. He took a few wary steps, and then rushed him. Suddenly startled, Yee snapped his head around, and Roycer froze in mid-stride. His muscles shuddered horribly as Jemmi leaned the force of her mind against Yee's.

Blood trickled down Roycer's chin from where his jaw had clenched on his tongue.

"Is this the best you can do, child?" Yee sneered. "Use the last gasp of an exhausted puppet against me? Countless others with real weapons have made the attempt, and they have all failed." His stoop disappeared, and he became a towering presence in the white chamber. "I am the immortal Andrew Constantin Fujiwara Borsanyi, founder of the Cosmopolis, eternal First Lord of the League of Man, and architect of all mankind's history. Who are you?"

Jemmi had no answer to that.

She released her pressure on Roycer, and he fell backwards towards her across the invisible floor. Instead, she reached out to Sara. She had to grope because she no longer knew where to find her, but at last they touched, and Jemmi's urgency roused Sara's attention. Jemmi concentrated all her awareness on the launch bay, dead Albiorix, and Yee standing next to the shuttle.

He's the one! She flung the rage and fear towards Sara. *He killed Albiorix! And now he'll do worse—*

The thought suddenly bloomed in Jemmi's mind that the most clever and crucial thing she could do was get down on her knees and bow her head. She welcomed the idea as an inspired stroke of brilliance, and rushed to kneel in submission. She heard Yee's footsteps snap against the crystal floor as he sauntered towards her, and it did not trouble her.

They felt the rumbling through the walls and the floor then. It started hushed and far off, a sustained roll of thunder that rushed up and overtook them.

Yee cocked his head and frowned, and then his eyes widened as he identified the sound: Sara had spasmed her entire boneless body in a long rolling wave, like a rope snapped across miles of ground. It was the roar of an earthquake, focused and aimed right at him.

Jemmi grabbed Roycer and spurred him with an intensity that sent him scrabbling maniacally past her into the cover of the stairwell. She dove in after him.

Yee dropped the canister and extended his arms overhead, not to fend off Sara's body, but to reach into her mind. He stood there for the space of a heartbeat, but there was no time to learn to contact her, and he abruptly broke and fled for the stairwell, all gangly arms and legs.

He snatched at Jemmi's ankle, and from somewhere she found the where-withal to shout, "Your nanos!" throwing all the weight and urgency she could into the thought. Yee stared at her and hesitated a moment—perhaps it was the power of her suggestion, or perhaps it was the age-old habit of cherishing his burden—and then spun back into the launch bay.

At that moment the living ceiling of the chamber lurched high up with a great solid heave that pulled the air screaming past their ears and whiplashed back down into the launch bay. It hammered against the invisible floor in an paroxysm of violence that obliterated Jemmi's scream. The shuttle and its equipment, which could bear the forces of vacuum, fire and ice and had stood unmarked for centuries, were instantly pulverized into a thin stratum of wreckage. Yee, standing among them, was mashed into nothing.

The wave rolled off again just as quickly, trailed by the sound of receding thunder. A stunning silence stretched for several minutes, punctuated as bits of unrecognizable debris rained down towards the stars from where they were embedded in Sarasvati's side, clattering or splatting to a stop against the crystal.

Jemmi pressed her face hard against the stairwell wall and waited until the world had stopped reverberating. It took a long time before she judged it was safe to move.

"Let's go, then," she said to Roycer—no compulsion, just an order. "Ah, wait."

She threaded her way into the launch bay and picked through the ankle-high detritus until she found Yee's canister. It was dented and scraped, but almost none of the paste had been spilled. She took it.

"Now we can go." She led Roycer back into Sarasvati, and up the long stairs. She was careful not to touch his thoughts again. Near the top of the climb, he stumbled to his knees, and clear-minded for the first time in weeks, sobbed with horror and loss. Jemmi sat several steps above him with her arms wrapped around her shins and waited patiently, mindful of all the things Roycer had seen and done, allowed no feeling but solicitude for Yee's needs. He doubled over and retched. When he began glaring at her during his pauses for breath, Jemmi picked herself up and continued climbing. He hurried to follow.

Jemmi stepped out through the ragged hole at the surface and climbed to the top of the mound. The air tasted to her as if it were filled with pain and righteous fury. A raw pink line now ran from the end of Sarasvati, crossing over the stairwell, and continuing deep into her interior. A strip of ground more than a hundred paces wide had wrenched itself clear, exposing the bare flesh beneath it. Trees, stones, earth and bits of homes lay tossed and scattered to either side for as far as she could see. In the hazy distance, a series of aftershocks or convulsions raised dust clouds and sent ripples running back towards them. Jemmi's own body burned in aggrieved empathy. She would never let anyone hurt Sara again.

Roycer joined her on the rubble and surveyed the destruction.

"What *are* you?" he asked.

Jemmi blinked for a moment, and while she considered, he shifted his weight and raised his fists to strike her. She flicked his mind and he went still. And that gave Jemmi her answer.

"Bow down," she told Roycer. "Get on your knees and bow down before me. I am the priestess of Sarasvati. I have come, and everything will change now."

With that, as her boy knelt with earnest awe and reverence, Jemmi walked to the place where Sara's wound was the worst, and poured the contents of Yee's canister out into it.

BOOJUM

ELIZABETH BEAR & SARAH MONETTE

The ship had no name of her own, so her human crew called her the *Lavinia Whateley*. As far as anyone could tell, she didn't mind. At least, her long grasping vanes curled—affectionately?—when the chief engineers patted her bulkheads and called her "Vinnie," and she ceremoniously tracked the footsteps of each crew member with her internal bioluminescence, giving them light to walk and work and live by.

The *Lavinia Whateley* was a Boojum, a deep-space swimmer, but her kind had evolved in the high tempestuous envelopes of gas giants, and their offspring still spent their infancies there, in cloud-nurseries over eternal storms. And so she was streamlined, something like a vast spiny lionfish to the earth-adapted eye. Her sides were lined with gasbags filled with hydrogen; her vanes and wings furled tight. Her color was a blue-green so dark it seemed a glossy black unless the light struck it; her hide was impregnated with symbiotic algae.

Where there was light, she could make oxygen. Where there was oxygen, she could make water.

She was an ecosystem unto herself, as the captain was a law unto herself. And down in the bowels of the engineering section, Black Alice Bradley, who was only human and no kind of law at all, loved her.

Black Alice had taken the oath back in '32, after the Venusian Riots. She hadn't hidden her reasons, and the captain had looked at her with cold, dark, amused eyes and said, "So long as you carry your weight, cherie, I don't care. Betray me, though, and you will be going back to Venus the cold way." But it was probably that—and the fact that Black Alice couldn't hit the broad side of a space freighter with a ray gun—that had gotten her assigned to Engineering, where ethics were less of a problem. It wasn't, after all, as if she was going anywhere.

Black Alice was on duty when the *Lavinia Whateley* spotted prey; she felt the shiver of anticipation that ran through the decks of the ship. It was an odd sensation, a tic Vinnie only exhibited in pursuit. And then they were underway, zooming down the slope of the gravity well toward Sol, and the screens all around Engineering—which Captain Song kept dark, most of the time, on the theory that swabs and deckhands and coal-shovelers didn't need to know where they were, or what they were doing—flickered bright and live.

Everybody looked up, and Demijack shouted, "There! There!" He was right: the blot that might only have been a smudge of oil on the screen moved as Vinnie banked, revealing itself to be a freighter, big and ungainly and hopelessly outclassed. Easy prey. Easy pickings.

We could use some of them, thought Black Alice. Contrary to the e-ballads and comm stories, a pirate's life was not all imported delicacies and fawning slaves. Especially not when three-quarters of any and all profits went directly back to the *Lavinia Whateley*, to keep her healthy and happy. Nobody ever argued. There were stories about the *Marie Curie*, too.

The captain's voice over fiberoptic cable—strung beside the *Lavinia Whateley's* nerve bundles—was as clear and free of static as if she stood at Black Alice's elbow. "Battle stations," Captain Song said, and the crew leapt to obey. It had been two Solar since Captain Song keelhauled James Brady, but nobody who'd been with the ship then was ever likely to forget his ruptured eyes and frozen scream.

Black Alice manned her station, and stared at the screen. She saw the freighter's name—the *Josephine Baker*—gold on black across the stern, the Venusian flag for its port of registry wired stiff from a mast on its hull. It was a steelship, not a Boojum, and they had every advantage. For a moment she thought the freighter would run.

And then it turned, and brought its guns to bear.

No sense of movement, of acceleration, of disorientation. No pop, no whump of displaced air. The view on the screens just flickered to a different one, as Vinnie skipped—apported—to a new position just aft and above the *Josephine Baker*, crushing the flag mast with her hull.

Black Alice felt that, a grinding shiver. And had just time to grab her console before the *Lavinia Whateley* grappled the freighter, long vanes not curling in affection now.

Out of the corner of her eye, she saw Dogcollar, the closest thing the *Lavinia Whateley* had to a chaplain, cross himself, and she heard him mutter, like he always did, *Ave, Grandaevissimi, morituri vos salutant*. It was the best he'd be able to do until it was all over, and even then he wouldn't have the chance to do much. Captain Song didn't mind other people worrying about souls, so long as they didn't do it on her time.

The Captain's voice was calling orders, assigning people to boarding parties port and starboard. Down in Engineering, all they had to do was monitor the *Lavinia Whateley's* hull and prepare to repel boarders, assuming the freighter's crew had the gumption to send any. Vinnie would take care of the rest—until the time came to persuade her not to eat her prey before they'd gotten all the valuables off it. That was a ticklish job, only entrusted to the chief engineers, but Black Alice watched and listened, and although she didn't expect she'd ever get the chance, she thought she could do it herself.

It was a small ambition, and one she never talked about. But it would be a hell of a thing, wouldn't it? To be somebody a Boojum would listen to?

She gave her attention to the dull screens in her sectors, and tried not to crane her neck to catch a glimpse of the ones with the actual fighting on them. Dogcollar was making the rounds with sidearms from the weapons locker, just in case. Once the *Josephine Baker* was subdued, it was the junior engineers and others who would board her to take inventory.

Sometimes there were crew members left in hiding on captured ships. Sometimes, unwary pirates got shot.

There was no way to judge the progress of the battle from Engineering. Wasabi put a stopwatch up on one of the secondary screens, as usual, and everybody glanced at it periodically. Fifteen minutes on-going meant the boarding parties hadn't hit any nasty surprises. Black Alice had met a man once who'd been on the *Margaret Mead* when she grappled a freighter that turned out to be carrying a divisions-worth of Marines out to the Jovian moons. Thirty minutes on-going was normal. Forty-five minutes, upward of an hour on-going, and people started double-checking their weapons. The longest battle Black Alice had ever personally been part of was six hours, forty-three minutes, and fifty-two seconds. That had been the last time the *Lavinia Whateley* worked with a partner, and the double-cross by the *Henry Ford* was the only reason any of Vinnie's crew needed. Captain Song still had Captain Edwards' head in a jar on the bridge, and Vinnie had an ugly ring of scars where the *Henry Ford* had bitten her.

This time, the clock stopped at fifty minutes, thirteen seconds. The *Josephine Baker* surrendered.

Dogcollar slapped Black Alice's arm. "With me," he said, and she didn't argue. He had only six weeks seniority over her, but he was as tough as he was devout, and not stupid either. She checked the Velcro on her holster and followed him up the ladder, reaching through the rungs once to scratch Vinnie's bulkhead as she passed. The ship paid her no notice. She wasn't the captain, and she wasn't one of the four chief engineers.

Quartermaster mostly respected crew's own partner choices, and as Black Alice and Dogcollar suited up—it wouldn't be the first time, if the *Josephine Baker*'s crew decided to blow her open to space rather than be taken captive—

he came by and issued them both tag guns and x-ray pads, taking a retina scan in return. All sorts of valuable things got hidden inside of bulkheads, and once Vinnie was done with the steelship there wouldn't be much chance of coming back to look for what they'd missed.

Wet pirates used to scuttle their captures. The Boojums were more efficient.

Black Alice clipped everything to her belt and checked Dogcollar's seals.

And then they were swinging down lines from the *Lavinia Whateley*'s belly to the chewed-open airlock. A lot of crew didn't like to look at the ship's face, but Black Alice loved it. All those teeth, the diamond edges worn to a glitter, and a few of the ship's dozens of bright sapphire eyes blinking back at her.

She waved, unselfconsciously, and flattered herself that the ripple of closing eyes was Vinnie winking in return.

She followed Dogcollar inside the prize.

They unsealed when they had checked atmosphere—no sense in wasting your own air when you might need it later—and the first thing she noticed was the smell.

The *Lavinia Whateley* had her own smell, ozone and nutmeg, and other ships never smelled as good, but this was . . . this was . . .

"What did they kill and why didn't they space it?" Dogcollar wheezed, and Black Alice swallowed hard against her gag reflex and said, "One will get you twenty we're the lucky bastards that find it."

"No takers," Dogcollar said.

They worked together to crank open the hatches they came to. Twice they found crew members, messily dead. Once they found crew members alive.

"Gillies," said Black Alice.

"Still don't explain the smell," said Dogcollar and, to the gillies: "Look, you can join our crew, or our ship can eat you. Makes no never mind to us."

The gillies blinked their big wet eyes and made fingersigns at each other, and then nodded. Hard.

Dogcollar slapped a tag on the bulkhead. "Someone will come get you. You go wandering, we'll assume you changed your mind."

The gillies shook their heads, hard, and folded down onto the deck to wait.

Dogcollar tagged searched holds—green for clean, purple for goods, red for anything Vinnie might like to eat that couldn't be fenced for a profit—and Black Alice mapped. The corridors in the steelship were winding, twisty, hard to track. She was glad she chalked the walls, because she didn't think her map was quite right, somehow, but she couldn't figure out where she'd gone wrong. Still, they had a beacon, and Vinnie could always chew them out if she had to.

Black Alice loved her ship.

She was thinking about that, how, okay, it wasn't so bad, the pirate game, and it sure beat working in the sunstone mines on Venus, when she found a locked cargo hold. "Hey, Dogcollar," she said to her comm, and while he was turning to cover her, she pulled her sidearm and blastered the lock.

The door peeled back, and Black Alice found herself staring at rank upon rank of silver cylinders, each less than a meter tall and perhaps half a meter wide, smooth and featureless except for what looked like an assortment of sockets and plugs on the surface of each. The smell was strongest here.

"Shit," she said.

Dogcollar, more practical, slapped the first safety orange tag of the expedition beside the door and said only, "Captain'll want to see this."

"Yeah," said Black Alice, cold chills chasing themselves up and down her spine. "C'mon, let's move."

But of course it turned out that she and Dogcollar were on the retrieval detail, too, and the captain wasn't leaving the canisters for Vinnie.

Which, okay, fair. Black Alice didn't want the *Lavinia Whateley* eating those things, either, but why did they have to bring them *back*?

She said as much to Dogcollar, under her breath, and had a horrifying thought: "She knows what they are, right?"

"She's the captain," said Dogcollar.

"Yeah, but—I ain't arguing, man, but if she doesn't know . . . " She lowered her voice even farther, so she could barely hear herself: "What if somebody *opens* one?"

Dogcollar gave her a pained look. "Nobody's going to go opening anything. But if you're really worried, go talk to the captain about it."

He was calling her bluff. Black Alice called his right back. "Come with me?"

He was stuck. He stared at her, and then he grunted and pulled his gloves off, the left and then the right. "Fuck," he said. "I guess we oughta."

For the crew members who had been in the boarding action, the party had already started. Dogcollar and Black Alice finally tracked the captain down in the rec room, where her marines were slurping stolen wine from broken-necked bottles. As much of it splashed on the gravity plates epoxied to the *Lavinia Whateley*'s flattest interior surface as went into the marines, but Black Alice imagined there was plenty more where that came from. And the faster the crew went through it, the less long they'd be drunk.

The captain herself was naked in a great extruded tub, up to her collarbones in steaming water dyed pink and heavily scented by the bath bombs sizzling here and there. Black Alice stared; she hadn't seen a tub bath in seven years. She still dreamed of them sometimes.

"Captain," she said, because Dogcollar wasn't going to say anything. "We think you should know we found some dangerous cargo on the prize."

Captain Song raised one eyebrow. "And you imagine I don't know already, cherie?"

Oh shit. But Black Alice stood her ground. "We thought we should be *sure*."

The captain raised one long leg out of the water to shove a pair of necking pirates off the rim of her tub. They rolled onto the floor, grappling and clawing, both fighting to be on top. But they didn't break the kiss. "You wish to be sure," said the captain. Her dark eyes had never left Black Alice's sweating face. "Very well. Tell me. And then you will know that I know, and you can be *sure*."

Dogcollar made a grumbling noise deep in his throat, easily interpreted: *I told you so.*

Just as she had when she took Captain Song's oath and slit her thumb with a razorblade and dripped her blood on the *Lavinia Whateley*'s decking so the ship might know her, Black Alice—metaphorically speaking—took a breath and jumped. "They're brains," she said. "Human brains. Stolen. Black-market. The Fungi—"

"Mi-Go," Dogcollar hissed, and the Captain grinned at him, showing extraordinarily white strong teeth. He ducked, submissively, but didn't step back, for which Black Alice felt a completely ridiculous gratitude.

"Mi-Go," Black Alice said. Mi-Go, Fungi, what did it matter? They came from the outer rim of the Solar System, the black cold hurtling rocks of the Öpik-Oort Cloud. Like the Boojums, they could swim between the stars. "They collect them. There's a black market. Nobody knows what they use them for. It's illegal, of course. But they're . . . alive in there. They go mad, supposedly."

And that was it. That was all Black Alice could manage. She stopped, and had to remind herself to shut her mouth.

"So I've heard," the captain said, dabbling at the steaming water. She stretched luxuriously in her tub. Someone thrust a glass of white wine at her, condensation dewing the outside. The captain did not drink from shattered plastic bottles."The Mi-Go will pay for this cargo, won't they? They mine rare minerals all over the system. They're said to be very wealthy."

"Yes, captain," Dogcollar said, when it became obvious that Black Alice couldn't.

"Good," the captain said. Under Black Alice's feet, the decking shuddered, a grinding sound as Vinnie began to dine. Her rows of teeth would make short work of the *Josephine Baker*'s steel hide. Black Alice could see two of the gillies—the same two? she never could tell them apart unless they had scars—flinch and tug at their chains. "Then they might as well pay us as someone else, wouldn't you say?"

• • •

Black Alice knew she should stop thinking about the canisters. Captain's word was law. But she couldn't help it, like scratching at a scab. They were down there, in the third subhold, the one even sniffers couldn't find, cold and sweating and with that stench that was like a living thing.

And she kept wondering. Were they empty? Or were there brains in there, people's brains, going mad?

The idea was driving her crazy, and finally, her fourth off-shift after the capture of the *Josephine Baker*, she had to go look.

"This is stupid, Black Alice," she muttered to herself as she climbed down the companion way, the beads in her hair clicking against her earrings. "Stupid, stupid, stupid." Vinnie bioluminesced, a traveling spotlight, placidly unconcerned whether Black Alice was being an idiot or not.

Half-Hand Sally had pulled duty in the main hold. She nodded at Black Alice and Black Alice nodded back. Black Alice ran errands a lot, for Engineering and sometimes for other departments, because she didn't smoke hash and she didn't cheat at cards. She was reliable.

Down through the subholds, and she really didn't want to be doing this, but she was here and the smell of the third subhold was already making her sick, and maybe if she just knew one way or the other, she'd be able to quit thinking about it.

She opened the third subhold, and the stench rushed out.

The canisters were just metal, sealed, seemingly airtight. There shouldn't be any way for the aroma of the contents to escape. But it permeated the air nonetheless, bad enough that Black Alice wished she had brought a rebreather.

No, that would have been suspicious. So it was really best for everyone concerned that she hadn't, but oh, gods and little fishes the stench. Even breathing through her mouth was no help; she could taste it, like oil from a fryer, saturating the air, oozing up her sinuses, coating the interior spaces of her body.

As silently as possible, she stepped across the threshold and into the space beyond. The *Lavinia Whateley* obligingly lit the space as she entered, dazzling her at first as the overhead lights—not just bioluminescent, here, but LEDs chosen to approximate natural daylight, for when they shipped plants and animals—reflected off rank upon rank of canisters. When Black Alice went among them, they did not reach her waist.

She was just going to walk through, she told herself. Hesitantly, she touched the closest cylinder. The air in this hold was so dry there was no condensation—the whole ship ran to lip-cracking, nosebleed dryness in the long weeks between prizes—but the cylinder was cold. It felt somehow grimy to the touch, gritty and oily like machine grease. She pulled her hand back.

It wouldn't do to open the closest one to the door—and she realized with that thought that she was planning on opening one. There must be a way to do it, a concealed catch or a code pad. She was an engineer, after all.

She stopped three ranks in, lightheaded with the smell, to examine the problem.

It was remarkably simple, once you looked for it. There were three depressions on either side of the rim, a little smaller than human fingertips but spaced appropriately. She laid the pads of her fingers over them and pressed hard, making the flesh deform into the catches.

The lid sprang up with a pressurized hiss. Black Alice was grateful that even open, it couldn't smell much worse. She leaned forward to peer within. There was a clear membrane over the surface, and gelatin or thick fluid underneath. Vinnie's lights illuminated it well.

It was not empty. And as the light struck the grayish surface of the lump of tissue floating within, Black Alice would have sworn she saw the pathetic unbodied thing flinch.

She scrambled to close the canister again, nearly pinching her fingertips when it clanked shut. "Sorry," she whispered, although dear sweet Jesus, surely the thing couldn't hear her. "Sorry, sorry." And then she turned and ran, catching her hip a bruising blow against the doorway, slapping the controls to make it fucking *close* already. And then she staggered sideways, lurching to her knees, and vomited until blackness was spinning in front of her eyes and she couldn't smell or taste anything but bile.

Vinnie would absorb the former contents of Black Alice's stomach, just as she absorbed, filtered, recycled, and excreted all her crew's wastes. Shaking, Black Alice braced herself back upright and began the long climb out of the holds.

In the first subhold, she had to stop, her shoulder against the smooth, velvet slickness of Vinnie's skin, her mouth hanging open while her lungs worked. And she knew Vinnie wasn't going to hear her, because she wasn't the captain or a chief engineer or anyone important, but she had to try anyway, croaking, "Vinnie, water, please."

And no one could have been more surprised than Black Alice Bradley when Vinnie extruded a basin and a thin cool trickle of water began to flow into it.

Well, now she knew. And there was still nothing she could do about it. She wasn't the captain, and if she said anything more than she already had, people were going to start looking at her funny. Mutiny kind of funny. And what Black Alice did *not* need was any more of Captain Song's attention and especially not for rumors like that. She kept her head down and did her job and didn't discuss her nightmares with anyone.

And she had nightmares, all right. Hot and cold running, enough, she fancied, that she could have filled up the captain's huge tub with them.

She could live with that. But over the next double dozen of shifts, she became aware of something else wrong, and this was worse, because it was something wrong with the *Lavinia Whateley*.

The first sign was the chief engineers frowning and going into huddles at odd moments. And then Black Alice began to feel it herself, the way Vinnie was . . . she didn't have a word for it because she'd never felt anything like it before. She would have said *balky*, but that couldn't be right. It couldn't. But she was more and more sure that Vinnie was less responsive somehow, that when she obeyed the captain's orders, it was with a delay. If she were human, Vinnie would have been dragging her feet.

You couldn't keelhaul a ship for not obeying fast enough.

And then, because she was paying attention so hard she was making her own head hurt, Black Alice noticed something else. Captain Song had them cruising the gas giants' orbits—Jupiter, Saturn, Neptune—not going in as far as the asteroid belt, not going out as far as Uranus. Nobody Black Alice talked to knew why, exactly, but she and Dogcollar figured it was because the captain wanted to talk to the Mi-Go without actually getting near the nasty cold rock of their planet. And what Black Alice noticed was that Vinnie was less balky, less *unhappy*, when she was headed out, and more and more resistant the closer they got to the asteroid belt.

Vinnie, she remembered, had been born over Uranus.

"Do you want to go home, Vinnie?" Black Alice asked her one late-night shift when there was nobody around to care that she was talking to the ship. "Is that what's wrong?"

She put her hand flat on the wall, and although she was probably imagining it, she thought she felt a shiver ripple across Vinnie's vast side.

Black Alice knew how little she knew, and didn't even contemplate sharing her theory with the chief engineers. They probably knew exactly what was wrong and exactly what to do to keep the *Lavinia Whateley* from going core meltdown like the *Marie Curie* had. That was a whispered story, not the sort of thing anybody talked about except in their hammocks after lights out.

The *Marie Curie* had eaten her own crew.

So when Wasabi said, four shifts later, "Black Alice, I've got a job for you," Black Alice said, "Yessir," and hoped it would be something that would help the *Lavinia Whateley* be happy again.

It was a suit job, he said, replace and repair. Black Alice was going because she was reliable and smart and stayed quiet, and it was time she took on more responsibilities. The way he said it made her first fret because that meant the Captain might be reminded of her existence, and then fret because she realized the Captain already had been.

But she took the equipment he issued, and she listened to the instructions and read schematics and committed them both to memory and her implants. It was a ticklish job, a neural override repair. She'd done some fiber optic bundle splicing, but this was going to be a doozy. And she was going to have to do it in stiff, pressurized gloves.

Her heart hammered as she sealed her helmet, and not because she was worried about the EVA. This was a chance. An opportunity. A step closer to chief engineer.

Maybe she had impressed the captain with her discretion, after all.

She cycled the airlock, snapped her safety harness, and stepped out onto the *Lavinia Whateley*'s hide.

That deep blue-green, like azurite, like the teeming seas of Venus under their swampy eternal clouds, was invisible. They were too far from Sol—it was a yellow stylus-dot, and you had to know where to look for it. Vinnie's hide was just black under Black Alice's suit floods. As the airlock cycled shut, though, the Boojum's own bioluminescence shimmered up her vanes and along the ridges of her sides—crimson and electric green and acid blue. Vinnie must have noticed Black Alice picking her way carefully up her spine with barbed boots. They wouldn't *hurt* Vinnie—nothing short of a space rock could manage that—but they certainly stuck in there good.

The thing Black Alice was supposed to repair was at the principal nexus of Vinnie's central nervous system. The ship didn't have anything like what a human or a gilly would consider a brain; there were nodules spread all through her vast body. Too slow, otherwise. And Black Alice had heard Boojums weren't supposed to be all that smart—trainable, sure, maybe like an Earth monkey.

Which is what made it creepy as hell that, as she picked her way up Vinnie's flank—though *up* was a courtesy, under these circumstances—talking to her all the way, she would have sworn Vinnie was talking back. Not just tracking her with the lights, as she would always do, but bending some of her barbels and vanes around as if craning her neck to get a look at Black Alice.

Black Alice carefully circumnavigated an eye—she didn't think her boots would hurt it, but it seemed discourteous to stomp across somebody's field of vision—and wondered, only half-idly, if she had been sent out on this task not because she was being considered for promotion, but because she was expendable.

She was just rolling her eyes and dismissing that as borrowing trouble when she came over a bump on Vinnie's back, spotted her goal—and all the ship's lights went out.

She tongued on the comm. "Wasabi?"

"I got you, Blackie. You just keep doing what you're doing."

"Yessir."

But it seemed like her feet stayed stuck in Vinnie's hide a little longer than was good. At least fifteen seconds before she managed a couple of deep breaths—too deep for her limited oxygen supply, so she went briefly dizzy—and continued up Vinnie's side.

Black Alice had no idea what inflammation looked like in a Boojum, but she would guess this was it. All around the interface she was meant to repair, Vinnie's flesh looked scraped and puffy. Black Alice walked tenderly, wincing, muttering apologies under her breath. And with every step, the tendrils coiled a little closer.

Black Alice crouched beside the box, and began examining connections. The console was about three meters by four, half a meter tall, and fixed firmly to Vinnie's hide. It looked like the thing was still functional, but something—a bit of space debris, maybe—had dented it pretty good.

Cautiously, Black Alice dropped a hand on it. She found the access panel, and flipped it open: more red lights than green. A tongue-click, and she began withdrawing her tethered tools from their holding pouches and arranging them so that they would float conveniently around.

She didn't hear a thing, of course, but the hide under her boots vibrated suddenly, sharply. She jerked her head around, just in time to see one of Vinnie's feelers slap her own side, five or ten meters away. And then the whole Boojum shuddered, contracting, curved into a hard crescent of pain the same way she had when the *Henry Ford* had taken that chunk out of her hide. And the lights in the access panel lit up all at once—red, red, yellow, red.

Black Alice tongued off the *send* function on her headset microphone, so Wasabi wouldn't hear her. She touched the bruised hull, and she touched the dented edge of the console. "Vinnie," she said, "does this *hurt*?"

Not that Vinnie could answer her. But it was obvious. She was in pain. And maybe that dent didn't have anything to do with space debris. Maybe—Black Alice straightened, looked around, and couldn't convince herself that it was an accident that this box was planted right where Vinnie couldn't . . . quite . . . reach it.

"So what does it *do*?" she muttered. "Why am I out here repairing something that fucking hurts?" She crouched down again and took another long look at the interface.

As an engineer, Black Alice was mostly self-taught; her implants were secondhand, black market, scavenged, the wet work done by a gilly on Providence Station. She'd learned the technical vocabulary from Gogglehead Kim before he bought it in a stupid little fight with a ship named the *V. I.*

Ulyanov, but what she relied on were her instincts, the things she knew without being able to say. So she *looked* at that box wired into Vinnie's spine and all its red and yellow lights, and then she tongued the comm back on and said, "Wasabi, this thing don't look so good."

"Whaddya mean, don't look so good?" Wasabi sounded distracted, and that was just fine.

Black Alice made a noise, the auditory equivalent of a shrug. "I think the node's inflamed. Can we pull it and lock it in somewhere else?"

"No!" said Wasabi.

"It's looking pretty ugly out here."

"Look, Blackie, unless you want us to all go sailing out into the Big Empty, we are *not* pulling that governor. Just fix the fucking thing, would you?"

"Yessir," said Black Alice, thinking hard. The first thing was that Wasabi knew what was going on—knew what the box did and knew that the *Lavinia Whateley* didn't like it. That wasn't comforting. The second thing was that whatever was going on, it involved the Big Empty, the cold vastness between the stars. So it wasn't that Vinnie wanted to go home. She wanted to go *out.*

It made sense, from what Black Alice knew about Boojums. Their infants lived in the tumult of the gas giants' atmosphere, but as they aged, they pushed higher and higher, until they reached the edge of the envelope. And then—following instinct or maybe the calls of their fellows, nobody knew for sure—they learned to skip, throwing themselves out into the vacuum like Earth birds leaving the nest. And what if, for a Boojum, the solar system was just another nest?

Black Alice knew the *Lavinia Whateley* was old, for a Boojum. Captain Song was not her first captain, although you never mentioned Captain Smith if you knew what was good for you. So if there *was* another stage to her life cycle, she might be ready for it. And her crew wasn't letting her go.

Jesus and the cold fishy gods, Black Alice thought. Is this why the *Marie Curie* ate her crew? Because they wouldn't let her go?

She fumbled for her tools, tugging the cords to float them closer, and wound up walloping herself in the bicep with a splicer. And as she was wrestling with it, her headset spoke again. "Blackie, can you hurry it up out there? Captain says we're going to have company."

Company? She never got to say it. Because when she looked up, she saw the shapes, faintly limned in starlight, and a chill as cold as a suit leak crept up her neck.

There were dozens of them. Hundreds. They made her skin crawl and her nerves judder the way gillies and Boojums never had. They were man-sized, roughly, but they looked like the pseudoroaches of Venus, the ones Black Alice still had nightmares about, with too many legs, and horrible stiff wings. They had ovate, corrugated heads, but no faces, and where their mouths ought to be sprouting writing tentacles

And some of them carried silver shining cylinders, like the canisters in Vinnie's subhold.

Black Alice wasn't certain if they saw her, crouched on the Boojum's hide with only a thin laminate between her and the breathsucker, but she was certain of something else. If they did, they did not care.

They disappeared below the curve of the ship, toward the airlock Black Alice had exited before clawing her way along the ship's side. They could be a trade delegation, come to bargain for the salvaged cargo.

Black Alice didn't think even the Mi-Go came in the battalions to talk trade.

She meant to wait until the last of them had passed, but they just kept coming. Wasabi wasn't answering her hails; she was on her own and unarmed. She fumbled with her tools, stowing things in any handy pocket whether it was where the tool went or not. She couldn't see much; everything was misty. It took her several seconds to realize that her visor was fogged because she was crying.

Patch cables. Where were the fucking patch cables? She found a two-meter length of fiberoptic with the right plugs on the end. One end went into the monitor panel. The other snapped into her suit comm.

"Vinnie?" she whispered, when she thought she had a connection. "Vinnie, can you hear me?"

The bioluminescence under Black Alice's boots pulsed once.

Gods and little fishes, she thought. And then she drew out her laser cutting torch, and started slicing open the case on the console that Wasabi had called the *governor.* Wasabi was probably dead by now, or dying. Wasabi, and Dogcollar, and . . . well, not dead. If they were lucky, they were dead.

Because the opposite of lucky was those canisters the Mi-Go were carrying.

She hoped Dogcollar was lucky.

"You wanna go *out*, right?" she whispered to the *Lavinia Whateley.* "Out into the Big Empty."

She'd never been sure how much Vinnie understood of what people said, but the light pulsed again.

"And this thing won't let you." It wasn't a question. She had it open now, and she could see that was what it did. Ugly fucking thing. Vinnie shivered underneath her, and there was a sudden pulse of noise in her helmet speakers: screaming. People screaming.

"I know," Black Alice said. "They'll come get me in a minute, I guess." She swallowed hard against the sudden lurch of her stomach. "I'm gonna get this thing off you, though. And when they go, you can go, okay? And I'm sorry. I didn't know we were keeping you from . . . " She had to quit talking, or she really was going to puke. Grimly, she fumbled for the tools she needed to disentangle the abomination from Vinnie's nervous system.

Another pulse of sound, a voice, not a person: flat and buzzing and horrible. "We do not bargain with thieves." And the scream that time—she'd never heard Captain Song scream before. Black Alice flinched and started counting to slow her breathing. Puking in a suit was the number one badness, but hyperventilating in a suit was a really close second.

Her heads-up display was low-res, and slightly miscalibrated, so that everything had a faint shadow-double. But the thing that flashed up against her own view of her hands was unmistakable: a question mark.

<?>

"Vinnie?"

Another pulse of screaming, and the question mark again.

<?>

"Holy shit, Vinnie! . . . Never mind, never mind. They, um, they collect people's brains. In canisters. Like the canisters in the third subhold."

The bioluminescence pulsed once. Black Alice kept working.

Her heads-up pinged again: <ALICE> A pause. <?>

"Um, yeah. I figure that's what they'll do with me, too. It looked like they had plenty of canisters to go around."

Vinnie pulsed, and there was a longer pause while Black Alice doggedly severed connections and loosened bolts.

<WANT> said the *Lavinia Whateley.* <?>

"Want? Do I *want* . . . ?" Her laughter sounded bad. "Um, no. No, I don't want to be a brain in a jar. But I'm not seeing a lot of choices here. Even if I went cometary, they could catch me. And it kind of sounds like they're mad enough to do it, too."

She'd cleared out all the moorings around the edge of the governor; the case lifted off with a shove and went sailing into the dark. Black Alice winced. But then the processor under the cover drifted away from Vinnie's hide, and there was just the monofilament tethers and the fat cluster of fiber optic and superconductors to go.

<HELP>

"I'm doing my best here, Vinnie," Black Alice said through her teeth.

That got her a fast double-pulse, and the *Lavinia Whateley* said, <HELP> And then, <ALICE>

"You want to help *me*?" Black Alice squeaked.

A strong pulse, and the heads-up said, <HELP ALICE>

"That's really sweet of you, but I'm honestly not sure there's anything you can do. I mean, it doesn't look like the Mi-Go are mad at *you*, and I really want to keep it that way."

<EAT ALICE> said the *Lavinia Whateley*.

Black Alice came within a millimeter of taking her own fingers off with the cutting laser. "Um, Vinnie, that's um . . . well, I guess it's better than being a brain in a jar." Or suffocating to death in her suit if she went cometary and the Mi-Go *didn't* come after her.

The double-pulse again, but Black Alice didn't see what she could have missed. As communications went, *EAT ALICE* was pretty fucking unambiguous.

<HELP ALICE> the *Lavinia Whateley* insisted. Black Alice leaned in close, unsplicing the last of the governor's circuits from the Boojum's nervous system. <SAVE ALICE>

"By eating me? Look, I know what happens to things you eat, and it's not . . . " She bit her tongue. Because she *did* know what happened to things the *Lavinia Whateley* ate. Absorbed. Filtered. Recycled. "Vinnie . . . are you saying you can save me from the Mi-Go?"

A pulse of agreement.

"By eating me?" Black Alice pursued, needing to be sure she understood.

Another pulse of agreement.

Black Alice thought about the *Lavinia Whateley*'s teeth. "How much *me* are we talking about here?"

<ALICE> said the *Lavinia Whateley*, and then the last fiber-optic cable parted, and Black Alice, her hands shaking, detached her patch cable and flung the whole mess of it as hard as she could straight up. Maybe it would find a planet with atmosphere and be some little alien kid's shooting star.

And now she had to decide what to do.

She figured she had two choices, really. One, walk back down the *Lavinia Whateley* and find out if the Mi-Go believed in surrender. Two, walk around the *Lavinia Whateley* and into her toothy mouth.

Black Alice didn't think the Mi-Go believed in surrender.

She tilted her head back for one last clear look at the shining black infinity of space. Really, there wasn't any choice at all. Because even if she'd misunderstood what Vinnie seemed to be trying to tell her, the worst she'd end up was dead, and that was light-years better than what the Mi-Go had on offer.

Black Alice Bradley loved her ship.

She turned to her left and started walking, and the *Lavinia Whateley*'s bioluminescence followed her courteously all the way, vanes swaying out of her path. Black Alice skirted each of Vinnie's eyes as she came to them, and each of them blinked at her. And then she reached Vinnie's mouth and that magnificent panoply of teeth.

"Make it quick, Vinnie, okay?" said Black Alice, and walked into her leviathan's maw.

Picking her way delicately between razor-sharp teeth, Black Alice had plenty of time to consider the ridiculousness of worrying about a hole in her suit. Vinnie's mouth was more like a crystal cave, once you were inside it; there was no tongue, no palate. Just polished, macerating stones. Which did not close on Black Alice, to her surprise. If anything, she got the feeling the Vinnie was holding her . . . breath. Or what passed for it.

The Boojum was lit inside, as well—or was making herself lit, for Black Alice's benefit. And as Black Alice clambered inward, the teeth got smaller, and fewer, and the tunnel narrowed. Her throat, Alice thought. I'm inside her.

And the walls closed down, and she was swallowed.

Like a pill, enclosed in the tight sarcophagus of her space suit, she felt rippling pressure as peristalsis pushed her along. And then greater pressure, suffocating, savage. One sharp pain. The pop of her ribs as her lungs crushed.

Screaming inside a space suit was contraindicated, too. And with collapsed lungs, she couldn't even do it properly.

alice.

She floated. In warm darkness. A womb, a bath. She was comfortable. An itchy soreness between her shoulderblades felt like a very mild radiation burn.

alice.

A voice she thought she should know. She tried to speak; her mouth gnashed, her teeth ground.

alice. talk here.

She tried again. Not with her mouth, this time.

Talk . . . here?

The buoyant warmth flickered past her. She was . . . drifting. No, swimming. She could feel currents on her skin. Her vision was confused. She blinked and blinked, and things were shattered.

There was nothing to see anyway, but stars.

alice talk here.

Where am I?

eat alice.

Vinnie. Vinnie's voice, but not in the flatness of the heads-up display anymore. Vinnie's voice alive with emotion and nuance and the vastness of her self.

You ate me, she said, and understood abruptly that the numbness she felt was not shock. It was the boundaries of her body erased and redrawn.

!

Agreement. Relief.

I'm . . . in you, Vinnie?

=/=

Not a"no." More like, this thing is not the same, does not compare, to this other thing. Black Alice felt the warmth of space so near a generous star slipping by her. She felt the swift currents of its gravity, and the gravity of its satellites, and bent them, and tasted them, and surfed them faster and faster away.

I am you.

!

Ecstatic comprehension, which Black Alice echoed with passionate relief. Not dead. Not dead after all. Just, transformed. Accepted. Embraced by her ship, whom she embraced in return.

Vinnie. Where are we going?

out, Vinnie answered. And in her, Black Alice read the whole great naked wonder of space, approaching faster and faster as Vinnie accelerated, reaching for the first great skip that would hurl them into the interstellar darkness of the Big Empty. They were going somewhere.

Out, Black Alice agreed and told herself not to grieve. Not to go mad. This sure beat swampy Hell out of being a brain in a jar.

And it occurred to her, as Vinnie jumped, the brainless bodies of her crew already digesting inside her, that it wouldn't be long before the loss of the *Lavinia Whateley* was a tale told to frighten spacers, too.

LEHR, REX

JAY LAKE

Captain Lehr's face had been ravaged by decades under the coruscating emanations of this forgotten world's overbright sun. The angry star, a rare purple giant, dominated the daysky with visible prominences that sleeted hard radiation through every human bone and cell that walked beneath its glare. Still, one could see the spirit of command which had once infused him, present even now in the lines and planes of his face as rough and striated as the great, crystalline cliffs which marched toward the horizon sparkling azure and lavender under the hard light. His eyes were marbled with a blindness which had come upon him in the long years, victim perhaps of some alien virus, until with his blank visage appeared to be chiseled from the planet's sinews as much the very rocks themselves.

How he and whoever yet lived among his crew had survived this hellish gravity well for close to half a human lifetime was a mystery to me, which yet remained to be truckled, but survive they had. The old man was king of all he surveyed with his blind eyes, soul shuttered behind milky shields, ruling from his seat in a shattered palace comprised of the main hull frame series of INS *Broken Spear*. The baroque pillars which had once bounded the great rays of energy required to leap between the stars now served to do little more than support a roof to keep off the rare rains, and cast a penumbra against the pitiless glare. The place had a gentle reek of aging plastic laying over the dank dance of stone on shadowed stone, but otherwise was little different from a cavern fitted out for the habitation of men.

We did not yet know where the rest of his benighted vessel had come to her grave, but she had certainly fulfilled her ill-starred name. Finding the balance of her remains was critical, of course, in the niggardly time allotted our expedition by Sector Control and the unsympathetic laws of physics. That mankind had bent our way around the speed of light was miracle enough, but we had not yet broken past the photons cast so wide in nature's bright net, and so must live with the twinned constraints of relativity and simultaneity.

"Golly, skipper, he's a real mess," whispered Deckard behind me. "Just like his ship."

I waved my idiot engineer to silence.

Allison Cordel, a woman still beautiful amid age and hard use, stood yet beside her commanding officer, loyal as any starman's wife though it was the two of them together lost so far from home. Our own records, copies of dusty personnel files laboriously thermaxed from ancient microfilm, had shown that despite the natural disadvantages of her sex Cordel had risen to Executive Officer of *Broken Spear* before that late ship's collapse from heaven. Most of the girl officers who came into the service under the Navy's occasional outbreaks of gender-rebalancing soon enough yielded to destiny and their biological imperatives and found more suitable work as service wives, competing as hostesses to aid their chosen man's rise to Admiral in the no-less vicious battlefields of the salon and ballroom. Not for Commander Cordel these sharp-nailed sham combats. In the time I had studied her file, I had developed a fond respect for her, nurtured amid the hope that she had been one of the survivors mentioned in the desperate longwave help signal which had finally arrived at Gloster Station after laboring at lightspeed across the echoing darkness between the stars.

Now I cast my eyes upon this woman who had served as sort of a shadow idol to me in the months of our journey to this unnamed place, Girl Friday to the great Captain's Robinson Crusoe. Had it been her footprints which disturbed the bright, brittle dust outside as she found whatever resources had sustained them all these years? At any rate, she was yet slim as any message torpedo, her rough-spun tunic cut in homage to a uniform doubtless long worn to raveling threads but still hinting at womanly charms beneath. Her eyes gleamed bright with genius as any worthy man's, her charming chestnut hair in an unbecoming style fit only for such a primitive place, shot through with a silver when lent her gravitas beyond her gender.

"So, Captain de Vere," she said, her voice like vacuum frost on a lander's struts, "you are come among us. Even in the face of our pleas for you to keep your distance."

Despite myself I nearly bowed, so elegant was her manner. Were there women this controlled, this powerful, even among the silk-walled drawing rooms at the core of the Empire? I strongly doubted it. She might have been a duke's consort had she remained in society, or even dowager-duchess of some cluster of lucky planets. Though I supposed this woman who had fought so hard for the twinned comets of her rank would hardly shed her uniform for the love of either a man or politics.

I settled on a salute. "My orders are all too plain, ma'am."

Cordel favored Lehr with a look in which I fancied I espied the smoldering ashes of prior argument, though the flash in her eyes was lost upon his sightless gaze. She then returned her attention to me, with a focus as tight as any comm laser. "So you have told us. 'Search and rescue with all despatch survivors and assets of *Broken Spear*.' Did it never occur to you that the survivors and assets might have made their peace with fate after all these years?"

Behind me, snickers broke out amid the ranks of my contact team. Those men would pay, later, with a thrashing or a discipline parade depending on how my temper had settled by then. I knew Heminge would rat out the culprit, and satisfied myself with a promise of a pointed discussion later on.

"Ma'am . . . " I chose my words with care and some precision, allowing for the sort of dauntless ego which had to be in the makeup of any woman of Cordel's achievements. "Commander, rather. With respect, it was your broadcast seeking assistance which summoned us to this place. *Broken Spear* was stricken from the ship list twenty-eight years ago, after she'd been missing thirty-six months from her last known course and heading." I drew myself up, tapping the deep well of pride in the service which had always been an inspiration to me. "The Imperial Navy does not leave starmen behind."

"Nor starwomen, apparently," she said with that chill still in her tone. I did fancy that a smile ghosted at the edge of her stern but striking face, even as another snicker escaped behind me.

It would be a thrashing, I thought, and a good one, down in the ship's gymnasium, something to make those monkeys remember respect.

"Enough," said Lehr. His voice was as ravaged as his expression, a mountain slipface given over to gravity's claims until there was only rough gravel and rude streams left to trap the unwary. "You are here. Perhaps you will profit thereby." He leaned forward on his throne—and throne it was, for all that his seat had been the captain's chair salvaged from *Broken Spear*'s bridge, the toggles and interfaces embedded in its generous arms long gone dark as the spark within their commander's eyes. Rocks, perhaps uncut gems, had been applied to the surfaces, creating strange patterns and half-recognizable friezes which his hand stroked as he spoke. Comfort, or some fingered language, a geological Braille reserved for his special use?

Lehr's blank gaze met my face is if he were still blessed with the gift of sight. That confident stone stare clamped a hard chill upon my spine, which I sought not to show as weakness before the captain's formidable executive officer. "We are upon a time of change here, Captain de Vere. It may be well enough that you are come among us."

It was a voice and manner that would recall any starman to his days as the rawest recruit, all left feet and ten-thumbed hands, much like a man grown and bearded might be yet a quaking boy before the echo of wrath bursting from an aging father. Nonetheless, my duty to my command and my orders sustained me against this unexpected onslaught of primitive emotion. "Indeed sir, and what would this time of change be?"

The captain's laugh was as rough as his speech, a sort of stony chuckle that gathered momentum until another layer was stripped from the gravel of his voice in a wheezing hack. The look with which Cordel favored me would have chilled a caloric insulator, but I resolutely ignored her, awaiting her commander's pleasure.

"I am dying, de Vere," he finally managed to say. "And dying I divide my kingdom among my daughters." His arm, still great-muscled and long enough to strike any man with the fist of authority, swept outward to encompass what lay behind my shoulders—the open end of his hall, where the cataclysm of *Broken Spear*'s demise had left a gap through which an enterprising man could have driven a herd of banths. "These green and pleasant lands which we have wrested from the anger of this world must be husbanded against the days of our children."

I turned slowly, staring out past the strips of thermal cloth and fabric scraps which made a curtain insufficient to hide the glowing glass desert beyond. If anything the color of a Terran field prospered under than hideous giant sun, it was outside my reckoning. My team—Deckard the engineer, Heminge the security man, Beaumont the political and Marley the doctor—stared as well, each then turning to cast a shadowed look towards me.

When I once more faced the captain, Cordel's face was twisted into a mask of silent misery, like a widow's crumpled handkerchief. She betrayed nothing in her breathing, but a slight shake of her head confirmed what I already knew: to humor the ancient, failed madman in deference to his years of service and impending demise was the far better course than to slaughter his final, feeble hopes with the hard light of truth.

"Indeed, sir," I said slowly, holding her gaze with mine. Could this gray-eyed Valkyrie be yet a natural woman beneath the veneer of discipline? "It is a fair world you have brought forth." In that moment, a thought surfaced, blazing bright betrayal of my just-coined policy of polite fable. I am not a man to leave a thing alone, even in face of a desirable woman's desperation, but surely he had not breached the chain of command so horribly as to get children upon his exec. There were no other women among *Broken Spear*'s crew list.

"Who are your daughters, sir?" I asked.

Like a metastable solution leaping to a crystalline state at the tap of a technician's stirring rod, Cordel's face hardened to wrath in that moment. Lehr, oblivious to anything beyond the soft stones of his eyes, said nothing.

A long minute of silence passed, underscored by the whistling of the hot wind outside and the slow, steady hiss of dustfall within, before I saluted again and excused myself and my party. We retreated beneath twin masks of blind indifference and bloody hatred, heading for the forge of sunlight beyond the shadows of this ruined starship palace.

We returned with all due haste to my own ship, INS *Six Degrees*. As an expeditionary cruiser, she was designed and built for descents into the treacherous territory of planetary gravity wells. The constraints of naval architecture generally kept ships in orbit, safe from weather, natural disaster or the less sophisticated forms of civil disturbance. Not *Six Degrees*. She was wrought as a great disc, capable of sliding through atmosphere layers without expending overmuch power, but now sitting balanced on tripodal struts atop a karst outcrop some kilometer and a half from Lehr's location. It was a natural vantage for defense, with a view of the broken valleys that led toward the crystalline cliffs, and a clear line of sight to the dull bulk that had once been *Broken Spear*.

When aboard, I abandoned my resolve to enforce justice among my officers in favor of a swift council of war with respect to the soon-to-be-late Captain Lehr and the matter of his ship. We had reviewed a dozen major action plans in the long, cold months of transit to this system, but none of our contingencies had included finding any of the crew alive.

I had secret orders, that not even the weasel Beaumont had seen, pertaining to the handling of *Broken Spear* and her cargo. *Six Degrees* carried a planet-buster in her number two hold, most unusual armament indeed for an expeditionary cruiser, but some of the outcomes modeled in the files of my sealed orders suggested that I might be called upon to execute that most awful responsibility of command—ordering wholesale death to be visited upon an entire world. Even if all we eliminated was the buzz of strange arthropods, it would still be acknowledged a great and terrible crime

It did not rank among my ambitions to be recorded in history as de Vere the Planetkiller. But *Broken Spear*'s secrets needed to stay lost—a determination which I was given to understand had been reached among the highest of the ivory-screened chambers of the Imperial House.

But no one had imagined that Lehr yet lived, king of a broken kingdom, attended upon by Cordel. And who were his so-called daughters?

My sons, as it were, surrounded me. Deckard, wiseacre but loyal, stood at one end of the ward room, his head deep in the hood of an inform-o-scanner brought in for our purposes.

Heminge, stolid as his pistol but equally reliable as both peacekeeper and weapon, sat at the conference table which had been pulled up from the deck and secured into place, a red marker in hand as he reviewed reconnaissance photography of this world, still damp from the imaging engines. The good

Doctor Marley, paler and more slightly built than the rest of us, sly and twisty as ever, a master of challenge without quite rising to the level of insubordination, was down in the sick bay, making notes about his observations of Lehr and Cordel with a promise to return shortly.

And of course there was Beaumont. My Imperial Bureau of Compliance liaison, by courtesy holding rank of Lieutenant Commander, and serving without apparent qualification or experience as executive officer on my ship, forced upon me by the nature of this mission. I would have been unsurprised to find that despite my sealed orders he had separate knowledge of my charge with respect to the planet-buster. Here was a man created by Nature to climb the ladders of power like a weasel in a hydroponics farm. Were I free to do so, I would have strapped him to that bloody bedamned bomb and dropped them both into the nearest star. Instead, he currently sat opposite me, his face set in that secretive smirk which seemed to be his most ordinary expression, hands steepled before his lips as if in prayer, his black eyes glittering.

Beaumont spoke into his fingertips: "So, Captain de Vere, such a pretty trail you have set yourself to. Do you plan to offer aid and comfort to *Broken Spear*'s survivors?"

"Imperial Military Code is clear enough," I replied. "We are required to render such assistance as our capabilities permit, and evacuate however many survivors we can accommodate, so long as those left behind are not so reduced in numbers or required skills as to be in peril of their lives."

"Codex three, chapter seven, subchapter twenty one. Good enough, Captain."

"I'm so pleased to have your approval, *Commander*. I misdoubt me that they will come. They were not pleased to see us."

Heminge interrupted without looking up from his photographs, though he was most certainly listening intently. "Where is the command section? The portions of *Broken Spear* which are identifiably hull down on this world do not include the command section."

"Does it matter?" snapped Beaumont.

Heminge looked up, met the political officer's eyes. "Yes. It does matter. *Sir.* Captain Lehr was sitting in a command chair. That means the command section was either at one time on the surface, having since departed, or that it survived undamaged in orbit long enough for interior components to be removed and brought down by other means."

Deckard spoke from the depths of his viewing hood, his voice only somewhat muddled. "There are several metallic bodies in high orbit. One might assume they represented missing sections of *Broken Spear*."

"Which suggests Lehr allowed the ship to be broken apart in orbit, and made an emergency landing with the main hull section," I said. The cargo-at-issue on board *Broken Spear* had been carried in the captain's safe, immediately behind the bridge on that hull type. Had they landed the command section as well and taken the cargo off? Or moved it to the main hull section before bringing that down?

It had been a terribly dangerous thing to do, whatever the reason. And the nature of Lehr's throne underscored that the object of my search could be anywhere.

I considered my regret for the planet-buster in the belly of *Six Degrees*. Marley bustled into the ward room, speaking quickly as he always did: "Only one woman on that ship, de Vere, which is one more than our lot has got. Don't know why he thinks he has daughters—Allison Cordel hasn't been gravid any more than I have. Not here, she'd never carry to term." Marley slid into a chair. "Lehr's dying, I'm fairly certain. In this environment, one must assume cancer or radiation poisoning. How he lasted this long is more than a small mystery. Delusional, of course, too, seeing green fields beyond his inner horizon. Gentlemen, what are we about now?"

"Shut up," Beaumont suggested.

"We are being signaled," Deckard added, emerging from his hood. He touched the personal comm unit strapped to his wrist. A cluster of microphones and screens and speaker grilles unfolded from the overhead.

"Attention *Six Degrees*," said a strange, flat voice, the caller devoid of emotion or inflection. I could scarce determine whether it was a man or woman who spoke. "Do you copy?"

"This is *Six Degrees*, de Vere commanding," I replied in my crispest training academy voice, waving madly at Deckard to indicate that he should track the source of the signal. "Please identify yourself."

"I am Ray Gun."

I exchanged glances with my command crew. Beaumont's face was sour and pinched . . . he never had either a sense of humor or an imagination. The others displayed varying degrees of thoughtful interest, though Marley was smiling strangely behind his hand.

"And you are whom and where . . . ?"

Deckard flashed one of Heminge's photo prints, an image of one hemisphere of this world as shot from our approach to the planet. He circled it with his finger.

Orbit? I mouthed.

My chief engineer nodded.

How could that be? But an unknown agency of Lehr's in orbit was no stranger than what we had already seen. The associated comm lag explained the strange rhythm of this conversation, for one.

"Ray Gun. I am one of Lehr's daughters. Bound to Cathar, who loves me as the stars love the horizons of evening."

Marley twirled one index finger around his temple.

For a woman, Ray Gun had a remarkably sexless voice. Not for her the tingling tones of Cordel's strong contralto, intertwined womanly charm and matronly discipline that went straight to my gut. And other parts. Ray Gun's strangeness made me wonder about this Cathar.

"And you are in orbit, Ray Gun?" I said. "How may I help you?"

Deckard shook his head, while Beaumont looked increasingly sour. I knew perfectly well what both of my officers were about—trying to puzzle how there were more women in this place. Unless Lehr had begat children on Cordel shortly after their arrival. But who would place a girl-child in orbit, and *how*? Why? This world was a conundrum and then some.

"My father has divided his kingdom between the best of his daughters," said Ray Gun primly. "We who love him most shall carry his standard. It is I who rule the skies above."

Deckard was back under the sensor hood, Marley made more notes, while Beaumont now stalked the deck in angry thought, glaring at me as Heminge watched him carefully. I glared back. Perhaps I could leave him here with the madmen and women.

"I'm very pleased to hear that," I told her.

"Good." Ray Gun's voice fell silent a moment. Then: "Do not listen to Cordel. She will betray the king my father's dream. You should leave. Cathar says so, and he is never wrong."

I was leaning toward Marley's theory. "Thank you for the information."

"Cathar and Kern will move against her soon. Best you stay away. Leave now, *Six Degrees*, while your purpose and dignity are intact."

Who the hell was Kern? "I shall take your remarks under advisement."

"Ray Gun out."

I looked at my command crew. They stared back at me, Deckard emerging from the sensor hood.

"That was very strange," Heminge said.

Deckard nodded. "I got a signal lock. It's one of those metallic objects I found earlier. Command section would seem to be likely."

"So who is Ray Gun? Not to mention Cathar and Kern?"

Beaumont swung around, breaking the momentum of his pacing to face me with barely-suppressed menace, as if he thought I was to be intimidated by a darker sort of passion mixed with the threat of his connection to the secretive political puppet masters of the Empire. "This is stupid, de Vere. All of it. You know what do. Everything else is just pointless theater of the mind."

Heminge's voice was quiet. "The bomb?"

Though my orders were in strictest confidence, the planet-buster itself was hardly a secret aboard my ship. It filled the number two hold, a modified re-entry vehicle designed to be launched from orbit. Any man could deduce its intended use. A smart man wouldn't comment on it. Especially not in front of Beaumont.

"Yes, the bomb, you moron," snapped Beaumont.

"So whatever is in our secret orders," Heminge put his hand up, palm out, "and don't get excited, we *must* have secret orders, since we're not carrying that thing on a cargo manifest, and it is fully commissioned. As I was saying, whatever is in our secret orders must be very important indeed, for you to take such disregard for the lives of *two commissioned officers of the Imperial Navy*. Not to mention crew and dependents, regardless as to their number or sanity."

"They're dead." Beaumont's voice was flat. "They've been legally dead since *Broken Spear* was taken off the ship list. Lehr and Cordel are walking around breathing, but their commissions lapsed twenty-eight baseline years ago."

"So whatever *it* is, this great, terrible secret is worth their lives, without any respect to their legal existence?"

I stood, took a deep breath. "Yes. Though it burns me to agree with my good Lieutenant Commander Beaumont." I cast him another sidelong glare, sickened by the look of triumph on his face. "Our view of the outcomes may be the same, but our view of the process differs. I prefer to dance a few measures in this theater of the mind. Our Captain Lehr holds secrets behind the marble of his blind eyes, gentlemen, and I propose to have them out of him if possible. They might just save his life at that."

Heminge nodded, his eyes still on Beaumont as he spoke. "How long, Captain?"

"On my authority," Beaumont said, one hand straying to the pistol at his belt, "a day."

"No." I stared him down. "I command here. You may have my commission when we get home, but until then the decision is mine." The orders had been clear enough. We weren't to spend time on site, lest we become contaminated too. I'd already consigned *Six Degrees* and her crew to extensive quarantine on our return, simply by landing and approaching Lehr in person—a fact as yet understood by no one but Beaumont, though I suspected Marley of either knowing or deducing it for himself. "As long as it takes."

Beaumont refused to flinch. "A time limit, de Vere."

Sadly, he was right. "Seventy-two hours, then."

Deckard walked across the ward room, slammed his shoulder into Beaumont, knocking the political officer backwards, though they were of a height and build. "Excuse me, *sir*. My clumsiness." He turned back toward me. "If time is short, we should be working."

"As you were, Beaumont," I shouted, before he could spring up off the deck. "We're going back out. I want to speak to Cordel." About these daughters, I told myself. The old man himself was useless, lost in the hallucination of a green world and decades of blind introspection.

"I'll bet you do," Beaumont muttered, picking himself up with a slow, false dignity. "I'll just bet you do."

We trudged across the dry crystal beds, gravel washed down from the distant cliffs. They smelled like talcum, with the astringent overlay of this world's native organics, stirred by the hot winds to a sort of dehydrated atmospheric soup which would eventually damage our lungs if breathed too long. The sun glinted hot, mauve steel in the sky, hiding the mysterious Ray Gun somewhere behind its glare.

Ray Gun had to be inhabiting *Broken Spear*'s missing command section. I glanced upward, shading my eyes from the daystar's killing brilliance. Where was she?

It.

Of course. Ray Gun was an "it."

"Deckard," I said, picking my way past a shining bush that resembled a fan of coral rendered by a drunken glassblower. "Did *Broken Spear* have onboard AI support?" Intelligence-boosted systems went in and out of fashion over the decades in a sort of endless tug-of-war between the inherent instability of such self-aware entities, prone to mental collapse after a brief, hot life-cycle, and the high value of an intelligence not subject to the disorientations of supraluminal travel nor the stresses of high acceleration.

"Depends," puffed my engineer.

"Depends on what?" asked Beaumont nastily.

I heard Deckard grunt, almost as if struck, but he could take care of himself. He chose the high road: "On whether she was pre- or post-Yankelov Act. Her ship class originally did, but there was a refit wave after the AI regs changed, right around the time *Broken Spear* was lost."

I thought that over. "So Ray Gun might be Lehr's ship's systems. All alone up there in orbit all these years."

"Crazy as an oxygen miner three days after a comet claim," said Marley.

"Indeed. And one of Lehr's daughters."

"Maybe Cathar's the other one," Heminge said.

A stranger stepped from behind a pillar of stacked rubble and glittering silica. "Cathar is a traitor," he declared.

Heminge and Beaumont both drew their weapons. I kept my own hands away from my holstered pistol and the swift death it could deal like the sword of justice. This was not my courtroom. Instead, I studied the stranger as he studied me, ignoring the armed threat my men presented.

He was whipcord thin, naked as the landscape and much like the sullen world around us covered with white dust that sparkled and flecked as he moved. That coating matched the sparse, silvered hair upon his head and about his shriveled penis, and the thousand-kilometer stare in his eyes, which seemed to bore right through me from beneath his hooded brows. Here was a man who looked across years, and bore their wounds upon his body. I could count his ribs, and the cords on his neck twitched as he spoke. He was no better armed than the wind.

"Another one rises from the earth," I said mildly. "Of the crew?"

"Lieutenant Fishman," he replied. His voice was as cracked as his skin, also a thing of this world. What this place had done to people, I thought. He raised his hands. "You should go. Before Granny Rail finds you."

"Surely you mean Ray Gun?"

"No." He laughed, a mirthless chuckle dry as an old bone. "She has taken the sky from my Captain. Granny Rail has taken the world. Lehr lives on sustained only by the love of Lady Cordel and myself."

Beaumont shoved forward, pistol in his hand. "Granny Rail. You're as cracked as that old rummy, Lieutenant Fishman. Go back to your hole in the soil and count yourself lucky to have any days remaining in your life."

Fishman shifted his long-range stare to drill through Beaumont. "You wouldn't understand loyalty, would you, man? Count yourself lucky to have any minutes remaining in your life."

Three gouts of dark fluid spouted in Beaumont's chest, grim flowers bringing color to this drab and barren landscape even as his final words died in his mouth. A smile quirked across Fishman's taut face as the rest of us dropped, but the great, gray-silver spider thing which erupted from the ground ignored him completely.

It whirled, clattering, a motile version of the crystalline plants of this world, except for the well-worn but fully functional Naval-issue assault rifles in two claws. Rolling up against a back-breaking jag of rocks, I drew my own pistol, but the blunted flechettes intended for antipersonnel use in vacuum-constrained environments would have very little effect on this bright, spinning monster.

Heminge moved past me, firing his much more deadly meson pistol. The rays gleamed with an eerie anti-light, the air ripping as the weapon sundered the very molecules that sustained us all, dust particles flashing into component atoms in the same moment to create an eye-bending sparkle which distracted even our ferocious many-limbed assailant.

One rifle exploded, taking the tip end of an arm with it in a shower of glass, accompanied by an ammoniac ordure very much at odds with the gleaming destruction. The other rifle swung to Heminge as he collided with the fast-moving legs, tumbling amid their silver-gray stems like a man in a twisting cage.

I launched myself after him, noting out of the corner of my eye Deckard taking a headshot on Beaumont, even as Marley scrambled for better cover, his medical kit already in his hand. Ever an optimist, the doctor, thinking about who might live to be the recipient of his attentions. The rifle spat again and something burned my thigh with the fire of a solar prominence, but then I was in among the legs, pressing the bell of my flechette pistol against a joint and firing even as Heminge shouted something unintelligible and loosed his meson pistol into the dented, dull ball which seemed to serve as nerve center and balance point for our enemy.

The very air ripped once more and my hair caught fire, then the thing exploded in a clattering shower of legs.

For a moment there was only the patter of debris and the whirl of dust devils, the ammonia scent of local death mixing with the stench of my burnt hair. I looked up, for somehow I was not standing any more, to see the long legs of Fishman above me.

"Granny Rail will be angry," he said, smiling enough to show shattered teeth that gleamed even within the shadows of his mouth.

I was amazed that I could hear him. I struggled for my voice, choking on dust, some thick, pooling liquid, and—though it shamed me—fear. "I want Cordel," I said, my finger crooking on the trigger of my pistol.

Marley bent over me while Deckard gathered pieces of the monster. Heminge, who unaccountably still had all his hair, grabbed at Fishman's arm. "We will find her."

A few minutes later my leg was bandaged and splinted. Deckard had the pieces of the monster laid out in roughly their original relationship, albeit disjointed and unmotivated now, studying them with the intensity of a mystic at the feet of their god. Marley squatted on his heels and watched me just as carefully.

"What is it we came to kill?" the doctor finally asked me. "Surely not these madmen with excessively high survival quotients?"

I could not be certain that I wasn't dying—Heminge's meson pistol had done more to my head than simply burn my hair off, either that or our assailant had struck me a chance blow there amidst the battle. Beaumont was dead unmourned, and so would not report me for treasonous speech. I could see him, steaming slightly, something wrong even with his blood. *Broken Spear,* I said, finding the words difficult. My mind formed them well enough, but something was wrong with my mouth and throat. "*Broken Spear* . . . carried . . . biologicals. Templates."

Marley's mouth twisted, his eye thoughtful. "Combat viruses?"

I tried to nod, but that was worse than speaking. "Uh huh. Tactical . . . population . . . con . . . control."

He glanced around. "If they're loose, we're all already infected. We may never go home."

"Planet . . . buster. We . . . have . . . quarantine . . . arr . . . angements."

"I can imagine. Well, whatever it is didn't kill *all* of these people. There's at least three of these lunatics left, after several decades. Which makes me wonder if the virus ever got into the wild."

My voice was coming back to me. "Not much . . . population control . . . there."

The doctor grinned. "You're returning to us, captain. Had me worried for a minute or two."

Deckard wandered over, a broken crystal rod in his hand. He cocked his head, stared at me as he wrinkled his nose. "You going to live, sir?"

"Yes." I wasn't ready to sit up, though.

"That thing was a highly modified Naval recon drone. Cyborged, if that's the right word, with components from the local ecosystem. Somebody's spent a lot of time over the years."

"Somebody's *had* a lot of time," I managed. Then: "Bury Beaumont, will you? Please?"

They exchanged glances.

Cordel came to me at last, trailed by Heminge with his pistol still in his hand and Fishman wearing a truculent expression. The ancient Lieutenant seemed to be so much furniture to his superior officer, but even I could see that when his eyes turned toward her, that thousand-kilometer stare came into bright focus.

I knew how he felt.

"I am sorry about your man," she said.

"I'm too tired to fence." My voice was quiet and slow. Marley and Deckard had propped me up against a rock, for the sake of my dignity. I had refused to be moved back to the ship until after I'd met Cordel, here, on open ground. The spider-thing still smoked nearby, evidence of someone's perfidy, and the pulsing sunlight seemed a better choice to me than the oily-aired, whispering corridors of *Six Degrees*. "So I will simply ask, on your life, ma'am. What has become of the biologicals *Broken Spear* was carrying in the captain's safe?"

Her puzzlement was genuine, as best as I could tell. "Biologicals? We carried no biologicals, Captain de Vere. Not beyond the standard cultures in our sick bay."

"You've been here thirty years and Lehr never mentioned this?"

She folded her knees, bending down to speak to me at eye level. I could have watched her legs move, stork-scissors, for hours. And had she opened to me, a little, some sense of engagement in those gray eyes? In that moment, I was ashamed of the reek of my injuries. "Captain," Cordel said. "I emptied the safe the one time Ray Gun landed on the surface. There was nothing of the kind, I assure you. Wherever did you come to think we were carrying something like that?"

I turned her statements over in my head. Why *was* I sent to crack a world to cinders? "What is *Broken Spear*'s terrible secret, then?"

"Ah," she said, her face shuttering. "Perhaps you should speak to my captain once more."

"He is too busy gazing at green fields beyond," I muttered.

"Indeed." She stood. "Fishman, gather this man up with all due gentleness and bring him to Lehr."

Deckard and Marley stepped forward together to object, but Cordel turned her glare, now pure ice, upon them. "Granny Rail will not bother Fishman. Hands free, you two might be able to win through with your lives if we are attacked once more by her servants."

And so we went, my head lolling back as I stared into the deepening colors of evening and tried to remember why I'd ever wanted to come to this world.

Approaching Lehr's palace, Deckard and Heminge were attacked by another of the spider-monsters. It lurched out of a stand of the crystalline growth, brushed past Marley and headed straight for the other two. I watched from my curious angle of repose in Fishman's arms—I am not light at all, which gave me cause to wonder at the Lieutenant's strength, especially in his advanced age—as Heminge snapped off a meson bolt which sheared two legs, while Deckard pumped flechettes into a high-stepping joint. Heminge's second shot slagged the underslung central core, proving that the creatures' advantage lay in surprise, which advantage they had now surrendered.

It was almost too easy, though I wondered why the attacker had not gone for Marley first. Perhaps because he carried no armament?

Then we swept through the curtains and into the hall of the blind king of this world. Lehr leaned forward on his throne, chin set upon his hand in an attitude of thoughtful repose. "Welcome, de Vere," he said, staring toward our little party at a height somewhat above my own angled head.

So, the great man did not know I was being carried wounded to be laid before his throne.

I tugged at Fishman to set me down. Deckard stepped forward to support me upright, that I might rise to meet the gaze of this shattered king, while Heminge made no subtle secret of covering one then another of our adversaries with his meson pistol. Only Marley held back, somewhere behind me, breathing louder than the rest of us.

"Captain," I replied, in my best voice. "Once more I greet you. Your executive officer has suggested we speak as commander to commander."

"My ship is broken," he intoned. "My kingdom divided among my loyalmost daughters." Cordel winced but held her tongue at this. "My time is nearly finished, de Vere. What will you of me?"

"I must know sir, to carry out my own duties. What secret did your ship carry?"

He stared a while, silent, almost unbreathing. Only the wind stirred, changing tone with the coming of night in the world beyond this shattered hull. I could hear Marley panting like some dog, though Deckard and Heminge were quiet enough. The moment grew close, some great truth waiting to emerge.

What had I been sent to kill?

"The mind," Lehr finally said. "The mind. We were first sworn then forsworn, de Vere. As you have been in turn."

What was he getting at? "The biologicals . . . they affect mental templates?"

"*Minds.* Admiral Yankelov feared much, and set us to testing in a faraway place. I broke my own ship, captain, rather than return, for I could not carry out the mission which had been laid upon me."

Yankelov, of the AIs. "Machine minds."

"Exactly. *Broken Spear* was set to test a crew of machine minds. Could a warship be flown, and fought, without a fleshly hand at the helm? What do you think, de Vere?"

I thought that I did not like this line of reasoning.

"And when my mission failed, when the minds grew fractious and independent, too powerful to be obedient, too disobedient to be entrusted with power, I was to terminate them." He leaned forward, hands shaking, and somehow found my face once more with his blind stare. "But I could not. They had become my children. My daughters."

And so I had been sent, *Six Degrees* beneath my feet, planet-buster in my hold, to make sure this plague of independence did not flow back into the Empire. No wonder they had emasculated the ships after the Yankelov Act. Starships with their weapons could not sail under the command of rebellious machines any more than they could sail under the command of rebellious men.

"I am sorry, sir."

"Not so sorry as you think, de Vere." Lehr shifted on his throne. "Ray Gun circles the skies, and Granny Rail walks the soil. Why do you think I have kept Cordel close, for all her disloyalties, and Fishman, who in the end is fit for little but screaming into the night?"

Behind me, Marley's breathing changed. The good doctor stirred, moved toward some end I did not yet fathom. In that moment I was glad that it was Heminge who held the meson pistol.

"Because they are all who are left you of your crew," I said. "It is clear enough."

Lehr shook his head. "We would never survive here. Even if I had gotten an infant on Cordel, before all our gonads were cooked by that wicked star, what of it? Only the children of the mind could live here. They have built me a green world I soon go to, and they will outlive us to inherit this one."

"I do not think so, sir. This cannot be."

"But why do you question?" Lehr seemed surprised. "You are one of them."

"What?" My ears buzzed, as if I had been struck on the head again.

Marley grabbed my shoulder. "Back to the ship, sir. You've had enough."

I shook him off. "No. I will hear him out."

"Sir—"

Lehr, again, loudly now as he rose on trembling legs. "I am king here, I know who passes my marches. Granny Rail's spiders do not assault the meat, only the mind. They patrol for sports, escapists, invaders." A hand rose, pale finger with cracked, black nail pointing in a shivering palsy toward my chest. "Much like yourselves. You, sir, are a machine."

Leaning on Deckard, I rolled up my sleeve.

"Sir," said Marley again, and his voice was desperate.

"No." I took my knife from my belt, unfolded it, and set the tip against the skin of my inner forearm. The blade slid in with a slight stretching and a fiery bolt of pain. Blood welled. Dark blood, dark as Beaumont's had been.

Black blood, smelling of oil, like the air of my ship.

"A test," said Marley quietly. "Which you are now failing, my friend."

I looked at him. He was smaller, paler than me. Deckard, Heminge, the late Beaumont, we all four were of a height, with space-dark skin and faces nearly the same. Marley was different. As for the rest of *Six Degrees'* crew, they were . . .

I knew my ship to be filled with petty officers and ratings and lieutenants, to be more than just my command crew, but in that moment I could not recall a single face or name. Just a shuffling crowd of uniforms.

"I never was," I said to Marley. "Nothing was real until we came here, was it?"

He shook his head. "No, I—"

Heminge's meson pistol blasted Marley into glittering pink fog. No one flinched except Cordel, perhaps the only true human left among us depending on where madness had deposited the good Lieutenant Fishman.

"Back to the ship, sir," my security officer said brusquely, with a glance at Lehr. "The king has his appointment with the country of the green, and we have our mission."

"Our own appointment," I said sadly.

Lehr continued to fix his blind gaze upon me. I appealed to him, the one authority who understood. In some indirect sense, my own father. "Sir . . . " I shuffled forward, supported by Deckard, and let my face tip into his hands. They trembled, warm and tinged with honest sweat. He stroked my hair a moment, a blessing.

Then: "Go, de Vere. Find your own fate as I shall soon find mine."

And so I went, followed by my unbreathing crew. The last I saw of Lehr, Cordel and Fishman were closed around him, angels fluttering to the aid of a dying god.

Six Degrees was empty, of course. Though the companionways and cabins were where my memory had said they should be, they were unpeopled. Decorated, sets for a play that the actors had abandoned. The ship even smelled empty, except for the vague stench of my burnt hair which preceded our every step. How had we ever believed ourselves surrounded by men?

Down in the number one hold we found four coffins. Or perhaps crates. Our names were stenciled on the lids, an accusation: Beaumont, de Vere, Deckard, Heminge.

"Marley flew us here, alone," said Deckard into the echoing, oily silence. "He pulled us out, filled us with memory, thought and faith, and here we are."

That was true enough. I remembered meetings, back in Sector Control, though when I strained for details they slipped away like eels in a recycling tank. Memories of memories, rather than the real thing.

Like being a copy of a real person. Was anything I knew true? "Why?" I asked, leaning ever more heavily on Deckard.

"A new generation of machines, I suppose," Heminge said bitterly. "It all makes a sort of twisted. Recasting the lessons of Lehr and *Broken Spear*. Fitting enough to send us here in pursuit. Convenient enough to lose us here if need be. It worked for them."

"So who was the sixth?"

"Sixth what?" asked Heminge.

"*Six Degrees*, this hollow ship is named. Four of us, Marley the doctor and director of our little act. Who was the sixth?"

Deckard cleared his throat. "Lehr. Father and king to us all. His is our sixth."

I turned this in my head. "Are we real . . . somewhere? Are we copies, of someone?" We must have been, I realized. Who would bother to create a Beaumont from nothing?

"I am my own man," said Deckard. He grinned at my stare. "So to speak."

Heminge stroked his coffin. "Do we bust the planet, or do we break the ship?"

"Or do we sail home and ask for an accounting?"

Deckard looked thoughtful. "Lehr's green fields are out there somewhere."

"In his mind."

"But we are all creatures of mind. That is all we are."

"Then go," I told him.

Heminge handed Deckard the meson pistol, then took my weight against his shoulder. "Good luck, man. You might need it."

We struggled to the bridge, where we waited til the engineer was gone, then sealed the hatches. On the viewscreens the world outside glittered in the pallid moonlight, stars glinting. Wind scrabbling at the hull.

Which parts were real?

"Anything could be true," Heminge said, obviously sharing my thought. "Marley could have programmed the planet-buster to blow if we lifted without some escape code. The bomb could be a dummy. This entire ship could be a dummy, just like all those empty cabins, something big and bad waiting in orbit to blast us."

"Anything could be true," I agreed. "That is what it means to be human."

I reached for the launch button, a great red roundel that glowed slightly. "To green fields beyond, then."

Heminge nodded. "And long life to Lehr."

Still feeling the set of my father's hands upon my brow, I pressed the button, hoping like any man for the future.

CRACKLEGRACKLE

JUSTINA ROBSON

Many times Mark Bishop read the assignment, but it never made more sense to him. He was to interview the Greenjack Hyperion, make an assessment of the claims made for it, and return his report. That part was simple. But after it, the evidence supplied by the Forged and human witnesses . . . this he couldn't manage more than a line or two of. Panic rose and the black and white print became an unknown language. He could see it hadn't changed, but simply by moving his eyes across it his mind redshifted and all meaning sped away from him.

He poured the one-too-many scotch from the concession bottle by his elbow just as the hostess was about to whisk it away, and drank it down. The burn was impersonal and direct. It did exactly what it always promised, and shot the pain where it hurt. He rubbed his eyes and tried again.

He disliked the sight of the document on his screen. It struck him suddenly that the paragraphs were too long. The white spaces between them loomed in violent stripes. Missing things were there. All of the unknown inlets holding the truth that the print struggled to express. The punctuation was a taunt, an assault that declared in black and white that the subject's defeat of his reason was absolute. Even the title was loathsome: Making A Case For The Intuitive Interpretation Of Full Spectrum Data In Unique Generative Posthuman Experience. Usually he had no bother with jargon, or any scientific melee, but what the hell did that mean? What did it mean to the person it referred to? Had they titled it or was it just the bureaucrat's pedantic label for something they could read but not comprehend?

A final slug of scotch ended his attempt. He only understood that there was no escape from meeting the Greenjack, as he had promised, as his job demanded: meet, interview, assess, report. That was all. It was easy. He'd done it a hundred times. More. He was an expert. That's why the government had hired him and kept him on the top payroll all these years. They trusted him to judge rightly, to know truth, to detect mistakes and delusions, to be sure.

Bishop tried to read the document once more. His eyes hurt and finally, after a forced march across the first few paragraphs, he felt a cluster headache come on and halt them with a fierce spasm of pain as if something had decided to drill invisible holes into his head via the back of his eyeballs. He lay back in the recline seat of the lift launcher and closed his eyes. The attendants circled and took away his cup, secured his harness and spoke pleasantly about the safety of the orbital lift system and the experience of several gs of force during acceleration—a song and dance routine he already knew so well he could have done it himself. He briefly remembered being offered a ride up on one of the Heavy Angels, explaining he didn't want it to the secretary. She couldn't understand his reluctance. Then in the background she heard some colleague whisper, "Mars." She'd gone red, then white.

But it wasn't just the difficulty of talking to the Forged now, he'd never liked the idea of being inside a body. It was too much like being eaten, or some form of unwilling sex. So he'd made his economy-excuse, a polite no, a don't-want-to-be-a-bother smile and now he was waiting for take off, no time left, unprepared for the big meeting, his mouth dry with all the things he'd taken to avoid doing anything repulsively human, like being sick.

The lift was moved into position by its waldos, attached to the cable, tested. The slight technicalities passed him in a blur of nauseating detail and then there was the stomach-leaving, spine shrinking hurl of acceleration in the back of his legs. The headache peaked. Weightlessness came as they soared above the clouds into the blue and then the black. He felt like lead. When the time came to unclip and get out, he half expected that he'd be set in position, a statue, and surprised himself by seeing his hands reach out and competently move him along the guiderails. He didn't hit anyone. The other passengers were all busy talking to each other or into their mikes. Then the smell filled his nostrils.

It was a mysterious animal tang that reminded him of the hot hides of horses, a drooling, dozing camel he had once attempted to ride, and, on top of that, the ocean. Bishop gripped on tight, knowing that all his juvenile, ancient spine-root superstitions had caught up with him. His interviewee had come to meet him in an act of unwanted courtesy. He would have to greet and speak to it . . . why had he forgotten its name suddenly? Why did it have to smell like that? But he was now holding up the queue. The stewardess mistook his hesitation for ignorance and started talking about freefall walking. All that remained was to turn himself towards the smooth, white-lit exit chute that led to the Offworld Destinations Lounge, and follow that telltale scent of primeval beast.

The other passengers sniffed curiously as they passed him, "so-sorrying" their way around his stalled self. He fiddled with his recorder, checking his microphone and switching everything on. It made him feel secure in the same way he imagined old world spies had once felt secure by their illicit link to someone somewhere who would at least hear their final moments. It wasn't exactly like being accompanied, but it was enough of a shield to let the prickling under his arms stop and for his headache to recede.

The thought came to him that he hadn't been himself lately. It was only natural after the conclusion of the enquiry and its open verdict. Too much stress. He ought to stop, cry off, take a holiday. Nobody would be surprised. But the thought of not having his job, the idea of having nothing to do but walk the familiar coast near Pismo Beach or under the tall silence of the redwoods—that made him pull himself along all the faster to escape the hum, the static darkness, the horror that was waiting there for him, that was already here in the notion of that place. He gritted his teeth and pushed that aside. The scotch made it easy. Why the hell hadn't he thought to bring some more?

He pulled himself forward into the glide that felt graceful even when it wasn't, and swallowed with difficulty. That smell! It was so curious here, where all the smells were ground out of existence quickly in the filtration of the dry air so that humans and their descendants, the Forged, could meet without the animal startle reflexes scent caused the humans. But the grace would only last a minute or two here, in the neutral zone of the Lift Centre. And why could he smell *this* one so clearly? It must reek—and as he thought this, he saw it/him, a tall, gangling, ugly creature that resembled a gargoyle from some mighty gothic cathedral whose creator had been keen on all the Old Testamentary virtues. It could easily have featured in his nightmares. He wouldn't have been surprised to discover that it had been modelled with an artistic eye to that effect. The Pangenesis Tupac, brooder, sculptor, creator in flesh and metal, enjoyed her humour at all levels of creation. The word *anathema* sat in his head, alone, as he bravely put on a smile of greeting.

"Mark Bishop?" said the gargoyle in an old English gentleman's voice, as fitting and unexpected as rain in Death Valley.

"I am." He found conviction, was so glad the other didn't offer his hand, and glanced down and saw it was a fistful of claws.

"My name is Hyperion. I am pleased to meet you. I have read many of your articles in the more popular academic journals and the ordinary press. Your reputation is well founded." It made a slight bow and the harsh interior lights shone off its bony eyelids.

It was shamefully difficult not to marvel at the sight and sound of a talking gryphon-thing, or want to see if those yellow eyes were real. Hyperion's voice seemed to indicate enjoyment, but who knew, with the Forged? Mark, ashamed of his hatred, gushed, "Forgive me, I'm having a lot of trouble with this assignment. I don't believe in the supernatural and . . . "

" . . . and you are nervous around the Forged. Most humans are, and pretend not to be. You have always been clear about your limitations in your previous work. I am not deterred. You have come this far. Let us complete the journey." Feathers rustled on it. Its face was scaled, beaked. How it managed speech was beyond him, and yet it spoke remarkably well. But parrots did too, Bishop reasoned, so why not this?

It took him almost a minute to understand what it'd said, not because it was unclear, but because he was so confused by the storm of feeling inside himself. Repulsion, aggression, fear. The stink, he realised at last with a shock of guilt, was himself.

Hyperion took hold of the guide rails delicately and spun itself away, tail trailing like a kite's. It's comfort with weightlessness spoke of many years spent there, in the cramped airlocks and crabbed tunnels of the old stations. In its wake, Bishop followed, slipping, and after a too brief eternity found himself at the entrance hatch that looked entirely machine, though there was no disguising the chitinous interior into which he was able to peer and see seats of the strange kind made for space travel—ball like concoctions of soft stuff that moved against tethers and into which one had to crawl like a mouse into a nest. He made himself concentrate only on mechanics, move a hand, a foot, that's all—it was the only thing that kept his control of himself intact.

Of course it was Forged. The only machines that travelled the length of the system were robotically controlled cargo carriers whose glacial pace was utterly unsuitable for this trip or most any other if you didn't have half a lifetime to spare. For local traffic to the moon and the various towed-in asteroids that had been clustered nearby to form the awkward mineral suburb of Rolling Rock, all travel was undertaken in the purpose built, ur-human creatures of the Flight. Every last one of them was a speed freak.

"Ironhorse Alacrity Valhalla has agreed to take us to our location." Hyperion made the introduction as he waited for Bishop to precede him into the dimly lit interior chitoblast and become a helpless parasite inside a being he couldn't even see or identify,but which had a mind, apparently rather like his own, only connected by the telepathy of contemporary electronic signalling to every other Forged mind—whereas he was quite alone. He checked his mike and gave Hyperion a sickly smile that he had intended to be professional and cheering. The creature blinked at him slowly, quite relaxed, and he saw that it had extraordinary eyes. They were large, as large as his fist in its big head, but beyond the clear, wet sclera lay an iris so complex and dazzling . . . another blink brought him to his senses. Yellow eyes. It was demonic. What idiot had made them that colour?

He was able to manage quite well, and put himself into the seatsack without any foolish struggling or tangles, even though now he was feeling slightly drunk. Cocooned next to each other, they were able to see one another's heads easily. Stuck to the side of each sack, a refreshment package waited. Within the slings, toilet apparatus was easy to find. There was a screen in the ceiling, if it was the ceiling—without gravity it hardly mattered—showing some pleasant views of pastoral Earth scenes, like a holiday brochure. Bishop figure it was for his benefit and tried to be comforted as a Hawaiian beach glowed azure at him, surrounded by thick, fleshy webbing that pulsed slightly in erratic measure.

Common lore said it was all right for old humans not to attempt talking to their host carrier at this point. The gargoyle could have been rabbitting on to the ship all the time of course, there was no knowing. His mind fussed around what they might say. It blurred hopelessly as he attempted to drag up anything about the task at hand. He couldn't bring any thought into focus long enough to articulate it.

The door sealed up behind them and was immediately lost in the strange texture of the wall. There were no ports. He wouldn't be seeing the stars unless the Alacrity wanted to show him images from outside on the holiday channel.

"Where are we going?" he asked, though it had been in the damn notes.

"To the spot you requested," Hyperion said with some puzzlement. "Don't you recall?" Bishop flushed hot with embarrassment, started sweating all over again. He didn't remember. Then there was a vague hint that he might have made a call, no, written a request, a secret note . . . had he? He checked the screen inventory of his mail. Nothing. Inside the cocoon of the webbing, he experienced a stab of shocking acuteness in the region of his guts and heart. He felt that he was losing his mind and that it was paying him back with this lance, this polearm of pure fear. What had he requested?

"No." He wanted to lie but his mouth wouldn't do it.

The Greenjack was quiet for a moment. "I think that we should talk a little on the way there, Mr. Bishop, if you don't mind." Its voice was gentle now, and had a rounded, richness that reminded Bishop of leather chairs, wood panelling, pipe tobacco, twilight, and cognac. Above the line of the cocoon, he could see its feet twitching gently, flexing their strangely padded digits. Dark claws, blunted from walking, were just visible. "I am well aware of the way my claims must appear to scientists such as yourself. Energies beyond human perception existing within our own spacetime perhaps is not too outlandish in itself. But my observations of their behaviour, and what it seems to mean for their interactions with us, that is the stuff of late night stories. Believe me, Mr. Bishop, I have studied them for many years before making these statements. And I would welcome any remarks."

Charlatan, Bishop thought. Must be. He'd thought it from the get go, when he first read about it.

• • •

Bishop had been in doubt on other assignments, though none of them like this one. Mostly, he wrote for journals about science or current affairs based on Earth. He was one of the more popular and able writers who could turn complicated and difficult notions into the kind of thing that most well educated people could digest with breakfast. Normally, he avoided all discussions about the Forged and their politics, but, of course, it had caught up with him as it must with everyone in the end, he reasoned. And his expertise had led to him being selected by the government to come and make a judgement out here about this odd person and its extraordinary claims, its illegal and incomprehensible existence. The Greenjack Cylenchar Hyperion was a member of a class created by the Forged themselves, by the Motherfather, Tupac, whose vast body had bred all the spacefarers and most of the Gravity Bound. It was a class she claimed was scientifically essential, though he had serious doubts. The Greenjacks were there to confront the boundaries of the perceivable universe, and to try and apprehend what, to ordinary human eyes, was beyond sight. Hyperion, in particular, was said to be able to perceive every frequency there was, and had been given adaptations to allow his mind to be able to cope with the information. Hyperion didn't just see, he *watched*. Recently, he'd been making dramatic claims about his visions that had been in all the papers.

Bishop struggled, but the panic was choking, he wasn't able to say the sensible thing he had in mind—namely, "Yes, but just because *you* can detect these things, why aren't they verified by machines?"

The Greenjack paused, just the length of time it would have taken him to make this reply, and added, "Machine verification has confirmed erratic frequency fluctuations in localised areas, but, obviously, they can't put an interpretation on these anomalies. We have successfully managed to get some mappings of areas and frequency variations that confirm my own sensory perceptions are accurate."

This was news. Bishop jerked as his screen recovered the files being zapped across to it and vibrated to alert him—all the data was there, already witnessed and verified by independent bodies . . . He felt himself breathing steadily. The scotch seemed to have made it out of his stomach. The pills he'd taken still worked hard on fooling his head that it knew which way was up. Better, that was better. Statistics. Facts. Good.

"But if you are too distressed we can delay this," the Cylenchar said suddenly. "Mr. Bishop?"

"No, we have to go," he didn't know where they had to go, though apparently he was determined. His panic returned.

"May I speak frankly?"

Into Bishop's agonised silence, Hyperion said clearly, "I think you have asked me to go to Mars because of your daughter. You are hoping that I will be able to find her where the inquest has failed. Is that right?"

A cold drench of sweat covered him from head to foot, as memory returned, cold, clear. He couldn't breathe. He was drowning. Mars. Tabitha. The unsolved mystery of the routine survey expedition vanishing without trace. Oh a sandstorm, a dust ocean, a flood of sand, a mighty sirocco that blew them away . . . what had it been and where was she? Nobody could answer. Not even the equipment returned a ping. But how? And when the months dragged on and the company pulled out and sent its condolences and added their names to the long list of people who'd gone missing on Mars during the fierce years of its terraforming, and then this assignment came, what else to do? Bring the creature who, above all, had been *made* to see. No frequency, no signal, no energy that the Greenjacks can't decipher, right? Of course, if she's there . . . and if she's dead, then this one will say so. It claims that some of the things it can sense aren't people but are what people leave or make somehow in the unseen fields they move in; trails and marks. It says some are like the wizards of story, able to make things with shape, with form, with intent that is almost conscious. Some can leave memories like prints on the empty air. Oh. But a man of strict science does not believe in that.

"Yes." Bishop said. He was small then, in his mouse nest, hanging, damp and suddenly getting the chills. He was afraid that the 'Jack would say no.

"I will be glad to look," it said instead, and Mark Bishop fell into a deep sleep on the spot.

Sleep was one of the many skills the 'Jack had learned in its long years of waiting for things that might not appear. It closed its eyes and shared a warm goodnight with Valhalla, who was more than curious to know the outcome now, and sang towards the red world with fire and all the winds of the sun.

They joined one another in a shared interior space, a private dreamtime. It was cosy. Valhalla whispered, "Sometimes I am flying in the sunlight, and there is nothing there, but I feel a cold, a call, a kind of falling. Is that real? Are the monsters from under the bed out at sea too?"

"Wake me if it happens," Hyperion said. "And we'll see."

He co-created a kind romance with Valhalla, in which they saw huge floating algal swarms of deep colour and shadow populate the fathoms beyond the stars. They named them in whispers, and with childish fingers measured their shapes in the sky, and then pinched them out of existence, snuff, snuff, snuff.

"There," Hyperion said, "they may be here, but they have no power. They can only hurt you if you let them. They live in the holes of the mind, and eat the spirit. Cracklegrackle. Just pinch them out." They got back into bed and closed the window, drew the shades. The Valhalla was happy again and drove on all the faster in his sleep.

Bishop was woken by the Valhalla's cheerful cry, "Mars!" The Ironhorse made orbit and scanned the surface to find the small outpost where the Gaiaform Nikkal Raven, chief developer of Mars, had built a human-scale shelter with its Hands in the lee of a high cliff. "Nobody's there now. If it's a graveyard or a ghost town, it's empty for sure, but with a bit of effort there's probably power and some basics that you could get going." For politeness, they contacted the Gaiaform.

"That's funny," Valhalla said, as Bishop struggled to change his clothes. "She sounds annoyed, or at least, she doesn't want to discuss the place."

The Nikkal's voice was grumpy on the intercom. She grated on Bishop's exposed nerves and wore out his fragile strip of patience almost at once. "My Hands got lost there too. Given up sending more. Thought I'd get to it later, after the planting on the south faces was finished. Just a minor space really, full of gullies."

They all recognised the feeling this rationale covered. "We don't need your help," Bishop grated. "Just want to get there and look around. That's all."

"But if anything happens it's on my watch," the Nikkal countered.

"Tupac knows we're here," Hyperion suggested. "We won't stay long. A day at the most."

" . . . as long as it takes . . . " Bishop said. He was in clean clothes. His panics were gone. He felt old and thin and shelterless, and looked around for something he could hold. He found only his small bag and his recorder, and filled his hands with them. A panic would have been welcome. Their fury was better than this deadly flat feeling that had taken their place. It was clear now. He was here, Thorson's Gullies, the last known location. Every step was a puppet step his body took at the behest of some will named Mark that wouldn't let it rest, but there was no more struggle between them. He felt that he did not inhabit these arms, these legs. They were his waldos, his servos, they were his method. Only his guts were still his own, a liquid concentration waiting for a mould.

"Come on, Mark," Hyperion called from the drop capsule.

Since when had they become friends? Bishop didn't know how, but he climbed inside the small fruit shape of the vehicle. Mars had lift cable, but no system in place. Cargo was simply clipped on and set going under whatever power it was able to muster. They were attached to the line and given a good shove by Valhalla. The new atmosphere buffeted them, warmed them, cooked them almost, and then they were down, Bishop still surprised, still too frozen to even be sick with either motion nausea or relief at their arrival. The capsule detached, put out its six wheeled legs like a bored insect and began to trundle the prescribed steady course towards the gullies. Hyperion opened the ventilation system and they sniffed the Martian air. It was thin, and even though it had been filtered a million ways, somehow gritty.

" . . . it's the names that are part of the trouble," Bishop said, staring out at the peculiar sight of Mars's tundra, red ochre studded with the teal green puffs of growing things in regular patterns. "Good and Evil. Why did you call them that?"

"There are more," Hyperion said. "There is Eater and Biter and Poison and Power and Luck and Fortune and Benificence, and the Cracklegrackle. I expect there are many more. But these are the commonest major sorts."

"But why? Couldn't you name them Energy Number One and so forth?"

"I could, but that wouldn't be accurate. Their names is what they are."

"How they seem to *you*. The one person who can see them."

"That's not exactly right. I think we can all perceive them, but only I can see them as easily as I can see you."

"And you say they are everywhere."

"Scattered, but everywhere in known space, I think."

"And some are spontaneous, but others are man made?"

"Yes. Few of the major arcana are manmade, like those. It takes a very powerful person to create one. Or a large group of people. There are many manmade minor arcana and many naturally occurring ones like that, but they are very shortlived, a day or two at most."

"You see my problem is that I can believe in this kind of thing at a symbolic level, within the human world, acting at large and small scales. We're creatures of symbolic meaning. But you're saying there's *physical* stuff, and that it has a real, external, distinct existence."

"Yes. I am saying it exists as patterns within the same energy fields that give rise to matter."

"Consciousness is material?"

"No. It has a material interaction that is more than simply the building of a house from a plan or the singing of a song, is what I am saying."

"And these things . . . patterns . . . can influence people?"

"Influence them, infect them, live inside them, alter them perhaps. Yes, I think so." The creature stared at him for the longest time, unblinking. "Yes."

"And just like that, we are expected to accept this—theory of material mind?"

Hyperion shrugged, as if he didn't much care either way. "I report what I see, but I say what it is for me. Otherwise, I would report nothing more than machines can report. When you look at a landscape, you don't list a bunch of coordinates and say they are mid green, then another list grey, another list white, and so on. You say, I see a hill with some trees, a river, a house in the distance."

"But you're making claims about the nature of this stuff, linking it to subjective values. Hills aren't subjective."

"They are. True, there is some rock that exists independently of you, some sand, some dust, but without *you*, it is no hill, and however the hill seems is how all hills seem to you, large or small—not mountains, not flat, perhaps even with traits that are more personal. If your home is among the hills, then they seem well known; if not, then they provoke suspicion."

They were trundling at high speed, balanced in their gyrobody between the capsule's six legs, seeming to float like thistledown between the rocks of this region of Mars; Thorson's Plot. Plot was something of a misnomer, as the area, already claimed by an Earth corporate, was some fifteen thousand square miles. The gullies, which made it a cheaper piece of real estate, and complicated to sow—hence the surveying team—were near the western edge and ran in a broad scar north-south along the lines of the mapping system. Thorsons had hoped to find watery deposits deep in the gullies, or perhaps some useful mineral, or who knows what down in the cracked gulches where twisting runnels of rock hid large areas from the sun and most of the wind which had scoured the planet for millennia. All around them were hills of varying sizes, some no more than dunes, others rising with rugged defiance in scarps and screes. Occasionally, small pieces of metal flashed the sunlight back at them as they moved between light and the shade of the thin high cloud that now streaked the sky white.

"The remains of Hands," the Greenjack said with interest, of course able to tell what everything was at any distance. "How interesting. And there is some debris from attempts to seed here, some markers, some water catchers. All wrecked. And . . . "

"And?" Bishop leapt on the hesitation.

"What I would call distress residue. A taint in the energy, very slight."

"What energy?'

"The subtle fields. You will find them referenced a great deal in my submitted thesis. Vibrationary levels where human perception is only infrequently able, or not able at all. When trauma occurs, bursts of energy are thrown off the distressed person into these fields, and although they decay quite rapidly, they leave a trace pattern behind which is very slow to fade."

"A disturbance in the Force," Bishop said bitterly. He felt nothing except the dread which had clutched at him in place of his panic.

"It might be only the natural upset of someone experiencing an unlucky accident," Hyperion said, unruffled. "It's hard to say without extreme observation and immersion on the site. You ought to be glad, Mr. Bishop, rather than contemptuous. Why else are you here?"

Mark gripped the arms of his seat. He was furious and full of nervous agitation. He ought to be civil, but he felt the need to destroy this creature's claims even as he wanted them to be right for his own sake. He didn't want to know about some spiritual plane, not after all the time it had taken to rid the human race of its destructive superstitions. Even if it existed, what difference did it make to those who were, in the shaman's own words, unable to interact with it. He could see no good coming of it. But he longed for it to be true. Somewhere in his fevered mind, where fragments of the shaman's testimony had lodged in spite of his allergic reaction to reading them, he recalled there being quite specific traces of people and moments stuck in this peculiar aether like flies in amber. Not always, not everywhere, but sometime and somewhere it acted as a recorder for incidents and individuals. It could. It *might have*.

The capsule lurched to a halt. They had arrived at the last known point of the survey team's wellbeing. A couple of waymarkers and a discarded, empty water canister pegged down beside them were the only visible remnants now. Without further talk, Hyperion and Bishop disembarked.

They fitted their facemasks—the air was still too thin for comfort—and Bishop put on his thin wind jacket and new desert boots. Hyperion sank a little in the fine grit on his four limbs, but otherwise he went as always, naked save for his fur, feathers, scales, and quills.

Wrestling the faceplate straps to get a good fit, Bishop noticed all the strange little fetishes the creature had attached to itself. Necklaces with bits of twig and bone . . . it looked like it had come off the set of a voodoo movie. He recalled now that it had labelled its profession on its passport as "shaman." He was so exhausted by his nervous disorders, however, that he didn't have the energy to muster a really negative response anymore. He was deadened to it. At last, the mask was tested and his spare oxygen packs fitted to the bodysuit that went over his clothes. Hyperion wore goggles and a kind of nosebag over his beak. He made a desultory symbol in the dust and smoothed it out again with one forepaw. The capsule, obeying commands from its uplink with Valhalla, folded up its spider legs and nestled down in a small hollow, lights dimming to a gleam as it moved into standby operation. All around, and as far as he could see in any direction, save for the shaman, Bishop was alone.

"There are very few true disappearances in human history, these days," Hyperion said after a moment when they both cast about in search of a direction. It moved closer to one of the markers and read the tags left there. "And this is not an unusual place, like those twisty spaces close to black holes for example. It is just a planet with a regular geology. The common assumption about this team's fate is that they absconded with the help of the Nikkal. From there, a number of possible avenues continue, most leading to the far system frontiers, where they were able to drop off the networks."

Bishop licked his lips, already starting to crack. The news was full of the asteroid bayous beyond the sphere of Earth's police influence and the renegade technology that festered there, unregulated. There was a lot of Unity activity. A lot of illegal, unethical, criminal work. "She had no reason to go."

"Perhaps not, but if the rest of them wanted to go they could hardly leave her behind. What would be easier for you, Mr. Bishop, to have her forcibly made into one of the Frontiersmen, or to have her dead here somewhere?"

How odd, he thought, that the 'Jack had no trouble voicing what inhabited his own awareness as a black hum beyond reckoning. Hearing the words aloud was startling, but it diminished the power of the awful feelings that gripped him inside.

"Let's start looking," Bishop said, standing still. All around them, their small dip radiated gullies that twisted and wound. The sun was beginning to go down and the high rocky outcrops cast sharp edged purple shadows.

Hyperion was exacting, his research both instantaneous and meticulous in a way that made Bishop simply envious. "The marker, as the police report indicates, says they started southwest with a view to making a loop trail back here within a six hour period, the route is marked in the statutory map." The shaman sniffed and the nosebag huffed. "All the searches have concentrated on following this route and found a scatter of personal belongings and the remains of a Finger of the Terraform, which was carrying the survey equipment. All of that was recovered intact." It held the two windbeaten Tags in its paw and rubbed them for a short time, thoughtfully. "But they did not go that way. Only the Finger took the trail."

"How do you know?"

Hyperion turned. "I can see it. I think it is time I showed you." It came across to him and held out one large, scaly arm. "Please, your screen viewer. I will adapt it to show some of the details I can see over its normal camera range. This will not be what *I* see, you understand, as I don't see it with my eyes. But it is the best I can do for you."

Reluctantly, Bishop handed over the precious viewer. It was his recorder too. His everything. "Don't mess up the record settings. It's on now."

The Greenjack inclined its head politely and slid one of its broad clawlike nails into one of the old style input ports. Bishop felt a chill. He'd never get used to how capable the Forged were with technology. They could interface directly with any machine.

"The signals I use to communicate with the device will cause some interference with my tracking," Hyperion said calmly. "So I will not use it all the time. If you see nothing, you may assume I am watching and listening. I will also shut the device down if its working interferes with the process, and I may ask you to move away at times." It handed the screen back, and Bishop checked it, panning it around in front of him. The camera showed whatever he pointed it at, recording diligently; it was really just like holding a picture frame up over the landscape. "I don't see anything."

"Look at the markers and the route."

He turned. From the tag line, he could now see a strange kind of coloration in the air, like points of deep shade. They were small. It was really almost like broken pixellation.

"That is the pattern left by the output of the Finger's microreactor projecting microbursts of decaying particles into the energy field. Radiation containment is generally good these days, so this is all you can find. It is also in the standard police procedurals. They mistakenly assumed it confirmed that all the travellers took the same path, since the Finger was carrying all the technical equipment and the others had only their masks and gas, their personal refreshments and devices. I would say it is certain that they *intended* to disappear here, as in fact all their individual communications gear has been accounted for along the Finger's trail."

Like a path cut with three-dimensional leaf shadows, the trail wound into the first gully, followed the obvious way along it, and vanished around the first turn.

"We can follow that and verify there was no other person with the Finger if you like," the shaman suggested.

"Parts of a Forged internal device unit were found," Bishop said, brain clicking in at last.

Hyperion shrugged.

"Or?" Bishop started to pan around. He soon found patches and bursts of odd colour washes everywhere, as if his screen were subject to a random painting class.

"Or we can follow the others and find out what they did, starting here."

"What is all this?"

"This is energy field debris."

As he moved around, Bishop could see that there was a huge glut of the stuff where they were, but traces of it were everywhere in fact, even in the distance. "Why so much of it?"

"There was a lot of activity here. The rest is down to regular cosmic interference, or perhaps . . . I am not actually sure what all of it is. The energy fields transect time and space, but they are linked to it, so while some of this is attached to the planet's energy sphere, some of it, as you see, is moving."

Streaks shot across the screen. A readout indicated that he was not seeing them in real time, as that would have been too fast for him to notice. The simulation and the reality overlay each other on the image, however, and the difference there was undetectable.

"I believe that the streaks are bonded to the spatial field, and that they are therefore stationary relative to absolute coordinates in space—thus as Mars traverses, so these things pass through." The creature cocked its head, a model of intellectual speculation.

Bishop relaxed his tired arms so that the screen pointed at the ground, saw the streaks shooting through his feet. "Through us?"

Hyperion nodded. "As with much cosmic ray debris. It moves too fast for me to say anything about it. I would need to move out into deep space and be on a relatively static vessel, in order to discover more about them."

'No such ship exists,' Bishop snorted. "Well, only . . . "

"Yes, only a Unity ship perhaps," the shaman said. "I shall ask for one soon."

They shared a moment of silence in which the subject of Unity, the newly discovered alien technology, rose and passed without further comment. Bishop would have loved to go into it at any other time. The surge of hysteria it had engendered had almost died down nowadays, with it being limited to offworld use, restricted use, or use far enough away from Earth and her concerns that it wasn't important to most humans, whatever strange features it possessed. FTL drives, or whatever they were, were only the half of it. It was under review. He'd seen some of the evidence. Now he let it go, and lifted the screen again. If Tabitha had gone on one of those ships, she could be anywhere. It would take years to get into Forged Space by ordinary means. Even an Ironhorse Accelerator couldn't go faster. She could have been there since the day it happened, almost a year ago. "This is just a mess."

"No," Hyperion said. He lowered his head and sniffed again, a hellish kind of hound. "There were four individuals here, all human, and one Forged, Wayfarer Jackalope McKnight."

"Bread Zee Davis, Bancroft Wan, Kialee Yang . . . " Bishop said, the names so often in his mind that they came off his tongue like an old catechism.

" . . . and Tabitha Bishop."

"I am sure which is the Forged," Hyperion said, "but the humans are harder to label. They are distinct, however."

"They'd worked together almost a year," Bishop said, wishing he'd kept his silence, but it was leaking. "No trouble. She sent me a postcard."

"May I see it?"

He hesitated, then fiddled the controls and handed over the screen. It had been shown so often during the inquest that he knew every millimetre of it better than he knew the lines in his own hand.

The object was small, almost really postcard-sized in the Greenjack's heavy paw. "Kialee is the Han girl, I am guessing."

"And Wan is the one with the black Mohawk. Davis is the wannabe soldier in all that ex military stuff." He knew every detail of that postcard. What most mystified him about it was how friendly they all seemed, how relaxed, the girls leaning on each other, the guys making silly faces, beer in hand; around them, the dull red of the tenting, and, in the background, a portable generator and a jumble of oxygen tanks. It could have been a snap of two couples on holiday, and not of students on work assignment. He wasn't sure if they'd been dating, or if dating was a concept that had gone out with dinosaurs like him.

The Greenjack was stock-still. It looked intently and then handed back the screen. "Thank you. In that case, I can now say that there was a struggle here. Bishop and Yang are surprised, but Davis and Wan are both agitated throughout. Only McKnight is calm."

"He was new. Newish. Their old Wayfarer went to another job."

The colours illumined as the shaman talked, showing Bishop warped fields of light that were as abstract as any randomly generated image. "McKnight and the men remain close together. There is a conflict with the women. There is a struggle; I think at this point the women are forced to give up their personal devices to Terraform Raven's Finger. I believe they are tied, at least at the hands. McKnight is armed with explosive charges for the survey. But he's also more than big enough to overpower and threaten them. I guess this is what happened. Davis and Wan dislike the events a great deal but they are willing participants. That's what I see. Then there's another argument, here, the men and McKnight. It's brief. Blood and flesh scraps from McKnight are found near here."

Bishop saw the oddest nebula of greys, streaked with black and bright red. "There was some kind of struggle . . . the Wayfarer was defending . . . " But the gargoyle shaman was shaking its head.

"He cuts out his own external comms unit," Hyperion said precisely. "In the Wayfarer, this is located at the back of the skull and embedded in the surface beneath a minor chitinous plate. To remove it would be painful and messy, but it is perfectly possible and certainly not lethal. But all communication is cut before this, so there is no official account of how it was removed. The only person who can account for that is Raven, and she claims that there was a local network dropout. I would have to question her directly to be sure of her account." The implication was stark.

The air, already bitter, felt suddenly colder. "So Davis and Wan made him do it?"

"I cannot say for certain. But he does it. Any other method risks it being hijacked by signals that would give away his position. He's hidden it somewhere around here, I'd bet. Or given it to the Finger, who lost it in the gullies way before it signalled a breakdown. We should look for it. Then they leave." Hyperion pointed Northwest. "That way.'"

Bishop thought of the evidence of the Finger's call. Raven's voice said, "They've gone. Just gone." And with that phrase, she'd ushered in an entire cult of people convinced that Mars harboured ghosts, or aliens, or fiends. As if their numbers needed adding to! But Bishop couldn't keep up his anger. The pictures continued.

There was a faint coloration like a long tunnel or a tube made of the faintest streaks of yellow, grey, and ashy white. It was almost pretty against the deepening red of the Martian afternoon. The tunnel down which Tabitha had vanished. So the shaman said.

"I hardly know anything about these people," Bishop protested with distress. He didn't understand how the creature drew its conclusions.

"It is all right, Mr. Bishop," the shaman said calmly, setting off in this new direction. "I know everything about them that I need to know."

For the first time in the time that he can remember lately, Mark Bishop has enough energy to hurry in the Greenjack's wake. "But how? Just from some picture?"

"Yes."

"But you can't tell anything just from a picture!"

"You can tell everything from a single look. For instance, I know that you, Mr. Bishop, had it in mind that if you found me a fraud here, you might use your gun to shoot me dead. And then yourself. We would be a memorial in this unpleasant spot, the monument of your surrender to despair and your inability to remain rational in the face of my abominable supernatural exploitation of both your grief and reputation." It continued walking steadily.

Bishop had no answer to that. He'd never verbalised or reified that intent, but he couldn't entirely dismiss it. His gun was in his holster pocket. Everyone had them. He couldn't say that the thought hadn't been his secondary insurance. That and the recorder, of course. It would have told the sad tale to those who came to find out what happened. The notion had been discarded a long time before they even landed, though, he realised, and now, the recorder was instead preserving this vision of Hyperion's skinny ass slowly wandering along a trackless gully through soft dirt and Bishop's labored breathing.

"Anyone can see these things," Hyperion mumbled as he went. "But they don't know how to tune in, to refine and translate and *know* them."

"Don't start on the psychic stuff." What the hell had those boys and that monster done with his little girl? "Tell me about Wan."

"Bancroft. He is idealistic, practical, yet ordinary. Bread is determined, focused, and he has been somehow thwarted in the past, which has made him bitter, though he hides this with great charm. McKnight is an entrepreneur, comfortable with criminal ways."

"McKnight is the leader, then?"

"Wan is the leader, Mr. Bishop, whoever's foot may seem to go first. As for the women, neither of them are involved in this plan except by accident. It is simply unfortunate that they were in this team when Wan met McKnight. I am certain that McKnight was the catalyst for what occurred here. Wan is too poor, too badly connected, and too ignorant to plan this venture alone. Possibly he didn't think of it until McKnight arrived to put the idea in his head. He isn't creative."

"You're quite the detective." Bishop didn't mean it quite as bitter as it sounded.

"I would like to be. But it isn't my intuition working so much as the patterns that I see."

Bishop gave a cursory glance at his screen. A twisting tube of colours, some bleeding others sharp, was all he could see; bad art on a tiresome landscape. "If you say so." In spite of himself, he had no trouble believing the Greenjack now. "Are the girls all right?"

"They are physically unharmed at this point. They are talking here . . . " the shaman indicated their way and the stretch ahead. He moved off alone for some distance, then narrated, "I feel terror and anger. I believe they were attempting to bargain an escape or discover the real plans. McKnight is all for telling them. He is enjoying the action. Wan forbids him. McKnight doesn't mind this, but Davis is getting edgy. He has never liked the involvement of the Terraform. His fear of retaliation is keeping him quiet now."

Bishop stopped suddenly, rooted in the unmade earth. He had realised that he was walking through time, and his sudden confidence in the shaman's analysis made him fear where the future led, even though it had already happened. He attempted to rally some criticism, some countermeasure to the rigorous story unfolding, to prove at least to himself that there was a chance that most of it was simply the shaman's whimsical interpretation of some very dry facts, but he struggled to do so.

Ahead of him, the large creature stopped in its own dusty tracks and turned about. It seemed patient and concerned. Every time he looked into its peculiar yellow eyes, he expected the disturbance of an alien encounter, but instead he felt that he was understood, and the feeling made him desperately uneasy. Who knew what confidence trickery it was capable of, after all? But for the life of him, he couldn't figure out a motive.

"When we get to the end of this," Bishop said hoarsely, coughing, "what will we do?"

"That depends on the end."

"I mean, if she isn't dead, if she was taken somewhere . . . will you help me? You said you'd ask for a Unity ship. I guess that means you know someone."

"I will find your daughter, Mr. Bishop," Hyperion said. "I already promised to. If you prefer I will say no more about the events that passed this way. No doubt you must wonder how I can know, and there is no way to tell you how, any more than you can explain how you do most things you do that are your nature. I expect that some greater analysis will be able to detail the process, but I am not interested to do it myself. I see these people and I feel what they have been feeling, as if I can watch it in a moving storybook. There are other things present, besides the people now. These disruptions in such a quiet area have acted as an attractorl, and some of the energies I spoke about earlier are beginning to converge on the scene. As yet, they are only circling. You may see . . ."

"These stains? I thought they were just bad rendering or the light or something. They're so faint. Watermarks."

"They are the ones. You will see them circle and converge, then scatter and reform. They may merge. Ignore them. They are not important."

"But they . . . " But the Greenjack was already moving on. The shadows were lengthening into early evening, and a slight cooling was in the air. Bishop kept one eye on the trail and the other on the screen, but the silence was too much for him. "Talk," he said.

"They are not speaking here," the shaman replied over its shoulder. "Yang is looking for a way to escape. Bishop is locked in her thoughts. She is angry with McKnight for his betrayal of their friendship, or what she thought was their friendship. She is questioning her assessment of the others. McKnight is leading, he is content. Wan and Davis are in the rear, pushing the women on. Wan is excited. Davis is starting to lose trust in him. Davis has a weak personality. He believes that he ought to be leader and Wan is beginning to annoy him. He is starting to form a strong resentment."

"What is that cloud?"

"He is forming negative energy vortices. This kind of personality often does. Their energy scatters out from the holes in their energy bodies. It is an interesting feature of humans that they create negative energy attractors much more readily and strongly than positive ones. I am not sure why this is, but I believe it is because damaged individuals are *leaky*, prone to influence and loss, whereas healthy types do not shed these frequencies without some deliberate effort. They are impervious to wild influence and create almost no disturbances. I must consult with the other Greenjacks when they are done travelling."

Bishop was silent for a while and they plodded on some quarter kilometre more as he checked his recordings. It was an ecology he was seeing, if it were true. A psychic kind of ecology. He couldn't help but notice it, even as it wasn't part of his concern. Just a peripheral. If the Greenjack had tried to convince him about all this any other way, he could probably have thought of a good hole or two to poke in things, but as it was . . . he shook his head and struggled on. He wasn't fit, and although gravity was lighter and walking easier, it was a long time since he'd hiked further than his back yard. He found himself stopped suddenly, almost walking onto Hyperion's tail. The Forged was still as a statue.

Bishop looked at the screen quickly. A darkening storm of purples and reds like a miniature cyclone was all around him. He waited, then Hyperion said, "They stop here. McKnight signals offworld. Wan and Davis start arguing again. Yang tries to escape. She just runs. Bishop tried to stop her. McKnight notices. Davis starts to run after her, but Wan says no. He was willing to leave her. He wants to. Davis catches Yang. Wan says to McKnight they should leave them both. He knows Davis is trouble, Yang he doesn't want anyway; they have some history . . . it's minor . . . he'd rather leave her for some reason I don't . . . Anyway. Bishop protests. Yang becomes hysterical. McKnight knocks her unconscious. Now Wan gets angry with McKnight. Davis's antagonism towards Wan crystallises. He threatens to turn them all in. McKnight doesn't like that. McKnight threatens Wan and Davis. Wan tries to calm things down. Bishop is raging. Wan ties up both women, hands and feet. Yang is injured, there is blood here. They wait. Quite a long time. I think an hour must pass or so. Davis is now focused entirely on Wan. Hates him. McKnight is the only calm one. Wan is furious but he's too smart to let it out. A ship comes. It lands over there . . . "

Mark Bishop got up and followed the Greenjack over to the place across the long shadows that had nearly covered the whole ground.

There was no sign of a landing, but then, given the weather, there wouldn't be. He recorded dutifully. The colored waterworld had gone. He watched the Greenjack circle and look, and pause. It returned from a small exploration and said, "This is the end of the trail here. The ship has come. It's a Forged craft. I don't know its name, but if I ever meet it, I'll know it by its energy signatures. It is one of three types of Ironhorse currently operating between the Far System and Earth. Can't say more. They all embark, except Yang. She's dead."

Bishop half wanted to ask for more, certain it was hiding things, but then he decided that it was enough, he didn't want to know. Everything inside him had stopped, waiting. What the shaman had just said was a testable claim, unless it meant some kind of spiritual residue. Beneath his coat, he felt the hairs on his neck stand on end. His heart gave an extra beat. "Are you sure?"

"Yes." Hyperion paused and then made a brief gesture with its head. Bishop followed the line, recorder in hand first. He saw nothing, just the usual Mars stuff, but then the shaman walked him out another hundred metres to a small mound that Bishop or anyone else would just have taken for one of the billion shifting dunes. "She is here."

Bishop took measurements, readings. They were still technically well within Thorson's Gullies. Nobody would have come here for a long, long time. Perhaps never. The land was bad, useless. This zone had already been mapped. There were no deposits of use. Then, with the shaman's help, he set up his recorder and began the process of moving the sand aside. He used his shoe as a spade. It didn't take long before he bumped something. Without ceremony, they uncovered a part of a desiccated human body, just enough to see the identifying badges on the suit, and then they covered it up again.

Bishop moved away a short distance and sat for a while, drinking water and watching the sun go down. It got very cold. His feet and hands ached. He wished for the scotch again, fervently, avidly, relentlessly. Hyperion sat beside him like a giant dog.

Bishop's hand strayed to the machine but he left it alone. He stumbled over the words, "Do you see her?" He was braced for any fool answer. He wanted there to be one, a good one.

"She was here," it said. "But now she has gone."

Bishop nodded. He wasn't going to ask for the details. He wasn't ready yet. Leave it at the cryptic stage until . . . "We should go."

"I suggest we walk back to the capsule rather than make any transmissions the Terraform might interpret. Also we must now consider this a murder investigation. What would you like to do? We could report it to the police and let them . . . "

"No. They got it all wrong the first time." Bishop was surprised by the force of his own hatred, but the shaman didn't skip a beat.

"Then we should not discuss this with Valhalla. We need help from sources that don't mind being accomplice to criminal acts."

Belatedly, Mark realised that by this it meant their failure to inform. Anything that wasted time now didn't matter to him. "Can you track them from here?"

"Not directly, but their intentions are reasonably clear. McKnight is at least guilty of manslaughter and kidnap. Wan and Davis of kidnap, misuse of corporate properties, perversion of the course of justice. The Terraform is on their side. They have every chance to make a good escape, but they couldn't head sunward—there's nothing there except Earth and the high population satellite systems, full of officials and the law. They have gone to the Belt—no Forged ship could take them further without at least stopping there for supplies. We will find something out that way." It seemed completely confident, almost resigned to its own cold certainty.

Bishop ignored the bleakness in its tone and waded forwards grimly in its wake, a squire to a weird and uncomforting King Wenceslas of the sands.

It was a long, hard, cold, and lonely passage. Bishop struggled all the way not to ask all the questions that were hunting him, but he didn't ask them, and at last they retraced all the path, and the Valhalla's Hand opened its thousand eyes and let them in. He couldn't afford to indulge his fears.

"Where to?" the Valhalla asked as it left orbit, swinging away in an arc that would return it to the sunward side so that it could pick up extra heat.

"Just to the lift station again," Hyperion said with a sigh, as though the journey had been tiring and a disappointment.

It made some small talk with Valhalla as Bishop settled himself in. He intended to check his recordings and prepare some method for transmitting them safely in case something happened to him, but before he was able to do any of that, exhaustion took over and he fell asleep. He slept all the way to the port, and woke feeling drained and thin. Hyperion led him through their formalities, and then they were sitting in the cafeteria, Bishop facing a reconstituted dinner with a dry mouth.

"An ordinary journey to the Belt is a three year stretch," the shaman said. He was lying like a giant dog on the smooth tiled floor next to Bishop's table, resting his head on a plastic plant pot beneath the convincing fake fronds of a plastic grass. "The fastest available transport can make it in one year. But Unity ships can make it instantly."

"Interference," Bishop croaked. He had managed a mouthful. It wasn't bad but he was so hungry even cardboard would have seemed delicious. Hungry or not, he was loath to think about Unity travel. They said it interfered with you at a fundamental level. They were not sure what the long-term implications would be.

"I will search here, perhaps they came this way." It was unconvincing. Nobody in their right mind would come this way if they wanted to get the hell out of Earth's influence.

Bishop surrendered to his curiosity and need. "You said you could get a Unity ship." He said it quietly. They weren't illegal, but they also weren't allowed this close to Earth space.

"I can ask a favor," Hyperion agreed. "I feel convinced that they have taken that route. I do not see how any legally operating taxi would be involved, and the illegal ones all come from midspace, and most have Unity drives. The most likely destination is Turbulence, the port on Hygeia. The majority of transfers take place there and there's only lipservice paid to the law at any level. It is Forged space and mostly rebel Forged at that."

"You think Wan wanted to remake himself?" Some humans wanted to experience addons that were better than just a comms set. It seemed ludicrous to Bishop, insane, an extreme form of self mutilation beyond tattoos and piercings, some kind of primal denial of one's self. It frightened him.

"I think there are lots of opportunities for all kinds of profit out there. Especially for those already on the run."

Bishop crumpled the wrapper his cutlery had come in. Unity technology was infectious. Even passengers aboard craft operating the technology were at risk. So far, in the years it had been around, its effects had proved relatively benign, but theorists guessed that this might be a product of a much more significant infiltration process. To use it was to risk something that could be a living death. Fanatics spoke of puppetry and zombies, aliens operating behind the scenes. He'd heard . . . "Perhaps they'd just abandon her."

"She was a witness," the shaman said. "A Terraform is complicit in crimes bringing severe penalties. Murder and human trafficking. The foundation of Mars, no less, is at stake. If they went with Raven's blessing, then they didn't go alone."

"Get your ship."

The creature got up slowly, "I will be back soon."

Bishop finished that meal, and then another as he waited, forking up food, watching the news on the cafeteria wall, not thinking now that there was no need to think any more. When he got there, when something happened, then he'd think.

They took an ordinary ship out to deep Mars orbit again, and were set adrift in a cargo pod with barely enough oxygen to survive. Something picked them up at the allotted minute and second, as displayed on Bishop's illuminated screen. Something cast them off again. There was rattling and clanking. After a few minutes of struggle, they emerged into the unloading bay of a large port. There was no trace of whoever had brought them there. There was no gravity, just the sickly spin of centrifuge. It was a struggle to keep the dinners inside him, but he did, though they felt as if they'd been in his stomach for the three year journey he'd skipped. The Greenjack helped him to get his spacelegs and then went off, sniffing.

Bishop sat in a rented cubic room at the port's only hotel and watched what Hyperion transmitted to his screen. For a few days, this was their pattern. The shaman didn't find the ship he was looking for, nor any trace of it, nor traces of the passengers. There were a lot of other things Bishop saw that disturbed him, but he was protected, by his distance, the recorder, and the fact that these troubling things were not his immediate mission. There were many shadows here, like the inkstained Mars twilight, moving splatters that now and again coagulated around a place or a person. He started to type, wrote "haunted"? He managed to read the report in bits and pieces. He struggled to wash, to shave, to function in between. He drank something called scotch that was alcohol with synthetic flavouring. It was good. It did the job. Beside "haunted," he copied the most loathsome and mysterious of the names of things that Hyperion had identified. Cracklegrackle. His nerves jangled. He tried turning the screen on himself, but only when the Jack wasn't there. He looked old. A fucking wreck, to be honest. He was amazed.

"They only affect those who wish to be affected," the shaman insisted as they ate together on their last, fruitless night.

"But how?" Bishop pushed his food around the bag it had come in, squashing it between his fingers and thumb.

The answer was so unexpected and ridiculous that it silenced him. "Through the hands and feet, the crown or base of the spine. Never mind that. These rumours of laboratories open in the midstream; any surgery is available there. We should look into that."

Bishop agreed; what else could he do? They moved to a lesser port, and then a lesser one, the last place that pretended to commercial operations. There was no hotel, just some rented rooms in a storehouse. Bishop began to run out of money, and sanity. He couldn't bring himself to contact work and explain his absence. He thought only about Tabitha. He drank to avoid feeling. He took pills for regimented sessions of oblivion. Sometimes he watched the Mars journey again on his screen. Those strange floating films of colour absorbed his attention more and more. The more he watched them, the more he saw that their movements seemed sinister and far from random. He saw himself pass through them and tried to remember if they had changed him.

He'd felt nothing. Nothing. Hyperion's statements about the people, seemed more and more unlikely. He felt it was a goosechase. Perhaps he had been paid to lead Bishop out here where he couldn't make trouble, and strand him. Perhaps the Terraform had bought the Greenjack off. This ran through his mind hourly. Only the transmissions of the 'Jack's travels kept him going.

Then one day, months after they had set out, he got the call.

"I found her."

"Is she . . ."

"Alive."

He scrabbled to get clean clothes, to clean himself, to get sober. He was full of joy, full of terror. The hours passed like aeons. The 'Jack brought a ship—one he saw this time, an Ironhorse Jackrabbit with barely enough space to fit them aboard. It yawned and they walked into its sharklike mouth. It held them there, one bite from vacuum death, and blinked them to the cloudstreams of Jupiter. He barely noticed.

"Are those things here?"

"Everywhere, Mr. Bishop," Hyperion said.

"What things?" the Jackrabbit asked.

"Energies," the Greenjack said. "Nothing for you to worry about."

There was some bickering about the return journey. Bishop couldn't make sense of it.

"Where is she?" he gripped the Greenjack's thorny arm. Its scaly skin was like a cat's tongue, strangely abrasive. Around him, floating, the few human visitors to this place looked lost. Tabitha was none of them. They all looked through portholes into the gauzy films of the planet's outer atmosphere streaming past below their tiny station. It looked like caramel coffee. Outside, various Forged were docked and queued. People had conversations in the odd little cubicles, like airlocks, that dotted the outside of the structure. Sometimes the doors flashed and then opened. People came out, went in, on both sides of the screen wall that separated the two environments of instation and freezing space from one another.

"This way," the jack said. He reached out and laid his tough paw across the back of Bishop's gripping hand for a second, then led him with a kick and drift through the slight pull of the planet's gravity well to one of those lit doorways.

Bishop peered inside, looking for her. The shaman followed him in. The room was empty.

He turned, "She's not here!"

The shaman pointed at the panel in the reinforced floor. Some Jupiterian Forged was on the other side.

Bishop looked at Hyperion because he didn't want to look at the window, but he floated towards it, his hands and feet betraying him as they pressed suddenly against the clear portal, and, on the far other side, across six sheets of various carbonates, glass, and vacuum, the Forged pressed its own hands towards his open palms.

Jupiter was no place for a human being. They died there in droves. Even the Forged, who had been engineered before birth to thrive in its vicious atmosphere and live lives as glorified gas farmers fell prey to its merciless storms. The upper cloud layer was never more than minus one twenty Celsius. Large creatures didn't operate that well at those temperatures, even ones that were mostly made of machine and chemical technologies so far removed from the original human that they were unrecognisable components of life. But Tupac, the motherfather, was able to create children who lived here, even some who dived far down to the place where hydrogen was a metal; scientists with singleminded visions. Tupac's efforts had advanced human knowledge and experience to the limit of the material universe.

Bishop's senses didn't stretch that far. He stared into eyes behind shields of methane ice that were nothing like his own, in a face that was twice the size of his, blue, bony, and metallic and more like the faceplate of a robot fish than anything else. Narrow arms, coated in crablike exoskeletal bone reached out for him. The hands were five-digit extensions, covered in strange suckerlike skin that clung easily to the glass. Behind that, the body was willowy, ballooning, tented like clothes in the wind, patterned like a mackerel. Jellyfishes and squid were in its history somewhere, microprecise fibre engineering and ultracold processor tech its true parents.

"She has a connection to Uluru," Hyperion said quietly, naming the virtual reality which all the Forged shared. When their bodies could not meet, in mind they could get together anytime. "I can put it to your screen."

Bishop turned then. "You're not seriously suggesting this . . . thing . . . is my daughter?"

"There is a market for living bodies of any kind in the Belt. Old humans are particularly preferred for the testing of adaptive medical transformation. Technicians there have a mission to press beyond any restraint and develop their skills to make and remake any living tissues . . . "

He exploded with a kind of laugh. "But you can't *make* Forged. Not like that."

Hyperion was silent for a moment. "They say it is important to become self-adaptive, that they are the next step beyond Forged. They will be able to remake themselves in any fashion without experiencing discontinuity of consciousness. Any flesh or machine will be incorporated if it is willed. The Actualised . . . "

"But it can't be her!" His stare at the shaman was too wide. His eyes hurt. Against his will, he found himself turning, looking through the walls at the creature's blinkless stare. Its face had no expression. It had no mouth or nose. Gill-like extensions fluttered behind its head like ruffles of voile. Its octopid hands pressed, pressed. Its nose touched the plate. Hyperion was holding the screen out to him.

He took it in nerveless hands. They were so limp he could hardly turn it.

"Davis tried to turn Wan in, once they reached Volatility, that port on Ceres. But the Forged Police there are all sympathisers. Wan and McKnight sold him, split the money . . . "

On the screen was the standard summer garden that Uluru created for all such meetings, a place for avatars to stand in simulated sunlight amid the shelter of shrubs and trees. Running through it, watermarked, was the background that Bishop could really see, the reality he was standing in. In front of the monstrous creature attached to the window stood Tabitha, in jeans and the yellow T-shirt with the T-Rex on it that he bought her at some airport lounge some lifetime ago. Her soft brown hair moved in the nonexistent breeze. He touched the screen to feel the texture of her perfect skin.

"Daddy." The lips moved to whisper. Through her hazel eyes, the great void eyes of the fish stared.

It was only an avatar. You could make these things easily. The photographs were even in his recorder. The voice was only like hers, it wasn't really hers. There must be hundreds of standard tracks of her in the archives somewhere. These things were simple to fake.

He thrust the screen back at Hyperion, though it was his, and tried to muster some shred of dignity. "Summon the ship."

The creature didn't move from its floating position at his side. "Mr. Bishop . . ."

"You've fooled me long enough with your chat and your lines and your little premade adventure complete with faked body, but I see through it now, if you can stand the irony of that, and I'm going. I find no evidence to confirm any of your ridiculous suggestions." He was so angry that he could barely speak. Bits of spit flew off him and floated, benign and silly bubbles in the slowly circulating air. "Really, this was one step too far! I bought it hook line and sinker until now. I suppose you were trying to see how far I could be drawn. Well, a long way! Perhaps you were going to get some money for bringing the Institute into disrepute and scandal when I made some case with it for your insane claims about good and evil and possession and . . . your goosechase. Yes. You took advantage of me. I was weak . . . " There was a sound in his head, that black hum. He could hear something in it. An identifiable noise. Definite. Sure.

"Bishop," the creature snapped.

" . . . daddy!" came the faint call from the screen as it tumbled down past the shaman's side and clattered against the cabin wall.

The black hum was laughing at him, a dreadful sound. It hurt his chest. It hurt everywhere. He was furious. His skin was red hot, he couldn't think of where to go. What a fool he'd been. "How dare you. How dare you . . . "

Suddenly, the hideous gargoyle hissed, a low, menacing sound. "I have done what I said I would. I have found your daughter. I have no interest in your views . . . "

Bishop was glaring around wildly. He made a shooing motion. "Get away! You won't mock me anymore! Stupid, hideous creatures!" He began to thump the glass panels where the Jupiter creature's hands were stuck. It didn't move, just stared at him with its hidden, empty eyes. "You!" he turned on Hyperion. "Make it go away!"

The Greenjack looked at him flatly, and even with its expressive handicap, he could feel its disgust. "Mr. Bishop, I urge you to look again, and *listen*. Your daughter . . . "

"It's not even possible!" Bishop kicked strongly for the door. Behind him, the recorder tumbled, ricocheting, out of control, the voice that came out of it growing fainter.

"Daddy!"

The door controls, they were too complicated for him. He couldn't figure them out. He turned and lashed out wildly, thinking the Greenjack was closer than it was. It caught the recorder easily from its spin and held it out to him, contempt in its every line.

Bishop took the little machine and smashed it against the wall until it stopped making any noise.

Beyond the clear wall, the Jupiterian was letting go slowly, suckers peeling off one by one. Its eyes had frosted over strangely, white cracks visible across the ice surfaces, spreading until they shrouded the whole orbit. Its head moved back from the pane and dipped. At the same moment, the door opened.

Bishop was out in a second. He couldn't breathe. Not at all. His chest was tight. There was no damn oxygen. There must have been a malfunction. He gripped the handrails, gasping, the blood pounding in his eyes. "Oxygen!" he he cried out. "There's no air!" In his ears was the black hum.

Hyperion passed him, gliding slowly. He was holding the recorder, and ignored Bishop's outburst. He started talking, and as Bishop had to listen to him, unable to go anywhere, he heard the black sound forming itself into a shape.

"I think that although you have broken the speakers and the screen, the memory is probably unharmed. It will not be possible to locate and arrest Davis as he has been scrapped for parts. Tabitha says that Wan and McKnight disposed of him first, before they went into the Belt proper. Wan wanted her to be rendered as well, but McKnight said there would be a lot more for a whole live subject. They were planning out how to create a trafficking chain and where to get more people for it from. She was taken to some facility about one twenty degrees off Earth vector. They wanted to make her as far from the original human as possible, to prove their accomplishments, but also because they thought it was fitting for humans to end up like the Forged out here have all ended, as slave workers in the materials industry. She isn't like the other Forged of course, she's just a fabrication. Her links to Uluru are very limited. She has no real contact other than voice and some vision with anyone else. And the Forged here are mostly rebel sympathisers. She tried to call you, but the networks out this way are very bad and none of the regular channels would carry her messages anyway because she is marked as a risk to the survival of the Actualist movement. It took a great deal of trouble to get her to come here. It is dangerous. She risked everything. And she didn't want to see you. It took days to persuade her that if you came there might be sufficient evidence to reopen the case and bring the Earthside Police out here to pursue it."

Bishop gulped. "You've done a very thorough job, I'll give you that."

The Greenjack made a clacking noise. It spoke in a calm, reasonable manner, as if Bishop were perfectly lucid. "I have not been able to trace the routes of Davis, Wan, or McKnight yet but I think they will be easy to find. I hope you understand, Mr. Bishop, that I do not require your permission to pursue the investigation or to make my findings known to the authorities. I also advise against your attempting to return to Earth alone. Many of the Forged here who would have you believe that they are honest taxis are pirates like Wan has aspired to become. The going rate for a live Old Monkey human in the Belt is upward of fifty thousand standard dollars. I doubt you have the finances to buy yourself out of trouble, even if they wanted you to."

The terrible pulse of the black hum wouldn't let him think. Bishop reeled against the bulkhead, the rail gripped in his slippery fingers. He was heroic. "We must rescue her. We can take her back. Find a way. I can raise the money on Earth. The Police can arrest those responsible and the government will . . ."

"The government is well aware of the situation," Hyperion said. "Returning Tabitha Earthside and attempting remodelling would be tantamount to a declaration of civil war out here. They will do no such thing. You know it as well as I do. Pull yourself together." It handed him his screen, which it had repaired somehow. Aside from a cracked screen and broken speakers, it seemed all right. "This is your evidence. It is our only hard evidence, aside from the Uluru recording I have made, but, of course, those involved are Forged, so they are suspect." This admission of bigotry in the judicial system seemed to make it tired. "If you do not act, there will be no justice of any kind."

Bishop held the screen without turning beyond the home page. He heard his own voice babbling, "We could kill them. McKnight, you can find him . . ."

Hyperion waited a few moments. "Tabitha is an extraordinary person, Mr. Bishop. Although it is a mystery how she has sprung from you. She understands your feelings. You have hurt her deeply and this makes me dislike you very much. After what she has been through, your rejection is by far the most damaging thing that has happened here. And now, you are seeking to spread misery further by your stupidity. The energy wells out here are all very dark. A few lights shine. Tabitha Bishop is one of them. You are now claiming that one of the energies is responsible for your weakness. I find that contemptible. Pull yourself together!"

"You! You could find them and kill them and you won't do it! Just this

superstitious, religious babble. You bring me here to show me . . . to show me
. . . Here, here!" He tried to get the screen to focus on him. "Show me now. I
know it's there. That thing. Show . . . " but Bishop could not finish. The words
had cannoned into each other behind his tongue and exploded there into an
unpronounceable summons for hell. Cracklegrackle.

He wanted very much to be dead. The shame was unbearable. He could not
carry it. On Earth, he would have been on his face, on his knees; here he was
floating, curled up tight into a ball.

The shaman waited. "You are not possessed, Mark. You are simply
hysterical. Your future with your daughter is your own choice. However, we
must take the recording back to Earth and submit it to the Police there. Then
we will have done our part. I, at least, will do so. You must hurry. She has to
leave in a moment."

Behind Bishop's eyes, the blackness was shot with red. He snarled at
Hyperion, silently, and then, inch by inch, he hauled himself to the cubicle
door, again with that will that wasn't his, no it wasn't.

His joints hurt. His throat was so tight. He couldn't breathe. Inside. The
rails. The flat expanse of glass. The slices of clear shielding. The coffee-coloured
clouds miles below, as soft and gentle as thistledown. Dirt on the floor. They
ought to clean this place. It was so hard to see through the handmarks, the
footprints, the wear and tear on the old polycarbonate. It was so hard to see
through the glass and the frozen methane that melted and ran to keep her
sight clear, then froze, then melted again so that she was always half blind. It
was so hard to see through his tears.

HIDEAWAY

ALASTAIR REYNOLDS

⊸✦⊷

Part One

There was, Merlin thought, *a very fine line between beauty and terror.* Most certainly where the Way was concerned. Tempting as it was to think that the thing they saw through the cutter's windows was only a mirage, there would always come a point when the mysterious artifact known as the syrinx started purring, vibrating in its metal harness. Somehow it was sensing the Way's proximity, anxious to perform the function for which it had been designed. It seemed to bother all of them except Sayaca.

"Krasnikov," she mouthed, shaping the unfamiliar word like an oath.

She was the youngest and brightest of the four disciples who had agreed to accompany Merlin on this field trip. At first the others had welcomed her into Merlin's little entourage, keen to hear her insights on matters relating to the Way and the enigmatic Waymakers. But in the cutter's cramped surroundings Sayaca's charms had worn off with impressive speed.

"Krasnikov?" Merlin said. "Sorry, doesn't mean anything to me either." He watched as the others pulled faces. "You're going to have to enlighten us, Sayaca."

"Krasnikov was . . . " she paused. "Well, a human, I suppose—tens of kiloyears ago, long before the Waymakers, even before the Flourishing. He had an idea for moving faster than light, one that didn't involve wormholes or tachyons."

"It can't work, Sayaca," said a gangly, greasy-scalped adolescent called Weaver. "You can't move faster than light without manipulating matter with negative energy density."

"So what, Weaver? Do you think that would have bothered the Waymakers?"

Merlin smiled, thinking that the trouble with Sayaca was that when she made a point it was almost always a valid one.

"But the Way doesn't actually allow faster-than-light travel," said one of the others. "That much we do know."

"Of course. All I'm saying is that the Waynet might have been an attempt to make a network of Krasnikov tubes, which didn't quite work out the way the builders intended."

"Mm," Merlin said. "And what exactly is a Krasnikov tube?"

"A tube-shaped volume of altered spacetime, light-years from end to end. Just like one branch of the Waynet. The point was to allow round-trip journeys to other star systems in arbitrarily short objective time."

"Like a wormhole?" Weaver asked.

"No; the mathematical formulation's utterly different." She sighed, looking to Merlin for moral support. He nodded for her to continue, knowing that she had already alienated the others beyond any reasonable point of return. "But there must have been a catch. It's clear that two neighboring Krasnikov tubes running in opposite directions violate causality. Perhaps when that happened . . . "

"They got something like the Waynet?"

Sayaca nodded to Merlin. "Not a static tube of restructured spacetime, but a rushing column of it, moving at a fraction below lightspeed. It was still useful, of course. Ships could slip into the Way, cross interstellar space at massive tau factors, and then decelerate instantaneously at the other end simply by leaving the stream."

"All very impressive," Weaver said. "But if you're such an expert, why can't you tell us how to make the syrinx work properly?"

"You wouldn't understand if I did," Sayaca said.

Merlin was about to intervene—tension was one thing, but he could not tolerate an argument aboard the cutter—when his glove rescued him. It had begun tickling the back of his hand, announcing a private call from the mothership. Relieved, he unhitched from a restraint harness and kicked himself away from the four adolescents. "I'll be back shortly," he said. "Try not to strangle each other, will you?"

The cutter was a slender craft only forty meters long, so it was normal enough that tempers had become frayed in the four days that they had been away from the *Starthroat*. The air smelled edgy, too: thick with youthful pheromones he did not remember from the last trip. The youngsters were all getting older, no longer his unquestioning devotees.

He pushed past the syrinx. It sat within a metal harness, its long axis aligned with the ship's. The conic device was tens of thousands of years old, but its matte-black surface was completely unmarred. It was still purring, too, like a well-fed cat. The closer they got to the Way, the more it would respond. It wanted to be set free, and shortly—Merlin hoped—it would get its wish.

The seniors would not be pleased, of course.

Beyond the syrinx was a narrow, transparent-walled duct which led back to Merlin's private quarters. He kicked himself along the passage, comfortable in freefall after four days of adaptation. The view was undeniably impressive; as always he found himself slowing to take it in.

The stars were clumped ahead, shifted from their real positions and altered in hue and brightness by the aberration caused by the cutter's motion. They were moving at nine-tenths of the speed of light. Set against this distorted starfield, far to one side, was the huge swallowship—the *Starthroat*—that Merlin's people called home. The swallowship was far too distant to see as anything other than a prick of hot blue light pointing aft, like a star that had been carelessly smudged. Yet apart from the four people with him here, every other human he knew was inside *Starthroat*.

And then there was the Way.

It lay in the opposite hemisphere of the sky, stretching into the infinite distance fore and aft. It was like a ghostly pipeline alongside which they were flying—a pipeline ten thousand kilometers thick and thousands of light-years long. It shimmered faintly—twinkling as tiny particles of cosmic debris annihilated themselves against its skin. Most of those impacts were due to dust specks that only had rest velocities of a few kilometers a second against the local stellar rest frame—so the transient glints seemed to slam past at eye-wrenching velocities. Not just a pipeline, then—but a glass pipeline running thick with twinkling fluid that flowed at frightening speed.

And perhaps soon they would relearn the art of riding it.

He pushed into his quarters, confronting his brother's image on the comms console. Although they were not twins—Gallinule was a year younger—they still looked remarkably alike. It was almost like looking in a mirror.

"Well?" Merlin said. "Trouble, I'm afraid."

"Let me guess. It has something to do with Quail."

"Well, the captain's not happy, let's put it like that. First you take the syrinx without authorization, then the cutter—and then you have the balls not to come back when the old bastard tells you." The face on the screen was trying not to smile, but Merlin could tell he was quietly impressed. "But that's not actually the problem. When I say trouble I mean for all of us. Quail wants all the seniors in his meeting room in eight hours."

Just time, Merlin thought, for him to drop the syrinx and make it back to *Starthroat*. Not as good as having time to run comprehensive tests, but still damnably tempting. It was almost suspiciously convenient.

"I hadn't heard of any crisis on the horizon."

"Me neither, and that's what worries me. It's something we haven't thought of."

"The Huskers stealing a lead on us? Fine. I expect to be comfortably senile by the time they get within weapons range."

"Just be there, will you? Or there'll be two of us in trouble." Merlin smiled. "What else are brothers for?"

The long oval meeting room was hundreds of meters inside *Starthroat's* armored hull. Covered in a richly detailed fresco, the walls enclosed a hallowed mahogany table of ancient provenance. Just as the table's extremities now sagged with age, time had turned the fresco dark and sepia. In one corner a proctor was slowly renovating the historic artwork, moving with machine diligence from one scene of conflict to another, brightening hues; sharpening brush-strokes that had become indistinct with age.

Merlin squeezed past the squat machine.

"You're late," Quail said, already seated. "I take it your trip was a fruitful one?" Merlin started to compose an answer, but Quail was already speaking again. "Good. Then sit down. You may take it as a very bad omen that I am not especially minded to reprimand you."

Wordlessly Merlin moved to his own chair and lowered himself into it.

What could be that serious?

In addition to the gaunt, gray-skinned captain, there were fifteen ship seniors gathered in the chamber. Apart from Merlin they were all in full ceremonial dress; medals and sigils of rank to the fore. This was the Council: the highest decision-making body in the ship save for Quail himself. One senior for every dozen subseniors, and one subsenior for every hundred or so crewmembers. These fifteen people represented somewhat less than fifteen thousand others working, relaxing, or sleeping elsewhere in the swallowship's vast confines. And much of the work that they did was concerned with tending the two hundred thousand people in frostwatch: frozen refugees from dozens of systems. The burdens of responsibility were acute; especially so given that the swallowship had encountered no other human vessel in centuries. No one became a senior by default, and all those present—Merlin included—had earned the right to sit with Quail. Even, Merlin thought, his enemies on the Council. Like Pauraque, for instance. She was a coldly attractive woman who wore a stiff-necked black tunic, cuffs and collar edged in complicated black filigrees. She tapped her fingers against the table's ancient wood, black rings clicking together.

"Merlin," she said. "Pauraque. How are you?"

She eyed him poisonously. "Reports are that you took one of the final two syrinxes without the express authorization of the Council Subdivision for Waynet Studies." Merlin opened his mouth, but Pauraque shook her head crisply. "No; don't even think of weaseling out of it. I'll see that this never happens again. At least you brought the thing back unharmed this time . . . didn't you?"

He smiled. "I didn't bring it back at all. It's still out there, approaching the Way." He showed Pauraque the display summary on the back of his glove. "I placed it aboard an automated drone."

"If you destroy it . . . " Pauraque looked for encouragement at the doleful faces around her. "We'll have you court-martialed, Merlin . . . or worse. It's common knowledge that your only reason for studying the syrinxes is so that you can embark on some ludicrous quest . . . "

Quail coughed. "We can discuss Merlin's activities later, Pauraque. They may seem somewhat less pressing when you've heard what I have to say." Now that he had their attention, the old man softened his tone of voice until it was barely a murmur. "I'm afraid I have remarkably bad news."

It would have to be, Merlin thought.

"For as long as some of us remember," Quail said, "one central fact has shaped our lives. Every time we look to stern, along the way we've come, we know that *they* are out there, somewhere behind us. About thirty light-years by the last estimate, but coming steadily closer by about a light-year for every five years of shiptime. In a century and a half we will come within range of their weapons." Quail nodded toward the fresco, one particularly violent tableau that showed ships exchanging fire above a planet garlanded in flames. "It won't be pretty. At best, we might take out one or two elements of the swarm before they finish us. Yet we live with this situation, some days hardly giving it more than a moment's thought, for the simple reason that it lies so far in our future. The youngest of us may live to see it, but I'll certainly not be among them. And, of course, we cling to the hope that tomorrow will offer us an escape route we can't foresee today. Better weapons, perhaps—or some new physics that enables us to squeeze a little more performance from our engines, so that we can outrun the enemy."

True enough. This was the state of things that they had known for years. It was the reality that had underpinned every waking thought for just as long. No one knew much about the Huskers except that they were ruthless alien cyborgs from somewhere near the Galaxy's center. Their only motive seemed to be the utter extermination of humanity from all the niches it had occupied since the Flourishing. This they prosecuted with glacial patience, in a war that had already lasted many kiloyears.

Quail took a sip of water before continuing. "Now I must disclose an alarming new discovery."

Stars winked into existence above the table: hundreds and then thousands of them, strewn in lacy patterns like strands of seaweed. They were looking at a map of the local stellar neighborhood—a few hundred light-years in either direction—with the line of the Way cutting through it like a blue laser. The swallowship's position next to the Way was marked, as was the swarm of enemy ships trailing it.

And then a smudge of radiance appeared far ahead, again near the Way. "That's the troubling discovery," Quail said.

"Neutrino sources?" Merlin said, doing his best to convince the room that his attention was not being torn between two foci.

"A whole clump of them in our path, about one hundred light-years ahead of us. Spectroscopy says they're more or less stationary with respect to the local stellar neighborhood. That means it isn't a swarm coming to intercept us from the front—but I'm afraid that's as good as the news gets."

"Husker?" said Gallinule.

"Undoubtedly. Best guess is we're headed straight toward a major operational concentration—hundreds of ships—the equivalent of one of our motherbases or halo manufactories. Almost certainly armed to the teeth and in no mood to let us slip past unchallenged. In short, we're running from one swarm toward another, which happens to be even larger."

Silence while the seniors—including Merlin—digested this news.

"Well, that's it then," said another senior, white-bearded, bald Crombec, who ran the warcrèches. "We've got no choice but to turn away from our current path."

"Tactically risky," Gallinule said.

Crombec rubbed his eyes, red with fatigue. Evidently he had been awake for some time—perhaps privy to this knowledge longer than the others, grappling with the options. "Yes. But what else can we do?"

"There is something," Merlin said. As he spoke he saw the status readout on his glove change; the sensors racked around the syrinx finally recording some activity. Considering what he was about to advocate, it was ironic indeed. "A crash-program to achieve Way-capability. Even if there's an ambush ahead, the Huskers won't be able to touch a ship moving in the Way."

Pauraque scoffed. "And the fact that the Cohort's best minds have struggled with this problem for kiloyears in no way dents your optimism?"

"I'm only saying we'd have a better than zero chance."

"And I suppose we could try and find this superweapon of yours while we're at it?"

"Actually," said Quail, raising his voice again, "there happens to be a third possibility, one that I haven't drawn your attention to yet. Look at the map, will you?"

Now Quail added a new star—one that had not been displayed before. It lay directly ahead of them, only a few tens of light-years from their current position. As they moved their heads to establish parallax, they all saw that the star was almost exactly aligned with the Way.

"We have a chance," he said. "A small one, but very much better than nothing. This system has a small family of worlds: a few rocky planets and a gas giant with moons. There's no sign of any human presence. In nearly every respect there's nothing remarkable about this place. Yet the Way passes directly through the system. It might have been accidental . . . or it might have been the case that the Waymakers wanted to have this system on their network."

Merlin nodded. Extensive as the Waynet was, it still only connected around ten million of the Galaxy's stars. Ten million sounded like a huge number, but what it meant was that for every single star on the network there were another *forty thousand* that could only be reached by conventional means.

"How far away?" he said.

Quail answered: "Without altering our trajectory, we'll reach it in a few decades of worldtime whatever we do now. Here's my suggestion. We decelerate, stop in the system and dig ourselves in. We'll still have thirty years before the Huskers arrive. That should give us time to find the best hiding places and to camouflage ourselves well enough to escape their detection."

"They'll be looking for us," Crombec said.

"Not necessarily." He made a gesture with his hands, clasping them and then drawing them slowly apart. "We can split *Starthroat* into two parts. One will continue moving at our current speed, with its exhaust directed back toward the Huskers. The other, smaller part will decelerate hard—but it'll be directing its radiation away from the aliens. We can fine-tune the beam direction so that the swarm ahead of us doesn't see it either."

"That's . . . ambitious," Merlin said. He had his gloved hand under the table now, not wanting anyone else to see the bad news that was spilling across it. "If hiding's your style."

"It's no one's style . . . just our only rational hope." Quail looked around the room, seeming older and frailer than any captain ought to be; rectangles of shadow etched beneath his cheekbones.

Crombec spoke up. "Captain? I would like to take command of the part of the ship that remains in flight."

There were a few murmurs of assent. Clearly Crombec would not be alone in preferring not to hide, even if the majority might choose to follow Quail.

"Wait," Pauraque said. "As soon as we put people on a decoy, with knowledge of what has happened earlier, we run the risk of the Huskers eventually learning it all for themselves."

"We'll take that risk," Quail snapped.

"There won't be one," said Crombec. "You have my word that I'll destroy my ship rather than risk it falling into Husker possession."

"Merlin?" the captain asked. "I take it you're with us?"

"Of course,"he said, snapping out of his gloomy reverie. "I support your proposal fully . . . as I must. Doubtless we'll have time to completely camouflage ourselves and cover our tracks before the swarm comes past. There's just one thing . . . "

Quail rested his head to one side against his hand, like a man close to exhaustion. "Yes?"

"You said the system was almost unremarkable . . . is it simply the presence of the Waynet that makes it otherwise?"

"No," Quail said, his patience wearing fatally thin. "No . . . there was something else—a small anomaly in the star's mass-luminosity relationship. I doubt that it's anything very significant. Look on the bright side, Merlin. Investigating it will give you something to do while the rest of us are busying ourselves with the boring work of concealment. And you'll have your precious syrinxes, as well—not to mention close proximity to the Waynet. There'll be plenty of time for all the experiments you can think of. I'm sure even you will be able to make two syrinxes last long enough . . . "

Merlin glanced down at his glove again, hoping that the news he had received earlier had in some way been in error, or his eyes had deceived him. But neither of those things proved to be the case.

"Better make that one," he said.

Naked, bound together, Sayaca and Merlin seemed to float in space, kindling a focus of human warmth between them. The moment when the walls of the little ship had vanished had been meant to surprise and impress Sayaca. He had planned it meticulously. But instead she began to shiver, though it was no colder than it had been an instant earlier. He traced his hand across her thigh, feeling her skin break into goose bumps.

"It's just a trick," he said, her face half-buried in his chest. "No one can see us from outside the cutter."

"Force and wisdom; it feels so cold now, Merlin. Makes me feel so small and vulnerable, like a candle on the point of flickering out."

"But you're with me."

"It doesn't make any difference, don't you understand? You're just a man, Merlin—not some divine protective force."

Grudgingly, but knowing that the moment had been spoiled, Merlin allowed the walls to return. The stars were still visible, but there was now quite clearly a shell of transparent metasapphire, laced with control graphics, to hold them at bay.

"I thought you'd like it," he said. "Especially now, on a day like this one."

"I just wasn't quite ready for it, that's all." Her tone shifted to one of reconciliation. "Where is it, anyway?"

Merlin issued another subvocal command to the ship, instructing it to distort and magnify the starfield selectively, until the object of Sayaca's interest sprang into focus. What they saw was the swallowship splitting into two uneven parts, like an insect undergoing some final, unplanned metamorphosis. Six years had passed since the final decision had been made to implement Quail's scheme. Sayaca and Merlin had become lovers in that time; Quail had even died.

The separation would have been beautiful, were so much not at stake. *Starthroat* did not exist anymore. Its rebuilding had been a mammoth effort that had occupied all of them in one way or another. Much of its mass had been retained aboard the part that would remain cruising relativistically. She had been named *Bluethroat* and carried roughly one-third of the frostwatch sleepers, in addition to Crombec and the small number of seniors and subseniors who had chosen to follow him. Needless to say there had been some dispute about Crombec getting most of the weapons, chiefly from Pauraque . . . but Merlin could not begrudge him that.

The smaller part they had named *Starling*. This was a ship designed to make one journey only, from here to the new system. It was equipped with a plethora of nimble, adaptable in-system craft, necessary for exploring the new system and finding the securest hiding places. Scans showed that a total of six worlds orbited the star they had now named Bright Boy. Only two were of significance: a scorched, airless planet much the same size as fabled Earth, which they named Cinder, and a gas giant they named Ghost. It seemed obvious that the best place to hide would be in one of these worlds, either Cinder or Ghost, but no decision had yet been made. Sayaca thought Cinder was the best choice, while Pauraque advocated using Ghost's thick atmosphere for concealment. Eventually a choice would be made, they would dig in, establish a base, and conceal all evidence of their activities.

The Huskers might slow down, curious—but they would find nothing.

"You were there, weren't you," Sayaca said. "When they decided this."

Merlin nodded—remembering how young she had seemed then. The last few years had aged them all. "We all thought Quail was insane . . . then we realized even an insane plan was the best we had. Except for Crombec, of course . . ."

Bluethroat was separating now; its torch still burning clean and steady, arcing back into the night along the great axis of the Way. Far behind—but far less than they had once been—lay the swarm, still pursuing Merlin's people.

"You think Crombec's people will die, don't you?" Sayaca said.

"If I thought he had the better chance, that's where I'd be. With his faction, rather than under Pauraque."

"I thought about following him, too," Sayaca said. "His arguments seemed convincing. He thinks we'll all die around Bright Boy."

"Maybe we will. I still think the odds are slightly more in our favor."

"Slightly?"

"There's something I don't like about our destination, Sayaca. Bright Boy doesn't fit into our normal stellar models. It's too bright for its size, and it's putting out far too many neutrinos. If you're going to hide somewhere, you don't do it around a star that stands out from the crowd."

"Would it make any difference if Quail had put you in charge rather than Pauraque? Or if the Council had not forbidden you to test the final syrinx?"

Conceivably, he thought, it might well have made a difference. He had been very lucky to retain any kind of seniority after what had happened back then. But the loss of the second syrinx had not been the utter disaster his enemies had tried to portray. The machine had still rammed against the Way in a catastrophic manner, but for the first time in living memory, a syrinx had seemed to do something else in the instants before that collision . . . chirping a series of quantum-gravitational variations toward the boundary. And the Way had begun to respond: a strange local alteration in its topology ahead of the syrinx. Puckering, until a dimple formed on the boundary, like the nub of a severed branch on a tree trunk. The dimple was still forming when the syrinx hit.

What, Merlin wondered, would have happened if that impact had been delayed for a few more instants? Might the dimple have finished forming, providing an entry point into the Way?

"I don't think it made any difference to me."

"They say you hated Quail."

"I had reasons not to like him, Sayaca. My brother and I both did."

"But they say Quail rescued you from Plenitude, that he saved your lives while everyone else died."

"That's true enough."

"And for that you *hated* him?"

"He should have left us behind, Sayaca. No; don't look at me like that. You weren't there. You can't understand what it was like."

"Maybe if I spoke to Gallinule, he'd have more to say about it." Subtly, she pulled away from him. A few minutes earlier it would have signified nothing, but now that tiny change in their spatial relationship spoke volumes. "They say you're alike, you and Gallinule. You both look alike, too. But there isn't as much similarity as people think."

Part Two

"There are definitely tunnels here," Sayaca said, years later.

Their cutter was parked on an airless plain near Cinder's equator, squatting down on skids like a beached black fish. Bright Boy was almost overhead; a disk of fierce radiance casting razor-edged shadows like pools of ink. Merlin moved over to Sayaca's side of the cabin to see the data she was projecting before her, sketched in ruddy contours. Smelling her, he wanted to bury his face in her hair and turn her face to his before kissing her, but the moment was not right for that. It had not been right for some time.

"Caves, you mean?" Merlin said.

"No; *tunnels*." She almost managed to hide her irritation. "Like I always said they were. Deliberately excavated. Now do you believe me?"

There had been hints of them before, from orbit, during the first months after the arrival around the star. *Starling* had sent expeditionary teams out to a dozen promising niches in the system, tasking them to assess the benefits of each before a final decision was made. Most of the effort was focussed around Cinder and Ghost—they had even put space stations into orbit around the gas giant—but there were teams exploring smaller bodies, even comets and asteroids. Nothing would be dismissed without at least a preliminary study. There were even teams working on fringe ideas like hiding inside the sun's chromosphere.

And for all that, Merlin thought, *they still won't allow me near the other syrinx*.

But at least Cinder was a kind of distraction. Mapping satellites had been dropped into orbits around all the major bodies in the system, measuring the gravitational fields of each body. The data, unraveled into a density-map, hinted at a puzzling structure within Cinder—a deep network of tunnels riddling the lithosphere. Now they had even better maps, constructed from seismic data. One or two small asteroids hit Cinder every month. With no atmosphere to slow them down, they slammed into the surface at many kilometers per second. The sound waves from those impacts would radiate through the underlying rock, bent into complex wave fronts as they traversed density zones. They would eventually reach the surface again, thousands of kilometers away, but the precise pattern of arrival times—picked up across a network of listening devices studding the surface—would depend on the route that the sound waves had taken.

Now Merlin could see that the tunnels were definitely artificial. "Who do you think dug them?"

"From here, there's no way we'll ever know." Sayaca frowned, puzzling over something in her data, and then seemed to drop the annoyance, at least for now, rather than have it spoil her moment of triumph. "Whoever it was, they tidied up after themselves. We'll have to go down—get into them."

"Perhaps we'll find somewhere to hide."

"Or find someone else already hiding." Sayaca looked into his face, her expression one of complete seriousness.

"Maybe they'll let us hide with them."

She turned back to her work. "Or maybe they'd rather we left them alone."

Several months later Merlin buckled on an immersion suit, feeling the slight prickling sensation around the nape of the neck as the suit hijacked his spinal nerves. Vision and balance flickered—there was a perceptual jolt he never quite got used to—and then suddenly he was back in the simulated realm of the Palace. He had to admit it was good; much better than the last time he had sampled Gallinule's toy environment.

"You've been busy," he said.

Gallinule's image smiled. "It'll do for now. Just wait till you've seen the sunset wing."

Gallinule led him through the maze of high-ceilinged, baroquely walled corridors that led from the oubliette to the other side of the Palace. They ascended and descended spiral staircases and crossed vertiginous inner chambers spanned by elegantly arched stonework bridges, delicate subtleties of masonry highlighted in sunset fire. The real Palace of Eternal Dusk had been ruined along with every other sign of civilization when the Huskers had torched Plenitude. This simulation was running in the main encampment inside Cinder, but Gallinule had spread copies of it around the system, wherever he might need a convenient venue for discussion.

"See anything that looks out of place?" Gallinule said.

Merlin looked around, but there was nothing that did not accord with his own memories. Hardly surprising. Of the two of them, Gallinule had always been the one with the eye for detail.

"It's pretty damned good. But why? And how?"

"As a test-bed. Aboard *Starthroat,* we never needed good simulation techniques. But our lives depend upon making the right choices around Bright Boy. That means we have to be able to simulate any hypothetical situation and experience it as if it were totally real."

Merlin agreed. The discovery that the tunnels in Cinder were artificial had enormously complicated the hideaway project. They had been excavated by a hypothetical human splinter group, which Sayaca had dubbed the Diggers. No one knew much about them. Certainly they had been more advanced than any part of the Cohort, but while their machines—lining the tunnels like a thick arterial plaque—seemed unfathomably strange, they were not quite strange enough to suggest that they had been installed by the Waymakers. And they were quite clearly human: markings were in a language that the linguists said had ancient links to Main. The Diggers were simply one of the thousands of cultures that had ascended to heights of technical prowess without making any recognizable dent on human history.

" . . . anyway, who knows what nasty traps the Diggers left us,"Gallinule was saying. "With simulations, we'll at least be able to prepare for the more obvious surprises." His youthful image shrugged. "So I initiated a crash program to resurrect the old techniques. At the moment we have to wear suits to achieve this level of immersion, but in a year or so we'll be able to step into simulated environments as easily as walking from one room to another."

They had reached a balcony on the sunset side of the Palace of Eternal Dusk. He leaned over the balustrade as far as he dared, seeing how the lower levels of the Palace dropped away toward the rushing sea below. The Palace of Eternal Dusk circled Plenitude's equator once a day, traveling with the line that divided day from night. Its motion caused Plenitude's sun to hang at the same point in the sky, two-thirds of its swollen disk already consumed by the sea. Somewhere deep in the keel of rock which the Palace rode lay throbbing mechanisms that both sustained the structure's flight—it had been flying for longer than anyone remembered—and generated the protective bubble that held it in a pocket of still air, despite its supersonic velocity relative to the ground.

Merlin's family had held the Palace for thirteen hundred years, after a short Dark Age on Plenitude. The family had been among the first to rediscover powered flight, using fragile aircraft to reach the keel. Other contenders had come, but the family had retained their treasure across forty generations, through another two Dark Ages.

Finally, however, the greater war had touched them.

A damaged Cohort swallowship had been the first to arrive, years ahead of a Husker swarm. The reality of interstellar travel was still dimly remembered on Plenitude, but those first newcomers were still treated with suspicion and paranoia. Only Merlin's family had given them the benefit of the doubt . . . and even then, not fully heeded the warning when it was given. Against their ruling mother's wishes, the two brothers had allowed themselves to be taken aboard the swallowship and inducted into the ways of the Cohort. Their old names were discarded in favor of new ones, in the custom of the swallowship's crew. They learned fluency in Main.

After several months, Merlin and Gallinule had been preparing to return home as envoys. Their plan was simple enough. They would persuade their mother that Plenitude was doomed. That would not be the easiest of tasks, but their mother's co-operation was vital if anything was to be saved. It would mean establishing peace among the planet's various factions, where none had existed for generations. There were spaces in the swallowship's frostwatch holds for sleepers, but only a few hundred thousand, which would mean that each region must select its best. It would not be easy, but there were still years in which to do it. "None of it will make any difference," their mother had said. "No one will listen to us, even if we believe everything Quail says."

"They have to."

"Don't you understand?" she said. "You think of me as your mother, but to fifty million of Plenitude's inhabitants I'm a *tyrant*."

"They'll understand," Merlin said, half-believing it himself.

But then the unthinkable had happened. A smaller element of the swarm had crept up much closer than anyone had feared, detected only when it was already within Plenitude's system. The swallowship's captain made the only decision he could, which was to break orbit immediately and run for interstellar space.

Merlin and Gallinule fought—pleaded—but Quail would not allow them to leave the ship. They told him all they wanted was to return home. If that meant dying with everyone else on Plenitude, including their mother, so be it.

Quail listened, and sympathized, and still refused them. It was not just their genes that the Cohort required, he said. Everything else about them: Their stories. Their hopes and fears. The tiniest piece of knowledge they carried, considered trivial by them, might prove to be shatteringly valuable. It was many decades of shiptime since they had found another pocket of humanity. Merlin and Gallinule were simply too precious to throw away.

Even if it meant denying them the right to die with valor.

Instead, on *Starthroat*'s long-range cameras, relayed from monitoring satellites sown around Plenitude, they watched the Palace of Eternal Dusk die, wounded by weapons it had never known before, stabbing deep into the keel on which it flew, destroying the engines that held it aloft. It came down slowly, grinding into the planetary crust, gouging a terrible scar across half of one scorched continent before it came to rest, ruined and lop-sided.

And now Gallinule had made this.

"If you can do all this now . . . " Merlin mused. He left the remark hanging, knowing his brother would take the bait.

"As I said, full immersion in a year or so. Then we'll need better methods to deal with the time-lag for communications around Bright Boy. We can't even broadcast signals for fear of them being intercepted by the Huskers, which limits us to line-of-sight comms between relay nodes sprinkled around the system. Sometimes the routing will add significant delays. That's why we need another kind of simulation. If we can create semblances—"

Merlin stopped him. "Semblances?"

"Sorry. Old term I dug from the troves. Another technique we've forgotten aboard *Starthroat*. We need to be able to make convincing simulacra of ourselves, with realistic responses across a range of likely stimuli. Then we can be in two places at once—or as many as we want to be. Afterward, you merge the memories gathered by your semblances."

Merlin thought about that. Many cultures known to the Cohort had developed the kind of technology Gallinule was referring to, so the concept was not unfamiliar to him.

"These wouldn't be conscious entities, though?"

"No; that's far down the line. Semblances would just be mimetic software: clever caricatures. Of course, they'd seem real if they were working well. Later . . . "

"You'd think of adding consciousness?"

Gallinule looked around warily. It was a reflex, of course—there could not possibly have been eavesdroppers in this environment he had fashioned—but it was telling all the same. "It would be useful. If we could copy ourselves entirely into simulation—not just mimesis, but neuron-by-neuron mapping— it would make hiding from the Huskers very much easier."

"Become disembodied programs, you mean? Sorry, but that's a definite case of the cure being worse than the disease."

"Eventually it won't seem anywhere near as chilling as it does now. Especially when our other options for hiding look less and less viable."

Merlin nodded sagely. "And you'd no doubt do all in your power to make them seem that way, wouldn't you?"

Gallinule shrugged. "If Cinder's tunnels turn out to be the best place to hide, so be it. But it's senseless not to explore other options." Merlin watched the way his knuckle tightened on the stone balustrade, betraying the tension he tried to keep from his voice.

"If you make an issue of this," Merlin said carefully, "you'd better assume I'll fight you, brother or not."

Gallinule touched Merlin's shoulder. "It won't come to a confrontation. By the time the options are in, the correct path will be clear to us all . . . you included."

"The correct path's already clear to me. And it doesn't involve becoming patterns inside a machine."

"You'd prefer suicide instead?"

"Of course not. I'm talking about something infinitely better than hiding." He looked hard into his brother's face. "You have more influence on the Council than I do. You could persuade them to let me examine the syrinx."

"Why not ask Sayaca the same thing?"

"You know well why not. Things aren't the same between us these days. If you . . . oh, what's the point." Merlin removed Gallinule's hand from his shoulder. "Nothing that happens here will make the slightest difference to your plans."

"Spare me the self-righteousness, Merlin. It's not as though you're any different." Then he sighed, looking out to sea. "I'll demonstrate my commitment to the cause, if that's what you want. You know that Pauraque's still exploring the possibility of establishing a camouflaged base inside Ghost's atmosphere?"

"Of course."

"What you probably don't know is our automated drones don't work well at those depths. So we're going in with an exploration team next month. It'll be dangerous, but we have the Council's say-so. We know there's something down there, something we don't understand. We have to find out what it is."

Merlin had heard nothing about anything unexpected inside Ghost, but he feigned knowledge all the same.

"Why are you telling me this?"

"Because I'm accompanying Pauraque. We've equipped a two-person cutter for the expedition, armored to take thousands of atmospheres of pressure." Gallinule paused and clicked his fingers out to sea, making the blueprints of the ship loom large in the sky, sharp against the dark blue zenith. The blueprint rotated dizzyingly. "It's nothing too technical. Another ship could be adapted before we go down there. I'd be happy to disclose the mods."

Merlin studied the schematic, committing the salient points to memory. "This is a goad, isn't it?"

"Call it what you will. I'm just saying that my commitment to the greater cause shouldn't be in any doubt." Another finger click and the phantom ship vanished from the sky. "Where yours fits in is another thing entirely."

Part Three

For days Ghost had loomed ahead: a fat sphere banded by delicate equatorial clouds, encircled by moons and rings. Now it swallowed half the sky, cloud decks reaching up toward him; castellations of cream and ochre stacked hundreds of kilometers high. His approach was queried by the orbiting stations, but they must have known what the purpose of his visit was. His brother and Pauraque were already down there in the clouds. He had a faint fix on their ship as it steered itself into the depths.

The seniors around Cinder had been eager to get him out of their hair, so it had not taken much to persuade them to give him a ship of his own. He had customized it according to Gallinule's specifications and added a few cautious refinements of his own . . . and then named it *Tyrant*.

The hull creaked and sang as it reshaped itself for transatmospheric travel. The navigational fix grew stronger. With Merlin inside, the ship fell, knifing down through cloud layers. The planet had no sharply defined surface, but there came a point where the atmospheric pressure was exactly equivalent to the air pressure inside *Tyrant*. Below that datum, pressure and temperature climbed steadily. Gravity was an uncomfortable two gees, more or less tolerable if he remained in his seat.

The metasapphire hull creaked again, reshaping itself. Merlin had descended more than a hundred kilometers below the one-atmosphere datum, and the pressure outside was now ten times higher. Above fifty atmospheres, the hull would rely on internal power sources to prevent itself buckling. Merlin did his best not to think about the pressure, but there was no ignoring the way the light outside had dimmed, veiled by the masses of atmosphere suspended above his head. Down below it was oppressively dark, like the sooty heart of a thunderstorm wrapped around half his vision. Only now and then was there a stammer of lightning, which briefly lit the cathedrals of cloud below for hundreds of kilometers, down to vertiginous depths.

If there'd been more time, he thought, *we'd have come with submarines, not spacecraft . . .*

It was a dismal place to even think about spending any time in. But in that respect it made perfect sense. The thick atmosphere would make it easy to hide a modestly sized floating base, smothering infrared emissions. They would probably have to sleep during the hideaway period, but that was no great hardship. Better than spending decades awake, always knowing that beyond the walls was that crushing force constantly trying to squash you out of existence.

But there was something down here, Gallinule had said. Something that might count against using Ghost as a hideaway.

They had to know what it was.

"Warning," said *Tyrant*. "External pressure now thirty bars. Probability of hull collapse in five minutes is now five percent."

Merlin killed the warning system. It did not know about the augmentations he had made to the hull armoring, but it was still unnerving. Yet Pauraque and Gallinule were lower yet, and their navigational transponder was still working.

If they were daring him to go deeper, he would accept.

"Merlin?" said his brother's voice, trebly with echoes from the atmospheric interference. "So you decided to join us after all. Did you bring Sayaca with you?"

"I'm alone. I didn't see any point in endangering two of us."

"Shame. Well, I hope you implemented those hull mods, or this is going to be a brief conversation."

"Just tell me what it is we're expecting to see down here. You mentioned something unexpected."

Pauraque's voice now. "There's a periodic pressure phenomenon moving through the atmosphere, like a very fast storm. What it is, we don't know. Until we understand it, we can't be certain that hiding inside Ghost will work."

Merlin nodded, suddenly seeing Gallinule's angle. His brother would want the phenomenon to prove hazardous just so that his plan could triumph over Pauraque's. It was an odd attitude, especially as Pauraque and Gallinule were now said to be lovers, but it was nothing unusual as far as his brother was concerned.

"I take it you have a rough idea when we can expect to see this thing?"

"Reasonably good," Pauraque said. "Approach us and follow our vector. We're going deeper, so watch those integrity readings."

As if to underline her words, the hull chose that moment to creak—a dozen alerts sounding. Merlin grimaced, silencing the alarms, and gunned *Tyrant* toward the other ship.

Ghost was a classical gas giant, three hundred times more massive than Cinder. Most of the planet was hydrogen in its metallic state, overlaid by a deep ocean of merely liquid hydrogen. The cloud layers, which seemed so immense—and which gave the world its subtle bands of color—were compressed into only a few hundred kilometers of depth. Less than a hundredth of the planet's radius, yet those frigid, layered clouds of ammonia, hydrogen, and water were as deep as humans could go. Pauraque wanted to hide at the lowest layer above the transition zone where the atmosphere thickened into a liquid hydrogen sea, under a crystal veil of ammonium hydro-sulfide and water-ice.

Ahead now, he could see the glint of the other ship's thrusters, illuminating sullen cloud formations as it passed through them. Only a few kilometers ahead.

"You mentioned that the phenomenon was periodic,"Merlin said. "What exactly did you mean by that?"

"Exactly what I said," came Pauraque's reply, much clearer now. "The pressure wave—or focus—moves around Ghost once every three hours."

"That's much faster than any cyclone."

"Yes." The icy distaste in Pauraque's voice was obvious. She did not enjoy having a civil conversation with him. "Which is why we consider the phenomenon sufficiently—"

"It could be in orbit."

"What?"

Merlin checked the hull readouts again, watching as pressure hotspots flowed liquidly from point to point. Rendered in subtle colors, they looked like diffraction patterns on the scales of a sleek, tropical fish.

"I said it could be in orbit. If one of Ghost's moons was in orbit just above the top of the cloud layer, three hours is how long it would take to go around.

The time would only be slightly less for a moon orbiting just below the cloud layer, where we are."

"Now you've really lost it," Gallinule said. "In orbit? *Inside* a planet?"

Merlin shrugged. He had thought about this already and had a ready answer, but he preferred that Gallinule believed him to be thinking the problem through even as they spoke. "Of course, I don't really think there's a moon down there. But there could still be something orbiting."

"Such as?" Pauraque said.

"A black hole, for instance. A small one—say a tenth of the mass of Cinder, with a light-trapping radius of about a millimeter. We'd have missed that kind of perturbation to Ghost's gravitational field until now. It wouldn't feel the atmosphere at all, not on the kind of timescales we're concerned with. But as the hole passed, the atmosphere would be tugged toward it for hundreds of kilometers along its track. Any chance that's your anomaly?"

There was a grudging silence before Pauraque answered. "I admit that at the very least it's possible. We more or less arrived at the same conclusion. Who knows how such a thing ended up inside Ghost, but it could have happened."

"Maybe someone put it there deliberately."

"We'll know soon enough. The storm's due any moment now."

She was right. The storm focus—whatever it was—moved at forty kilometers per second relative to Ghost's core, but since Ghost's equatorial cloud-layers were already rotating at a quarter of that speed, and in the same sense as the focus, the storm only moved at thirty kilometers per second against the atmosphere. Which, Merlin thought, was still adequately fast.

He told the cabin windows to amplify the available light, gathering photons from beyond the visible band and shifting them into the optical. Suddenly it was as if the overlaying veils had been stripped away; sunlight flooded the canyons and crevasses of cloud through which they were flying. The liquid hydrogen ocean began only a few tens of kilometers below them, under a transition zone where the atmospheric gases became steadily more fluidic. It was blood-hot down there; pressures nudged toward one hundred atmospheres. Not far below the sea they would climb into the thousands, at temperatures hot enough to melt machines.

And now something climbed above the horizon to the west. *Tyrant* began to shriek alarms, its dull machine-sentience comprehending that there was something very wrong nearby, and that it was a wrongness approaching at ferocious speed. The storm focus gathered clouds as it moved, tugging them violently out of formation. To Merlin's eyes, the way it moved reminded him of something from his childhood, something glimpsed moving through Plenitude's tropical waters with predatory swiftness: a darting mass of whirling tentacles.

"We're too high," Pauraque said. "I'm taking us lower. I want to be much closer to the focus when it arrives."

Before he could argue, Merlin saw the violet thrust spikes of the other ship. It slammed away, dwindling into the soupy stillness of the upper transition zone. He thought of a fish descending into some lightless ocean trench, into benthic darkness.

"Watch your shielding," he said, as he dove his own ship after them.

"Pressure's still within safe limits," Gallinule said, though they both knew that what now constituted safe was not quite the usual sense of the word. "I'll pull up if the rivets start popping, trust me."

"It's not just the pressure that worries me. If there's a black hole in that focus, there's also going to be a blast of gamma rays from the matter being sucked in."

"We haven't seen anything yet. Maybe the flux is masked by the clouds."

"You'd better hope it is."

Merlin was suited up, wearing the kind of high-pressure mobility armor he had only ever worn before in warcrèche simulations. The armor was prized technology, many kiloyears old; nothing like it now within the Cohort's technical reach. He hoped Gallinule and Pauraque were similarly prudent. If the hull gave in, the suits might only give them a few more minutes of life, but near something as unpredictable and chaotic as a miniature black hole, there was no such thing as too much shielding.

"Merlin?" Gallinule said. "We've lost a power node. Damn jury-rigged things. If there's a pressure wave before the focus we might start to buckle . . . "

"You can't risk it. Pull up and out. We can come back again on the next pass, three hours from now."

He had seen accretion disks, the swirls of matter around stellar-mass black holes and neutron stars, and what he saw near the storm's focus looked very similar: a spiraling concentration of cloud, tortured into rainbow colors as strange, transient chemistries came into play. They were so deep in the transition zone here that only tiny pressure changes were enough to condense the air into its fluid state. Lightning cartwheeled across the focus, driven by static differentials in the moving air masses. Merlin checked the range: close now, less than two hundred kilometers away.

And something was wrong.

Pauraque's ship was sinking too far, drifting too close to the heart of the storm. They were above it now, but their rate of descent would bring them close to the focus by the time it arrived.

"Force and wisdom; I told you to pull up, not go deeper!"

"We have a problem. Can't reshape the hull on our remaining nodes. No aerodynamic control." Gallinule's voice was calm, but Merlin knew his brother was terrified.

"Vector your thrust."

"Hell's teeth, what do you think I'm trying to do?"

No good. He watched the violet spikes of the other ship's thrusters stab in different directions, but there was nothing Gallinule could do to bring them out of their terminal descent. Merlin thought of the mods Gallinule had recommended. Unless he had added some hidden improvements, the other ship would implode in ten or fifteen seconds. There would be no surviving that.

"Listen to me," Merlin said. "You have to equalize pressure with the outside, or that hull's going to implode."

"We'll lose the ship that way."

"Don't argue, just do it! You have no more than ten seconds to save yourselves!"

He closed his eyes and hoped they were both suited. Or perhaps it would be better if they were not. To die by hull implosion would be swift, after all. The inrushing walls would move faster than any human nerve impulses.

On the magnified view of the other ship he saw a row of intakes flicker open along the dorsal line. Soup-thick atmosphere would have slammed in like an iron fist. Maybe their suits were good enough to withstand that shock.

He hoped so.

The thrust flames died out. Running lights and fluorescent markings winked out. A moment later he watched the other ship come apart like something fashioned from gossamer. Debris lingered for an instant before being crushed toward invisibility.

And two bulbously suited human figures fell through the air, drifting apart as they were caught in the torpid currents that ran through the transition zone. For a moment the suits were androform, but then their carapaces flowed liquidly toward smooth egg-shapes, held rigid by the same principle that still protected Merlin's ship. They were alive—he was sure of that—but they were still sinking, still heavier than the air they displaced. The one that was now falling fastest would pass the storm at what he judged to be a safe distance. The other would fall right through the storm's eye.

He thought of the focus of the storm: a seething eye of flickering gamma rays, horrific gravitational stress, and intense pressure eddies. They had not seen it yet, but he could be sure that was what it would be like. A black hole, even a small one, was no place to be near.

"Final warning," *Tyrant* said, bypassing all his overrides. "Pressure now at maximum safe limit. Any further increase in . . ."

He made his decision.

Slammed *Tyrant* screaming toward the survivor who was headed toward the eye. It would be close—hellishly so. Even the extra margins he had built into this ship's hull would be pushed perilously close to the limit. On the cabin window, cross-hairs locked around the first falling egg. Range: eleven kilometers and closing. He computed an approach vector and saw that it would be even closer than he had feared. They would be arcing straight toward the eye by the time he had the egg aboard. Seven kilometers. There would not be time to bring the egg aboard properly. The best he could do would be to open a cavity in the hull and enclose it. Frantically he told *Tyrant* what he needed; by the time he was done, range was down to three kilometers.

He felt faint, phantom deceleration as *Tyrant* matched trajectories with the egg and brought itself in for the rendezvous. The egg left a trail of bubbles behind it as it dropped, evidence of the transition to ocean. Somewhere on *Tyrant*'s skin, a cavity puckered open, precisely shaped to accept the egg. They tore through rushing curtains of cloud. In a few moments he would be near enough to see the eye, he knew. One kilometer . . . six hundred meters. Three hundred.

The faintest of thumps as the egg was captured. Membranes of hull locked over the prize and resealed. Whoever he had saved was as safe now as Merlin.

Which was really saying very little.

"Instigate immediate pull-up. Hull collapse imminent. Severe pressure transition imminent."

He was through the eye now, perhaps only two or three kilometers from the sucking point of the black hole. He had expected to see the clouds drawn into a malignant little knot, with a flickering glint of intense light at the heart of the whirlpool, but there was nothing, just clear skies. There was a local gravitational distortion, but it was nowhere near as severe as he had expected. Merlin glanced at the radiation alarms, but they were not showing anything unusual.

No hint of gamma radiation.

He wanted time to think, wanted to work out how he could be this close to a black hole and feel no radiation, but what was coming up below instantly demanded his attention. There was the other egg, tumbling below, wobbling as if in a mirage. Pressure was distorting it, readying to crush it. And down below, slumbering under the transition zone, was the true hydrogen sea. In a few seconds the other egg would be completely immersed in that unimaginably dense blackness and it would all be over. For a moment he considered swooping in low; trying to snatch the egg before it hit. He ran the numbers and saw the chilling truth.

He would have to enter the sea as well.

Merlin gave *Tyrant* its orders and closed his eyes. Even in the cushioning embrace of his suit, the hairpin turn as the ship skimmed the ocean would still not be comfortable. It would probably push him below consciousness. Which, he thought, might turn out to be the final mercy.

The sea's hazy surface came up like a black fog.

Thought faded for an instant, then returned fuzzily; and now through the windows he saw veils of cloud toward which he was climbing. The feeling of having survived was godlike. Yet something was screaming. The ship, he realized. It had sloughed millimeters of hull to stay intact. He prayed that the damage would not prevent him getting home.

"The second egg . . . " Merlin said. "Did we get it?"

Tyrant was clever enough—just—to know what he meant. "Both eggs recovered."

"Good. Show me . . . "

Proctors carried the first egg into the cabin, fiddling with it until they persuaded it to revert to androform shape. When the facial region became transparent he saw that it was Gallinule that this egg had saved, although his brother was clearly unconscious. Not dead though: he could tell that from the egg's luminous readouts. He felt a moment of pure, unadulterated bliss. He had saved Gallinule, but not selfishly. He had not known which of the two eggs had been falling toward the eye. In fact, he did not even know that this was that egg. Had he plucked his brother from the sea, instants before the ocean would have crushed him?

But then he saw the other egg. The proctors, stupid to the end, had seen fit to bring it into the cabin. They carried it like a trophy, as if it were something he would be overjoyed to see. But it was barely larger than a space helmet.

Part Four

"I think I know what killed her," Sayaca said.

The three of them had agreed to meet within the Palace of Eternal Dusk. Sayaca had arranged a demonstration, casting into the sky vast projected shapes, which she orchestrated with deft gestures.

"It wasn't a black hole, was it?" Gallinule said.

"No." She took his hand in both of hers, comforting him as they dug through the difficult memory of Pauraque's death. It had happened months ago, but the pain of it was still acute for Gallinule. Merlin watched from one side, lingeringly resentful at the tenderness Sayaca showed his brother. "I think it was something a lot stranger than a black hole. Shall I show you?"

A double helix writhed in the sky, luminous and serpentlike against Plenitude's perpetual pink twilight.

Releasing Gallinule's hand, Sayaca lifted a finger and the DNA coil swelled to godlike size, until the individual base pairs were themselves too large to discern as anything other than blurred assemblages of atoms, huger than mountains. But atoms were only the beginning of the descent into the world of the vanishingly small. Atoms were assembled from even tinier components: electrons, protons, and neutrons, bound together by the electroweak and -strong forces. But even those fundamental particles held deeper layers of structure. All matter in the universe was woven from quarks or leptons; all force mediated by bosons.

Even that was not the end.

In the deepest of deep symmetries, the fermions—the quarks and leptons—and the bosons—the messengers of force—blurred into one kind of entity. Particle was no longer the right word for it. What everything in the universe seemed to boil down to, at the very fundamental level, was a series of loops vibrating at different frequencies, embedded in a multidimensional space.

What, Sayaca said, scientists had once termed *superstrings*.

It was elegant beyond words, and it explained seemingly everything. But the trouble with superstring theory, Sayaca added, was that it was extraordinarily difficult to test. It was likely that the theory had been reinvented and discarded dozens or hundreds of times in human history, during each brief phase of enlightenment. Undoubtedly the Waymakers must have come to some final wisdom as to the ultimate nature of reality . . . but if they had, they had not left that verdict in any form now remembered. So from Sayaca's viewpoint, superstring theory was at least as viable as any other model for unifying the fundamental particles and forces.

"But I don't see how any of this helps us understand Pauraque's Storm," Merlin said.

"Wait," said Sayaca's semblance. "I haven't finished. There's more than one type of superstring theory, understand? And some of those theories make a special prediction about the existence of something called shadow matter. It's not the same thing as antimatter. Shadow matter's like normal matter in every respect, except it's invisible and insubstantial. Objects made of normal and shadow matter just slip through each other like ghosts. There's only one way in which they sense each other."

"Gravity," Merlin said.

"Yes. As far as gravity's concerned, there's nothing to distinguish them."

"So what are you saying, that there could be whole universes made of shadow matter coexisting with our own?"

"Exactly that." She went on to tell them there was every reason to suppose that the shadow universe was just as complex as the normal one, with exactly analogous particle types, atoms, and chemistry. There would be shadow galaxies, shadow stars, and shadow worlds—perhaps even shadow life.

Merlin absorbed that. "Why haven't we encountered anything like shadow matter before?"

"There must be strong segregation between the two types across the plane of the Galaxy. For one reason or another, that segregation has broken down around Bright Boy. There seems to be about half a solar mass of shadow matter gravitationally bound to this system—most of it sitting in Bright Boy's core."

Merlin tightened his grip on the balustrade. "Tell me this answers all our riddles, Sayaca."

Sayaca told them the rest, reminding Merlin how they had probed Cinder's interior via sound waves, each sonic pulse generated by the impact of an in-falling meteorite; the sound waves tracked as they swept through Cinder, gathered at a network of listening posts sprinkled across the surface. It was these seismic images that had first elucidated the fine structure of the Digger tunnels. But—unwittingly—Sayaca had learned much more than that.

"We measured Cinder's mass twice. The first time was when we put our own mapping satellites into orbit. That gave us one figure. The seismic data should have given us a second estimate that agreed to within a few percent. But the seismic data said there was only two-thirds as much mass as there should have been, compared with the gravitational mass estimate." Sayaca's semblance paused, perhaps giving the two of them time to make the connection themselves. When neither spoke, she permitted herself to continue. "If there's a large chunk of shadow matter inside Cinder, it explains everything. The seismic waves only travel through normal matter, so they don't see one-third of Cinder's composition at all. But the gravitational signature of normal and shadow matter is identical. Our satellites felt the pull of the normal *and* shadow matter, just as we did when we were walking around inside Cinder."

"All right," he said. "Tell me about Bright Boy, too."

"It makes just as much sense. Most of the shadow matter in this system must be inside the star. Half a solar mass would be enough for Bright Boy's shadow counterpart to become a star in its own right—burning its own shadow hydrogen to shadow helium, giving off shadow photons and shadow neutrinos, none of which we can see. Except just like Bright Boy it would be an astrophysical anomaly—too bright and small to make any kind of sense, because its structure is being affected by the presence of an equal amount of normal matter from *our* universe. Both stars end up with hotter cores, since the nuclear reactions have to work harder to hold up the weight of overlying stellar atmosphere."

Sayaca thought that the two halves of Bright Boy—the normal and shadow mass suns—had once been spatially separated, so that they formed the two stars of a close binary system. That, she said, would have been something so strange that no passing culture could have missed it, for the visible counterpart of Bright Boy would have seemed to be locked in orbital embrace with an invisible partner, signaling its oddity across half the Galaxy. Over the ensuing billions of years, the two stars had whirled closer and closer together, their orbital motions damped by tidal dissipation, until they had merged and settled into the same spatial volume. *Whoever comes after us,* Merlin thought, *we won't be the last to study this cosmic mystery.*

"Then tell me about Pauraque's Storm," he said, flinching at the memory of her crushed survival egg.

Gallinule nodded. "Go on. I want to know what killed her."

Sayaca spoke now with less ease. "It must be another chunk of shadow matter—about the mass of a large moon, squashed into a volume no more than a few tens of kilometers across. Of course, it wasn't the shadow matter itself that killed her. Just the storm it caused by its passage through the atmosphere."

And not even that, Merlin thought. It was his decision that killed her; his conviction that it was more vital to save the first egg, the one falling into the storm's eye. Afterward, discovering that there was no gamma-ray point there, he had realized that he could have saved both of them if he had saved Pauraque first.

"Something that massive, and that small . . . " Gallinule paused. "It can't be a moon, can it?"

Sayaca turned away from the sunset. "No. It's no moon. Whatever it is, it was made by someone. Not the Huskers, I think, but someone else. And I think we have to know what it was they had in mind."

Nervously, Merlin watched seniors populate the auditorium—walking in or simply popping into holographic existence, like card figures dropped into a toy theater. Sayaca had bided her time before announcing her discovery to the rest of the expedition, but eventually the three of them had gathered enough data to refute any argument. When it became clear that her news would be momentous, seniors had flown in from across the system, leaving the putative hideaways they were investigating. A few of them even sent their semblances, for the simulacra were now sophisticated enough to make many physical journeys unnecessary.

The announcement would take place in the auditorium of the largest orbiting station, poised above Ghost's cloud-tops. An auroral storm was lashing Ghost's northern pole, appropriately dramatic for the event. He wondered if Sayaca had scheduled the meeting with that display in mind.

"Go easy on the superstring physics,"Gallinule whispered in Sayaca's ear, as she sat between the two men. "You don't want to lose them before you've begun. Some of these relics don't even know what a quark is, let alone a baryon-to-entropy ratio." Gallinule was right to warn Sayaca. It would be like her to begin her announcement by projecting a forest of equations on the display wall.

"Don't worry," Sayaca said. "I'll keep it nice and simple; throw in a few jokes to wake them up."

Gallinule kept his voice low. "They won't need waking up, once they realize what the implications are. Straightforward hiding's no longer an option, not with something as strange as the Ghost anomaly sitting in our neighborhood. When the Huskers arrive they're bound to start investigating. They're also bound to find any hideaway we construct, no matter how well camouflaged."

"Not if we dig deep enough," Merlin said.

"Forget it. There's no way we can hide now. Not the way it was planned, anyway. Unless . . . "

"Don't tell me; we'd be perfectly safe if we could store ourselves as patterns in some machine memory?"

"Don't sound so nauseated. You can't argue with the logic. We'd be nearly invulnerable. The storage media could be physically tiny, distributed in many locations. Impossible for the Huskers to find them all."

"The Council can decide," Sayaca said, raising a hand to shut the two of them up. "Let's see how they take my discovery, first."

"It was Pauraque's discovery," Merlin said quietly. "Whatever."

She was already walking away from them, crossing the auditorium's floor toward the podium where she would address the congregation. Sayaca walked on air, striding across the clouds. It was a trick, of course: the real view outside the station was constantly changing because of the structure's rotation, but the illusion was flawless.

"It may have been Pauraque who discovered the storm," Gallinule said, "but it was Sayaca who interpreted it."

"I wasn't trying to take anything away from her."

"Good."

Now she stepped up to the podium, the hem of her electric-blue gown floating above the clouds. She stood pridefully, surveying the people who had gathered here to hear her speak. Her expression was one of complete calm and self-assurance, but Merlin saw how tightly she grasped the edges of the podium. He sensed that beneath that shell of control she was acutely nervous, knowing that this was the most important moment in her life, the one that would make her reputation among the seniors and perhaps shape all of their destinies.

"Seniors . . . " Sayaca said. "Thank you for coming here. I hope that by the time I've finished speaking, you'll feel that your time wasn't wasted." Then she extended a hand toward the middle of the room and an image of Ghost sprang into being. "Ever since we identified this system as our only chance of concealment, we've had to ignore the troubling aspects of the place. Bright Boy's anomalous mass-luminosity relationship, for instance. The seismic discrepancies in Cinder. Pauraque's deep-atmospheric phenomenon in Ghost. Now the time has come to deal with these puzzles. I'm afraid that what they tell us may not be entirely to our liking."

Promising start, Merlin thought. She had spoken for more than half a minute without using a single mathematical expression.

Sayaca began to speak again, but she was cut off abruptly by another speaker. "Sayaca, there's something we should discuss first." Everyone's attention moved to the interjector. Merlin recognized who it was immediately: Weaver. Cruelly handsome, the boy had outgrown his adolescent awkwardness in the years since Merlin had first known him as one of Sayaca's class.

"What is it?" she said, only the tiniest hint of suspicion in her voice.

"Some news we've just obtained." Weaver looked around the room, clearly enjoying his moment in the limelight while attempting to maintain the appropriate air of solemnity. "We've been looking along the Way, as a matter of routine, monitoring the swarm that lies ahead of us. Sometimes off the line of the Way, too—just in case we find anything. We've also been following the *Bluethroat*."

It was so long since anyone had mentioned that name that it took Merlin an instant to place it. Of course, the *Bluethroat*. The part of the original ship that Crombec had flown onward, while the rest of them piled into *Starling* and slowed down around Bright Boy. It was not that anyone hated Crombec or wished to bury him and his followers from history, simply that there had been more than enough to focus on in the new system.

"Go on . . . " Sayaca said.

"There was a flash. A tiny burst of energy light-years from here, but in the direction we know Crombec was headed. I think the implications are clear enough. They met Huskers, even in interstellar space."

"Force and wisdom," said Shikra, the archivist in charge of the Cohort's most precious data troves. "They can't have survived."

Merlin raised his voice above the sudden murmur of debate. "When did you find this out, Weaver?"

"A few days ago."

"And you waited until now to let us know?"

Weaver shifted uncomfortably, beginning to sweat. "There were questions of interpretation. We couldn't release the news until we were sure of it." Then he nodded toward Sayaca. "You know what I mean, don't you?"

"Believe me, I know exactly what you mean,"she said, shaking her head. She must have known that the moment was no longer hers; that even if she held the attention of the audience again, their minds would not be fully on what she had to say.

She handled it well, Merlin thought.

But irrespective of what she had found in Ghost, the news was very bad. The deaths of Crombec and his followers could only mean that the immediate volume of space was much thicker with Husker assets than anyone had dared fear. Forget the two swarms they had already known about; there might be dozens more, lurking quietly only one or two light-years from the system. And perhaps they had learned enough from Crombec's trajectory to guess that there must be other humans nearby. It would not take them long to arrive.

In a handful of years they might be here.

"This is gravely serious," one of the other seniors said, raising her voice above the others. "But it must not be allowed to overshadow the news Sayaca has for us." He nodded at her expectantly. "Continue, won't you?"

Months later, Merlin and Gallinule were alone in the Palace, standing on the balcony. Gallinule was toying with a white mouse, letting it run along the balustrade's narrow top before picking it up and placing it at the start again. They had put Weaver's spiteful sabotage long behind them, once it became clear that it had barely dented the impact of Sayaca's announcement. Even the most conservative seniors had accepted the shadow-matter hypothesis, even if the precise nature of what the shadow matter represented was not yet clear.

Which was not to say that Weaver's own announcement had been ignored, either. The Huskers were no longer a remote threat, decades away from Bright Boy. The fact that they were almost certainly converging on the system brought an air of apocalyptic gloom to the whole hideaway enterprise. They were living in end times, certain that no actions they now took would really make much difference.

It's been centuries since we made contact with another human faction, another element of the Cohort, Merlin thought. *For all we know, there are no more humans anywhere in the Galaxy. We are all that remains; the last niche which the Huskers haven't yet sterilized. And in a few years we might all be dead as well.*

"I almost envy Sayaca," Gallinule said. "She's completely absorbed in her work in Cinder again. As if nothing else will ever affect her. Don't you admire that kind of dedication?"

"She thinks she'll find something in Cinder that saves us all."

"At least she's still optimistic. Or desperate, depending on your point of view. She sends her regards, incidentally."

"Thanks," Merlin said, biting his tongue.

Gallinule had just returned from Cinder, his third and longest trip there since Sayaca had left Ghost. Once the shadow-matter hypothesis had been accepted, Sayaca had seen no reason to stay here. Other gifted people could handle this line of enquiry while she returned to her beloved tunnels. Merlin had visited her once, but the reception she had given him had been no more than cordial. He had not gone back.

"Well, what do you think?" Gallinule said.

Suspended far out to sea was a representation of what they now knew to be lurking inside Ghost. It was the sharpest view Merlin had seen yet, gleaned by swarms of gravitational-mapping drones swimming through the atmosphere. What the thing looked like, to Merlin's eye, was a sphere wrapped around with dense, branching circuitry. The closer they looked, the sharper their focus, the more circuitry appeared, on steadily smaller scales, down to the current limiting resolution of about ten meters. Anything smaller than that was simply blurred away. But what they saw was enough. They had been right, all those months ago: this was nothing natural. And it was not quite a sphere, either: resolution was good enough now to see a teardrop shape, with the sharp end pointed more or less parallel to the surface of the liquid hydrogen ocean.

"I think it scares me," Merlin said. "I think it shows that this is the worst possible place we could ever have picked to hide."

"Then we have to accept my solution," Gallinule said. "Become software. It can be done, you know. In a few months we'll have the technology to scan ourselves." He held up the mouse again. "See this little fellow? He was the first. I scanned him a few days ago."

Merlin stared at the mouse.

"This is really him," Gallinule continued. "Not simply a projection of a real mouse into the Palace's environment, or even a convincing fake. Slice him open and you'd find everything you'd expect. He only exists here now, but his behavior hasn't changed at all."

"What happened to the real mouse, Gallinule?"

Gallinule shrugged. "Died, of course. I'm afraid the scanning procedure's still fairly destructive."

"So the little catch in your plan for our salvation is that we'd have to die to get inside your machine?"

"If we don't do it, we die anyway. Not much to debate, is there?"

"Not if you put it in those terms, no. We could of course experiment with the final syrinx and find a better way to escape, but I suppose that's too much of an imaginative leap for anyone to make."

"Except you, of course."

They were silent for long moments. Merlin stared out to sea, the Palace's reality utterly solid to him now. He did not think that it felt any less real to the mouse. This was how it could be for all of them, if Gallinule had his way: inhabiting any environment they liked until the Husker threat was over. They could skip over that time if they wished, or spend it exploring a multitude of simulated worlds. The trouble was, would there be anything to lure them back into the real world when the danger had passed? Would they even bother remembering what had come before? The Palace was already tantalizing enough. There had been times when Merlin had found it difficult to leave the place. It was like a door into his youth.

"Gallinule . . . " Merlin said. "There's something I always meant to ask you about the Palace. You've made it as real as humanly possible. There isn't a detail out of place. Sometimes it makes me want to cry, it's so close to what I remember. But there's something missing. Someone, to be exact. Whenever we were here—back in the real Palace, I mean—then she was always here as well."

Gallinule stared at him in something like horror. "You're asking me if I ever thought of simulating Mother?"

"Don't tell me it didn't cross your mind. I know you could have done it as well."

"It would have been a travesty."

Merlin nodded. "I know. But that doesn't mean you wouldn't have thought of it."

Gallinule shook his head slowly and sadly, as if infinitely disappointed at his brother's presumption. In the silence that followed, Merlin stared out at the shadow-matter object that hung over the sea. Whatever happened now, he thought, things between him and Gallinule could never be quite the same. It was not simply that he knew Gallinule was lying about their mother. Gallinule would have tried recreating her; anything less would have been an unforgivable lapse in his brother's devotion to detail. No; what had truly come between them was Sayaca. She and Gallinule were lovers now, Merlin knew, and yet this was something that he had never discussed with his brother. Time had passed and now there seemed no sensible way to broach the subject. It was simply there—unavoidable, like the knowledge that they would probably all die before very long. There was nothing to be done about it, so no point in discussing it. But in the same moment he realized something else, something that had been nagging at the back of his mind since the very earliest maps of the anomaly had been transmitted.

"Expand the scale," he said. "Zoom out, massively."

Gallinule looked at him wordlessly, but obeyed his brother all the same. The anomaly shrunk toward invisibility.

"Now show the anomaly's position within the system. All planetary positions to be exactly as they are now."

A vast, luminous orrery filled the sky: concentric circles centered on Bright Boy, with nodal points for the planets.

"Now extend a vector with its origin in the anomaly, parallel to the anomaly's long axis. Make it as long as necessary."

"What are you thinking?" Gallinule said, all animosity gone now.

"That all the anomaly ever was, was a pointer, directing our attention to the really important thing. Just do it, will you?"

A straight line knifed out from Ghost—the anomaly insignificant at this scale—and cut across the system, toward Bright Boy and the inner worlds.

Knifing straight through Cinder.

Part Five

"I wanted you to be the first to know," Sayaca said, her semblance standing regally in his quarters like a playing-card monarch. "We've found signals coming from inside the planet. Gravitational signals—exactly what we'd expect if someone in the shadow universe was trying to contact us."

Merlin studied the beautiful lines of her face, reminding himself that all he was speaking to was a cunning approximation of the real Sayaca, who was light-hours of communicational timelag down-system.

"How do they do it? Get a signal across, I mean."

"There's only one way: you have to move large masses around quickly, creating a high frequency ripple in spacetime. They're using black holes, I think: miniature ones, like the thing you first thought we'd found in Ghost. Charged up and oscillated, so that they give off an amplitude-modulated gravitational wave."

Merlin shrugged. "So it wasn't such a stupid idea to begin with."

Sayaca smiled tolerantly. "We still don't know how they make and manipulate them. But that doesn't matter for now. What does is that the message is clearly intended for us. It's only commenced since we reached into Cinder's deeper layers. Somehow that action alerted them—whoever *they* are—to our presence."

Merlin shivered despite himself. "Is there any chance that these signals could be picked up by the Huskers as well?"

"Every chance, I'd say—unless they stop before they get here. Which is why we've been working so hard to decode the signal."

"And you have?"

Sayaca nodded. "We identified recurrent patterns in the gravitational signal, a block of data that the shadow people were sending over and over again. Within this block of data were two kinds of bits: a strong gravitational pulse and a weaker one, like a one and zero in binary notation. The number of bits in the signal was equal to the product of three primes—definitely not accidental—so we reassembled the data-set along three axes, forming a three-dimensional image." Sayaca paused and lifted her palm. What appeared in midair was a solid rectangular form, slab-sided and featureless. It rotated lazily, revealing its blankness to the audience.

"Doesn't look like much," Merlin said.

"That's because the outer layer of the solid is all ones. In fact, only a tiny part of its volume is made up of zeroes at all. I'll remove the ones and display only the zero values . . . "

A touch of showmanship: the surface of the box suddenly seemed to be made out of interlocking birds, frozen in formation for an instant before flying in a million different directions. Suddenly what she was showing him made a lot more sense. It was like a ball of loosely knotted string. A map of Cinder's crustal tunnels, plunging more deeply toward the core than their own maps even hinted. Five or six hundred kilometers into the lithosphere.

"But it doesn't tell us anything we wouldn't have learned eventually . . . " Merlin said.

"No; I think it does." Sayaca made the image enlarge, until she was showing him the deep end of one particular tunnel. It was capped by a nearly spherical chamber. "All the other shafts end abruptly, even those that branch off from this one at higher levels. But they've clearly drawn our attention to this chamber. That has to mean something."

"You think there's something there, don't you."

"We'll know soon enough. By the time this semblance speaks to you, Gallinule and I will have almost reached that chamber. Wish us the best of luck, won't you? Whatever we find in there, I'm fairly certain it'll change things for us."

"For better or for worse?"

The semblance smiled. "We'll just have to wait and see, won't we?"

End times, Merlin thought again. He could taste it in the air: quiet desperation. The long-range sensors sprinkled around the system had picked up the first faint hints of neutrino emission, which might originate with Husker craft moving stealthily toward Bright Boy from interstellar space. And the main swarms up and down the length of the Way had not gone away.

One or two humans had undergone Gallinule's fatal scanning process now, choosing to go ahead of the pack rather than wait for the final stampede. Their patterns were frozen at the moment, but before very long Gallinule's acolytes would weave a simulated environment which the scanned could inhabit. Then, undoubtedly, others would follow. But not many. Merlin was not alone in flinching at the idea of throwing away the flesh just to survive. There were some prices that were simply too high, simply too alien.

Do that, he thought, *and we're halfway to being Husker ourselves.*

What could he do to save himself, if saving the rest of them was out of the question? He thought of stealing the syrinx. He had not learned enough to use it safely yet, but he knew he was not far from being able to do so. But it was tightly guarded, under permanent Council scrutiny. He had asked Gallinule and Sayaca to apply persuasion to the others, but while they might have had the necessary influence, they had not acceded to his wishes.

And now Sayaca was back from Cinder, bearing tidings. She had convened a meeting again, but this time nobody was going to steal her thunder.

Especially as she had brought someone with her.

It was the semblance of a woman: a female of uncertain age but from approximately the same genetic background as everyone present. That was nothing to be counted on; since the Flourishing there had been many splinters of humanity, which seemed monstrously strange to those who had remained loyal to the old phenotype. But had this woman changed her clothes, make-up, and hairstyle, she could have walked among them without attracting a second glance. Except perhaps for her beauty: something indefinably serene in her face and bearing that seemed almost supernatural.

Her expression, before she began speaking, was one of complete calm.

"My name is Halvorsen," she said. "It's an old name, archaic even in my own time . . . I have no idea how it will sound to your ears, or if you can even understand a word of what I'm saying. We will record versions of this message in over a thousand languages, all that we hold in our current linguistics database, in the hope that some distant traveler will recognize something, anything, of use."

Merlin raised a hand. "Stop . . . stop her. Can you do that?"

Sayaca nodded, causing Halvorsen to freeze, mouth open. "What is she?" Merlin said.

"Just a recording. We triggered her when we arrived in the chamber. It wasn't hard to translate her. We already knew that the Diggers' language would later evolve into Main, so it was just a question of hoping that one of the recordings would be in a tongue that was also in our records."

"And?"

"Well, none of her messages were in languages we knew moderately well. But three were in languages for which we had fragments, so we were able to patch together this version using all three threads. There are still a few holes, of course, but I don't think we'll miss anything critical."

"You'd better hope not. Well, let her—whoever she is—continue."

Halvorsen became animated again. "Let me say something about my past," she said. "It may help you establish the time frame in which this recording was made. My ancestors came from Earth. So did yours—if you are at all human—but in my case I even met someone who had been born there, although it was one of her oldest memories, something as faint and tiny as an image seen through the wrong end of a telescope. She remembered a time before the Flourishing, before the great migrations into the Orion Arm. We rode swallowships for ten thousand years, cleaving close to lightspeed. Then came wars. Awful wars. We hid for another ten thousand years, until our part of the Galaxy was quiet again. We watched many cultures rise and fall, learning what we could from them; trading with those who seemed the least hostile. Then the Waymakers came, extending their transit network into our region of space. They were like gods to us as well, although we stole some of their miracles and fashioned them to our own uses. After thousands of years of careful study we learned how to make syrinxes and to use the Waynet." She paused. "We had a name for ourselves, too: the Watchers."

Halvorsen's story continued. She told them how a virus had propagated through their fleets, subtly corrupting their most ancient data heirlooms. By the time the damage was discovered, all their starmaps had been rendered useless. They no longer knew where Earth was. At first, the loss seemed of minimal importance, but as time passed, and they came into contact with more and more cultures, it became clear that the Watchers' records had probably been the *last* to survive uncorrupted.

"That was when she died, the oldest of us. I think until then she had always clung to some hope that we would return to Earth. When she knew it could never happen, she saw no reason to continue living."

Then they entered a long Dark Age. The Waymakers had gone; now, unpoliced, terrors were roaming the Galaxy. Marauders sought the technological wisdom that the Watchers had acquired over slow millennia. The Watchers fled, pursued across the light-years in much the same manner as the Cohort now found itself, hounded from star to star. Like the Cohort, too, they found Bright Boy. They were exploring it, trying to understand the system's anomalies; hoping that the understanding would bring new power over their enemies. They had excavated the tunnel system into Cinder and created the machines that lined the terminal chamber. They, too, had detected signals from the shadow universe, although the contents of the messages proved much harder to decode.

"They were alien," Halvorsen said. "Truly alien: automated transmissions left behind half a billion years earlier by a group of creatures who had crossed over into the shadow universe. They had been fleeing the fire that was about to be unleashed by the merger of a pair of binary neutron stars only a few hundred light-years away. They left instructions on how to join them. We learned how to generate the same kinds of high-frequency gravitational waves that they were using to signal us. Then we learned how to encode ourselves into those wave packets so that we could send biological information between universes. Although the aliens were long gone, they left behind machines to tend for us and to take care of our needs once we were reassembled on the other side."

"But the Marauders are long gone,"Merlin said. "Our oldest records barely mention them. Why didn't Halvorsen and her people return here?"

"There was no need," Sayaca said. "We tend to think of the shadow universe as a cold, ghostly place, but once you're mapped into it, it looks much like our own universe—the sky dotted with bright suns, warm worlds orbiting them. Theirs for the taking, in fact. Halvorsen's people had been late-players in a Galaxy already carved up by thousands of earlier factions. But the shadow universe was virgin territory. They no longer had to skulk around higher powers, or hide from outlaw clades. There was no one else there."

"Except the aliens . . . the—" Merlin blinked. "What did she call them?"

Sayaca paused before answering. "She didn't. But their name for them was the . . . " Again, a moment's hesitation. "The Shadow Puppets. And they were long gone. They'd left behind machines to assist any future cultures who wanted to make the crossing, but there was no sign of them now. Maybe they moved away to settle some remote part of the shadow Galaxy, or maybe they returned to our universe when the threat from the merger event had passed."

"Halvorsen's people trusted these creatures?"

"What choice did they have? Not much more than us. They were in as much danger from the Marauders as we are from the Huskers."

It was Halvorsen who continued the story. "So we crossed over. We expanded massively; extended a human presence around a dozen nearby systems on the other side. Star travel's difficult because there's no Waynet, but the social templates we acquired during the time before the Marauders have served us well. We've been at peace for one thousand years at the time of this message's recording. Many more thousands of years are likely to have passed before it reaches you. If we attempted to communicate with you gravitationally, then you can be sure that we're still alive.

By then we will have studied you via the automated systems we left running in Cinder. They will have told us that you are essentially peaceable; that we are ready to welcome you."

Halvorsen's tone of voice changed now. "That's our invitation, then. We've opened the gateway for you; provided the means for information to pass into the shadow universe. To take the next step, you must make the hardest of sacrifices. You must discard the flesh; submit yourselves to whatever scanning techniques you have developed. We did it once, and we know it's a difficult journey, but less difficult than death. For us, the choice was obvious enough. With you, it may not be so very different." Halvorsen paused and extended a hand in supplication. "Do not be frightened. Follow us. We have been waiting a long time for your company."

Then she bowed her head and the recording halted.

Merlin could feel the almost palpable sense of relief sweeping the room, though no one was undignified enough to let it show. A swelling of hope, after so many months of staring oblivion in the face. Finally, there was a way out. A way to survive, which was something other than Gallinule's route to soulless immortality in computer memory. Even if it also meant dying . . . but it would only be a transient kind of death, as Halvorsen had said. Waiting for them on the other side was another world of the flesh, into which they would all be reborn.

A kind of promised land.

It would be very difficult to resist, especially when the Huskers arrived. But Merlin just stared hard at the woman called Halvorsen, certain that he knew the truth and that Sayaca had, on some level, wanted him to know it as well.

She was lying.

Tyrant fell toward empty space, in the general direction of the Way. When Merlin judged himself to be a safe distance from Cinder he issued the command that would trigger the twenty nova-mines emplaced in the lowermost chamber. He looked down on the world and nothing seemed to happen, no stammer of light from the exit holes of the Digger tunnel system. Perhaps some inscrutable layer of preservation had disarmed the nova-mines.

Then he saw the readouts from the seismic devices that Sayaca had dropped on the surface, what seemed like half a lifetime earlier. He had almost forgotten that they existed—but now he watched each register the detonation's volley of sound waves as they reached the surface. A few moments later, there was a much longer, lower signal—the endless roar of collapsing tunnels, like an avalanche. Some sections of the tunnels would undoubtedly remain intact, but it would be hard to cross between them. He was not yet done, though. First he directed missiles at the tunnel entrances, collapsing them, and then assigned smaller munitions to destroy Sayaca's seismic instruments, daubing the surface in nuclear fire.

There must be no evidence of human presence here; nothing to give the Huskers a clue as to what had happened—

That everyone was gone now: crossed over into the shadow universe. Sayaca, Gallinule, all the others. Everyone he knew, submitting to the quick, clean death of Gallinule's scanning apparatus. Biological patterns encoded into gravitational signals and squirted into the realm of shadow matter.

Except, of course, Merlin.

"How did you guess?" Sayaca had asked him, just after she had presented Halvorsen's message.

They had been alone, physically so, for the first time in months. "Because you wanted me to know, Sayaca. Isn't that the way it happened? You had to deceive the others, but you wanted me to know the truth. Well, it worked. I guessed. And I have to admit, you and Gallinule did a very thorough job."

"Do you want to know how much of it was true?"

"I suppose you're going to tell me anyway."

Sayaca sighed. "More of it than you'd probably have guessed. We did detect signals from the shadow universe, just as I said."

"Just not quite the kind you told us."

"No . . . no." She paused. "They were much more alien. Enormously harder to decode in the first place. But we managed it, and the content of the messages was more or less what I told the Council: a map of Cinder's interior, directing us deeper. There we encountered other messages. By then, we had become more adept at translating them. It wasn't long before we understood that they were a set of instructions for crossing over into the shadow universe."

"But there was never any Halvorsen."

Sayaca shook her head. "Halvorsen was Gallinule's idea. We knew that crossing over was the only hope we had left, but no one would want to do it unless we could make the whole thing sound more, well . . . palatable. The aliens were just too alien—shockingly so, once we began to understand their nature. Not necessarily hostile, or even unfriendly . . . but unnervingly strange. The stuff of nightmares. So we invented a human story. Gallinule created Halvorsen and between us we fabricated enough evidence so that no one would question her reality. We manufactured a plausible history for her and then pasted her story over the real one."

"The part about the aliens fleeing the neutron star merger?"

"That was completely true. But they were the only ones who ever crossed over. No humans ever followed them."

"What about the Diggers?"

"They found the tunnels, explored them thoroughly, but it seems that they never intercepted the signals. They helped though; without them it would have been a lot harder to make Halvorsen's story sound convincing." She paused, childlike in her enthusiasm. "We'll be the first, Merlin. Isn't that thrilling in a way?"

"For you, maybe. But you've always stared into the void, Sayaca. For everyone else, the idea will be chilling beyond words."

"That's why they couldn't know the truth. They wouldn't have agreed to cross over otherwise."

"I know. And I don't doubt that you did the right thing. After all, it's a matter of survival, isn't it?"

"They'll learn the truth eventually," Sayaca said. "When we've all crossed over. I don't know what'll happen to Gallinule and me then. We'll either be revered or hated. I suppose we'll just have to wait and see, but I suspect it may be the latter."

"On the other hand, they'll know that you had the courage to face the truth and hide it from the others when you knew it had to be hidden. There's a kind of nobility in that, Sayaca."

"Whatever we did, it was for the good of the Cohort. You understand that, don't you?"

"I never thought otherwise. Which doesn't mean I'm coming with you."

Her mouth opened the tiniest of degrees. "There's nothing for you here, Merlin. You'll die if you don't follow us. I don't love you the way I used to, but I still care for you."

"Then why did you let me know the truth?"

"I never said I did. That must have been Gallinule's doing." She paused. "What was it, then?"

"Halvorsen," Merlin said. "She was created from scratch; a human who had never lived. You did a good job, as well. But there was something about her that I knew I'd seen before. Something so familiar I didn't see it at first. Then, of course, I knew."

"What?"

"Gallinule based her on our mother. I always suspected he'd tried simulating her, but he denied it. That was another lie, as well. Halvorsen proved it."

"Then he wanted you to know. As his brother." Merlin nodded. "I suppose so."

"Then will you follow us?"

He had already made his mind up, but he allowed a long pause before answering her. "I don't think so, Sayaca. It just isn't my style. I know there's only a small chance that I can make the syrinx work for me, but I prefer running to hiding. I think I'll take that risk."

"But the Council won't let you have the syrinx, Merlin. Even after we've all crossed over, they'll safeguard it here. Surround it with proctors who'll kill you if you try and steal it. They'll want it unharmed for when we return from the shadow universe."

"I know."

"Then why . . . oh, wait. I see." She looked at him now, all empathy gone; something of the old Sayaca contempt showing through. "You'll blackmail us, won't you. Threaten to tell the Council if we don't provide you with the syrinx."

"You said it, not me."

"Gallinule and I don't have that kind of influence, Merlin."

"Then you'd better find it. It's not much to ask, is it? A small token of your gratitude for my silence. I'm sure you can think of something." Merlin paused. "After all, it would be a shame to spoil everything now. Halvorsen's story seemed so convincing, too. I almost believed it myself."

"You cold, calculating bastard." But she said it with half a smile, admiring and loathing him at the same time.

"Just find a way, Sayaca. I know you can. Oh, and one other thing."

"Yes?"

"Look after my brother, will you? He may not have quite my streak of brilliance, but he's still one of a kind. You're going to need people like him on the other side."

"We could use you too, Merlin."

"You probably could, but I've got other business to attend to. The small matter of an ultimate weapon against the Huskers, for instance. I'm going to find it, you know. Even if it takes me the rest of my life. I hope you'll come back and see how I did one day."

Sayaca nodded, but said nothing. They both knew that there were no more words that needed to be said.

And, true to his expectations, Sayaca and Gallinule had come through. The syrinx was with him now—an uninteresting matte-black cone that held the secrets of crossing light-years in a few breaths of subjective time—sitting in its metal harness inside *Tyrant*. He did not know exactly how they had persuaded the Council to release it. Quite possibly there had been no persuasion at all, merely subterfuge. One black cone looked much like another, after all.

This however was the true syrinx, the last they had.

It was unimaginably precious now, and he would do his best to learn its secrets in the weeks ahead. Countless millions had died trying to gain entry to the Waymakers' transit system, and it was entirely possible that Merlin would simply be the next. But it did not have to be like that. He was alone now—possibly more alone than any human had ever been—but instead of despair what he felt was a cold, pure elation: he now had a mission, one that might prove to be soul-destroyingly difficult, even futile, but he had the will to accomplish it.

Somewhere behind him the syrinx began to purr.

ISABEL OF THE FALL

IAN McLEOD

Once, in the time which was always long ago, there lived a girl. She was called Isabel and—in some versions of this tale, you will hear of the beauty of her eyes, the sigh of her hair, the falling of her gaze which was like the dark glitter of a thousand wells, but Isabel wasn't like that. In other tellings, you will learn that her mouth stuck out like a seapug's, that she had a voice like the dawn-shriek of a geelie. But that wasn't Isabel, either. Isabel was plain. Her hair was brown, and so, probably, were her eyes, although that fact remains forever unrecorded. She was of medium height for the women who then lived. She walked without stoop or any obvious deformity, and she was of less than average wisdom. Isabel was un-beautiful and unintelligent, but she was also un-stupid and un-ugly. Amid all the many faces of the races and species which populate these many universes, hers was one of the last you would ever notice.

Isabel was born and died in Ghezirah, the great City of Islands which lies at the meeting of all the Ten Thousand and One Worlds. Ghezirah was different then, and in the time which was always long ago, it is often said that the animals routinely conversed, gods walked the night and fountains filled with ghosts. But, for Isabel, this was the time of the end of the War of the Lilies.

Her origins are obscure. She may have been a child of one of the beggars who, then as now, seek alms amid the great crystal concourses. She may have been daughter of one of the priestess soldiers who fought for their Church. She may even have been the lost daughter of some great matriarch, as is often the way in these tales. All that is certain is that, when Isabel was born in Ghezirah, the many uneasy alliances which always bind the Churches had boiled into war. There were also more men then, and many of them were warriors, so it is it even possible that Isabel was born as a result of rape rather than conscious decision. Isabel never knew. All that she ever remembered, in the earliest of the fragmentary records which are attributed to her, is the swarming of a vast crowd, things broken underfoot, and the swoop and blast overhead of what might have been some kind of military aircraft. In this atmosphere of panic and danger, she was one moment holding onto a hand. Next, the sky seemed to ignite, and the hand slipped from hers.

Many people died or went mad in the War of the Lilies. Ghezirah itself was badly damaged, although the city measures things by its own times and priorities, and soon set about the process of healing its many islands which lace to form the glittering web which circles the star called Sabil. Life, just as it always must, went on, and light still flashed from minaret to minaret each morning with the cries of the cries of Dawn-Singers, even if many of the beauties of which they sang now lay ruined beneath. The Churches, too, had to heal themselves, and seek new acolytes after many deaths and betrayals. Here, tottering amid the smoking rubble, too young to fend for herself, was plain Isabel. It must have been one of the rare times in her life that she was noticed, that day when she was taken away with many others to join the depleted ranks of the Dawn Church.

The Dawn Church has its own island in Ghezirah, called Jitera, and Isabel may have been trained there in the simpler crafts of bringing light and darkness, although it is more likely that she would have attended a small local academy, and been set to the crude manual tasks of rebuilding one of the many minarets which had been destroyed, perhaps hauling a wheelbarrow or wielding a trowel. Still, amid the destruction which the War of the Lilies had visited on Ghezirah, every Church knew that to destroy the minarets which bore dawn across the skies would have been an act beyond folly. Thus, of all the Churches, that of the Dawn had probably suffered least, and could afford to be generous. Perhaps that was the reason that Isabel, for all her simple looks and lack of gifts, was apprenticed to become a Dawn-Singer as she grew towards womanhood. Or perhaps, as is still sometimes the way, she rose to such heights because no one had thought to notice her.

Always, first and foremost in the Dawn Church, there is the cleaning of mirrors: the great reflectors which gather Sabil's light far above Ghezirah's sheltering skies, and those below; the silver dishes of the great minarets which dwarf all but the highest mountains; the many, many lesser ones which bear light across the entire city each morning with the cries of the Dawn-Singers. But there is much else which the apprentices of the Dawn Church must study. There is the behaviour of the light itself, and the effects of lenses; also the many ways in which Sabil's light must be filtered before it can safely reach flesh and eyes, either alien of or human. Then there are the mechanisms which govern the turning of all these mirrors, and the hidden engines which drive them. And there is the study of Sabil herself, who waxes and wanes even though her glare seems unchanging. Ghezirah, even at the recent end of the War of Lilies, was a place of endless summer and tropic warmth, where the flowers never wilted, the trees kept their leaves for a lifetime, and the exact time when day and night would flood over the city with the cries of the Dawn-Bringers was decreed in the chapels of the Dawn Church by the spinning of an atomic clock. But, in the work of the young apprentices who tended the minarets, first and always, there was the cleaning of the mirrors.

Isabel's lot was a hard one, but not unpleasant. Although she had already risen far in her Church, there were still many others like her. Each evening, after prayers and night-breakfast, and the study of the photon or the prism, Isabel and her fellow apprentices scattered to ascend the spiral stairs of their designated local minaret. Some would oil the many pistons and flywheels within, or perhaps tend to the needs of the Dawn-Singer herself, but most clambered on until they met the windy space where what probably seemed like the whole of Ghezirah lay spread glittering beneath them, curving upwards into the night. There, all through the dark hours until the giant reflectors far above them inched again towards Sabil, Isabel pulled doeskin pouches over her hands and feet, unfolded rags, wrung out sponges, unwound ropes and harnesses, and saw with all the other apprentices to polishing the mirrors. Isabel must have done well, or at least not badly. Some of her friends fell from her minaret, leaving stripes of blood across the sharp edge of the lower planes which she herself had to clean. Others were banished back to their begging bowls. But, for the few remaining, the path ahead was to become a Dawn-Singer.

To this day, the ceremonies of induction of this and every other Church remain mostly secret. But now, if she hadn't done so before, Isabel would have travelled by tunnel or shuttle to the Dawn Church's island of Jerita, and touched the small heat of the clock which bore the unchanging day and night of eternal summer to all Ghezirah. There would have been songs of praise and sadness as she was presented to the senior acolytes of her Church. Then, after they had heard the whisper of deeper secrets, Isabel's fellow apprentices were all ritually blinded. Whatever the Eye of Sabil is, it must filter much of the star's power until just enough rays of a certain type remain to destroy vision, yet leave the eyes seemingly undamaged. The apprentices of the Dawn Church all actively seek this moment as a glimpse into the gaze of the Almighty, and it is hard to imagine how Isabel managed to avoid it. Perhaps she simply closed her eyes. More likely, she was forgotten in the crowd.

Thus Isabel, whose eyes were of a colour remains forever unrecorded, became a Dawn-Singer, although she was not blind, and—somehow—she was able to survive this new phase of her life undetected. She probably never imagined that she was unique. Being Isabel, and not entirely stupid, but certainly not bright, she probably gave the matter little deep thought. In this new world of the blind, where touch and taste and sound and mouse-like scurryings of new apprentices were all that mattered, Isabel, with all her limited gifts, soon discovered the trick of learning how not to see.

She was given tutelage of a minaret on the island of Nashir, where the Floating Ocean hangs as a blue jewel up on the rising horizon. Nashir is a beautiful island, and a great seat of learning, but it was and is essentially a backwater. Isabel's minaret was small, too, bringing day and night to a cedar valley of considerable beauty but no particular significance save the fact that to the west it overlooked the rosestone outer walls of the Cathedral of the Word. Before dawn as she lay in her high room, Isabel would hear laughter and the rumble of footsteps as her mirror-polishing apprentices finished their duties, and would allow a few more privileged ones to pretend to imagine they had woken her with their entrance, and then help her with her ablutions and prayers. Always, she gazed through them. Almost always now, she saw literally nothing. She thought of these girls as sounds, names, scents, differing footsteps and touches. Borne up with their help onto her platform where, even atop this small minaret, the sense of air and space swam all around her, Isabel was strapped to her crucifix in solemn darkness, and heard the drip-tick of the modem which received the beat of Jerita's atomic clock, and sensed the clean, clear waiting of the freshly-polished mirrors around and above her as, with final whispers and blessings, the apprentices departed to their quarters down by the river, where, lulled by birdsong, they would sleep through most of the daylight their mistress would soon bring.

The drip-tick of the modem changed slightly. Isabel tensed herself, and began to sing. Among the mirrors' many other properties, they amplified her voice, and carried it down the dark valley towards her departing apprentices, and to the farmsteads, and across the walls of the Cathedral of the Word. It was a thrilling, chilling sound, which those who had morning duties were awakened by, and those who did not had long ago learned to sleep though. Far above her, in a rumble like distant thunder, the great mirrors within Ghezirah's orbit poised themselves to turn to face the sun. Another moment, and the modem's drip-tick changed again, and with it Isabel's song, as, in dazzling pillars, Sabil's light bore down towards every minaret. Isabel tensed in her crucifix and moved her limbs in the ways she had learned; movements which drove the pulleys and pistons that in turn caused the mirrors of her minaret to fan their gathered rays across her valley. Thus, in song and light, each day in Ghezirah is born, and Isabel remained no different to any other Dawn-Singer, but for the one fact that, at the crucial moment when first light flashed down to her, she had learned to screw up her eyes.

A typical day, and her work was almost done then until the time came to sing the different songs which called in the night. Sometimes, if there were technical difficulties, or clouds drifted out over from the Floating Ocean, or there was rain, Isabel would have to re-harness herself to her crucifix and struggle hard to keep her valley alight. Sometimes, there were visitors or school parties, but mostly now her time was her own. It wasn't unknown for Dawn-Singers to plead with their apprentices to leave some small job undone each night so they could have the pleasure of absorbing themselves in it through the following day. But, for Isabel, inactivity was easy. She had the knack of the near simple-minded of letting time pass through her as easily as the light and the wind.

One morning, Isabel was inspecting some of the outer mirrors. Such minor tasks, essentially checking that her apprentices were performing their duties as they should, were part of her life. Any blind Dawn-Singer worth her salt could tell from the feel of the air coming off a particular mirror whether it had been correctly polished, and then set at the precise necessary angle on its runners and beds. Touching it, the smear of a single bare fingertip, would have be sacrilege, and sight, in this place of dazzling glass, was of little use. Isabel, in the minaret brightness of her lonely days, rarely thought about looking, and when she did, what she saw was a world dimmed by the blotches which now swam before her eyes. In a few more months, years at the most, she would have been blinded by her work. But as it was, on this particular nondescript day, and just as she had suspected from a resistance which she had felt in the left arm of her crucifix, a mirror in the western quadrant was misaligned. Isabel studied it, feeling the wrongness of the air. It was Mirror 28, and the error was a matter of fractions of second of a degree, and thus huge by her standards. The way Mirror 28 was, it scarcely reflected Sabil's light at all, and made the corner of her minaret where she stood seem relatively dim. Thus, as Isabel wondered whether to try to deal with the problem now or leave it for her apprentices, she regained a little more of her sight.

The valley spread beneath her was already shimmering in those distant times of warm and sudden mornings, and the silver river flashed back the light of her minaret. The few dotted houses were terracotta and white. Another perfect day, but for a slight dullness in the west caused by the particular faulty mirror. The effect, Isabel thought as she strained her aching eyes, was not unpleasing. The outer rosestone walls of the Cathedral of the Word, the main structure of which lay far beyond the hills of this valley, had deep, pleasant glow to them. The shadows seemed fuller. Inside the walls, there were paved gardens, trees and fountains. Dove clattered, flowers bloomed, insects hummed, statues gestured. Here and there, for no obvious reason, were placed slatted white boxes. Nothing and nobody down there seemed to have noticed that she had failed them today in her duties. Isabel smiled and inhaled the rich, pollen-scented air. It was a minor blemish, and she still felt proud of her work. Near the wall, beside a place where its stones dimpled in towards a gateway, there was a pillared space of open paving. This, too, was of rosestone. Isabel was about to shut her eyes so she could concentrate better on the scene when she heard, the sound carrying faint on the breeze, the unmistakable slap of feet on warm stone. She peered down again, leaning forward over Mirror 28, her unmemorable face captured in reflection as she saw a figure moving far below across the open paving. A young girl, by the look of her. Her hair was flashing gold bands, as were her arms and ankles. She was dancing, circling, in some odd way which made no sense to Isabel, although she looked graceful in a way beyond anything Isabel could explain.

That night, after she had sung in the darkness, Isabel neglected to mention the fault with Mirror 28 to her apprentices. The next morning, breathing the same warm air at the same westerly corner of her minaret, she listened again to shift and slap of feet. It was a long time before she opened her eyes, and when she did, her vision seemed clearer. The girl dancing on the rosestone paving far below had long black hair, and she was dressed in the flashing silks which Isabel associated with alien lands and temples. Rings flashed from her fingers. A bindi glittered at her forehead. Isabel breathed, and watched, and marvelled.

The next blazing day, the day after, Isabel watched again from the top of her minaret beside faulty Mirror 28. It was plainly some ritual. The girl was probably an apprentice, or perhaps a minor acolyte. She was learning whatever trade it was which was practised in the Cathedral of the Word. Isabel remembered, or tried to remember, her own origins. That swarming crowd. Then hunger, thirst. What would have happened if she had been taken instead to this place beyond the wall? Would she have ever been this graceful? Isabel already knew the answer, but still the question absorbed her. In her dreams, the hand which she held as the fighter plane swooped became the same oiled olive colour as that girl's flashing skin. And sometimes, before the thundering feet of her apprentices awakened her to another day of duty, Isabel almost felt as if she, too, was dancing.

One day, the air was different. The Floating Ocean which hung on the horizon was a place of which Isabel understood little, although it was nurtured in Sabil's reflected energies by a specialist Order of her Church. Sometimes, mostly, it was blue. Then it would glitter and grey. Boiling out from it like angry thoughts would come clouds and rain. At these times, as she wrestled on her crucifix, Isabel imagined shipwreck storms, heaving seas. At other times, the clouds which drifted from it would be light and white, although they also interfered with the light in more subtle and often more infuriating ways. But on this particular day, Isabel awoke to feel dampness on her skin, clammy but not unpleasant, and a sense that every sound and creak of this minaret with which she was now so familiar had changed. The voices of her apprentices, even as they clustered around her, were muffled, and their hair and flesh smelled damp and cold. The whole world, what little she glimpsed of it as she ascended the final staircase and was strapped to her crucifix, had turned grey. The wood at her back was slippery. The harnesses which she had cured and sweated and strained into the shapes of her limbs were loose. She knew that most of the minaret's mirrors were clouding in condensation even before the last of murmuring senior apprentices reported the fact and bowed out of her way.

The sodden air swallowed the first notes of her song. With the mechanisms of the whole minaret all subtly changed, Isabel struggled as she had never struggled before to bring in the day. Sabil's pillar was feeble, and the mirrors were far below their usual levels of reflectivity. Still, it was for mornings such as this for which she had been trained, and she caught this vague light and fanned it across her valley even though she felt as if she was swimming through oceans of clay. And her song, as she finally managed to achieve balance and the clouding began to dissolve in the morning's heat, grew more joyous than ever in her triumph, such that people in the valley scratched the sleep from their heads and thought as they rarely thought; *Ah, there is the Dawn-Singer, bringing the day!* Despite the cold white air, they probably went about their ablutions whistling, confident that some things will never change.

It was several more hours before Isabel was sure that the smaller minds and mechanisms of the minaret had reached their usual equilibrium, and could be trusted to run themselves. But the world, as she climbed down from her crucifix, was still shrouded. *Fog*—she had learned the word in her apprenticeship, although she had thought of it as one of those mythical aberrations, like a comet-strike. But here it was. She wandered the misted balconies and gantries. The light here was diffuse, but ablaze. Soon, she guessed, the power she had brought from her sun would burn this moist white world away. But in the west, there was a greater dimness, which was amplified today. Here, the air was almost as chill as it had been before daybreak. Isabel bit her lip and ground her palms. She cursed herself, to have allowed this to come about. What would her old training mistress say! Too late now to attempt to rectify the situation at Mirror 28, with the planes beaded wet and the pistons dripping. She would have to speak to her apprentices this evening, and do her best to pretend sternness. It was what teachers generally did, she had noticed: when they had failed to deal with something, they simply blamed their class. Isabel tried to imagine the scene to the invisible west below. That dancing girl beyond the walls of the Cathedral of the Word would surely find this near-darkness a great inconvenience. The simple, the obvious—the innocent—thing seemed to be to go down and apologise to her.

Isabel descended the many stairways of her minaret. Stepping out into the world outside seemed odd to her now—the ground was so *low*!—but especially today, when, almost mimicking the effects of her fading sight, everything but her minaret which blazed above her was dim and blotched and silvered. She walked between the fields in the direction of the rosestone walls, and heard but didn't see the animals grazing. Brushing unthinkingly and near-blindly as now habitually did against things, she followed close to the brambled hedges, and, by the time she felt the dim fiery glow of the wall coming up towards her, her hands and arms were scratched and wet. The stones of the wall were soaked, too. The air here was a damp presence. Conscious that she was entering the dim realm which her own inattention had made, Isabel felt her way along the wall until she came to the door. It looked old and little-used; the kind of door you might find in a story. She didn't know whether to feel surprise when she turned the cold and slippery iron hoop, and felt it give way.

Now, she was in the outer gardens of the Cathedral of the Word, and fully within the shade of faulty Mirror 28. It was darker here, certainly, but her senses and her sight soon adjusted, and Isabel decided that the effect wasn't unpleasant, in some indefinable and melancholy way. In this diffuse light, the trees were dark clouds. The pavements were black and shining. Some of the flowers hung closed, or were beaded with silver cobwebs. A few bees buzzed by her, but they seemed clumsy and half-asleep in this half-light as well. Then, of all things, there was a flicker of orange light; a glow which Isabel's half-ruined eyes refused to believe. But, as she walked towards it, it separated itself into several quivering spheres, bearing with them the smell of smoke, and the slap of bare feet on wet stone.

The open courtyard which Isabel had gazed down on from her minaret was impossible to scale as she stood at the edge of it on this dim and foggy day, although the surrounding pillars which marched off and vanished up into the mist seemed huge, lit by the flicker of the smoking braziers placed between them. Isabel moved forward. The dancer, for a long time, was a sound, a disturbance of the mist. Then, sudden as a ghost, she was there before her.

"*Ahlan wa sahlan* . . . " She bowed from parted knees, palms pressed together. She smelled sweetly of sweat and sandalwood. Her hair was long and black and glorious. "And who, pray, are you? And what are you doing here?"

Isabel, flustered in a way which she had not felt in ages, stumbled over her answer. The minaret over the wall . . . She pointed uselessly into the mist. This dimness—no, not the mist itself, but the lack of proper light . . . The dancer's kohled and oval eyes regarded her with what seemed like amusement. The bindi on her brow glittered similarly. Although the dancer was standing still, her shoulders rose and fell from her exertions. Her looped earrings tinked.

"So, you bring light from that tower?"

Isabel, who perhaps still hadn't made the matter as clear as she should have, nodded in dizzy relief that this strange creature was starting to understand her. "I'm so *sorry* it's so dark today. I've—I've heard your dancing from my tower, and I—thought . . . I thought that this oversight would be difficult for you."

"Difficult?" The girl cocked her head sideways like a bird to consider. The flames were still dancing. Their light flicked dark and orange across her arms. "No, I don't think so. In fact, I quite like it. My name's Genya, by the way. I'm a beekeeper . . . " She gave a liquid laugh and stepped forward, back, half-fading. "Although, thanks to you, there are few enough bees today need keeping."

"Beekeeper—but I thought these were the gardens of the Cathedral of the Word? I thought you were—"

"—Oh, I'm a *Librarian* as well. Or at least, a most senior apprentice. But some of us must also learn how to keep bees."

Isabel nodded. "Of course. For the honey . . . "

Again, Genya laughed. There seemed to be little Isabel could do which didn't cause her amusement. "Of no! Never for *that*! We give the honey away the poor at our main gates on moulid days. We keep bees because they teach us how to find the books. Do you want me to show you?"

Isabel was shown. That first day, the misty gardens were nothing but a puzzle to her. There were flowering bushes which she was told by Genya bore within each their cells whole libraries of information about wars fought and lost. There were stepped crypt-like places beyond creaky iron gates where, through other doors which puffed open once Genya made a gesture, lay bound books of the histories of things which had never happened in this or any other world. They were standing, Genya whispered, reaching up to take down a silvery thing encased in plastic, merely at the furthest shore of the greatest oceans of all possible knowledge. Yet some of these clear, bright, artificially lit catacombs were as big as all but the finest halls of the Dawn Church's own seats of learning.

"What *is* that, anyway?"

It was a rainbowed disk. After a small struggle, Genya opened the transparent box which contained it. "I think it contains music." Isabel had to gasp when Genya placed the fingertips upon the surface, so closely did it resemble a mirror. But Genya's fingers moved rapidly in a caressing, circling motion. Her eyes closed for a moment. She started humming. "Yes. It *is* music. An old popular song about fools on hills. It's lovely. I wish I had the voice like you to sing it."

"You can *hear* it from that?"

Genya nodded. "It's something which is done to us Librarians. To our fingers. See . . . " She raised them towards Isabel's gaze. Close to the end, the flesh seemed raw, like fresh scar tissue. "We're given extra optic nerves. Small magnetic sensors ... Processors ... Other things ... " She snapped the rainbow disk back into its case. "It makes life a lot easier." She tried to demonstrate the same trick with a brown ribbon of tape, the spool of which instantly took off on its own down the long corridor in which they were standing. She hummed, once they had caught up with it, another tune.

"It's all part of being a Librarian, having tickly fingers," Genya announced as she slotted the object back on its shelf. "By the way . . . " She turned back towards Isabel. "I was under the impression that there was a far worse excruciation for you Dawn-Singers ... " Genya leaned forward with a dancer's gaze, peering as no one ever had into the forgotten shade of Isabel's eyes. "You're supposed to be *blind*, aren't you? But it's plain to even the stupidest idiot that you're not ... "

Next dawn, the skies were clear again. Once more, the Floating Ocean was calm and distant and blue. Those in that valley who cared to listen to Isabel's song might have thought that day that it sounded slightly perfunctory. But ordinary daybreaks such as these were easy sport for Isabel now. She was even getting used to the different feel of the minaret which came from the fault in Mirror 28. Under blue skies which only a connoisseur or an acolyte would have noticed a slight darkening of in the western quadrant, she hurried across the fields towards the rosestone walls of the Cathedral of the Word.

Even though their prosecutors were able to argue the facts convincingly the other way, neither Isabel not Genya ever thought that their acts in those long ago days of Ghezirah's endless summer amounted to betrayal. They knew that their respective Churches guarded their secrets with all the paranoid dread of the truly powerful, who are left with much to loose and little to gain. They knew, too, of the recent terrors of the War of the Lilies. But their lives had been small. Further up the same rosestone wall, if Isabel had cared to follow it beyond her valley, she would have eventually have found that its fine old blocks was pockmarked with sprays of bullets; further still, the stone itself dissolved into shining heaps of dream-distorted lava, and the gardens still heaved with the burrowing teeth of trapmoles. Yet Nashir had suffered far less in the War of the Lilies than many of Ghezirah's islands. In the vast lattice of habitation which surrounded Sabil, there were still huge rents and floating swathes of spinning rubble. Seventeen years is little time to recover from a war, but peace and youth and endless summer are heady brews, and lessons doled out in the Church classrooms by the rap of a mistress's cane sometimes remain forever wrapped in chalkdust and boredom. Day brilliant after day in that backwater of a backwater, Isabel and Genya wandered deeper into the secrets of Cathedral of the Word's cloisters and gardens. Day after day, they betrayed the secrets of their respective Churches.

The Cathedral and its environs are vast, and the farms and villages and towns and the several cities of Nashir which surround it are mostly there, in one way or another, to serve its needs. Beyond the ridge of the Isabel's valley, standing at the lip of stepped gardens which went down and down so far that the light grew blue and hazed, they saw a distant sprawl of stone, glass, spires on the rising horizon.

"Is that the Cathedral?"

Not for the first time that day, Genya laughed. "Oh no! It's just the local Lending Office . . . " They walked on and down; waterfalls glittering beside them in the distant blaze of, far greater, minaret than Isabel's. Another day, rising to the surface from the tunnels of a catacomb from which it had seemed they would never escape, Isabel saw yet another great and fine building. Again, she asked the same question. Again, Genya laughed. Still, within those grounds with their wild white follies and statues a shrines to Dewey, Bliss and Ranganathan, there were many compensations.

As their daily journeys grew further, it became necessary to travel by speedier methods if Isabel was to return to her minaret in time to sing in the night. The catacombs of books were too vast for any Librarian to categorise even the most tightly defined subject without access to rapid transport. So, on the silk seats of caleches which buzzed on cushions of buried energy, they swept along corridors. The bookshelves flashed past them, the titles spinning too fast to read, until the spines themselves became indistinguishable and the individual globelights blurred into a single white stripe overhead. Isabel and Genya laughed and whooped as they urged their metal craft into yet greater feats of speed and manoeuvrability. The dusty wisdoms of lost ages cooled their faces.

They rarely saw anyone, and then only as faint figures tending some distant stack of books, or the trails of aircraft like scratches across the blue roof of the Ghezirahan sky. Genya's training, the dances and the indexing and—for an exercise, the sub-categorising of the lesser tenses of the verb meaning *to blink* in sixty eight lost languages—came to her through messages even more remote than the tick of Isabel's modem. Sometimes, the statues spoke to her. Sometimes, the flowers gave off special scents, or the furred leaves of a bush communicated something in their touch to her. But, mostly, Genya learned from her bees.

One day, Isabel succumbed to Genya's repeated requests and led her to the uppermost reaches of her minaret. Genya laughed as she peered down from the spiralling stairways as they ascended. The drops, she claimed, leaning far across the worn brass handrails, were dizzying. Isabel leaned over as well; she'd never thought to *look* at her minaret in this way. Seen from the inside, the place was like a huge vertical tunnel, threaded with sunlight and dust and the slow tickings of vast machinery, diminishing down towards seeming infinity.

"Why is it, anyway, that you Dawn-Singers need to be blinded?" Genya asked as they climbed on, her voice by now somewhat breathless.

"I suppose it's because we become blind soon enough—a kind of mercy. That, and because we have access to such high places. We Dawn-Singers know how to combine lenses . . . " Isabel paused on a stairs for a moment as a new thought struck her, and Genya bumped into her back. "So perhaps the other Churches are worried about what, looking down, we might see . . . "

"I'm surprised anyone ever gets to the top of this place without dying of exhaustion. Your apprentices must have legs like trees!" But they did reach the top, and Isabel felt the pride she always felt at her minaret's gathered heat and power, whilst Genya, when she had recovered, moved quickly from silvery balcony to balcony, exclaiming about the view. Isabel was little used to seeing anything up here, but she saw through her fading eyes many reflected images of her friend, darting mirror to mirror with her pretty silks trailing behind her like flocks of coloured birds. Isabel smiled. She felt happy, and the happiness was different to the happiness she felt each dawn. Chasing the reflections, she finally found the real Genya standing on the gantry above Mirror 28.

"It's darker here."

"Yes. This mirror has a fault in it."

"This must have been where you first saw me . . . " Genya chuckled. "I thought the light had changed. The colours were suddenly deeper. For a while, it even had the bees confused. Sometimes, the sunlight felt almost cool as I danced though it—more soothing. But I suppose that was your gaze . . . "

They both stared down at the gardens of the Cathedral of the Word. They looked glorious, although the pillared space where Genya had danced seemed oddly vacant without her. Isabel rubbed her sore eyes as bigger blotches than usual swam before them. She said, "You've never told me about that dance."

"It's supposed to be a secret."

"But then, so are many things."

They stood there for a long time amid the minaret's shimmering light, far above the green valley and the winding rosestone wall. Today felt different. Perhaps they were growing too old for these trysts. Perhaps things would have to change . . . The warm wind blew past them. The Floating Ocean glittered. The trees murmured. The river gleamed. Then, with a rising hum like a small machine coming to life, a bee which had risen the thermals to this great height blundered against Isabel's face. Somehow, it settled there. She felt its spiky legs, then the brush of Genya's fingers as she lifted the creature away.

"I'll show you the dance now, if you like."

"Here? But—"

"—just watch."

From her cupped hands, Genya laid the insect on the gapped wooden boards. It sat there for a moment in the sunlight, slowly shuffling its wings. It looked stunned. "This one's a white-tail. Of course, she's a worker—and a *she*. They do all the work, just like in Ghezirah. Most likely she's been sent out this morning as a scout. Many of them never come back, but the ones that do, and if they've found some fine new source of nectar, tell the hive about it when they return . . . " Genya stooped. She rubbed her palms, and held them close to the insect and breathed their scent towards it, making a sound as she did so—a deep-centred hum. She stepped back. "Watch . . . " The bee preened her antennae and quivered her thorax and shuffled her wings. She wiggled back, and then forwards, her small movements describing jerky figures of eight. "They use your minaret as a signpost . . . " Genya murmured as the bee continued dancing. Isabel squinted; there *was* something about its movements which reminded of Genya on the rosestone paving. "That, and the pull and spin of all Ghezirah. It's called the waggly dance. Most kinds of social bees do it, and its sacred to our Church as well."

Isabel chuckled, delighted. "The waggly dance?!"

"Well, there are many longer and more serious names for it."

"No, no—it's lovely . . . Can you tell where's she been?"

"Over the wall, of course. And she can't understand why there's hard ground up here, up where the sun should be. She thinks we're probably flowers, but no use for nectar-gathering."

"You can tell all of *that*?"

"What would be the point, otherwise, in her dancing? It's the same with us Librarians. Our dance is a ritual we use for signalling where a particular book is to be found."

Isabel smiled at her friend. The idea of someone dancing to show where a book lay amid the Cathedral of the Word's maze of tunnels, buildings and catacombs seemed deliciously impractical, and quite typical of Genya. The way they were both standing now, Isabel could see their two figures clearly reflected in Mirror 28's useless upper convex. She was struck as she always was by Genya's effortless beauty—and then by her own plainness. Isabel was dull as a shadow, even down to the greyed leather jerkin and shorts she was wearing, her mosey hair which had been cropped with blind efficiency, and then held mostly back by a cracked rubber band. She could, in fact, almost have been Genya's shade. It was a pleasant thought—the two of them combined in the light which she brought to this valley each day—but at the same time, the reflection bothered Isabel. For a start, Mirror 28 poured darkness instead of light from her minaret. Even its name felt cold and steely, like a premonition . . .

Isabel mouthed something. A phrase: *the fault in Mirror 28*. It was a saying which was to become popular throughout the Ten Thousand and One Worlds, signifying the small thing left undone from which many other larger consequences, often dire, will follow . . .

"What was that?"

"Oh . . . Nothing . . ."

The bee, raised back into the air by Genya's hands, flew away. The two young women sat talking on the warm decking, exchanging other secrets. There were intelligent devices, Isabel learned, which roamed the aisles of the Cathedral of the Word, searching, scanning, reading, through dusty centuries in pursuit of some minor truth. They were friendly enough when you encountered them, even if they looked like animated coffins. Sometimes, though, if you asked them nicely, they would put aside their duties and let you climb on their backs and take you for a ride . . .

The modem was ticking. Another day was passing. It was time for Genya to return beyond the walls of the Cathedral of the Word. Usually, the two young women were heedlessly quick with their farewells, but, on this blazing afternoon, Isabel felt herself hesitating, and Genya reached out, tracing with her ravaged and sensitive fingers the unmemorable outlines of her friend's face. Isabel did so too. Although her flesh then was no more remarkable than she was, she had acquired a blind person's way of using touch for sight.

"Tomorrow . . . ?"

"Yes?" They both stepped back from each other, embarrassed by this sudden intimacy.

"Will you dance for me—down on that paving? Now that I know what it's for, I'd love to watch you dance again."

Genya smiled. She gave the same formal bow which she had given when they had first met, then turned and began her long descent of the minaret's stairs. By the time she had reached the bottom, Isabel had already strapped herself into her crucifix and was saying her preliminary prayers as she prepared to sing out another day. Unstarry darkness beautiful as the dawn itself washed across all Ghezirah, and Isabel never saw her friend again.

Of the many secrets attributed to the Dawn Church, Isabel still knew relatively few. She didn't know for example, that light, modulated in ways beyond anything she could feel with her human senses, can bear immense amounts of data. As well as singing in the dawn each day from her crucifix, she also heedlessly bore floods of information which passed near-instantly across the valley, and finally, flashing minaret to minaret, returned to the place where it had mostly originated, which was the gleaming island of Jerita, where all things pertaining to the Dawn Church must begin and end. Even before Isabel had noticed it herself, some part of the great Intelligence which governed the runnings of her Church had noted, much as a great conductor will notice the off-tuning of a single string in an orchestra, a certain weakness in the returning message from the remote but nevertheless important island of Nashir where the Cathedral of the Word spread it vast roots and boughs. To the Intelligence, this particular dissonance could only be associated with one minaret, and then to a particular mirror, numbered 28. The Intelligence had many other concerns, but it began to monitor the functioning of that minaret more closely, noticing yet more subtle changes which could not be entirely ascribed to the varying weather or the increasing experience of a new acolyte. In due course, certain human members of the Church were also alerted, and various measures were put in hand to establish the cause of this inattention, the simplest of which involved a midday visit to the dormitories beside the river in Isabel's valley, where apprentices were awoken and quietly interrogated about the behaviour of their new mistress, then asked if they might be prepared to forgo sleep and study their mistress from some hidden spot using delicate instruments with which would, of course, be provided.

The morning after Isabel had watched the bee's dance dawned bright and sweet as ever. The birds burst into song. The whole valley, to her fading eyes, was a green fire. Still, she was sure that, if she used her gaze cautiously, and looked to the side which was less ravaged, she would be able to watch Genya dance. Her breath quickened as she ascended the last stairway. She felt as if she was translucent, swimming through light. Then, of all things, and amplified by mechanisms which mimicked the human inner ear, the doorway far at the base of her minaret sounded the coded knock which signified the urgent needs of another member of her Church. In fact, there were two people waiting at Isabel's doorway. One bore a stern and sorrowful demeanour, whilst the other was a new acolyte, freshly blinded. Even before they had touched hands and faces, Isabel knew that this acolyte had come to replace her. Although she was standing on the solid ground of Ghezirah, she felt as if she was falling.

Unlike many other details of Isabel's life, facts of her trial are relatively well recorded. Strangely, or perhaps not, the Church of the Word is less free in publishing its proceedings, although much can be adduced from secondary sources. The tone of the press reports, for example, is astonishingly fevered. Even before they had had the chance to admit their misdeeds, Isabel and Genya were both labelled as criminals and traitors. They were said to be lovers, too, in every possible sense apart from the true one. They were foolhardy, dangerous—rabid urchins who had been rescued from the begging-bowl gutters of Ghezirah by their respective Churches, and had repaid that kindness with perfidy and deceit. Did people really feel so badly towards them? Did anyone ever really imagine that what they had done was any different to the innocent actions of the young throughout history? The facts may be plain, but such questions, from this distance of time, remain unanswerable. It should be remembered, though, that Ghezirah was still recovering from the War of the Lilies, and that the Churches, in this of all times, needed to reinforce the loyalty of their members. It was time for an example to be made—and for the peace to be shown for what it really was, which was shaky and incomplete and dangerous. For this role, Isabel and Genya were chosen.

As a rule, the Churches do not kill their errant acolytes. Instead, they continue to use them. Isabel, firstly, had her full sight, and then more, returned to her in lidless eyes of crystal which could never blink. Something was also done to her flesh which was akin to the operations which had been performed on Genya's fingertips. Finally, but this time in a great minaret on the Church's home island of Jerita, she was returned to her duties as a Dawn-Singer. But dawn for her now became a terrible thing, and the apprentices and clerks and lesser acolytes who lived and worked for their Church around the forested landscapes of the Windfare Hills returned from their night's labours to agonised screams. Still, Isabel strove to perform her duties, although the light was pure pain to the diamonds of her lidless eyes and the blaze of sunlight was molten lead to flesh which now felt the lightest breeze as a desert gale.

No one's mind, not even Isabel's, could sustain such torment indefinitely. As the years passed, it is probable that the portions of her brain which suffered most were slowly destroyed even though the sensors in her scarred and shining flesh continued working. Isabel in her decline became a common sight amid the forests and courtyards of the lesser academies of the Windfare Hills; a stooped figure, wandering and muttering in the painful daylight which she had brought, wrapped in cloths and bandages despite the summer's endless warmth; an object lesson in betrayal, her glittering eyes always shaded, averted in pain. She was given alms. Everyone knew her story, and felt that they had suffered with her—or at least that she had suffered for them. She was treated mostly with sadness, kindness, sympathy. The nights, though, were Isabel's blessing. She wandered under the black skies almost at ease, brushing her fingers across the cooling stones of statues, listening to the sigh of the trees.

Perhaps she remembered Mirror 28, or that day of fog when she first met Genya. More likely, being Isabel, there was no conscious decision involved in the process of bringing, slowly, day by day and year by year, a little less light across to the stately rooftops and green hills of this portion of Jerita other than a desire to reduce her own suffering. People, though, noted the new coolness of the air, the difference of the light amid these hills, and, just as Genya and Isabel had once done, they found it pleasantly melancholy. The Church's Intelligence, too, must have been aware in its own way of these happenings, although this was perhaps what it had always intended. People began to frequent the Windfare Hills because of these deeper shadows, the whisper of leaves from the seemingly dying trees blowing across lawns and down passageways. They lit fires in the afternoons to keep themselves warm, and found thicker clothes. It is likely that few had ever travelled beyond Ghezirah, or were even aware of the many worlds which glory in the phenomena called *seasons*. Only the plants, despite all the changes which had been wrought on them, understood. As Isabel, who had long had nothing to loose, one day took the final step of letting darkness continue to hang for many incredible moments hang over Windfare whilst all the rest of Jerita ignited with dawn, the trees clicked their branches and shed a few more leaves into the chill mists, and remembered. And waited.

This, mostly, is the story of Isabel of the Fall as it is commonly told. The days grew duller across the Windfare Hills. The nights lengthened. A ragged figure, failing and arthritic, Isabel finally came to discover, by accidentally thrusting her hand into the pillar of Sabil's light which poured into her minaret, that the blaze which had caused her so much pain could also bring a blissful end to all sensation. She knew by then that she was dying. And she knew that her ruined, blistered flesh—as she came to resemble an animated pile of the charcoal sticks of the leavings of autumnal fires—was the last of the warnings with which her Church had encumbered her. Limping and stinking, she wandered further afield across Dawn Church's island of Jerita. Almost mythical already, she neglected her duties to the extent that her minaret, probably without her noticing in the continuing flicker of short and rainy days, was taken from her. The desire for these seasons had spread by now across Ghezirah. Soon, as acolytes of the Green Church learned how to reactivate the genes of plants which had once coped with such conditions, spring was to be found in Culgaith, and chill winter in Abuzeid. The spinning islands of Ghezirah were changed forever. And, at long last, in this world of cheerful sadness and melancholy joy which only the passing of seasons can bring, the terrors of the War of the Lilies became a memory.

One day, Isabel of the Fall was dragging herself and what remained of her memories across a place of gardens and fountains. A cool wind blew. The trees here were the colour of flame, but at the same time, she was almost sure that the enormous building which climbed ahead of her could only be the Cathedral of the Word. She looked around for Genya and grunted to herself—she was probably off playing hide and seek. Isabel staggered on, the old wrappings which had stuck to her burnt flesh dragging behind her. She looked, as many how now remarked, like a crumpled leaf; the very spirit of this new season of autumn. She even smelled of decay and things burning. But she still had the sight which had been so ruthlessly given to her, and the building ahead . . . The building ahead seemed to have no end to its spires . . .

Cold rains rattled across the lakes. Slowly, day by day, Isabel approached the last great citadel of her Church, which truly did rise all the way to the skies, and then beyond them. The Intelligence which dwelt there had long been expecting her, and opened its gates, and refreshed the airs of its corridors and stairways which Isabel, with the instincts of a Dawn-Singer, had no need to be encouraged to climb. Day and darkness flashed through the arrowslit windows as she ascended. Foods and wines would appear at turns and landings, cool and bland for her wrecked palate. Sometimes, hissing silver things passed her, or paused to enquire if they could carry her, but Isabel remained true to the precepts and vanities of her Church, and disdained such easy ways of ascension. It was a long, hard climb. Sometimes, she heard Genya's husky breath beside her, her exclamations and laughter as she looked down and down into the huge wells which had opened beneath. Sometimes, she was sure she was alone. Sometimes, although her blackened face had lost all sensation and her eyes were made of crystal, Isabel of the Fall was sure she was crying. But still she climbed.

The roof which covers the islands of Ghezirah is usually accessed, by the rare humans and aliens who do such things, by the use of aircraft and hummingbird caleches. Still, it had seemed right to the forgotten architects of the Dawn Church that there should be one last tower and staircase which ascended all of the several miles to the top of Ghezirah's skies. By taking the way which always led *up*, and as the other towers and minarets fell far beneath her, Isabel found that way, that last spire, and followed it. Doorways opened. The Intelligence led her on. She never felt alone now, and even her pain fell behind her. Finally, though, she came to a doorway which would not open. It was a plain thing, round-lipped and with a wheel at its centre which refused to turn. A light flashed above it. Perhaps this was some kind of warning. Isabel considered. She sat there for many days. Food appeared and disappeared. She could go back down again, although she knew she would never survive the journey. She could go on, but that light . . . Over to her left, she saw eventually, was some sort of suit. A silvered hat, boots, a cape. They looked grand, expensive. Surely not for her? But then she remembered the food, the sense of a presence. She pulled them on over her rags, or rather the things pulled themselves over her when she approached them. Now, the wheel turned easily, even before she had reached out to it. Beyond was disappointing; a tiny space little more than the size of a wardrobe. But then there was a sound of hissing, and a door similar to one which had puzzled her span its wheel, and opened. Isabel stepped out.

The great interior sphere of Ghezirah hung spinning. Everywhere within this glittering ball, there were mirrors wide as oceans. Everywhere, there was darkness and light. And Sabil hung at the centre of it, pluming white; a living fire. Isabel gasped. She had never seen anything so beautiful—not even Genya dancing. She climbed upwards along the gantries through stark shadows. Something of her Dawn-Singer's knowledge told her that these mirrors were angled for night, and that, even in the unpredictable drift of these new seasons, they would soon bring dawn across Ghezirah. She came to the lip of one vast reflector, and considered it. At this pre-dawn moment, bright though it was, its blaze was a mere ember. Then, leaning over it as she had once leaned over Mirror 28 with Genya, Isabel did something she had never done before. She touched the surface of the mirror. There was no sense left in her ravaged hands, but, even through the gloves of her suit and Sabil's glare and hard vacuum, it felt smooth, cool, perfect. The mirror was vast—the size of small planet—and it curved in a near endless parabola. Isabel understood that for such an object to move at all, and then in one moment, it could not possibly be made of glass, or any normal human substance. But at the same time, it looked and felt solid. Without quite knowing what she was doing, but sensing that the seconds before dawn were rapidly passing, Isabel climbed onto the edge of the mirror. Instantly, borne by its slippery energies, she was sliding, falling. The seconds passed. The mirror caught her. Held her. She waited. She thought of the insects which she sponged from so many mirrors in her nights as an apprentice, their bodies fried by the day's heat. But dawn was coming . . . For the last time, as all the mirrors moved in unison to bear Sabil's energies towards the sleeping islands of Ghezirah below, Isabel spread her arms to welcome her sun. Joyously, as the light flashed bear on her, she sang in the dawn.

In some versions of this tale, Isabel is said to have fallen towards Sabil, and thus to have gained her name. In others, she is called simply Isabel of the Autumn and her final climb beyond the sky remains unmentioned. In some, she is tragically beautiful, or beautifully ugly. The real truth remains lost, amid much else about her. But in the Dawn Church itself Isabel of the Fall is still revered, and amid of its many mysteries it is said that one of Ghezirah's great internal reflectors still bears the imprint of her vaporised silhouette, which is the only blemish on all of its mirrors which the Church allows. And somewhere, if you know where to look amid all of Ghezirah's many islands, and at the right time of day and in the correct season, there is a certain wall in a certain small garden where Isabel's shape can be seen, pluming down from the minarets far above; traversing the hours brick to mossy brick as a small shadow.

As for Genya, she is often forgotten at the end of this story. She touches Isabel's face for a last time, smiles, bows and vanishes down the stairways of the minaret towards oblivion. But the fact that she was also punished by her Church remains beyond doubt, and the punishment was as cruel and purposeful in its own way as that which was visited on Isabel. Genya retained all her senses, her special fingertips, even briefly her skills as a dancer; what her Church took from her was the ability to *understand*. She was then set the task of transcribing many manuscripts from one dead language to another, dictating, recording, endlessly reading and reciting with every input of her eyes and flesh. There were urrearth stories of princess and dragons, equations over which geniuses would have wept, but the meaning of them all passed though Genya unnoticed. Genya became a stupid but useful vessel, and she grew ancient and proficient and fat in a pillowed crypt in the far depths of the Cathedral of the Word, where the windows look out on the turning stars and new acolytes were taken to see her—the famous Genya who had once loved Isabel and betrayed her Church; now white and huge, busy and brainless as a maggot as she rummaged through endless torrents of words. But there are worse fates, and Genya lacked the wisdom to suffer. And she wasn't soulless— somewhere, deep within the rolls of fat and emptiness, all those spinning words, she was still Genya. When she died, muttering the last sentence of an epic which no other Librarian or machine could possibly have transcribed, that part of her passed on with the manuscript to echo and remain held forever somewhere amid all the vast cliff-faces of books in the Cathedral of the Word. To this day, within pages such as these, Genya can still sometimes be found, beautiful as she once was, dancing barefoot across the warm rosestone paving on an endless summer's morning in the time which was always long ago.

PRECIOUS MENTAL

ROBERT REED

The man came to Port Beta carrying an interesting life.

Or perhaps that life was carrying him.

Either way, he was a strong plain-faced human, exceptionally young yet already dragging heavy debt. Wanting honest, reliable employment, he wrestled with a series of aptitude tests, and while scoring poorly in most categories, the newcomer showed promise when it came to rigor and precision and the kinds of courage required by the mechanical arts. Port Beta seemed like a worthy home for him. That was where new passengers arrived at the Great Ship, cocooned inside streakships and star taxis, bomb-tugs and one-of-a-kind vehicles. Long journeys left most of those starships in poor condition. Many were torn apart as salvage, but the valuable and the healthiest were refurbished and then sent out again, chasing wealthy travelers of every species.

A local academy accepted the newcomer, and he soon rose to the most elite trade among technicians. Bottling up suns and antimatter was considered the highest art. Drive-mechanics worked on starship engines and dreamed about starship engines, and they were famous for jokes and foul curses understandable only to their own kind. Their work could be routine for years, even decades, but then inside the monotony something unexpected would happen. Miss one ghost of a detail and a lasting mistake would take hold, and then centuries later, far from Port Beta, a magnificent streakship would explode, and the onboard lives, ancient and important, were transformed into hard radiation and a breakneck rain of hot, anonymous dust.

That was why drive-mechanics commanded the highest wages.

And that was why new slots were constantly opening up in their ranks.

According to official records, the academy's new student was born on the Great Ship, inside a dead-end cavern called Where-Peace-Rains. Peculiar humans lived in that isolated realm, and they usually died there, and to the soul, they clung to preposterous beliefs, their society and entire existence woven around one linchpin idea:

The multiverse was infinite.

There was no denying that basic principle. Quantum endlessness was proven science, relentless and boundless and beautiful. Yet where most minds saw abstractions and eccentric mathematics, those living inside Where-Peace-Rains considered infinity to be a grand and demanding gift. Infinity meant that nothing could exist just once. Whatever was real, no matter how complicated or unlikely, had no choice but to persist forever.

In that way, souls were the same as snowflakes.

A person's circumstances could seem utterly, yet he was always surviving in limitless places and dying in limitless places, and he couldn't stop being born again in every suitable portion of the All.

Life had its perfect length. Most humans and almost every sentient creature believed in living happily for as long as possible. But the archaic souls inside that cave considered too much life to be a trap. One or two centuries of breathing and sleeping were plenty. Extend existence past its natural end, and the immortal soul was debased, impoverished, and eventually stripped of its grandeur. Only by knowing that you were temporary could life be stripped of illusion and the cloaks of false-godhood, and then the blessed man could touch the All, and he could love the All, and if his brief existence proved special, a tiny piece of his endless soul might earn one moment of serene clarity.

Where-Peace-Rains constantly needed babies. Like primitive humans, its citizens were built from water and frail bone and DNA full of primate instincts. The outside world called them Luddites—an inadequate word, part insult and part synonym for madness. But the young drive-mechanic was remarkable because he grew up among those people, becoming an important citizen before relinquishing their foolish ways.

Stepping alone into the universe, the man was made immortal.

But immortality was an expensive magic.

It had to be.

Archaic muscles and organs needed to be retrofitted. The body had to be indifferent to every disease, ready to heal any wound. Then the soggy soft and very fragile human brain was transformed into a tough bioceramic wonder, complex enough to guarantee enough memory and quick intelligence to thrive for eons.

But transformation wasn't the only expense. The boundless life never quit needing space and food and energy. Eternal, highly gifted minds relished exotic wonders, yet they also demanded safety and comfort—two qualities that were never cheap. That's why the Great Ship's captains demanded huge payments from immortals. Passengers who never died would never stop needing. And that was why the one-time Luddite was impressive: Fresh inside his new body, consumed by his many debts, he was using a new brain to learn how to repair and rebuild the most spectacular machines built by any hands.

Every student was soon hired as a low-wage trainee. The newcomer did small jobs well, but more importantly, he got out of the way when he wasn't needed. People noticed his plain, unimpressive face. It was a reasonable face; fanatics didn't need beauty. The man could be brusque when displeased, and maybe that quality didn't endear him with his superiors. But he proved to have an instinct for stardrives, and he knew when to buy drinks for his colleagues, and he was expert in telling dry old jokes, and sometimes, in a rare mood, he offered stories about Where-Peace-Rains. Audiences were curious the cavern and its odd folk, the left-behind family and their ludicrous faith. Years later, co-workers thought enough their colleague to attend his graduation, and if the man didn't show enough pride with the new plasma-blue uniform, at least he seemed comfortable with the steady work that always finds those who know what they are doing.

Decades passed, and the reformed Luddite acquired responsibilities and then rank, becoming a dependable cog in the Tan-tan-5 crew.

Then the decades were centuries.

One millennium and forty-two years had steadily trickled past. Port Beta remained a vast and hectic facility, and the Great Ship pushed a little farther along its quarter-million year voyage around the galaxy, and this man that everybody knew seemed to have always been at his station. His abandoned family had died long ago. If he felt any interest in the generations still living inside Where-Peace-Rains, he kept it secret. Skill lifted him to the middle ranks, and he was respected by those that knew him, and the people who knew him best never bothered to imagine that this burly, plain-faced fellow might actually be someone of consequence.

2

His name used to be Pamir.

Wearing his own face and biography, Pamir had served as one of the Great Ship's captains. Nothing about that lost man was cog-like. In a vocation that rewarded charm and politics, he was an excellent captain who succeeded using nothing but stubborn competence. No matter how difficult the assignment, it was finished early and without fuss. Creativity was in his toolbox, but unlike too many high-gloss captains, Pamir used rough elegance before genius. Five projects wearing his name were still taught to novice captains. Yet the once-great officer had also lost his command, and that was another lesson shared with the arrogant shits who thought they deserved to wear the captains' mirrored uniform: For thousands of years, Pamir was a rising force in the ranks, and then he stupidly fell in love with an alien. That led to catastrophes and fat financial losses for the Ship, and although the situation ended favorably enough, passengers could have been endangered, and worse than that, secrets had been kept from his vengeful superiors.

Sitting out the voyage inside the brig was a likely consequence, but dissolving into the Ship's multitudes was Pamir's solution. The official story was that the runaway captain had slipped overboard thirty thousand years ago, joining colonists bound for a new world. As a matter of policy, nobody cared about one invisible felon. But captains forgot little, and that's why several AIs were still dedicated to Pamir's case—relentless superconductive minds endlessly sifting through census records and secret records, images dredged up from everywhere, and overheard conversations in ten thousand languages.

Every morning began with the question, "Is this the day they find me?"

And between every breath, some piece of that immortal mind was being relentlessly suspicious of everyone.

"Jon?"

Tools froze in mid-task, and the mechanic turned. "Over here."

"Do you have a moment?"

"Three moments," he said. "What do you want, G'lene?"

G'lene was human, short and rounded with fat—a cold-world adaptation worn for no reason but tradition. One of the newest trainees, she was barely six hundred years old, still hunting for her life's calling.

"I need advice," she said. "I asked around, and several people suggested that I come to you first."

The man said nothing, waiting.

"We haven't talked much before," she allowed.

"You work for a different crew," he said.

"And I don't think you like me."

The girl often acted flip and even spoiled, but those traits didn't matter. What mattered was that she was a careless technician. It was a common flaw worn by young immortals. Carelessness meant that the other mechanics had to keep watch over her work, and the only question seemed when she would be thrown out of the program.

"I don't know you much at all," said Pamir. "What I don't like is your work."

She heard him, took a quick breath, and then she pushed any embarrassment aside. "You're the Luddite, aren't you?"

There were various ways to react. Pamir told the nearest tool to pivot and aim, punching a narrow hole through the center of his palm.

Blood sprayed, and the hole began to heal instantly.

"Apparently not," he said.

G'lene laughed like a little girl, without seriousness, without pretense.

Pamir didn't fancy that kind of laugh.

"Jon is a popular name with Luddites," she said.

Pamir sucked at the torn flesh. He had worn "Jon" nearly as long as he had worn this face. Only in dreams was he anybody else.

"What kind of advice are you chasing?" he asked.

"I need a topic for my practicum."

"Ugly-eights," he said.

"That's what you're working on here, isn't it?"

He was rehabilitating the main drive of an old star-taxi. Ugly-eights were a standard, proven fusion engine. They had been pushing ships across the galaxy longer than most species were alive. This particular job was relentlessly routine and cheap, and while someone would eventually find some need for this old ship, it would likely sit inside a back berth for another few centuries.

"Ugly-eights are the heart of commerce in the galaxy," said Pamir.

"And they're ugly," she said.

"Build a new kind of ugly," he said. "Tweak a little function or prove that some bit or component can be yanked. Make this machine better, simpler or sexier, and a thousand mechanics will worship you as a goddess."

"Being worshipped," she said. "That would be fun."

She seemed to believe it was possible.

The two of them were standing in the middle of an expansive machine shop. Ships and parts of ships towered about them in close ranks. Port Beta was just ten kilometers past the main doors, and the rest of Pamir's crew and his boss were scattered, no other face in sight.

"I know what you did for your practicum," said G'lene. "You built a working Kajjas pulse engine."

"Nobody builds a working Kajjas pulse," he said. "Not even the Kajjas."

"You built it and then went up on the hull and fired the engine for ninety days."

"And then my luck felt spent, so I turned it off."

"I want to do something like that," she said. "I want something unusual."

"No," he said. "You do not, no."

She didn't seem to notice his words. "It's too bad that we don't have any Kajjas ships onboard. Wouldn't it be fun to refab one of those marvels?"

Kajjas space had been left behind long ago. Not one of their eccentric vessels was presently berthed inside Beta. But the Great Ship had five other ports, reserved for the captains and security forces. Did G'lene know facts that weren't public knowledge? Was the girl trying to coax him into some kind of borderline adventure?

"So you want to play with a real Kajjas ship," Pamir said.

"But only with your help. I'm not a fool."

Pamir had never given much thought to G'lene's mind. What he realized then, staring at that pretty ageless and almost perfectly spherical face, was that she didn't seem to be one thing or another. He couldn't pin any quality to his companion.

"The Kajjas are famous explorers," she said.

"They used to be, but the wandering urge left them long ago."

"What if I knew where to find an old Kajjas starship?"

"I'd have to ask where it's hiding."

"Not here," she said.

The way she spoke said a lot. "Not here." The "here" was drawn out, and the implications were suddenly obvious.

"Shit," said Pamir.

"Exactly," she said.

"It's not on the Great Ship, is it?"

The smile brightened, smug and ready for the next question.

"Who are you?" he asked.

"Exactly who I seem to be," she said.

"A lipid-rich girl who is going to fail at the academy," he said.

To her credit, she didn't bristle. Poise held her steady, and she let him stare at her face a little longer before saying, "Maybe I was lying."

"You aren't talking about your practicum, are you?"

"Not really," she said. "No, I have friends who need to hire a drive-mechanic."

"Friends," he said.

"Best friends," she said. "And like all best friends, they have quite a lot of money."

Pamir said, "No."

"Take a leave of absence," she said. "The bosses like your work. They'll let you go. Then in a little while ... well, a long while ... you can come back again with enough money to wipe away all of your debts."

"What do you know about my debts?"

The smile sharpened. "Everything," she said.

"No, I don't want this," he said.

Then a little meanness crept into her laugh. "Is it true what they say?"

"It often is."

"Luddite minds are better than others," she said. "They work harder because they have to start out soft and simple."

"We all start simple," he said.

"You need to go with me," she insisted.

There was a threat woven into the words, the tone. Pamir started to gauge his surroundings as well as this peculiar creature, but he never heard the killer's approach. One moment, the drive-mechanic was marshaling his tools for some ad hoc battle, but before he was ready, two impossibly strong hands were clasped around his neck, reaching from behind, calmly choking the life out of a thousand year-old body.

3

The Kajjas home sun was a brilliant F-class star circled by living worlds, iron-fattened asteroids, and billions of lush comets. Like humans, the Kajjas evolved as bipeds hungry for oxygen and water, and like most citizens of the galaxy, biology gave them brief lifespans and problematic biochemistries. Independent of other species, they invented the usual sciences, and after learning the principles of the Creation, they looked at everything with new eyes. But their solar system happened to be far removed from the galactic plane. The nearest star was fifty light-years away. Isolated but deeply clever, the Kajjas devised their famous pulse engines—scorching, borderline-stable rockets built around collars of degenerate matter. Kajjas pulses were as good as the best drives once they reached full throttle, but stubborn physics still kept them from beating the relativistic walls. Every voyage took time, and worse still, those pulse engines had the irksome habit of bleeding radiation. Even the youngest crew would die of cancers and old age before the voyage was even half-finished.

Faced the problem of spaceflight, every species realized that there were no perfect answers, at least so long as minds were mortal and the attached bodies were weak.

A consensus was built among the Kajjas. Alone, they began reengineering their basic nature. With time they might have invented solutions as radical as their relentless star-drives, but not long after the project began, a river of laser light swept out at them from the galaxy's core—a dazzling beacon carrying old knowledge, including the tools and high tricks necessary to build the bioceramic mind.

A similar beacon would eventually find the Earth, unleashing the potentials of one wild monkey.

But that event was a hundred million years in the future.

Human history was brief and complicated—a few hundred thousand years of competing, combustible civilizations. By comparison, the Kajjas built exactly one technological society. War and strife were unimaginable. Unity rode in their blue blood. Once armed with immortal minds and the infamous engines, their starships rained down across a wide portion of the galaxy, setting up colonies and trade routes while poking into ill-explored corners. The Kajjas were curious and adaptable explorers, and it was easy to believe that they would eventually rule some fat portion of local space. But the species reached its zenith while the dinosaurs still ran over one tiny world, and then their slow decline began. Colonies withered. Their starships began keeping to the easy, well-mapped routes. Some of the Kajjas never even went into space. And what always bothered Pamir, and what always intrigued him, was that these ancient creatures had no clear idea what had gone wrong.

A few Kajjas rode onboard the Great Ship. They were poorer than the typical passenger, but each had a love for brightly lit taverns, and in moderation, drinks made from hot spring waters and propanol salted liberally with cyanide.

Philosophers by nature and cranky philosophers at that, the Kajjas made interesting company. Pamir approved of their irritable moods. He liked cryptic voices and far-sighting reflections. This was a social species with clear senses of hierarchies. If you wanted respect, it was important to sit near your Kajjas friend, near enough to taste the poison on his breath, and to wring the best out of the experience, you had to act as if he was the master of the table and everyone sitting around it.

Pamir's favorite refugee was ageless to the eye, but eyes were easily fooled.

"We were courageous voyagers," said the raspy voice.

"You were," Pamir agreed.

His companion had various names, but in human company, he preferred to be called "Tailor."

"Do you realize how many worlds we visited?"

"No, Tailor, I don't."

"You do not know, and we can only guess numbers." The words were tumbling out of an elderly, often repaired translator. "Ten million planets? Twenty billion? I can't even count the places that I have walked with these good feet."

The Kajjas suddenly propped his legs on the tabletop.

Knowing what was proper, Pamir leaned between the toe-rich, faintly kangaroo-style feet. "I would tolerate your stories, if you could tolerate my boundless interest."

The alien's head was narrow and extremely deep, like the blade of a hatchet. Three eyes surrounded a mouth that chewed at the air, betraying suspicion. "Do I know you, young human?"

"No," Pamir lied. "We have never met."

He was wearing that new face and the name Jon, and he was cloaked in a fresh life story too.

"You seem familiar to me," said the Kajjas.

"Because you're ancient and full of faces, remembered and imagined too."

"That feels true."

"I beg to know your age," Pamir said.

The question had been asked before, and Tailor's answer was always enormous and never repeated. If the alien felt joyous, he claimed to be youthful forty million years old. But if angry or despairing, he painted himself as being much, much older.

"I could have walked along your Cretaceous shoreline," said Tailor that evening, hinting at a very dark disposition.

"I wish you had," said Pamir.

"Yet I can do that just the same," the Kajjas said, two eyes turning to mist as the mind wove some private image.

Pamir knew to wait, sipping his rum.

The daydream ended, and the elderly creature leaked a high trilling sound that the translator turned into a despairing groan.

"My mind is full," Tailor declared.

"Should I envy you?"

Iron blades rubbed hard against one another—the Kajjas laugh. "Fill your mind with whatever you wish. Envy has its uses."

"Should my species envy yours?"

Every eye cleared. "Are you certain we haven't met?"

"Nothing is certain," said Pamir.

"Indeed. Indeed."

"Perhaps you know other humans," Pamir said.

"I have sipped drinks with a few," Tailor said. "Usually male humans, as it happens. One or two of them had your bearing exactly."

The focus needed to be shifted. "You haven't answered me, my master. Should humans envy your species' triumphs?"

A long sip of poison turned into a human-style nod. "You should envy every creature's success. And if you wish my opinion—"

"Yes."

"In my view, our greatest success is the quiet grace we have shown while making our plunge back to obscurity. Not every species vanishes so well as the Kajjas."

"Humans won't," said Pamir.

"On that, we agree."

"And why did your plunge begin?" the human asked. "What went wrong for you, or did something go right?"

Pamir had drunk with this entity many times over the millennia. Tailor gave various answers to this question, each delivered without much faith in the voice. Usually he claimed that living too long made an immortal cowardly and dull. Too many of his species were ancient, and that antediluvian nature brought on lethargy, and of course lethargy led to a multifaceted decline.

Wearing the Jon face, Pamir waited for that reliable excuse again.

But the alien said nothing, wiggling those finger-like toes. Then with an iron laugh, fresh words climbed free of his mouth.

"I think the secret is our minds," he began.

"Too old, are they?" asked Pamir.

"I am not talking about age. And while too many memories are jammed inside us, they are not critical either."

"What is wrong with your mind?"

"And yours too." Tailor leaned forward. A hand older than any ape touched Pamir's face, tracing the outlines of his forehead. "Your brain and mine are so similar. In its materials and the nanoscopic design, and in every critical detail that doesn't define our natures."

"True, true," said the worshipful Pamir.

"Does that bother you?"

"Not at all."

"Of course not, no," said the alien. "But have you ever asked yourself . . . has that smart young mind of yours ever wondered . . . why doesn't this sameness leave you just a little sick in your favorite stomach?"

4

Choke an immortal man, pulverize the trachea and neck bones and leave the body starved of oxygen, and he dives into a temporary coma. But the modern body is more sophisticated than machines, including star-drives, and within their realm, humans can be far more durable, more self-reliant. Choke the man and a nanoscopic army rises from the mayhem, knitting and soothing, patching and building. Excess calories are warehoused everywhere, including inside the bioceramic mind, and despite the coma and the limp frame, nothing about the victim is dead. Pamir wasn't simply conscious. He was lucid, thoughts roaring, outrage in full stride as he guessed about enemies and their motives and what he would do first when he could move again, and what he would do next, and depending on the enemies, what color his revenge would take.

But there were many states between full life and true death.

He was sprawled out on the shop floor, and standing over him, somebody said, "Done."

Then he felt himself being lifted.

A woman said, "Hurry."

G'lene?

His body was carried, but not far. There was a maze of storage hangers beneath the shop. Pamir assumed that he was taken into one of those rooms, and once set down again he found the strength to strike a careless face, once and then twice again before someone shoved a fat tube down his ruined throat.

Fiery chemicals cooked his flesh.

Too late, he tried to engage his nexuses. But their voices had been jammed, and all that came back to him was white noise and white deathly light.

In worse ways than strangling, his body was methodically killed.

Deafness took him, and his sense of smell was stripped away, and every bit of skin went numb. In the end, the only vision remaining was imagination. A body couldn't be left inside a storage hanger. Someone would notice. That's why he imagined himself being carried, probably bound head to toe to keep him from fighting again. But he didn't feel any motion, and nothing changed. Nothing happened. Lying inside blackness, his thoughts ran on warehoused power, and when no food was offered those same thoughts began to slow, softening the intensities of each idea, ensuring a working consciousness that could collapse quite a bit farther without running dry.

The streakship's launch was never noticed, and the long, fierce acceleration made no impression.

But Pamir reasoned something like that would happen. Clues and a captain's experience let him piece together a sobering, practical story. If any Kajjas ship was wandering near the Great Ship, it would have been noticed. That news would have found him. And since it wasn't close, and since the universe was built mostly from inconvenient trajectories, the streakship would probably have to burn massive amounts of fuel just to reach the very distant target—assuming it didn't smash into a comet while plunging through interstellar space.

This kind of mission demanded small crews and fat risks, and Pamir was going to remain lost for a very long time.

"Unless," he thought. "Unless I'm not lost at all."

Paranoia loves darkness. Perhaps this ugly situation was a ruse. Maybe the relentless AI hunters had finally found him, but nobody was quite sure if he was the runaway captain. So instead of having him arrested, the captains decided to throw the suspect inside a black box, trying to squeeze the secrets out of him.

Bioceramic minds were tiny and dense and utterly unreadable.

But a mind could be worn down. A guilty man or even an innocent man would confess to a thousand amazing crimes. Wondering if prison was better than dying on some bizarre deep-space quest, Pamir found the temptation to say his old name once, just to see if somebody had patched into his speech center. But as time stretched and the thoughts slowed even more, he kept his mind fixed on places and days that meant something to a man named Jon. He pictured Port Beta and the familiar machinery. He spoke to colleagues and drank with them, the routine, untroubled life of the mechanic lingering long past his death. Then when he was miserably bored, he imagined Where-Peace-Rains, spending the next years with a life and beliefs that before this were worn only as camouflage.

For the first time, he missed that life that he had never lived.

Decades passed.

Oxygen returned without warning, and flesh warmed, and new eyes opened as a first breath passed down his new throat.

A face was watching him.

"Hello, Jon," said the face, the hint of a smile showing.

Pamir said, "Hello," and breathed again, with relish.

G'lene appeared to be in fine health, drifting above the narrow packing crate where his mostly dead body had been stowed.

Pamir sat up slowly.

A thoroughly, wondrously alien ship surrounded them. Its interior was a cylinder two hundred meters in diameter and possibly ten kilometers long. Pamir couldn't see either end of this odd space. The walls were covered with soft glass threads, ruddy like the native Kajjas grass, intended to give the Kajjas good purchase for kicking when they were in zero gravity, like now. But when the ship's engines kicked on, the same threads would come alive, lacing themselves into platforms where the crew could work and rest, the weaves tightening as the gees increased. That was standard Kajjas technology. Kajjas machines were scattered about the curved, highly mobile landscape, each as broken as it was old. There were control panels and what looked like immersion chambers, none of them working, and various hyperfiber boxes were sealed against the universe. Every surface wore a vigorous coat of dust. Breathing brought scents only found in places that had been empty forever. Rooms onboard the Great Ship smelled this way. But the air and the bright lights felt human, implying that his abductors had been onboard long enough to reconfigure the environment.

G'lene kept her distance. "How do you feel, Jon?"

"Can you guess?" he asked.

She laughed quietly, apparently embarrassed.

In the distance, three entities were moving in their direction. Two of them were human.

"Our autodoc just spliced a fast-breaker pipe into your femoral," she said. "You'll be strong and ready in no time."

Pamir studied legs that didn't look like his legs, and he looked at a rib-rich chest and a stranger's spidery hands. Starvation and nothingness had left him eroded, brittle and remarkable.

"Our captain wants you to start repairing the pulse drive," G'lene said.

"And I imagine that our captain wants enthusiasm on my part."

She blinked. She said, "Hopefully."

"You know a little something about machines," he said. "How does the old engine look?"

"I'm no expert, as you like to tell me. But it looks like the last crew put everything to sleep in the best ways. Unfortunately there's no fuel onboard, and none of the maintenance equipment is functioning."

"I hope our captain considered these possibilities."

"We brought extra fuel and tools, yes."

"Enough?"

She stared at his skinny legs.

Pulse engines, like flesh, were adaptable when it came to nutrition. Any mass could be fed through the collars, transformed into plasma and light.

Pamir wiggled his bare toes.

The other crewmembers were kicking closer.

"I'm guessing that the Kajjas crew is also missing," he said.

"Oh, yes," she said.

"How long missing?"

The question made her uneasy.

"How long have we been here?" he asked.

That was another difficult topic, but she nodded when she said, "Nineteen days."

The autodoc beneath him was a small field model, serviceable but limited. Pamir studied it and then the girl, and then he flexed one leg while leaving the other perfectly still. Asked to work, the atrophied muscles took the largest share of the new food, and the leg grew warmer, sugars burning and lipids burning until the slippery blood began to glow.

"How about the sovereigns?" he asked.

"Sovereigns?"

"The ship's AIs." Most species patterned their automated systems after their social systems, and the Kajjas preferred noble-minded machines in charge of the automated functions.

"We've tried talking to the AIs," said G'lene. "They don't answer."

Tossing both legs out from the tiny growth chamber, Pamir dragged the fast-break pipe with them. "And what are we? A salvage operation?"

She said, "Yes."

"And at the end of the fun, am I paid? Or am I murdered for good?"

"Paid," she blurted. "The offer from me was genuine, Jon. There's a lot of money to be made here."

"For a badly depleted Kajjas ship," he said, sighing. "It's more than hopeful, believing this derelict can earn much on the open market."

She said nothing.

"But it is exceptionally old, isn't it?"

"That's what our captain says."

"Sure, the Kajjas sent missions everywhere," he said. "They were even happy to poke far outside the Milky Way."

"Which makes this a marvelous relic," she said.

"To a species inflicted with hard times. Nobody with a genuine purse would give a little shit about this lost wreck."

The two other humans were arriving—a woman and a man. They were closely related, or they loved to wear faces that implied some deep family bond.

"This is Maxx," G'lene said, referring to the man.

"And I'm Rondie," the woman offered.

Powerful people, each as muscular as G'lene was round, their every motion and the flash of their eyes proved they were youngsters.

Pamir wondered whose hands had strangled him.

"It's great to finally meet you," Maxx said, nothing but pure, undiluted happiness in his voice. "We keep hearing that you can make this ship healthy again."

"Who says that?" Pamir asked.

"The only one who matters," the fellow said, laughing amiably.

What was more disturbing: Being kidnapped for a mission that he didn't want to join, or being trapped in the company of three earnest, inexperienced near-children?

Next to the humans, the drive-mechanic was utterly ancient.

But compared to their captain, Pamir was a newborn.

"Hello to you, Jon," said the Kajjas.

"Why me?" Pamir asked. "You should know how to fix your own beast."

One last kick made the glass crinkle and flow, bringing the captain into the group. The sound of grinding iron preceded the words, "I have never mastered the peculiar genius to be a worthy engineer."

"Too bad," said Pamir.

Then Tailor touched his own head above the eyes. "And to learn the necessary talents now would require empty spaces inside my head, which means discarding some treasured memories. And how could I do such to pieces of my own self?"

• • •

5

Pamir knew that nobody was clever enough or worthy enough, much less lucky enough to truly disappear.

The tiniest body still possessed mass and volume, shadow and energy.

And a brilliant mind was never as clever as three average minds sniffing after something of interest.

The wise fugitive always kept several new lives at the ready.

But every ready-made existence carried risks of its own, including the chance that someone would notice the locker jammed with money and clothes, the spare face and a respectable name never used.

Like real lives, each false life had its perfect length, and there was no way to be sure how long that was.

No matter how compromised the current face, transitions always brought the most perilous days.

Paranoia was a fugitive's first tool.

But panic could make the man break from cover at the worst possible moment.

Love meant trust, which meant that no face should be loved.

Most of all, the wanted man should be acutely suspicious of the face in the mirror.

Patterns defined each life, and old patterns were trouble.

Except acquiring the new walk and voice, pleasures and hates was the most cumbersome work possible. And even worse, fine old strategies could be left behind, and the best instincts were corroded by the blur of everything new.

In a crowd of ten million strangers, nobody cared about the human who used to be many things, including a captain. And among the millions were four exceptions, or perhaps one hundred and four, or just that one inquisitive soul standing very close.

Now look into that sea of faces, stare at humans and aliens, machines and the hybrids between. Look hard at everything while pointing one finger—a finger that has been worn for some little while—and now against some very long odds, pick out which of those souls should be feared.

Humans found the derelict machine drifting outside the Milky Way, and after claiming the Great Ship as their own, loyal robots proceeded to map the interior. Each cavern was named using elaborate codes. Even excluding small caves and holes, there were billions of caverns on the captains' maps. Positions and volumes were included each name, but there was also quite a lot of AI free verse poetry. Then as the Great Ship entered the galaxy, one paronomasia-inspired AI savant was ordered to give a million caverns better designations—

words that any human mouth could manage—and one unremarkable hole was named:

Where-Peace-Rains.

Peace ruled inside the dark emptiness, but there was no rain. Remote and unspectacular, the cavern remained silent for long millennia. Communities of archaic humans were established in other locations. Some failed, others found ways to prosper. Mortal passengers had one clear advantage; being sure to die, they paid relatively small sums to ride the Great Ship. And unlike their eternal neighbors, they could pay a minimal fee to have one child. Three trifling payments meant growth, and the captains soon had to control populations through laws and taxes as well as limiting the places where those very odd people could live.

Forty-five thousand years ago, human squatters claimed Where-Peace-Rains, setting up the first lights and a hundred rough little homes in the middle of the bare granite floor. They told themselves they were clever. They assured each other that they were invisible, stealing just a trickle of power from the Ship. But an AI watchdog noticed the theft, and once alerted to the crime, the Master Captain sent one of her more obstinate officers to deal with the ongoing mess.

Pamir was still a captain—an entity full of authority and the ready willingness to deploy his enormous powers.

Wearing a mirrored uniform, he walked every street inside the village, telling the strangers that they were criminals and he wasn't happy. He warned that he could order any punishment that could be imagined, short of genocide. Then he demanded that the Luddites meet him in the round at the village's heart, bags packed, and ready for the worst.

Three hundred people, grown and young, assembled on the polished red granite.

"Explain your selves," the captain demanded.

A leader stepped forward. "We require almost nothing," the old/young man began, his voice breaking at the margins. "We are simple and small, and we ask nothing from the captains or the sacred Ship."

"Shut up," said Pamir.

Those words came out hard, but what scared everyone was the captain's expression. Executions weren't possible, but a lot of grim misery lay between slaughter and salvation, and while these people believed in mortality, they weren't fanatics chasing martyrdom or some ill-drawn afterlife.

Nobody spoke.

Then once again, the captain's voice boomed.

"Before anything else, I want you to explain your minds to me. Do it now, in this place, before your arbitrary day comes to an end."

Nobody was allowed to leave and reset the sun. With little time left, a pretty young woman was pressed into service. Perhaps the other squatters thought she would look appealing to the glowering male officer. Or maybe she was the best, bravest voice available. Either way, she spoke about the limits of life and the magic of physics and the blessings of the eternal, boundless multiverse. Pamir appeared to pay attention, which heartened some. When she paused, he nodded. Could they have found an unlikely ally? But then with a low snort, he said, "I like numbers. Give me mathematics."

The woman responded with intricate, massive numbers wrapped around quantum wonders, invoking the many worlds as well as the ease with which fresh new universes sprang out of the old.

But the longer she spoke, the less impressed he seemed to be. Acting disgusted, then enraged, Pamir told the frightened community, "I know these theories. I can even believe the crazy-shit science. But if you want this to go anywhere good, you have to make me believe what you believe. You have to make me trust the madness that we aren't just here. There are an infinite number of caves exactly like this stone rectum, and infinite examples of you, and there is no measurable end of me. And all of us have assembled in these endless places, and this meeting is happening everywhere exactly as it is here.

"Convince me of that bullshit," he shouted.

The woman's infinite future depended on this single performance. Tears seemed like a worthy strategy. She wept and begged, dropping to her knees. Her skin split and the mortal blood flowed against the smooth stony ground, and every time she looked up she saw an ugly immortal dressed in that shiny garb, and every time she looked down again, the world seemed lost. No words could make this blunt, brute of a man accept her mind. No action or inaction would accomplish any good. Suddenly she was trying only to make herself worthy in the eyes of the other doomed souls, and that was the only reason she stood again, filling her body with pride, actively considering the merits of rushing the captain to see if she could bruise that awful face, if only for a moment or two.

Yet all that while, Pamir had a secret:

He had no intention of hurting anyone.

This was a tiny group. A captain of his rank had the clout to give each of them whatever he wished to give them. And later, if pressed by his superiors, Pamir could blame one or two colleagues for not adequately defending this useless wilderness. Really, the scope of this crime was laughably, pathetically tiny—a mild burden more than an epic mess, regardless what these bright terrified eyes believed.

Out of fear or born from wisdom, the woman didn't assault him.

Then the captain reached into a pocket on his uniform.

The object hadn't been brought by chance. Pamir came with a plan and options, and eons later, novice captains would stand in their classroom, examining all the aspects of the captain's scheme.

Out from the pocket came his big hand, holding what resembled a sphere.

He explained, "This is a one hundred-and-forty-four faced die, diamond construction, tear-shaped weights for a rapid settling, each number carrying its own unique odds."

Luddite faces stared at the object.

Nobody spoke.

"I'm going to toss it high," said Pamir. "And then you, baby lady . . . you call out any number. And no, I won't let you look at the die first. You'll make your guess, and you will almost certainly lose. But then again, as you understand full well, any fraction of the endless is endless. And regardless of my toss, an infinite number of you are going to win this game."

Swallowing, the woman discovered a thin smile.

"And if I am right?" she asked.

"You stay here. And your people stay here. The entire cavern is granted to you, under my authority. But you aren't allowed to steal power from our reactors, and your water has to be bought on the common markets, and you will be responsible for your food and your mouths, and if you overpopulate this space, the famines and plagues will rest on your little shoulders.

"Is that understood?" he asked.

Everybody nodded, and everybody had hope.

But when Pamir threw the die, the girl offered the most unlikely number.

"One," she shouted.

One was riding on the equator, opposite 144—the smallest facets on the diamond face.

Up went the die.

And then was down, rattling softly as it struck, bouncing and rolling, slowing as sandals and boots and urgent voices pulled out of the way.

Looking at the number was a formality.

The cave would soon be empty and dark.

Yet odd as it seemed, Pamir wasn't particularly surprised to find the simplest number on top, in plain view: As inevitable as every result must be.

6

Reaching with a nexus, Pamir discovered an elaborate star chart waiting for him. The galaxy was stuffed inside a digital bottle, the nearest million suns translated into human terms and human clocks. At the center was the Kajjas ship—a long dumbbell-shaped body with a severely battered shield at one end, the pulse engine and drained fuel tanks behind. Its hull was slathered with black veneers and stealth poxes and what looked like the remnants of scaffolding. The captains never spotted this relic; too many light-years lay between their telescopes and this cold wisp of nothing. Even the Great Ship was too distant to deserve any size—the core of a jovian world rendered as a simple golden vector. Sixty years had been invested reaching the Kajjas vessel, and home was receding every moment. Hypothetical courses waited to be studied. Pamir gave them enough of a look to understand the timetables, and then he seasoned the quiet with a few rich curses.

A second nexus linked him to this ship's real-time schematics. Blue highlights showed areas of concern. An ocean's worth of blue was spread across the armored, badly splintered prow. High-velocity impacts had done their worst. Judging by ancient patches, smart hands had once competently fixed the troubles. But then those hands stopped working—a million years ago, or twenty million years ago. Since then the machine had faithfully chased a line that began in the deepest, emptiest space, only recently slicing its way across the Milky Way.

Pamir referred back at the star chart, discovering that it was far larger than he assumed. The blackness and the stars encompassed the Local Group of galaxies, and some patches were thoroughly charted.

A quiet, respectful curse seemed in order.

A small streakship was tethered to the dumbbell's middle. Pamir knew the vessel. It arrived at Port Beta in lousy shape, where it was rehabbed but never rechristened. Someone higher ranking than the mechanics decided that nothing would make the vessel safe, which was when the high-end wreck was dragged inside a back berth, waiting for an appropriately desperate buyer.

Tailor.

Pamir warmed the air with blasphemies and moved on to the manifests.

And all along, the Kajjas had been watching him.

"I remember a different boy," the alien said. "You aren't the polite, good-natured infant with whom I drank."

"That boy got strangled and packed up like cargo."

"Each of us flew in hibernation," said Tailor. "There was no extra space, no room for indulgences. I was very much like you."

Pamir cursed a fourth time, invoking Kajjas anatomy.

The alien reacted with silence, every eye fixed on the angry mechanic.

"Your streakship is tiny and spent," Pamir said. "Something half again better than this, and we could have strapped this artifact on its back and used those young engines to carry us home quickly."

"Except our financing was poor," said Tailor.

"No shit."

"We have rich options," said Tailor. "We will use our remaining fuel and then carve up the streakship like a sweet meat, dropping its pieces through the pulse engine."

"With a troop of robots, that's easy work," Pamir said.

Tailor remained silent.

"Only you neglected to bring any robots, didn't you?"

"Worthy reasons are in play."

"I doubt that."

The other humans were watching the conversation from a safe distance.

"So why?" asked Pamir. "Why is this fossil so important?"

Two eyes went pale.

"You're going to tell me," the human said.

"Unless I already have, Jon. I explained, but you chose not to hear me."

Scornful laughter chased away the quiet, and then Pamir turned his attentions elsewhere. The manifest was full of news, good and otherwise. "At least you spent big for tools and fuel."

"They were important," the alien said.

Pamir chewed his tongue, tasting blood.

"I am asking for your expert opinion," said Tailor. "Can we meet our goals and return to the Ship?"

"There is an answer, but I damn well don't know it."

"You aren't the boy with whom I drank."

Pamir said nothing.

"Perhaps I should have cultivated that boy's help at the outset," said Tailor. "He could have plotted my course and devised my methods too."

"That would have been smart."

Tailor showed his plate-like teeth, implying concern. "I cannot help but notice, sir. You have been studying our ships and vectors, but you have barely paid attention to either engine."

"Engines aren't the worst problem."

"But your specialty is the drive machinery," said Tailor. "That should be your first concern. Instinct alone should put your eyes and mind on those elements, not the state of a hull that has survived quite well on its own."

Pamir looked away. The other humans looked confident, relaxed, flashing little smiles when they whispered to one another. Maxx and Rondie did most of the whispering. G'lene floated apart from the others, and she smiled the most.

"Are they supposed to help me?" Pamir asked.

"Each will be useful, yes," said Taylor. "The twins are general starship mechanics, and they have other training too."

"I don't recognize them. They haven't worked near Beta."

Silence.

"So they must be from a different port, different background. Probably military. Soldiers love to be strong, even if their bulk gets in the way."

Tailor started to reply.

"Also, I see six thousand kilos that's blue-black on the manifest," Pamir continued. "You're not letting me see this. But since indulgences were left behind, the mass is important. So I'll guess that we're talking about weapons."

"I will admit one truth to you, Jon. About you, sir, I have a feeling."

"Is that feeling cold blue dread?"

Iron clawed against iron. "There never was a boy, it occurs to me. I think that you are somewhat older than your name claims, and maybe, just perhaps, we have met each other in the past."

"Who's the enemy?" Pamir asked.

"If only I knew that answer," the alien began.

Then Tailor said nothing more, turning and leaping far away.

7

Forty-four thousand years was a sliver of time. The galaxy had moved only in little ways since people dared slip inside Where-Peace-Rains, and nothing inside but the least stubborn, most trivial details had changed within the cave. The same genetics and honored language were in play. Stock beliefs continued to prosper. And there was still a round expanse of cool red granite where the captain had once played one round of chance, the stone dished in at the middle by generations of worshippers and their mortal feet.

Of course there were many more faces, and there was far less peace. Following the terms of the ancient agreement, archaics produced their own power and clean water and rough, edible foodstuffs. Carefully invested funds had allowed them to purchase a scrap star-drive—an ugly-eight reconfigured to generate electricity, not thrust. The drive was set on the cavern floor, not a thousand meters from the holy place where a chunk of diamond determined the world. The machinery was designed to run forever without interruption, provided that it was maintained regularly. And the ugly-eight had run for thousands of years without trouble. But it was being used in an unusual capacity, and not all of its wastes were bottled up. Lead plates and hyperfiber offered shielding, but the occasional neutron and gamma blast found ways to escape, and the childless men working nearby were prone to murderous cancers.

One engineer had worked fifty years in the most critical job in the world. A bachelor named Jon, he was still holding out hope that the tumor in his liver could be cut out of him, and then smarter, friendlier radiations would have a fighting chance to kill the cancers that had broken loose.

Jon lived inside a small apartment within walking distance of the reactor.

Everyone in Where-Peace-Rains lived in a small apartment, and everyone lived close to their important places.

Jon arrived home early. The foreman told him that he looked especially tired and needed to sleep, and Jon had agreed with the prognosis. Nothing felt unusual when he arrived. A key worn smooth by his fingers went into the lock, and the lock gave way with a solid click. But as the door swung inwards, he smelled a stranger, and a strange voice spoke out of the darkness.

"Just be aware," it said. "You're not alone."

Robberies weren't uncommon in the world, and sometimes thieves turned violent. But this was no robbery. The intruder was sitting in Jon's best chair, the seat reserved for guests. The human was relaxed enough to appear lazy. That was the first quality Jon noticed as the room's single light came on. The second detail was the man's appearance, which was substantial, and the beautiful face, even and clean-shaven. His clothes looked like the garb worn by fancy hikers and novice explorers who occasionally passed through the local caverns. Some of those people asked to come inside the archaic community. A few of the immortal passengers were intrigued by archaics, and the best of the interlopers left behind money and little favors.

But there were bad immortals too. They came for one reason, to coax people out of their home, out into the true world—as if one place was truer than another, and as if a person could simply choose his life.

"I let myself in," the stranger said.

Jon took off the daily dosage badge. "You want something," he guessed.

"Yes, I do."

"From me."

"Absolutely, yes."

Nuclear engineers earned respectable salaries, but nobody in this world was wealthy. Jon's fanciest possession was an old ceramic teapot, precious to him because it had been in his family for three thousand years.

The stranger was surely older than the pot.

Stories came back to Jon, unlikely and probably crazy stories. He had never believed such things could involve him, but when he met the man's blue eyes, something passed between them. Suddenly they had an understanding, the beginnings of a relationship. Jon found himself nodding. He knew what this was. "You think that I am dying," he said.

"You are dying."

"But how could you know?"

The immortal shifted his weight, perhaps a little uncomfortable with the subject. Or maybe quite a lot was balanced on the next moments, and he was making his rump ready for whatever Fate saw fit to throw at them.

"I've seen your doctor's files," the man said. "She tells you that you might survive to the end of the year, but I know she's being generous."

Jon had sensed as much. Yet it hurt to hear the news. A new burden, massive and acidic, was burning through his frail, middle-aged body.

He dropped into his own chair.

"I'm sorry," said the man.

Maybe he was sorry, because he sounded earnest.

"You want my life," Jon said.

The pretty face watched him, and after a moment he said, "Maybe."

"Why maybe?"

"Or if you'd rather, I'll pay for your treatments elsewhere."

"I can't abandon Peace," said Jon. "And even if I did, your doctors and your autodocs can't legally cure me."

"Cancer is not the problem," the man said. "I am talking about full treatments. I'm ready to give you that gift, if you want it. Leave your realm and live forever anywhere you want inside the Great Ship, inside the endless universe . . . except for here . . . "

"No."

Did Jon think before answering? He wasn't sure.

But giving the offer serious consideration, he said, "Never, no."

"Good," the stranger said.

Jon leaned forward. The room was small and the chairs were close together, and now they were close enough to kiss. "Are you wearing a mask?"

"Not much of one, if you can see it," said the man, laughing.

"You want my life," Jon repeated.

"Apparently you don't want to hold onto it. Why shouldn't I ask the question?"

They sat and stared at one another. Next door, a newborn was starting to feel her empty stomach, and her cry quickly built until there was no other sound in the world.

Suddenly she fell silent, her mouth full of nipple.

Jon thought about that mother's fine brown nipple. Then he wasn't thinking about anything, waiting for whatever happened next.

Out from a hiker's pocket came a weapon—a sleek gun designed by alien hands. "Except it's not a gun," the man explained. "In my realm, this is a camper's torch and portable grill. For me, the worst burns would heal inside an hour. But the torch can transform ninety kilos of your flesh and bone into a fine white ash, and I can place your remains in whatever garden or sewage plant you want on my way out of town."

Jon stared at the alien machine.

The man dropped it into Jon's lap, and then he sat back.

Its weight was a surprise. The machine was more like a sketch of a weapon, lightweight to the brink of unreal.

"I won't use the tool on you," the stranger promised. "You'll have to use it on yourself."

"No."

Did he think that time?

Jon hadn't, and after hard deliberation, he said, "Maybe."

"And for your trouble," the man began.

He stopped talking.

"I would want something," Jon said.

Not only did his companion have an offer waiting, he knew everything about Jon's living family. Nuclear technicians didn't dare make babies, what with mutations and cancers and the genuine fear that their sons and sons-in-law would follow them into this grim business. But he had siblings and cousins and a dozen nephews, plus even more nieces. Accepting this illegal arrangement meant that each limb of his family would receive enough extra money, dressed up in various excuses, and their lives would noticeably improve.

Jon passed the fierce machine from one hand to the other.

What looked like a trigger was begging to be tugged.

"No, not like that," the man said, patiently but not patiently. Something in this business was bothering him. "And when you do it, if you do it," he said, "stand in the middle of the room. We don't want to set a wall on fire."

Jon considered standing and then didn't.

The man watched him, weighing him, probably using an outsider's magic as well as his eyes.

"It's not enough," Jon said at last.

"It probably isn't," the man agreed.

"If I do this, you walk out of here with my life. Is that what happens?"

"Yes."

"So this isn't nearly enough. Everybody that I will think . . . they'll have no choice but believe . . . that I abandoned them and our cause . . . "

"That can't be helped," the man said. "It sucks, but what other way is there?"

Jon studied the machine once more.

"I picked you and just you," said the man. "Nobody else fits my needs. And sure, yes, the others will be free to tell themselves that you got weak and gave up. But you know that won't be true, and I'll live forever knowing that it wasn't true. And besides, when I give up this life of yours, I can send a confession back here. I'll tell them that you died in your home. Hell, if you want, I can tell the world that I murdered you, which will sure make everybody smile."

Jon started to hand back the alien hardware.

He paused.

The stranger reached up, and in one sloppy motion he tore off the mask, revealing a new face, a genuine face. It was Jon's face, rendered completely— the washed-out, hollow-eyed face already halfway to ash.

"Now I have one more gift, if you want it," said the man.

"What is that?"

"I'll tell you who I am."

Jon shrugged. "What do I care? Your real name doesn't matter."

Reaching into a pocket, his tormentor and salvation brought out a diamond with one hundred and forty-four faces.

Jon jumped up, and then he nearly keeled over, fainting. The alien machine hit the dirty carpet, humming for a moment, leaving an arc of charred fiber.

"Careful," said the one-time captain.

"Let me hold it," Jon said.

The man placed the diamond into his palm and closed the hand around it. The immortal's flesh was exactly as cool and sick as Jon's flesh, which was another wonderful detail.

"Is this the same die?" Jon asked.

"No, that trinket got left behind long ago," Pamir said.

Inspiration came to the dying man. Forcing the diamond into the fugitive's hand, he said, "Throw it. Or roll it. Pick your number either way, and if she stands on top, I will do whatever you want."

Pamir closed his hand.

He breathed once, deeply.

"No, I played that game once," the lost captain said, and with that he dropped the diamond back into his pocket. "I'm done letting chance run free."

8

Three hours of sleep and the humans were sharing the day's first meal. Tailor wasn't with them. Since boarding on the fossil ship, the alien had spent most of his time cuddling with a distant control panel, trying to coax the sovereigns into saying one coherent word. But despite ample power and reassuring noise, the AIs remained lost, crazy or rotted and probably gone forever.

G'lene felt sorry for the old beast, chasing what wasn't there.

And that was where her empathy ended. Like most aliens, the Kajjas man was a mystery and always would be. She accepted that fact. Dwelling on what refused to make sense was senseless. What G'lene cared about, deeply and forever, were human beings. That was true onboard the Great Ship, and her desires were even more urgent here in the wilderness.

But her three human companions were burdens, odd and vexing, usually worse than useless. The twins never stopped whispering in each other's ears.

They went so far as creating their own language, and deciphering their private words was a grave insult. Yet despite their vaunted closeness, they did nothing sexual. With a defiant tone, Rondie claimed that sex was an instinct best thrown aside. "That's what my brother did, and I did, and you should too." Preaching to a woman who couldn't imagine any day without some lustful fun, the muscle-bound creature said, "Each of us would be stronger and five times happier if we gave up every useless habit."

G'lene was entitled to feel sorry about her loneliness. That's why she kept smiling at Jon, the Luddite. She smiled at him one hundred times every day. Not that it helped, no. But he was the only possibility in a miserably poor field, and she reasoned that eventually, after another year or maybe a decade, she would wear some kind of hole in his cold resolve.

This was Jon's third breakfast as a living crewmember.

G'lene smiled as always, no hope in her heart. Yet this morning proved to be different. The odd homely conundrum of a man suddenly noticed her expression. At least he met her eyes, answering with what might have been the slyest grin that had ever been tossed her way.

She laughed, daring to ask, "Are you in a good mood, Jon?"

"I am," he said. "I'm in a lovely, spectacular mood."

"Why's that?"

"Last night, I realized something very important."

"Something good, I hope."

"It is. And do want to you know what my epiphany was?"

"Tell it," she said, one hand scratching between her breasts.

But then Jon said, "No," and his eyes wandered. "I don't think that you really do want to know."

G'lene knew thousands of people, but this Luddite was the most bizarre creature, human or otherwise.

The twins were sharing their breakfast from the same squeeze-bowl. They stopped eating to laugh with the same voice, and then Rondie said, "Give up the game, dear. That boy doesn't want you."

What a wicked chain of words to throw at anyone.

"But you can tell us your epiphany," Maxx said.

Jon glanced at the twins.

G'lene felt uneasy in so many ways, and she had no hope guessing why.

Tipping her head, Rondie said, "Whisper your insight inside my ear. I promise I won't share it with anyone."

Her brother gave a hard snort, underscoring her lie.

"No, I think I should tell everyone," said Jon. "But first, I want to hear a confession from you two. Which one of you strangled me?"

Maxx laughed, lifting a big hand.

But his sister grabbed his arm, bracing her feet inside the glass strands before flinging him aside. "No, I'm quieter, and I have the better grip. So I did it. I broke your little neck."

Jon nodded, and then he glanced at G'lene.

"All right, that's done," G'lene said. "What's the revelation?"

"Starting now," said Jon, "we are changing priorities."

"Priorities," Maxx repeated, as if his tongue wanted to play with the word.

"You've been spending your last few days assembling weapons," Jon said to the twins. "That crap has to stop."

Similar faces wore identical expressions, puzzled and amused but not yet angry.

"Our enemies won't arrive inside a starship," said Jon. "Unless I'm wrong, and then I doubt that we could offer much of a fight."

"Our enemies," Maxx repeated.

"Do you know who they are?" G'lene asked.

Jon shook his head. "I don't. Do any of you?"

Nobody spoke.

Jon teased a glob of meal-and-milk from his breakfast orb, spinning the treat before flicking it straight into his mouth.

The ordinary gesture was odd, though G'lene couldn't quite see why.

"Tailor claims that we have to be ready for an attack," said Jon. "Except our sovereign isn't particularly forthcoming about when and where that might happen. His orders tell us nothing specific, and that's why they tell us plenty. For instance, this crazy old wreck is worth nothing, which means that it's carrying something worth huge risks and lousy odds."

The twins didn't look at each other. Thinking the same thoughts, they glanced at G'lene, and she tried to offer a good worried smile. And because it sounded a little bit reasonable, she said, "That Kajjas is so old and so strange. I just assumed that he's just a little paranoid. Isn't that what happens after millions of years?"

"My experience," said Jon. "It doesn't take nearly that long."

"You want to change priorities," Rondie said, steering the subject.

"Change them how?" Maxx asked.

"Forget munitions and normal warfare," said the Luddite. "We have one clear job, and that's to finish loading the fuel and dismantling the streakship. Its entire mass has to be ready to burn, when the time comes."

"That would be crazy," said Maxx. "If you can't get the pulse engine firing, then the other ship becomes our lifeboat."

"Except we aren't going to fly any streakship," said Jon. "Streakships are brilliant and very steady and we love them because of it. But if we have enemies, then they'll spot us at a distance, and believe me, streakships are easy targets.

On the other hand, the Kajjas pulse engine is a miserable mess full of surges and little failures. Teaching us will be a very difficult proposition. And that's why today, in another ten minutes, I want the two of you to start mapping the minimum cuts to make that other ship into a useable corpse."

"But you promised," said Maxx. "Our enemies aren't coming inside a warship."

"What I promised is that we can't beat them if they do come. We don't have the munitions or armor to offer any kind of fight. My little epiphany, for what it's worth, is that our foes, if they are real, will have one of two strategies: They don't want anybody to have this ship or its cargo, which means they destroy us out here, in deep space. In which case, boarding parties are a waste. Or they want to have whatever we have here, and that's why we have to make ourselves a lousy target."

Rondie scoffed. "Again, we know nothing."

"Or there's nothing worth knowing," G'lene added.

"Physics and tactics," Jon said. "I see our advantages as well as our weaknesses, which is why my plan is best."

"Impressive," said Maxx with a mocking tone, one leg kicking him a little closer to Jon.

G'lene didn't like anybody's face. Where was Tailor? In the distance, hands and long feet working at a bank of controls—controls that hadn't been used since she was a broth of scattered DNA running in the trees, waiting for mutations and the feeble tiny chance to become human.

Jon's gaze was fixed in the middle of the threesome.

"You know quite a lot for a simple drive-mechanic," Maxx said.

"Simple can be good." Jon winked at that empty spot of air. "Now ask yourselves this: Why did our captain hire children?"

"We're not children," Rondie said.

Maxx said.

But G'lene sighed, admitting, "I wondered that too."

"Real or imagined, Tailor's enemy is treacherous," said Jon. "Our Kajjas wants youth. He brought only humans, which is a very young species. And he wants humans that aren't more than a thousand years old, give or take. That way he could study our entire lives, proving to his satisfaction that we aren't more than we seem to be."

"I'm not a little girl," said Rondie.

"You're not," Maxx said.

But Jon was a thousand and the siblings weren't even five centuries old, making them the babies in this odd group.

G'lene watched the angry faces and Jon's face, alert but weirdly calm. Then she noticed the twins' sticky breakfast floating free of its orb. G'lene was born on the Great Ship. Everybody had been. This was their first genuine experience with zero-gee, and she hated it. Without weight, everything small got lost inside the same careless moment, and she didn't know how to move without thinking, and she wasn't moving now, remembering how the Luddite so easily, so deftly, made that bite of his breakfast spin and drift into his waiting mouth.

Jon had been in zero gravity before this.

When?

She nearly asked. But then Maxx said, "I'm going back to work. Plasma guns need to be secured and powered up."

"No, you're not," said Jon.

Rondie kicked closer to the Luddite, hands flexing. "Who put you in charge?" she asked.

"Life," Jon said.

Everybody laughed at him.

But then he asked, "Do you know what I did last night? While you slept, I changed the pass-codes on every gun. Nothing warms an egg without my blessing."

The twins cursed.

Jon shrugged and said, "By the way, I've convinced our human-built AIs that the only voice of reason here is me. Me."

The twins wrapped some brutal words around, "Luddite," and "mutiny."

The mysterious human showed them nothing. He didn't brace for war or smile at his victory. The milky water from a glacier was warmer and far more impatient. Then the twins' anger finally ebbed, and Jon looked at G'lene. Again, from somewhere, he found the sly grin that unsettled her once more. But it also had a way of making her confident, which she liked.

"You never were a Luddite," she blurted.

Jon didn't seem to notice. "Sleep is an indulgence," he told everyone. "We're working hard and smart from this instant, and we'll launch eighteen days earlier than you originally planned. Everybody can sleep, but only when we're roaring back to the Great Ship."

"You're somebody else entirely," she said. "Who are you?"

"I'm Jon, the drive-mechanic," he told them. "And I'm Jon, the temporary captain of this fossil ship.

"Everything else is electrons bouncing inside a box."

9

The field kitchen had no trouble generating propanol and cyanide, and for that matter, spitting out passable rum—an archaic drink that Pamir had grown fond of. What was difficult was finding the moment when the ship's new captain and the Kajjas could drink without interruption. The streakship was being gutted and sliced up, each piece secured against the scaffolding on the old ship's hull. Pamir's three-body crew was working with an absence of passion, but they were working. When everything was going well enough, he offered some calibrated excuse about his lifesuit malfunctioning. Then alone, he slipped back inside the long interior room, grabbing the refreshments and joining Tailor, drifting before that bank of murmuring and glowing, deeply uncooperative machines.

"For you, my sovereign," said the human, handing over a bulb of poison.

The Kajjas was fondling the interfaces, using hands and bare toes, using touch and ears. But his eyes were mist and dream, and the long neck held the head back in a careless fashion that hinted at deep anguish.

The bulb drifted beside him, unnoticed.

Pamir cracked his bulb, sipping the liquor as he waited.

Then the eyes cleared, but Tailor continued to stare into the machinery.

"I have two questions," said the human.

"And I have many," the Kajjas said. "Too many."

" 'The army is one body masquerading as many,' " Pamir quoted. " 'You are at war with one puzzle, and it just seems like a multitude.' "

"Whose expression is that?"

"Harum-scarums use it," Pamir said.

"I know a few harum-scarums," said Tailor. "They are a spectacularly successful species."

"You should have hired them, not us."

"Perhaps I should have."

Pamir sipped the rum again.

"I'm not oblivious, blind or stupid," the alien said. "I understand that you have taken control of my ship and its future."

"Your plans were weak, and I did what was necessary. Do you approve?"

"Have I contested this change?"

"Here is your chance," said Pamir.

Tailor steered the conversation back where it began. "You wish to ask two questions."

"Yes."

Tailor claimed the other bulb, sipping deeply. "You wish to know if I am making progress."

"I don't care," Pamir said.

"You are lying."

"I have a talent in that realm."

Iron crashed against iron, leaving the air ringing. "Well, I am enjoying some small successes. According to the rough evidence, this is a cargo vessel transporting something precious. But the various boxes and likely cavities are empty, and the sovereigns' language began ancient and then changed over time, and meanwhile these machines have descended into codes or madness, or both."

"How old are you?" Pamir asked.

The Kajjas' three eyes were clear as gin, and each one reached deep inside the head, allowing light to pour into a shared cavity where images danced within a tangle of lenses and mirrors, modern neurons and tissues older than either species.

"You have posed that question before," Tailor said. "You've asked more than once, if my instincts are true."

Pamir confessed how many times they had met over drinks.

"Goodness." Laughter followed, and a sip. "I have noticed. You are suddenly acting and sounding like a captain. Maybe that was one of your disguises, long ago."

"There was no disguise," he said. "I was a fine captain."

"Or there was, and you were fooled as well."

Pamir liked the idea. He didn't believe it, but the meme found life inside him, cloying and frightening and sure to linger.

"I'm a few centuries older than ninety-three million years," Tailor said. "And while I can't claim to have walked your earth, I have known souls—Kajjas and other species—who saw your dinosaurs stomping about on your sandy beaches."

"Lucky souls."

The Kajjas preferred to say nothing.

"I'm waking our engine tomorrow," Pamir said.

"According to your own schedule, that's far too soon."

"It is. But I've decided that we can fly and cut apart the streakship at the same time. We'll use our hydrogen stocks until they're nine-tenths gone, and then we'll throw machine parts down the engine's mouth."

"Butchering the other ship will be hard work, under acceleration."

"Which brings me to my second question: Will you help my crew do the essential labor?"

"And give my important work its sleep," Tailor said.

"Unless you can do both at once."

The mouth opened to speak, but then it closed again, saying nothing as two eyes clouded over.

Pamir finished his drink, the bulb flattened in his hand.

Tailor spoke. Or rather, his translator absorbed the soft musical utterances, creating human words and human emotions that struggled to match what could never be duplicated. Honest translations were mythical beasts. On its best day, communication was a sloppy game, and Pamir was lucky to know what anyone meant, including himself.

"This starship," said the alien. "It is older than me."

"How do you know?"

"There are no markings, no designations. I have looked, but there is no trace of any name. Yet the ship is identical to vessels built while my sun was far outside the galaxy. Those ships were designed for the longest voyages that we could envision, and then they were improved beyond what was imaginable. They had one mission. They were to carry brave and very patient crews into the void, out beyond where anyone goes, in an effort to discover our galaxy's sovereigns."

"Our galaxy's sovereigns," Pamir repeated. "I don't understand."

"But the concept is obvious."

"Someone rules the galaxy?"

"Of course someone does."

"And how does leaving the galaxy prove anything?"

"That's a third question," Tailor pointed out.

"It's your query, not mine. Not once in my life have I ever thought that way."

"And which life is that?"

"Talk," said Pamir.

"Onboard your Great Ship, I once met a Vozzen historian of considerable age and endless learning. The two of us spent months discussing the oldest species of intelligent life, those bold first examples of technological civilizations, and what caused each to lose its grip on Forever and die away. The historian's mind was larger and far wiser than mine. I admit as much. But you can appreciate how the same principles are at work inside both of us, and inside you. The bioceramic mind is the standard for civilized worlds. It was devised early, and several founding worlds have been given credit, although none of them exist anymore. And since the mind's introduction into the galaxy, no one has managed more than incremental improvements on its near-perfection."

"The brain works," said Pamir.

"One basic design is shared by twenty million species. Of course intellect and souls and the colors of our emotions vary widely, even inside the human animal. At first look and after long thought, one might come to the conclusion that it is as you say: We have what's best, and there isn't any reason to look farther."

"We don't look farther," Pamir agreed.

"Humans don't. But the Kajjas once did. That is point: Our nameless fleet was buried inside a great frozen dwarf world, every pulse engine blazing, driving that shrinking world toward our Second Eye, your Andromeda. The survivors of that epic were under orders to investigate what kind of minds those natives employed, and if another, perhaps worthier mind was found, the fleet would return home immediately.

"At the very most," said Tailor, "that mission would have demanded eight million years. I was born near the end of that period, and I spent my youth foolishly watched for those heroes to return and enlighten us. But they did not appear, even as an EM whisper. Ten and twenty and then fifty million passed, yet just by their absence, much was learned. We assumed that they were dead and the ships were lost, or the explorers had pushed farther into the void, seeking more difficult answers.

"Few civilizations ever attempt such wonders. I have always believed that, and the Vozzen happily agreed with my assessment.

"Don't you find that puzzling? Intriguing? Wrong? The resources of a galaxy in hand, and few of us ever attempt such a voyage.

"But my brethren did. And afterward, living inside my galaxy, I have tried my best to answer the same questions. It is the burden and blessing of being Kajjas: Each of us knows that he rules only so much, and every ruler has worthy masters of his own, wherever they might hide."

"Sovereigns to the galaxy," said Pamir, his voice sharpening.

"You don't believe in them," Tailor said.

"Have you found them?"

"Everywhere, and nowhere. Yes." The laugh was brief, accompanied by a sad murmuring from the translator. "Everywhere that I travel, there are rumors of deeds that claim no father, legends of creatures that wear any face and any voice. There is even talk about invisible worlds and hidden realms, conspiracies and favored species and species that diminish and succumb to no good opponent.

"About our masters, I have little to say. Except that they terrify me, and because I am Kajjas, I wish that I could lie between their mighty feet and beg for some little place at their table."

Pamir had too many questions to ask or even care about. His crew was noticing his absence. One nexus rewarded him with a string of obscenities from the twins, and with those words, promises to turn him over to the Great Ship's captains as soon as they arrived home.

It was no secret that Pamir could hear them, and Rondie and Maxx didn't care.

And all that while, G'lene said nothing.

"Suddenly," said Tailor, almost shouting the word.

"What?"

"Just two million years ago, suddenly and with the barest of warnings, our old fleet began to return home."

Pamir nodded, and waited.

"The ships appeared as individuals. I won't explain how a person might know in advance where such a derelict will show itself, but there is a pattern and we have insights, and there have been some little successes in finding them before anyone else. The crews are always missing. Dead, we presume. But 'missing' is a larger, finer word. Empty ships return like raindrops, scattered and almost unnoticed, and their AIs are near death, and nothing is learned, and sometimes tragic events find the salvage teams that come out to meet these relics."

"Your enemies strike," Pamir said.

"Yet disaster isn't certain," the alien said. "That might imply that there are no masters of the galaxy. Or it means that they are the ultimate masters, and better than us, they know what is and is not a threat to their powers."

Pamir drifted closer, placing his body in a submissive pose.

Long feet pulled away from the display panel, surrounding the human head. "The old fleet had one additional command," Tailor said. "If no equal or at least different mind could be found in the wilderness, then the Kajjas had to assemble at some sunless world, preferably a large moon stirred by a brown dwarf sun, and there, free of interference and ordinary thoughts, our finest minds would build a colony. Then in that nameless place, they and their offspring would kill preconceptions and create something else."

"They were to build a different way of thinking, yes.

"And that is what they were to send home, however they could and in the safest way possible."

Approximating the Kajjas language, the human said, "Shit."

Tailor stroked the panel with one hand, watching a thousand shades of blue swirl into fancy shapes that collapsed as soon as the fingers lifted. "I don't know this language," he said. "It is older than me and full of odd terms, and maybe it has been corrupted. There are fine reasons to believe that there is no meaning inside these machines. But it is possible, weak as the chance seems, that the truth stands before me, and my ordinary mind, and yours, are simply unable to see what is."

The alien was insane, Pamir hoped.

The hand released the display, and Tailor said, "Yes."

"Yes what?"

"I will help make the ship ready for flight. Obviously, nothing I do here can be confused for good."

• • •

10

A brick of metallic hydrogen plunged into the first collar, the widest collar, missing the perfect center by the width of a small cold atom. Compression accompanied the hard kick of acceleration, and then a second collar grabbed hold, flinging it through ten of its brothers. Neutronium wire wrapped inside high-grade hyperfiber made the choke points, each smaller and more massive than the ones before, and the cycle continued down to where the brick was burning like a sun—a searing finger of dense plasma that still needed one last inspiration to become useful, reliable fuel.

Pulse engines relied on that final collar of degenerate matter. From outside, the structure looked like a ceramic bottle shaped by artisan hands—a broad-mouthed bottle where it began and then tapering to a point that magically dispensed the ultimate wine. Plasma flowed into the bottle's interior, clinging to every surface while being squeezed. But what was smooth to the eye was vast and intricately shaped at the picometer scale—valleys and whorls, high peaks and sudden holes. Turbulence yielded eddies. The birth of the universe was replicated in tiny realms, and quantum madness took hold. Casimir fields and antiproton production triggered a lovely apocalypse that ended with the obliteration of mass and a majestic blast of light and focused neutrinos.

Then the next moment arrived, bringing another brick of hydrogen.

Twelve thousand and five bricks arrived in order. There were no disasters, but the yields proved fickle. Then the ship's captain killed the engine, invoking several wise reasons for recertifying a control system that was, despite millions of years of sleep, running astonishingly well.

But who knew what a healthy pulse engine could accomplish?

The human captain wasn't sure, and he confessed that loudly, often and without any fear of looking stupid.

Pamir had settled into a pattern. His nameless ship would accelerate hard, pushing at four gees for ten minutes or three days. Bodies ached. Muscles grew in response to the false weight. Then they would coast for a few minutes or for an hour, except the time they drifted for a week, every easy trajectory slipping out of reach.

The ship's sovereigns must have done this good work once, but they remained uncooperative. The streakship's AIs had been salvaged to serve as autopilots, but they weren't confident of their abilities. Pamir gave his crew reasons that wanted to be believed. He offered technical terms and faked various solutions that were intended to leave the children scared of this ancient, miserably unhappy contraption. Tailor required a bit more honesty, and that was why the captain invoked the Kajjas' faceless enemies. Pamir explained that he didn't want other eyes knowing where they would be tomorrow and thirty years from now. "The wounded bandelmoth is hunted by a flock of ravenous tangles," Pamir explained. "The moth flies a quick but utterly random course, letting chance help fend off the inevitable."

"Why not tell the others what you tell me?" the Kajjas asked. "Why invent noise about 'damned stuck valves' and 'damned chaotic flows'?"

"I don't trust my crew," he said flatly.

The Kajjas tapped one foot, agreeing with the sentiment.

"If our children thought they could fly home, they might try it."

"But what I wish to know: Do you have faith in our new captain?"

"More than I have in the rest of you," Pamir said. "I don't believe what you believe, old friend. Not about the galaxy's mysterious rulers. Not about the peculiar sameness of our brains. Not about mysterious foes diving out of the darkness to kill us."

"I believe quite a lot more than that," Tailor said.

"Of course our enemy could be more treacherous than you can imagine. For example, maybe toxic memes have taken control over me, and that's why I took charge of this primordial ship."

"I hope that isn't the case," said the Kajjas.

"And I'll share that wish, or I'll pretend to."

"And what's your impression of Tailor?"

Pamir shrugged. "The ancient boy dances with some bold thoughts. He sounds brave and a little wise, and on his best days profound. But really, I consider him to be the dodgiest suspect of all."

"Then we do agree," said Tailor. "I trust none of us."

They laughed for a moment, quietly, without pleasure.

"But again," Pamir concluded. "I don't accept your galactic sovereigns. Except when I make myself believe in them, and even then, I always fall back on the lesson that every drive-mechanic understands."

"Which lesson?"

"A reliable star-drive doesn't count every hydrogen atom. The machinery doesn't need to know the locations of every proton and electron. No engineer, sane or pretending to be, would design any engine that attempts to control every element inside its fire. And for all of their chaos and all of their precision, star-drives are far simpler than any corner of the galaxy.

"Maybe I'm wrong. You're right, and some grand game is being played with the Milky Way and all of us. But you and I, my friend: We are two atoms of hydrogen, if that. And no engine worth building cares about our tiny, tiny fates."

Robots could have been trusted with this work, if someone brought them and trained them and then insulated each of them from clever enemies. No, maybe it was better that the crew did everything. They worked through the boost phases, and they picked up their pace during the intervals of free fall. G'lene was the weakest: Clad in an armored lifesuit, suffering from the gees, she could do little more than secure herself to the hull's scaffolding, slicing away at the scrap parts set directly in front of her. Complaining was a crucial part of her days, and she spent a lot of air and imagination sharing her epic miseries. By comparison, the twins were stoic soldiers who reveled in their strength, finding excuses to race one another between workstations and back to the airlock at the end of the day. But Tailor proved to be the marvel, the prize. The Kajjas world was more massive than the earth, but his innate physical power didn't explain his dependability or the polish of his efforts. Pamir told him what needed to be cut and into what shapes and where the shards needed to be stored, and looking at the captain as his sovereign, he never grumbled, and every mistake was his own.

One day, Tailors' shop torch burped and burnt away his leg. He reacted with silence, sealing the wound with the same flame before dragging himself inside, stripping out of the lifesuit and eating one of the bottled feasts kept beside the airlock, waiting to supercharge any healings.

"Captains have a solemn duty," the twins joked afterwards. "They should sacrifice the same as their crew."

"Yeah, well, my leg stays on," said Pamir.

The laughter was nearly convincing.

Two years were spent slowly dismantling the streakship. Every shard of baryonic matter had been shaped and put away, waiting to be shoved down the engine's throat after the hydrogen was spent. The only task left was to carve up the streakship's armored prow. Better than hydrogen, better than any flavor of baryonic matter, a slender smooth blade of hyperfiber would ignore compression and heat, fighting death until its instantaneous collapse and a jolt of irresistible power. But hyperfiber was a better fuel in mathematics than it was in reality, subject to wildness and catastrophic failure—a measure waiting for desperate times.

Shop torches were too weak. Sculpting hyperfiber meant deploying one of their plasma guns. Pamir ordered his crew to remaining indoors, the humans maintaining the lights and atmosphere while Tailor was free to return to his obsessions. For five months, Pamir began every day by passing through the airlock to wake a single gun. A block of armor was fixed into a vice, waiting to be carved into as many slips of fuel as possible. The work lasted until his nerves were shot. Then the gun had to be secured, and he crawled back inside the ship. G'lene always threw a smile at him. The twins pretended to ignore him, their curses still echoing in the bright air. Tailor was muttering to the sovereigns or searching for cargoes that didn't exist, or he did nothing but sit and think. Pamir needed to sit and think. But first he had to kick his way to the engine, attacking its inevitable troubles.

When the sixth month began, the twins stopped cursing him.

Even worse, they started to smile. They called him, "Sir," and without prompting, they did their duties. One evening Rondie was pleasant, almost charming, grinning when she said that she knew that his jobs were difficult and she was thankful, like everyone, for his help and good sense.

Pamir wasn't sure what to believe, and so he believed everything.

Tailor continued fighting with the sovereigns.

"I have a verdict," he said one day.

"And that is?" asked Pamir.

"These machines are not insane. They pretend madness to protect something from someone. And the problem is that they won't tell me what either might be."

"Can you break through?"

"If I was as wise as my ancestors, I would, yes." The Kajjas laughed. "So I am convinced and a little thankful that I never will be."

Three years and a month had passed since their launch, the voyage barely begun. Pamir shook himself out of a forty minute nap, ate a quick breakfast and then donned a lifesuit that needed repairs. But the hyperfiber harvest would end in another nine days, and the suit was still serviceable. So alone, he trudged through the airlock and onto a gangway. The plasma gun was locked where he had left it six hours ago. The gun welcomed him with a diagnostic feed, and while it was charging, Pamir used three nexuses to watch the interior. The twins were sleeping. G'lene was studying a mechanic's text, boredom driving her toward competency. And Tailor was staring into a display panel, trying to guess the minds of his ancestors.

Sensors were scattered around the huge cabin. Some were hidden, others obvious. And a few were self-guided, wandering in random pathways that would surprise everyone, including the captain who let them roam.

The peace had held for months.

But Pamir had been strangled and packed away with the luggage, and every day, without fail, he considered the smart clean solution to his worries. Three minutes, and the problem would be finished, with minimal fuss.

Kill the crew before they killed him.

Temporarily murder them, of course.

But those cold solutions had to be avoided. Despite temptations, he clung to the idea that kindness and compassion were the paths to prove your sanity.

Everybody seemed to hold that opinion. G'lene still flirted with the only available man. Maxx offered to drink heavily with his friend Jon, once his hard work was done. And just last week, his sister tried defining herself to this tyrannical captain: Rondie and her brother shared very weak but wealthy parents. They had wanted strong children. Genes were tweaked, giving both of them muscles and strong attitudes. Rondie said that she was beautiful even if nobody else thought so. She said that her parents had wisely kept their wealth away from their children, which was why they joined the military. And then in the next breath, the girl confessed to hating those two ageless shits for being so wise and looking out for their souls.

At that point she laughed. Pamir couldn't tell at whom.

He said, "In parts of the multiverse, both of you are weak and happy."

"A Luddite perspective," she said.

"It is," he agreed.

"Who are you really?" she asked.

"I'm you in some other realm."

"What does that mean?"

"Think," he said, liking the notion then and liking it more as he let it percolate inside his old mind.

That was a good day, and so far this day had proved ordinary.

The twins slept but that didn't keep them from conversing—secret words bouncing between each other's dreams. Tailor was on a high platform, muttering old words that his translator didn't understand. G'lene was the quiet one. She studied. She fell asleep. Then she was awake and reading again, and that was when the pulse engine fell silent.

Pamir lifted from the gangway. Then he caught himself and strapped his body down, focusing on the white-hot shard of hyperfiber before him.

The airlock opened.

He didn't notice.

Three average people, working in concert, could easily outthink the weary fugitive. Pamir saw nothing except what his eyes saw and what the compromised sensors fed to him. The twins slept, and while studying, G'lene played with herself. Pamir looked away, but not because of politeness. At this point, those other bodies were as familiar and forgettable as his. No, his eyes and focus returned to the brilliant slip of hyperfiber that had almost, almost achieved perfection.

From a distant part of the cabin, Tailor called out.

The shout was a warning, or he was giving orders. Or maybe this was just another old word trying to subvert the security system, and it didn't matter in the end.

The ex-soldiers had cobbled together several shop torches, creating two weak plasma guns. The first blast struck Pamir in his left arm, and then he had no arm. But Maxx had responsibility for the captain's right arm, and the boy tried too hard to save the plasma gun. Wounded, Pamir spun as the second blue-white blast peeled back the lifesuit's skin, scorching his shoulder but leaving his right hand and elbow alive.

Quietly and deliberately, Pamir aimed with care and then fired.

Charged and capable, his weapon could have melted the ship's flank. But it was set for small jobs, and killing two muscular humans was a very small thing.

The first blast hit Rondie in her middle, legs separating from her arms and chest. Cooked blood exploded into the frigid vacuum while the big pieces scattered. Maxx dove into the blood cloud to hide, and he fired his gun before it could charge again, accomplishing nothing but showing the universe where he was hiding.

Pamir turned two arms into ash and a gold-white light.

But where was G'lene?

Pamir spun and called out, and then he foolishly tried to kick free of the gangway. But he forgot the tie-downs. Clumsier than any bouncing ball, he lurched in one direction and dropped again, and G'lene shot him with a series of kinetic charges. Lifesuits were built to withstand high-velocity impacts, but the homemade bullets had hyperfiber jackets tapering to needles that pierced the suit's skin, bits of tungsten and iron diving inside the man's flailing sorry body.

The plasma gun left Pamir's grip, spinning as it fled the gangway.

A woman emerged from shadow, first leaping for the gun and securing it. She was crying, and she was laughing. The worst possibilities had been avoided, but she still had the grim duty of retrieving body parts. The plasmas hadn't touched the twins' heads, and they remained conscious, flinging out insults in their private language, even as their severed pieces turned calm, legs and organs and one lost hand saving their energies for an assortment of futures.

G'lene grabbed Maxx first, sobbing as she tied the severed legs to his chest.

Rondie said, "Leave," and then, "Him."

"You're next," G'lene promised.

"No no look," Rondie muttered.

Too late, the crying woman turned.

Every lifesuit glove was covered with high-grade hyperfiber. Pamir was holding his own dead limb with living fingers, using those dead fingers like a hot pad. That was how he could control the slip of hyperfiber that he had been carving on. A kiss from the radiant hyperfiber was enough to cut the tie-downs that secured him, and then he leaped at G'lene. The crude blade was hotter than any sun. He jabbed it at her belly, aiming for the biggest seam, missing once and then planting his boots while shoving harder, searing heat and his fine wild panic helping to punch the beginnings of a hole into the paper-thin armor.

G'lene begged for understanding, not mercy, and she let go of body parts, trying to recover her own weapon.

Pamir shoved again, and he screamed, and the blade vanished inside the woman.

Flesh cooked, and G'lene wailed.

He let her suffer. With his flesh roaring in misery, Pamir set to work tying down body parts and weapons. All the while the girl's round body was swelling, the fire inside turning flesh into gas, and then empathy stopped him. He finally removed her helmet, the last scream emerging as ice, the round face freezing just before a geyser of superheated vapor erupted out of her belly.

"You had some role," Pamir said.

They were sharing a small platform tucked just beneath the ship's prow. The alien had been crawling through an access portal where nothing had ever been stowed. The glass threads had pulled together, building the platform that looked like happy red grass. Pamir hated that color just now. The alien's eyes were clear, and he didn't pretend to look anywhere but at the battered, mostly-killed human.

"Each of us has a role," Tailor said.

"You helped them," said the captain.

"Never," he said.

"Or you carefully avoided helping, but you neglected to warn me."

"I could have done more," the creature admitted. "But why are you distressed? They intended a short death for you, just long enough for you to reconsider."

Every situation had options. The captain's first job was to sweep away the weakest options.

What remained was grim.

"I should kill you too," he said.

"Can you fly this ship alone?"

"It's an experiment that I am willing to run."

Tailor had fewer options, and only one was reasonable. "Secure me," he said. "Each day, please, you can tie me to one place. I'll work where you trap me. If I can go nowhere, what harm do I pose?"

"What if you talk to the sovereigns? You could turn them against me."

"Or you can separate their influences with the ship," the Kajjas said. "Feed them power, of course. But please, let this conundrum have its way with me."

"No."

The three eyes went opaque, blind.

"No," Pamir repeated.

"You once said something important," Tailor said.

"Once?"

"I overheard you. When you came back to life the last time, you were talking to the children. You claimed that there was a reason why youthful souls interested me."

"Young minds can't hide secrets," Pamir said.

"But that isn't their major benefit." Iron knives struck one another inside that long throat. "Just finding the treasure may not be enough. A young mind, unburnished and willing, often proves more receptive to mystery."

"And to madness," Pamir said.

Tailor let one eye clear. "Whoever you are, you hold a strong mind."

"Thank you," Pamir said.

"On the whole," said the Kajjas, "I believe that strength is our universe's most overprized trait."

11

Of course there were sovereigns. Pamir always knew that. The sovereigns were vast and relentless, and they were immortal, and he knew their faces: The kings of vacuum and energy, and their invincible children, time and distance. Those were the masters of everything. Their stubborn uncharitable sense of the possible and the never-can-be was what ruled the Creation. All the rest of the players were little souls and grand thoughts, and that was the way it would always be.

The Great Ship was obeying the kings. It remained no better than a point, a conjecture, crossing one hundred thousand kilometers every second. Reaching the Ship was life's only purpose. Pamir thought of little else. The human-made AIs thought of nothing else. The hydrogen had been consumed until only a thin reserve remained, and then the streakship's corpse was thrown to oblivion, each bit unique in shape and composition. Calculations demanded to be made. Adjustments never ended. Slivers of a cabin wall exploded differently than the plumbing ripped out of fuel pump, and while the Kajjas engine ate each gladly, there was sloppiness, and sometimes the magic would fail, leading to silence as the nameless ship once again began to drift.

Every day had its sick machines.

No week was finished without the engine dying unexpectedly, ruining the latest trajectory.

Anyone less competent than Pamir would have been defeated. Anyone more talented would have known better and given up in this idiot venture on the first day. A soul less proud or more clear-headed would have happily aimed for one of the solar systems on the Kajjas' charts—a living place that would accept the relic starship and two alien species of peculiar backgrounds. But Pamir clung to his stations, and the AIs found new solutions after every hiccup, while Tailor filled his lucid moments moving from platform to cubbyhole, talking to the madness.

Several decades of furious work brought them halfway home.

And then the engine was silenced on purpose, and their ship was given half a roll, preparing to slow its momentum before intercepting the Great Ship.

"You have to pay attention to me," said Tailor.

Pamir was in earshot, barely. But his companion was talking to himself, or nobody.

"I see your stares," the Kajjas said.

Pamir ignored him. From this point on, they had even less play in their trajectories and the remaining time. The Great Ship was swift, but the Kajjas ship had acquired nearly twice its velocity. Very few equations would gently drop them into the berth at Port Beta, while trillions of others shot them ahead the Great Ship, or behind.

"Do you hear me?" Tailor asked.

Yes, but Pamir pressed on. His companion was another one of the thousand tasks that he could avoid for the time being, and maybe always. What the captain needed to do next was prepare a test-firing of the hyperfiber fuel, and the fuel feeds begged to be recalibrated, and one of his AIs had developed an aversion to an essential algorithm, and he hadn't eaten his fill in three days, and meanwhile the small, inadequate telescopes riding the prow had to be physically carried to the stern and fixed to new positions so that they could look ahead, eating the photons and neutrinos that never stopped raining and never told him enough.

Eating was the first priority.

Pamir was finishing a huge meal when the first note of a warning bell arrived, followed immediately by two others.

Those bells were announcing intruders.

Pamir made himself enjoy his dessert, a slab of buttery janusian baklava, and then, keeping his paranoia in check, he examined the data and first interpretations. The half-roll had revealed a different sky. The telescopes had spotted three distinct objects traversing local space. None were going to collide with Pamir, yet each could well have been aimed at this ship while it moved on an earlier tangent. Each was plainly artificial. The smaller two were the most distant, plunging from different directions, visible only because they were using their star-drives. Measuring masses and those fires, Pamir guessed about likely owners. An enormous coincidence was at hand, three strangers appearing at the perfect place for an attack. The roll-over left him predictable, exposed. It would be smart to conjure up a useful dose of fear. But the fear didn't come. Pamir wasn't calm, and he couldn't recall the last time when he was happy. But he wasn't properly worried either. A thousand ships could be lurking nearby, each with their engines off—invisible midges following his every possible course. But that possibility didn't scare him. His heartbeat refused to spike, right up until the nearest vessel suddenly unleashed a long burn.

Their neighbor was a huge, top-of-the-line streakship, and if Pamir followed the best available trajectory, that luxury ship and his own thumping heart would soon pass within twenty million kilometers of one another.

But the heart was quiet, and Pamir knew why: The universe did not care about him, or this relic, or even crazy old Tailor.

A loud transmission arrived thirteen hours later, straight from the streakship. In various languages and in data, its owners were named as well as the noble species onboard, both by number and their accumulated wealth. Then a synthetic voice asked for Pamir's identity, and with words designed to sound friendly to as many species as possible, it asked if the two of them were perhaps heading toward the same destination? "Are we joining on the Great Ship together, my lovely friend?"

Pamir invented new lies, but he didn't use them. Instead, he identified himself as Human Jon. With his own weary voice, he explained that this was a salvage operation and he was alone, and his ship was little better than a bomb. That's why he kept trying to maneuver out from the path of others. Invoking decency, he decided to delay his test firings, watching the interloper, wondering what it would do in response.

Devoted to its own course, the other voice wished him nothing but the best and soon blasted into the lead.

And three weeks later, the streakship's central engine went wrong. Containment failed or some piece of interstellar trash pierced the various armors. Either way, the universe was suddenly filled with one spectacular light, piercing and relentless, along with the wistful glow from a million distant suns.

Pamir knew a thousand sentient species well enough to gather with them, drinking and eating with them, absorbing natures and histories and the good jokes while sharing just enough of his blood and carefully crafted past. Bioceramic minds didn't merely absorb memories. They organized the past well enough that sixty thousand years later, a bored man doing routine work could hear the song from a right-talisman harp and the clink of heavy glasses kissing each other, and with the mind's eye he saw the face of the most peculiar creature sitting across from him: A withered face defined by crooked teeth and scars, fissures where the skin sagged and sharp bones where muscle had once lived.

That Pamir was younger than many captains, while his companion was a fraction his age and probably no more than ten years from death. She was as human as Pamir, though he had trouble seeing her that way. Archaics living on the stormy shore of the Holiday Seas had sent delegates to meet with this captain. These citizens were to come to terms on tiny matters of babies and fees paid for those babies, and where their people could travel, and where the other passengers could not.

Pamir already possessed the famous snarl.

"You're stranger to me than most aliens," said the novice captain, finishing his first Mist-of-Tears. "If I try, I understand an extraterrestrial's thought process. But if I look at you and try to figure you out, I get tangled. I end up wanting to scream."

The archaic was drinking rum. Maybe it was the taste in the old woman's mouth, or maybe it was his words. Or perhaps she enjoyed the music coming from an exotic instrument. Whatever the reason, she offered a smile, and then looking down at the swirling dark liquor, she told the glass, "Scream. You won't hurt my feelings."

"You're dying. Right in front of me, you are dying."

The grin lifted. "And you feel for me, how dear."

"A hundred years isn't enough time." Pamir wouldn't scream, but he couldn't sit comfortably either. "I know what you people believe, and it's crazy. Religious scared mad foolish shit-for-brains crazy."

"I'm one hundred and forty years-old," she said with her slow, careful voice. Then after a weirdly flirtatious wink, she added, "I personally believe in modest genetic engineering, ensuring good health and a swift decline at the end."

"Good for you," he said.

She sipped and said nothing.

The young captain ordered another round. Their bartender was a harum-scarum, gigantic, covered with scales and spines and a sour-temper, ready to battle any patron who gave her any excuse. Pamir felt closer and much warmer toward that creature than he did to the frail beast beside him.

"There is another way for you," he told her.

A little curious, the old woman looked at him.

"Employ limited bioceramic hardware. A single thread is all that you'd need. Thinner than a hair, planted deep inside that fatty organ of yours, and you could spend one hundred and forty years learning everything quickly and remembering all of it. Then you'd die, just like you want, and your family could have their funeral. A ceremony, an ornate spectacle, and your grandchildren could chop the implant out of your skull. Maybe they could pretend it was a treasure. Wouldn't that be nice? They can drop your intellect into a special bottle and set it on some noble high shelf, and if they ever needed your opinion, about anything, they could bring you down for a chat. That's the better way to live like a primitive."

Cheerfully, almost giggling, the old woman said "I am not a Luddite."

Pamir hadn't used the word, and he didn't intend to use it now.

" 'Archaic' isn't an adequate word either," she said.

"What's the best word?" he asked.

"Human," she said instantly, without hesitation or doubt.

Pamir snorted and leaned forward, wondering if this unfriendly back-and-forth was going to help their negotiations. Probably not, he decided. Oh well, he decided. "If that's what you are, what am I?" he asked.

"A machine," she said.

He leaned back, hard. "Bullshit."

The old woman shrugged and smiled wistfully.

"Is that the word you use? When we're not present, do you call us cyborgs?"

With a constant, unnerving cheeriness, she said, "Cyborgs are partly human, and you are not. Your minds, and your flesh, and the basic nature of your bones and brains: Everything about you is an elaborate manifestation of gears and electrical currents with just enough masquerading in place to keep you ignorant of your own nature."

"I don't like you," said the young captain.

"Try the rum," she said.

He played with the mirrored hat on his head.

Then she said, "But as you helpfully pointed out, I shouldn't be around much longer. So really, what can my opinion weigh?"

Theory claimed that hyperfiber would make a potent fuel. But every theory involved modeling and various flavors of mathematics and usually a fair share of hope. Truth demanded tests, which was why Pamir dropped a single blade of fuel into the ship's mouth. And when the engine survived that experiment, he sent in three others, followed by a hundred more closely-packed slivers.

The old model proved wildly pessimistic.

Yields were at the high end of predictions, and more importantly, each explosion was set inside a tiny piece of time. Brutal kicks passed through the Kajjas ship. Plasmas were spewed ahead, velocities pushing against light-speed, and Pamir let himself breathe while the AIs celebrated with party paradoxes and new models of annihilation, plus fresh crops of trajectories that took into account this unexpected power.

Pamir began slowing the ship with high-gee burns, randomly spaced, and despite premonitions for the worst, the old engine never complained.

Was this how the vanished Kajjas explored the far galaxies? Building hyperfiber only to burn it again?

Three months into the deceleration, the ship was in a coasting phase. Glass strands were pulled to the round cabin walls while Pamir worked on another recalibration. Space appeared normal, benign and cold and vast, and then suddenly an adjacent portion of space became hot. Distant lasers were firing on wandering comets and dust, and the nameless grit responded by boiling, turning to gas and wild ions. Within minutes, a billion cubic kilometers had been engulfed by a bright cobalt glow that looked lovely to the scared human eye.

The Kajjas was wearing smart-manacles and three watchdog sensors. The nearest display panel was busy, gold and mauve wrapped around symbols that looked like a genuine language. But Tailor was standing apart from every machine, closely watching something in one hand, something quite small. Pamir had to call his name several times to be noticed.

The clear eyes rose, and the alien called out, "This is a wondrous day."

"But not especially pleasant," said Pamir. "Somebody is shooting at us, and now I'm starting to believe you."

"Then this day is even better," the creature proclaimed.

A single strand of red glass was dangling from his hand. At a distance and even up close, it looked like every other stalk of fake grass.

Pamir didn't ask about glass or symbols.

"I'm here to warn you," was all that he had time to say. "We're still aiming for the Great Ship. I'm not giving that up. But no sane predictable brain would ever try it this way."

12

Modern bodies didn't easily rot.

Trillions of bacteria lived inside the guts and pores, but they weren't simple beasts waiting for easy meals. Every microbe was a sophisticated warrior tailored to serve its host. Service meant protecting the flesh in life, and if that life was cut to pieces by a plasma blast, then the surviving trillions worked as one, fending off wild bacteria while pulling out the excess moisture, rendering the temporarily dead man as a collection of perfectly mummified pieces.

Even broken, Maxx was a tough looking fellow. Pamir gave the autodoc every chunk, every burnt shred, and he kept close tabs on the progress. Dried tissues were rehydrated and then fed. Stem cells cultured themselves, and they built what was missing, and two days later the growth chamber was filled to overflowing with a naked man, hairless and massive. An earthly gorilla would be proud of that body. Leaving Maxx trapped inside the chamber seemed wise, but there was little choice. Pamir opened the lid before the boy was ready to move, and he stood over him, starting to explain what he wanted.

Maxx interrupted. "Where's my sister?"

"She'll be next," the captain promised. "But only after you make a promise, or you lie well enough to fool me."

Too soon, Maxx tried to sit up.

Two fingers and a quiet, "Stay," were enough to coax him back down again.

"I was awake," the boy said. "When I was dead, I was thinking."

"Thinking about Rondie," Pamir guessed.

"Not always, no."

The words carried implications.

Pamir quickly explained what had happened since their fight and what might happen if they held the same conventional course. He said that he had considered using Tailor, but the alien was useless. An insight had infected him, and he was even crazier than usual. As a precaution, Pamir had limited his tools and chained him nearby.

Maxx glanced at the Kajjas.

Then with a slower voice, the captain laid out the basics of his mad plan.

Some part of Maxx listening. Yet more compelling matters had to be considered. The boy's voice was uneasy, shrill at the edges when he asked, "When will my sister be back?"

Rondie's remains were more numerous and in worse condition, and the autodoc was limited. "Six days, or with luck, five," he said.

"Take your time," Maxx advised.

Pamir said, "I don't do sloppy work."

"That isn't what I mean." Then with a shy smile, Maxx said, "I rather liked it, being alone."

"Solitude has its pleasures," Pamir said.

"Yeah, I promise, I'll do whatever you want me to do," said the resurrected man. "Just please, don't tell my sister what I just confessed to you."

The ship had rolled again, and denying every commonsense vector, it was once more accelerating, hard.

Pamir and Maxx were out of sight, out of reach. Tailor wore manacles and tethers, and an ordinary tool kit was in easy reach. Standing took too much work. Against the thundering engine, it was better to sit deep in the grassy glass. The drill lay between his feet, recharging itself. Five times, the Kajjas had ordered the drill to cut a single precise hole, and then with his own trembling hands, he fed one of the treasures into the breach.

Momentous times, that's what these were. His species had labored for one hundred million years, searching for enlightenment. Tailor couldn't remember when he wasn't preparing for this day. And at long last, he broken every code and deciphered old, vanished technologies. No barriers remained. The magic had no choice but work, and that's what he was doing.

Five times he overrode the drill's safeties, coaxing a slender beam of high-UV light to evaporate his flesh and then his bone before eating slowly, carefully into the living template of his mind.

Each hole was perfect.

Into each hole went one of the rare treasures.

During the first four attempts, he emptied his mind of thought, making ready for lightning and epiphanies. Tailor was relaxed and rested, fortunate beyond all measure, thinking about nothing, ready to be seized by truth in whatever serene form it came. And something did happen. Four times, there were sensations, the painful roiling of electrons that became familiar and intense to a point where much more was promised . . . and then the intensity slackened and slipped, nothing remaining but the residues one endures when rising from a deep, perishable dream.

On the fifth attempt, Tailor changed tactics.

He purposefully thought about quite a lot. Perhaps engaging old memories would open the necessary gateway. Who knew? That's why he built lost rooms in his head, and why he spoke to family members who were dead or so distant that they might as well be. He recalled his first journey in space and his first new sun, and buried inside that flood of old, rarely-touched remembrance he discovered a nameless world, watery and deliciously warm but not available to colonize. Why was that? Because there were rules, yes. Supposedly the galaxy had no sovereigns, but the rising civilizations, young and otherwise, had carved laws and punishments out of the potential. This wet world was too promising to be claimed. The furry souls hiding inside their burrows and up on the high tree branches held promise—just enough of this and not too much of that—and their world was stable enough to survive comet blasts and the next half billion years. That was why the Kajjas scout team was just visiting. It had already been decided to move to another nearby solar system, harsher and far more promising.

Tailor couldn't remember when he last thought about that world.

It might have been the human homeland. Who would know? The galaxy never stopped moving, suns marching in every direction. Certainty would take work and patience, and he didn't have either to spare.

He considered calling to Jon. This memory would be a gift.

But the scorching laser had burrowed deep into his mind, much deeper than the others, and the fifth thread had to be eased into position and then sealed in place. Tailor accomplished both tasks with fingers and a torch. The thread only looked like the red glass. Years had been spent walking on the cargo, sleeping with it and ignoring it, and he never suspected: One strand in eight million was glass on the outside, mimicking their mates, but it was bioceramic at the core. Each core employed an architecture that was nothing like the standard mind. How it worked was just another mystery. Tailor had found six odd threads already, there were probably several hundred more, and this thread was inside him and talking to his soul, bringing nothing but pain, pure simple dumb pain, as the brain felt the grievous injury, more and more of his ancient memories thrown to oblivion.

Tailor dipped his head, and the translator transformed his noble sobs into sick human sobs.

All the while, their nameless ship was filled with motion, with purpose. The invincible engine was eating hyperfiber and shitting out the remnants. And Jon and Maxx were far away, making ready for the last portion of this desperate scheme.

Despair was a shroud, and through the shroud came a human voice.

"What are you doing?" she asked.

"Healing," the Kajjas said.

The new patient was lying inside the growth chamber. The autodoc had lifted its lid, allowing her flesh to grow while she breathed freely.

Rondie turned onto her side.

With a paternal voice, the autodoc told its patient to do nothing but rest.

"Shut up," she said.

Tailor laughed, but not because of her.

"Where's my brother?" she asked.

"Helping our insane captain," he said. "Jon has decided to harvest our own ship's armor and employ it as fuel."

"No," she said.

"It is a strange tactic, yes," he said.

"I mean, why isn't Maxx with me?"

Looking at any human, looking at the beast deeply and with all of his experience, it often occurred to Tailor that each of these creatures was a species onto herself. "Human" was just a convenience applied to a pack of disagreeable, dissimilar fur-bearers.

"You look strong," he said.

She said, "I'm feeling better."

"Wonderful," he said. "Can you climb out of that device now?"

Rondie was exceptionally powerful. Even unfinished, she sat up easily and the naked legs came out without much trouble. But death had made her cautious, and she moved slowly until an alarm sounded, the autodoc trying to coax her to behave with nothing but loud, brash sounds.

She jumped free and slapped the controls, earning silence.

"Come here," Tailor said.

Five slivers were inside him, and he had no idea what enlightenments they were carrying.

"When will my Maxx come back?" she asked.

Tailor said, "Come here and I will call your brother."

She took slow steps against the thundering of the engine. "So our bastard captain tied you down," she said, looking at the manacles and tethers.

"This is a verdict which I deserved and embraced." Then he reached with one hand and a foot, which was a blunder.

Rondie stopped, keeping out of his reach.

"You look as if you're hurting," she said.

"A few wounds, yes. But the mind is durable and profound, and I will heal soon enough."

"I'm going to get dressed," she said. "I want to find Maxx."

"But first," said Tailor.

She stared at him, waiting.

"G'lene is waiting inside the box, that packing crate lying just past the autodoc." The sixth thread felt light and cool in his palm and between his long fingers. "Would you unpack G'lene for me, please?"

"Let the bastard cure her."

"But I don't want you to feed her to the autodoc," he said. "No, I very much want the girl for myself. And I have a good reason, if that matters."

She shrugged, absolutely unmotivated.

"If you did this," he said, "the Luddite will be exceptionally angry with you. I promise."

"Okay," she allowed.

And as she walked toward the boxes, Tailor called out, "If it is easier, you may cut off the head. I desire nothing else."

13

The mad plan was to burn up their original fuel stocks in order to bring them home on a short vector. All that while, they would carve away a portion of the ship's prow, holding back those shards for later. If they survived the boost phase, the ship would be rolled again at the last possible moment, and then the engine's muscle and endurance would be severely tested. Hyperfiber would be shoved into oblivion and expelled before them—a long spike of plasma and radiations slicing through the blackness. Every local eye would see their arrival, and that was part of Pamir's scheme: If someone tried to kill this ship, it would be a loud public act, a revealing act. If some secret power was at large, it would surely prefer to settle this matter in more private ways.

Pamir had explained his plan, and to one degree or another, the others accepted his rule if not his logic. Besides, everyone knew that they were far off course, and at this velocity and in this place, there was simply no other route home.

Every hand was needed. The original crew was at work, infuriating yet predictable. But now a second crew shared the ship with them. The twins could follow their usual script, sometimes for a full day or two. But then the boy suddenly begged to be left alone, please. Except his sister came out of death lonely, famished for more touches than ever and private words known only to her and maybe even the first stirrings of lust for the only object of value in her brief life.

The Kajjas remained the ancient puzzle. Freed of manacles and his studies, Tailor helped slice apart the least critical portions of the ship's armor. But without warning, he would suddenly turn fearless, risking millions of years of existence by stepping onto the open prow. Grains of dust would explode on all sides while he did nothing but sing, throwing old songs into the vacuum, eyes gazing up at the blue-shifted starlight that fell inside his joyous soul.

Even Pamir was two people. Long habit and the ingrained personality usually held him where he belonged—a blunt strong-willed soul that could sleep minutes every day and push three day's work into two. He ruled a minor realm inside the boundless universe governed by faceless, amoral laws. Those laws were too powerful and too perfect to give a shit about little him, and wasn't that the least awful existence imaginable?

But the other Pamir, the new man, was much less certain about everything.

Invisible, potent sovereigns held sway over the galaxy. Except in Pamir's mind, they weren't Kajjas sovereigns. They wore the faces and attitudes of captains. They were bold opinionated creatures looking splendid in their bright uniforms, each one ambitious, each a rival to all of the others, and somewhere there sat a world-sized Master Captain holding a godly feast every million years, just to prove to her nervous self that she was genuinely in charge.

The imagery had its charms, its humor.

Laughing, he could deny everything. One senile alien from a vanquished race was not much of an authority, and there were explanations waiting to be invoked. Their ship was nothing but a derelict, and its sovereigns were crazy, and nothing here was worth two drops of blood or any reputation. Those bits of glass that Tailor found were just that. They were glass. The alien had installed them, and what changed about him? The new boldness was nothing but Tailor's anguish for a thoroughly wasted life. The streakship following them was one mild coincidence, and its detonation was another. And that final attack—the wild flash of laser light—was just some local species running experiments in deep space, or a factory ionizing the dust to harvest it, or maybe someone was trying to kill them. But what did that mean? There were endless reasons to destroy another ship, and saving the universe for the sovereigns was far down on the list.

Wild thoughts kept running where they wanted inside the captain's exhausted mind. But he suppressed the worst of them, and he learned to ring the humor out of the paranoia and push on.

But whatever his burdens, G'lene's were immeasurably worse.

Through his nexuses, Pamir had watched Rondie cut the woman's head off of her boiled corpse. Then she handed the head to Tailor, and he watched what Tailor did with that gift. But the prow was far away and the high-gee acceleration had to be maintained. It took only minutes to carve a fresh hole into G'lene's mind, and then the final thread—one last piece of glass—was implanted.

Change the time or change the circumstances, and Pamir would not have brought her back to life. Better autodocs onboard the Great Ship would repair the damaged intellect first. But he needed G'lene's hands, her back. He fit the surviving pieces inside the growth chamber, and they remembered their original self, knitting together and building connections, swelling with water and fat until the girl emerged on schedule, seemingly unharmed.

Pamir didn't tell her about the rough surgery. As far as he could see, nobody else mentioned it either. The inserted glass had done nothing to change the girl's complaining attitude, and she still had bouts of laziness. But there was a quiet that had gotten inside her and wouldn't let her free. She stopped flirting, and more alarming, she stopped masturbating too.

Dreaming, she wept.

Awake, the girl used her nexuses for most peculiar functions. Everybody was near the prow, everybody carving hyperfiber, but her attentions were focused on textbooks and general how-to files. She used to fitfully study. Now she acted focused if not happy. She said that she was the same, by feeling and by thought, except she had a sudden passion for stardrives and the ships that surrounded those engines. Pamir asked why. Everyone asked. Explaining herself, G'lene claimed that she had to think about something while she was dead. Contemplating her life seemed reasonable. And in the darkness, she told herself: "Quit making a mess of your existence and do your damned work."

It was easy to accept the girl's reasoning. Pamir took the role of tutor, if only to keep close tabs on her progress. Each month, G'lene researched a different drive, exhausting its basics before trying to master some subsystem that other drive-mechanics found cumbersome or boring. She wasn't notably smarter than before, and her memory was no sharper. She would still be one of the weakest students in any class. But G'lene was focusing her skills on rockets and power sources, and the months became several years, and then suddenly, without comment, she quit accessing the texts and manuals.

Pamir mentioned the change.

The girl shrugged and finished polishing the latest slip of hyperfiber. Then she stepped away, saying, "I realized. I'll never be good doing your job."

"No?"

With a slow, untroubled voice, she said, "If we survive this, I will quit the program."

Her captain had ever seen her make any smart choice, until now.

During those intense years, their ship ate the last of its hydrogen stocks and the final bits of the streakship guts, and then most the streakship's hyperfiber was tossed into oblivion. No invisible hand tried to murder them. No truly vital system failed. The ship's huge prow was degraded, pierced with tunnels and little caverns, and several lumps of comet ice managed to punch deep. But the frame remained sound, and the engine was in fair shape when they gave it one fast rest, and as the slow final roll-over began, the captain decided that this was the moment when their ship deserved to finally wear some kind of name.

He let Tailor master the honor.

A moment of consideration led to a Kajjas phrase—an honored term meaning wisdom and deep, profound sanity. Then with a most respectful voice, the translator said, "Precious Mental."

They wrote that name on various bare surfaces, in a thousand distinct languages.

"I don't know this tongue," G'lene said.

She was reading over Pamir's shoulder. "The language is mine," he said. "It's the dialect we use inside Where-Peace-Rains."

She touched the lettering, and a painful murmur came out of her.

"I've been watching you," he said.

"All of you keep staring at me."

"Do you know why?"

"Because you're worried."

"There's a lot to worry about," he said.

She tried to leave.

"Stay here," he said.

"Is that an order?"

"If it keeps you here, it is." Pamir didn't want to touch her, but a hand to the shoulder seemed important. Then he forgot that he was holding her, saying, "I know what you're studying now."

"You know everything," she said, bristling slightly.

"Mathematics," he said.

"Yes."

"But not just any numbers," Pamir said. "You're dabbling with the big, scary conundrums, the old problems about existence and the shape of the universe."

"Yes," she said.

He kept quiet, waiting.

"What's wrong with that?" she asked.

"Why are you?" he asked.

She shrugged. "I've also developed a taste for poetry."

"Bleak poems about death," he said. "Yeah, I'm eavesdropping. Each of us is worried about you, G'lene."

"Including me."

He waited for a long moment. Then he quietly asked, "What happened? When you were dead in the box, what happened?"

"I thought about you," she said calmly. "I could have killed you on the gangway, and you could have killed me. Again and again, I relived all of that. And then at the end, just before you put me inside the autodoc—just before the darkness broke—this idea came to me. From the middle of my regrets and stupidity, it came."

"What idea?"

She shook her head.

"Tell me," Pamir insisted.

She looked at her captain and then at the archaic words—white lines smoothly drawn across a coal-black housing. "Have you ever noticed, sir? There are so many ways to push a ship across space. Dozens of engines are popular, and thousands have been tried at least once. But most of us wear the same basic brain. And shouldn't thought be more important than action?"

"Is that your epiphany?" he asked.

"No," she said. "That's me wishing that my brain was smarter."

He nodded, weighing his next words.

But then she pushed aside her doubts. "I was alive but only barely, trapped inside a room without light or ends," she said. "I was thinking about you, Jon. You're not the person that you pretend to be. You're no Luddite or drive-mechanic, but you're doing a very fine job of pretending.

"And then all of the sudden, out of nowhere, I thought: 'What if everyone is the same as Jon?

" 'What if everything is that way?

" 'Not just people, but the universe?' I thought. 'What if everything we see and everything we know is one grand lie, an extraordinary mask, and waiting behind the mask is something else entirely?' "

• • •

14

The Great Ship was close enough to see and close enough to fear.

Approaching from behind, the Kajjas ship was tracing a rigorous line, a very peculiar line, and if nothing changed their tiny vessel would miss every Port and the emergency landing sites on the hull. If the pulse engine never fired, the five of them would pass in front of their home and continue onwards, eventually leaving the galaxy for places that not even Tailor's charts would show.

But if their engine ignited, a collision was possible. That's why they were studied, and that's why various voices called out to them. Captains demanded to know the ship's history and intentions. The Great Ship's best weapons were directed forwards, fending off lost moons and the like. But there was ample firepower on the backside, ready to eviscerate their little craft. Pamir assured his crew that crosshairs were locked on them, probably for some time. He also confessed that ignoring the first pleas was his strategy. Those captains needed to feel ignored, which made them worry. There was a tradition to command and rank and the corrosive strategies of those who wore the mirrored uniforms. Worry was what helped the five of them. A captain's responsibilities grew heavier when nobody was listening. And then at the ripe moment, Pamir told their audience a story—a sweet balance of truth and lie, pieces of it practiced for a thousand years.

Early on, Pamir had considered making a full confession.

But what would that help? A nervous captain might believe him too well, and smelling commendations, sprinkle the space between them with arrest warrants and nuclear mines.

No, he was still Jon. He was the drive-mechanic hired to bring home one lost ship. Playing to every bias held by those mirrored uniforms, he admitted that he was an idiot far from his native habitat. Taking no credit for himself, he thanked his AIs for finding this odd route home. Captains would always accept genius in machines before genius in a tool-bearing grunt. Then as the pivotal moment approached, Pamir added a long, faintly sentimental message aimed at his descendants wearing his blood and his name. And for no reason but that it felt true, he told Where-Peace-Rains that he was miserably sorry for his crime of living far too long.

The rest of Pamir's crew was in place, waiting. Each wore the best available lifesuit, and each suit was set on a tall bed of shock absorbers. Those beds would do almost nothing, and the glassy grass heaped around them was mostly for show. Gee-forces of this magnitude would kill most machines. Hyperfiber and bioceramics would survive, if barely. There was only the slenderest of room for error, but then again, as experienced showed, some guesses were pessimistic, and if you took a risk, sometimes the results were golden.

Pamir was inside his suit, securing himself to his bed.

Nearby, Rondie said private words to Maxx.

Her brother responded with silence.

Injured, she said his name twice, and then Maxx spoke out, but not to her. "So Jon," he said with a loud, clear voice. "For the record, what's your real name?"

He said it. For the first time in decades, he said, "Pamir," aloud, and then added, "If you survive and I survive, turn me in. There's going to be an ample reward."

The man laughed. "If I survive, that's the reward."

Mournfully, Rondie said, "Maxx."

"If we live, I mean," he said.

Then the twins were talking again, dancing with words devised in just the last few hours.

Tailor was closer to him, and G'lene was the closest.

"Thank you," said the Kajjas. "Without you, nothing ends properly."

Pamir made polite noise about helping hands and interesting conversations.

G'lene said nothing.

Pamir said her name.

Nothing.

He repeated the word, but with a captain's tone behind it.

She sniffed once, and then very quietly, almost sweetly, she admitted, "I can't get comfortable yet. How much longer will this be?"

Quite a lot occurred, most of it happening slowly.

And seven months later, a famous man returned to his childhood home.

Every citizen wanted to see him, but of course that was impossible. A lottery identified the luckiest few, and certain people of power bought slots or invented places for themselves, and of course there were cameras in position, feeding views to every apartment and tavern and even the hospital beds. The energy demands were enormous. The old stardrive was laboring at ninety percent capacity. But if anything should go wrong, some joked, at least they had an expert on hand who could fix the machine, probably with his eyes closed.

Yet despite fame and warm feelings, Jon sensed the doubts that came with the crowd. They were staring at a creature that had left their ranks long ago. Every face resembled his face, except he was something else. He was a machine. He was a monster and a traitor to the most suspicious ones, and Pamir was ready to admit as much to anyone who wanted to start a brawl.

"I'm not like you," he began. "And anymore, after everything, I don't know who I resemble."

The story they wanted was spectacular, and like most good stories, it was already known to everyone, here and throughout the Great Ship. So that's where Pamir began: He was a lump of tissue and fear inside a lifesuit, and following preprogrammed instructions, the Kajjas ship let loose with its one old engine. But unlike every other firing, there were no millisecond breaks between each sliver of fuel. Tons and tons of hyperfiber passed through the collars and out the magic wine bottle, and a blaze that rivaled the Great Ship's engines slowed their descent, twisting their motion into a course that could be adjusted only in the tiniest, most fractional ways.

The storyteller remembered nothing after the first damning jerk of the engine.

Encased inside hyperfiber, his body turned to mush and then split apart, dividing according to density. Teeth settled at the bottom of the suit, pulverized bits of bone laid over them. And floating on top was the water that began inside his body, inside his cells—a dirty brew distinctly unlike the stuff that ran out of pipes and that fell as rain, denser and stranger in a realm where gravity was thousands of times stronger than was right.

In the end, good wise captains were debating what to do about this unwelcomed piece of museum trash. Do they shoot it apart to be careful, or shoot it apart as a warning to whoever tried to repeat this maneuver? But Pamir had been very careful about his aim, and once his destination was assured, the argument ended. A few moments later, Precious Mental rode down on the last gasps of its engine, entering the centermost nozzle of the Ship's own rockets.

Each nozzle was impervious to these whiffs of heat and raw light.

Three kilometers off target, the old ship touched down and split wide, the debris field larger than the floor of this old cavern.

Jon was pulled from the rubble, his lifesuit cracked but intact.

Four more suits were found, but only two other survivors.

"My friend Tailor died," he told his audience. "And my very good friend G'lene was killed too. Their minds had recently undergone surgery. The nanofractures spread and grew, and everything shattered. Bioceramic is a wonderful substance, right up until it breaks. And nothing brings anyone back from that kind of damage."

His sadness was theirs. His grief and anguish made every face hurt. At that point, Pamir could have ended this chore. His plan was to walk out of this place and invent his death, using a stand-in body and fake damage from the crash landing. But the earnest smart watchful faces didn't want him to leave, and he didn't want solitude just now.

He was standing in the middle of the red granite round.

At the edge of the crowd was one young woman. She was Jon's relative. This many generations after his leaving, everybody was part of his family. And in her hand was a teapot that someone had remembered. Careful hands had taken it off its shelf and cleaned it up, and there was even cold tea inside, ready to be given in some little ceremony devised for this very peculiar occasion.

Pamir smelled the tea, and at that moment, for endless good reasons, he confessed.

No, he didn't name himself. Nor did he mention that his namesake died more than ten centuries ago. What he told them was the story that he had revealed only in pieces to the investigators and the overseeing captains. He told about Tailor's quest for enlightenment, and he described a fleet of exploratory ships racing out to neighboring galaxies. With minimal detail and words, he explained how the Kajjas was afraid of invisible sovereigns, and Jon admitted that he was temporarily sick with that fear, but then at the end, waiting for the engine to fire once more, he decided that there was no ground or heart to any of these wild speculations.

It took weeks for his pulverized body to be made into something living, and then into a man's shape, and finally into his old body.

After months of care, he was finally awake again. He was eating again. His attendant was a harum-scarum. The alien told him that two of his companions were sharing a room nearby, each a little farther in the healing than he was, and when the human asked about the other two, a grave sound emerged from the attendant's eating mouth. Then she explained that both had died instantly, and they had felt nothing, which was a sorry way to die, oblivious to the moment.

But his two wonderful friends had not died, of course.

In that bed, restrained by lousy health and the watchful eyes of doctors, Jon could suddenly see everything clearly. G'lene's own words came back to him. Why would the galaxy have a thousand stardrives but only one basic mind? And how can the thousand or ten thousand original civilizations all vanish together in the remote past? Why can't there be forces at work and different minds at work, hidden in myriad ways?

Jon paused.

Where-Peace-Rains listened to his silence.

He coughed weakly into a shaking fist, and the girl, urged by others, started forward with her offering of cold water infused with ordinary tea.

He stopped her.

"It's like this," he said. "If there are hidden captains, and in one measure or another they are steering our galaxy, then how can I deny the possibility—the distinct probability—that they would be naturally curious about some one hundred million year-old vessel that was getting washed up on our shore? Tailor believed that this mission was his, but that doesn't make it so. Maybe it never was. And in the end, our masters got exactly what they wanted, which was a viable sample of novel technologies, and with G'lene, a creature with whom they could talk to and perhaps learn from."

When did the man begin to cry?

Jon wasn't certain, but he was definitely crying now.

Encouragement was offered, and once again, the girl and the tea came forward. She had a nice smile. He had seen that same smile before, more than forty millennia ago. He was crying and then he had stopped crying, wiping his face dry with a sleeve, and he said to the girl, "Give me the pot. I want to hold, like old times."

She was happy to relinquish the chore.

But as she pulled back, she saw what was in her hands now. She felt the glass threads squirming of their own volition. Laughing nervously, she said, "What are these things?"

He offered his best guess.

Everybody wanted to see, including the cameras.

But he waved the others off, and then just to her, he muttered, "They could be a danger. G'lene had one inside her, and it made her halfway crazy. Tailor found several hundred more before we crashed, but on my own, on the sly, I found a few. I never told anybody, and that's five of them. You keep them. Put them somewhere safe, and give them to your next thousand generations. Please."

The girl nodded solemnly, putting the threads into her best pocket.

"What if?" he said.

"What if what, Jon?" she asked.

He sighed and nodded

"What if this brain of mine is designed to be stupid?" he asked. "What if the obvious and important can't be seen by me, or by anyone else?"

A sorrowful face made her prettier. She wasn't yet twenty, which was nothing. It was barely even born by the man's count. But after struggling for something to say—something kind or at least comforting—she touched the man with her cool little hand. "Maybe you're right," she said. "But when you talk about that poor friend of yours, the girl and her suffering . . . I wonder if perhaps there is no treachery, no conspiracy. Maybe it is a kindness, making all of you a little foolish.

"Letting you forget the awful truth about the universe.

"Isn't that what you do with children, lending them the peace that lets them sleep through their nights . . . ?"

THE TWO SISTERS IN EXILE

ALIETTE DE BODARD

In spite of her name (an elegant, whimsical female name which meant Perfumed Winter, and a reference to a long-dead poet), Nguyen Dong Huong was a warrior, first and foremost. She'd spent her entire life in skirmishes against the pale men, the feathered clans and the dream-skinners: her first ship, *The Tiger Lashes with His Tail*, had died at the battle of Bach Nhan, when the smoke-children had blown up Harmony Station and its satellites; her second had not lasted more than a year.

The Tortoise in the Lake was her fourth ship, and they'd been together for five years, though neither of them expected to live for a further five. Men survived easier than ships—because they had armour, because the ships had been tasked to take care of them. Dong Huong remembered arguing with *Lady Mieng's Dreamer*, begging the ship to spare itself instead of her; and running against a wall of obstinacy, a fundamental incomprehension that ships could be more important than humans.

For the Northerners, however, everything would be different.

"We're here," *The Tortoise in the Lake* said, cutting across Dong Huong's gloomy thoughts.

"I can see nothing."

There came a low rumble, which distorted the cabin around her, and cast an oily sheen on the walls. "Watch."

Outside, everything was dark. There was only the shadow of *The Two Sisters in Exile*, the dead ship that they'd been pulling since Longevity Station. It hung in space, forlorn and pathetic, like the corpse of an old woman; although Dong Huong knew that it was huge, and could have housed her entire lineage without a care.

"I see nothing," Dong Huong said, again. The ground rumbled beneath her, even as her ears popped with pressure—more laughter from *The Tortoise in the Lake*, even as the darkness of space focused and narrowed—became the shadow of wings, the curve on vast surfaces—the hulls of two huge ships flanking them; thin, sharp, like a stretch of endless walls—making *The Tortoise in the Lake* seem small and insignificant, just as much as Dong Huong herself was small and insignificant in comparison to her own ship.

A voice echoed in the ship's vast rooms, harsh and strong, tinged with the Northerners' dialect, but still as melodious as declaimed poetry. "You wished to speak to us. We are here."

All Dong Huong knew about Northerners were dim, half-remembered snatches of family stories that were almost folk-tales: the greater, stronger part of the former Dai Viet Empire; the pale-skinned people of the outer planets, a civilisation of graceful cities and huge habitats, of wild gardens on mist-filled hillsides, of courtly manners and polished songs.

She was surprised, therefore, by the woman who disembarked onto *The Tortoise in the Lake*. Rong Anh was indeed paler than she was under her makeup, but otherwise ordinary looking: though very young, barely old enough to have bonded to a ship in Nam society, she bore herself with a poise any warrior would have envied. "You have something for us."

Dong Huong made a gesture, towards the walls of the room; the seething, ever-shifting mass of calligraphy; the fragments of poems, of books, of sutras, a perpetual reminder of the chaos underpinning the universe. "I . . . apologise," she said at last. "I've come to bring one of your ships back to you." To appease them, her commander had said. To avoid a declaration of war from a larger and more developed empire, a war which would utterly destroy the Nam.

Anh did not move. "I saw it outside. Tell me what happened."

"It was an accident," Dong Huong said. *The Two Sisters in Exile*—a merchant vessel from the Northerners' vast fleet—had just happened to cross the line of fire at the wrong time. "A military exercise that went wrong. I'm sorry."

Anh hadn't moved; but the ceruse on her face looked less and less like porcelain, and more and more like bleached bone. "Our ships don't die," she said, slowly.

"I'm sorry," Dong Huong said, again. "They're as mortal as anyone, I fear." The vast majority of attacks on a ship would do little but tear metal: a ship's vulnerable point was the heartroom, where the Mind that animated it resided. Unlike Nam ships, Northerner ships were large and well shielded; and no pirate had ever managed to hack or pierce their way into a heartroom.

But fate could be mocking, uncaring: as *The Two Sisters in Exile* passed by Dong Huong's military exercise, a random lance of fire had gone all the way to the heartroom on an almost impossible trajectory—searing the Mind in its cradle of optics. They'd heard the ship's Mind scream its pain in deep spaces long after the lance had struck; had stood in stunned silence, knowing that the Mind was dying and that nothing would stop that.

Anh shook her head; looked up after a while, and her mask was back in place, her eyebrows perfectly arched, like moths. "An accident."

"The people responsible have been . . . dealt with." Swiftly, and unpleasantly; and firmly enough to make it clear this would be not tolerated. "I have come to bring the body back, for a funeral. I'm told this is the custom of your people."

Nam ships and soldiers didn't get a funeral, or at least not one that was near a planet. They lay frozen where they had fallen—stripped of all vital equipment, the cold of space forever preserving them from decay, a permanent monument; a warning to anyone who came; a memory of glory, which the spirits of the dead could bask into all the way from Heaven. It would be Dong Huong's fate; *The Tortoise in the Lake*'s fate, in a few years or perhaps more if Quan Vu, God of War, saw fit to extend His benevolence to them both. Dong Huong had few expectations.

"It is our custom." Anh inclined her head. Her eyes blinked, minutely: it looked as if she was engaged elsewhere, perhaps communicating with her own ships. "We will bring her back where she was born, and bury her with the blessing of her descendants. You will come."

It wasn't a question, or even an invitation; but an order. "Of course," Dong Huong said. She hesitated, then said, "The military exercise was under my orders. If you want to clear my blood debt . . . "

Anh paused, halfway through one of the ship's dilating doors. "Blood debt?" Her head moved up, a fraction, making her seem almost inhuman. "What would we do with your life?"

Take it as a peace offering, Dong Huong thought, biting her tongue. She couldn't say it; she'd been forbidden. Never admit what you'd come from; say just what was needed. Admit your guilt but say nothing about your hopes, lest they betray you as everything in life was bound to do.

"Did you know her?" she asked.

Anh did not move. At long last, still not looking at Dong Huong, she said, "She was of my lineage."

"Kin to you," Dong Huong said, unsure of the implications. Minds were borne within a human womb before being implanted in their ships: this made them part of a lineage, as much as human children.

"Yes," Anh said. "I've known her since I was a child." Her hand had clenched on the wall; but she walked away without saying anything more.

After Anh was gone, Dong Huong opened her usual book of poetry, one of the only treasures she'd brought on board the ship. But the words blurred in her eyesight, slid away from her comprehension like raindrops on polished jade; and, rather than bringing her peace as they always did, the poems only frustrated her.

Instead, she turned off the lights, and lay back in the darkness, thinking of Xuan and Hai—of their faces, frozen in the instant before she ordered *The Tortoise in the Lake* to fire, and transfixed them as surely as their ships had transfixed *The Two Sisters in Exile*—she saw them, falling, fading from her ship's views—leaving nothing but the memory of their shocked gazes, weighing her, accusing her.

She'd had to do it. Quickly, decisively, as she'd done everything in life; as she'd parted from her husband when he failed to uphold the family's honour; as she'd forged her path in the military, never looking back, never regretting. And, as she'd told Anh, the matter had been closed: the perpetrators punished, order and law upheld, justice dealt out.

But still . . .

"You're brooding," *The Tortoise in the Lake* said.

Dong Huong said nothing. She felt the weight of her armour on her body; the cold touch of metal on her skin; the solidity of everything around her, from the poetry on the wall to the folded clothes besides her bed. The present, which was the only thing that mattered. "I'm the officer whose crew shot the ship in the first place. By my presence here, I endanger everything," she said.

"Nonsense." The room seemed to contract, become warmer and more welcoming, down to the words palpitating on the walls; the ship's voice grew less distant. "Have you not seen their ships?"

"I have. They're huge."

"They're weaponless." There was a tinge of contempt in *The Tortoise in the Lake*'s voice. "Cargo transport, with a little reserve against pirates; but even less well-armed than the smoke-children."

Dong Huong shivered, in the darkness. "Did you have to pick that example?"

"No," the ship said, after a while. "You're right, I didn't think."

"I saw her face," Dong Huong said at last. "She looks young, but doesn't act like it."

"Rejuvenation treatments?"

"Among other things." Dong Huong shivered. The Nam were a small, fractured empire; beset on all sides by enemies. The Northerners, on the other hand . . . They were large; they hadn't fought a large-scale war in centuries; and they had had time to develop everything from medical cures to advanced machinery. If they wanted war, the South, for all its warrior heritage, would be badly outgunned and outnumbered.

"They love their peace," the ship said. "Go to sleep, younger sister. There will be plenty of time in the morning."

Younger sister. Nothing more than convention by now; though the Mind of her first ship, *The Tiger Lashes with His Tail*, had shared blood with her: the mother that had borne it in her womb had been a cousin of Dong Huong's own father.

She did sleep, in the end. In her dreams, she walked in the lineage house again: on ochre ground, amidst cacti and shrunken bushes, and shrieking children playing rhyme-games in the courtyards. The smell of lemongrass and garlic rose from the kitchens like a balm to her soul, a reminder of the future she was fighting for; of what it meant to safeguard the Empire against its enemies. She saw her aunt, the mother of *The Tiger Lashes with His Tail*, standing tall and proud—her face unmoving as she learnt of the ship's fall at Bach Nhan, her eyes dark and dry; as if she'd already wept beforehand.

Surely she had known, or suspected. Ships didn't live long; but then, neither did human children. They both spread their wings like butterflies, like phoenixes, and ascended into the Heavens with the ancestors, watching over the Nam people. Dong Huong had tried to whisper such platitudes to her aunt; but nothing had come; and in her dreams—which were not real, not a true recollection—she stood looking into her aunt's eyes, and saw the tears welling up, as black and opaque as ink from a broken brush.

Dong Huong didn't come from a family of warriors, but from a very old lineage of scholars, who had turned merchants rather than bond to ships and take up knives and guns. Fifth Uncle, her favourite when she was a child, regularly went to Northern planets; and he would speak to her of Northern wonders, always with the same misty, open-eyed sense of awe. He would remind her that the Northerners hadn't fallen from grace, that they still remembered the original Dai Viet Empire and its culture that had stretched from one end of the galaxy to another; that they still had literature and poetry about beauty and dreams, and knew a life that wasn't a succession of one battle after another.

As a child, Dong Huong had drunk those words like tea or sugar cane juice. As an adult, within her combat unit, she had dismissed them. A civilisation that barely knew war would be weak, a stunted, dying flower rather than the magnificent blossoming her relatives described.

But the view beneath her now, as she and Anh descended in a shuttle towards the planet . . . As vast and as overwhelming as the two Northerner ships that had been her first contact—continents of chrome and verdant trees, sweeping away from her, seas glittering a vivid turquoise, with the glint of ten thousand boats on the waves—and, around them, in the atmosphere, a ballet of ships, as numerous as birds in the skies—a few huge spaceships like her own, carrying a Mind in their heartrooms; and myriad simple shuttle ships, manually driven, that nevertheless wove in and out of each other's way, dancing like the rhythms of a song, the words of a poem—

"You seem impressed," Anh said. "Have you never seen a planet?"

"Not—" Dong Huong swallowed, unable to dispel a memory of her own barren homeworld. "Not this kind, I'm afraid."

Anh smiled, indulgently. "Come. Let's get you to the funeral."

After disembarking from the shuttle, Dong Huong felt . . . naked, a warrior without a sword. She had her gun at her hip, and her armour on her; Anh hadn't even attempted to remove it from her, as if it all didn't matter much. She also had the voice and video loop of *The Tortoise in the Lake* to carry in her thoughts, but still . . . the higher gravity was grinding her bones against one another; and unfamiliar people, each dressed in more elaborate clothes than the previous one, turned and stopped, staring at her with the same odd expression on their faces—appraisal, disapproval?

Everything around her was freakish, different: buildings that were too tall, streets that were too wide, crisscrossed by alien vehicles. Everything was stately, orderly, so far from the chaotic traffic that marked Nam streets. Even the sky above was out of place; a deep, impossible blue with a thin, gleaming overlay: weather control, Anh said indulgently, as if it were the most natural thing in the world.

Weather control. Dong Huong breathed in rain, and the distant smell of flowers; and thought of the gardens of her home planet—ochre ground, cacti breaking out in large, breathtaking flowers—but nowhere as rich, nowhere as pointlessly complicated.

The funeral place was huge. Dong Huong had expected a funeral hall; a temple or a larger complex. But certainly not a city within the city, a whole area of tall buildings sprouting the white flags of mourning: every street filled with a stream of people in hempen garments, all wearing the strip of cloth that denoted the family of the dead.

When Dong Huong fell in battle—as she must, for it was the fate of all warriors—her lineage would weep for her. Her husband and her husband's brothers as well, perhaps, and that was all: two dozen people at the most, perhaps fifty if one included the more distant cousins. "Who are they?" she asked.

Anh paused at the entrance to a slender, white spire, and smiled. "I told you. Her descendants."

"The—"

"She was old," Anh said. Her voice was low, hushed. "Her mother was born in the Hieu Phuc reign; and she bore a Mind and four human children; and the children in turn had children of their own; and the children had children, on and on through the generations . . . "

"How—" Dong Huong moistened her tongue, tried again. "How long had it lived?" *The Tortoise in the Lake* was ten years old, a veteran by Nam standards.

"Four centuries. Our ships live long; so do our stations. How else shall we maintain our link to the past?"

"The shuttles?" Dong Huong asked, at last, her voice wavering, breaking like a boat in a storm.

Anh nodded, gravely. "Their pilots, yes. I told you that she had many descendants. And many friends."

Within Dong Huong's thoughts, *The Tortoise in the Lake* recoiled, watching the ballet of the dozen largest ships in the skies. Every one of them had a Mind; every one of them was as old as *The Two Sisters in Exile*. Every one of them . . .

"Is this her?" The speaker was a man, who, like Anh, didn't look a day older than sixteen—a face Dong Huong ached to see older, more mature—less naive about the realities of the war.

"Minh. I see you were waiting for us." Anh did not smile.

Minh's eyes were wide, almost shocked. "News gets around. Is it true?"

Anh gestured upwards, to the ballet of ships in the sky. "Do you think we'd all gather, if it wasn't true?"

Dong Huong hadn't said anything, waiting to be recognised. At last, Minh turned to her.

"Dong Huong, this is Teacher Minh," Anh said. "He leads our research programs."

Minh's gaze was on her, scrutinising her as one might look at a failed experiment. "Dong Huong. A beautiful name. It ill-suits you."

"It's been said before," Dong Huong said.

Minh sighed. He looked at Anh, and back at her. "She's so . . . hard, Anh. Too young to be that callous."

"Nam," Anh said, with the same tinge of contempt to her voice. "You know how they are. Shaped by war."

Minh's face darkened. "Yes. There is that."

"You disapprove?" Dong Huong felt a need, a compulsion to challenge him, to see him react in anger, in fear.

"Life is sacred," Minh said, leading her towards a double-panel door, with Anh in tow. "As we well know. Our bodies are a gift from our parents and our ancestors, and they shan't be wasted."

"Wasted?" Dong Huong shook her head. "You mistake us. We give them back, in the most selfless fashion possible. We live for our families, for the Empire. We give our lives so that they might remain safe, unconquered."

Minh snorted. "You are such children," he said. "Playing with forces you don't understand. Which is what brings us here, isn't it?"

The spire led into a hall vaster than the Northern ships; the walls were decked with images of outside, of the two ships dragging the carcass of *The Two Sisters in Exile*. And it was full—of grave people in rich clothes, of mourners with tears streaming on their faces. She'd never seen so many people gathered together; and suspected that she would never see them again.

Minh and Anh led Dong Huong to the front, ignoring her protestations, and introduced her to the principal mourner: an old, frail woman who looked more bewildered than sad. "It's never happened before," she said. "Ships don't die. They never do . . . "

"No," Minh said, slowly, gently. "They never do." He wasn't looking at Dong Huong. "I remember, the summer I came home from the Sixth Planet. She was docked in Azure Dragon Spaceport, looking so grand and beautiful— she'd used the trip to go in for repairs. She laughed on my comms, told me that now she looked as young as me, that she felt she could race anywhere in the universe. She . . . " His voice broke; he raised a hand, rubbing at reddened eyes.

"It's our fault," Dong Huong said. "That's why I've come, to offer amends."

"Amends." Minh didn't blink. "Yes, of course. Amends." He sounded as though he couldn't understand any of the words, as though they were an entirely alien concept.

Anh steered Dong Huong away from Minh, and towards her place in the front. "I don't know anything about this," Dong Huong protested.

"You'll watch. You said 'amends', didn't you? Consider this the start of what you owe the ship," Anh said, firmly planting her at the front of the assembly.

Dong Huong stood, feeling like a particularly exotic animal on display— with the weight of everyone's gaze on her nape, the growing wave of shock, anger, incomprehension in the room. The ceremony was still going on in the background: monks had joined the mourners, their chanted mantras a continuous drone in the background, and the smell of incense was rising everywhere in the room. She clenched her hand on her gun, struggling to remember her composure.

On the screens, the ship had been towed to what looked like its final destination; while a seething mass of smaller flyers gathered—not ships, not shuttles, but round spheres that looked like a cloud of insects compared to the *The Two Sisters in Exile*. The old woman took up her place at the lectern amidst the growing silence. "We're all here," she said at last. "Gathering from our planets, our orbitals, our shuttles, dancing in the skies to honour her. Her name was *The Two Sisters in Exile*, and she knew every one of our ancestors."

Dong Huong had expected anger; or grief; but not the stony, shocked silence of the assembly. "She was assembled in the yards of the Twenty-First Planet, in the last days of the Dai Viet Empire." Her voice shivered, and became deeper and more resonant—no, it was a ship, speaking at the same time as her, its voice heavy with grief. "Her Grand Master of Design Harmony was Nguyen Van Lien; her Master of Wind and Water Khong Tu Khinh; and her beloved mother Phan Thi Quynh. She was born in the first year of the reign of Emperor Hieu Phuc, and died in the forty-second year of the Tu Minh reign. Dong Huong of the Nam brought her here."

The attention of the entire hall turned to Dong Huong, an intensity as heavy as stone. No hatred, no anger; but merely the same shock. This didn't happen; not to them, not to their ships.

"Today, we are gathered to honour her, and to fill the void that she lives in our lives. She'll be—missed." The voice broke; and the swarm of spheres that had gathered in space shuddered and broke, wrapping themselves around the corpse of *The Two Sisters in Exile*—growing smaller and smaller, slowly eating away at the corpse until nothing remained, just a cloud of dust that danced amongst starlight.

"Missed." The entire hall was silent now, transfixed by the ceremony. Someone, somewhere, was sobbing; and even if they hadn't been, the spreading wave of shock and grief was palpable.

Four centuries old. Her descendants, more numerous than the leaves of a tree, the birds in the sky, the grains of rice in a bowl. A life, held sacred; more valuable than jade or gold. Dong Huong watched the graceful ballet in the sky; the ceremony, perfectly poised, with its measured poetry and recitations from long-dead scholars; and, abruptly, she knew the answer she'd take back to her people.

Graceful; scholarly; cultured. The Northerners had forgotten what war was; what death for ships was. They had forgotten that all it took was a lance or an accident to sear away four centuries of wisdom.

They had forgotten how capricious, how arbitrary life was, how things could not be prolonged or controlled. And that, in turn, meant that this—this single death, this incident that would have had no meaning among the Nam—would have them rise up, outraged, bringing fire and wind to avenge their dead, scouring entire planets to avenge a single life.

They would say no, of course. They would speak of peace, of the need for forgiveness. But something like this—a gap, a void this large in the fabric of society—would never be filled, never be forgiven. Minh's research programs would be bent and turned towards enhancing the weapons on the merchant ships; and all those people in the hall, all those gathered descendants, would become an army on a sacred mission.

In her mind, Dong Huong saw the desert plains of her home planet; the children playing in the ochre courtyard of her lineage house; the smell of lemongrass and garlic from the kitchens—saw it all shiver and crinkle, darkening like paper held to a flame.

Quan Vu watch over us. They're coming.

LODE STARS

LAVIE TIDHAR

The Illuminati starship *Trinity* was three light years away from the Orbitals and decelerating when the message reached Mikhaila Petrova that her father had died. For her it was only a month since she had last seen him, but that time was relative: back home in the Orbitals, over three years had passed.

He must have died almost as soon as she left for the Third Eye. She stared at the screen and re-ran the message, watching her aunt as she spoke. There was a new, discreet scar under her aunt's left eye and her skin bulged, just slightly, below the ear. Adapted Martian bioware. She must have got *that* pretty quickly, too.

"Mikhaila," Aunt Alexandra said, "your father's gone into God's eye." She stared into the camera and nodded slowly. Her lips were surprisingly fat in the thin, ascetic face. "I know this will come as a shock."

Three light-years away, Mikhaila stared at her aunt's image and the same sense of dislike filled her that always did where her father's older sister was concerned. Dislike, followed swiftly by an anger that tried to mask the pain beneath.

On screen, Alexandra shrugged, looking momentarily helpless. "He was alone in the Cyclop around the eye, meditating. In recent years, Mikki, your father had developed some strange ideas. I must confess I was relieved when you took command of the *Trinity* and took her to Third Eye. Your father's ideas . . . were a cause for concern. When you left he began to spend much of his time in the Cyclop, skirting close to the gravitational pull of the eye. He must have simply come too close, found out too late that he couldn't turn back." She sighed and said, "I know he went gladly when he realised, knowing he will be seen by God."

Mikhaila sat alone and watched Aunt Alexandra twist on screen. That sudden piousness at the end, too, was unlike the woman she remembered, and Mikhaila wondered numbly what else had changed back home in the last three years.

"Your father's gone into God's eye." The polite Illuminati way of saying, "He's dead." But her father had really gone into God's eye: she bit her lower lip until she felt pain, tasted a drop of blood like the taste of dull metal. Father, alone in the tiny Cyclop, suddenly too close to the gravitational field: the brief realization that there is no going back. Then the tides, tearing him and the ship into individual atoms, sucking them in until they passed the event horizon and disappeared forever from the visible universe. She didn't think it would hurt, much, being torn apart like this: but then again, she couldn't know. When an Illuminati was sent to the Eye it was a funereal occasion, and the tides tore only at already-dead flesh, while the mourners watched from the Orbitals and performed the rituals and, later, got drunk.

"Don't come back," Aunt Alexandra said on screen. "There is nothing that you can do. Mikki . . . " did the voice quaver a little? "I'm sorry."

The recording ceased and the screen faded back into being a wall. Mikhaila sat back and thought of her father again, alone as he was swallowed by the black hole. But for her father to die this way just didn't make sense. There was no way the Cyclop would be unable to determine the safety parameters around the eye. So what had really happened? Why had her father died?

Her throat felt sore, tingled with swallowed tears. She stared at the wall for a long moment more before rising, and stepped into the corridor outside, heading to the ship's control room.

The *Trinity*'s deceleration brought it down from 99.99% of the speed of light to a more conventional ten percent. At this speed time dilation still affected the crew but the differences between ship time and that of Third Eye's Orbitals were minimal: Mikhaila felt the pressure that had built up over the past month amongst the crew begin to dissipate when the screen lit up with an image of the Orbitals that wasn't Doppler-shifted. Three years, in the space of a month. It was a difficult transition to make.

The Orbitals ringed the Third Eye like dark clams, a wide chain of habitats worn around the neck of the black hole. Lights burned from a thousand human dwellings and local net traffic was rambunctious. And yet the chain was incomplete, and many of the Orbitals appeared to be drifting away—like a miniature Diaspora, Mikhaila thought. On screen the view changed, zoomed away from the Eye onto the star field beyond, and was then replaced by the eye-and-pyramid symbol.

"Incoming message," Rochiro Yuki said from her communications Conch. "From Grandmistress Ortega of Third Eye." She paused, then added, "Time delay is currently at eight point five minutes."

"Put her on," Mikhaila said, and a moment later Grandmistress Ortega's blunt, nut-brown face appeared on the wide screen. The Grandmistress wore an organic eye-patch that seemed to crawl over her face and it startled Mikhaila, who had just seen another Grandmistress who also carried evidence of new Martian bioware augmentation. She filed it away in her mind. Nothing the Grand Lodge members did was likely to be a coincidence.

Ortega didn't waste time on small talk: she introduced herself briskly before launching into the real reason for the call. "Captain Petrova," she said, "you arrive at an inauspicious time. The Eye has been causing us some considerable concern in the past year, with increased emissions of Hawking radiation and an increase in gravitational force that have forced us to a distance from the Eye we had not had to take for a millennium. I understand—" her right, unaugmented eye stared directly into the camera so that she appeared to be looking down directly at Mikhaila—"that you are here to conduct several specialised experiments in the vicinity of the Eye. When you left, there was no need to inquire more closely as to the nature of the experiments." The eye blinked. The Martian eye-patch rippled like jelly over the left. "That is no longer the case. I expect a full operations plan to be broadcast to me immediately. You will now direct your ship to the Grand Lodge Orbital where you will be my guests until a decision has been made whether to allow you access to the Eye." She stopped, blinked. Mikhaila watched as right eye closed and left eye rippled. It made her want to punch the Martian eye-patch, the way one squashes a leech. "I may have a different assignment for you."

She disappeared, replaced on screen by the eye-and-pyramid logo.

"What the hell did that mean?" Sandor said from his Conch. His head stuck out of the immersion tank and he peered at Mikhaila with the slight bafflement that seemed to always surround the tall scientist.

"I expect some of the people living around Third Eye are becoming concerned enough to think of a little trip," Mikhaila said. She had to force herself to concentrate: a mental image of her father being torn apart with the Cyclop kept enveloping her mind. "To Homelight, most likely."

"She can't *commandeer* the ship," Sandor said. "Just so people can run away to a *world*!"

Like all Orbital dwellers he held those of Homelight, the Illuminati's only planetoid, with a mixture of hidden envy and openly-displayed contempt. Mikhaila remembered her one visit to Homelight for her initiation ceremony; all that she remembered clearly was the one view of the impossibly-tall, lizard-green pyramids that rose like volcanoes from the surface of the world. Homelight had no atmosphere; it was nothing more than a wandering moon until it was found by the Illuminati and dragged back to the three

Eyes, and Mikhaila spent her entire time there in a small part of the Grand
Lodge Pyramid, only granted that one fleeting look at the world from above.
"*Grandmistress* Ortega can do what she wants," Mikhaila said, a little stiffly.
"If she decides to send us off to Homelight or Second Eye or even back home
there's absolutely nothing we can do about it."

"Well, *I* can't see it coming to that," Rochiro said. "Though it isn't such a
bad idea, you know. We could charter the ship and get ourselves a round trip
to the world." The sound of laughter emerged from her Conch. "Everybody
knows Third Eyers are rich."

"We'll see," Mikhaila said. Then that she told them about her father.

The Grand Lodge Orbital was a small moon with its own ring of smaller
orbiting habitats. Mikhaila was surprised it was so close to the Eye. She was
also concerned.

The *Trinity* decelerated gently into the Third Eye system until reaching a
near-stationary position on the edge of the Grand Lodge's hangers-on: some
of them have evidently been around for a very long time. A nearby orbital
was a miniature stellar system composed of three hollowed-out asteroids, a
Ring and two more modern—though still several centuries old—constructed
orbitals, all linked together into a makeshift web. There was even a small
pyramid, growing on the back of the smallest asteroid like a bright green
tumour.

If Ortega was telling the truth about the recent, unexplained activity
of the Eye, then why were the Grand Lodge and its followers so close to
the Eye's gravitational pull? And if Ortega, for whatever reason, wasn't
telling the truth, and there *was* no danger, then the question changed and
became a big *why*. Why would Ortega lie about the activity of the Eye? No,
Mikhaila decided, Grandmistress Ortega would not lie about that and, in
fact, Sandor had already confirmed the unusual activity of the Eye as they
decelerated, as did Rochiro's analysis of the local net traffic. But perhaps
she wasn't telling them all of the truth, and she knew more than she was
admitting or telling. Mikhaila wondered if the Grandmistress knew what
the small crew of the *Trinity* really wanted to achieve here, three long light
years away from home. It was a game she wasn't sure how well she could
play. For now, she filed away the speculations and concentrated on the ride
to the orbital.

She and Sandor got into their individual Cyclops; she always thought of the
release from the ship as the image of a fish, blowing bubbles. She and Sandor
were the bubbles: Rochiro had renounced flesh life several years before and
had become a Conch, living entirely inside the immersion tank and she rarely
now left the ship.

"I'll pick up some information about stuff back home," she said. "As well as the local situation. You keep your ears open too."

A hole opened in the Grand Lodge orbital, and the two Cyclops were swallowed by it and entered one of the orbital's giant hangars. A delegation of two recent Initiates welcomed them and led the way to the meeting with Ortega.

In person, the Grandmistress was surprisingly short, and her Martian bioware augmentation even more repulsive. Mikhaila's father had never trusted the biological artefacts that were created from the forced evolution of the few microbiological traces discovered on Mars, back in pre-Exodus days. The alien genetic code itself was fascinating—Mikhaila took a few basic modules of Martian Bio Programming her first year at the Magdalen Orbiter—but the results always carried with them a strange, alien sense that made her feel uncomfortable.

"Captain Petrova," Ortega said. Her hand was brown and calloused and her grip was firm as she shook Mikhaila's hand. The eye patch rippled as she spoke. "I am sorry to hear about your loss."

Surprise mingled with shock; perhaps seeing that in Mikhaila's face the Grandmistress said, "I expect I received the message from First Eye at the same time as you. Again, I am sorry. Your aunt Alexandra was very fond of your father."

Mikhaila forced herself to smile, said something about "Dear aunt Alexandra," while in her mind she saw again the unwelcome image of her father, sucked into the Eye. "I was not aware you knew each other."

"No?" Ortega said. Something in her voice suggested she did not quite believe Mikhaila. "We were initiated into the Mysteries together on Homelight. Your aunt is now a powerful figure at the First Eye Grand Lodge; you must know we keep a permanent feed between the Eyes."

"Of course," Mikhaila said. "I'm sorry. The news . . . it is something of a shock."

Grandmistress Ortega nodded. "I understand." A small smile touched the corners of her mouth and she touched Mikhaila lightly on her shoulder. "If you need to talk please come to me. The loss of your father is a loss to all Illuminati."

Mikhaila nodded, bit down on a reply. Instead, she said, "Have you had a chance to look at the research proposal I forwarded?"

Ortega's thin smile withdrew. "Yes. I'm afraid that under the current circumstances it would not be advisable."

Anger warmed Mikhaila's face. "And why not?"

An unreadable expression settled on Ortega's face. "Because right now, I don't need any more casualties like your father."

The words hang between them, riding a tense, growing silence as the two women locked eyes. "I demand access to the Eye," Mikhaila said. Her voice was soft, barely audible, but it affected the Grandmistress like a physical blow.

"You can demand nothing," Ortega said. "Don't forget your position, Captain. Do you reject the authority of the Lodge?"

"I spent three *years* travelling here," Mikhaila said. "I will *not* turn back now."

The thin smile returned to Ortega's lined face. "I'm afraid," she said, equally softly, "that you don't really have a choice at all." She turned away from Mikhaila and gestured to a wide screen where the Orbitals were displayed from a distant camera. "The Eye is growing," she said quietly. "Only by tiny increments, but it is growing as if it is being fed matter on a large scale. *Something* is causing that, and as we don't know what then the Grand Lodge has no choice but to see it as a potentially hostile activity."

"Hostile?" Disgust almost made her choke. "What could possibly threaten the Illuminati?"

On Ortega's face the Martian eye patch shivered and began to migrate across her face, revealing a grotesque hole where her left eye should have been. "I don't know," she said. She had pitched her voice low still, but the anger in it was unmistakable. "And until I do, no one—and that means *no one*, Captain—is allowed access to the Eye. Do I make myself understood?"

The eye patch now nestled in the space between Ortega's left shoulder and her neck. It looked like a sleepy, obese beetle.

"Yes," Mikhaila said. Cold settled in the bottom of her stomach and spread, enveloping her until she felt as if she were made entirely of ice. "Quite, quite clear."

"Is the woman mad?" Rochiro said loudly in Mikhaila's ear. Mikhaila was in her allocated rooms at the Grand Lodge: she didn't plan to stay there long. "She is going directly against the Mysteries!"

"I don't think she is mad," Mikhaila sub-vocalized. "But I do wonder what she's playing at. I did notice all the local feeds aimed at the Eye don't appear to be operating. What's net traffic like?"

"The same," Rochiro admitted. "Everything is being re-routed on direct links cutting out the Godfeeds, narrow beam, minimal loss—it's strange. Much more efficient, obviously, but how will God see us?"

"I don't think it's God that's being blinded," Mikhaila said. She massaged her face, feeling a growing pain in the bridge of her nose. "I think . . . I think my father was successful." She didn't complete her thought aloud, conscious that the conversation was most likely monitored. *I think the Eye is talking back.*

"How's Sandor?" Rochiro said, changing the subject.

Mikhaila laughed. "Grumpy. He demanded permission to run his experiments from Grandmistress Ortega. *Demanded*. It didn't go very well from there."

"What *are* we going to do, Captain?"

"I have an idea," Mikhaila said. The pain spread up to her eyes now. "But we'll talk about it back on the ship. Meantime, how are the backpackers?"

"Most of them are gone already," Rochiro said. "I mentioned a possible Homelight flight and a few are sticking around for it. Willing to pay, too."

"Is that Ran one of them?"

"Raz. Yeah."

Mikhaila wondered briefly about Rochiro's complicated sex life then shook the thought from her head. Who—or *how*—her comms. officer spent her off time was none of her business. And it was always good to have a few backpackers around, if only for morale.

"Ortega didn't mention anything to me," Mikhaila said. "Yet. I have a meeting with her in a few hours. I'm going to try and get some sleep first. Hopefully she'll let us go after that."

"Sleep well, then," Rochiro said, and the connection ended.

Mikhaila lay back on the bed and thought about her father; and about what it was that she thought he had done.

She felt only a little better after her sleep, and worse after her meeting with Ortega. But now, as she was gliding through space in her Cyclop—a round, compact craft whose shell could be made to allow through harmless light and turn the entire vehicle transparent—and saw the *Trinity* she felt better. Smaller craft hovered all over the *Trinity*'s shell, attaching themselves like flies to flesh. Ships came and went in a complicated dance: there were never that many starships and whenever one went cross-system (or cross-Eyed, which as a joke dated back nearly two millennia) it had plenty to carry. The two Cyclops wove themselves into the elaborate dance and soon Mikhaila and Sandor were standing back in the command room of the *Trinity* with Rochiro.

"Ortega wants us to go to Homelight," Sandor said the moment he saw her. He blinked at the command room as if searching for a place to vent anger. "I'd say it was just her way of getting rid of us, but there were a hell of a lot of people came up to me asking about a place."

"Three," Mikhaila said, and Sandor grimaced. "It's indicative of a wider trend."

Mikhaila smiled.

"So what's the plan, Captain?" Rochiro said. "Seeing as we can't dump anything into the Eye for the foreseeable future . . . "

"No," Mikhaila said. "We can't. But we *can* monitor the Hawking radiation that's being emitted."

"You think . . . ?" Rochiro said, and Mikhaila said, "Can you do it?"

"Sure. Don't know if it would be political to send out a few probes but I can probably get all the data directly off of Third Eye Mirror."

"Just make sure you confirm its authenticity," Sandor said darkly. "Something doesn't feel right about any of this."

"Yes, *sir*," Rochiro said. "Captain, is there anything else?"

"Yes," Mikhaila said. "I want you to delay the *Trinity* for as long as you can. Come up with some technical problems to keep us stationary. And find me someone on the, um, *unofficial* channels who knows about Martian biotech."

"Might take a few days to make a contact," Rochiro said. Mikhaila thought about the Grandmistress' eye patch, of her aunt's own new augmentation hidden beneath her skin. "That's fine," she said. "Just make sure it's not traceable."

"I'll see what I can do." The silence that followed from the communications Conch carried a strong sense of irritation. Mikhaila almost smiled: Rochiro was convinced that as a Conch she was a true Illuminati, one of the few truly Enlightened who always knew what was *really* going on. She'd be eating up bandwidth following anything she could sniff out. "I'm sorry," she said, feeling suddenly tired again, "you know what you're doing."

The three of them fell into a silence. It was the comfortable silence of people who knew each other well, and Mikhaila felt that she was setting something raw and unpredictable into that unit, *her* unit, when she broke it and said, "Sandor, I want you to wake up Leibniz."

The Martian expert lived in Ghostown.

It took seven ship-days (by now aligned with Third Eye's own calendar-time arrangement) to locate him. When Rochiro at last told Mikhaila she had sounded sheepish.

"A *hobbyist*?" Mikhaila had said. "I said unofficial channels and you got me some guy who plays with a backyard evolution kit?"

"Mr. Alvarez," Roshiro had said, each word enunciated clearly, "is an *expert* on Martian bio-coding. An expert, moreover, who is not affiliated with any official Lodge corporations."

Mikhaila nodded. Under the circumstances she couldn't really complain. "Fine. When can I see him?"

The hidden Rochiro, the part of her that was flesh and blood might have smiled. "Any time you like." Then she told her where Mr. Alvarez lived.

Cocooned in the Cyclop, Mikhaila now watched as the distant lights of

Ghostown lit up a complex—yet essentially random—pattern against the darkness of Eyeless space. They twinkled in and out of existence, inscribing messages for God that had no meaning to anyone but, perhaps, the ghosts.

The Cyclop floated closer and Ghostown came into naked-eye view; Mikhaila drew in breath as the giant, elongated structure filled up her field of vision. It was like a rock the size of a moon that had been stretched across space into a wide baguette shape, pan-fried and old: even from a distance she could see that the outer shell was crawling with insects. A black-metal beetle emitting ionised particles from its rear approached the Cyclop and for a moment the view blanked. The beetle was the size of her fist. In that brief glimpse it looked fat and well-fed.

When the screen cleared a hole was opening in the side of the rock, expelling out both air and mechanoid insects; she heard their angry buzzing as they flooded the local channels. The Cyclop slid into the opening.

Ghostown's rotation created only a very low gravity. Mikhaila found herself inside a tomb-like space, almost floating in the thin air. It smelled dry, with only a distant taste of something human, like smoke or the lingering traces of frying onion. Here there were no bugs: all around her and as far away as she could see stood a vast and open forest of columns that rose from the rocky ground, gleaming in hues of matt black and cold metallic blue and disappeared into the impossibly-high ceiling.

She took another breath; the ghosts began whispering to her.

Their whispers had an almost physical touch, and as she walked away from the Cyclop they grew it tone and volume until some of the trapped souls screeched and others begged her: to touch the columns, to let them ride her body, to help them. Some of the columns shifted and changed their look, revealing a hidden, virtual world beneath, and some of the ghosts manifested on the makeshift screens, some men and some women and some no longer recognisable as human.

She had never before seen a ghost, and she found the experience distressing. Ghostown was the end result of an ancient belief: back in the pre-Exodus solar system of which Earth was a part many people—some of them Illuminati—talked about the possibility of an event they called a Singularity, and of something else called Upload culture. The idea was that human minds could be transported to digital systems, neuron-networks copied, neuron by painstaking neuron, until an exact, digital copy of the mind resided in a virtual environment where it could live like a god, at least a demi-god.

The idea was not impossible, and so, some centuries after the Illuminati fleet discovered the three Eyes and settled around three *real* singularities, a splinter group around Third Eye built the complex that eventually became known as Ghostown. It was an honourable experiment: the men and women who worked on it had wanted to transcend as a way of coming closer to God, that unexplained, unknown force that resided in the ur-universe from which all other universes grew, and watched this particular universe—so the Illuminati reasoned—through the only eyes it had: the singularities that hid at the heart of every black hole.

"Mikhaila Petrova?"

The voice startled her. It was deep and strangely homely, and the man who stepped out of what appeared to her for a moment as just another screen was small and deeply tanned, with sparse white hair and deep, brown eyes. "Mr. Alvarez?"

He nodded. "Shmuel," he said. He gestured, his arm encompassing the "What do you think of it?"

"It's . . . " Mikhaila said, and then wasn't sure what answer he expected, "disconcerting."

Shmuel Alvarez nodded. He stepped forward and, now that she could see him more clearly, Mikhaila discerned the patches of Martian bioware on his nearly-naked body. His body itself was muscled and seemed younger than his face, and he wore only a small loincloth that—she realised with a start—was not cloth but another Martian bio-construct. As she watched the loincloth opened a lazy, inhuman eye and winked at her.

"It takes you that way," Alvarez said quietly. "Sometimes I think it would be merciful if we just pointed it at the Eye and sent the ghosts directly to God. But I am afraid that is not a course of action the Grand Lodge would ever tolerate. Come with me."

He led Mikhaila through the cavern of columns, and all the time the ghosts whispered to her and cried for her to save them. She saw faces whose features were distinct and different from each other, who spoke in old dialects and laughed and cried and shouted her name, which they had picked up from Alvarez's speech.

She tried not to show how she felt. Disgust, which she hadn't expected to feel, and pity, which she had. The ghosts surprised her, and she couldn't tell why. They made her think of her father, and she wondered again about what she thought he tried to achieve, and if he, too, was a ghost in some form. The Illuminati who were involved in the Upload project did not consider that the human brain would have a problem existing in isolation, that it was evolved to function in a human body, and that sensory input—of a specific kind—was needed. In other words, a human brain needed a human body—and what happened when a mind was trapped in a virtual environment was apparent all around her.

"They killed themselves," Alvarez said. "The Upload process used a copy-

and-erase approach, to make sure no one would be left behind. That ghost—" he pointed at a column they were just passing. The fractured face of a once-beautiful woman stared at them from a thousand replicated shards. "—is now the only thing left of the woman she had once been."

"Why live here, Mr. Alvarez?"

They had reached a clearing in the forest of columns. It was a wide space that was fenced by light, flexible walls that were stretched from column to column and formed . . . a zoo. Mikhaila watched as strange compact bio-constructs walked and hopped and crawled across the rocky floor; some climbed the columns while others formed groups that more often than not merged gradually into one blob of mass before splitting again into different shapes. A creature the size of a small child ambled towards her and from its mouth came the shriek of a ghost encased in new-found flesh.

"Because it's private, Captain Petrova," Shmuel Alvarez said, and his hands moved as if to encompass the entire mini-habitat he had created. "And because I find there are inherent potentialities in the possible creation of a ghost-Martian interface."

"Feel you . . . touch you . . . taste you . . . smell you . . ." The possessed Martian construction moved towards Mikhaila and fell to all fours, developing an elongated snout in the process. "Make love . . . " Its voice sounded suddenly forlorn and lost.

"Enough," Alvarez said, and the ghost-ridden creature stiffened, and turned away without sound.

"You're not joking," Mikhaila said. She looked at Alvarez's creation and held down a shudder. She'd prefer to deal with the Grandmistresses themselves.

"No," Alvarez agreed. He led her to a small house erected in the centre of the clearing. When they got there she discovered the house was no more than a small room made of the same light material as the outer walls, and that it was empty. Alvarez closed the door. His loincloth shook and stretched itself around him, flesh-coloured and thin.

He tilted his head as if listening. Then, "No," he said again. "A ghost-Martian interface is a possibility that has significant implications for the deeper Mysteries. Your father understood that well, Mikhaila."

She drew back. "How do you know my father?"

There was a mesh of fine wrinkles at the corners of Shmuel Alvarez's eyes and they made his smile seem sad. "How do I know what he believed? Because I believe the same as him, Mikhaila. Because I, too, believe that there is life beyond the Eyes' event horizon."

She woke up into darkness, and the sweet faint smell of her lover's body pressed into her between the sheets. Ernesto's arm was lying on her chest, and when she pushed him off he muttered something intelligible and turned over.

Mikhaila rose and put on the loose informal trousers and shirt that were the sign of ship life: it made her smile, the thought of this super-advanced starship being piloted by people dressed in pyjamas.

The *Trinity* was on her way to Homelight, cargo hold converted to people-carrying. Beside the backpackers—Ernesto joined the ship at Third Eye while Rochiro's Raz remained with them, happy to follow Rochiro after his brief exploration of the Third Eye Orbitals—the ship thronged with Third Eye families who had decided to take the one and a half light years journey to the world. Mikhaila walked softly out of Ernesto's cabin and made her way through a service corridor (Crew Only) back to the control room, where Sandor waited.

"Leibniz's awake," he said, and nodded to a corner of the room where the Other's avatar sat calmly in an old-fashioned armchair.

Starships did not, as a rule, need overwhelmingly powerful computers. The very first space probes sent from Earth seemed to manage, just about, with two 8-bit processors and the Illuminati designers appreciated that fact. Nevertheless, the *Trinity* did carry with it one piece of complex machinery, a quantum computer with a DNA-coded interface and its own fortified cadaver of hulk-metal: more than any human, Leibniz was conscious of the possibility of permanent death and was determined to have nothing to do with it.

Leibniz's avatar stood up as she came into the room. It was over six feet tall, a silver-skinned, bald mannequin whose sexless body was undraped by clothes. If humans feared being Uploaded, the Others feared the opposite: being trapped in a human body, being *Downloaded* seemed to them perverse and frightening, and would drive the being so confined into a dangerous process of fragmentation and insanity.

"Petrova," Leibniz said. The voice came directly from the avatar's mouth, which did not move. As usual, it went straight to the point. Like most Others Leibniz could communicate with people, running a sort of low-level expert system that mimicked a human personality, but as he had said to Petrova the one time, what was the point? Others did not evolve from biological bodies but in the vast and disembodied breeding grounds of digital code, and subsequently did not have the drives and emotions, flesh-bound, that formed a human character. "If there is a code hidden in the Hawking radiation then I can't find it." The mannequin hesitated, then said, "Unless it is there and I can't see and understand it."

Mikhaila thought about what Alvarez had told her, back on Ghostown. She expected Leibniz's next words.

"Petrova," Leibniz said, and the voice coming from the mannequin changed, sounding like metal flashing in a dark room. "Why is there a ghost on the ship?"

"Ah."

The ghost was Alvarez's parting gift, as was the fat, amorphous Martian aug that she left in Rochiro's capable, if proverbial, hands as soon as she could. She didn't imagine the Other had missed the fact, or its implications. But it was giving her the chance to argue: it was all that she could hope for.

"I do not wish to interface with biological matter."

"It's only a different platform," Mikhaila said. She felt wide-awake; she slept deep for the first time in months. "It's *code*."

"Running a crazed human ghost riding shotgun? Mikhaila, self-preservation alone would forbid me from trying."

"Tell me," Mikhaila said. She stared at the avatar and it stared back, without expression. "How long have you been an Illuminati?"

The voice lost its inflection, became flat. "I came out of the breeding grounds about seven hundred years ago. I was initiated into the Mysteries shortly after."

"Do you believe that singularities, as the only places where the laws of the universe do not apply, are windows into the ur-universe, and that something we can only think of as God, a maker of universes, must exist there in some form?"

"It's a possibility," Leibniz said. "An intriguing one."

"Humbling?"

"I can emulate pride, but I can't be arsed to feel it," the Other said, and made Mikhaila suddenly laugh.

There was a short, comfortable silence.

"Think about it," Mikhaila said. "There's time. After Homelight . . . "

"After Homelight," Leibniz agreed. The Mannequin made a curious gesture with its left hand. "Then we'll see."

She woke up in the narrow bed feeling disoriented. The room was small and dark, and there were no windows. Mikhaila whispered an order and a soft light came on. She had been dreaming of black holes, and her head felt raw and strange, as if it belonged to someone else.

She sub-vocalized. "Sandor?"

The reply returned filled with static. "I'm at the Great Library. I'm glad you finally decided to get up."

"Did you find anything?"

A pause. Then, "Meet me at the apex in half an hour?"

She agreed. Got up, prepared genuine coffee from the reproduction-antique coffeemaker provided in her room. Screens around the room woke up to her movements and began showing images of the dark sky as seen from Homelight.

"Pretty," Leibniz said.

Mikhaila ignored him. She ordered one of the screens and it turned into a mirror. She stood and watched herself, and worried. Her image in the mirror seemed alien to her. Different. An ur-Mikhaila, a stranger wearing her face. The thumb on her left hand was flesh-coloured, only subtly different to the rest of her fingers. She had grafted Leibniz on just before the *Trinity* reached Homelight. Neither of them enjoyed it.

There were dark rings around her eyes. Her breasts felt raw to her, her nipples hurting, and on her ribs, less discreet than the Other, was a patch of red flesh that seemed to crawl on her flat stomach. The Martian bio-construct, its ghost made to sleep.

She kept seeing things from impossible angles. Slivers of light that formed fragmented pictures in her head, familiar images made startling and new.

Alien. She was turning into a fragment herself, something more, or perhaps less, than human. Something *different*. She turned away from the mirror, suddenly uncomfortable with her own naked figure, and dressed quickly before taking hold of the coffee.

Just drinking it was a problem. While the human part of her was tasting the coffee the Other was breaking it down into components, running pointless diagnostics on everything that entered her body. And through the Martian construct the coffee tasted different, a synesthesia of smells and colours that made her giddy, not helped by the insane dreams of the sleeping ghost riding the interface of flesh.

She didn't finish the coffee. Instead, she opened the door and stepped outside into the corridor. Here was the same level of silence, the same absence of noise: it ran all through the living quarters of the Grand Lodge Pyramid and extended to all its levels, a hush that permeated the air, whispering of mysteries.

Mikhaila thought about the Mysteries as she walked down empty corridors to the service elevators that would take her up, to the apex deck with its panorama of desolate views. The conviction that behind the creation of the universe lay God—lay an intelligence, a consciousness, a *something* that made the Big Bang happen, that gave the universe the constants it needed to support life, to create suns and planets and people—was what drove the early Illuminati in the Exodus. It took them on a wild ride through interstellar space, looking for a theoretical hole in the universe, for the tear in space and time where the laws and the constants no longer applied, and where God's eye was open, beyond the universe, and watched it in the slow speed of light . . .

The elevator took her, still within her own bubble of silence, to the apex. She recognized some of the people moving here—new immigrants from Third Eye brought on board the *Trinity*—but the majority were Illuminati scholars, members of the Grand Lodge or the Great Library, identified in the distinguished black robes of the scholars of Mystery.

Sandor was waiting for her beside one of the walls, his gaze lost in the panoramic vista of space and world, and she joined him and watched with him in silence. The green pyramids rose from the surface of Homelight like impossible temples, reaching for the dark night above, and the stars that met her eyes were strangers, the galaxy an unfamiliar ribbon fluttering in the great emptiness.

"We can talk now," Leibniz said.

Mikhaila turned away from the view and Sandor followed her.

"What did you find?"

Sandor looked tired, and there was a smell about him that took Mikhaila a moment to recognise: dusty paper and mock-leather, the smell of ancient books.

"What I didn't find," Sandor said. "There is nothing in the databases about the possibility of life beyond the Eyes. Not even speculation. Not a suggestion, not a theory, nothing."

"But we knew this," Mikhaila said. "My father . . . "

"Your father . . . " Sandor said. He wore his unpleasant smile, the one that said he was deeply irritated. " . . . does not seem to exist. Two papers, both from over thirty years ago, both about nothing in particular."

Mikhaila stood still, her fingers curling to balls. Then, "I expected that," she said.

"Did you?" He looked angry.

"Yes," Mikhaila said, feeling the same anger taking root. "He always warned me of the possibility. He suspected a conspiracy of the Lodges."

Sandor laughed, a frustrated bark. "An Illuminati suspecting a conspiracy. Conspiracies are what we *do*, Mikhaila. Take ten for the price of one. Take your pick. Choose a card, any card."

"Sandor, calm down," Leibniz said. He spoke through Mikhaila's mouth, and she felt her body freezing in protest as the Other utilised her vocal cords. The sense of alienation rose in her, threatening to suffocate her. "We did not expect to find anything in the archives. I've been running duplicate agents on the digital side since we landed. Now what did you find?"

Sandor looked away, drawn back to the view of Homelight beyond the window. "I found a book."

"What book?" Leibniz again, silencing Mikhaila's own question.

Sandor laughed again. "A children's book. From eight hundred years ago. A collection of legends. Everything else is off-limits, or just been borrowed, or doesn't exist, or digitised and destroyed. Guess no one thought there'd be any harm in letting me browse the children's archives."

Mikhaila felt Leibniz throbbing on her hand, and in the hidden patch below her own robe the Martian bio-construct stirred, the ghost inside it trying to wake up. She felt both of the influences like sharp, medical pains, and a phantom smell of spirits tickled her nose. "*What* book?"

"*The Legend of Aldus Trismegistus.*"

Mikhaila stilled. The name, dimly familiar, evoked in her a certain dread that she could feel pumping up from her abdomen. And the ghost was nearly roused now, the name of the book acting as a drug on its fragile consciousness. She felt Leibniz's reaction even before he spoke. "Who was Aldus Trismegistus and what was the manner of his death?" and then she remembered.

It was an old riddle, a children's nursery rhyme, learnt on the playground, separated from her now by both space and time. "Who was Aldus Trismegistus and what was the manner of his death?"

"He was a man," Sandor said, "who entered a joining with an Other. He slept . . . "

"For a thousand years," Mikhaila said, remembering. "As the ships left Earth system and went searching for God. And he was woken up only when the First Eye was found, and then . . . "

"He killed himself. *Them*selves. Three-times Aldus, who joined with an Other, and merged with a Martian aug. He threw himself into First Eye, three thousand years ago. That's what the book tells."

"And?" Mikhaila said. A headache was blossoming inside her, and the ghost was whispering to her, dribbling of sex and the flesh and something else, too: an old memory of childhood and of singing an even older rhyme.

"And that's it," Sandor said. "In the nursery rhyme."

"But not in the book."

"No." The word was flat and heavy, like an old, forgotten tombstone. "You see, the book doesn't end with Aldus' death. In the story, Aldus never died at all."

"He still lives," Leibniz said, "is that it?" But Mikhaila already knew he was right, and she took control over her vocal cords and said, "he went into the Eye, but he didn't die—" and the old rhyme returned to her, like a persistent shard of music, and she saw in Sandor's eye the same wild thought as he completed the words: "—Aldus Trismegistus was one and three times alive."

There were words expressing sorrow at her loss, quiet warnings about the futility of hope, words of advice about grieving, and about letting go of the dead. The room, high up on the Southern corner of the Grand Lodge

Pyramid, twinkled with light; a fine mist fell from the high ceiling onto lush, transparent vegetation of a kind she had never seen before. Designer plants, sucking up the mist and turning all the colours of the rainbow.

"Your father was a good man," Grand Master Rune said to her, his hand enveloping a rolled crystal leaf containing an amber drink. "He would be proud of you. You did good to come here and bring us the new immigrants. You're a true Illuminati, Mikhaila. Remember we must all serve."

Grand Master Rune was short and hairless, his head a shaven dome. His eyes were deep-set and ordinary brown. His fingers were bitten, the skin around the nails raw and red. Earlier he said, "We were initiated together, me and your father. I was sorry to hear of the accident."

The words of the old riddle still echoed in her head. "Who was Aldus Trismegistus and how did he die?" and she felt it reverberating through her new components. The Martian aug crawled across her stomach and wrapped itself around a breast, shivering. She was going insane; or perhaps, she thought, not sure which part of her the thought came from, she was becoming Aldus.

"You don't look well," Rune said and he released his drink into the air, the leaf unfurling and sailing away on an invisible breeze. His gaze took her in, all of her: she saw him note the Other on her hand and his eyes lingered for longer than necessary on her breasts, as if knowing there was something alien there that did not belong.

Or maybe, she thought, he's just looking at your tits.

"Sit down," he said. He guided her away from the throngs of people to a quiet corner. Two giant leaves unfolded from a stem and they sat down, the leaves moulding themselves around their bodies. "Mikhaila," he said, and his voice abandoned its mere-human tones and took on the aspect of a Grand Master, stern and impersonal and powerful. "Whatever you are doing to yourself, don't. Do not meddle with things you do not understand."

Mikhaila tried to smile. "I'm an Illuminati," she said. "It's what we *do*."

The Grand Master shook his head in an old gesture of negation. "You are not high up enough in the study of the Mysteries. Don't go seeking conspiracies where none exist. Look at you." He gestured to Leibniz, but the gesture seemed to take in more than that, hinting at the Martian biomass and its ghostly rider. "You're killing yourself."

"Like Aldus Trismegistus?" Mikhaila said, feeling a sense of relief as the words were out, a challenge. Time to put down your cards, she thought.

Rune blinked. She noticed his own discreet Martian aug, a faint red line running down his neck, behind his ear. And he too, she saw, had an Other, though this one was in his left earlobe and was so discreet she had to know it was there to see it. "If you like."

"What would you have me do?" Mikhaila asked. "Tell me the truth. Tell me why Third Eye is becoming inhospitable. Tell me why I was not allowed to study the Eye. Tell me . . . " the thought remained unformed in speech.

Tell me why my father died.

"Go home," Rune said instead. "Say goodbye to your father. Mikhaila—" he paused, then said, "The Grand Lodge has been concerned for some time—for several hundred years, in fact—with the possibility that life this close to the Eyes might become even more dangerous." He turned to her and his eyes took hers in, forcing her to pay him attention. "We have decided to organise . . . an expedition. For the first time in two millennia, we would like to expand—and to re-establish contact with other parts of humanity, if any exist in the direction we once came from."

Mikhaila drew in breath, imagining the oxygen rushing through her blood-stream, cleansing her. She felt her pulse race up despite the air she was inhaling. Leibniz warned her, *sotto voce*, to be careful.

"As one of our finest starship captains," the Grand Master said, and for the first time since she met him Rune smiled, "we would like you and the *Trinity* to be a part of the expedition."

Mikhaila found she was unable to speak. She felt a fever rise in her and inside her the voices of her body's co-habitants threatened to drown her own thoughts, which were of journeys, and strangeness, and adventure.

"Think about it," Rune said. He rose and the leaf he was sitting on furled back on itself. "But go home first. Your aunt misses you."

He walked away, but Mikhaila remained sitting, and all the while Leibniz was whispering to her about bribes, and about carrots and sticks.

The fever burned her. Her body had become a battle-ground, a clash of entities too alien to co-exist. The Martian *thing* was tight around her waist and seemed to be spreading, growing over her stomach and breasts. And the ghost that haunted it was fully awake now, and insane. Its jabbering hurt her like thousands of internal cuts.

Leibniz kept quiet. The Other throbbed where her thumb had been, as if barricading himself against the mayhem in her body though with little success. Her mind became a screen where sequences of different and alien codes clashed and competed, a miniature breeding ground of Human and Martian and Other.

When she gained partial consciousness she felt she was on fire, the bedsheets heavy with sweat, and she caught snatches of conversation as if from far away. She heard Sandor talking about carrots and sticks, and understood from what he said that at some point before leaving Homelight the *Trinity*'s systems had been carefully wiped of the Hawking Radiation data they had collected at Third Eye. Rochiro seemed completely upset about this invasion of her domain, more than she seemed at Mikhaila's condition. Sandor spoke in short angry bursts and Rochiro was a sequence of longer notes against him.

When she dreamed she saw evolutions. She went through condensed minutes of Martian evolution as it may have been, the alien genetic code producing an ecology of stunning complexity; and she dreamed the ghost's dreams, in which she walked through an ancient temple and schemed to become Uploaded and saw shadows wherever she turned.

She felt herself changing. Somewhere inside her codes began to match, to mutate into each other. To communicate.

The fever burned her. She felt as if she was no longer human. And when the voices in her head merged at last into one she knew what she had to do.

She no longer needed the erased data. As they approached First Eye, the heaviest and largest of the three black holes the *Illuminati* had discovered at the end of their immensely long journey, her new eyes began to see the quantum radiation leaking and her new mind was on the verge of deciphering it.

It was . . . strange. As if a mathematics that felt somehow wrong had become a series of deferred signifiers, operating within an exotic Saussurean *langue*. She couldn't comprehend it; but gradually, she began to discern places where the alien nature of the code abated, became almost human. She began listening for those moments, for their rhythm as they trickled out of the Eye like tears.

When Mikhaila woke up the *Trinity* was already decelerating towards First Eye and her aunt was demanding that she speak to her. It had been seven years since she had been home; though to her it was only a year. She made a good impression of the old Mikhaila and told her aunt that she needed time alone.

Then she took her Cyclop and stole away from the *Trinity*.

She floated alone and invisible, the black hole a piece of darkness in a universe of stars, and she listened to it talk.

She thought she could hear her father's voice, sometimes, in between the too-alien code. She thought he said her name, but she couldn't be sure.

She could hear other voices, too. She thought she heard her mother, who was sent into the Eye when Mikhaila was only a girl. She remembered the day of the funeral, the way her father almost didn't cry.

She thought about the idea they had come up with, this small group of *Illuminati* within *Illuminati*: that life may have evolved beyond the Eye's event horizon, in that relative band of stable space-time. A kind of life that sat inside God's eye, caught between a universe they could only see and a place where the world ended. All matter is information, her father said, all matter is data. We always thought we went straight to God, but maybe there's a stop on the way.

There was only one way to know. The Cyclop rode the pull of the Eye, heading lazily towards the massive gravity well. Mikhaila hardly paid attention, she was listening so hard. It was like reading signals in the sand, wiped away too quickly by the rushing water.

She thought she felt the tides as they began to pull her body apart, but when she looked outside she saw it was a sleek dark ship and that it was forcing her to it and she could have cried.

She *almost* understood the message. She felt her eyes growing heavy as she approached the ship, and then she blacked out.

She knew something was being done to her, both to her body and to her mind. A breaking up, a separation. She felt the moment the Otherness was gone, felt Leibniz as he was re-formed beside her, a lone and separate entity. After a while she could no longer feel the ghost, and when she woke up and looked down at herself all that remained of the blind Martian construct were pale bands of skin, like bars across her chest and stomach. She woke up grieving. It was a failure. She had hoped for transcendence, and she failed.

Gradually she began to recognise the images that were coming through her eyes, though her seeing felt limited, singular and uneasy. The first thing she saw was Aunt Alexandra's face. The Grand Mistress was looking down on her with a frown. Mikhaila began to form a word but couldn't and her aunt's face changed: an expression of concern that touched Mikhaila unexpectedly.

She slept, and didn't dream.

When she woke up her aunt was there again.

"You were being driven mad," Aunt Alexandra said to her. Mikhaila was trying to sit up and finding it difficult. "How could you think of jumping into a black hole before it's your time?"

"What have you got to hide?" Mikhaila said, the words coming slow and unfamiliar. "That something lives inside? That we could *talk* to it?"

"Yes," her aunt said, "something lives inside," and this sudden admission, most of all, lifted away an old weight in Mikhaila's mind, and made her light-headed. "But can we talk to it? To them? You tried, and you were ready to kill yourself."

"I would have . . . lived inside," Mikhaila whispered. Her eyes wouldn't focus. "All matter is information. They would have re-built me, like they did my father."

"Mikhaila . . . " Aunt Alexandra looked into her eyes and sighed. "You think there are ghosts beyond the event horizon? The *Illuminati* dead risen in heaven? You tried to understand them—they, it, whatever we can try and call whatever is inside there—and even augmented as you were in the strands of three evolutions you failed. The simple truth is we don't understand what's behind the event horizon but we treat it with respect—and with caution."

"It's a conspiracy," Mikhaila said, but discovered that she couldn't feel much about it. She remembered the children's book Sandor had discovered and it nearly made her smile. "Is that why Aldus Trismegistus died? Is that the answer to the riddle?"

"No," another voice said. "*That* was a story." The face of a man appeared beside her aunt. No, not a man. An avatar. "I managed to control my three components. I was two centuries older than you back then. And a time came when the human and Martian parts of me remained only in their pure code, and I migrated almost entirely into my Other body." He paused. "But I never died."

"Three-times Aldus, who joined with an Other, and merged with a Martian aug," Mikhaila half sang, and found that, though she didn't know why, she believed him.

"The song got it wrong," the avatar said, a little stiffly. "Aldus was the Other. The name of the human was Scott."

Aunt Alexandra coughed. "You can consider yourself initiated into the Greater Mysteries, as of now," she said. "You know almost as much as we do. I tried to tell my brother to wait and that he wasn't ready, but he didn't listen. He did the same thing as you, and it drove him insane. Is he there? Sometimes I think he is. I listen to the Eye and I can almost hear him talking to me. But if he is, then he is too alien now. Since Aldus's time we did a lot of research on three-way interfaces. I'm . . . changed. Perhaps too much. But it isn't working. It isn't enough."

She thought of the way she was driven towards the Eye. Was that what happened to her father? She tried to remember back, looking for signs: he must have already been augmented before she left. And she thought, he must have dealt with Alvarez.

She felt chilled, now, having experienced that same painful imperfect joining. Did he have marks on his skin? Was he wearing long clothes? She thought he did but could no longer be sure.

"We need something more, Mikhaila," Aldus said. "We need another element. Another way of seeing. Another form of life. That's why we're sending out the starships. Not to go back, but to go further." The avatar's eyes were almond-shaped, a too-detailed reproduction of a human eye. "To find new life, and join with them."

"That's enough," Aunt Alexandra said. "She needs to rest."

Aldus looked at her and inclined his head. "Sleep well," he said, "Grandmistress."

Mikhaila, head suddenly full of starships and stars, let herself close her eyes at the words; and sleep claimed her immediately. Her dreams felt lighter, and belonged to her alone; for she knew now that, whatever happened, she was once more herself, and the memories receded and she only dreamed, a dream that would in the coming years recur to her, that she was floating: a being of peace, a child of pure light, shining into the watching God's eyes.

SILENT BRIDGE, PALE CASCADE

BENJANUN SRIDUANGKAEW

The knife of her consciousness peeling off death in layers: this is how she wakes.

She is General Lunha of Silent Bridge, who fought one war to a draw as a man, and won five more a woman against adversaries who commanded miniature suns.

The knowledge reconstitutes piecemeal in the flexing muscles of her memory, in the gunfire-sear of her thoughts as she opens her eyes to a world of spider lilies skirmishing in flowerbeds, a sky of fractal glass. She is armed: an orchid-blade along one hip, a burst-pistol along the other. She is armored: a helm of black scarabs on her head, a sheath of amber chitin on her limbs and torso. There is no bed for her, no casket enclosing her. She comes to awareness on her feet, at ease but sharp. The way she has always been.

Grass crackles and hisses. She draws the blade, its petals unfurling razor mouths, and recognizes that this weapon is personal to her. All generals have them: a bestiary of blades and a gathering of guns, used to an edge and oiled to a sheen. She maintained a smaller collection than most; this was one she always kept at her side.

The grass is stilled, coils of circuits and muscles and fangs, petroleum stains on Lunha's sword. She fires a shot into its vitals to be certain. A detonation of soundless light.

Her datasphere snaps online. Augmens bring one of the walls into sharp focus, an output panel. At the moment, audio alone.

"We had to make sure you were physically competent." A voice keyed to a register of neutrality, inflection and otherwise; she cannot tell accent, preferred presentation, or much else. "It is our pleasure to welcome you back, General Lunha."

"My connection is restricted. Why is this?"

"There have been some changes to data handling at your tier of command. We'll send you the new protocols shortly. It is routine. You'll want a briefing."

"Yes." Lunha attempts to brute-force access, finds herself without grid privileges that ought to have been hers by right.

"Your loyalty to the Hegemony has never been questioned."

"Thus I've proven," said Lunha, who in life served it for sixty years from cadet to general.

"We will not question it now." The panel shimmers into a tactical map. "This world would offer its riches and might to our enemies. Neutralize it and the woman who lures it away from Hegemonic peace. Peruse her dossier at your leisure."

The traitor planet is Tiansong, the Lake of Bridges, which in life was Lunha's homeworld.

Their leader is Xinjia of Pale Cascade, who in life was Lunha's bride.

Naturally she questions whether she is Lunha, rebuilt from scraps of skin and smears, or a clone injected with Lunha's data. The difference is theoretical beyond clan altars; in practice the two are much the same. There is a family-ghost copy of her floating about in Tiansong's local grid, but that too is a reconstruction from secondary and tertiary sources, no more her soul or self than her career logs.

The grid enters her in a flood, though like all Hegemonic personnel above a certain rank Lunha is partitioned to retain autonomous consciousness. For good measure she runs self-diagnostics, which inform her that she is not embedded with regulators or remote surveillance. Perhaps it is a sign of trust; perhaps the reconstruction is experimental, and the biotechs did not want to risk interfering with her implants. She entertains the thought that she never died—severe injury, a long reconstruction, an edit of her memory to remove the event. The report is sealed, either way.

They've given her a tailored habitat: one section for rest, one for contemplation, one for physical practice. Being in this profession, she has few personal effects; most are accounted for. Not merely equipment but also the keepsakes of conquests. Here the gold-veined skeletons of Grenshal wolves, there the silver-blossom web of live Mahing spiders. A Silent Bridge shrine for the memories of elders, compressed snapshots of their accomplishments, proverbs and wisdom. Lunha did not consult them often, does not consult them now, and examines the altar only to ensure her family-ghost does not number among them.

Her grid access continues to be tight. She may listen in on military broadcasts of all levels when she cares to, but she can't communicate. Public memory is a matter of course and she checks that for civilian perception of

Tiansong. To the best of their knowledge Tiansong embroiled itself in civil war, during which a new religion emerged, spearheaded by Xinjia. A dispatch would be sent to return Tiansong to peace.

Reports on classified channels are somewhat different.

Out of habit she evaluates troop strength, positions, resources: this is impersonal, simply the way her mind works. She estimates that with Tiansong's defenses it'd require less than a month to subdue her homeworld with minimal damage. In a situation where that isn't a concern, it would be under a week. Quick strike rather than campaign, and entirely beneath her.

For three days she is left in isolation—no other being shares her space and she lacks social access. The void field around the compound forbids her to step far beyond the garden. On the fourth day, she stirs from meditation to the hum of moth engines, the music of shields flickering out to accommodate arrival. She does not go forth to greet nor move to arm herself; it seems beside the point.

Her handler is purebred Costeya stock, a statuesque neutrois with eyes the color of lunar frost. They wear no uniform, introduce themselves simply as Operative Isren.

"From which division?" Lunha tries to write to Isren, the right of any general to alter the thoughts and memory of lesser officers. She can't.

"Operative," Isren says, and nothing else. They bow to her in the Tiansong manner, hand cupped over fist, before saluting her. "Your situation's unique."

"Why am I required? It is no trouble to flatten Tiansong."

Isren has knelt so they are level; they have a trick of arranging their bearing and their limbs so that the difference in height doesn't intimidate. "A bloodless solution is sought."

"There are other Tiansong personnel in active service."

When Isren smiles there's something of the flirt in the bend of their mouth. "None so brilliant as you. Xinjia of Pale Cascade is a labyrinthine opponent. She has brought awareness of the public sync to her world and had the opportunity to spread the idea before we imposed embargo. She boasts . . . disconnect. In essence she's become an infection."

"Has she achieved it? Disconnect?"

A shard of silence pinched between Isren's professional circumspection and the situation's need for candor. When they do speak it is delicately, around the edge of this balance. "Not through the conventional methods. Her way entails ripping out network nodes and reverse-engineering them. Fifty-fifty chance for cerebral damage. Five to eight thousand have been incapacitated, at last count."

Lunha browses through available reports. Risk of brain death or not, Xinjia has gained traction, so much that she has been made First of Tiansong. It's not unanimous; nearly half the clans posited against her. But nearly half was not half, and Silent Bridge tipped the scale. Her plans have been broadcast to twenty independent worlds. "Removing her won't suffice."

"No. You are invested in keeping Tiansong well, Xinjia alive, and that's why we brought you back."

"Let me travel there. I would assess the situation on the ground."

"That was anticipated," Isren says. "We are on Tiansong."

When Lunha last visited her homeworld she was a man. Among family she's celebrated only as daughter and niece, for all that she flows between the two as water over stone. Whatever her gender, General Lunha's face—pride of several clans—is too well known, and so she puts on a mesh to hollow out her cheeks, broaden her nose, slope out her brow.

She travels light, almost ascetically. One firearm, one blade. Tiansong currency, but not too much. Her one concession to luxury is a disruptor array to guard against targeting and deep scans. Isren does not accompany her in person; on the pristine sea of Tiansong phenotypes, Isren's Costeya face would be an oil slick. The operative has no objection to blending in, but on so short a notice, adjusting musculature, complexion and facial tells is beyond even Isren.

Lunha avoids air transports and their neural checks, keeping to the trains and their serpent-tracks. She takes her time. It is a leave of absence—the idea amuses and she catches herself smiling into the scaled window, her reflection momentarily interrupting art ads. One of them urges her to see a production of *The Pearl Goddess and the Turtle,* done by live actors and performed in a grid-dead auditorium. No recording, no interruptions.

At one clan-hold she says she is a daughter of Razor Garden; at another, in different clothes and with a voice deepened by mods, Lunha introduces himself as a groom newly marrying into Peony Aqueduct. At each Lunha is received with courtesy and invited to evening teas, wedding dinners, autumn feasts. Despite the tension of embargo they are hospitable, but none will so much as breathe Xinjia's name.

Her breakthrough comes while she sits in a kitchen sipping plum tea, legs stretched out and listening to an elderly cook who fancies she resembles his middle son, long lost to a gambling addiction. "You want to destroy a nemesis, you teach their child to gamble," the cook is saying as he spoons chives and onions into dumpling skin.

"So the ancestors say." Lunha's enemies tend toward a more direct approach. She takes pride in having survived some two hundred assassination attempts, though it doesn't escape her that she might've failed to foil the final one. "These days there are quicker ways."

The cook chuckles like dry clay cracking. "These days you point the young, impressionable son to Pale Cascade."

"Ah, it is but half a chance of ruin. I thought they hosted guests no more, having become grudging on hospitality of late? Since we can't get off-world it was my hope to at least visit every hold before matrimony binds me . . . "

He shrugs, pinches the last dumpling shut, and begins arranging them in the steamer. On Tiansong no one trusts replicants to get cuisine right. "If you know someone who knows someone in Silent Bridge."

"Is that so. Many thanks, uncle."

She catches the next finned, plumaged train bound for her ancestral home.

The public sync, the great shared memory, is an instrument to maintain peace. Even after learning of it and what it does, Lunha continued to believe this, as she does now. It doesn't do much for freedom of thought; it comes with all the downsides of information regulated under the state's clenched fist and the grid usurps perception of the real. But it functions, stabilizes. The Costeya Hegemony has existed in equilibrium for centuries.

It is useful now as she edits herself into the distant branches of Silent Bridge rather than its primary boughs, as her true birth order dictates. The specifics make her hesitate. She settles on female, for convenience more than anything, and picks childless Ninth Aunt as her mother. No sibling, less dissonance to having a sudden sister where once there was none. Those reactions cannot be overridden. Emotions cannot be molded.

When she arrives at the entrance bridge suspended between the maws of pearl-clasping dragons, Ninth Aunt comes to greet her. "My girl," her aunt says uncertainly, "what kept you so long in Razor Garden?"

"Grand nuptials, Mother, and I earned my board helping." A bow, proper. An embrace, stiff. Having a daughter is merely a fact, the gestures Ninth Aunt makes merely obligation.

Her edits have it that she's been away three months; in truth she hasn't been home for as long as—her mind stumbles over the rut of her death. But not counting that it's been five years. Silent Bridge hasn't changed. A central pagoda for common worship. Sapphire arches and garnet gates twining in conversation to mark the city's boundaries. Tiansong cities have always been less crowded than most, and there's never that density of lives in the habitat towers here as on Costeya birthworlds. A wealth of space, a freedom of aesthetics. Barely a whisper of the Hegemony.

Far better off than many Costeya subjects, Lunha knows for a fact; there are border planets that remain in ruins even to this day after their annexation. She cannot understand Xinjia.

• • •

When they first met Xinjia wore masks and prosthetic arms; she danced between folded shadows of dragons and herons, only parts of her visible in infrared. Like all thespians of her caliber, Xinjia never appeared in off-world broadcasts. Tiansong makes a fortune out of its insularity—foreigners wishing to enjoy its arts must come to the source and pay dearly, though there are always rogues and imitators.

Lunha in the audience, breathless from applause. A friend who knew a friend brokered her an introduction. Offstage, Xinjia shed the mask but kept the dress, paper breastplate and bladed belts. In the custom of shadow-thespians she wore her face plain, bare, without mods. It made Lunha touch her own, self-conscious of the optic overlays, the duochrome cast to her jawline, replicant-chic.

They talked quickly, amidst the noise of departing spectators; they talked again later, in the quiet of the staff's lounge where the furniture, retrogressive, did not contour to their bodies.

"You talk drama like a layperson," Xinjia remarked once, between sips of liquid gold and jellyfish garnished in diced ivory.

"I don't have a background."

"Officer school doesn't teach fine arts?" The actor drew a finger across Lunha's knuckles. "A soldier with a passion for theater."

"Not before tonight." Lunha caught herself, succeeded in not blushing.

"Soldiers fascinate me," Xinjia said, absently. "The juxtaposition of discipline and danger. Violence and control."

Tiansong marriage lasts five years, at the end of which spouses and family members evaluate one another: how well they fit, how well they belong. A collaborative project.

They wedded on a barge, surrounded by family, blessed by avatars of thundering war-gods with their quadruple arms and spears and battle-wheels. Given that Silent Bridge and Pale Cascade were old rivals, neither Xinjia nor Lunha expected it to last—and it came a surprise to all involved that the marriage was extended past the first five years into the second, then the third.

Divorce came after Lunha made lieutenant-colonel. By then they'd been spouses for nineteen years.

The ivory tiles and the redwood walls of the great house hum with trackers. Lunha sets her array to nullify ones that would gene-match her.

Silent Bridge has always been one of the more—paranoid, she supposes other clans would say—but it's never been like this. A city-wide security lockdown. Anyone not family has been ejected; off-worlders are long gone, scared away by a non-existent epidemic just before the embargo fell.

Xinjia anticipated that sanction. Lunha considers the possibility that she found a way to manipulate the sync. It unsettles.

She keeps up desultory small talk with Ninth Aunt, with cousins who tentatively say they have missed her. It is the thing to say to a relative months unseen. They do it carefully, unsure of the words, of regarding her as family.

To pretend to be a stranger pretending to be of Silent Bridge. Lunha buried away entirely, like the haunting she is, the ghost she should be.

"Is that all you have?" Ninth Aunt says, trying to be a mother. "The clothes on your back and not much else?"

"I've always traveled light." Lunha nods. "You know that, Mother."

"You've never taken care of yourself, more like."

It always surprises Lunha what people imagine to fill up the gaps, patch up the cracks of recall brought by the blunt impact of edit. A defense mechanism, army psychologists liked to tell her, to ward off mental dissolution. There are Hegemonic facilities devoted to research into that, the sync's effects. What it can do. What it can't.

Isren has gifted her with a spy-host; Lunha activates it with a visualization of tadpoles bursting through deep water. She avoids contact. There are disconnected people in Silent Bridge. They would know Ninth Aunt has never had children.

After days of self-imposed house arrest, she steals to the streets.

In the hours of thought and ancestors, the walkways are burnished gold. A low whisper of overhead vehicles like memory, a gleam of pearl from atmospheric stations like moons. Lunha inhales not air but the quiet.

She wanders first aimless, then with a direction as she cross-references the host's eavesdropped data. From the security measures she assumed it would be the great house, the halls in which Silent Bridge primaries make governance and cast laws. Two of them her mothers. They are proud of Lunha, but they always expected her rise through the ranks, her conquests of fifteen worlds in Costeya's name, and if she'd been or done any less it would have been a blot on a lineage of prodigies.

An old shrine, turtle tiles and turtle roof, stone monks enclosing a garden of fern and lavender. The scriptorium is guarded by wasp drones. She inputs a bypass code, stop-motion images of blue heron spearing silver fish. A murmur of acknowledgment and they give way; these are all Hegemonic make, and she has been reinstated as general. They've been reverse-engineered, but not deep enough to keep her out. She can't quite fault the Tiansong techs; less than a thousand in the Hegemony command her level of access.

Between shelves showing paper books in augmens visuals, Lunha waits. She passes the time reading poetry, immersing herself in Huasing's interlocking seven-ten stanzas, Gweilin's interstitial prose-sculpture telling of the sun-archer and her moon-wife. They eel through her awareness, comforting, the balm of familiarity.

Xinjia arrives, eventually. It is where she comes to think when she needs solitude, and from what Lunha can tell solitude is precious to her these days, too rare.

The scriptorium is large, and Lunha did not go sixty years in the army without learning stealth. She finds a space to occupy, a blind spot where Xinjia will not look, and for a time simply observes.

Xinjia looks at peace, striding easily to the mat and the bar. She sheds her slippers, most of her clothes, until she is down to pastel secondskin, lavender shifting to gray as she moves. Hands on the bar she arches backward, stretching until her neck cords, the muscles in her torso pushing out in bas-relief.

Lunha turns off vocal mods and says, in her own voice, "Xinjia."

Her former wife straightens quickly, supple—sinuous. They had elaborate pet names for each other once. Bai Suzhen for Xinjia, after the white snake of legend.

A precipice moment, but Xinjia does not fall. "General Lunha is dead. What are you?"

"A ghost." Lunha reaches into Tiansong's grid. Of course there's a copy of her in the archive of primaries, her knowledge and victories turned to clan wisdom. "But you would be familiar with that."

"Shall I offer you tea?"

"No," Lunha says, though she follows when Xinjia leads her to the low table, the cushions. "How have you been?"

"You'd be familiar with updates on me."

"First of Tiansong."

"It was necessary to obtain that title to do what needs doing." Xinjia calls up the ghost: Lunha's face, serene. Feminine. Xinjia did not much like it when, on rare occasions, Lunha was a man. "This contains much of how you planned, how you dealt with your enemies."

"The data they sent home would be scoured of classified information." A jar of ashes, after a fashion.

"I was more interested in how you thought. Strange, but I don't think I ever knew you so well as posthumously." The secondskin has absorbed sweat, leaves only a trace of clean, saline scent. Xinjia has never worn perfume. Offstage she goes through the world strictly as herself. "There were votes to input your data to a replicant. I overrode it."

"We haven't been spouses for a long time."

"I remarried," Xinjia says, "into Silent Bridge. And so we are family, which gives me some rights over managing your image. Your mothers agreed with me the replicant idea was . . . abhorrent. May I touch you?"

Lunha nods and watches Xinjia's thumb follow the line of her jaw, her nose, her mouth. There Xinjia stops, a weight of consideration, a pressure of shared recall.

"Is it surgery or are you wearing something over your face?"

"The latter," she says against Xinjia's finger and entertains the thought of their first time together, feeding each other slices of persimmon, licking the sweetness off each other's hand. Slick fabrics that warmed to them, braids of sheet slithering against hips and thighs and ankles. For sex Xinjia never liked a still bed. "Why have you undertaken this?"

"A glitch," Xinjia says, in that detached way. Her hand has drifted away to rest—as though incidentally—on Lunha's knee. "A glitch that left some out of sync, myself among them. What was it? Something happening on Yodsana, an explosion at a resort. Just a tidbit of news, insignificant, nothing to do with us. I think I was looking up Yodsana puppet theater, or else I'd never have noticed. To me the resort was operating as usual. To everyone else it'd gone up in flames, fifty tourists dead. I made a note to myself. Except a few days later I couldn't remember why or what it was about. What did I care?"

"That happens." Rarely. Beyond rare.

Xinjia smiles, faint. "I followed some leads, made discoveries, gained contacts. It isn't just me, Lunha. As we speak disconnect is happening on more worlds than you realize, one or two persons at a time. I've only taken it to a larger scale."

"You will take all of Tiansong with you."

"Enough of Tiansong wanted this that they elected me First. Can you imagine how I felt when—" Xinjia blinks, pulls away. A command brings up a floor compartment: a set of cups, a dispenser. "When did they let you . . . ?"

"General. After three successful campaigns." At this point it seems senseless to keep unsaid. "I underwent preparatory conditioning to minimize dissonance, though at the time I didn't realize what it was for."

"Hegemonic personnel must've let it slip. To friends, loved ones."

"Seldom. Easily overwritten." Easily detected. The penalties exorbitant.

"You are all right with this?" Xinjia pours. Chrysanthemum steam, the tea thick with tiny black pearls harvested from Razor Garden orchards. "Sixty years in service, an illustrious career. You can't understand at all why I'm doing this, why others want me to do this?"

"In principle I can guess. In practice—this is not wise."

A cup is slid toward her. "They can take all we are from us. They can rob us of our languages, our cities, our names; they can make us strangers to ourselves and to our ghosts, until there's no one left to tend the altars or follow the hour of thought or sweep the graves."

Lunha sips. She misses touch, not just any human contact but Xinjia's specifically. "The Hegemony has no cause to do that. The amount of rewriting it'd take would be colossal."

"It would cost them less to reduce Tiansong to scorch marks than to process that much. Yes. Should they find a reason though, my soldier, they will do it. Changing us a little at a time. Perhaps one day we'll stop lighting the incenses, the next we'll have Costeya replicants cooking for us. After a month, no one dances anymore the way I do. Instead: Costeya scripts, chrome stages and replicants performers, like on Imral and Salhune. They've this hold on our . . . everything. That I cannot abide." Her former wife, someone else's now, looks up. "I believed that neither would you."

"Xinjia. Bai Suzhen." Lunha does not reach out, still, will not be the one to yield tenderness. They haven't been spouses for so long. "Eighty years ago there was a conflict between Iron Gate and Crimson Falls. It was escalating. It'd have torn Tiansong apart, a field of ruins and carcasses, until the Hegemony intervened. A thorough edit. Now no one remembers that; now Iron Gate and Crimson Falls are at peace. You may not believe it, but that is what soldiers fight for—to preserve equilibrium, to bring stability."

"To enforce the Hegemonic definition of that."

"It's one that works."

"And the massacres of Tiansong empresses when Costeya first took over, what about that? Is that stability; is that peace? Or is it bygones simply because it's been all of three centuries? No. Don't answer that."

"There are planets *now* which suffer much worse. I've been there; I've ordered their ruin and the execution of their citizens." Lunha knows that she has failed, already. That there was never a way to win. Not here.

"You are not yourself," Xinjia says softly.

"I am. I have always been myself."

"Then there is no ground on which we can meet. Perhaps there never has been."

Lunha drinks until there's no more in her cup, tea or pearl. "I will find a way to keep Tiansong safe."

In the end neither of them surrenders. They do not touch; they do not kiss. A parting of strangers' courtesy.

"Isren."

It takes no more than that, on their unique frequency, to summon the operative. A link, with visuals to let her know Isren remains in the habitat. "Yes, General?"

"I could not dissuade First of Tiansong."

"In that case please head for Iron Gate. There'll be a shuttle keyed to one of our ships in orbit."

"No." Lunha gazes out through the round window, makes it widen to take up the whole wall. Silent Bridge at midday is platinum. "Bring me armor. I expect it within seventy-two hours. Are you authorized to officiate a duel?"

Her handler's expression does not change, save for a rapid blink. "That's not what we had in mind, General."

"A duel minimizes collateral damage. Tiansong's representative wins and we leave it under embargo, to limit the influence of disconnect. If Xinjia is assassinated, apprehended or otherwise forcibly stopped there will be others, and not on this world alone. It'll be almost impossible to track the unsynchronized." It is not a certainty, but it is how Xinjia would have learned to plot from Lunha's image. "I win and Tiansong gives up its schemes, surrenders to reintegration. I don't lose, Operative Isren."

"You invoke an archaic statute."

"I invoke it correctly, and this is not the first time I've pushed to resolve by single combat. This is a situation where military destruction is untenable, diplomatic solution impossible."

"If you lose, General, I'll be overriding the result." Isren is silent for a moment. "A duel to the death."

"So it goes."

She sends word to Xinjia to choose a single-combat proxy, briskly outlining the terms. Xinjia accepts them immediately. They are the best that can be had, under the circumstances.

Lunha revokes the edits she made and takes off the facial mesh. She spends some time cleaning, hot water this side of scalding, balm and pigments to smooth away marks left by the mesh. Tiansong commanders of old did that, purify mind and body before going into battle, and Lunha has always followed suit. Not much time for the mind, but few engagements ever gave her the leisure.

Isren's arrival is not covert, and Silent Bridge is prepared. Lunha watches a feed from the operative's eyes as the primaries greet the neutrois, coolly formal. Isren's readouts telling who is disconnected: Lunha's mothers, two other primaries, distant cousins Lunha doesn't know—too young.

They escort Isren, courteous. Lunha does not admit them into her room. Her mothers catch a glimpse of her face—her own, the face she was born and grew up with—and Mother Yinliang's eyes widen, stricken.

Isren unpacks armor, dress uniform, more weapons. "I assumed you'd want this to be ceremonious. I've obtained authorization for your . . . tactical decision."

Perhaps she should've found time to speak to her mothers, Lunha thinks, but it is too late, she moved too fast. Odd, that. In battle there's never been such a thing as *too fast*. "I appreciate it."

"Do you want to talk about it?" Isren tilts their head, just enough to emphasize a pale throat notched by a jeweled implant.

"I don't intend to become familiar with you, Operative."

The neutrois' laugh is ambiguous. "I'm married, quite happily. A career soldier like you, though she's not half as feted. There's an advantage to partnering within the ranks. Fewer secrets to keep. Speaking of that, has the First of Tiansong gone entirely offline, physically removed the neural implants? Can she still interface with the grid?"

"She's kept the implants."

Isren inclines their head. "I've sent you a program. Experimental. It'll reintegrate her into sync. The infiltration method is the best of what we have; all you need is to establish a link with her and it'll latch on."

"Side-effects?" Lunha grips the helm in her hands and decides against it. She'll show her face.

"So far as it's been tested, none. The worst that could happen is that it won't work."

No side-effects. A program that forces neural interface back into the grid, and Isren would have her believe there are no side-effects. Isren wears no immediately visible protection, but they are not without. Lunha calculates her odds of avoiding the nerve toxins and disabling Isren before the operative's nanos activate. Aloud she says only, "I'll take that into account, Operative Isren. My thanks."

At night, Silent Bridge is sapphires. All the colors that sapphires can be, the finest grade and luster.

Under her armor the dress uniform is snug; at her hip the orchid-blade rests with the ease of her own limbs. The winds cut harsh enough to sting and the summit of the great house is sheer, the tiles under them smooth.

Mother Yinliang has no expression anymore; Mother Fangxiu never did. Xinjia merely looks abstract, her gaze apathetic save when it rests on her proxy. A broad woman, sleek and muscled like a fox, veteran champion of Iron Gate pits. An insult, when it comes down to it, though Lunha does not underestimate.

Each pair of eyes records and broadcasts. The uniform, the armor. She is a Hegemonic general. Except for her and Isren there is no hint of Costeya anywhere in Silent Bridge.

Still time to execute that program, General. Isren's voice through the private band.

Lunha strides forward to pay her mothers respect. Bending one knee, head bowed, the submission of a proper child. Neither answers her; neither touches her head. She accepts that and rises to face the pit fighter.

The first trickle of adrenaline. Her reflexes coil and her mind settles into that space of faceted clarity, the interior of her skull arctic and luminous.

She unsheathes her orchid-blade, its mouths baring teeth to the wind, its teeth clicking hunger to the cold.

They begin.

THE TEAR

IAN McDONALD

Ptey, sailing

On the night that Ptey voyaged out to have his soul shattered, eight hundred stars set sail across the sky. It was an evening at Great Winter's ending. The sunlit hours raced toward High Summer, each day lavishly more full of light than the one before. In this latitude, the sun hardly set at all after the spring equinox, rolling along the horizon, fat and idle and pleased with itself. Summer-born Ptey turned his face to the sun as it dipped briefly beneath the horizon, closed his eyes, enjoyed its lingering warmth on his eyelids, in the angle of his cheekbones, on his lips. To the summer-born, any loss of the light was a reminder of the terrible, sad months of winter and the unbroken, encircling dark.

But we have the stars, his father said, a Winter-born. *We are born looking out into the universe.*

Ptey's father commanded the little machines that ran the catamaran, trimming sail, winding sheets, setting course by the tumble of satellites; but the tiller he held himself. The equinoctial gales had spun away to the west two weeks before and the catboat ran fast and fresh on a sweet wind across the darkening water. Twins hulls cut through the ripple-reflections of gas-flares from the Temejveri oil platforms. As the sun slipped beneath the huge dark horizon and the warmth fell from the hollows of Ptey's face, so his father turned his face to the sky. Tonight, he wore his Steris Aspect. The ritual selves scared Ptey, so rarely were they unfurled in Ctarisphay: births, namings, betrothals and marriages, divorces and deaths. And of course, the Manifoldings. Familiar faces became distant and formal. Their language changed, their bodies seemed slower, heavier. They became possessed by strange, special knowledges. Only Steris possessed the language for the robots to sail the catamaran and, despite the wheel of positioning satellites around tilted Tay, the latitude and longitude of the Manifold House. The catamaran itself was only run out from its boathouse, to strong songs heavy with clashing harmonies, when a child from Ctarisphay on the edge of adulthood sailed out beyond the outer mole and the fleet of oil platforms to have his or her personality unfolded into eight.

Only two months since, Cjatay had sailed out into the oily black of a late winter afternoon. Ptey was Summer-born, a Solstice boy; Cjatay a late Autumn. It was considered remarkable that they shared enough in common to be able to speak to each other, let alone become the howling boys of the neighborhood, the source of every broken window and borrowed boat. The best part of three seasons between them, but here was only two moons later, leaving behind the pulsing gas flares and maze of pipe work of the sheltering oil-fields, heading into the great, gentle oceanic glow of the plankton blooms, steering by the stars, the occupied, haunted stars. The Manifolding was never a thing of moons and calendars, but of mothers' watchings and grand-mothers' knowings and teachers' notings and fathers' murmurings, of subtly shifted razors and untimely lethargies, of deep-swinging voices and stained bedsheets.

On Etjay Quay, where the porcelain houses leaned over the landing, Ptey had thrown his friend's bag down into the boat. Cjatay's father had caught it and frowned. There were observances. Ways. Forms.

"See you," Ptey had said.

"See you." Then the wind caught in the catamaran's tall, curved sails and carried it away from the rain-wet, shiny faces of the houses of Ctarisphay. Ptey had watched the boat until it was lost in the light dapple of the city's lamps on the winter-dark water. See Cjatay he would, after his six months on the Manifold House. But only partially. There would be Cjatays he had never known, never even met. Eight of them, and the Cjatay with whom he had stayed out all the brief Low Summer nights of the prith run on the fishing staithes, skinny as the piers' wooden legs silhouetted against the huge sun kissing the edge of the world, would be but a part, a dream of one of the new names and new personalities. Would he know him when he met him on the great floating university that was the Manifold House?

Would he know himself?

"Are they moving yet?" Steris called from the tiller. Ptey shielded his dark-accustomed eyes against the pervasive glow of the carbon-absorbing plankton blooms and peered into the sky. *Sail of Bright Anticipation* cut two lines of liquid black through the gently undulating sheet of biolight, fraying at the edges into fractal curls of luminescence as the sheets of microorganisms sought each other.

"Nothing yet."

But it would be soon, and it would be tremendous. Eight hundred stars setting out across the night. Through the changes and domestic rituals of his sudden Manifolding, Ptey had been aware of sky-watch parties being arranged, star-gazing groups setting up telescopes along the quays and in the campaniles, while day on day the story moved closer to the head of the news. Half the world—that half of the world not blinded by its extravagant axial tilt—would be looking to the sky. Watching Steris rig *Sail of Bright Anticipation*, Ptey had felt cheated, like a sick child confined to bed while festival raged across the boats lashed beneath his window. Now, as the swell of the deep dark of his world's girdling ocean lifted the twin prows of *Sail of Bright Anticipation*, on his web of shock-plastic mesh ahead of the mast, Ptey felt his excitement lift with it. A carpet of lights below, a sky of stars above: all his alone.

They were not stars. They were the eight hundred and twenty six space habitats of the Anpreen Commonweal, spheres of nano-carbon ice and water five hundred kilometers in diameter that for twice Ptey's lifetime had adorned Bephis, the ringed gas giant, like a necklace of pearls hidden in a velvet bag, far from eye and mind. The negotiations fell into eras. The Panic; when the world of Tay became aware that the gravity waves pulsing through the huge ripple tank that was their ocean-bound planet were the bow-shocks of massive artifacts decelerating from near light-speed. The Denial, when Tay's governments decided it was Best Really to try and hide the fact that their solar system had been immigrated into by eight hundred-and-some space vehicles, each larger than Tay's petty moons, falling into neat and proper order around Bephis. The Soliciting, when it became obvious that Denial was futile—but on our terms, our terms. A fleet of space probes was dispatched to survey and attempt radio contact with the arrivals—as yet silent as ice. And, when they were not blasted from space or vaporized or collapsed into quantum black holes or any of the plethora of fanciful destructions imagined in the popular media, the Overture. The Sobering, when it was realized that these star-visitors existed primarily as swarms of free-swimming nano-assemblers in the free-fall spherical oceans of their eight hundred and some habitats, one mind with many forms; and, for the Anpreen, the surprise that these archaic hominiforms on this backwater planet were many selves within one body. One thing they shared and understood well. Water. It ran through their histories, it flowed around their ecologies, it mediated their molecules. After one hundred and twelve years of near-light speed flight, the Anpreen Commonweal was desperately short of water; their spherical oceans shriveled almost into zero gravity teardrops within the immense, nano-tech-reinforced ice shells. Then began the era of Negotiation, the most prolonged of the phases of contact, and the most complex. It had taken three years to establish the philosophical foundations: the Anpreen, an ancient species of the great Clade, had long been a colonial mind, arranged in subtle hierarchies of self-knowledge and ability, and did not know who to talk to, whom to ask for a decision, in a political system with as many governments and nations as there were islands and archipelagos scattered across the world ocean of the fourth planet from the sun.

Now the era of Negotiation had become the era of Open Trade. The Anpreen habitats spent their last drops of reaction mass to break orbit around Bephis and move the Commonweal in-system. Their destination was not Tay, but Tejaphay, Tay's sunward neighbor, a huge waterworld of unbroken ocean one hundred kilometers deep, crushing gravity, and endless storms. A billion years before the seed-ships probed the remote star system, the gravitational interplay of giant worlds had sent the least of their number spiraling sunwards. Solar wind had stripped away its huge atmosphere and melted its mantle of water ice into a planetary ocean, deep and dark as nightmares. It was that wink of water in the system-scale interferometers of the Can-Bet-Merey people, half a million years before, that had inspired them to fill their night sky with solar sails as one hundred thousand slow seed-ships rode out on flickering launch lasers toward the new system. An evangelically pro-life people were the Can-Bet-Merey, zealous for the Clade's implicit dogma that intelligence was the only force in the universe capable of defeating the physical death of space-time.

If the tens of thousand of biological packages they had rained into the world-ocean of Tejaphay had germinated life, Tay's probes had yet to discover it. The Can-Bet-Merey did strike roots in the afterthought, that little blue pearl next out from the sun, a tear spun from huge Tejaphay.

One hundred thousand the years ago, the Can-Bet-Merey had entered the post-biological phase of intelligence and moved to that level that could no longer communicate with the biological life of Tay, or even the Anpreen.

"Can you see anything yet?" A call from the tiller. *Sail of Bright Anticipation* had left behind the carbon-soaked plankton bloom, the ocean was deep dark and boundless. Sky and sea blurred; stars became confused with the riding lights of ships close on the horizon.

"Is it time?" Ptey called back.

"Five minutes ago."

Ptey found a footing on the webbing, and, one hand wrapped in the sheets, stood up to scan the huge sky. Every child of Tay, crazily tilted at 48 degrees to the ecliptic, grew up conscious that her planet was a ball rolling around the sun and that the stars were far, vast and slow, almost unchanging. But stars could change; Bephis, that soft smudge of light low in the south-east, blurred by the glow of a eight hundred moon-sized space habitats, would soon be once again the hard point of light by which his ancestors had steered to their Manifoldings.

"Give it time," Ptey shouted. Time. The Anpreen were already voyaging; had switched on their drives and pulled out of orbit almost an hour before. The slow light of their embarkation had still not reached Tay. He saw the numbers spinning around in his head, accelerations, vectors, space and time all arranged around him like fluttering carnival banners. It had taken Ptey a long time to understand that not everyone could see numbers like him and reach out and make them do what they wanted.

"Well, I'll be watching the football," Cjatay had declared when Teacher Deu had declared a Special Class Project in conjunction with the Noble Observatory of Pteu to celebrate the Anpreen migration. "We're all jumping up and down, Anpreen this, Anpreen that, but when it comes down to it, they aliens and we don't know what they really want, no one does."

"They're not aliens," Ptey had hissed back. "There *are* no aliens, don't you know that? We're all just part of the one big Clade."

Then Teacher Deu had shouted at them quiet you boys and they had straightened themselves at their kneeling-desks, but Cjatay had hissed,

"So if they're our cousins, why don't they give us their star-crosser drive?"

Such was the friendship between Ptey and Cjatay that they would argue over nodes of free-swimming nanotechnology orbiting a gas giant.

"Look! Oh look!"

Slowly, very slowy, Bephis was unraveling into a glowing smudge, like one of the swarms of nuchpas that hung above the waves like smoke on High Summer mornings. The fleet was moving. Eight hundred worlds. The numbers in his skull told Ptey that the Anpreen Commonweal was already at ten percent of lightspeed. He tried to work out the relativistic deformations of space-time but there were too many numbers flocking around him too fast. Instead, he watched Bephis unfurl into a galaxy, that cloud of stars slowly pull away from the bright mote of the gas giant. Crossing the ocean of night. Ptey glanced behind him. In the big dark, his father's face was hard to read, especially as Steris, who was sober and focused, and, Ptey had learned, not particularly bright. He seemed to be smiling.

It is a deep understanding, the realization that you are cleverer than your parents, Ptey thought. Behind that first smirking, satisfied sense of your own smartness comes a more profound understanding; that smart is only smart at some things, in some situations. Clever is conditional: Ptey could calculate the space-time distortion of eight hundred space habitats, plot a course across the dark, steepening sea by the stars in their courses, but he could never harness the winds or whistle the small commands to the machines, all the weather-cleverness of Steris. That is how our world has shaped our intelligences. A self for every season.

The ravel of stars was unwinding, the Anpreen migration flowing into a ribbon of sparkles, a scarf of night beyond the veils of the aurora. Tomorrow night, it would adorn Tejaphay, that great blue guide star on the edge of the world, that had become a glowing smudge, a thumbprint of the alien. Tomorrow night, Ptey would look at that blue eye in the sky from the minarets of the Manifold House. He knew that it had minarets; every child knew what the Manifold House and its sister houses all round the world, looked like. Great hulks of grey wood gone silvery from salt and sun, built over upon through within alongside until they were floating cities. Cities of children. But the popular imaginations of Teacher Deu's Grade Eight class never painted them bright and loud with voices; they were dark, sooty labyrinths sailing under a perpetual cloud of black diesel smoke that poured from a thousand chimneys, taller even than the masts and towers. The images were sharp in Ptey's mind, but he could never see himself there, in those winding wooden staircases loud with the cries of sea birds, looking out from the high balconies across the glowing sea. Then his breath caught. All his imaginings and failures to imagine were made true as lights disentangled themselves from the skein of stars of the Anpreen migration: red and green stars, the riding lights of the Manifold House. Now he could feel the thrum of its engines and generators through the water and the twin hulls. Ptey set his hand to the carbon nanofiber mast. It sang to deep harmonic. And just as the stars are always further than you think, so Prey saw that the lights of the Manifold House were closer than he thought, that he was right under them, that *Sail of Bright Anticipation* was slipping through the outer buoys and nets, and that the towers and spires and minarets, rising in his vision, one by one, were obliterating the stars.

Nejben, swimming

Beneath a sky of honey, Nejben stood hip deep in water warm as blood, deep as forgetting. This High Summer midnight, the sun was still clear from the horizon, and in its constant heat and light, the wood of the Manifold House's old, warped spires seemed to exhale a spicy musk, the distilled pheromone of centuries of teenage hormones and sexual angsts and identity crises. In cupped hands, Nejben scooped up the waters of the Chalybeate Pool and let them run, gold and thick, through his fingers. He savored the sensuality, observed the flash of sunlight through the falling water, noted the cool, deep plash as the pool received its own. A new Aspect, Nejben; old in observation and knowledge, for the body remained the same though a flock of selves came to roost in it, fresh in interpretation and experience.

When Nejben first emerged, shivering and anoxic, from the Chalybeate Pool, to be wrapped in silvery thermal sheets by the agisters, he had feared himself mad. A voice in his head, that would not go away, that would not be shut up, that seemed to know him, know every part of him.

"It's perfectly normal," said agister Ashbey, a plump, serious woman with the blackest skin Nejben had ever seen. But he remembered that every Ritual Aspect was serious, and in the Manifold House the agisters were never in any other Aspect. None that the novices would ever see. "Perfectly natural. It takes time for your Prior, your childhood Aspect, to find its place and relinquish the control of the higher cognitive levels. Give it time. Talk to him. Reassure him. He will feel very lost, very alone, like he has lost everything that he ever knew. Except you, Nejben."

The time-free, sun-filled days in the sunny, smoggy yards and cloisters of the First Novitiate were full of whisperings; boys and girls like himself whispering goodbye to their childhoods. Nejben learned his Prior's dreads, that the self that had been called Ptey feared that the numbers, the patterns between them, the ability to reduce physical objects to mathematics and see in an instant their relationships and implications, would be utterly lost. He saw also that Nejben in himself scared Ptey: the easy physicality, the unselfconscious interest in his own body, the awareness of the hormones pumping like tidewater through his tubes and cells; the ever-present, ever-tickling nag of sex; everywhere, everywhen, everyone and thing. Even as a child-self, even as shadow, Ptey knew that the first self to be birthed at the Manifold House was the pubescent self, the sexual self, but he felt this growing, aching youth to be more alien than the disembodied, mathematical Anpreen.

The tiers led down into the palp pool. In its depths, translucencies shifted. Nejben shivered in the warm High Summer midnight.

"Hey! Ptey!"

Names flocked around the Manifold House's towers like sun-gulls. New selves, new identities unfolded every hour of every day and yet old names clung. Agister Ashbey, jokey and astute, taught the social subtleties by which adults knew what Aspect and name to address and which Aspect and name of their own to wear in response. From the shade of the Poljeri Cloister, Puzhay waved. Ptey had found girls frightening, but Nejben liked them, enjoyed their company and the little games of admiring insult and flirting mock-animosity he played with them. He reckoned he understood girls now. Puzhay was small, still boy-figured, her skin Winterborn-pale, a Janni from Bedenderay, where at midwinter the atmosphere froze. She had a barbarous accent and continental manners, but Nejben found himself thinking often about her small, flat boy-breasts with their big, thumbable nipples. He had never thought when he came to the Manifold House that there would be people here from places other than Ctarisphay and its archipelago sisters. People—girls—from the big polar continent. Rude girls who cursed and openly called boys' names.

"Puzhay! What're you doing?"

"Going in."

"For the palps?"

"Nah. Just going in."

Nejben found and enjoyed a sudden, swift swelling of his dick as he watched Puzhay's breasts taunten as she raised her arms above her head and dived, awkward as a Bedenderay land-girl, into the water. Water hid it. Sun dapple kept it secret. The he felt a shiver run over him and he dived down, deep down. Almost he let the air rush out of him in a gasp as he felt the cool cool water close around his body; then he saw Puzhay in her tight swim-shorts that made her ass look so strong and muscley turn in the water, tiny bubbles leaking from her nose, to grin and wave and beckon him down. Nejben swam down past the descending tiers of steps. Green opened before him, the bottomless emerald beyond the anti-skray nets where the Chalybeate pond was refreshed by the borderless sea. Between her pale red body and the deep green sea was the shimmering curtains of the palps.

They did not make them we did not bring them they were here forever. Ten thousand years of theology, biology, and xenology in that simple kinder-group rhyme. Nejben—all his people—had always known their special place; stranger to this world, spurted into the womb of the world-sea as the star-sperm, the seed of sentience. Twenty million drops of life-seed swam ashore and became humanity, the rest swam out to sea and met and smelled and loved the palps, older than forever. Now Nejben turned and twisted like an eel past funny, flirting, heartbreaking Puzhay, turning to show the merest glimpse of his own sperm-eel, down toward the palps. The curtain of living jelly rippled and dissolved into their separate lives. Slick, cold, quivering jelly slid across his sex-warm flesh. Nejben shivered, quivered; repelled yet aroused in a way that was other than sex. The water took on a prickle, a tickle, a tang of salt and fear and ancient ancient lusts, deep as his first stiff dream. Against sense, against reason, against three million years of species wisdom, Nejben employed the tricks of agister Ashbey and opened his mouth. He inhaled. Once he gagged, twice he choked, then he felt the jellied eeling of the palps squirm down his throat: a choke, and into the lungs. He inhaled green salt water. And then, as the palps demurely unraveled their nano-tube outer integuments and infiltrated them into his lungs, his bronchial tubes, his bloodstream, he *became*. Memories stirred, invoked by olfactory summonings, changed as a new voice, a new way of seeing, a new interpretation of those memories and experiences, formed. Nejben swam down, breathing memory-water, stroke by stroke unraveling.

There was another down there, far below him, swimming up not through water but through the twelve years of his life. A new self.

Puzhay, against the light of a three o'clock sky. Framed in the arch of a cell window, knees pulled up to her chest. Small budding breasts; strong, boy jawline, fall and arc of hair shadow against lilac. She had laughed, throwing her head back. That first sight of her was cut into Nejben's memory, every line and trace, like the paper silhouettes the limners would cut of friends and families and enemies for Autumn Solstice. That first stirring of sex, that first intimation in the self of Ptey of this then-stranger, now-familiar Nejben.

As soon as he could, he had run. After he had found out where to put his bag, after he had worked out how to use the ancient, gurgling shit-eater, after agister Ashbey had closed the door with a smile and a blessing on the wooden cell—his wooden cell—that still smelled of fresh-cut timber after hundreds of years on the world-ocean of Tay. In the short season in which photosynthesis was possible, Bedenderay's forests grew fast and fierce, putting on meters in a single day. Small wonder the wood still smelled fresh and lively. After the midnight walk along the ceramic lanes and up the wooden staircases and through the damp-smelling cloisters, through the gently undulating quadrangles with the sky-train of the Anpreen migration bright overhead, holding on, as tradition demanded, to the bell-hung by a chain from his agister's waist; after the form filling and the photographings and the registering and the this-is-your-ident-card this is your map I've tattooed onto the back of your hand trust it will guide you and I am your agister and we'll see you in the east Refectory for breakfast; after the climb up the slimy wooden stairs from *Sail of Bright Anticipation* on to the Manifold House's quay, the biolights green around him and the greater lamps of the great college's towers high before him; when he was alone in this alien new world where he would become eight alien new people: he ran.

Agister Ashbey was faithful; the tattoo, a clever print of smart molecules and nanodyes, was meshed into the Manifold House's network and guided him through the labyrinth of dormitories and cloisters and Boy's Pavilions and Girlhearths by the simple, aversive trick of stinging the opposite side his map-hand to the direction in which he was to turn.

Cjatay. Sea-sundered friend. The only other one who knew him, knew him the moment they had met outside the school walls and recognized each other as different from the sailing freaks and fishing fools. Interested in geography, in love with numbers, with the wonder of the world and the worlds, as the city net declared, beyond. Boys who looked up at the sky.

As his burning hand led him left, right, up this spiral staircase under the lightening sky, such was Ptey's impetus that he never thought, would he know Cjatay? Cjatay had been in the Manifold House three months. Cjatay could be—*would* be—any number of Aspects now. Ptey had grown up with his father's overlapping circles of friends, each specific to a different Aspect, but he had assumed that it was a grown up thing. That couldn't happen to him and Cjatay! Not them.

The cell was one of four that opened off a narrow oval at the head of a tulip-shaped minaret—the Third Moon of Spring Tower, the legend on the back of Ptey's hand read. Cells were assigned by birth-date and season. Head and heart full of nothing but seeing Cjatay, he pushed open the door—no door in the Manifold House was ever locked.

She was in the arched window, dangerously high above the shingled roofs and porcelain domes of the Vernal Equinox division. Beyond her, only the wandering stars of the Anpreen. Ptey had no name for the sudden rush of feelings that came when he saw Puzhay throw back her head and laugh at some so-serious comment of Cjatay's. Nejben did.

It was only at introductory breakfast in the East Refectory, where he met the other uncertain, awkward boys and girls of his intake, that Ptey saw past the dawn seduction of Puzhay to Cjatay, and saw him unchanged, exactly as he had had been when he had stepped down from Etjay Quay into the catamaran and been taken out across the lagoon to the waste gas flares of Temejveri.

She was waiting crouched on the wooden steps where the water of the Chalybeate Pool lapped, knees pulled to her chest, goose flesh pimpling her forearms and calves in the cool of after-midnight. He knew this girl, knew her name, knew her history, knew the taste of a small, tentative kiss stolen among the crowds of teenagers pushing over 12th Canal Bridge. The memory was sharp and warm, but it was another's.

"Hi there."

He dragged himself out of the water onto to the silvery wood, rolled away to hide his nakedness. In the cloister shadow, Ashbey waited with a sea-silk robe.

"Hi there." There was never any easy way to tell someone you were another person from the one they remembered. "I'm Serejen." The name had been there, down among the palps, slipped into him with their mind-altering neurotransmitters.

"Are you?"

"All right. Yes, I'm all right." A tickle in the throat made him cough, the cough amplified into a deep retch. Serejen choked up a lungful of mucus-stained palp-jelly. In the early light, it thinned and ran, flowed down the steps to rejoin its shoal in the Chalybeate Pool. Agister Ashbey took a step forward. Serejen waved her away.

"What time is it?"

"Four thirty."

Almost five hours.

"Serejen." Puzhay looked coyly away. Around the Chalybeate Pool, other soul-swimmers were emerging, coughing up lungfuls of palp, shivering in their thermal robes, growing into new Aspects of themselves. "It's Cjatay. He needs to see you. Dead urgent."

Waiting Ashbey folded new-born Serejen in his own thermal gown, the intelligent plastics releasing their stored heat to his particular body temperature.

"Go to him," his agister said.

"I thought I was supposed to . . . "

"You've got the rest of your life to get to know Serejen. I think you should go."

Cjatay. A memory of fascination with starry skies, counting and numbering and betting games. The name and the face belonged to another Aspect, another life, but that old lust for numbers, for discovering the relationships between things, stirred a deep welling of joy. It was as rich and adult as the swelling of his dick he found in the bright mornings, or when he thought about Puzhay's breasts in his hands and the tattooed triangle of her sex. Different; no less intense.

The shutters were pulled close. The screen was the sole light in the room. Cjatay turned on hearing his lockless door open. He squinted into the gloom of the stair head, then cried excitedly,

"Look at this look at this!"

Pictures from the observation platforms sent to Tejaphay to monitor the doings of the Anpreen. A black-light plane of stars, the blinding blue curve of the water world stopped down to prevent screen-burn. The closer habitats showed a disc, otherwise it was moving lights. Patterns of speed and gravity.

"What am I looking at?"

"Look look, they're building a space elevator! I wondered how they were going to get the water from Tejaphay. Simple, duh! They're just going to vacuum it up! They've got some kind of processing unit in stationary orbit chewing up one of those asteroids they brought with them, but they using one of their own habitats to anchor it."

"At twice stationary orbit," Serejen said. "So they're going to have to build down and up at the same time to keep the elevator in tension." He did not know where the words came from. They were on his lips and they were true.

"It must be some kind of nano-carbon compound," Cjatay said, peering at the screen for some hint, some elongation, some erection from the fuzzy blob of the construction asteroid. "Incredible tensile strength, yet very flexible. We have to get that; with all our oil, it could change everything about our technology. It could really make us a proper star-faring people." Then, as if hearing truly for the first time, Cjatay turned from the screen and peered again at the figure in the doorway. "Who are you?" His voice was high and soft and plaintive.

"I'm Serejen."

"You sound like Ptey."

"I was Ptey. I remember him."

Cjatay did a thing with his mouth, a twisting, chewing movement that Serejen recalled from moments of unhappiness and frustration. The time at his sister's nameday party, when all the birth family was gathered and he had shown how it was almost certain that someone in the house on Drunken Chicken Lane had the same nameday as little Sezjma. There had been a long, embarrassed silence as Cjatay had burst into the adult chatter. Then laughter. And again, when Cjatay had worked out how long it would take to walk a light-year and Teacher Deu has asked the class *does anyone understand this?* For a moment, Serejen thought that the boy might cry. That would have been a terrible thing; unseemly, humiliating. Then he saw the bag on the unkempt bed, the ritual white clothes thrust knotted and fighting into it.

"I think what Cjatay wants to say is that he's leaving the Manifold House," agister Ashbey said, in the voice that Serejen understood as the one adults used when they had uncomfortable things to say. In that voice was a hidden word that Ashbey would not, that Serejen and Puzhay could not, and that Cjatay never would speak.

There was one in every town, every district. Kentlay had lived at the bottom of Drunken Chicken Lane, still at fortysomething living with his birth-parents. He had never married, though then-Ptey had heard that some did, and not just others like them. Normals. Multiples. Kentlay had been a figure that drew pity and respect alike; equally blessed and cursed, the Lonely were granted insights and gifts in compensation for their inability to manifold into the Eight Aspects. Kentlay had the touch for skin diseases, warts, and the sicknesses of birds. Ptey had been sent to see him for the charm of a dangling wart on his chin. The wart was gone within a week. Even then, Ptey had wondered if it had been through unnatural gifts or superstitious fear of the alien at the end of the wharf.

Cjatay. Lonely. The words were as impossible together as *green sun* or *bright winter*. It was never to be like this. Though the waters of the Chalybeate Pool would break them into many brilliant shards, though there would be other lives, other friends, even other wives and husbands, there would always be aspects of themselves that remembered trying to draw birds and fishes on the glowing band of the Mid Winter Galaxy that hung in the sky for weeks on end, or trying to calculate the mathematics of the High Summer silverlings that shoaled like silver needles in the Lagoon, how they kept together yet apart, how they were many but moved as one. *Boiling rain. Summer ice. A morning where the sun wouldn't rise. A friend who would always, only be one person.* Impossibilities. Cjatay could not be abnormal. Dark word. A vile word that hung on Cjatay like an oil-stained tarpaulin.

He sealed his bag and slung it over his shoulder.

"I'll give you a call when you get back."

"Yeah. Okay. That would be good." Words and needs and sayings flocked to him, but the end was so fast, so sudden, that all Serejen could do was stare at his feet so that he would not have to see Cjatay walk away. Puzhay was in tears. Cjatay's own agister, a tall, dark-skinned Summer-born, put his arm around Cjatay and took him to the stairs.

"Hey. Did you ever think?" Cjatay threw back the line from the top of the spiral stair. "Why are they here? The Anpreen." Even now, Serejen realized, Cjatay was hiding from the truth that he would be marked as different, as not fully human, for the rest of his life, hiding behind stars and ships and the mystery of the alien. "Why did they come here? They call it the Anpreen Migration, but where are they migrating *to*? And what are they migrating *from*? Anyone ever ask that? Ever think about that, eh?"

Then agister Ashbey closed the door on the high tower-top cell.

"We'll talk later."

Gulls screamed. Change in the weather coming. On the screen behind him, stars moved across the face of the great water.

Serejen could not bear to go down to the quay, but watched *Sail of Bright Anticipation* make sail from the cupola of the Bright Glance Netball Hall. The Manifold House was sailing through a plankton-bloom and he watched the ritual catamaran's hulls cut two lines of bioglow through the carpet of carbon-absorbing microlife. He stood and followed the sails until they were lost among the hulls of huge ceramic oil tankers pressed low to the orange smog-glow of Ctarisphay down under the horizon. Call each other. They would always forget to do that. They would slip out of each other's lives—Serejen's life now vastly more rich and populous as he moved across the social worlds of his various Aspects. In time, they would slip out of each other's thoughts and memories. So it was that Serejen Nejben ex-Ptey knew that he was not a child any longer. He could let things go.

After morning Shift class, Serejen went down to the Old Great Pool, the ancient flooded piazza that was the historic heart of the Manifold House, and used the techniques he had learned an hour before to effortlessly transfer from Serejen to Nejbet. Then he went down into the waters and swam with Puzhay. She was teary and confused, but the summer-warmed water and the physical exercise brightened her. Under a sky lowering with the summer storm that the gulls had promised, they sought out the many secret flooded colonnades and courts where the big groups of friends did not go. There, under the first crackles of lightning and the hiss of rain, he kissed her and she slipped her hand into his swimsuit and cradled the comfortable swell of his cock.

Serejen, loving.

Night, the aurora and sirens. Serejen shivered as police drones came in low over the Conservatorium roof. Through the high, arched windows, fires could still be seen burning on Yaskaray Prospect. The power had not yet been restored, the streets, the towering apartment blocks that lined them, were still dark. A stalled tram sprawled across a set of points, flames flickering in its rear carriage. The noise of the protest had moved off, but occasional shadows moved across the ice beneath the mesmerism of the aurora; student rioters, police security robots. It was easy to tell the robots by the sprays of ice crystals thrown up by their needle-tip, mincing legs.

"Are you still at that window? Come away from there, if they see you they might shoot you. Look, I've tea made."

"Who?"

"What?"

"Who might shoot me? The rioters or the police?"

"Like you'd care if you were dead."

But he came and sat at the table and took the bowl of thin, salty Bedenderay maté.

"But sure I can't be killed."

Her name was Seriantep. She was an Anpreen Prebendary ostensibly attached to the College of Theoretical Physics at the Conservatorium of Jann. She looked like a tall, slim young woman with the dark skin and blue-black hair of a Summer-born Archipelagan, but that was just the form that the swarm of Anpreen nano-processor motes had assumed. She hived. Reris Orhum Fejannan Kekjay Prus Rejmer Serejen Nejben wondered how close you had to get before her perfect skin resolved into a blur of microscopic motes. He had had much opportunity to make this observation. As well as being his notional student—though what a functionally immortal hive-citizen who had crossed one hundred and twenty light years could learn from a fresh twenty-something meat human was moot—she was his occasional lover.

She drank the tea. Serejen watched the purse of her lips around the delicate porcelain bowl decorated with the ubiquitous Lord of the Fishes motif, even in high, dry continental Jann. The small movement of her throat as she swallowed. He knew a hundred such tiny, intimate movements, but even as she cooed and giggled and gasped to the stimulations of the Five Leaves, Five Fishes ritual, the involuntary actions of her body had seemed like performances. Learned responses. Performances as he made observations. Actor and audience. That was the kind of lover he was as Serejen.

"So what is it really like to fuck a pile of nano-motes?" Puzhay had asked as they rolled around with wine in the cosy warm fleshiness of the Thirteenth Window Coupling Porch at the ancient, academic Ogrun Menholding. "I'd imagine it feels . . . fizzy." And she'd squeezed his cock, holding it hostage, *watch what you say, boy.*

"At least nano-motes never get morning breath," he'd said, and she'd given a little shriek of outrage and jerked his dick so that he yelped, and then they both laughed and then rolled over again and buried themselves deep into the winter-defying warmth of the piled quilts.

I should be with her now, he thought. The months-long winter nights beneath the aurora and the stars clouds of the great galaxy were theirs. After the Manifold House, he had gone with her to her Bedenderay and her home city of Jann. The City Conservatorium had the world's best theoretical physics department. It was nothing to do with small, boyish, funny Puzhay. They had formalised a partnering six months later. His parents had complained and shivered through all the celebrations in this cold and dark and barbarous city far from the soft elegance of island life. But ever after winter, even on the coldest mornings when carbon dioxide frost crusted the steps of the Tea Lane Ladyhearth where Puzhay lived, was their season. He should call her, let her know he was still trapped but that at the first sign, the very first sign, he would come back. The cell net was still up. Even an email. He couldn't. Seriantep didn't know. Seriantep wouldn't understand. She had not understood that one time when he tried to explain it in abstracts; that different Aspects could—should—have different relationships with different partners, love separately but equally. *That as Serejen, I love you, Anpreen Prebendary Seriantep, but as Nejben, I love Puzhay.* He could never say that. For an immortal, starcrossing hive of nano motes, Seriantep was very singleminded.

Gunfire cracked in the crystal night, far and flat.

"I think it's dying down," Seriantep said.

"I'd give it a while yet."

So strange, so rude, this sudden flaring of anti-alien violence. In the dreadful dead of winter too, when nothing should rightfully fight and even the trees along Yaskaray Prospect drew down to their heartwood and turned to ice. Despite the joy of Puzhay, Serejen knew that he would always hate the Bedenderay winter. *You watch out now,* his mother had said when he had announced his decision to go to Jann. *They all go dark-mad there.* Accidie and suicide walked the frozen canals of the Winter City. No surprise then that madness should break out against the Anpreen Prebendaries. Likewise inevitable that the popular rage should be turned against the Conservatorium.

The university had always been seen as a place apart from the rest of Jann, in summer aloof and lofty above the sweltering streets, like an over-grand daughter; in winter a parasite on this most marginal of economies. Now it was the unofficial alien embassy in the northern hemisphere. There were more Anpreen in its long, small-windowed corridors than anywhere else in the world.

There are no aliens, Serejen thought. *There is only the Clade. We are all family.* Cjatay had insisted that. The ship had sailed over the horizon, they hadn't called, they had drifted from each other's lives. Cjatay's name occasionally impinged on Serejen's awareness through radio interviews and opinion pieces. He had developed a darkly paranoid conspiracy theory around the Anpreen Presence. Serejen, high above the frozen streets of Jann in deeply abstract speculation about the physical reality of mathematics, occasionally mused upon the question of at what point the Migration had become a Presence. The Lonely often obsessively took up narrow, focused interests. Now the street was listening, acting. Great Winter always was a dark, paranoid season. *Here's how to understand,* Serejen thought. *There are no aliens after you've had sex with them.*

Helicopter blades rattled from the walls of the College of Theoretical Physics and then retreated across the Central Canal. The silence in the warm, dimly-lit little faculty cell was profound. At last, Serejen said, "I think we could go now."

On the street, cold stabbed even through the quilted layers of Serejen's great-coat. He fastened the high collar across his throat and still he felt the breath crackle into ice around his lips. Seriantep stepped lightly between the half bricks and bottle shards in nothing more than the tunic and leggings she customarily wore around the college. Her motes gave her full control over her body, including its temperature.

"You should have put something on," Serejen said. "You're a bit obvious."

Past shuttered cafés and closed up stores and the tall brick faces of the student Hearths. The burning tram on the Tunday Avenue junction blazed fitfully, its bitter smoke mingling with the eternal aromatic hydrocarbon smog exhaled by Jann's power plants. The trees that lined the avenue's centre strip were folded down into tight fists, dreaming of summer. Their boot heels rang loud on the street tiles.

A darker shape upon the darkness moved in the narrow slit of an alley between two towering tenement blocks. Serejen froze, his heart jerked. A collar turned down, a face studying his—Obredajay from the Department of Field Physics.

"Safe home."

"Aye. And you."

The higher academics all held apartments within the Conservatorium and were safe within its walls; most of the research staff working late would sit it out until morning. Tea and news reports would see them through. Those out on the fickle streets had reasons to be there. Serejen had heard that Obredajay was head-over-heels infatuated with a new manfriend.

The dangers we court for little love.

On the intersection of Tunday Avenue and Yaskaray Wharf, a police robot stepped out of the impervious dark of the arches beneath General Gatoris Bridge. Pistons hissed it up to its full three meters; green light flicked across Serejen's retinas. Seriantep held up her hand, the motes of her palm displaying her immunity as a Prebendary of the Clade. The machine shrank down, seemingly dejected, if plastic and pumps could display such an emotion.

A solitary tea-shop stood open on the corner of Silver Spider Entry and the Wharf, its windows misty with steam from the simmering urns. Security eyes turned and blinked at the two fleeing academics.

On Tannis Lane, they jumped them. There was no warning. A sudden surge of voices rebounding from the stone staircases and brick arches broke into a wave of figures lumbering around the turn of the alley, bulky and shouldering in their heavy winter quilts. Some held sticks, some held torn placards, some were empty handed. They saw a man in a heavy winter coat, breath frosted on his mouth-shield. They saw a woman almost naked, her breath easy, unclouded. They knew in an instant what she saw. The hubbub in the laneway became a roar.

Serejen and Seriantep were already in flight. Sensing rapid motion, the soles of Serejen's boots extended grips into the rime. As automatically, he felt the heart-numbing panic-rush ebb, felt himself lose his grip on his body and grow pale. Another was taking hold, his flight-or-fight Aspect; his cool, competent emergency service Fejannen.

He seized Seriantep's hand.

"With me. Run!"

Serejen-Fejannen saw the change of Aspect flicker across the tea-shop owner's face like weather as they barged through his door, breathless between his stables. Up to his counter with its looming, steaming urns of hot hot water. This tea-man wanted them out, wanted his livelihood safe.

"We need your help."

The tea-man's eyes and nostrils widened at the charge of rioters that skidded and slipped around the corner in to Silver Spider Entry. Then his hand hit the button under the counter and the shutters rolled down. The shop boomed, the shutters bowed to fists striking them. Rocks banged like gunfire from metal. Voices rose and joined together, louder because they were unseen.

"I've called the police," Seriantep said. "They'll be here without delay."

"No, they won't," Fejannen said. He pulled out a chair from the table closest the car and sat down, edgily eying the grey slats of the shutter. "Their job is to restore order and protect property. Providing personal protection to aliens is far down their list of priorities."

Seriantep took the chair opposite. She sat down wary as a settling bird.

"What's going on here? I don't understand. I'm very scared."

The café owner set two glasses of maté down on the table. He frowned, then his eyes opened in understaidng. An alien at his table. He returned to the bar and leaned on it, staring at the shutters beyond which the voice of the mob circled.

"I thought you said you couldn't be killed."

"That's not what I'm scared of. I'm scared of you, Serejen."

"I'm not Serejen. I'm Fejannen."

"Who, what's Fejannen?"

"Me, when I'm scared, when I'm angry, when I need to be able to think clearly and coolly when a million things are happening at once, when I'm playing games or hunting or putting a big funding proposal together."

"You sound . . . different."

"I *am* different. How long have you been on our world?"

"You're hard. And cold. Serejen was never hard."

"I'm not Serejen."

A huge crash—the shutter bowed under a massive impact and the window behind it shattered.

"Right, that's it, I don't care what happens, you're going." The tea-man leaped from behind his counter and strode towards Seriantep. Fejannen was there to meet him.

"This woman is a guest in your country and requires your protection."

"That's not a woman. That's a pile of . . . insects. Things. Tiny things."

"Well, they look like mighty scared tiny things."

"I don't think so. Like you said, like they say on the news, they can't really die."

"They can hurt. *She* can hurt."

Eyes locked, then disengaged. The maté-man returned to his towering silos of herbal mash. The noise from the street settled into a stiff, waiting silence. Neither Fejannen nor Seriantep believed that it was true, that the mob had gone, despite the spearing cold out there. The lights flickered once, twice.

Seriantep said suddenly, vehemently, "I could take them."

The tea-man looked up.

"Don't." Fejannen whispered.

"I could. I could get out under the door. It's just a reforming."

The tea-man's eyes were wide. A demon, a winter-grim in his prime location canal-side tea shop!

"You scare them enough as you are," Fejannen said.

"Why? We're only here to help, to learn from you."

"They think, what have you got to learn from *us*? They think that you're keeping secrets from us."

"Us?"

"Them. Don't scare them any more. The police will come, eventually, or the Conservatorium proctors. Or they'll just get bored and go home. These things never really last."

"You're right." She slumped back into her seat. "This fucking world . . . Oh, why did I come here?" Seriantep glanced up at the inconstant lumetubes, beyond to the distant diadem of her people's colonies, gravid on decades of water. It was a question, Fejannen knew, that Serejen had asked himself many times. A post-graduate scholar researching space-time topologies and the cosmological constant. A thousand-year-old post-human innocently wearing the body of a twenty-year-old woman, playing the student. She could learn nothing from him. All the knowledge the Anpreen wanderers had gained in their ten thousands year migration was incarnate in her motes. She embodied all truth and she lied with every cell of her body. Anpreen secrets. No basis for a relationship, yet Serejen loved her, as Serejen could love. But was it any more for her than novelty; a tourist, a local boy, a brief summer loving?

Suddenly, vehemently, Seriantep leaned across the table to take Fejannen's face between her hands.

"Come with me."

"Where? Who?"

"Who?" She shook her head in exasperation. "Ahh! Serejen. But it would be you as well, it has to be you. To my place, to the Commonweal. I've wanted to ask you for so long. I'd love you to see my worlds. Hundreds of worlds, like jewels, dazzling in the sun. And inside, under the ice, the worlds within worlds within worlds . . . I made the application for a travel bursary months ago, I just couldn't ask."

"Why? What kept you from asking?" A small but significant traffic of diplomats, scientists, and journalists flowed between Tay and the Anpreen fleet around Tejaphay. The returnees enjoyed global celebrity status, their opinions and experiences sought by think-tanks and talk shows and news-site columns, the details of the faces and lives sought by the press. Serejen had never understood what it was the people expected from the celebrity of others but was not so immured behind the fortress walls of the Collegium, armoured against the long siege of High Winter, that he couldn't appreciate its personal benefits. The lights seemed to brighten, the sense of the special hush outside, that was not true silence but waiting, dimmed as Serejen replaced Fejannen. "Why didn't you ask?"

"Because I though you might refuse."

"Refuse?" The few, the golden few. "Turn down the chance to work in the Commonweal? Why would anyone do that, what would I do that?"

Seriantep looked long at him, her head cocked slightly, alluringly, to one side, the kind of gesture an alien unused to a human body might devise,

"You're Serejen again, aren't you?"

"I am that Aspect again, yes."

"Because I thought you might refuse because of *her*. That other woman. Puzhay."

Serejen blinked three times. From Seriantep's face, he knew that she expected some admission, some confession, some emotion. He could not understand what.

Seriantep said, "I know about her. We know things at the Anpreen Mission. We check whom we work with. We have to. We know not everyone welcomes us, and that more are suspicious of us. I know who she is and where she lives and what you do with her three times a week when you go to her. I know where you were intending to go tonight, if all this hadn't happened."

Three times again, Serejen blinked. Now he was hot, too hot in his winter quilt in this steamy, fragrant tea-shop.

"But that's a ridiculous question. *I* don't love Puzhay. *Nejben* does."

"Yes, but you *are* Nejben."

"How many times do I have to tell you . . . ." Serejen bit back the anger. There were Aspects hovering on the edge of his consciousness like the hurricane-front angels of the Bazjendi Psalmody; selves inappropriate to Seriantep. Aspects that in their rage and storm might lose him this thing, so finely balanced now in this tea-shop. "It's our way," he said weakly. "It's how we are."

"Yes, but . . . " Seriantep fought for words. "It's *you*, there, that body. You say it's different, you say it's someone else and not you, not Serejen, but how do I know that? How *can* I know that?"

You say that, with your body that in this tea-shop you said could take many forms, any form, Serejen thought. Then Fejannen, shadowed but never more than a thought away in this besieged, surreal environment, heard a shift in the silence outside. The tea-man glanced up. He had heard it too. The difference between *waiting* and *anticipating*.

"Excuse me, I must change Aspects."

A knock on the shutter, glove-muffled. A voice spoke Fejannen's full name. A voice that Fejannen knew from his pervasive fear of the risk his academic Aspect was taking with Seriantep and that Serejen knew from those news reports and articles that broke through his vast visualisations of the topology of the universe and that Nejben knew from a tower top cell and a video screen full of stars.

"Came I come in?"

Fejannen nodded to the tea-man. He ran the shutter up high enough for the bulky figure in the long quilted coat and boots to duck under. Dreadful cold blew around Fejannen.

Cjatay bowed, removed his gloves, banging rime from the knuckles and made the proper formalities to ascertain which Aspect he was speaking to.

"I have to apologise; I only recently learned that it was you who were caught here."

The voice, the intonations and inflections, the over-precisions and refinements—no time might have passed since Cjatay walked out of Manifold House. In a sense, no time *had* passed; Cjatay was caught, inviolable, unchangeable by anything other than time and experience. Lonely.

"The police will be here soon," Seriantep said.

"Yes, they will," Cjatay said mildly. He looked Seriantep up and down, as if studying a zoological specimen. "They have us well surrounded now. These things are almost never planned; what we gain in spontaneity of expression we lose in strategy. But when I realised it was you, Fejannen-Nejben, I saw a way that we could all emerge from this intact."

"Safe passage," Fejannen said.

"I will personally escort you out."

"And no harm at all to you, politically."

"I need to distance myself from what has happened tonight."

"But your fundamental fear of the visitors remains unchanged?"

"I don't change. You know that. I see it as a virtue. Some things are solid, some things endure. Not everything changes with the seasons. But fear, you said. That's clever. Do you remember, that last time I saw you, back in the Manifold House. Do you remember what I said?"

"Nejben remembers you asking, where are they migrating to? And what are they migrating from?"

"In all your seminars and tutorials and conferences, in all those questions about the shape of the universe—oh, we have our intelligences too, less broad than the Anpreen's, but subtler, we think—did you ever think to *ask* that question: why have you come here?" Cjatay's chubby, still childish face was an accusation. "You are fucking her, I presume?"

In a breath, Fejannen had slipped from his seat into the Third Honorable Offense Stance. A hand on his shoulder; the teashop owner. No honor in it, not against a Lonely. Fejannen returned to his seat, sick with shuddering rage.

"Tell him," Cjatay said.

"It's very simple," Seriantep said. "We are refugees. The Anpreen Commonweal is the surviving remnant of the effective annihilation of our sub-species of Panhumanity. Our eight hundred habitats are such a minuscule percentage of our original race that, to all statistical purposes, we are extinct. Our habitats once englobed an entire sun. We're all that's left."

"How? Who?"

"Not so much *who*, as *when*," Cjatay said gently. He flexed cold-blued fingers and pulled on his gloves.

"They're coming?"

"We fear so," Seriantep said. "We don't know. We were careful to leave no traces, to cover our tracks, so to speak, and we believe we have centuries of a headstart on them. We are only here to refuel our habitats, then we'll go, hide ourselves in some great globular cluster."

"But why, *why* would anyone do this? We're all the same species, that's what you told us. The Clade, Panhumanity."

"Brothers disagree," Cjatay said. "Families fall out, families feud within themselves. No animosity like it."

"Is this true? How can this be true? Who knows about this?" Serejen strove with Fejannen for control and understanding. One of the first lessons the Agisters of the Manifold House had taught was the etiquette of transition between conflicting Aspects. A war in the head, a conflict of selves. He could understand sibling strife on a cosmic scale. But a whole species?

"The governments," Cjatay said. To the tea-man, "Open the shutter again. You be all right with us. I promise." To Serejen, "Politicians, some senior academics, and policy makers. And us. Not you. But we all agree, we don't want to scare anyone. So we question the Anpreen Prebendaries on our world, and question their presence in our system, and maybe sometimes it bubbles into xenophobic violence, but that's fine, that's the price, that's nothing compared to what would happen if we realised that our guests might be drawing the enemies that destroyed them to our homes. Come on. We'll go now."

The tea-man lifted the shutter. Outside, the protestors stood politely aside as Cjatay led the refugees out on to the street. There was not a murmur as Seriantep, in her ridiculous, life-threatening house-clothes, stepped across the cobbles. The great Winter Clock on the tower of Alajnedeng stood at twenty past five. The morning shift would soon be starting, the hot-shops firing their ovens and fry-pots.

A murmur in the crowd as Serejen took Seriantep's hand.

"Is it true?" he whispered.

"Yes," she said. "It is."

He looked up at the sky that would hold stars for another three endless months. The aurora coiled and spasmed over huddling Jann. Those stars were like crystal spearpoints. The universe was vast and cold and inimical to humanity, the greatest of Great Winters. He had never deluded himself it would be otherwise. Power had been restored, yellow street light glinted from the helmets of riot control officers and the carapaces of counterinsurgency drones. Serejen squeezed Seriantep's hand.

"What you asked."

"When?"

"Then. Yes. I will. Yes."

Torben, melting.

The Anpreen shatter-ship blazed star-bright as it turned its face to the sun. A splinter of smart-ice, it was as intricate as a snow-flake, stronger than any construct of Taynish engineering. Torben hung in free-fall in the observation dome at the centre of the cross of solar vanes. The Anpreen, being undifferentiated from the motes seeded through the hull, had no need for such architectural fancies. Their senses were open to space; the fractal shell of the ship was one great retina. They had grown the blister—pure and perfectly transparent construction-ice—for the comfort and delight of their human guests.

The sole occupant of the dome, Torben was also the sole passenger on this whole alien, paradoxical ship. Another would have been good. Another could have shared the daily, almost hourly shocks of strange and new and wonder. His other Aspects had felt with Torben the breath-catch of awe, and even greater privilege, when he had looked from the orbital car of the space elevator—the Anpreen's gift to the peoples of Tay—and seen the shatter-ship turn out of occultation in a blaze of silver light as it came in to dock. They had felt his glow of intellectual vindication as he first swam clumsily into the star-dome and discovered, with a shock, that the orbital transfer station was no more than a cluster of navigation lights almost lost in the star fields beyond. No sense of motion. His body had experienced no hint of acceleration. He had been correct. The Anpreen could adjust the topology of spacetime. But there was no one but his several selves to tell it to. The Anpreen crew—Torben was not sure whether it was one or many, or if that distinction had any meaning—was remote and alien. On occasion, as he swam down the live-wood panelled corridors, monoflipper and web-mittens pushing thick, humid air, he had glimpsed a swirl of silver motes twisting and knotting like a captive waterspout. Always they had dispersed in his presence. But the ice beyond those wooden walls, pressing in around him, felt alive, crawling, aware.

Seriantep had gone ahead months before him.

"There's work I have to do."

There had been a party; there was always a party at the Anpreen Mission among the ever-green slopes of generous, volcanic Sulanj. Fellow academics, press and PR from Ctarisphay, politicians, family members, and the Anpreen Prebendaries, eerie in their uniform loveliness.

"You can do the research work on *Thirty-Third Tranquil Abode*, that's the idea," Seriantep had said. Beyond the paper lanterns hung in the trees and the glow of the carbon-sink lagoon, the lights of space-elevator cars rose up until they merged with the stars. She would ride that narrow way to orbit within days. Serejen wondered how he would next recognise her.

"You have to go." Puzhay stood in the balcony of the Tea Lane Ladyhearth, recently opened to allow spring warmth into rooms that had sweated and stifled and stunk all winter long. She looked out at the shooting, uncoiling fresh green of the trees along Uskuben Avenue. Nothing there you have not seen before, Nejben thought. Unless it is something that is the absence of me.

"It's not forever," Nejben said. "I'll be back in year, maybe two years." *But not here*, he thought. He would not say it, but Puzhay knew it. As a returnee, the world's conservatoriums would be his. Bright cities, sun-warmed campuses far from the terrible cold on this polar continent, the winter that had driven them together.

All the goodbyes, eightfold goodbyes for each of his Aspects. And then he took sail for the ancient hospice of Bleyn, for sail was the only right way to come to those reefs of ceramic chapels that had clung to the Yesger atoll for three thousand hurricane seasons.

"I need . . . another," he whispered in the salt-breezy, chiming cloisters to Shaper Rejmen. "The curiosity of Serejen is too naive, the suspicion of Fejannen is too jagged, and the social niceties of Kekjay are too too eager to be liked."

"We can work this for you," the Shaper said. The next morning, he went down into the sweet, salt waters of the Othering Pots and let the programmed palps swarm over him, as he did for twenty mornings after. In the thunder-heavy gloaming of a late spring night storm, he awoke to find he was Torben. Clever, inquisitive, wary, socially adept and conversationally witty Torben. Extreme need and exceptional circumstances permitted the creation of Nineths, but only, always. temporarily. Tradition as strong as an incest taboo demanded that the number of Aspects reflect the eight phases of Tay's manic seasons.

The Anpreen shatter-ship spun on its vertical axis and Torben Reris Orhum Fejannan Kekjay Prus Rejmer Serejen Nejben looked on in wonder. Down, up, forward: his orientation shifted with every breath of air in the observation dome. An eye, a monstrous eye. Superstition chilled him, childhood stories of the Dejved whose sole eye was the eye of the storm and whose body was the storm entire. Then he unfolded the metaphor. An anti-eye. Tejaphay was a shield of heartbreaking blue, streaked and whorled with perpetual storms. The Anpreen space habitat *Thirty-Third Tranquil Abode*, hard-docked these two years past to the anchor end of the space elevator, was a blind white pupil, an anti-pupil, an unseeing opacity. The shatter-ship was approaching from Tejaphay's axial plane, the mechanisms of the orbital pumping station were visible beyond the habitat's close horizon. The space elevator was a cobweb next to the habitat's three-hundred kilometre bulk, less even than a thread compared to enormous Tejaphay, but as the whole assemblage turned into daylight, it woke sparkling, glittering as sun reflected from its billions of construction-ice scales. A fresh metaphor came to Torben: the sperm of the divine. *You're swimming the wrong way!* he laughed to himself, delighted at this infant Aspect's unsuspected tendency to express in metaphor what Serejen would have spoken in math, Kekjay in flattery, and Fejannen not at all. No, it's our whole system it's fertilising, he thought.

The Anpreen ship drew closer, manipulating space-time on the centimetre scale. Surface details resolved from the ice glare. The hull of *Thirty-Third Tranquil Abode* was a chaotic mosaic of sensors, docks, manufacturing hubs, and still less comprehensible technology, all constructed from smart-ice. A white city. A flight of shatter-ships detached from docking arms like a flurry of early snow. Were some of those icy mesas defensive systems; did some of those ice canyons, as precisely cut as a skater's figures, conceal inconceivable weapons? Had the Anpreen ever paused to consider that to all cultures of Tay, white was the colour of distrust, the white of snow in the long season of dark?

Days in free-gee had desensitised Torben sufficiently so that he was aware of the subtle pull of nanogravity in his belly. Against the sudden excitement and the accompanying vague fear of the unknown, he tried to calculate the gravity of *Thirty-Third Tranquil Abode,* changing every hour as it siphoned up water from Tejaphay. While he was still computing the figures, the shatter-ship performed another orientation flip and came in to dock at one of the radial elevator heads, soft as a kiss to a loved face.

On tenth days, they went to the falls, Korpa and Belej, Sajhay and Hannaj, Yetger and Torben. When he stepped out of the elevator that had taken him down through thirty kilometres of solid ice, Torben had imagined something like the faculty of Jann; wooden-screen cloisters and courts roofed with ancient painted ceilings, thronged with bright, smart, talkative students boiling with ideas and vision. He found Korpa and Belej, Sajhay, Hannaj, and Yetger all together in a huge, windy construct of cells and tunnels and abrupt balconies and netted-in ledges, like a giant wasps' nest suspended from the curved ceiling of the interior hollow.

"Continuum topology is a tad specialised, I'll admit that," Belej said. She was a sting-thin quantum-foam specialist from Yeldes in the southern archipelago of Ninnt, gone even thinner and bonier in the attenuated gravity of *Thirty-Third Tranquil Abode.* "If it's action you're looking for, you should get over to *Twenty Eighth.* They're sociologists."

Sajhay had taught him how to fly.

"There are a couple of differences from the transfer ship," he said as he showed Torben how to pull up the fish-tail mono-tights and how the plumbing vents worked. "It's lo-gee, but it's not *no*-gee, so you will eventually come down again. And it's easy to build up too much delta-vee. The walls are light but they're strong and you will hurt yourself. And the nets are there for a reason. Whatever you do, don't go through them. If you end up in that sea, it'll take you apart."

That sea haunted Torben's unsettled, nanogee dreams. The world-sea, the two hundred and twenty-kilometer diameter sphere of water, its slow, huge nanogee waves forever breaking into globes and tears the size of clouds. The seething, dissolving sea into which the Anpreen dissipated, many lives into one immense, diffuse body which whispered to him through the paper tunnels of the Soujourners' house. Not so strange, perhaps. Yet he constantly wondered what it would be like to fall in there, to swim against the tiny but non-negligible gravity and plunge slowly, magnificently, into the boil of water-borne motes. In his imagination, there was never any pain, only the blissful, light-filled losing of self. So good to be free from the unquiet parliament of selves.

Eight is natural, eight is holy, the Bleyn Shaper Yesger had whispered from behind ornate cloister grilles. *Eight arms, eight seasons. Nine must always be unbalanced.*

Conscious of each other's too-close company, the guest scholars worked apart with their pupils. Seriantep met daily with Torben in a bulbous chapter house extruded from the mother nest. Tall hexagon-combed windows opened on the steeply downcurving horizons of *Thirty-Third Tranquil Abode*, stippled with the stalactite towers of those Anpreen who refused the lure of the sea. Seriantep flew daily from such a tower down around the curve of the world to alight on Torben's balcony. She wore the same body he had known so well in the Jann Conservatorium, with the addition of a pair of functional wings in her back. She was a vision, she was a marvel, a spiritual creature from the aeons-lost motherworld of the Clade: an *angel*. She was beauty, but since arriving in *Thirty Third Tranquil Abode*, Torben had only had sex with her twice. It was not the merman-angel thing, though that was a consideration to metaphor-and-ludicrous-conscious Torben. He didn't love her as Serejen had. She noticed, she commented.

"You're not . . . the same."

Neither are you. What he *said* was, "I know. I couldn't be. Serejen couldn't have lived here. Torben can. Torben is the only one who can." *But for how long, before he splits into his component personalities?*

"Do you remember the way you . . . he . . . used to see numbers?"

"Of course I do. And before that, I remember how Ptey used to see numbers. He could look up into the night sky and tell you without counting, just by *knowing*, how many stars there were. He could see numbers. Serejen could make them *do* things. For me, Torben; the numbers haven't gone away, I just see them differently. I see them as clearly, as absolutely, but when I see the topospace transformations, I see them as words, as images and stories, as analogies. I can't explain it any better than that."

"I think, no matter how long I try, how long any of us try, we will never understand how your multiple personalities work. To us, you seem a race of partial people, each a genius, a savant, in some strange obsessive way."

Are you deliberately trying to punish me? Torben thought at the flicker-wing angel hovering before the ice-filled windows.

True, he was making colossal intuitive leaps in his twisted, abstruse discipline of spacetime geometry. Not so abstruse: the Anpreen space drives, that Taynish physicists said broke the laws of physics, reached into the elevenspace substrate of the universe to locally stretch or compress the expansion of spacetime—foreshortening ahead of the vehicle, inflating it behind. Thus the lack of any measurable acceleration, it was the entire continuum within and around the shatter-ship that had moved. Snowflakes and loxodromic curves had danced in Torben's imagination: he had it, he had it. The secret of the Anpreen: relativistic interstellar travel, was now open to the peoples of Tay.

The *other* secret of the Anpreen, that was.

For all his epiphanies above the spherical ocean, Torben knew that seminars had changed. The student had become the teacher, the master the pupil. *What is you want from us?* Torben asked himself. *Truly want, truly need?*

"Don't know, don't care. All I know is, if I can find a commercial way to bubble quantum black holes out of elevenspace and tap the evaporation radiation, I'll have more money than God," said Yetger, a squat, physically uncoordinated Oprann islander who relished his countrymen's reputation for boorishness, though Torben found him an affable conversationalist and a refined thinker. "You coming to the Falls on Tennay?"

So they set off across the sky, a little flotilla of physicists with wine and sweet biscuits to dip in it. Those older and less sure of their bodies used little airscooter units. Torben flew. He enjoyed the exercise. The challenge of a totally alien language of movement intrigued him, the fish-tail flex of the flipper-suit. He liked what it was doing to his ass muscles.

The Soujourners'-house's western windows gave distant views of the Falls, but the sense of awe began twenty kilometres out when the thunder and shriek became audible over the constant rumble of sky traffic. The picnic party always flew high, close to the ceiling among the tower roots, so that long vistas would not spoil their pleasure. A dense forest of inverted trees, monster things grown kilometres tall in the nanogee, had been planted around the Falls, green and mist-watered by the spray. The scientists settled on to one of the many platforms sculpted from the boulevard-wide branches. Torben gratefully peeled off his fin-tights, kicked his legs free, and spun to face the Falls.

What you saw, what awed you, depended on how you looked at it. Feet down to the world-sea, head up to the roof, it was a true fall, a cylinder of falling water two hundred metres across and forty kilometres long. Feet up, head down, it was even more terrifying, a titanic geyser. The water was pumped through from the receiving station at near supersonic speeds, where it met the ocean-bead the joined waters boiled and leaped kilometres high, broke into high looping curls and crests and globes, like the fantastical flarings of solar prominences. The roar was terrific. But for the noise-abatement properties of the nanoengineered leaves, it would have meant instant deafness. Torben could feel the tree branch, as massive as any buttress wall of Jann fortress-university, shudder beneath him.

Wine was opened and poured. The biscuits, atavistically hand-baked by Hannaj, one of whose Aspects was a master pastry chef, were dipped into it and savoured. Sweet, the light sharpness of the wine and the salt mist of another world's stolen ocean tanged Torben's tongue.

There were rules to Tennays by the Falls. No work. No theory. No relationships. Five researchers made up a big enough group for family jealousy, small enough for cliquishness. Proper topics of conversation looked homeward; partnerships ended, children born, family successes and sicknesses, gossip, politics, and sports results.

"Oh. Here." Yetger sent a message flake spinning lazily through the air. The Soujourners'-house exfoliated notes and message from home onto slips of whisper-thin paper that peeled from the walls like eczema. The mechanism was poetic but inaccurate; intimate messages unfurled from unintended walls to turn and waft in the strange updrafts that ran through the nest's convoluted tunnels. It was the worst of forms to read another's message-scurf.

Torben unfolded the rustle of paper. He read it once, blinked, read it again. Then he folded precisely in eight and folded it away in his top pocket.

"Bad news?" For a broad beast of a man, Yetger was acute to emotional subtleties. Torben swallowed.

"Nothing strange or startling."

Then he saw where Belej stared. Her gaze drew his, drew that of everyone in the picnic party. The Falls were failing. Moment by moment, they dwindled, from a deluge to a river, from a river to a stream to a jet, a hiding shrieking thread of water. On all the platforms on all the trees, Anpreen were rising into the air, hovering in swarms, as before their eyes the Falls sputtered and ceased. Drops of water, fat as storms, formed around the lip of the suddenly exposed nozzle to break and drift, quivering, down to the spherical sea. The silence was profound. Then the trees seemed to shower blossoms as the Anpreen took to the air in hosts and choirs, flocking and storming.

Numbers and images flashed in Torben's imagination. The fuelling could not be complete, was weeks from being complete. The ocean would fill the entire interior hollow, the stalactite cities transforming into strange reef communities. Fear gripped him and he felt Fejannen struggle to free himself from the binding into Torben. *I need you here, friend,* Torben said to himself, and saw the others had made the same calculations.

They flew back, a ragged flotilla strung across kilometres of airspace, battling through the ghostly aerial legions of Anpreen. The Soujourners' house was filled with fluttering, gusting message slips shed from the walls. Torben snatched one from the air and against all etiquette read it.

Sajhay are you all right what's happening? Come home, we are all worried about you. Love Mihenj.

The sudden voice of Suguntung, the Anpreen liaison, filled every cell of the nest, an order—polite, but an order—to come to the main viewing lounge, where an important announcement would be made. Torben had long suspected that Suguntung never left the Soujourners' house, merely deliquesced from hominiform into airborne motes, a phase transition.

Beyond the balcony nets, the sky seethed, an apocalypse of insect humanity and storm clouds back as squid ink rolling up around the edge of the world ocean.

"I have grave news," Suguntung said. He was a grey, sober creature, light and lithe and androgynous, without any salting of wit or humour. "At 12:18 Taynish Enclave time, we detected gravity waves passing through the system. These are consistent with a large numbers of bodies decelerating from relativistic flight."

Consternation. Voices shouting. Questions questions questions. Suguntung held up a hand and there was quiet.

"On answer to your questions, somewhere in the region of thirty eight thousand objects. We estimate them at a range of seventy astronomical units beyond the edge of the Kuiper belt, decelerating to ten percent lightspeed for system transition."

"Ninety three hours until they reach us," Torben said. The numbers, the coloured numbers, so beautiful, so distant.

"Yes," said Suguntung.

"Who are they?" Belej asked.

"I know," Torben said. "Your enemy."

"We believe so," Suguntung answered. "There are characteristic signatures in the gravity waves and the spectral analysis."

Uproar. By a trick of the motes, Suguntung could raise his voice to a roar that could shout down a crowd of angry physicists.

"The Anpreen Commonweal is making immediate preparations for departure. As a matter of priority, evacuation for all guests and visitors has been arranged and will commence immediately. A transfer ship is already waiting. We are evacuating the system not only for our own protection, but to safeguard you as well. We believe that the Enemy has no quarrel with you."

"*Believe*?" Yetger spat. "Forgive me if I'm less than completely reassured by that!"

"But you haven't got enough water," Torben said absently, mazed by the numbers and pictures swimming around in his head, as the message leaves of concern and hope and come-home-soon fluttered around. "How many habitats are fully fuelled? Five hundred, five hundred and fifty? You haven't got enough, even this one is at eighty percent capacity. What's going to happen to them?"

"I don't give a fuck what happens to them!" Hannaj had always been the meekest and least assertive of men, brilliant but forever hamstrung by self-doubt. Now, threatened, naked in space, pieced through and through by the gravity waves of an unknowable and power, his anger burned. "I want to know what's going to happen to *us*."

"We are transferring the intelligences to the interstellar-capable habitats." Suguntung spoke to Torben alone.

"Transferring; you mean copying," Torben said. "And the originals that are left, what happens to them?"

Suguntung made no answer.

Yetger found Torben floating in the exact centre of the viewing lounge, moving his tail just enough to maintain him against the microgee.

"Where's your stuff?"

"In my cell."

"The shatter-ship's leaving in an hour."

"I know."

"Well, maybe you should, you know . . . "

"I'm not going."

"You're *what*?"

"I'm not going, I'm staying here."

"Are you insane?"

"I've talked to Suguntung and Seriantep. It's fine. There are a couple of others on the other habitats."

"You have to come home, we'll need you when they come . . . "

"Ninety hours and twenty five minutes to save the world? I don't think so."

"It's home, man."

"It's not. Not since *this*." Torben flicked the folded note of his secret pocket, offered it to Yetger between clenched fingers.

"Oh."

"Yes."

"You're dead. We're all dead, you know that."

"Oh, I know. In the few minutes it takes me to reach wherever the Anpreen Migration goes next, you will have aged and died many times over. I know that, but it's not home. Not now."

Yetger ducked his head in sorrow that did not want to be seen, then in a passion hugged Torben hugely to him, kissed him hard.

"Goodbye. Maybe in the next one."

"No, I don't think so. One is all we get. And that's a good enough reason to go out there where none of our people have ever been before, I think."

"Maybe it is." Yetger laughed, the kind of laughter that is on the edge of tears. Then he spun and kicked off up through the ceiling door, his duffel of small possessions trailing from his ankle.

For an hour now, he had contemplated the sea and thought that he might just be getting the way of it, the fractal patterns of the ripples, the rhythms and the micro-storms that blew up in squalls and waves that sent globes of water quivering into the air that, just as quickly, were subsumed back into the greater sea. He understood it as music, deeply harmonised. He wished one of his Aspects had a skill for an instrument. Only choirs, vast ensembles, could capture the music of the water bead.

"It's ready now."

All the while Torben had calculated the music of the sea, Seriantep had worked on the smart-paper substrate of the Soujourners'-house. Now the poll was complete, a well in the floor of the lounge. *When I leave, will it revert?* Torben thought, the small, trivial wit that fights fear. *Will it go back to whatever it was before, or was it always only just Suguntung?* The slightest of gestures and Seriantep's wisp-dress fell from her, The floor ate it greedily. Naked and wingless now in this incarnation, she stepped backward into the water, never for an instant taking her eyes from Torben.

"Whenever you're ready," she said. "You won't be hurt."

She lay back into the receiving water. Her hair floated out around her, coiled and tangled as she came apart. There was nothing ghastly about it, no decay into meat and gut and vile bone, no grinning skeleton fizzing apart in the water like sodium. A brightness, a turning to motes of light. The hair was the last to go. The pool seethed with motes. Torben stepped out of his clothes.

I'm moving on. It's for the best. Maybe not for you. For me. You see, I didn't think I'd mind, but I did. You gave it all up so easily, just like that, off into space. There is someone else. It's Cjatay. I heard what he was saying, and as time went by, as I didn't hear from you, it made sense. I know I'm reacting. I think I owe you that, at least. We're all right together. With him, you get everything, I find I can live with that. I think I like it,. I'm sorry Torben, but this is what I want.

The note sifted down through the air like a falling autumn leaf to join the hundreds of others that lay on the floor. Torben's feet kicked up as he stepped down into the water. He gasped at the electrical tingle, then laughed, and, with a great gasp, emptied his lungs and threw himself under the surface. The motes swarmed and began to take him apart. As the *Thirty-Third Tranquil Abode* broke orbit around Tejaphay, the abandoned space elevator coiling like a severed artery, the bottom of the Soujourners'-house opened, and, like a tear, the mingled waters fell to the sea below.

Jedden, running.

Eighty years Jedden had fallen, dead as a stone, silent as light. Every five years, a few subjective minutes so close to light-speed, he woke up his senses and sent a slush of photons down his wake to see if the hunter was still pursuing.

Redshifted to almost indecipherability, the photons told him, *Yes, still there, still gaining.* Then he shut down his senses, for even that brief wink, that impact of radiation blueshifted to gamma frequencies on the enemy engine field, betrayed him. It was decades since he had risked the scalarity drive. The distortions it left in space-time advertised his position over most of a quadrant. Burn quick, burn hot and fast, get to lightspeed if it meant reducing his reaction mass perilously close to the point where he would not have sufficient ever to brake. Then go dark, run silent and swift, coasting along in high time dilation where years passed in hours.

Between wakings, Jedden dreamed. He dreamed down into the billions of lives, the dozens of races and civilizations that the Anpreen had encountered in their long migration. The depth of their history had stunned Jedden, as if he were swimming and, looking down, discovered beneath him not the green water of the lagoon but the clear blue drop of the continental shelf. Before they englobed their sun with so many habitats that it became discernible only as a vast infra-red glow, before even the wave of expansion that had brought them to that system, before even they became motile, when they wore mere bodies, they had been an extroverted, curious race, eager for the similarities and differences of other sub-species of PanHumanity. Records of the hundreds of societies they had contacted were stored in the spin-states of the quantum-ice flake that comprised the soul of Jedden. Cultures, customs, ways of being human were simulated in such detail that, if he wished, Jedden could have spend aeons living out their simulated lives. Even before they had reached the long-reprocessed moon of their homeworld, the Anpreen had encountered a light-sail probe of the Ekkad, three hundred years out on a millennium-long survey of potential colony worlds. As they converted their asteroid belts into habitat rings, they had fought a savage war for control of the high country against the Okranda asteroid colonies that had dwelled there, hidden and unsuspected, for twenty thousand years. The doomed Okranda had, as a final, spiteful act, seared the Anpreen homeworld to the bedrock, but not before the Anpreen had absorbed and recorded the beautiful, insanely complex hierarchy of caste, classes, and societies that had evolved in the baroque cavities of the sculpted asteroids. Radio transmission had drawn them out of their Oort cloud across two hundred light years to encounter the dazzling society of the Jad. From them, the Anpreen had learned the technology that enabled them to pload themselves into free-flying nanomotes and become a true Level Two civilization.

People and beasts, machines and woods, architectures and moralities, and stories beyond counting. Among the paraphernalia and marginalia of a hundred races, were the ones who had destroyed the Anpreen, who were now hunting Jedden down over all the long years, closing metre by metre.

So he spent hours and years immersed in the great annual eisteddfod of the Barrant-Hoj, where one of the early generation of seed ships (early in that it was seed of the seed of the seed of the first flowering of mythical Earth) had been drawn into the embrace of a fat, slow hydrocarbon-rich gas giant and birthed a brilliant, brittle airborne culture, where blimp-cities rode the edge of storms wide enough to drown whole planets and the songs of the contestants—gas-bag-spider creatures huge as reefs, fragile as honeycomb—belled in infrasonic wavefronts kilometers between crests and changed entire climates. It took Barrant-Hoj two hominiform lifetimes to circle its sun—the Anpreen had chanced upon the song-spiel, preserved it, hauled it out of the prison of gas giant's gravity well, and given it to greater Clade.

Jedden blinked back into interstellar flight. He felt—he imagined—tears on his face as the harmonies reverberated within him. Cantos could last days, chorales entire weeks. Lost in music. A moment of revulsion at his body, this sharp, unyielding thing of ice and energies. The hunter's ramscoop fusion engine advertised its presence across a thousand cubic light-years. It was inelegant and initially slow, but, unlike Jedden's scalarity drive, was light and could live off the land. The hunter would be, like Jedden, a ghost of a soul impressed on a Bose-condensate quantum chip, a mote of sentience balanced on top of a giant drive unit. The hunter was closing, but was no closer than

Jedden had calculated. Only miscalculation could kill you in interstellar war. The equations were hard but they were fair.

Two hundred and three years to the joke point. It would be close, maybe close enough for the enemy's greed to blind him. Miscalculation and self-deception, these were the killers in space. And luck. Two centuries. Time enough for a few moments rest.

Among all the worlds was one he had never dared visit: the soft blue tear of Tay. There, in the superposed spin states, were all the lives he could have led. The lovers, the children, the friends and joys and mudanities. Puzhay was there, Cjatay too. He could make of them anything he wanted: Puzhay faithful, Cjatay Manifold, no longer Lonely.

Lonely. He understood that now, eighty light years out and decades to go before he could rest.

Extraordinary, how painless it had been. Even as the cells of Torben's body were invaded by the motes into which Seriantep had dissolved, even as they took him apart and rebuilt him, even as they read and copied his neural mappings, there was never a moment where fleshly Torben blinked out and nanotechnological Torben winked in, there was no pain. Never pain, only a sense of wonder, of potential racing away to infinity on every side, of a new birth—or, it seemed to him, an anti-birth, a return to the primal, salted waters. As the globe of mingled motes dropped slow and quivering and full as a breast toward the world-ocean, Torben still thought of himself as Torben, as a man, an individual, as a body. Then they hit and burst and dissolved into the sea of seething motes, and voices and selves and memories and personalities rushed in on him from every side, clamouring, a sea-roar. Every life in every detail. Senses beyond his native five brought him impression upon impression upon impression. Here was intimacy beyond anything he had ever known with Seriantep. As he communed, he was communed with. He knew that the Anpreen government—now he understood the reason for the protracted and ungainly negotiations with Tay : the two representations had almost no points of communication—were unwrapping him to construct a deep map of Tay and its people—rather, the life and Aspects of one under-socialised physics researcher. Music. All was music. As he understood this, Anpreen Commonweal Habitat *Thirty Third Tranquil Abode*, with its five hundred and eighty two companions, crossed one hundred and nineteen light years to the Milius 1183 star system.

One hundred and nineteen light years, eight months subjective, in which Torben Reris Orhum Fejannan Kekjay Prus Rejmer Serejen Nejben ceased to exist. In the mote-swarm, time, like identity, could be anything you assigned it to be. To the self now known as Jedden, it seemed that he had spent twenty years of re-subjectivized time in which he had grown to be a profound and original thinker in the Commonweal's physics community. Anpreen life had only enhanced his instinctive ability to see and apprehend number. His insights and contributions were startling and creative. Thus it had been a pure formality for him to request a splinter-ship to be spun off from *Thirty Third Tranquil Abode* as the fleet entered the system and dropped from relativistic flight at the edge of the Oort cloud. A big fat splinter ship with lots of fuel to explore space-time topological distortions implicit in the orbital perturbations of inner Kuiper Belt cubewanos for a year, a decade, a century, and then come home.

So he missed the annihilation.

Miscalculation kills. Lack of circumspection kills. Blind assumption kills. The Enemy had planned their trap centuries ahead. The assault on the Tay system had been a diversion; the thirty-eight thousand drive signatures mostly decoys; propulsion units and guidance systems and little else scattered among a handful of true battleships dozens of kilometres long. Even as lumbering, barely mobile Anpreen habitats and Enemy attack drones burst across Tay's skies, so bright they even illuminated the sun-glow of high summer, the main fleet was working around Milius 1183. A work of decades, year upon year of slow modifications, staggering energies, careful careful concealment and camouflage, as the Enemy sent their killing hammer out on its long slow loop.

Blind assumption. The Anpreen saw a small red sun at affordable range to the ill-equpped fleet. They saw there was water there, water; worlds of water to re-equip the Commonweal and take it fast and far beyond the reach of the Enemy in the great star clouds that masked the galactic core. In their haste, they failed to note that Milius 1183 was a binary system, a tired red dwarf star and a companion neutron star in photosphere-grazing eight hour orbit. Much less then did they notice that the neutron star was missing.

The trap was perfect and complete. The Enemy had predicted perfectly. Their set-up was flawless. The hunting fleet withdrew to the edges of system, all that remained were the relays and autonomous devices. Blindsided by sunglare, the Anpreen sensoria had only milliseconds of warning before the neutron star impacted Milius 1183 at eight percent light speed.

The nova would in time be visible over a light-century radius. Within its spectrum, careful astronomers might note the dark lines of hydrogen, oxygen, and smears of carbon. Habitats blew away in sprays of plasma. The handful of stragglers that survived battled to reconstruct their mobility and life-support systems. Shark-ships hidden half a century before in the rubble of asteroid belts and planetary ring systems woke from their long sleeps and went a-hunting.

Alone in his splinter ship in the deep dark, Jedden, his thoughts outwards to the fabric of space-time and at the same time inwards to the beauty of number, the song within him, saw the system suddenly turn white with death light. He heard five hundred billion sentients die. All of them, all at once, all their voices and hearts. He heard Seriantep die, he heard those other Taynish die, those who had turned away from their home world in the hope of knowledge and experience beyond anything their world could offer. Every life he had ever touched, that had ever been part of him, that had shared number or song or intimacy beyond fleshly sex. He heard the death of the Anpreen migration. Then he was alone. Jedden went dark for fifty years. He contemplated the annihilation of the last of the Anpreen. He drew up escape plans. He waited. Fifty years was enough. He lit the scalarity drive. Space-time stretched. Behind him, he caught the radiation signature of a fusion drive igniting and the corresponding electromagnetic flicker of a scoopfield going up. Fifty years was not enough.

That would be his last miscalculation.

Twenty years to bend his course away from Tay. Another ten to set up the deception. *As you deceived us, so I will fool you*, Jedden thought as he tacked ever closer to lightspeed. *And with the same device, a neutron star.*

Jedden awoke from the sleep that was beyond dreams, a whisper away from death, that only disembodied intelligences can attain. The magnetic vortex of the hunter's scoopfield filled half the sky. Less than the diameter of a light-minute separated them. Within the next ten objective years, the Enemy ship would overtake and destroy Jedden. Not with physical weapons or even directed energy, but with information: skullware and dark phages that would dissolve him into nothingness or worse, isolate him from any external sense or contact, trapped in unending silent, nerveless darkness.

The moment, when it came, after ninety light-years, was too fine-grained for hominiform-intelligence. Jedden's sub-routines, the autonomic responses that controlled the ship that was his body, opened the scalarity drive and summoned the dark energy. Almost instantly, the Enemy responded to the course change, but that tiny relativistic shift, the failure of simultaneity, was Jedden's escape and life.

Among the memories frozen into the heart of the Bose-Einstein condensate were the star-logs of the Cush Né, a fellow migrant race the Anpreen had encountered—by chance, as all such meets must be—in the big cold between stars. Their star maps charted a rogue star, a neutron dwarf ejected from its stellar system and wandering dark and silent, almost invisible, through deep space. Decades ago, when he felt the enemy ramfield go up and knew that he had not escaped, Jedden had made the choice and the calculations. Now he turned his flight, a prayer short of light-speed, towards the wandering star.

Jedden had long ago abolished fear. Yet he experienced a strange psycho-somatic sensation in that part of the splinter-ship that corresponded to his testicles. Balls tightening. The angle of insertion was so precise that Jedden had had to calculate the impact of stray hydroxyl radicals on his ablation field. One error would send him at relativistic speed head on into a neutron star. But he did not doubt his ability, he did not fear, and now he understood what the sensation in his phantom testicles was. Excitement.

The neutron star was invisible, would always be invisible, but Jedden could feel its gravity in every part of his body, a quaking, quailing shudder, a music of a hundred harmonies as different parts of the smart-ice hit their resonant frequencies. A chorale in ice and adrenaline, he plunged around the neutron star. He could hope that the hunting ship would not survive the passage, but the Enemy, however voracious, was surely never so stupid as to run a scoop ship through a neutron star's terrifying magnetic terrain with the drive field up. That was not his strategy anyway. Jedden was playing the angles. Whipping tight around the intense gravity well, even a few seconds of slowness would amplify into light-years of distance, decades of lost time. Destruction would have felt like a cheat. Jedden wanted to win by geometry. By calculation, we live.

He allowed himself one tiny flicker of a communication laser. Yes. The Enemy was coming. Coming hard, coming fast, coming *wrong*. Tides tore at Jedden, every molecule of his smart-ice body croaked and moaned, but his own cry rang louder and he sling-shotted around the neutron. *Yes!* Before him was empty space. The splinter-ship would never fall of its own accord into another gravity well. He lacked sufficient reaction mass to enter any Clade system. Perhaps the Enemy had calculated this in the moments before he too entered the neutron star's transit. An assumption. In space, assumptions kill. Deep in his quantum memories, Jedden knew what was out there. The slow way home.

Fast Man, slowly

Kites, banners, pennants, and streamers painted with the scales and heads of ritual snakes flew from the sun rigging on the Festival of Fast Children. At the last minute, the climate people had received budgetary permission to shift the prevailing winds lower. The Clave had argued that the Festival of Fast Children seemed to come round every month and a half, which it did, but the old and slow said, *not to the children it doesn't.*

Fast Man turned off the dust road on to the farm track. The wooden gate was carved with the pop-eyed, O-mouthed hearth-gods, the chubby, venal guardians of agricultural Yoe Canton. As he slowed to Parent Speed, the nodding heads of the meadow flowers lifted to a steady metronome tick. The wind-rippled grass became a restless choppy sea of current and cross-currents. Above him, the clouds raced down the face of the sun-rod that ran the length of the environment cylinder, and in the wide yard before the frowning eaves of the ancient earthen manor, the children, preparing for the ritual Beating of the Sun-lines, became plumes of dust.

For three days, he had walked up the eternal hill of the cylinder curve, through the tended red forests of Canton Ahaea. Fast Man liked to walk. He walked at Child-Speed and they would loop around him on their bicycles and ped-cars and then pull away shouting, you're not so fast, Fast Man! He could have caught them, of course, he could have easily outpaced them. They knew that, they knew he could on a wish take the form of a bird, or a cloud, and fly away from them up to the ends of the world. Everyone in the Three Worlds knew Fast Man. He needed neither sleep nor food, but he enjoyed the taste of the highly seasoned, vegetable-based cuisine of the Middle Cantons and their light but fragrant beer, so he would call each night at a hostel or township pub. Then he would drop down into Parent Speed and talk with the locals. Children were fresh and bright and inquiring, but for proper conversation, you needed adults.

The chirping cries of the children rang around the grassy eaves of Toe Yau Manor. The community had gathered, among them the Toe Yau's youngest, a skipping five year-old. In her own speed, that was. She was months old to her parents; her birth still a fresh and painful memory. The oldest, the one he had come about, was in his early teens. Noha and Jehau greeted Fast Man with water and bread.

"God save all here," Fast Man blessed them. Little Nemaha flickered around him like summer evening bugs. He heard his dual-speech unit translate the greeting into Children-Speech in a chip of sound. This was his talent and his fame; that his mind and words could work in two times at once. He was the generational ambassador to three worlds.

The three great cylinders of the Aeo Taea colony fleet were fifty Adult Years along in their journey to the star Sulpees 2157 in the Anpreen categorisation. A sweet little golden star with a gas giant pressed up tight to it, and, around that gas world, a sun-warmed, tear-blue planet. Their big, slow lathe-sculpted asteroids, two hundred kilometres long, forty across their flats, had appeared as three small contacts at the extreme edge of the Commonweal's sensory array. Too far from their flightpath to the Tay system and, truth be told, too insignificant. The galaxy was festering with little sub-species, many of them grossly ignorant that they were part of an immeasurably more vast and glorious Clade, all furiously engaged on their own grand little projects and empires. Races became significant when they could push lightspeed. Ethnologists had noted as a point of curiosity a peculiar time distortion to the signals, as if everything had been slowed to a tenth normal speed. Astrogators had put it down to an unseen gravitational lensing effect and noted course and velocity of the lumbering junk as possible navigation hazards.

That idle curiosity, that moment of fastidiousness of a now-dead, now-vaporised Anpreen who might otherwise have dismissed it, had saved Jedden. There had always been more hope than certainty in the mad plan he had concocted as he watched the Anpreen civilization end in nova light. Hope as he opened up the dark energy that warped space-time in calculations made centuries before that would only bear fruit centuries to come. Hope as he woke up, year upon year in the long flight to the stray neutron star, always attended by doubt. The slightest miscalculation could throw him off by light-years and centuries. He himself could not die, but his reaction mass was all too mortal. Falling forever between stars was worse than any death. He could have abolished that doubt with a thought, but so would the hope have been erased to become mere blind certainty.

Hoping and doubting, he flew out from the slingshot around the neutron star.

Because he could hope, he could weep; smart-ice tears when his long range radars returned three slow-moving images less than five light-hours from the position he had computed. As he turned the last of his reaction mass into dark energy to match his velocity with the Aeo Taea armada, a stray calculation crossed his consciousness. In all his redefinitions and reformations, he had never given up the ability to see numbers, to hear what they whispered to him. He was half a millennium away from the lives he had known on Tay.

For ten days, he broadcast his distress call. *Help, I am a refugee from a star war.* He knew that, in space, there was no rule of the sea, as there had been on Tay's world ocean, no Aspects at once generous, stern, and gallant that had been known as SeaSelves. The Aeo Taea could still kill him with negligence. But he could sweeten them with a bribe.

Like many of the country houses of Amoa ark, Toe Yau Manor featured a wooden belvedere, this one situated on a knoll two fields spinward from the old house. Airy and gracious, woven from genetweak willow plaits, it and its country cousins all across Amoa's Cantons had become a place for Adults, where they could mix with ones of their own speed, talk without the need for the hated speech convertors around their necks, gripe and moan and generally gossip, and, through the central roof iris, spy through the telescope on their counterparts on the other side of the world. Telescope parties were the latest excuse for Parents to get together and complain about their children.

But this was their day—though it seemed like a week to them—the Festival of Fast Children, and this day Noha Toe Yau had his telescope trained not on his counterpart beyond the sun, but on the climbing teams fizzing around the sun-riggings, tens of kilometres above the ground, running out huge monoweave banners and fighting ferocious kite battles high where the air was thin.

"I tell you something, no child of mine would ever be let do so damn fool a thing," Noha Toe Yau grumbled. "I'll be surprised if any of them make it to the Destination."

Fast Man smiled, for he knew that he had only been called because Yemoa Toe Yau was doing something much more dangerous.

Jehau Toe Yau poured chocolate, thick and cooling and vaguely hallucinogenic.

"As long as he's back before Starship Day," she said. She frowned down at the wide green before the manor where the gathered Fast Children of the neighbourhood in their robes and fancies were now hurtling around the long trestles of festival foods. They seemed to be engaged in a high-velocity food fight. "You know, I'm sure they're speeding the days up. Not much, just a little every day, but definitely speeding them up. Time goes nowhere these days."

Despite a surprisingly sophisticated matter-anti-matter propulsion system, the Aeo Taea fleet was limited to no more than ten percent of lightspeed, far below the threshold where time dilation became perceptible. The crossing to the Destination—Aeo Taea was a language naturally given to Portentous Capitalizations, Fast Man had discovered—could only be made by generation ship. The Aeo Taea had contrived to do it in just one generation. The strangely slow messages the Anpreen had picked up from the fleet were no fluke of space-time distortion. The voyagers' bodies, their brains, their perceptions and metabolisms, had been in-vitro engineered to run at one-tenth hominiform normal. Canned off from the universe, the interior lighting, the gentle spin gravity and the slow, wispy climate easily adjusted to a life lived at a snail's pace. Morning greetings lasted hours, that morning a world-week. Seasons endured for what would have been years in the outside universe, vast languorous autumns. The three hundred and fifty years of the crossing would pass in the span of an average working career. Amoa was a world of the middle-aged.

Then Fast Man arrived and changed everything.

"Did he give any idea where he was going?" Fast Man asked. It was always the boys. Girls worked it through, girls could see further.

Jehau pointed down. Fast Man sighed. Rebellion was limited in Amoa, where any direction you ran lead you swiftly back to your own doorstep. The wires that rigged the long sun could take you high, kilometres above it all in your grand indignation. Everyone would watch you through their telescopes, up there high and huffing, until you got hungry and wet and bored and had to come down again. In Amoa, the young soul rebels went *out*.

Fast Man set down his chocolate glass and began the subtle exercise that reconfigured the motes of his malleable body. To the Toe Yaus, he seemed to effervesce slightly, a sparkle like fine silver talc or the dust from a moth's wings. Jehau's eyes widened. All the three worlds knew of Fast Man, who had brought the end of the Journey suddenly within sight, soothed generational squabbles, and found errant children—and so everyone though they knew him personally. Truly, he was an alien.

"It would help considerably if they left some idea of where they were going," Fast Man said. "There's a lot of space out there. Oh well. I'd stand back a little, by the way." He stood up, opened his arms in a little piece of theatre, and exploded into a swarm of motes. He towered to a buzzing cylinder that rose from the iris at the centre of the belvedere. *See this through your telescopes on the other side of the world and gossip.* Then, in a thought, he speared into the earth and vanished.

In the end, the Fast Boy was pretty much where Fast Man reckoned he would be. He came speed-walking up through the salt-dead city-scape of the communications gear just above the convex flaring of the drive shield, and there he was, nova-bright in Fast man's radar sight. A sweet, neat little cranny in the main dish gantry with a fine view over the construction site. Boys and building. His complaining to the Toe Yaus had been part of the curmudgeonly image he liked to project. Boys were predictable things.

"Are you not getting a bit cold up there?" Fast Man said. Yemoa started at the voice crackling in his helmet phones. He looked round, helmet tilting from side to side as he tried to pick the interloper out of the limitless shadow of interstellar space. Fast Man increased his surface radiance. He knew well how he must seem; a glowing man, naked to space, toes firmly planted on the pumice-dusted hull and leaning slightly forward against the spin force. He would have terrified himself at that age, but awe worked for the Fast Children as amiable curmudgeon worked for their slow parents.

"Go away."

Fast Man's body-shine illuminated the secret roots. Yemoa Toe Yau was spindly even in the tight yellow and green pressure skin. He shuffled around to turn his back; a deadlier insult among the Aeo Taea than among the Aspects of Tay for all their diverse etiquettes. Fast Man tugged at the boy's safety lanyard. The webbing was unfrayed, the carabiner latch operable.

"Leave that alone."

"You don't want to put too much faith in those things. Cosmic rays can weaken the structure of the plastic: put any tension on them, and they snap just like that, just when you need them most. Yes sir, I've seen people just go sailing out there, right away out there."

The helmet, decorated with bright bird motifs, turned toward Fast Man.

"You're just saying that."

Fast Man swung himself up beside the runaway and settled into the little nest. Yemoa wiggled away as far as the cramped space would permit.

"I didn't say you could come up here."

"It's a free ship."

"It's not *your* ship."

"True," said Fast Man. He crossed his legs and dimmed down his self-shine until they could both look out over the floodlit curve of the star drive works. The scalarity drive itself was a small unit—small by Amoa's vistas; merely the size of a well-established country manor. The heavy engineering that overshadowed it, the towering silos and domes and pipeworks, was the transfer system that converted water and anti-water into dark energy. Above all, the lampships hovered in habitat-stationary orbits, five small suns. Fast Man did not doubt that the site hived with desperate energy and activity, but to his Child Speed perceptions, it was as still as a painting, the figures in their bird-bright skinsuits, the heavy engineers in their long-duration work armour, the many robots and vehicles and little jetting skipcraft all frozen in time, moving so slowly that no individual motion was visible, but when you looked back, everything had changed. A long time even for a Parent, Fast Man sat with Yemoa. Beyond the construction lights, the stars arced past. How must they seem to the adults, Fast Man thought, and in that thought pushed down into Parent Speed and felt a breathless, deeply internalised gasp of wonder as the stars accelerated into curving streaks. The construction site ramped up into action; the little assembly robots and skippers darting here and there on little puffs of reaction gas.

Ten years, ten grown-up years, since Fast Man had osmsoed through the hull and coalesced out of a column of motes on to the soil of Ga'atu Colony, and still he did not know which world he belonged to, Parent or Fast Children. There had been no Fast Children then, no children at all. That was the contract. When the Destination was reached, that was the time for children, born the old way, the fast way, properly adjusted to their new world. Fast Man had changed all that with the price of his rescue: the promise that the Destination could be reached not in slow years, not even in a slow season, but in hours; real hours. With a proviso; that they detour—a matter of moments to a relativistic fleet—to Fast Man's old homeworld of Tay.

The meetings were concluded, the deal was struck, the Aeo Taea fleet's tight tight energy budget would allow it, just. It would mean biofuels and muscle power for the travellers; all tech resources diverted to assembling the three dark energy scalarity units. But the journey would be over in a single sleep. Then the generous forests and woodlands that carpeted the gently rolling midriffs of the colony cylinders all flowered and released genetweak pollen. Everyone got a cold for three days, everyone got pregnant, and nine Parent months later, the first of the Fast Children was born.

"So where's your clip?"

At the sound of Yemoa's voice, Fast Man geared up into Child Speed. The work on the dazzling plain froze, the stars slowed to a crawl.

"I don't need one, do I?" Fast Man added, "I know exactly how big space is."

"Does it really use dark energy?"

"It does."

Yemoa pulled his knees up to him, stiff from his long vigil in the absolute cold. A splinter of memory pierced Fast Man: the fast-frozen canals of Jann, the months-long dark. He shivered. Whose life was that, whose memory?

"I read about dark energy. It's the force that makes the universe expand faster and faster, and everything in it, you, me, the distance between us. In the end, everything will accelerate away so fast from everything else that the universe will rip itself apart, right down to the quarks."

"That's one theory."

"Every particle will be so far from everything else that it will be in a universe of its own. It will *be* a universe of its own."

"Like I said, it's a theory. Yemoa, your parents . . . "

"You use this as a space drive."

"Your matter/anti-matter system obeys the laws of Thermodynamics, and that's the heat-death of the universe. We're all getter older and colder and more and more distant. Come on, you have to come in. You must be uncomfortable in that suit."

The Aeo Taea skinsuits looked like flimsy dance costumes to don in the empty cold of interstellar space but their hides were clever works of molecular technology, recycling and refreshing and repairing. Still, Fast Man could not contemplate the itch and reek of one after days of wear.

"You can't be here on Starship Day," Fast Man warned. "Particle density is very low out here, but it's still enough to fry you, at lightspeed."

"We'll be the Slow ones then," Yemoa said. "A few hours will pass for us, but in the outside universe, it will be fifty years."

"It's all relative," Fast Man said.

"And when we get there," Yemoa continued, "we'll unpack the landers and we'll go down and it'll be the new world, the big Des Tin Ay Shun, but our Moms and Dads, they'll stay up in the Three Worlds. And we'll work, and we'll build that new world, and we'll have our children, and they'll have children, and maybe we'll see another generation after that, but in the end, we'll die, and the Parents up there in the sky, they'll hardly have aged at all."

Fast Man draped his hands over his knees.

"They love you, you know."

"I know. I know that. It's not that at all. Did you think that? If you think that, you're stupid. What does everyone see in you if you think stuff like that? It's just . . . what's the point?"

None, Fast Man thought. *And everything. You are as much point as the universe needs, in your yellow and green skinsuit and mad-bird helmet and fine rage.*

"You know," Fast Man said, "whatever you think about it, it's worse for them. It's worse than anything I think you can imagine. Everyone they love growing old in the wink of an eye, dying, and they can't touch them, they can't help, they're trapped up there. No, I think it's so very much worse for them."

"Yah," said Yemoa. He slapped his gloved hands on his thin knees. "You know, it is freezing up here."

"Come on then." Fast Man stood up and offered a silver hand. Yemoa took it. The stars curved overhead. Together, they climbed down from the aerial and walked back down over the curve of the world, back home.

Oga, tearing.

He stood 1on the arch of the old Jemejnay bridge over the dead canal. Acid winds blew past him, shrieking on the honed edges of the shattered porcelain houses. The black sky crawled with suppressed lightning. The canal was a dessicated vein, cracked dry, even the centuries of trash wedged in its cracked silts had rusted away, under the bite of the caustic wind, to scabs and scales of slag. The lagoon was a dish of pure salt shimmering with heat haze. In natural light, it would have been blinding but no sun ever challenged the clouds. In Oga's extended vision, the old campanile across the lagoon was a snapped tooth of crumbling masonry.

A flurry of boiling acid rain swept over Oga as he turned away from the burning vista from the dead stone arch on to Ejtay Quay. His motes sensed and changed mode on reflex, but not before a wash of pain burned through him. Feel it. It is punishment. It is good.

The houses were roofless, floorless; rotted snapped teeth of patinated ceramic,: had been for eight hundred years. Drunken Chicken Street. Here Kentlay the Lonely had sat out in the sun and passed the time of day with his neighbours and visitors come for his gift. Here were the Dilmajs and the vile, cruel little son who had caught birds and pulled their feathers so that they could not fly from his needles and knives, street bully and fat boy. Mrs. Supris, a sea-widow, a baker of cakes and sweets, a keeper of mournings and ocean-leavings. All dead. Long dead, dead with their city, their world.

This must be a mock Ctarisphay, a stage, a set, a play-city for some moral tale of a prodigal, an abandoner. A traitor. Memories turned to blasted, glowing stumps. A city of ruins. A world in ruins. There was no sea any more. Only endless poisoned salt. This could not be true. Yet this was his house. The acid wind had no yet totally erased the carved squid that stood over the door. Oga reached up to touch. It was hot, biting hot; everything was hot, baked to an infra-red glow by runaway greenhouse effect. To Oga's carbon-shelled fingertips, it was a small stone prayer, a whisper caught in a shell. If the world had permitted tears, the old, eroded stone squid would have called Oga's. Here was the hall, here the private parlour, curved in on itself like a ceramic musical instrument. The stairs, the upper floors, everything organic had evaporated centuries ago, but he could still read the niches of the sleeping porches cast in the upper walls. How would it have been in the end days, when even the summer sky was black from burning oil? Slow, painful, as year upon year the summer temperatures rose and the plankton blooms, carefully engineered to absorb the carbon from Tay's oil-riches, died and gave up their own sequestered carbon.

The winds keened through the dead city and out across the empty ocean. With a thought, Oga summoned the ship. Ion glow from the re-entry shone through the clouds. Sonic booms rolled across the sterile lagoon and rang from the dead porcelain houses. The ship punched out of the cloud base and unfolded, a sheet of nano motes that, to Oga's vision, called memories of the ancient Bazjendi angels stooping down the burning wind. The ship beats its wings over the shattered campanile, then dropped around Oga like possession. Flesh melted, flesh ran and fused, systems meshed, selves merged. Newly incarnate, Oga kicked off from Ejtay Quay in a pillar of fusion fire. Light broke around the empty houses and plazas, sent shadows racing down the desiccated canals. The salt pan glared white, dwindling to the greater darkness as the light ascended. With a star at his feet, Oga punched up through the boiling acid clouds, up and out until, in his extended shipsight, he could see the infra-glow of the planet's limb curve against space. A tear of blood. Accelerating, Oga broke orbit.

Oga. The name was a festival. Father-of-all-our-Mirths, in subtly inflected Aeo Taea. He was Fast Man no more, no longer a sojourner; he was Parent of a nation. The Clave had ordained three Parent Days of rejoicing as the Aeo Taea colony cylinders dropped out of scalarity drive at the edge of the system. For the children, it had been a month of party. Looking up from the flat end of the cylinder, Oga had felt the light from his native star on his skin, subtle and sensitive in a dozen spectra. He masked out the sun and looked for those sparks of reflected light that were worlds. There Saltpeer, and great Bephis: magnifying his vision, he could see its rings and many moons; there Tejaphay. It too wore a ring now; the shattered icy remnants of the Anpreen

Commonweal. And there; there: Tay. Home. Something not right about it. Something missing in its light. Oga had ratcheted up his sight to the highest magnification he could achieve in this form.

There was no water in the spectrum. There was no pale blue dot.

The Clave of Aeo Taea Interstellar Cantons received the message some hours after the surface crews registered the departure of the Anpreen splinter ship in a glare of fusion light: *I have to go home.*

From five A.U.s out, the story became brutally evident. Tay was a silver ball of unbroken cloud. Those clouds comprised carbon dioxide, carbonic, and sulphuric acid and a memory of water vapour. The surface temperature read at two hundred and twenty degrees. Oga's ship-self possessed skills and techniques beyond his hominiform self; he could see the perpetual lighting storms cracking cloud to cloud, but never a drop of pure rain. He could see through those clouds, he could peel them away so that the charred, parched surface of the planet lay open to his sight. He could map the outlines of the continents and the continental shelves lifting from the dried ocean. The chains of archipelagos, once jewels around the belly of a beautiful dancer, were ribs, bones, stark mountain chains glowing furiously in the infra-dark.

As he fell sun-wards, Oga put the story together. The Enemy had struck Tay casually, almost as an afterthought. A lone warship, little larger than the ritual catamaran on which the boy called Ptey had sailed from this quay so many centuries before, had detached itself from the main fleet action and swept the planet with its particle weapons, a spray of directed fire that set the oil fields burning. Then it looped carelessly back out of the system, leaving a world to suffocate. They had left the space elevator intact. There must be a way out. This was judgment, not murder. Yet two billion people, two thirds of the planet's population, had died.

One third had lived. One third swarmed up the life-rope of the space elevator and looked out at space and wondered where they could go. Where they went, Oga went now. He could hear their voices, a low em-band chitter from the big blue of Tejaphay. His was a long, slow chasing loop. It would be the better part of a year before he arrived in parking orbit above Tejaphay. Time presented its own distractions and seductions. The quantum array that was his heart could as easily recreate Tay as any of scores of cultures it stored. The mid-day aurora would twist and glimmer again above the steep-gabled roofs of Jann. He would fish with Cjatay from the old, weather-silvered fishing stands for the spring run of prith. The Sulanj islands would simmer and bask under the midnight sun and Puzhay would again nuzzle against him and press her body close against the hammering cold outside the Tea Lane Womenhearth walls. They all could live, they all would believe they lived, *he* could, by selective editing of his consciousness, believe they lived again. He could recreate dead Tay. But it was the game of a god, a god who could take off his omniscience and enter his own delusion, and so Oga chose to press his perception down into a time flow even slower than Parent Time and watch the interplay of gravity wells around the sun.

On the final weeks of approach, Oga returned to world time and opened his full sensory array on the big planet that hung tantalisingly before him. He had come here before, when the Anpreen Commonweal hung around Tejaphay like pearls, but then he had given the world beneath him no thought, being inside a world complete in itself and his curiosity turned outwards to the shape of the universe. Now he beheld Tejaphay and remembered awe. Three times the diameter of Tay, Tejaphay was the true water world now. Ocean covered it pole to pole, a hundred kilometres deep. Immense weather systems mottled the planet, white on blue. The surviving spine of the Anpreen space elevator pierced the eye of a perpetual equatorial storm system. Wave trains and swells ran unbroken from equator to pole to smash in stupendous breakers against the polar ice caps. Oga drew near in sea meditation. Deep ocean appalled him in a way that centuries of time and space had not. That was distance. This was hostility. This was elementary fury that knew nothing of humanity.

Yet life clung here. Life survived. From two light minutes out, Oga had heard a whisper of radio communication, from the orbit station on the space elevator, also from the planet's surface. Scanning sub Antarctic waters, he caught the unmistakable tang of smart ice. A closer look: what had on first glance seemed to be bergs revealed a more complex structure. Spires, buttresses, domes, and sprawling terraces. Ice cities, riding the perpetual swell. Tay was not forgotten: these were the ancient Manifold Houses reborn, grown to the scale of vast Tejaphay. Closer again: the berg city under his scrutiny floated at the centre of a much larger boomed circle. Oga's senses teemed with life-signs. This was a complete ecosystem, and ocean farm, and Oga began to appreciate what these refugees had undertaken. No glimpse of life had ever been found on Tejaphay. Waterworlds, thawed from ice-giants sent spiralling sunwards by the gravitational play of their larger planetary rivals, were sterile. At the bottom of the hundred-kilometre deep ocean, was pressure ice, five thousand kilometres of pressure ice down to the iron core. No minerals, no carbon ever percolated up through that deep ice. Traces might arrive by cometary impact, but the waters of Tejaphay were deep and pure. What the Taynish had, the Taynish had brought. Even this ice city was grown from the shattered remnants of the Anpreen Commonweal.

A hail from the elevator station, a simple language algorithm. Oga smiled to himself as he compared the vocabulary files to his own memory of his native tongue. Half a millennium had changed the pronunciation and many of the words of Taynish, but not its inner subtleties, the rhythmic and contextual clues as to which Aspect was speaking.

"Attention unidentified ship, this is Tejaphay orbital Tower approach control. Please identify yourself and your flight plan."

"This is the Oga of the Aeo Taea Interstellar Fleet." He toyed with replying in the archaic speech. Worse than a breach of etiquette, such a conceit might give away information he did not wish known. Yet. "I am a representative with authority to negotiate. We wish to enter into communications with your government regarding fuelling rights in this system."

"Hello, Oga, this is Tejaphay Orbital Tower. By the Aeo Taea Interstellar Fleet, I assume you refer to the these objects." A sub-chatter on the data channel identified the cylinders, coasting in-system. Oga confirmed.

"Hello, Oga, Tejaphay Tower. Do not, repeat, do not approach the tower docking station. Attain this orbit and maintain until you have been contacted by Tower security. Please confirm your acceptance."

It was a reasonable request, and Oga's subtler senses picked up missile foramens unfolding in the shadows of the Orbital Station solar array. He was a runner, not a fighter; Tejaphay's defences might be basic fusion warheads and would need sustained precision hits to split open the Aeo Taea colony cans, but they were more than a match for Oga without the fuel reserves for full scalarity drive.

"I confirm that."

As he looped up to the higher ground, Oga studied more closely the berg cities of Tejaphay, chips of ice in the monstrous ocean. It would be a brutal life down there under two gravities, every aspect of life subject to the melting ice and the enclosing circle of the biosphere boom. Everything beyond that was as lifeless as space. The horizon would be huge and far and empty. City ships might sail for lifetimes without meeting another polis. The Taynish were tough. They were a race of the extremes. Their birthworld and its severe seasonal shifts had called forth a social response that other cultures would regard as mental disease, as socialized schizophrenia. Those multiple Aspects—a self for every need—now served them on the hostile vastnesses of Tejaphay's world ocean. They would survive, they would thrive. Life endured. This was the great lesson of the Clade: that life was hope, the only hope of escaping the death of the universe.

"*Every particle will be so far from everything else that it will be in a universe of its own. It will be a universe of its own*, a teenage boy in a yellow spacesuit had said up on the hull of mighty Amoa, looking out on the space between the stars. Oga had not answered at that time. It would have scared the boy, and though he had discovered it himself on the long flight from Milius 1183, he did not properly understand to himself, and in that gap of comprehension, he too was afraid. *Yes,* he would have said. *And in that is our only hope.*

Long range sensors chimed. A ship had emerged around the limb of the planet. Consciousness is too slow a tool for the pitiless mathematics of space. In the split second that the ship's course, design, and drive signature had registered on Oga's higher cognitions, his autonomic systems had plotted course, fuel reserves, and engaged the scalarity drive. At a thousand gees, he pulled away from Tejaphay. Manipulating space time so close to the planet would send gravity waves rippling through it like a struck gong. Enormous slow tides would circle the globe; the space elevator would flex like a crackled whip. Nothing to be done. It was instinct alone and by instinct he lived, for here came the missiles. Twenty nanotoc warheads on hypergee drives, wiping out his entire rearward vision in a white glare of lightweight MaM engines, but not before he had felt on his skin sensors the unmistakable harmonies of an Enemy deep-space scoopfield going up.

The missiles had the legs, but Oga had the stamina. He had calculated it thus. The numbers still came to him. Looking back at the blue speck into which Tejaphay had dwindled, he saw the engine-sparks of the missiles wink out one after the other. And now he could be sure that the strategy, devised in nanoseconds, would pay off. The warship was chasing him. He would lead it away from the Aeo Taea fleet. But this would be no long stern chase over the light decades. He did not have the fuel for that, nor the inclination. Without fuel, without weapons, he knew he must end it. For that, he needed space.

It was the same ship. The drive field harmonics, the spectrum of the fusion flame, the timbre of the radar images that he so gently, kiss-soft, bounced off the pursuer's hull, even the configuration he had glimpsed as the ship rounded the planet and launched missiles. This was the same ship that had hunted him down all the years. Deep mysteries here. Time dilation would compress his planned course to subjective minutes and Oga needed time to find an answer.

The ship had known where he would go even as they bucked the stormy cape of the wandering neutron star. It had never even attempted to follow him; instead, it had always known that it must lay in a course that would whip it round to Tay. That meant that even as he escaped the holocaust at Milius 1183, it had known who he was, where he came from, had seen through the frozen layers of smart-ice to the Torben below. The ship had come from around the planet. It was an enemy ship, but not the Enemy. They would have boiled Tejaphay down to its iron heart. Long Oga contemplated these things as he looped out into the wilderness of the Oort cloud. Out there among the lonely ice, he reached a conclusion. He turned the ship over and burned the last of his reaction in a hypergee deceleration burn. The enemy ship responded immediately, but its ramjet drive was less powerful. It would be months, years even, before it could turn around to match orbits with him. He would be ready then. The edge of the field brushed Oga as he decelerated at fifteen hundred gravities and he used his external sensors to modulate a message on the huge web, a million kilometres across: *I surrender.*

Gigayears ago, before the star was born, the two comets had met and entered into their far, cold marriage. Beyond the dramas and attractions of the dust cloud that coalesced into Tay and Tejaphay and Bephis, all the twelve planets of the solar system, they maintained their fixed-grin gazes on each other, locked in orbit around a mutual centre of gravity where a permanent free-floating haze of ice crystals hovered, a fraction of a Kelvin above absolute zero. Hidden amongst them, and as cold and seemingly as dead, was the splintership. Oga shivered. The cold was more than physical—on the limits of even his malleable form. Within their thermal casing, his motes moved as slowly as Aeo Taea Parents. He felt old as this ice and as weary. He looked up into the gap between ice worlds. The husband-comet floated above his head like a halo. He could have leaped to it in a thought.

Lights against the starlight twinkle of the floating ice storm. A sudden occlusion. The Enemy was here. Oga waited, feeling every targeting sensor trained on him.

No, you won't, will you? Because you have to know.

A shadow detached itself from the black ship, darkest on dark, and looped around the comet. It would be a parliament of self-assembling motes like himself. Oga had worked out decades before that Enemy and Anpreen were one and the same, sprung from the same nanotechnological seed when they attained Class Two status. Theirs was a civil war. *In the Clade, all war was civil war*, Oga thought. Panhumanity was all there was. More like a family feud. Yes, those were the bloodiest fights of all. No quarter and no forgiveness.

The man came walking around the small curve of the comet, kicking up shards of ice crystals from his grip soles. Oga recognised him. He was meant to. He had designed himself so that he would be instantly recognisable, too. He bowed, in the distances of the Oort cloud.

"Torben Reris Orhum Fejannan Kekjay Prus Rejmer Serejen Nejben, sir."

The briefest nod of a head, a gesture of hours in the slow-motion hypercold.

"Torben. I'm not familiar with that name."

"Perhaps we should use the name most familiar to you. That would be Serejen, or perhaps Fejannen, I was in that Aspect when we last met. I would have hoped you still remembered the old etiquette."

"I find I remember too much these days. Forgetting is a choice since I was improved. And a chore. What do they call you now?"

"Oga."

"Oga it shall be, then."

"And what do they call *you* now?"

The man looked up into the icy gap between worldlets. *He has remembered himself well*, Oga thought. *The slight portliness, the child-chubby features, like a boy who never grew up. As he says, forgetting is a chore.*

"The same thing they always have: Cjatay."

"Tell me your story then, Cjatay. This was never your fight, or my fight."

"You left her."

"She left *me*, I recall, and, like you, I forget very little these days. I can see the note still; I could recreate it for you, but it would be a scandalous waste of energy and resources. She went to you."

"It was never me. It was the cause."

"Do you truly believe that?"

Cjatay gave a glacial shrug.

"We made independent contact with them when they came. The Council of governments was divided, all over the place, no coherent approach or strategy. 'Leave us alone. We're not part of this.' But there's no neutrality in these things. We had let them use our system's water. We had the space elevator they built for us, there was the price, there was the blood money. We knew it would never work—our hope was that we could convince them that some of us had always stood against the Anpreen. They torched Tay anyway, but they gave us a deal. They'd let us survive as a species if some of us joined them on their crusade."

"They *are* the Anpreen."

"*Were* the Anpreen. I know. They took me to pieces. They made us into something else. Better, I think. All of us, there were twenty four of us. Twenty four, that was all the good people of Tay, in their eyes. Everyone who was worth saving."

"And Puzhay?"

"She died. She was caught in the Arphan conflagration. She went there from Jann to be with her parents. It always was an oil town. They melted it to slag."

"But you blame me."

"You are all that's left."

"I don't believe that. I think it was always personal. I think it was always revenge."

"You still exist."

"That's because you don't have all the answers yet."

"We know the kind of creatures we've become; what answers can I not know?"

Oga dipped his head, then looked up to the halo moon, so close he could almost touch it.

"Do you want me to show you what they fear so much?"

There was no need for the lift of the hand, the conjuror's gesture; the pieces of his ship-self Oga had seeded so painstakingly through the wife-comet's structure were part of his extended body. *But I do make magic here,* he thought. He dropped his hand. The star-speckled sky turned white, hard painful white, as if the light of every star were arriving at once. *An Olbers sky,* Oga remembered from his days in the turrets and cloisters of Jann. And as the light grew intolerable, it ended. Blackness, embedding, huge and comforting. The dark of death. Then Oga's eyes grew familiar with the dark, and, though it was the plan and always had been the plan, he felt a plaint of awe as he saw ten thousand galaxies resolve out of the Olbers dazzle. And he knew that Cjatay saw the same.

"Where are we? What have you done?"

"We are somewhere in the region of two hundred and thirty million light years outside our local group of galaxies, more precisely, on the periphery of the cosmological galactic supercluster known as the Great Attractor. I made some refinements to the scalarity drive unit to operate in a one dimensional array."

"Faster-than-light travel," Cjatay said, his upturned face silvered with the light of the ten thousand galaxies of the Great Atrractor.

"No, you still don't see it," Oga said, and again turned the universe white. Now when he flicked out of hyperscalarity, the sky was dark and starless but for three vast streams of milky light that met in a triskelion hundreds of millions of light years across.

"We are within the Bootes Supervoid," Oga said. "It is so vast that if our own galaxy were in the centre of it, we would have thought ourselves alone and that our galaxy was the entire universe. Before us are the Lyman alpha-blobs, three conjoined galaxy filaments. These are the largest structures in the universe. On scales larger than this, structure becomes random and grainy. We become grey. These are the last grand vistas, this is the end of greatness."

"Of course, the expansion of space is not limited by lightspeed," Cjatay said.

"Still you don't understand." A third time, Oga generated the dark energy from the ice beneath his feet and focused it into a narrow beam between the wife-comet and its unimaginably distant husband. *Two particles in contact will remain in quantum entanglement no matter how far they are removed,* Oga thought. *And is that true also for lives?* He dismissed the scalarity generator and brought them out in blackness. Complete, impenetrable, all-enfolding blackness, without a photon of light.

"Do you understand where I have brought you?"

"You've taken us beyond the visible horizon," Cjatay said. "You've pushed space so far that the light from the rest of the universe has not had time to reach us. We are isolated from every other part of reality. In a philosophical sense, we are a universe in ourselves."

"That was what they feared? You feared?"

"That the scalarity drive had the potential to be turned into a weapon of unimaginable power? Oh yes. The ability to remove any enemy from reach, to banish them beyond the edge of the universe. To exile them from the universe itself, instantly and irrevocably."

"Yes, I can understand that, and that you did what you did altruistically. They were moral genocides. But our intention was never to use it as a weapon—if it had been, wouldn't we have used it on you?"

Silence in the darkness beyond dark.

"Explain then."

"I have one more demonstration."

The mathematics were critical now. The scalarity generator devoured cometary mass voraciously. If there were not enough left to allow him to return them home . . . Trust number, Oga. You always have. Beyond the edge of the universe, all you have is number. There was no sensation, no way of perceiving when he activated and deactivated the scalarity field, except by number. For an instant, Oga feared number had failed him, a first and fatal betrayal. Then light blazed down on to the dark ice. A single blinding star shone in the absolute blackness.

"What is that?"

"I pushed a single proton beyond the horizon of this horizon. I pushed it so far that space and time tore."

"So I'm looking at . . . "

"The light of creation. That is an entire universe, new born. A new big bang. A young man once said to me, 'Every particle will be so far from everything else that it will be in a universe of its own. It will *be* a universe of its own.' An extended object like this comet, or bodies, is too gross, but in a single photon, quantum fluctuations will turn it into an entire universe-in-waiting."

The two men looked up a long time into the nascent light, the surface of he fireball seething with physical laws and forces boiling out. *Now you understand*, Oga thought. *It's not a weapon. It's the way out. The way past the death of the universe. Out there beyond the horizon, we can bud off new universes, and universes from those universes, forever. Intelligence has the last word. We won't die alone in the cold and the dark.* He felt the light of the infant universe on his face, then said, "I think we probably should be getting back. If my calculations are correct—and there is a significant margin of error—this fireball will shortly undergo a phase transition as dark energy separates out and will undergo catastrophic expansion. I don't think that the environs of an early universe would be a very good place for us to be."

He saw portly Cjatay smile.

"Take me home, then. I'm cold and I'm tired of being a god."

"Are we gods?"

Cjatay nodded at the microverse.

"I think so. No, I know I would want to be a man again."

Oga thought of his own selves and lives, his bodies and natures. Flesh indwelled by many personalities, then one personality—one aggregate of experience and memory—in bodies liquid, starship, nanotechnological. And he *was* tired, so terribly tired beyond the universe, centuries away from all that he had known and loved. All except this one, his enemy.

"Tejaphay is no place for children."

"Agreed. We could rebuild Tay."

"It would be a work of centuries."

"We could use the Aeo Taea Parents. They have plenty of time."

Now Cjatay laughed.

"I have to trust you now, don't I? I could have vaporized you back there, blown this place to atoms with my missiles. And now you create an entire universe . . ."

"And the Enemy? They'll come again."

"You'll be ready for them, like you were ready for me. After all, I am still the enemy."

The surface of the bubble of universe seemed to be in more frenetic motion now. The light was dimming fast.

"Let's go then," Cjatay said.

"Yes," Oga said. "Let's go home."

Oga, returning

BIOGRAPHIES

Yoon Ha Lee lives in Louisiana with her family and has not yet been eaten by gators. Her works have appeared in *Clarkesworld, Lightspeed, Tor.com, The Magazine of Fantasy and Science Fiction*, and other venues, and she authored the StoryNexus game Winterstrike (winterstrike.storynexus.com/s).

James Patrick Kelly has won the Hugo, Nebula and Locus awards; his fiction has been translated into twenty-two languages. He writes a column on the internet for *Asimov's Science Fiction Magazine* and is on the faculty of the Stonecoast Creative Writing MFA Program at the University of Southern Maine.

Gwyneth Jones is the author of many fantasy, horror novels and thrillers for teenagers using the name Ann Halam, and several highly regarded sf and fantasy novels for adults. She's won two World Fantasy awards, the James Tiptree Jr award, the Arthur C Clarke award, the Children of the Night award and the Philip K Dick award, among other honours. She lives in Brighton, UK, with her husband, some goldfish and two cats called Ginger and Milo; likes old movies, practices yoga, blogs at boldaslove.co.uk and has done some extreme tourism in her time, but now prefers short-haul travel.

Gareth L. Powell is a novelist from the UK. Although he has written two well-received space opera novels and numerous short stories, he is probably best known for his Ack-Ack Macaque trilogy, published by Solaris Books. He can be found online at: www.garethlpowell.com

Greg Egan is the author of more than fifty short stories and eleven science fiction novels. His most recent books are a trilogy, *The Clockwork Rocket, The Eternal Flame* and *The Arrows of Time*, set in a universe with different laws of physics than our own.

Although **Chris Willrich** loves a good space adventure, he's best known for his sword and sorcery characters Gaunt and Bone, who've appeared in *The*

Magazine of Fantasy & Science Fiction, Beneath Ceaseless Skies, Flashing Swords, and *Lightspeed*, and in the novels *The Scroll of Years* and *The Silk Map*, both from Pyr. He's also the author of *Pathfinder Tales: The Dagger of Trust*, from Paizo Publishing.

Michael F. Flynn is author of the Spiral Arm space opera series and the Hugo nominee, Eifelheim. His recent short fiction collection is *Captive Dreams*. A recipient of the Robert A. Heinlein Award, the Sidewise Award, and the Sturgeon prize, he has been several times a Hugo finalist. He holds a master's in mathematics and has worked as a consultant in quality management and applied statistics with clients both here and abroad.

Una McCormack is a *New York Times* bestselling author of eight novels based on *Star Trek* and *Doctor Who*. Her audio plays based on *Doctor Who* and *Blake's 7* have been produced by Big Finish, and her short fiction has been anthologised by Farah Mendlesohn, Ian Whates, and Gardner Dozois. She has a doctorate in sociology and teaches creative writing at Anglia Ruskin University, Cambridge.

David Moles has been writing and editing science fiction and fantasy since 2002, and is a past finalist for the Hugo Award, the World Fantasy Award, and the John W. Campbell Award for Best New Writer, as well as the winner of the 2008 Theodore Sturgeon Memorial Award, for the novelette "Finisterra," included in this volume. David's most recent book is the novella *Seven Cities of Gold*. He currently lives in California.

Naomi Novik is the *New York Times* bestselling author of the Temeraire series, and winner of the Campbell Award, the Locus Award, and the Compton Crook Award. She was born in New York in 1973, a first-generation American, and raised on Polish fairy tales, Baba Yaga, and Tolkien. She published *His Majesty's Dragon*, the first of the Temeraire novels, in 2006, and her latest, *Blood of Tyrants*, is the eighth. Naomi lives in New York City with her husband Charles Ardai and daughter Evidence and many purring computers. Her website is at naominovik.com.

Kage Baker (1952-2010) was the Nebula and Hugo Award-nominated and Locus Award-winning author of the Company series. In addition to the nine Company novels and dozens of Company short stories, her fiction includes novels, novellas, and short stories that span science fiction and fantasy. Her 2003 novel *The Anvil of the World* was a Mythopoeic Award finalist, and her 2004 short story collection, *Mother Aegypt and Other Stories*, was a Locus

Award nominee. *The House of the Stag* earned her a second *Romantic Times* Reviewer's Choice Winner in 2008 and a World Fantasy Award nomination. Her full bibliography can be found at kagebaker.com.

Elizabeth Bear was born on the same day as Frodo and Bilbo Baggins, but in a different year. When coupled with a childhood tendency to read the dictionary for fun, this led her inevitably to penury, intransigence, and the writing of speculative fiction. She is the Hugo, Sturgeon, Locus, and Campbell Award winning author of twenty-five novels (The most recent is *Steles of the Sky*, from Tor) and almost a hundred short stories. Her dog lives in Massachusetts; her partner, writer Scott Lynch, lives in Wisconsin. She spends a lot of time on planes.

Sarah Monette lives in a 106-year-old house in the Upper Midwest with a great many books, two cats, and one husband. Her first four novels were published by Ace Books. Her short stories have appeared in *Strange Horizons*, *Weird Tales*, and *Lady Churchill's Rosebud Wristlet*, among other venues, and have been reprinted in several Year's Best anthologies. (Jamie and Mick have, so far, appeared in two other short stories.) *The Bone Key*, a 2007 collection of interrelated short stories, was re-issued in 2011 in a new edition. A non-themed collection, *Somewhere Beneath Those Waves*, was published the same year. Sarah has written two novels (*A Companion to Wolves* and *The Tempering of Men*) and three short stories with Elizabeth Bear. Her novel, *The Goblin Emperor*, was recently published by Tor under the name Katherine Addison. Visit her online at www.sarahmonette.com.

Jay Lake lives in Portland, Oregon, where he works on numerous writing and editing projects. His books for 2013 and 2014 include *Kalimpura* and *Last Plane to Heaven* from Tor and *Love in the Time of Metal and Flesh* from Prime. His short fiction appears regularly in literary and genre markets worldwide. Jay is a winner of the John W. Campbell Award for Best New Writer, and a multiple nominee for the Hugo, Nebula and World Fantasy Awards. He blogs regularly about his terminal colon cancer on his website at jlake.com.

Justina Robson is the author of nine SFF novels and a history of the Transformers as well as numerous short stories. She particularly loves writing about AI, robotics, cyborgs and transhuman subjects.

Alastair Reynolds was born in Barry in 1966. He spent his early years in Cornwall, then returned to Wales for his primary and secondary school education. He completed a degree in astronomy at Newcastle, then a PhD in the same subject at St Andrews in Scotland. He left the UK in 1991 and spent the next sixteen years working in the Netherlands, mostly for the European Space Agency, although he also did a stint as a postdoctoral worker in Utrecht. He had been writing and selling science fiction since 1989, and published his first novel, *Revelation Space*, in 2000. He has recently completed his tenth novel and has continued to publish short fiction. His novel *Chasm City* won the British Science Fiction Award, and he has been shortlisted for the Arthur C Clarke award three times. In 2004 he left scientific research to write full time. He married in 2005 and returned to Wales in 2008, where he lives in Rhondda Cynon Taff.

Ian R. MacLeod grew up in the West Midlands, studied law, and worked for many years at his honing writing skills under his desk in the Civil Service before moving on to house-husbandry and education. His stories and novels at the more adventurous edges of the fantastic genres have won numerous awards and been translated into many languages. He now lives with his wife in the riverside town of Bewdley.

Robert Reed is the author of numerous SF works and a few hard-to-categorize ventures. His latest novel is a trilogy in one volume: *The Memory of Sky*, published by Prime Books, is set in Reed's best known creation, the universe of Marrow and the Great Ship. In 2007, Reed won a Hugo for his novella, "A Billion Eves." He lives in Lincoln, Nebraska with his wife and daughter.

Aliette de Bodard lives and works in a computer-infested living room in Paris, where she has a day job as a software engineer. In her spare time, she writes speculative fiction: her Aztec noir fantasy *Obsidian and Blood* is published by Angry Robot, and her short fiction has appeared in places like *Clarkesworld Magazine*, *Lightspeed* and *Interzone*. She won the BSFA Award for Best Short Fiction with "The Shipmaker," and has been a finalist for the Hugo and Nebula. Her SF novella "On a Red Station, Drifting" was published December 2012 from Immersion Press.

Lavie Tidhar is the World Fantasy Award winning author of *Osama*. He has also won a British Fantasy Award and a BSFA Award. His latest novel is *The Violent Century* and, forthcoming, *The Drummer*.

Benjanun Sriduangkaew enjoys writing love letters to cities real and speculative. Her work can be found in *Clarkesworld Magazine*, *Beneath Ceaseless Skies*, *The Dark*, and Jonathan Strahan's *The Best Science Fiction and Fantasy of the Year*.

• • •

Ian McDonald is the author of the 2011 Hugo Award-finalist *The Dervish House* and many other novels, including Hugo Award-nominees *River of Gods* and *Brasyl*, and the Philip K. Dick Award-winner *King of Morning, Queen for a Day*. He won a Hugo in 2006 for his novelette, "The Djinn's Wife," and has won the Locus Award and four British Science Fiction Awards. His short fiction, much of which was recently collected in *Cyberabad Days*, has appeared in magazines such as *Interzone* and *Asimov's* and in numerous anthologies. His most recent book is Empress of the Sun, part 3 of the Everness series for younger readers. His next novel for adults will be *Luna*. He lives just outside Belfast, in Northern Ireland.

PUBLICATION HISTORY

ABOUT THE EDITOR

Rich Horton is an Associate Technical Fellow in Software for a major aerospace corporation. He is also a columnist for *Locus* and for *Black Gate*. He edits a series of Best of the Year anthologies for Prime Books, and also for Prime Books he has co-edited *Robots: The Recent A.I.* and *War and Space: Recent Combat.*